W9-BYU-833

FEB - - 2015

THE
PROVIDENCE
OF FIRE

ALSO BY BRIAN STAVELEY

The Emperor's Blades

THE PROVIDENCE OF FIRE

Chronicle of the Unhewn Throne, Book II

BRIAN STAVELEY

A TOM DOHERTY ASSOCIATES BOOK
NEW YORK

WILLIAMSBURG REGIONAL LIBRARY
7770 CROAKER ROAD
WILLIAMSBURG, VA 23188

This is a work of fiction. All of the characters, organizations, and events portrayed in this novel are either products of the author's imagination or are used fictitiously.

THE PROVIDENCE OF FIRE

Copyright © 2014 by Brian Staveley

All rights reserved.

Map by Isaac Stewart

A Tor Book
Published by Tom Doherty Associates, LLC
175 Fifth Avenue
New York, NY 10010

www.tor-forge.com

Tor® is a registered trademark of Tom Doherty Associates, LLC.

The Library of Congress Cataloging-in-Publication Data is available upon request.

ISBN 978-0-7653-3641-5 (hardcover)
ISBN 978-1-4668-2844-5 (e-book)

Tor books may be purchased for educational, business, or promotional use. For information on bulk purchases, please contact the Macmillan Corporate and Premium Sales Department at 1-800-221-7945, extension 5442, or write to specialmarkets@macmillan.com.

First Edition: January 2015

Printed in the United States of America

0 9 8 7 6 5 4 3 2 1

For my wife

AN ACKNOWLEDGMENT

Last time, I made a list of names.

It seemed like the right approach, given that so many people had helped me in so many ways as I was writing *The Emperor's Blades*. This book is even bigger, and so one might expect a longer list, an even greater catalogue of names, but I've grown a bit suspicious of lists.

To make a list in the acknowledgments of a book is to say, *I know my debts*. And the truth is, I don't, not even half of them. For every great idea that I can trace to an actual person, to a specific conversation over beers, there are scores, hundreds of wonderful thoughts that people— some friends, some utter strangers, some in writing, some in casual conversation—have laid into my arms like little babies.

I've raised these ideas as though they were mine, tried to take good care of them, tucked them tight between the covers of this book. Some of them have lived with me a long time, and I've grown incredibly fond of them, possessive even, so much so that it takes the occasion of this formal acknowledgment to tell the truth: *I don't know where they all came from.*

Now, as they head back out into the world, I like to imagine that although they might be frightened at first, they will grow increasingly delighted at the sheer size of it all, the color, the freedom, that they might recognize the majesty of the place they came from. The world is so much larger than one writer's mind, and though these ideas have lived with me awhile, I was never their final home.

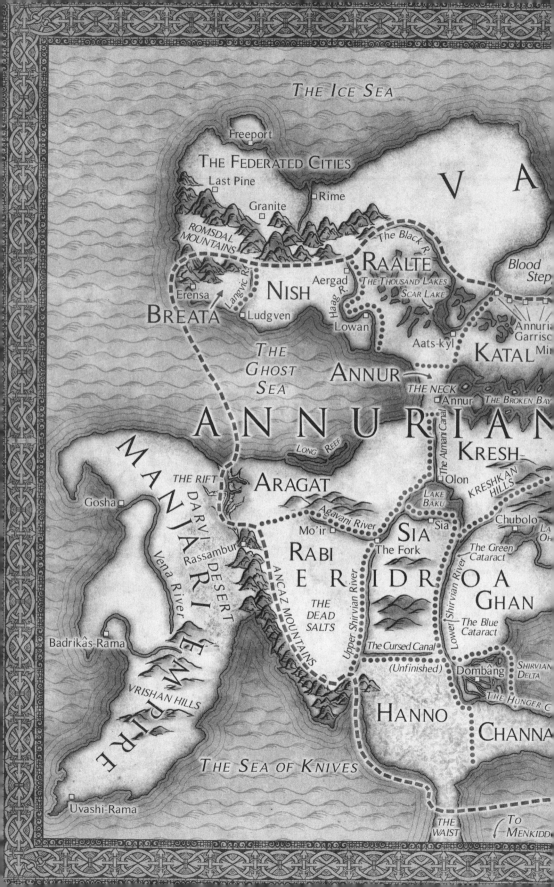

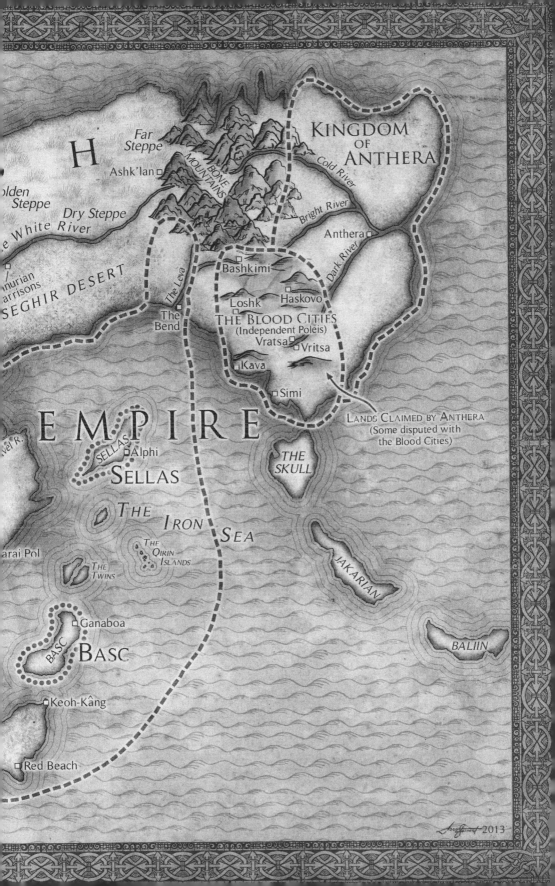

THE
PROVIDENCE
OF FIRE

PROLOGUE

By the time Sioan reached the tower's top, stepping from the last stair into the bitter chill of the night, the air in her lungs burned with a fury to match the fire raging in the streets below. The climb had taken hours—half the night, in fact. The guardsmen pacing her showed no visible strain, but then, the Aedolian Guard jogged the steps of Intarra's Spear in full armor once a moon. Keeping pace with a middle-aged Empress and three small children proved no great difficulty. She, on the other hand, felt ready to drop. Each landing invited her to stop, to sit, to lean against the wooden scaffolding that supported the stairs, close her eyes, and collapse into sleep.

I have grown too soft, she told herself again and again, self-reproach the only thing keeping her wobbling legs moving. *I have become a soft woman living among soft things.*

In truth, however, she worried more about her children than herself. They had all made the climb to the top of the Spear, but never with such urgency. A normal ascent might span two days, with breaks along the way for rest and refreshment, trays of food and generous mattresses laid out by an advance party of cooks and slaves. Those climbs were pleasant, celebratory; the children were too small for this furious charge. And yet Sioan's husband had insisted. One did not refuse the Emperor of Annur.

This is their city, Sanlitun told her. *The heart of their empire. This is something they must see. The climb will be the least of the difficulties they will one day face.*

Not that *he* had to climb the 'Kent-kissing tower. A Kettral Wing, five hard-eyed men and women in black, had whisked the Emperor to the top of the Spear beneath their massive, terrifying hawk. Sioan understood the urgency. Flames tore through the streets, and her husband needed the vantage to command the response. Annur could not afford to wait while he mounted tens of thousands of steps.

The Kettral had offered to come back for Sioan and the children, but she refused. Sanlitun claimed the birds were tame, but tame was not the same thing as domesticated, and she had no intention of abandoning her children to the talons of a creature that could rend oxen to ribbons with a single swipe.

And so, as the Emperor stood on the roof giving orders to stop the city from burning, Sioan had labored up the stairs, inwardly cursing her husband for insisting they join him, cursing herself for growing old. The Aedolians climbed silently, but the children, despite their initial enthusiasm, struggled. Adare was the oldest and strongest, but even she was only ten, and they hadn't climbed for long before she started to pant. Kaden and Valyn were even worse. The steps—a human construction built into the clear, ironglass shell of the ancient, impossible structure—were large for their short legs, and both boys kept tripping, purpling shins and elbows against the wooden treads.

For thirty floors, the wooden steps wound upward through level after level of administrative chambers and luxurious suites. The human builders of those chambers and suites had stopped at thirty floors. Though the shell of the tower stretched on above, so high that it seemed endless, only the stairs continued, spiraling up inside the vast emptiness, up and up, thin and trembling, suspended in the center of the impossible glass column. Hundreds of paces higher, the staircase pierced the solitary prison level—a single floor built of solid steel—then continued higher still. During the day, it was like climbing through a column of pure light. At night, however, the surrounding void was disorienting, even frightening. There was only the winding stair, the encompassing dark, and beyond the walls of the spear itself, the angry blaze of Annur burning.

For all her husband's insistence on haste, the city would burn whether or not the four of them were there to watch, and Sioan urged the children to stop each time they reached a landing. Adare, however, would fall down dead before she disappointed her father, and Valyn and Kaden, miserable though they were, trudged on grimly, shooting glances at each other, each clearly hoping the other would quit, neither willing to say the words.

When they emerged, finally, from the trapdoor, all three looked ready to fall over, and though a low wall ringed the top of Intarra's Spear, Sioan put her arms out protectively when the wind gusted. She need not have worried.

The Aedolians—Fulton and Birch, Yian and Trell—ringed the children, guarding, even here, against some constant, unseen threat. She turned to her husband, the curses ready on her tongue, then fell silent, staring at the blaze destroying the city below.

They had seen it from inside the Spear, of course—the furious red refracted through the glass walls—but from the impossible height of the tower's top, the streets and canals might have been lines etched on a map. Sioan could extend a hand and blot out whole quarters—Graves or Lowmarket, West Kennels or the Docks. She could not, however, blot out the fire. The report, when she started climbing, had put it on the very western edge of Annur, a vicious conflagration confined to half a dozen blocks. During their interminable ascent, however, it had spread, spread horribly, devouring everything west of the Ghost Road and then, fanned by a quick wind off the western sea, lapped its way east toward the far end of the Godsway. She tried to calculate the number of houses burned, the lives lost. She failed.

At the sound of the trapdoor clattering shut, Sanlitun turned. Even after years of marriage, his gaze still gave her pause. Though Adare and Kaden shared their father's burning irises, the fire in the children's eyes was warm, almost friendly, like the light from a winter hearth or the gaze of the sun. Sanlitun's eyes, however, burned with a frigid, unwavering flame, a light with no heat or smoke. No emotion showed on his face. He might have spent half the night watching the stars chart their course through the dark or the moonlight ribbing the waves rather than fighting a conflagration that threatened to consume his city.

Sanlitun considered his children, and Sioan felt Adare straighten at her side. The girl would collapse later, in the privacy of her own chambers, but now, in the presence of her father, legs trembling with the strain of the climb, she refused to lean on her mother. Kaden's eyes were wide as plates as he stared at the city below. He might have been alone on the roof, a child of seven facing the blaze all by himself. Only Valyn took her hand, sliding his small fingers into her grip as he looked from the fire to his father, then back.

"You arrived in time," the Emperor said, gesturing to the dark blocks of the city.

"In time for *what*?" Sioan demanded, her anger threatening to choke her. "To watch ten thousand people burn?"

Her husband considered her for a moment, then nodded. "Among other things," he replied quietly, then turned to the scribe at his side.

"Have them start another fire," he said. "The full length of Anlatun's Way, from the southern border of the city to the north."

The scribe, face intent, bent to the task, brushing the words over the parchment, holding the sheet in the air a moment to dry, rolling it quickly, tucking it into a bamboo tube, then slipping it into a chute running down the center of the Spear. It had taken Sioan half the night to ascend the 'Shael-spawned tower; the Emperor's orders would reach the palace below in a matter of moments.

The command away, Sanlitun turned to his children once again. "Do you understand?" he asked.

Adare bit her lip. Kaden said nothing. Only Valyn stepped forward, squinting against the wind and the fire both. He turned to the long lenses cradled in their brackets against the low wall, lifted one, and put it to his eye. "Anlatun's Way isn't burning," he protested after a moment. "The fire is still blocks to the west."

His father nodded.

"Then why . . ." He trailed off, the answer in his dark eyes.

"You're starting a second fire," Adare said. "To check the first."

Sanlitun nodded. "The weapon is the shield. The foe is the friend. What is burned cannot burn again."

For a long time the whole family stood in silence, staring at the blaze eating its way east. Only Sioan refused a long lens. She could see what she needed to see with her own eyes. Slowly, implacably, the fire came on, red and gold and horrible until, in a straight line across the western end of the city, a new set of fires burst out, discrete points at first, spreading together until an avenue of flame limned the western edge of the broad street that was Anlatun's Way.

"It's working," Adare said. "The new fire is moving west."

"All right," Sioan said abruptly, understanding at last what her husband wanted them to see, what he wanted them to learn; desperate, suddenly, to spare her children the sight and the knowledge both. "They have witnessed enough."

She reached out to take the long lens from Adare, but the girl snatched it away, training it on the twin fires once more.

Sanlitun met his wife's glare, then took her hand in his own. "No," he said quietly. "They have not."

It was Kaden, finally, who realized.

"The people," he said, gesturing. "They were running away, running east, but now they've stopped."

"They're trapped," Adare said, dropping her long lens and spinning to confront her father. "They're *trapped*. You have to *do* something!"

"He did," Valyn said. He looked up at the Emperor, the child's hope horrible in his gaze. "You already did, right? An order. Before we got here. You warned them somehow. . . ."

The boy trailed off, seeing the answer in those cold, blazing eyes.

"What order would I give?" Sanlitun asked, his voice soft and unstoppable as the wind. "Thousands of people live between those two fires, Valyn. Tens of thousands. Many will have fled, but how would I reach those who have not?"

"But they'll burn," Kaden whispered.

He nodded slowly. "They are burning even now."

"Why," Sioan demanded, not sure if the tears in her eyes were for the citizens screaming unheard in their homes so far below, or for her children, staring, horrified, at the distant flames. "Why did they need to see *this*?"

"One day the empire will be theirs."

"Theirs to rule, to *protect*, not to destroy!"

He continued to hold her hand, but didn't look away from the children. "They will not be ready to rule it," he said, his eyes silent as the stars, "until they are willing to see it burn."

1

Kaden hui'Malkeenian did his best to ignore both the cold granite beneath him and the hot sun beating down on his back as he slid forward, trying to get a better view of the scattered stone buildings below. A brisk wind, soaked with the cold of the lingering snows, scratched at his skin. He took a breath, drawing the heat from his core into his limbs, stilling the trembling before it could begin. His years of training with the monks were good for that much, at least. That much, and precious little else.

Valyn shifted at his side, glancing back the way they had come, then forward once more.

"Is this the path you took when you fled?" he asked.

Kaden shook his head. "We went that way," he replied, pointing north toward a great stone spire silhouetted against the sky, "beneath the Talon, then east past Buri's Leap and the Black and Gold Knives. It was night, and those trails are brutally steep. We hoped that soldiers in full armor wouldn't be able to keep up with us."

"I'm surprised they were."

"So was I," Kaden said.

He levered himself up on his elbows to peer over the spine of rock, but Valyn dragged him back.

"Keep your head down, Your Radiance," he growled.

Your Radiance. The title still sounded wrong, unstable and treacherous, like spring ice on a mountain tarn, the whole surface groaning even as it glittered, ready to crack beneath the weight of the first unwary foot. It was hard enough when others used the title, but from Valyn the words were almost unbearable. Though they'd spent half their lives apart, though both were now men in their own right, almost strangers, with their own secrets and scars, Valyn was still his brother, still his blood, and all the training, all the years, couldn't quite efface the reckless boy Kaden remembered from his childhood, the partner with whom he'd played blades and bandits, racing through the hallways and pavilions of the Dawn Palace. Hearing Valyn use the official title was like hearing his own past erased, his childhood destroyed, replaced utterly by the brutal fact of the present.

The monks, of course, would have approved. *The past is a dream,* they used to say. *The future is a dream. There is only now.* Which meant those same monks, the men who had raised him, trained him, were not men at all, not anymore. They were rotting meat, corpses strewn on the ledges below.

Valyn jerked a thumb over the rocks that shielded them, jarring Kaden from his thoughts. "We're still a good way off, but some of the bastards who killed your friends might have long lenses."

Kaden frowned, drawing his focus back to the present. He had never even considered the possibility of long lenses—another reminder, as if he needed another reminder, of how poorly his cloistered life at Ashk'lan had prepared him for this sudden immersion in the treacherous currents of the world. He could paint, sit in meditation, or run for days over rough trail, but painting, running, and meditation were meager skills when set against the machinations of the men who had murdered his father, slaughtered the Shin monks, and very nearly killed him as well. Not for the first time, he found himself envying Valyn's training.

For eight years Kaden had struggled to quell his own desires and hopes, fears and sorrows, had fought what felt like an endless battle against himself. Over and over the Shin had intoned their mantras: *Hope's edge is sharper than steel. To want is to lack. To care is to die.* There was truth to the words, far more truth than Kaden had imagined when he first arrived in the mountains as a child, but if he had learned anything in the past few days, days filled with blood, death, and confusion, he had learned the limits to that truth. A steel edge, as it turned out, was plenty sharp. Clinging to the self might kill you, but not if someone put a knife in your heart first.

In the space of a few days, Kaden's foes had multiplied beyond his own persistent failings, and these new enemies wore polished armor, carried swords in their fists, wielded lies by the thousands. If he was going to survive, if he was to take his father's place on the Unhewn Throne, he needed to know about long lenses and swords, politics and people, about all the things the Shin had neglected in their single-minded effort to train him in the empty trance that was the *vaniate*. It would take years to fill in the gaps, and he did not have years. His father was dead, had been dead for months already, and that meant, prepared or not, Kaden hui'Malkeenian was the Emperor of Annur.

Until someone kills me, he added silently.

Given the events of the past few days, that possibility loomed suddenly, strikingly large. That armed men had arrived with orders to murder him and destroy the monastery was terrifying enough, but that they were comprised of his own Aedolian Guard—an order sworn to protect and defend him—that they were commanded by high-ranking Annurians, men at the very top of the pyramid of imperial politics, was almost beyond belief. In some ways, returning to the capital and sitting the Unhewn Throne seemed like the surest way to help his enemies finish what they had started.

Of course, he thought grimly, *if I'm murdered in Annur, it will mean I made it* back *to Annur, which would be a success of sorts.*

Valyn gestured toward the lip of the rocky escarpment that shielded them. "When you look, look slowly, Your Radiance," he said. "The eye is attracted to motion."

That much, at least, Kaden knew. He'd spent enough time tracking crag cats and lost goats to know how to remain hidden. He shifted his weight onto his elbows, inching up until his eyes cleared the low spine of rock. Below and to the west, maybe a quarter mile distant, hunched precariously on a narrow ledge between the cliffs below and the vast, chiseled peaks above, stood Ashk'lan, sole monastery of the Shin monks, and Kaden's home.

Or what remained of it.

The Ashk'lan of Kaden's memory was a cold place but bright, scoured clean, an austere palette of pale stone, wide strokes of snow, vertiginous rivers shifting their glittering ribbons, ice slicking the north-facing cliffs, all piled beneath a hard, blue slab of sky. The Aedolians had destroyed it. Wide sweeps of soot smudged the ledges and boulders, and fire had lashed the junipers to blackened stumps. The refectory, meditation hall, and dormitory stood in ruins. While the cold stone of the walls had refused to burn, the wooden rafters, the shingles, the casings of the windows and broad pine doors had all succumbed to the flame, dragging sections of masonry with them as they fell. Even the sky was dark, smudged with oily smoke that still smoldered from the wreckage.

"There," Valyn said, pointing to movement near the northern end of the monastery. "The Aedolians. They've made camp, probably waiting for Micijah Ut."

"Gonna be a long wait," Laith said, sliding up beside them. The flier grinned.

Before the arrival of Valyn's Wing, all Kaden's knowledge of the Kettral, of Annur's most secretive and deadly soldiers, came from the stories he had lapped up as a child, tales that had led him to imagine grim, empty-eyed killers, men and women steeped in blood and destruction. The stories had been partly right: Valyn's black eyes were cold as last year's coals, and Laith—the Wing's flier—didn't seem at all concerned about the wreckage below or the carnage they had left behind. They were clearly soldiers, disciplined and well trained, and yet, they seemed somehow young to Kaden.

Laith's casual smile, his obvious delight in irritating Gwenna and provoking Annick, the way he drummed on his knee whenever he got bored, which was often—it was all behavior the Shin would have beaten out of him before his second year. That Valyn's Wing could fly and kill was clear enough, but Kaden found himself worrying, wondering if they were truly ready for the difficult road ahead. Not that he was ready himself, but it would have been nice to think that *someone* had the situation in hand.

Micijah Ut, at least, was one foe Kaden no longer needed to fear. That the massive Aedolian in all his armor had been killed by a middle-aged woman wielding a pair of knives would have strained belief had Kaden not seen the body. The sight had brought him a muted measure of satisfaction, as though he could set the weight of steel and dead flesh in the scales to balance, in some small part, the rest of the slaughter.

"Anyone want to sneak into their camp with Ut's body?" Laith asked. "We could prop him up somewhere, make it look like he's drinking ale or taking a leak? See how long it takes them to notice the fucker's not breathing?" He looked from Valyn to Kaden, eyebrows raised. "No? That's not why we came back here?"

The group of them had returned to Ashk'lan that morning, flying west from their meager camp in the heart of the Bone Mountains, the same camp where they had fought and killed the men chasing them down, Aedolians and traitorous Kettral both. The trip had occasioned a heated debate: there was broad agreement that someone needed to go, both to check for survivors and to see if there was anything to be learned from the Annurian soldiers who had remained behind when Ut and Tarik Adiv chased Kaden into the peaks. The disagreement centered on just *who* ought to make the trip.

Valyn didn't want to risk bringing anyone outside his own Wing, but Kaden pointed out that if the Kettral wanted to make use of the snaking network of goat tracks surrounding the monastery, they needed a monk familiar with the land. Rampuri Tan, of course, was the obvious choice— he knew Ashk'lan better than Kaden, not to mention the fact that, unlike Kaden, he could actually *fight*—and the older monk, despite Valyn's misgivings, seemed to consider his participation a foregone conclusion. Pyrre, meanwhile, argued that it was stupid to return in the first place.

"The monks are dead," she observed, "may Ananshael unknit their celibate souls. You can't help them by poking at the bodies."

Kaden wondered what it felt like to be the assassin, to worship the Lord of the Grave, to have lived so close to death for so long that it held no terror, no wonder. Still, it was not the bodies he wanted to go back for. There was a chance, however small, that the soldiers had captured some of the monks rather than killing them. It wasn't clear what Kaden could do if they had, but with the Kettral at his back it might be possible to rescue one or two. At the very least, he could look.

Tan had dismissed the notion as sentimental folly. The reason to go back was to observe the remaining Aedolians, to ferret out their intentions; Kaden's guilt was just further evidence of his failure to achieve true detachment. Maybe the older monk was right. A true Shin would have rooted out the coiling tightness that snaked about his heart, would have cut away, one by one, the barbs of emotion. But then, aside from Tan and Kaden himself, the Shin were dead: two hundred monks murdered in the night because of him, men and boys whose only goal was the empty calm of the *vaniate* burned and butchered where they slept to cover up an Annurian coup. Whatever waited at Ashk'lan, it had happened because of Kaden. He had to go back.

The rest was simple. Valyn commanded the Wing, Valyn obeyed the Emperor, and so, in spite of Tan's objections and Pyrre's, in spite of his own concerns, Valyn had bowed his head and obeyed, flying Kaden along with the rest of the Wing to discover what was left of his mountain home. They landed a little to the east, out of sight of the monastery, then covered the final miles on foot. The track was easy, mostly downhill, but the tension built in Kaden's chest as they drew closer.

The Aedolians hadn't bothered to hide their slaughter. There was no need. Ashk'lan lay well beyond the border of the empire, too high in the mountains for the Urghul, too far south for the Edish, too far from anywhere for merchants and traders, and so the brown-robed bodies had been left to litter the central courtyard, some burned, others cut down as they fled, dried blood staining the stones.

"Lots of monks," Laith pointed out, nodding toward the monastery. "All pretty dead."

"What about them?" Valyn asked, pointing toward a row of figures seated cross-legged on the far side of the ledge, staring out over the steppe. "Are they alive?"

Laith raised the long lens. "Nope. Stabbed. Right in the back." He shook his head. "Not sure why they're sitting there. No one tied them."

Kaden looked at the slumped men for a moment, then closed his eyes, imagining the scene.

"They didn't run," he said. "They sought refuge in the *vaniate*."

"Yeah . . ." the flier said, drawing out the syllable skeptically. "Doesn't look like they found it."

Kaden stared at the corpses, remembering the awesome emotional vacancy of the trance, the absence of fear, or anger, or worry. He tried to imagine what they had felt sitting there, looking out over the wide green steppe while their home burned a few paces behind them, watching the cold stars as they waited for the knife. "The *vaniate* might surprise you," he said quietly.

"Well, I'm tired of being surprised," Valyn growled. He rolled onto his side to look at Kaden, and once again Kaden found himself trying to see his brother—the brother he had once known—beneath the scars and lacerations, behind those unnaturally black eyes. Valyn the child had been quick to smile, to laugh, but Valyn the soldier looked harried, haunted, hunted, as though he distrusted the very sky above him, doubted his own battered hand and the naked sword it held.

Kaden knew the outlines of the story, how Valyn, too, had been stalked by those who wanted to bring down the Malkeenian line. In some ways, Valyn had had it worse than Kaden himself. While the Aedolians had struck suddenly and brutally into the heart of Ashk'lan, the soldiers had been strangers to Kaden, and the sense of injustice, of betrayal, remained abstract. Valyn, on the other hand, had seen his closest friend murdered by his fellow soldiers. He'd watched as the military order to which he'd devoted his life failed him—failed him or betrayed him. Kaden still worried about the possibility that the Kettral command, the Eyrie itself, was somehow complicit in the plot. Valyn had reason enough to be tired and wary, and yet there was something else in that gaze, something that worried Kaden, a darkness deeper than suffering or sorrow.

"We wait here," Valyn went on, "out of sight, until Annick, Talal, and Gwenna get back. If they don't find any monks, *living* monks, we hump out the way we came in, and get back on the 'Kent-kissing bird."

Kaden nodded. The tension from the walk in had lodged deep in his stomach, a tight knot of loss, and sorrow, and anger. He set about loosening it. He had insisted on coming back for the survivors, but it looked as though there were no survivors. The residual emotion was doing him no good; was, in fact, obscuring his judgment. As he tried to focus on his breath, however, the images of Akiil's face, of Pater's, of Scial Nin's, kept floating into his mind, startling in their immediacy and detail. Somewhere down there, sprawled among those blasted buildings, lay everyone he knew, and everyone, aside from Rampuri Tan, who knew him.

Someone else, someone without the Shin training, might find relief in the knowledge that those faces would fade over time, that the memories would blur, the edges soften; but the monks had taught him not to forget. The memories of his slaughtered friends would remain forever vivid and immediate, the shape of their sprawled forms would remain, carved in all their awful detail. *Which is why,* he thought grimly, *you have to unhitch the feeling from the fact.* That skill, too, the Shin had taught him, as though to balance the other.

Behind him, soft cloth scuffed over stone. He turned to find Annick and Talal, the Wing's sniper and leach, approaching, sliding over the wide slabs of rock on their bellies as though they'd been born to the motion. They pulled up just behind Valyn, the sniper immediately nocking an arrow to her bow, Talal just shaking his head.

"It's bad," he said quietly. "No prisoners."

Kaden considered the leach silently. It had come as a surprise to discover that men and women who would have been burned alive or stoned to death for their unnatural abilities anywhere else in Annur served openly with the Kettral. All Kaden's life he'd heard that leaches were dangerous and unstable, their minds warped by their strange powers. Like everyone else, he'd grown up on stories of leaches drinking blood, of leaches lying and stealing, of the horrifying leach-lords, the Atmani, who in their hubris shattered the very empire they had conspired to rule.

Another thing about which I know too little, Kaden reminded himself.

In the short, tense days since the slaughter and rescue, he had tried to talk with Talal, to learn something about the man, but the Kettral leach was quieter, more reserved than the rest of Valyn's Wing. He proved unfailingly polite, but Kaden's questions yielded little, and after the tenth or twelfth evasive response, Kaden started talking less, observing more. Before they flew out, he had watched Talal smudge the bright hoops in his ears with coal from the fire, then his bracelets, then his rings, working the char into the metal until it was almost as dark as his skin.

"Why don't you just take them off?" Kaden had asked.

"You never know," Talal had replied, shaking his head slowly, "what might come in handy out there."

His well, Kaden realized. Every leach had one, a source from which he drew his power. The stories told of men who could pull strength from stone, women who twisted the sharp grip of terror to their own ends. The metal hoops looked innocuous enough, but Kaden found himself staring at them as though they were venomous stone spiders. It took an effort to stamp out the emotion, to look at the man as he was, not as the tales would paint him. In fact, of all the members of Valyn's Wing, Talal seemed the most steady, the most thoughtful. His abilities were unnerving, but Valyn seemed to trust him, and Kaden didn't have so many allies that he could afford the prejudice.

"We could spend all week hunting around the rocks," Talal went on, gesturing to the serrated cliffs. "A couple of monks might have slipped the cordon—they know the territory, it was night. . . ." He glanced over at Kaden and trailed off, something that might have been compassion in his eyes.

"The whole southeastern quadrant is clear," Annick said. If Talal was worried about Kaden's feelings, the sniper seemed indifferent. She spoke in clipped periods, almost bored, while those icy blue eyes of hers scanned the rocks around them, never pausing. "No track. No blood. The attackers were good. For Aedolians."

It was a telling crack. The Aedolians were some of Annur's finest soldiers, handpicked and exhaustively trained to guard the royal family and other important visitors. How this particular group had been incited to betrayal, Kaden had no idea, but Annick's obvious disdain spoke volumes about her own abilities.

"What are they doing down there?" Valyn asked.

Talal shrugged. "Eating. Sleeping. Cleaning weapons. They don't know about Ut and Adiv yet. Don't know that we arrived, that we killed the soldiers chasing Kaden."

"How long will they stay?" Kaden asked. The slaughter seemed absolute, but some part of him wanted to descend anyway, to walk among the rubble, to look at the faces of the slain.

"No telling," Talal replied. "They've got no way to know that the smaller group, the one that went after you, is dead."

"They must have a protocol," Annick said. "Two days, three days, before searching or retreating."

Laith rolled his eyes. "It may shock you to discover, Annick, that some people aren't slaves to protocol. They might not actually *have* a plan."

"Which is why we would kill them," the sniper replied, voice gelid, "if it came to a fight."

Valyn shook his head. "It's not going to come to a fight. There've got to be seventy, eighty men down there. . . ."

A quiet but fierce cursing from behind them cut into Valyn's words.

"The 'Kent-kissing, Hull-buggering *bastard*," Gwenna spat, rolling easily over a spine of rock into a low, ready crouch. "That whoreson, slit-licking ass."

Valyn rounded on her. "Keep your voice down."

The red-haired woman waved off the objection. "They're a quarter mile off, Valyn, and the wind's blowing the wrong way. I could sing the 'Shael-spawned Kettral attack anthem at the top of my voice and they wouldn't notice."

This defiance, too, surprised Kaden. The soldiers he remembered from back in the Dawn Palace were all rigid salutes and unquestioned obedience. While it seemed that Valyn had the final call on decisions regarding his Wing, none of the others went out of their way to defer to him. Gwenna, in particular, seemed determined to nudge her toe right up to the line of insubordination. Kaden could see the irritation on his brother's face, the strain around his eyes, tension in the jaw.

"*Which* bastard are we talking about now?" Laith asked. "There are plenty to go around these days."

"That fancy prick Adiv," Gwenna said, jerking her head toward the northwest. "The one with the blindfold and the attitude."

"The Mizran Councillor," Kaden interjected quietly. It was one of the highest posts in the empire, and not a military position. Kaden had been surprised, even before the betrayal, when the man arrived with the contingent of Aedolians. Now it was just more evidence, as if he needed more, that the conspiracy had penetrated the most trusted quarters of the Dawn Palace.

"Whatever his job is," Gwenna replied, "he's over there, on foot, picking his miserable way out of the mountains. Couldn't have missed our bird by more than a few hundred paces."

Valyn sucked air between his teeth. "Well, we knew Tarik Adiv was alive when we didn't find the body. Now we know where he is. Any sign of Balendin?"

Gwenna shook her head.

"That's something, at least," Valyn replied.

"It is?" Laith asked. "No doubt Balendin's the more dangerous of the two."

"Why do you say that?" Kaden asked.

Laith stared. "Balendin's *Kettral*," he replied finally, as if that explained everything. "He trained with us. And he's a leach."

"Adiv is a leach himself," Talal pointed out. "That's how they kept up with Kaden in the mountains, how they tracked him."

"I thought they used those spider creatures for the tracking," Laith said.

Talal nodded. "But someone needed to control them, to handle them."

"It doesn't matter now," Valyn said. "Right now Balendin's missing and Adiv is here. Let's work with what we have."

"I've got eyes on him," Annick said.

While they were talking, the sniper had moved silently to a concealed spot between two boulders, half drawing her bowstring.

Kaden risked a glance over the ridge. At first he saw nothing, then noticed a figure limping down a shallow drainage three hundred paces off. He couldn't make out the councillor's face at that distance but the red coat was unmistakable, the gold at the cuffs and collar badly tarnished but glinting in the midday light.

"He made good time," Talal observed.

"He's had a night, a day, another night, and a morning," Gwenna said scornfully. "It's not more than seventy miles from where we lost him."

"As I said," Talal replied. "Good time."

"Think he cheated?" Laith asked.

"I think he's a leach," Talal said.

"So . . . yes," the flier concluded, grinning.

"Remind me not to 'cheat,'" Talal replied, fixing the flier with a steady stare, "the next time you're in a tight place."

"Take him down?" Annick asked. The bowstring was at her ear now, and though the strain must have been immense, she remained as still as stone.

Kaden glanced over the ridge again. At this distance he could barely make out the blindfold wrapping Adiv's eyes.

"Isn't he too far off?"

"No."

"Take the shot, Annick," Valyn said, turning to Kaden. "She'll make it. Don't ask me how."

"Stand by," the sniper responded after a pause. "He's passing behind some rock."

Kaden looked from Annick to Valyn, then to the small defile where Adiv had disappeared. After hours of lying on their bellies, waiting and watching, things were abruptly going too fast. He had expected the long wait to be followed by conversation, deliberation, a review of the facts and exchange of ideas. Suddenly, though, with no discussion at all, a man was about to die, a traitor and a murderer, but a man all the same.

The Kettral didn't seem concerned. Gwenna and Valyn were staring over the rock; the demolitions master eagerly, Valyn silent and focused. Laith was trying to make a wager with Talal.

"I'll bet you a silver moon she kills him with the first shot."

"I'm not betting against Annick," the leach replied.

The flier cursed. "What odds will you give me to take the other side? Ten to one for her to miss?"

"Make it fifty," Talal said, resting his bald head against the rock, considering the sky.

"Twenty."

"No," Kaden said.

"Fine. Twenty-five."

"Not the bet," Kaden said, putting a hand on Valyn's shoulder. "Don't kill him."

Valyn turned from the valley below to look at Kaden. "What?"

"Oh for the sweet love of 'Shael," Gwenna growled. "Who's running this Wing?"

Valyn ignored Gwenna. Instead, his black eyes bored into Kaden, drinking the light. "Adiv's behind all this, Your Radiance," he said. "He and Ut. They're the ones that killed the monks, that tried to kill you, not to mention the fact that they're clearly involved in our father's murder. With Ut gone, Adiv is the ranking commander down there. We kill him, we take a head off the beast."

"I have him again," Annick said.

"Don't shoot," Kaden insisted, shaking his head, trying to order his thoughts. Years earlier, while attempting to recapture a goat, he'd lost his footing above the White River, plunging down the rocks and into the current. It was all he could do to breathe, to keep his head above the roiling surface, to fend off the jagged boulders as they loomed up before him, all the time knowing that he had less than a quarter mile to pull himself clear of the torrent before it plunged him over a cliff. The immediacy of the moment, the inability to pause, to reflect, the absolute necessity of *action* had terrified him and when he finally caught hold of a fallen limb, clawing his way up and out, the feeling left him shaking on the bank. The Shin had taught him much about patience, but almost nothing of haste. Now, with the eyes of the entire Wing upon him, with the coal-smudged point of Annick's arrow fixed on Adiv, he felt that awful, ineluctable forward rush all over again.

"A few more seconds," Annick said, "and he'll be in the camp. It'll be more difficult to take him then."

"*Why?*" Valyn demanded, staring at Kaden. "Why do you want him alive?"

Kaden forced his eddying thoughts into a channel, the channel into speech. There would be no second chance to say what he had to say. The arrow, once loosed, would not be called back.

"We know him," he began slowly. "We need him. Back in Annur we can observe who he talks to, who he trusts. He'll help us to unravel the conspiracy."

"Yeah," Gwenna snapped, "and maybe he'll murder a few dozen more people on the way."

"I'm losing him," Annick said. "Decide now."

"Oh for 'Shael's sake," Laith grumbled. "Just kill him already. We can sort out the details later."

"No," Kaden said quietly, willing his brother to see past the present, to understand the logic. "Not yet."

Valyn held Kaden's gaze for a long time, jaw tight, eyes narrowed. Finally he nodded. "Stand down, Annick. We have our orders."

2

*P*lan might be too noble a word," Pyrre said, reclining against a large boulder, head back, eyes closed even as she spoke, "but I'd like to think we had some sort of vague *inclination*."

They'd made it back from the monastery easily enough, rejoining the rest of the group in the hidden defile where they'd set up camp. The other Kettral were checking over their weapons, the two monks sat cross-legged on the rough stone, while Triste fingered the long scab on her cheek, her wide eyes darting from one person to the next as though unsure where to look, who to trust.

Valyn studied the girl a moment, surprised all over again at the course of events that had led such a fragile, arresting young woman to this place, tangling her up in the same snare with soldiers and monks. She was a concubine, Kaden had said. Adiv had offered her to Kaden as a gift, one intended to distract the new emperor while the Aedolians made ready to murder him. Evidently, Triste wasn't a part of the plot, but she was plenty distracting all the same. Valyn felt like he could watch her forever, but then, she wasn't the one who needed watching. With an effort, he shifted his gaze to Pyrre Lakatur.

Valyn considered the woman, trying to figure her angle. He had always imagined the Skullsworn to be a sort of sinister mirror image of the Kettral—all blades and blacks and brusque efficiency. At the very least, he had expected the assassin-priests of the Lord of the Grave to be imposing. Pyrre, however, seemed more like a decadent atrep's wife. The woman was elegant, almost flashy; rings sparkled on her fingers, a bright cloth band held back her hair, hiding the flecks of gray at her temples, and her tunic and leggings, though badly tattered by the violence of the preceding week, were cut of fine wool to flatter her form. She didn't look like a killer, not at first glance, but the signs were there if you paid attention: the easy way she held her knives, switching readily between the standard grip and the Rabin; the way she always seemed to position herself, as now, with a cliff or boulder at her back; her apparent indifference to the bloodshed of the days before.

And then there was the way she smelled. Valyn still couldn't put words to some of the things he could sense since emerging from Hull's Hole. The slarn egg had changed him; the eggs had changed them all. That, evidently, had been the point of the final Kettral test, the reason all cadets were sent blind and bleeding into that endless cave on Irsk, scavenging the darkness for the eggs of those reptilian monsters. The eggs reversed the poison, but they did more, much more. Like the rest of the Kettral, any member of Valyn's Wing could now see in the shadows and hear things at the edge of hearing. They were all stronger than they had been, too, tougher, as though some of the slarn's wiry strength had been sewn into their flesh when they seized the eggs and drank. But only Valyn had found the dark egg, the one guarded by the king himself. Only Valyn drank the bilious tar while his body shook with the poison.

He was still struggling to understand what it had done to him. Like the others, he'd found his sight and hearing suddenly, if subtly, enhanced. He could hear small rocks clattering down the cliffside a hundred paces distant, could make out the pinions on the hawks that wheeled overhead . . . but there was more. Sometimes an animal fury clamped down on his heart, a savage desire, not just to fight and kill, not just to see the mission done, but to rend, to hack, to *hurt*. For the hundredth time, he remembered the slarn circling around and around him, eager claws scraping the stone. If they were now a part of his eyes and ears, were they also a part of his mind?

He set the question aside, focusing on the assassin. *Smell* wasn't quite the right word. He could smell more acutely, to be sure—the woman's sweat, her hair, even from two paces distant—but this vague sensation hovering at the edge of thought wasn't that. Or it was that, but *more*. Sometimes he thought he was losing his mind, imagining new senses for himself, but the sensation remained: he could *smell* emotion now: anger, and hunger, and fear in all its infinite variation. There was the raw musk of terror and pinched hint of frayed nerves. Everyone in their battered group shared the fear, at least to some extent. Everyone but Rampuri Tan and the Skullsworn.

According to Kaden, Pyrre had come to Ashk'lan because she was paid to make the trip, to save his life, and she *had* rescued Kaden several times over. Despite an inclination to provoke Tan and the Kettral, she made a formidable ally. Still, how far could you trust a woman whose sole allegiance was to the Lord of the Grave? How far could you trust a woman who seemed, from both her smell and demeanor, utterly indifferent to death?

"I have a plan," Kaden replied, glancing from Pyrre to Tan to Valyn.

Valyn stifled a groan.

⸸

The night before, after tethering the bird, walking the perimeter three times, and double-checking, to Gwenna's great irritation, the flickwicks and moles she had hidden to guard both approaches to the pass, Valyn had climbed to the top of a large boulder, a jagged shard of rock set apart from the rest of the group. Partly he wanted the high ground, a spot with a clear view of everything below, and partly he wanted to be alone, to try to make sense of the events of the last few days, of his own role in the brutal fighting that had taken place. Kaden found him there just as night's bleak stain leaked over the eastern peaks.

"Don't get up," Kaden said as he climbed the side of the rock. "If you start bowing now, I'll throw you off the mountain." His voice was quiet, ragged.

Valyn glanced over, hesitated, then nodded, returning his attention to the naked sword across his knees. His fight with Sami Yurl had left a tiny nick in the smoke steel halfway down the blade. He'd been at it with his stone for the better part of an hour, smoothing it out stroke by careful stroke.

"Have a seat," he said, gesturing with the stone, "Your Rad—"

"Not that either," Kaden groaned, perching cross-legged at the very lip of the boulder. "Save it for when someone else is listening."

"You *are* the Emperor," Valyn pointed out.

Kaden didn't say anything. After a few licks of the stone, Valyn looked up to find his brother staring with those fiery eyes out over the valley below. The depths of the ravine were already sunk in shadow, but the setting sun had caught the far rim, drenching it in bloody light.

"I am," Kaden said after what seemed like a long time. "Intarra help us all, I am the Emperor."

Valyn hesitated, uncertain how to respond. During the fight two days earlier, Kaden had been cold as midwinter ice, calm and ready as any Kettral. That certainty, however, seemed to have vanished. Valyn had witnessed something like it on the Islands, had seen men and women, twenty-year veterans returning from successful missions, fall to pieces the moment they set foot back on Qarsh. There was something about being safe again, about being finally and undeniably *alive* after living so close to death, that made soldiers, *good* soldiers, soldiers who held it together for days or weeks under the most brutal circumstances, dance like madmen, collapse sobbing, or drink themselves nearly to oblivion over on Hook.

There's no shame, the Kettral said, *in crying in your own rack.* The rest of the equation remained unspoken, axiomatic: you could cry all you wanted in your rack, provided you got up again in a day or two, provided that when you got up, you went back out, and that when you went back out, you were the baddest, fastest, most brutal motherfucker on the four continents. It wasn't at all clear whether or not Kaden had that kind of resilience, that kind of resolve.

"How are you?" Valyn asked. It was a stupid question, but every conversation had to start somewhere, and Kaden looked like he might sit cross-legged the whole night without saying another word. "After what we ran into down there?"

Valyn had seen scores of dead bodies in the course of his training, had learned to look at the hacked-up limbs and crusted blood the way another man, someone not raised by the Kettral, might consider a side of beef or a plucked rooster. There was even a certain satisfaction to be had in studying the aftermath of violence and seeing answers in the wreckage. As Hendran wrote in his *Tactics*: *The deader a man gets, the more honest he becomes. Lies are a vice of the living.* That was true enough, but Kaden hadn't been trained to pick over bodies, especially not the bodies of his friends and fellow monks. It must have been hard to encounter them— even from a distance—burned and cut to pieces.

Kaden took a long, slow breath, shuddered for a moment, then fell still. "It's not the older monks that bother me," he said finally. "They had all achieved the *vaniate,* had found a way to snuff out their fear."

Valyn shook his head. "No one escapes fear. Not really."

"These men would have surprised you," Kaden said, turning to look at him, face sober, composed. "The children, though, the novices especially . . ." He trailed off.

The wind had picked up as the sun set. It whipped around them, scrabbling at hair and clothes, tugging Kaden's robe, threatening to rip him off the rock. Kaden didn't seem to notice. Valyn searched for something to say, some comfort he might offer, but found nothing. The Shin novices were dead, and, if they were anything like everyone else, they had died in pain and terror, baffled, confused, and suddenly, utterly alone.

"I wonder," Kaden said quietly, "if I shouldn't let them have it."

It took Valyn a moment to find his bearings in the shifting conversation, but when he did, he shook his head curtly.

"The Unhewn Throne is yours," he said firmly, "as it was our father's. You can't surrender it because of a handful of murders."

"Hundreds," Kaden replied, voice harder than Valyn expected. "The Aedolians killed hundreds, not a handful. And the throne? If I'm so desperate to sit on top of a chunk of rock, there are plenty." He gestured into the night. "I could stay right here. The view is better and no one else would be killed."

Valyn glanced over his blade, ran a finger along the edge, feeling for the nick.

"Are you sure about that?"

Kaden laughed helplessly. "Of course I'm not sure, Valyn. Let me list for you the things I know for sure: the print of a brindled bear, the color of bruiseberries, the weight of a bucket of water . . ."

"All right," Valyn said. "I get it. We're not sure about anything."

Kaden stared at him, the fire in his irises so bright it had to hurt. "I know this: the Aedolians came for me. The monks died because of me."

"That's the truth," Valyn replied, "but it's not the end of the truth."

"You sound like a monk."

"The killing is aimed at you right now, but it won't *stop* with you. Let me tell you something *I* know: men are animals. Look anywhere you want: Anthera or the Blood Cities, the jungle tribes of the Waist, look at the fucking *Urghul,* for 'Shael's sake. People kill to get power, they kill to keep power, and they kill if they think they might lose it, which is pretty much always. Even if you and I both stay out of it, even if we both *die,* whoever came after us will *keep coming.* They'll find the next threat, the next worrisome voice, the next person with the wrong name or the wrong skin. Maybe they'll go after the rich for their coin or the peasants for their rice, the Bascans because they're too dark or the Breatans because they're too pale—it doesn't matter. People who will murder monks will murder any-one. I *trained* with bastards like this. They won't back off because you give up. They'll come on harder. Do you *get* that?"

Valyn fell silent, the words drying up as suddenly as they had come. He was panting, he realized. Blood slammed in his temples and his fingers had curled into fists so tight they hurt. Kaden was watching him, watching him the way you might watch a wild animal, wary and uncertain of its intent.

"We'll find him," Kaden said finally.

"Find who?"

"The Kettral leach. Balendin. The one who killed your friend. We'll find him, and we'll kill him."

Valyn stared. "This isn't about me," he protested. "That's my point."

"I know," Kaden replied. Somehow, the uncertainty had sloughed off of him. There was a distance in those burning eyes again, as though Valyn was seeing them from miles away. "I know it isn't."

They sat awhile, listening to a rockfall farther down the ridgeline. It sounded like a series of explosions, like Kettral munitions, only louder, boulders the size of houses loosened by winter ice losing their hold, shat-tering to pieces on the rocky slopes below.

"So," Valyn said warily, "no more bullshit about sitting the fight out on a piece of rock in the middle of the mountains."

Kaden shook his head.

"Good. Now what's the plan?"

Valyn had heard it once already, the outlines at least, but he hoped to Hull that a day and a night had been enough for Kaden to change his mind. That hope shattered after a glance at his brother.

"The way I told you," Kaden replied. "We split up. Tan and I go to the Ishien—"

"The Ishien," Valyn said, shaking his head. "A group of monastics even more secretive and strange than your Shin monks. A cadre of fanatics that you've never even met."

"They know about the Csestriim," Kaden replied. "They hunt the Cse-striim. It's what they do, why their order was founded. All those old stories about centuries of war, about humans fighting for their lives against armies of immortal, unfeeling warriors—most people think it's all just myth. Not the Ishien. For them, the war never ended. They are still fighting. If I'm going to survive, if we are going to *win,* I need to know what they know."

Valyn bore down on the stone, scraping it over the steel more roughly than he'd intended. He and his Wing had risked everything to come after Kaden, had thrown away their place on the Islands and their years of training both. Already they had been betrayed, captured, and almost killed, and there was a very real chance that by the time the whole thing had played out, more than one of them would be dead. That part was fine. They all understood the risks, had all accepted years earlier that they might die defending the Emperor and empire. To let Kaden wander off, however, to be *ordered* to stand aside while he threw himself into danger, was both stupid and insulting. The whole thing set Valyn's teeth on edge.

"Your monk friend doesn't seem to think too highly of the plan, and he's the one who spent some time with these bastards, right?"

Kaden blew out a long breath. "Rampuri Tan was one of the Ishien before he came to the Shin. For years."

"And then he *left*," Valyn pointed out, letting the last word hang in the air a moment. "Doesn't speak too highly of this private war of theirs."

"It's not a private war," Kaden replied. "Not anymore. Not if the Csestriim killed our father."

"All right," Valyn said. "I take the point. So let's fly there together. My Wing can watch your back while you learn what you need to learn, then we all go to Annur together."

Kaden hesitated, then shook his head. "I don't know how long I'll be with the Ishien, and I need you back in Annur as soon as possible. We don't know the first thing about what's going on in the capital."

"We know that that priest, Uinian, is locked up for Father's murder," Valyn replied.

"But what does that *mean*?"

Valyn found himself chuckling bleakly. "Well, either Uinian did it or he didn't. Maybe he's Csestriim, and maybe he's not. If he is involved, either he acted alone, or he didn't. My guess is that he had some sort of help—that would explain his ability to turn Tarik Adiv and Micijah Ut, to suborn at least a Wing of Kettral, but then again, maybe they all had a sudden upwelling of religious sentiment." He shook his head. "It's tough to see the situation clearly from atop this rock."

"That's why I need you in Annur," Kaden said. "So that when I return, I'll have some idea what I'm up against. Time is crucial here."

Valyn watched his brother. The first stars blazed in the eastern sky, but Kaden's eyes burned brighter, the only true light in the great dark of the mountains. There was something in the way he sat, in the way he moved or didn't move, something Valyn could apprehend only dimly. . . .

"That's not the only reason," Valyn said finally. "You want us in Annur, but that's not all. There's something else."

Kaden shook his head ruefully. "I'm supposed to be the one who's good at noticing things."

"What is it?" Valyn pressed.

Kaden hesitated, then shrugged. "There are gates," he said finally. "*Kenta*. I should be able to use them. It's why I was sent here in the first place, but I need to test them. I need to know."

"Gates?"

"A network of them, made by the Csestriim thousands of years ago and scattered across both continents." He hesitated. "Maybe *beyond* both continents for all I know. You step through one *kenta* and emerge from a different one hundreds of miles distant. Thousands of miles. They were a Csestriim weapon, and now they are entrusted to us, to the Malkeenians, to keep and to guard."

Valyn stared for a moment. "Slow down," he said finally, trying to make sense of the claim, to comprehend the full scope of the implications. Ancient Csestriim gates, portals spanning continents—it sounded like insanity, but then, pretty much everything since leaving the Islands had seemed insane. "Go back and tell it from the start."

Kaden remained silent a moment, gathering his thoughts, and then, as Valyn listened in disbelief, explained it all: the Blank God and the Csestriim leaches, the war against the humans and the founding of the empire, the *vaniate*—some strange trance that the Shin had somehow learned from the Csestriim, that Kaden himself had learned from the Shin—and the annihilation that threatened anyone who attempted to use the gates without achieving it. According to Kaden, Annur itself hinged on the network of *kenta,* hinged on the ability of the emperors to use them. The concept made tactical and strategic sense. The Kettral enjoyed a crushing advantage over their foes because the birds allowed them to move faster, to know more, to turn up suddenly where no one expected them to be. The gates, if they were real, would prove even more powerful. *If* they were real. If they actually worked.

"Have you seen one?" Valyn asked. "Have you seen anyone use one?"

Kaden shook his head. "But there's a *kenta* near here in the mountains, one that leads to the Ishien. I asked Tan about it earlier."

Valyn spread his hands. "Even if it's real, even if it does what the monk claims, it could kill you."

"Obliterate is more like it, but yes."

Valyn slid his sword back into its sheath, tucked the small stone into a pouch at his belt. The wind was cold, sharp, the stars like shards of ice scattered across the clear night.

"I can't let you do it," he said quietly.

Kaden nodded, as though he had expected the answer. "You can't stop me."

"Yes, I can. The whole thing is worse than foolish, and I know something about foolish." He ticked off the problems on his fingers. "Your monk is, at best, a mystery; these gates have the power to destroy entire armies; and the Ishien, given what little we know about them, sound like obsessive maniacs. It is a *bad decision,* Kaden."

"Sometimes there are no good decisions. If I'm going to thwart the Csestriim and rule Annur, I need the Ishien, and I need the gates."

"You can wait."

"While our foes consolidate their power?" Kaden turned to watch him. Valyn could hear his brother's breathing, could smell the dried blood on his skin, the damp wool of his robe, and beneath it, something else, something hard and unbending. "I appreciate you trying to keep me safe," he said quietly, laying a hand on Valyn's shoulder, "but you can't, not unless we live here in the mountains forever. Whatever path I take, there is risk. It comes with ruling. What I need from you most is not safety, but support. Tan doubts me. Pyrre challenges me. Your Wing thinks I'm an untrained, guileless recluse. I need *you* to back me."

They locked eyes. The plan was madness, but Kaden didn't sound mad. He sounded ready.

Valyn blew out a long, frustrated breath. "What happened to sitting on this rock while the Csestriim rule Annur?"

Kaden smiled. "You convinced me not to."

†

"The plan," Kaden said, facing down the group with more poise than Valyn would have expected, "is that Tan and I are going to the nearest *kenta*—he says there is one in the mountains northeast of here. We will all fly there, Tan and I will use the gate to reach the Ishien, and the rest of you will fly on to Annur. Once you're in the city, you can contact my sister,

Adare, and learn what she knows. Tan and I will meet you in the capital, at the Shin chapterhouse."

"In my experience," Pyrre drawled, "plans tend to be a little heavier on the 'hows' and the 'if, thens.' "

"Why don't we *all* just take this fucking *kenta* thing?" Gwenna demanded. Valyn's Wing had greeted Kaden's explanation of the gates first with amusement, then skepticism, then wariness, and though Valyn himself understood the response, shared it, in fact, he had promised Kaden his support.

"Gwenna . . ." he began.

"No, really!" she said, rounding on him. "If these things are real, we could save a whole lot of Hull's sweet time using them. They eat less than birds and I can't imagine they shit at all. . . ."

"The *kenta* would destroy you," Tan said, cutting through her words.

Pyrre raised an eyebrow. "How frightening. They sound like fascinating artifacts, but this is all beside the point. My contract stipulates I keep Kaden safe. Playing nursemaid for his brother might be entertaining, but it's not what I crossed half of Vash to accomplish."

Valyn ignored the jibe. "The Emperor has decided," he said. "It is ours to obey."

The words were true enough, but they did little to allay his misgivings. *Orders,* he reminded himself. *You're following orders.*

Orders hadn't been too much trouble for him back on the Islands—he had been a cadet then, and the men and women telling him what to do had earned their scars dozens of times over. Kaden, on the other hand, might be the rightful Emperor, but he was no soldier; he had none of the training, none of the instincts. Letting him get involved with the reconnaissance of Ashk'lan at an immediate, tactical level had been a mistake. Valyn's mistake. Not only had Kaden interfered with a crucial decision, he had put himself in harm's way to do so. And Adiv was alive. Valyn forced down the thought along with his mounting anger.

Kaden *was* the Emperor, and Valyn hadn't flown two thousand miles just to undermine his brother's nascent authority.

"I have told you before," Tan said, shaking his head slowly, "the Ishien are not like the Shin."

"As I recall," Kaden replied, "no one is like the Shin."

"You thought your training hard?" the older monk asked. "It was a pleasant diversion compared with what the Ishien endure. They have a different path and different methods, methods that lead to unpredictable results. It is impossible to know how they would respond to our arrival."

"You were one of them once," Kaden pointed out. "They know you."

"They knew me," Tan corrected. "I left."

"If you don't want the imperious young Emperor to go through the mysterious gate," Pyrre opined, flipping a knife in the air and catching it without opening her eyes, "then don't show him where the gate is."

Kaden turned to the Skullsworn. "Why does it matter to you what course I follow?"

She flipped the knife again. "As I've explained, I was paid to keep you safe. No one's stuck a blade in you yet, but I wouldn't call this"—she waved her knife at the surrounding peaks—"safe."

On that point, at least, she and Valyn agreed.

"I release you from your contract," Kaden said.

She chuckled. "You can't release me. I understand that you've had a very exciting promotion, but I serve a god, not an emperor, and Ananshael is quite clear about the honoring of contracts."

"And what," Valyn asked finally, unable to hold on to his silence any longer, "are the exact terms of your contract? To protect Kaden at Ashk'lan? To escort him back within the borders of Annur? Or is it a permanent thing—you have to follow him around the rest of his life, making sure no one sticks a knife in his back while he's eating braised duck or making love to his future empress? I'm not sure the Aedolians—let alone the empress—will appreciate a Skullsworn lurking around the halls."

Pyrre laughed a warm, throaty laugh. "One could be forgiven, after the recent performance of the Aedolian Guard, for thinking the new Emperor might prefer a change of personnel." She looked over at Kaden with that half smile of hers, raising an inquisitive eyebrow. When he didn't respond, she shrugged. "Sadly, I won't be fluffing his imperial feather bed or massaging his radiant buttocks. My task is to see him back to the city of Annur, to ensure that he reaches the Dawn Palace safely. After that, our time together, sweet though it has been, is finished."

Valyn studied the woman, trying to see past the careless façade, the casual bravado, past the very real fact of the 'Kent-kissing knife she kept flipping and flipping.

"Who hired you?" he asked.

She raised an eyebrow. "That would be telling."

"It's time to do some telling," Valyn said, shifting to put a little more space between himself and the Skullsworn.

She noticed the movement, caught her knife, and smiled. "Nervous?"

"Cautious," Valyn replied. "A Skullsworn shows up in the Bone Mountains, just about as far as you can get from Rassambur without hiring a ship, claiming she has come to guard an emperor when the whole world knows the Skullsworn pay no fealty to any state, kingdom, or creed but their own sick worship of death."

"Sick," she replied, a smile tugging at the corner of her mouth. "*Sick.* How uncharitable. There are priests and priestesses of Ananshael who would kill you for those words." She tapped the blade of her knife speculatively against her palm. "Are you interested in seeing how your Kettral training holds up against someone more skilled than those cumbersome Aedolians?"

Valyn measured the ground between them. The woman hadn't moved, hadn't even bothered to sit up, but a quick flick of the wrist would send that blade straight at his chest, and he didn't have any illusions about his ability to snatch daggers out of the air. She didn't smell scared. She smelled . . . amused.

"I am interested," he said, keeping his voice level, his anger in check, "in understanding why you are here. In knowing who hired a Skullsworn to guard an Annurian emperor."

She watched him carefully, almost eagerly, as though she were hoping he might reach for his blades, then shrugged and put her head back against the rock, closing her eyes.

"You haven't guessed?" she asked.

Valyn had plenty of guesses, but none of them made much sense. The Skullsworn were assassins, not saviors.

"My father," Kaden said quietly. "Sanlitun hired you."

Pyrre pointed at him without opening her eyes.

"He's not quite as hopeless as he looks, this new Emperor of yours."

Valyn glanced over at Kaden. "Why would Father send *Skullsworn*?"

"Maybe because the 'Kent-kissing Aedolian Guard turned out to be filled with traitors and idiots," Gwenna observed. "The men he sent to warn you got themselves killed, and the ones who came for Kaden came to *kill* him."

"It makes sense," Kaden said. "A strange sort of sense. He didn't know who was a part of the conspiracy, and so he tried to protect each of us in a different way. He sent his most trusted Aedolians after you, but one of them must have let the plan leak. For me, he decided to send people who weren't involved with imperial politics at all."

Valyn blew out a long, slow breath. It *did* make sense. It also spoke to Sanlitun's level of desperation. The Skullsworn, after all, had been hired in the past to murder Annurian emperors.

He shook his head. "Well, it's a good fucking thing whoever we're fighting against didn't hire their own batch of Skullsworn."

Pyrre chuckled. "They did. Who do you think killed the boatload of Aedolians dispatched to warn Valyn?"

Valyn stared. "You bastards are fighting on *both* sides of this thing?"

"Kill her," Gwenna said. "Let's just kill her and be done with it."

The assassin didn't even open her eyes at the threat. "I like meeting a young woman with a decisive cast of mind," she said. "I'd prefer not to offer you to the god just because you're feeling rash. And yes, we are, as you point out, on both sides, but only because to a worshipper of Ananshael, these *sides* don't matter. There are the living, and the dead. If a contract involves killing, and there is enough gold involved, we will take the contract, the keeping of which is an act of holy devotion. I am obliged to see Kaden to Annur, even if it means opening the throats of other priests and priestesses in the process."

"In that case," Kaden said, "my plan is the best for you, too. I get back to Annur faster, which means your work is over sooner."

Pyrre waved an admonitory finger at him. "In theory."

"The assassin is irrelevant," Tan cut in.

"The assassin takes issue with that statement," Pyrre shot back, "and she points out once again that if you don't want your precocious young leader to go through your secret gate, you could simply avoid showing him said gate."

For a moment Tan actually seemed to consider the suggestion, then shook his head. "Though his mind moves like a beast's, he is not a beast. To pen him would only delay the inevitable. He must reach these decisions on his own."

"I'm just waiting for you all to figure it out," Valyn said firmly, "but let's be really clear on one point: Kaden is the Emperor of Annur. He rules here, and if there's too much more talk about 'penning,' or 'beasts,' then either you"—he pointed at the assassin—"or you"—at Tan—"are going to end up dead in the bottom of a ravine."

"How spirited," Pyrre said, flipping her knife again, "and fraternal."

Tan ignored the warning altogether, and not for the first time Valyn found himself wondering about the monk's past. That Pyrre seemed indifferent to the presence of a Wing of Kettral made a certain sense—the Skullsworn supposedly left behind all fear of death in the process of their initiation. The monk, on the other hand, was an utter enigma. Evidently he'd destroyed a number of the freakish Csestriim creatures—*ak'hanath*, Kaden called them—in the fighting days earlier, but as Valyn never saw the things alive, he wasn't sure how difficult that would be. The monk carried his spear as though he understood how to use it, but there was no telling *where* he had learned. Perhaps among these Ishien that Kaden was so eager to visit.

"There's really only one question," Kaden said. "Will the Ishien help me?"

Tan considered the question. "Possibly."

"Then we go."

"Or they might not."

"Why? Their war is against the Csestriim, as is mine."

"But their path is not yours."

Kaden seemed about to respond, then took a deep breath, held it for a while before exhaling slowly as he gazed over the mountains. Partly, Valyn felt sorry for his brother. He himself had spent enough time trying to corral an unruly Wing that he understood the frustrations of thwarted command. Kaden had it even worse. At least Valyn's Wing, for all their difficulty, were as young and green as he was. Rampuri Tan had been Kaden's instructor, his teacher until the destruction of Ashk'lan, and wrangling the monk looked about as easy as hauling a boulder uphill. Tan appeared as indifferent to Kaden's imperial title as he did to Valyn's military rank and training. If the older monk was going to be convinced, it would be for reasons Valyn would never fathom.

"Then what do you suggest?" Kaden asked, showing impressive restraint.

"Fly me to the *kenta*," Tan replied. "I will visit the Ishien, learn what they know, while you return to the capital with your brother. We will all meet in Annur."

Kaden said nothing. He stared out over the western peaks so long that eventually even Pyrre propped up her head, squinting at him between slitted lids. Tan also remained motionless, also staring west. No one spoke, but Valyn could feel the tension between the two monks, a silent struggle of wills.

"No," Kaden said at last.

Pyrre rolled her eyes and dropped her head back against the rock. Tan said nothing.

"I will not be shepherded from place to place, kept safe while others fight my battles," Kaden said. "The Csestriim killed my father; they tried to kill me and Valyn. If I'm going to fight back, I need what the Ishien know. More, I need to meet them, to forge some sort of alliance. If they are to trust me, first they have to know me."

Tan shook his head. "Trust does not come easily to the men of the order I once served."

Kaden didn't flinch. "And to you?" he asked, raising his brows. "Do you trust me? Will you take me to the *kenta,* or do I need to leave you behind while Valyn flies me all over the Bones searching?"

The monk's jaw tightened. "I will take you," he said finally.

"All right," Valyn said, rolling to his feet. He didn't like the plan, but at least they were moving, at least they were finally doing something. All the sitting and talking was keeping them pinned down, making them easier to find, to attack. "Where are we going?"

"Assare," Tan replied.

Valyn shook his head. "Which is what . . . a mountain? A river?"

"A city."

"Never heard of it."

"It is old," Tan said. "For a long time it was dangerous."

"And now?"

"Now it is dead."

3

I t was her eyes that would get her killed.

Adare understood that well enough as she studied herself in the full-length mirror, safe behind the locked doors of her chambers inside the Crane. She had exchanged her ministerial robes for a servant's dress of rough wool, traded her silk slippers for serviceable traveling boots, discarded her silver rings and ivory bracelets, scrubbed the faint traces of kohl from her eyelids and ocher from her cheeks, scoured away the delicate perfume she had favored since her thirteenth year, all in the effort to eliminate any trace of Adare, the Malkeenian princess, the Minister of Finance, all in the hope of becoming no one, nothing.

Like killing myself, she brooded as she stared at her reflection.

And yet, there was no killing the flame in her eyes, a bright fire that shifted and burned even when she stood still. It seemed unfair that she should have to shoulder the burden of Intarra's gaze without any possibility of reaping the rewards, and yet, despite coming into the world three years prior to her brother, Adare would never sit the Unhewn Throne. It was Kaden's seat now. It didn't matter that Kaden was missing, that Kaden was ignorant of imperial politics, that Kaden knew none of the players nor any of the games; it was upon Kaden that the entire empire attended. The fire in his eyes would put him on that massive seat of stone while the flame in hers might see her murdered before the week was out.

You're being unreasonable, Adare chided herself silently. Kaden hadn't asked for his eyes any more than she had. For all she knew, the conspiracy that ended her father's life hadn't stopped there. Stranded among oblivious monks at the end of the earth, Kaden would make a pitifully easy target. By now, he, too, could be dead.

A contingent of the Aedolian Guard had departed months earlier, led by Tarik Adiv and Micijah Ut. At the time, the decision had surprised her.

"Why not send the Kettral?" she had asked Ran il Tornja. As *kenarang,* il Tornja was Annur's highest-ranking general, nominally in charge of both the Kettral and the Aedolian Guard, and as interim regent, he was responsible for finding Kaden, for seeing him returned safely to the throne. Dispatching a group of men by ship seemed a strange choice, especially for a leader who commanded an entire eyrie of massive flying hawks. "A Kettral Wing could be there and back in what . . . a week and a half?" Adare had pressed. "Flying's a lot faster than walking."

"It's also a lot more dangerous," the *kenarang* had replied. "Especially for someone who's never been on a bird."

"More dangerous than trekking through territory north of the Bend? Don't the Urghul pasture there?"

"We're sending a hundred men, Minister," he'd said, laying a hand on her shoulder, "all Aedolians, led by the First Shield and Mizran Councillor both. Better to do this thing slowly and to do it right."

It wasn't the decision Adare would have made, but no one had asked her to make the decision, and at the time, she'd had no idea that il Tornja himself had murdered her father. She, like everyone else, had pinned the death on Uinian IV, the Chief Priest of Intarra, and only months later, when she discovered the truth, did she think back to the conversation, dread curdling in her stomach like rancid oil. Maybe il Tornja hadn't sent the Kettral after Kaden because he *couldn't.* The conspiracy couldn't extend everywhere. If il Tornja wanted Kaden dead, the easiest place to do it would be in some 'Shael-forsaken mountains beyond the edge of the empire, and if the Kettral remained loyal to the Unhewn Throne, the regent would have to send someone else, a group he'd been able to deceive or suborn. That the Aedolians themselves, the order devoted to guarding the Malkeenians, might turn on her family seemed impossible, but then, so did her father's death, and he was dead. She had seen his body laid in the tomb.

The facts were stark. Il Tornja had murdered Sanlitun. He had also sent Ut and Adiv after Kaden. If they were part of the larger conspiracy, Kaden was dead, dead while Adare herself remained unmolested, unharmed, to all appearances tucked safely away in her comfortable chambers inside the Dawn Palace, protected by her irrelevance. Emperors were worth assassinating. Evidently their daughters or sisters were safe.

Only, she wasn't safe. Not really.

Her eyes strayed to the massive tome that was her father's only bequest: Yenten's cumbersome *History of the Atmani*. She had burned the message hidden inside, the terse warning in which Sanlitun fingered Ran il Tornja, Annur's greatest general, as his killer, but for some reason she had kept the book. It was suitably grim, 841 pages detailing the history of the immortal leach-lords who ruled Eridroa long before the Annurians, then went mad, tearing their empire apart like a damp map.

Is that what I'm about to do? Adare wondered.

She had considered a dozen courses of action, and discarded them all, all except one. The gambit on which she finally settled was risky, more than risky, riddled with danger and fraught with uncertainty, and for the hundredth time she considered *not* going, giving up her insane plan, keeping her mouth shut, continuing her ministerial duties, and doing her very best to forget her father's final warning. She had never set a foot outside the Dawn Palace without an entourage of Aedolians, never walked more than a mile on her own two feet, never bartered over the price of an evening meal or haggled for a room in a highway inn. And yet, to stay would mean returning to him, to il Tornja, would mean a daily miming of the love she had felt before she learned the truth.

The thought of going back to his chambers, to his bed, decided her. For a week after her horrifying discovery she had avoided him, pleading illness first, then absorption in her ministerial work. The labors of the Chief Minister of Finance, the post to which her father had appointed her in his final testament, might plausibly fill up a day or two, but she couldn't dodge il Tornja forever, not without arousing suspicion. He had already come looking for her twice, each time leaving behind a small bouquet of maidenbloom along with a note in his crisp, angular hand. He hoped her fever would soon pass. He had need of her counsel. He missed the softness of her skin beneath his fingers. *Skin like silk,* the bastard called it. A month earlier the words would have called a flush to her cheek. Now they curled her fingers into fists, fists that, with an effort, she unclenched as she watched them in the mirror. Even something as insignificant as those pale knuckles might draw attention.

For the hundredth time she slipped the narrow strip of muslin cloth from the pocket of her dress. That and a small purse of coin were the only things she could afford to take with her; anything else would be noticed when she left the palace. The rest of what she needed—pack, pilgrim's robes, food—she would have to purchase in one of the Annurian markets. Provided she could find the right stall. Provided her barter didn't give her away immediately. She coughed up a weak laugh at the absurdity of the situation: she was the Annurian Minister of Finance, hundreds of thousands of golden suns flowed through her offices every week, and yet she'd never bought so much as a plum for herself.

"No time like the present," she muttered, wrapping the muslin twice around her eyes, then tying it tight behind her head. Through the blindfold the edges of the world appeared softened, as though a heavy ocean mist had blown west off the Broken Bay, sifting between the shutters. She could see just fine, but it wasn't her *own* sight she was worried about. The purpose of the cloth was to hide the simmering fire of her eyes. She already knew it worked. She must have tried it out a dozen times already, in daylight and darkness, studying her face from every possible angle, searching for the glint that would see her dead until her eyes ached from the strain. In daylight, it worked perfectly, but at night, with the lamps snuffed, if she looked at herself straight on, she could see the faint glow of her irises. Maybe if she just . . .

With a snort of irritation she tugged the fabric free.

"You're stalling," she told herself, speaking the words out loud, using the sound to goad her into action. "You're a scared little girl and you're stalling. *This* is why the old vultures on the council think you're too weak for your post. *This,* what you're doing right now. Father would be ashamed. Now stuff the 'Shael-spawned cloth back in your pocket, leave off mugging at yourself in the mirror, and walk out the door."

Not that it was quite that easy. Beyond her outer door waited Fulton and Birch. The pair of Aedolians had watched over her each morning since she turned ten, their presence as reliable as the walls of the palace itself. She had always found them a comfort, two stones in the shifting currents of Annurian politics; now, however, she worried they might destroy her plan before she could set it in motion.

She had no reason to distrust them; in fact, she had thought long and hard about confiding in the two, about asking them to come with her when she fled. Their swords would make the long road that much safer, and the familiar faces would be dearly welcome. She *thought* she could rely on them, but then, she had relied on il Tornja, and he had killed her father. Fulton and Birch were sworn to guard her, but so were the men sent east to retrieve Kaden, and though they'd been gone for months, no one had heard anything from *him*.

Keep your own counsel, she reminded herself as she swung open the door. *Keep your own counsel and walk your own path.* At least she wouldn't get them killed if her whole plan collapsed.

The two soldiers nodded crisply as she stepped out.

"A new dress for you, Minister?" Fulton asked, narrowing his eyes at the sight of the rough wool.

"I understand wanting out of those miserable ministerial robes," Birch added with a grin, "but I thought you could have afforded something a little more stylish."

Birch was the younger of the two, a dashing portrait of military virility with his exotic blond hair and square jaw. He was pale, almost as pale as the Urghul, but Adare had seen plenty of bone-white northerners, mostly ministers and bureaucrats, come and go from the Dawn Palace. No one was likely to mistake Birch for a minister. The man was built beautifully as one of the sculptures lining the Godsway. Even his teeth were perfect, the kind of thing an artist might use as a model.

Fulton was older than his partner, and shorter, and uglier, but around the palace people whispered that he was the more deadly, and though Birch could be brash and outspoken around Adare—a familiarity earned after years dogging her footsteps—he deferred to the older man instinctively.

"I'm leaving the red walls," Adare replied, "and I don't want to be noticed."

Fulton frowned. "I wish you had informed me earlier, Minister. I would have had your full guard armored and ready."

Adare shook her head. "The two of you *are* my full guard, at least for today. I need to go to the Lowmarket, to check on the sale of gray goods for the ministry, and as I said, I don't want to be noticed."

"The Guard is trained in discretion," Fulton replied. "We won't draw undue attention."

"Half a dozen men in full armor lugging broadblades?" Adare replied, raising an eyebrow. "I never doubted your discretion, Fulton, but you blend with the good citizens of Annur about as well as a lion with housecats."

"We promise to purr," Birch added, winking.

"Allow me just a moment to send a slave to the barracks," Fulton said, as though the matter were already settled. "We will have a traveling contingent ready by the time you reach the gate. I will instruct them to wear cloaks over their plate."

"No," Adare replied. There was more stiffness in the word than she had intended, but everything hinged on this. Ditching Fulton and Birch would be difficult enough. If they managed to bring the full contingent, she'd be traveling inside a cordon of men like a fish caught in a loose net. "I understand that you're just looking out for my safety," she continued, trying to balance force with conciliation, "but I need an unvarnished view of what's happening in the Lowmarket. If the stallholders know I'm coming, all the illegal goods will disappear by the time I get there. We'll find a group of upstanding Annurian merchants hawking nothing more exciting than almonds and door fittings."

"Send someone else," Fulton countered, arms crossed. "You have an entire ministry under your command. Send a clerk. Send a scribe."

"I have sent clerks. I have sent scribes. There are some parts of the job I must do myself."

Fulton's jaw tightened. "I don't have to remind you, Minister, that the city is unsettled."

"Annur is the largest city of the largest empire in the world," Adare snapped. "It is always unsettled."

"Not like this," the Aedolian replied. "The priest who murdered your father was loved by thousands, tens of thousands. You revealed the truth about him, saw him killed, and then proceeded to force through a set of Accords that crippled his Church and his religion both."

"The people don't see it that way."

He nodded. "Many may not, but many is not all. The Sons of Flame . . ."

"Are gone, I disbanded the military order."

"Disbanded soldiers do not simply disappear," Fulton replied grimly. "They keep their knowledge, and their loyalties, and their blades."

Adare realized she had balled her hands into fists. The Aedolian had voiced her own secret hope—that the Sons of Flame were out there, and that they had kept their blades. In the stark light of day, her plan was madness. The Sons of Flame loathed her for what she had done to both their Church and their order. When Adare showed up in the southern city of Olon alone, unguarded, they were more likely to burn her than to hear her out, and yet she could see no other course.

If she was going to make a stand against il Tornja, she needed a force of her own, a well-trained military machine. Rumor out of the south suggested the Sons were regrouping. The force was there—hidden, but there. As for their loyalties . . . well, loyalties were malleable. At least she desperately hoped so. In any case, there was no point worrying the point further. She could wait in her chambers like a coddled lapdog, or she could take up the only weapon available to her and hope the blade didn't slice straight through her hand.

"I will do what needs doing," Adare said, forcing some steel into her voice. "Do you send a slave to guard my door each morning? No, you come yourself. A slave can polish your armor, but the heart of your duty can only be performed by you."

"Actually," Birch added, "he polishes his own armor, the stubborn goat."

"We're going out," Adare continued. "Just the three of us. I have every faith in your ability to keep me safe, especially given no one will know who I am. You can bring your blades and wear your armor, but put something over it, a traveling cloak, and *not* one with the Guard's 'Kent-kissing insignia emblazoned across it. I will meet you by the Low Gate at the next gong."

✝

Adare let out a long breath when she'd passed beneath the portcullis, crossed the wooden bridge spanning the moat, and slipped beyond the outer guardsmen into the turmoil beyond.

She risked a glance over her shoulder, unsure even as she turned whether she was checking for pursuit or stealing one final look at her home, at the fortress that had shielded her for more than two decades. It was difficult to appreciate the scale of the Dawn Palace from the inside: the graceful halls, low temples, and meandering gardens prevented anyone from seeing more than a sliver of the place at once. Even the central plaza, built to accommodate five thousand soldiers standing at attention, to awe even the most jaded foreign emissaries, comprised only a tiny fraction of the whole. Only from outside could one judge the palace's true scale.

Red walls, dark as blood, stretched away in both directions. Aside from the crenellations and guard towers punctuating their length, they might have been some ancient feature of the earth itself rather than the work of human hands, a sheer cliff thrust fifty feet into the air, impassable, implacable. Even unguarded, those walls would pose a serious problem to any foe, and yet, it was never the red walls that drew the eye, for inside them stood a thicket of graceful towers: the Jasmine Lance and the White, Yvonne's and the Crane, the Floating Hall, any one of them magnificent enough to house a king. In another city, a single one of those towers would have dominated the skyline, but in Annur, in the Dawn Palace, they looked like afterthoughts, curiosities, the whim of some idle architect. The eye slid right past them, past and above, scaling the impossible height of Intarra's Spear.

Even after twenty years in the Dawn Palace, Adare's mind still balked at the dimensions of the central tower. Partly it was the height. The spire reached so high it seemed to puncture the firmament, to scratch the blue from the sky. Climbing to the top of the Spear took the better part of a morning provided you started well before dawn, and in years past, some of Annur's aging emperors had been known to take days to make the trip, sleeping at way stations set up inside the structure.

The way stations were a later addition. *Everything* inside the tower—the stairs, the floors, the interior rooms—was an addition, human cleverness cobbled onto the inside of a tower older than human thought. Only the walls were original, walls cut or carved or forged from a substance clear and bright as winter ice, smooth as glass, stronger than tempered steel. From the chambers inside, you could look straight through those walls, out onto the streets and buildings of Annur and beyond, far beyond, well out over the Broken Bay and west into the Ghost Sea. People journeyed from across the empire, from beyond her borders, just to gape at this great, scintillating needle. As much as the legions or the fleet, Intarra's Spear, its presence at the very heart of the Dawn Palace, drove home the inevitability of Annurian might.

And it's all just a few hundred paces from this, Adare reflected as she turned her back on the palace.

Surrounding her, literally in the shadow of the immaculately maintained walls, hunkered a long row of wine sinks and brothels, teak shacks slapped together, their walls as much gap as wood, crooked doorways and windows hung with limp, ratty cloth. The juxtaposition was glaring, but it had its logic: the Malkeenians maintained the right to raze fifty paces beyond the moat in the event of an assault on the city. There had been no such assault in hundreds of years, but those citizens rich enough to want fine homes were cautious enough to build them elsewhere, far enough from the palace that no skittish emperor would burn them in the name of imperial security. And so, despite their proximity to the palace, the streets and alleys surrounding Adare were all squalor and noise, the scent of cheap pork grilled to burning, rancid cooking oil, shrimp paste and turmeric, and, threaded beneath it all, the salt bite of the sea.

In the past, as befit her station, Adare had always departed the palace by the Emperor's Gate, which opened westward onto the Godsway, and for a moment she simply stood, trying to get her bearings, trying to make sense of the cacophony around her. A man was approaching, she realized with a start, a hawker, the wooden bowl hung from his neck filled with some sort of blackened meat, the strips charred to their skewers. He was halfway into his pitch when Fulton stepped forward, shaking his grizzled head and grumbling something curt that Adare couldn't quite make out. The vendor hesitated, glanced at the pommel of the blade protruding through the Aedolian's cloak, then spat onto the pitted flags and moved away, already soliciting other business. Birch joined them a moment later.

"Over Graves?" he asked. "Or along the canal?"

"Graves would be safer," Fulton responded, looking pointedly at Adare. "No crowds, fewer lowlifes."

The district lay immediately to the west, rising steeply onto the hill that had once, as its name suggested, been given over entirely to funerary plots. As the city grew, however, and land became more precious, the well-to-do merchants and craftsmen who sold their goods in the Graymarket or along the Godsway had slowly colonized the area, building between the cemeteries until the entire hill was a patchwork of crypts and open land broken by rows of mansions with handsome views over the Dawn Palace and the harbor beyond.

"Graves would be longer," Adare said firmly. She had made it past the red walls, but their shadow loomed, and she wanted to be away, truly buried in the labyrinth of the city, and quickly. Unwilling to tip her hand to the Aedolians, she hadn't yet donned her blindfold, relying instead on the depth of her hood to hide her face and eyes. The meager disguise made her twitchy and impatient. "If we want to reach the Lowmarket and be back before noon, we'll need to take the canal. It's relatively straight. It's flat. I've traveled the canals before."

"Always with a full contingent of guards," Fulton pointed out. Even as they stood talking, his eyes ranged over the crowd, and his right hand never strayed far from his sword.

"The longer we stand here arguing," Adare countered, "the longer I'm outside the palace."

"And we're ducks here," Birch added, his earlier playfulness gone. "It's your call, Fulton, but I'd rather be moving than standing."

The older Aedolian growled something incomprehensible, stared long and hard at the canal snaking away to the west, then nodded gruffly. "Let's get across the bridge," he said. "Less traffic on the southern bank." He fell in on her left as they crossed the stone span, while Birch walked a few paces to the right, taking up a position between Adare and the waterway when they reached the far side.

The canal, like two dozen others coiling through the city, was as much a thoroughfare as the actual streets. Vessels crowded the channel, tiny coracles, barges, and slender snake boats, most loaded with wicker baskets or open barrels, most selling to the people on the shore, taking coin in long-handled baskets, and returning goods—fruit or fish, *ta* or flowers— with the same. People crowded both banks, leaning out over the low stone balustrades, shouting their orders to the boatmen. Every so often, something would drop into the water, and the half-naked urchins shivering on the bank would leap in, fighting viciously with one another in their eagerness to retrieve the sinking goods.

Without a score of palace guardsmen to clear a path, the walk took longer than Adare remembered. Though she stood taller than most women, almost as tall as Birch, she lacked the bulk necessary to force her way through the press of bodies. Fulton seemed to grow more tense, more wary, with every step, and Adare was starting to feel nervous herself, the relief of having slipped the noose of the red walls replaced by the constant pressure of sweating bodies all around her, the jostling and shouting, the hammering of a thousand voices.

By the time they broke into the relative tranquillity of the broad plaza facing the Basin, Adare could feel sweat slicking her back. Her breath was all bound up inside her chest and she let it out in a long, uneven sigh. Compared to the lanes fronting the canal, the plaza was wide and relatively empty, a huge sweep of stone flags dotted with knots of men and women. She could see more than two feet in front of her. She could move, breathe. How she would have managed the walk without Fulton and Birch she had no idea.

Well, you'd better figure it out soon, she told herself. *You can't take them with you.*

She glanced out over the Basin, the wide semi-lake where the Atmani Canal ended after hundreds of miles, ramifying into half a dozen smaller conduits that would carry water and boats to the various quarters of the city. Scores of narrow long-keels swung at anchor, divesting their cargo onto smaller rafts or bobbing barrel-boats, then topping up on stores for the return trip south toward Olon and Lake Baku.

For a moment Adare paused, eyeing those craft. Her journey would be so much simpler if she could just choose one, step aboard, pay a captain for food and a luxury cabin, then spend the trip south rehearsing her meeting with the secretly reunited Sons of Flame and their shadowy leader, Vestan Ameredad. In many ways, the boat would be safer than taking her chances walking the long road—no prying eyes, no brigands, almost no human interaction. The prospect was so alluring. . . . Alluring and utterly stupid.

Even at a distance, Adare could make out tax inspectors in their stiff uniforms, members of her own ministry, moving up and down the quays, looking over the off-loaded barrels and bales. She stood far enough off that there was no chance of discovery, but she shrank back into her hood all the same. Within a day Ran would discover that his tame pet had gone missing, and when he came after her, he would expect her to think like a pampered princess. By the next morning, the *kenarang*'s minions would be crawling through all the most expensive inns and guesthouses in the city. They would be interrogating ship captains down in the harbor, and they would be all over the Basin asking questions about a young woman with coin in her pocket and hidden eyes.

Adare's shoulders tightened at the thought of pursuit, hundreds of il Tornja's men scouring the city for her, and she almost yelped when Fulton stepped closer, taking her firmly by the elbow.

"Don't look over your shoulder, Minister," he said, voice low. "We are being followed." He glanced at his companion. "Birch, take second point, eyes on the northeast quadrant."

Adare started to turn, but Fulton jerked her forward ungently.

"Don't. Look," he hissed.

Tiny barbs of fear pricked Adare's skin. "Are you sure?" she asked. "Who is it?"

"Yes, and I don't know. Two tall men. They just stepped into a *ta* shop."

Instead of glancing back, Adare stared at the crowd moving and shifting around her. She had no idea how Fulton had picked two faces out of the chaos. There must have been thousands of people in the wide plaza— porters, bare-chested and bent nearly double beneath their loads; knots of garrulous women in bright silk, down from the Graves to pick over the newest goods before they reached market; beggars prostrated beside the fountains; wagon-drivers in broad straw hats prodding indifferent water buffalo through the press. Half an Annurian legion could have been following her through the crowd and Adare might not have noticed.

"There were hundreds of people moving west along the canal," Adare whispered. "This is the busiest hour for the Basin. It doesn't mean they're all stalking us."

"With due respect, Minister," Fulton replied, herding her surreptitiously to the south, toward one of the smaller streets leading out of the broad square, "you have your business and I have mine."

"Where are we going?" Adare demanded, risking a glance over her shoulder despite the Aedolian's orders. Birch had taken a dozen steps back, his boyish face serious as he scanned the storefronts. "We're headed south, not west."

"We're not going to the Lowmarket anymore. It's not safe."

Adare took a deep breath. Her entire plan hinged on going west, on getting through the broad plaza, then over the large bridge spanning the Atmani Canal. The fact that someone might have seen her leaving the Dawn Palace, that men might even now be tracking her through the city streets, only increased her urgency.

"Well, if someone *is* following, we have to go on," she said. "We can lose them in the Lowmarket."

Fulton glared at her.

"The Lowmarket is an assassin's dream—constant crowds, miserable sight lines, and enough noise that you can't hear yourself talk. I didn't want you traveling there in the first place, and you're certainly not going now. You can have me removed from my post when we return to the palace. Have me stripped of my steel, if you want, but until we return, until you do, it is my charge to guard you, and I intend to keep that charge." His grip tightened on her elbow. "Keep moving. Don't run."

He glanced over his shoulder toward Birch, who flicked a series of hand signs, too quick for Adare to follow. The younger Aedolian looked grim and Fulton nodded curtly as he shepherded her toward the nearest street.

"Where are we going?" Adare hissed again. A return to the Dawn Palace was impossible. Il Tornja would hear of her departure and the strange conditions surrounding it. He would learn that she had been disguised, that she had insisted on a minimal guard, and he would want answers she was ill prepared to give. Even if, through some miracle, Adare was able to keep the abortive journey a secret, the Aedolians would never allow her outside the red walls without a full escort again. "Where are you taking me?" she demanded, vaguely aware of panic fringing her voice.

"Safety," Fulton replied. "A storefront nearby."

"We'll be *trapped* in a 'Kent-kissing storefront."

"Not this one. We own it. Run it. Called a rabbit hole—for situations like this."

From out of the press, a vendor stepped toward them. He was a fat, genial man smiling a crack-toothed smile as he reached into the bulging cloth bag at his side.

"Firefruit, lady? Fresh from the Si'ite orchards and juicy as a kiss. . . ."

Before he could proffer the fruit in question, Fulton stepped forward. The Aedolian hadn't drawn his blade, but he didn't need to. His fist smashed into the vendor's soft throat, and the man crumpled.

Adare pulled back, aghast.

"He was just trying to *sell* me something," she protested.

The fruit seller rolled onto his side, a broken gargle escaping from his windpipe. Pain and panic filled his eyes as he tried to drag himself away on his elbows. The Aedolian didn't spare him a glance.

"I didn't swear an oath to guard *his* life. We are undermanned and far from the red walls. Keep moving."

Behind them, Birch flicked more signals with one hand, the other ready on his sword. Adare felt her breath thicken inside her chest, her stomach churn. In a city of a million souls, she was trapped. Fulton's firm hand on her elbow had seen to that. Once they left the plaza, there would be no way forward or back, nowhere to run. The Aedolians were only trying to keep her safe, but . . .

She stared at Fulton, at his grizzled face. What if they *weren't* trying to keep her safe? Away from familiar eyes, the Aedolians could drag her into any old alley and finish the job. She pulled up short. *They tried to keep you* inside *the palace,* a voice in her head reminded her, but her ears were ringing and Birch was shouting something, quickening his pace to a trot as he waved them forward.

It has to be now, she realized. Whether the Aedolians were innocent or not, whether someone was really following them or not, return meant discovery, and discovery meant failure.

My father is dead, she reminded herself, *and I am his last blade.* Then, all in a burst, she yanked free.

Surprise twisted Fulton's features. "Minister . . ." he began, but before he could finish, Adare turned and darted west, deeper into the plaza, toward the canal that emptied into the Basin. She needed to get over the bridge spanning that canal, then to the narrow watercourse draining away to the west. *Just a few hundred paces,* she thought, feet pounding on the wide stones. Just a few hundred paces and she'd be safe.

"Birch!" the Aedolian bellowed. The younger guardsman spun around, stretching out an arm to stop her, but he was too slow, baffled into momentary hesitation by her unexpected flight.

Adare ducked to the left, felt the fabric of the dress twist between her legs, and for a moment she was falling, careening toward the broad paving stones. She caught herself with an outstretched hand, pain tearing up her thumb and into her wrist, stumbled a few steps, heard Birch cursing behind her, and then she was running again, the treacherous dress hiked up above her knees.

Men and women paused to stare as she raced by, faces looming up one after the next, a series of still portraits: a startled child with wide brown eyes; a canal hand holding a long hook, half his face maimed by a vicious scar; a blond Edishman with a beard braided halfway down his chest. Her hood had fallen back revealing her face, revealing her eyes. People began to point, to exclaim. A few children even ran behind her hollering "princess" and "Malkeenian."

She risked a glance over her shoulder—whether for the Aedolians or her more mysterious pursuit, she wasn't sure. Fulton and Birch were charging after her, but they were a dozen paces back, and, with a flash of surprise, she realized that her plan, though battered, was actually working. The men were stronger than her by far, stronger and faster, but they wore a quarter of their weight in steel beneath those traveling cloaks. Adare had only her coin purse and the blindfold secreted beneath her robe.

Just a little farther, she told herself. *A little farther and it won't matter who saw.*

She wasn't sure how long she'd been running, but suddenly she was almost there, almost to the narrow spillover people called the Chute. The Chute wasn't a proper canal. Unlike the half-dozen waterways that spread out from the Basin to the north, east, and west, all wide enough to permit the narrow canal vessels for which they had been dug, the side channel was barely six paces across, a miniature waterfall constructed to drain off the excess power of the canal's current so that the other channels snaking through the city might flow more placidly.

On other visits to the Basin and the Lowmarket, Adare had seen grinning, naked children riding the Chute. They would leap in from the bridge above, then let the frothing current carry them away west, out of sight between buildings cantilevered out over the water. It had looked easy, fun. As she hoisted herself onto the wide, low balustrade, however, she froze, staring in dismay at the water below. She had remembered a short drop, maybe a few paces, into a swift, refreshing current. Her memory, evidently, had failed her.

Something had transformed the Chute from a giddy little overflow suitable for childish games into a churning, roiling current thrashing over and into itself, tossing foam a dozen feet into the air. Adare clung more tightly to the rail. There were no children in sight.

Autumn, she realized, her legs trembling from the frantic run and this new shock. She had seen the children swimming the Chute in early autumn, when the canals and the Basin itself sat at their lowest level. Now, though, it was the tail end of spring, and the current chewed ferociously at its banks like some hunger-maddened beast trying to break its bonds. Adare had learned to swim in the Emerald Pool back in the Dawn Palace. As a child, she had even prevailed upon her Aedolians to let her paddle around in the harbor on calm days. This, though—she wasn't even sure she *could* swim in that furious current, certainly not in her exhausted state, not with the weight of the wool dress pulling her down. She started to climb back from the rail. She could keep running, outdistance her pursuit on foot, lose them in the alleys and side streets of Annur, hide out somewhere. . . .

A shout from the base of the bridge froze her in place.

Fulton and Birch had already reached the span, the younger Aedolian one pace in front of his companion, both of them bellowing something incomprehensible. Both were red-faced and sweating, but both looked ready to run another mile. She wouldn't escape them on foot. She couldn't. It was the Chute or nothing. Adare stared as they approached, paralyzed by her fear, her indecision.

Do something, she snarled at herself, glancing once more at the raging current below. *Do something!*

And then, with a cry that was half sob, half defiance, she was over, tumbling uncontrollably toward the thundering current.

4

W ell, that's not on the 'Kent-kissing maps," Gwenna shouted from her perch on the Kettral's other talon, pitching her voice to carry above the wind's fury.

Valyn settled for a nod in response, not trusting himself to open his mouth without losing his tongue to his chattering teeth. Back in the Qirins it would be good swimming weather already, but late spring in the Bone Mountains would be called winter anywhere else, especially when you were flying three thousand paces up. Even Valyn's heaviest blacks did little to blunt the biting wind.

He squinted through frozen lashes, trying to make better sense of the valley beneath them, a gouge running east to west, so deep and narrow he could only see the bottom when they passed directly overhead. They'd been quartering this section of the peaks for the better part of the afternoon, searching the desolate gray stone and ice for some sign of Rampuri Tan's lost city. The monk had given Valyn a rough idea where to look, but the details were hazy.

"I have been there only twice," Tan told him earlier, his tone suggesting Valyn was a fool for pursuing the issue, "and I never approached from the air."

Which meant a long and very cold grid search. The Kettral had the most accurate maps in the world—coastlines and rivers were easy to chart from atop a soaring bird—but no one had bothered to explore deep into the Bone Mountains. The granite spires and high, snowbound valleys were too rugged and remote to be of any military interest: no one was taking an army through the Bones, and, aside from a few rough mining villages far to the south, no one was living there either.

Valyn would have said that large-scale habitation was impossible this far north, but he could just make out, carved into the sheer granite wall of the deep valley directly below, a series of rectangular holes and open ledges. The stonework was so ancient, so roughened by wind and weather, that it took him a moment to realize he was looking at stairs and chimneys, windows and balconies, all honeycombing the vertical side of the cliff. Assare, the dead city promised by Rampuri Tan.

About time, Valyn thought, clenching his jaw against the cold. He reached over to tap Kaden on the arm, then pointed.

Kaden took a firm hold on the overhead strap, then leaned out a little farther from the talon to get a better look. Despite his lack of training, he was handling these early kettral flights with surprising composure. Valyn himself had been terrified of the birds when he first arrived on the Islands, but Kaden, after asking a few straightforward questions about how best to mount, dismount, and position himself during flight, had endured the trip with no apparent anxiety, relaxing into the harness and watching the peaks with those impassive blazing eyes. When the bird completed a quarter pass over the valley, he turned back to Valyn and nodded.

Things had gone less smoothly over on the bird's opposite talon; Gwenna, irritated to be sharing a perch with Triste, spent half the flight prodding and repositioning the girl, frightening her while failing to make her either safer or more comfortable. It wasn't Triste's fault she didn't know the first thing about the riding of massive birds.

That she'd managed to stay alive, even to help when everything went into the shitter, said something about her resolve, her tenacity, but there were limits. The girl wasn't Kettral; she was a priestess of the Goddess of Pleasure, and a childhood in Ciena's temple learning about lutes, dancing, and fine wine had done little to prepare her for the rigors of Kettral travel.

Of course, Valyn reminded himself, *I'd look just as uncomfortable if someone demanded that I play the lute.* They each had their weaknesses. The difference was, you didn't die if you screwed up a passage on the lute.

After a while, Gwenna gave up her half-assed attempts to help, abandoning Triste to swing in the cold wind. Valyn looked over, watching the girl huddle into herself, dangling miserably in her harness. She'd exchanged her shredded gown for the too-large uniform of one of the dead Aedolians, and though it hung on her like laundry flapping on a line, the ludicrous clothing did nothing to obscure her raven-dark hair or violet eyes. Next to Triste, the other women in the group looked dull, drab. Not that Gwenna was likely to give a shit about that. Clearly it was the girl's incompetence she considered unforgivable.

And Valyn didn't even want to think about what was happening over on the other bird. They were lucky to have the second kettral, the one left behind when they'd killed Sami Yurl's traitorous Wing—Suant'ra couldn't have hauled the whole group on her own—but adding another bird forced Talal into a flier's role, leaving Rampuri Tan and Pyrre to Annick's dubious tutelage down below. At least Gwenna had bothered to berate Triste about her flying posture; as far as Valyn could make out, the sniper had neglected her charges entirely, her hard eyes fixed on the terrain below, bow half drawn, despite the frigid wind. Fortunately, both Rampuri Tan and Pyrre seemed to have found the knack of hanging in the harness while holding on to the straps above. They hadn't plummeted to their deaths, at least, which was something.

We'll be down soon, Valyn reminded himself, squinting at the ground below, trying to figure out the best spot for the drop.

It was clear why this valley, unlike the others, had been able to support human settlement: it was deeper, much deeper. Instead of the rough, V-shaped defiles that gouged the peaks all around, here the sheer granite walls fell away thousands upon thousands of feet, shadowing and sheltering a climate in the gorge below that was green rather than brown and gray, with real trees instead of the isolated and stunted trunks dotting the rest of the mountains. As they dipped below the upper rim, Valyn could feel the warmer, moister air. At the head of the valley, where the glaciers melted, a slender filament of waterfall tumbled over the lip, half hidden behind a veil of spray, shimmering, roiling, and reflecting the light, then splashing into a lake that drained out in a lazy river along the valley floor. Grass flanked the river; not the bunchy, ragged clumps he'd seen in the higher peaks, but real grass, green and even, if not particularly lush.

It was the city itself, however, the drew Valyn's eye, if *city* was even the right word. Valyn had never seen anything to compare to it. Stairs chipped from the stone face zigzagged from ledge to ledge, and while some of those ledges looked natural, as though huge shards of stone had simply peeled away, others were too regular, too neat, evidently chiseled out over years or decades. Ranks of rough, rectangular holes pierced the wall— windows into interior chambers. Other, smaller apertures might have served as chimneys or sockets for some lattice of wooden scaffolding long rotted away. It was difficult to gauge the scale, but the highest windows opened out at least a hundred paces above the valley floor, far higher than the tips of the blackpines below. It was a staggering accomplishment. Valyn tried to guess how long such a place would take to build, how many men and women had labored for how many years to hack their mountain home from the rock, but he was a soldier, not an engineer. Decades maybe. Centuries.

It was a beautiful spot. More importantly, you could defend it. The only approach into the gorge was from the east, up the horridly steep broken valley. Fifty men could hold the canyon mouth against an army with little need to do anything more than shove boulders down the scree. The flat land at the base of the cliffs offered plenty of space on which to graze animals and grow crops, and if an army somehow managed to force its way into the gorge, the city itself, adequately provisioned, looked capable of withstanding an indefinite siege. It was a good spot, a safe spot.

So why is it dead?

Rampuri Tan hadn't told them shit about the place, which was probably a good thing, since Valyn was having trouble believing the little he'd already heard. Evidently, the *kenta* was down there, somewhere. Evidently Kaden and Tan could use it to travel halfway around the world in a single step. The whole thing sounded ludicrous, but after eight years training with leaches, after seeing what Talal and Balendin could do with their strange powers, after Valyn's own experience in Hull's Hole, he was less ready to dismiss Kaden's story of the gates out of hand. Still, it would have helped to know what the 'Kent-kissing things *looked* like.

Valyn had hoped he might get a description of what they were searching for—dimensions, features—but Kaden didn't seem to know much more about the gates than the Csestriim bit, and all the monk would say was, "You find the city, and I will take us to the *kenta*."

"Well, here's the city," Valyn muttered, flexing his freezing sword hand to regain some motion while checking over his straps. He flicked a little hand sign at Gwenna: *aided dismount, short perimeter check.* She nodded impatiently, already loosening Triste's buckles for the drop. Valyn signaled to Laith with a few tugs on the straps, and the flier banked Suant'ra slightly to bring her down right at the base of the cliff, a few dozen paces from the stairs and windows.

This place had better *be dead,* Valyn thought, as the cracked stone loomed up beneath him.

The drops went better than he could have hoped. Both monks followed instructions perfectly, as though they'd spent days memorizing them; Triste was almost light enough to catch; and Pyrre, who looked like she was going to bust her head open, tucked into the fall at the last minute and rolled to her feet chuckling. Annick and Gwenna didn't wait for the others to regain their balance before darting off, blades out, to check the perimeter, one outward into the high grass, the other, after lighting a storm lantern, into the gaping mouth of the city itself.

"As I often say after a night of drinking," Pyrre remarked, glancing over to where Laith and Talal had landed the birds, "I would have enjoyed that more if we had done less of it."

"Long flights take a while to get used to," Valyn replied, careful to hide the fact that he, too, felt stiff and sore from hanging in the harness, wind-chapped and cold right down in his marrow. The assassin claimed to be on their side, but so far, the people who were supposed to be on their side had proven astoundingly eager to kill them, and Valyn had no desire to reveal more to the woman than he had to. He turned instead to Rampuri Tan.

"Tell me this is the place."

The monk nodded. "It is farther north than I realized."

"And this place is what, exactly?" Pyrre asked, tilting her head back to gaze up the looming cliff. "A part of Anthera?"

"I don't think it's part of anything," Kaden replied, turning slowly to take in the crumbling carved façade. "Not anymore."

Although there was at least an hour of daylight remaining in the high peaks, deep in the valley night was gathering already, and Valyn stared into the growing gloom, trying to fix the surrounding terrain in his mind: the waterfall, the small lake, the narrow river draining out to the east. Eons of rockfall had piled up in places along the cliff base, but a little farther out, stands of blackpine grew densely enough that he couldn't see more than a hundred paces in any direction.

He turned his attention back to the carved rock. A single entrance like a toothless mouth—the one through which Gwenna had disappeared—provided the only access at ground level, though a row of narrow slits glowered down on them from twenty or thirty feet above: arrow loops, scores of them. Rough carvings flanked the doorway, human shapes so eroded by wind and rain that Valyn could make out little more than the position of the bodies. Perhaps they had been triumphant once, but erosion had so twisted the forms that now they appeared frozen in postures of defeat or death. The remnants of rusted pintles protruded from the stone, but the hinges they once held were gone, as were the doors themselves, presumably rotted away. Whatever the place was, it had clearly been abandoned for a very long time.

Laith was going over Suant'ra, checking her pinions for damage, then the leading edges of her wings. Yurl's kettral waited a dozen paces off, feathers ruffled against the coming night, watching them all with one black, inscrutable eye. The birds would fly for anyone with the proper training, and in theory she wouldn't know or care that Valyn and his soldiers had been the ones to destroy Sami Yurl's Wing. That was the fucking theory, at least. Valyn hoped to Hull it was right.

"A night's rest will do them good, too," Laith said, combing through 'Ra's tailfeathers with his fingers.

Valyn shook his head. "They're not getting a rest."

The flier turned. "Excuse me?"

"You have the call-and-command whistles for Yurl's bird?" Valyn asked.

"Of course. She wouldn't be much good without them."

"I want them both in the air," Valyn said. "Circling. Yurl's bird can stay low, just above the trees, but I want 'Ra high. If we need to get out quick, we'll call them."

Laith shook his head. "She's tired, Val. They *both* are."

"So are we."

"And we're going to get some *sleep* tonight. Even with the thermals in this canyon, it'll be a strain to fly in circles half the night. The birds aren't any use to us if they're half dead."

"They're even less use to us completely dead," Valyn said. "We have to assume someone is following us. Hunting us. Another Kettral Wing, maybe two."

"*Why* do we have to assume that?"

Valyn stared. "We went rogue. We disobeyed a direct order when we left the Islands. We slaughtered another Kettral Wing. . . ."

"They tried to murder the Emperor," Talal pointed out quietly as he approached the group.

"No one knows that but *us*," Valyn said. "As far as the Eyrie is concerned, we're traitors."

"Unless *they're* the traitors," Laith said grudgingly. "Daveen Shaleel or the Flea or whoever. In which case we're just as screwed."

Valyn blew out a slow breath. "I don't think the Flea's part of it."

"You just said you think the bastard is *hunting* us."

"I do," Valyn said, "but I don't think he's part of the plot." He paused, trying to make sure he wasn't missing anything. "Think it through with me. Yurl and Balendin were bad, they were part of the conspiracy, and Shaleel sent them north."

"Ah," Talal said, nodding.

"Ah, what?" Laith demanded, looking from Valyn to the leach and back. "Someone spell it out for the idiot over here."

"If you were trying to murder the Emperor," Valyn said, "and you could send Yurl or the Flea, who would you send?"

"Ah," Laith said. "If the veteran wings were part of the plot, Shaleel would have sent them." He brightened. "Good news! Whoever's hunting us is on our side."

"But they don't know that," Valyn pointed out, "and they might fill us full of arrows before we can inform them."

"Bad news," Laith said, spreading his hands. "The ups and downs are killing me. Still, if it's all true, if we really are being stalked by the Kettral, that's all the more reason to have the birds rested. Listen to me, Valyn. I know kettral. There are only two better fliers than me back on the Islands: Quick Jak and Chi Hoai Mi. Jak failed the Trial and, if you're right, Chi Hoai's hunting us, so I'm the best you've got and I'm telling you to rest them."

Valyn frowned into the darkness, trying to imagine he were the Flea. The thought was ludicrous, but he kept at it. "This isn't a flying question, Laith, it's a tactics question. If I were them, I'd want to take out our birds first. Ground us. Without wings, we'd be at their mercy. I'm not letting that happen."

Laith spread his arms wide. "Have you *seen* the mountains we've been flying over? The whole fucking Eyrie could be here flying search grids and odds are no one would find us."

"I'm not concerned about the whole Eyrie," Valyn replied, keeping his voice level, "I'm concerned about the Flea. He and his Wing have a reputation, in case you weren't paying attention back on the Islands, for making a total hash of the odds. Put the birds in the air. One high, one low."

Laith locked eyes with him, then threw up his hands. "You're one worried son of a bitch, Valyn hui'Malkeenian."

"It's your job to fly," Valyn replied. "It's my job to worry."

The flier snorted. "Here," he said, tossing something overhand to

Valyn. "If you're going to worry, you may as well have one of the whistles. Yurl's Wing had two."

It took Laith a few more minutes to finish checking over the kettral. By the time he'd sent them into the air once more—silent black shapes slicing across the stars—Annick had returned, jogging out from behind a few pines with an arrow nocked to the string of her bow.

"Any company?" Valyn asked.

She shook her head. "No light, no smoke, no refuse or visible waste."

"It's not exactly thriving," he agreed, glancing around once more.

"As I told you," Tan interjected, "it is dead."

"I'll fucking say," Gwenna added, stepping out of the doorway, lantern held in one hand, a bared short blade in the other.

"Anything inside?" Valyn asked, ignoring the monk. It was all well and good for Rampuri Tan to have his opinions, but Valyn's carelessness had nearly cost him and his Wing their lives already. He had no intention of spending any time in a strange city, dead or not, without running through his own protocols.

Gwenna shrugged. "Stuff that doesn't rot: knives, pots, bracelets. Oh, and bones. A whole shitload of bones."

"Where?"

"Everywhere. It's like every poor bastard in the place was slaughtered as they sat down to breakfast."

Valyn frowned and turned back to the monk. "All right, so we can see for ourselves it's empty. Where are we? What killed the people who lived here?"

"This is Assare," Tan replied. "The first human city."

Gwenna let out a bark that might have been laughter. Valyn started to ask Tan how he knew all this, why the place didn't appear on any imperial maps, but night was nearly upon them, and they hadn't moved to any reliable cover. Gwenna and Annick were good scouts, but Valyn wanted the group holed up in a full defensive position before the darkness thickened further. He could see and move well enough in full darkness—in fact, it gave him a distinct advantage—but the other members of his Wing hadn't reaped quite the same benefit from their own time in Hull's Hole, and the rest of the party, the ones who weren't Kettral, would be essentially blind.

"Fine. We can talk about it later. Right now," he pointed to the cliff face, "we're going inside and up, someplace in front, with windows; I want to be able to keep eyes on the valley."

Laith raised an eyebrow, then jerked a thumb at Tan. "This guy says the city's older than dirt and you want to set up camp in a crumbling cliff? What about something less likely to fall on our heads?"

"I want the high ground," Valyn replied.

"For what? Hunting rats?"

Valyn bit back a sharp retort. "Yes, for hunting rats. It's a cliff, Laith. Cliffs don't just fall over."

The flier gestured to the scree scattered across the valley floor, some boulders the size of small houses.

"The cliff is sound," Tan said. "And the *kenta* is inside." As if that settled the whole matter.

"That's what we came for," Valyn said. "Now *move*. Light's wasting and we're standing out here like geese."

The Kettral set out at a light jog, while Pyrre and the monks fell in a few steps behind. Valyn had crossed half the distance before he realized that Triste wasn't following. She still stood in the broad, grassy clearing, staring around, eyes wide as lanterns in the crepuscular light, the too-large clothes clutched tight about her in one hand.

"Triste," Valyn called. "Let's go."

She seemed not to have heard him, and he turned back, cursing beneath his breath. It was bad enough when his own Wing questioned his decisions—at least they were capable fighters and good tactical thinkers—but if he had to play wet nurse to this girl all the way back to Annur . . . The thought evaporated as she turned to face him, face baffled, as though lost in the slow depths of dream.

"Triste," he said, studying her. "*Triste.*"

Finally she focused on him. Tears welled in her eyes, catching the gold of the fading light.

"Are you all right?" Valyn asked, putting a hand on her elbow.

She nodded, trembling. "Yes. I just . . . I don't know. It's such a *sad* place."

"You're cold. Tired. Let's get inside."

She hesitated, then turned toward the ancient city, allowing herself to be led.

†

From the outside, the cliff had appeared solid; the simple façade was chipped and worn, whatever once shuttered the windows long gone to dust, but the angles of the doorframe looked true, the crucial verticals more or less plumb. As they stepped beneath the engraved lintel, however, Valyn could see that here, too, time and decay had worked their quiet violence. Though the city's bones were bedrock, the chiseling and carving of the builders had allowed in both the wind and the water. Small rivulets spilled over the rock, draining from some impossible height. The water ran cold and clear now, but in the winter it would freeze, and centuries of ice had shattered whole sections of stone, prizing them from the walls and ceiling. A rock the size of a horse blocked part of the passage, while smaller chunks made the footing treacherous.

Valyn pushed deeper into the cave, the smell of damp stone and lichen filling his nostrils. After twenty claustrophobic paces guarded by arrow loops and murder holes, the corridor opened out into a high, wide space— half natural cavern, half carved—evidently an entrance hall of sorts. Recessed sconces for torches grooved the walls, and a wide basin, cracked but graceful, sat in the center. It must have been welcoming once, if not exactly grand, but now it felt empty, cold, and too large to easily defend.

Doorways radiated outward, black rectangles in the lesser gloom, while wide stone stairs rose along the walls on each side. One route looked as likely as the other, and Valyn turned to Tan.

"Which way?"

No one replied.

"You all might enjoy sightseeing," Valyn went on after a moment, glancing over at the others, "but there are a dozen doors off this hall, and we don't have the people to guard them or the tools to seal them up. So, if you're done admiring the architecture . . ."

"Valyn," Kaden said finally. "Do you have some sort of light? I can barely see my hand in front of my face in here."

Valyn almost snapped something impatient about getting up higher before they started worrying about lights, then realized that his brother wasn't exaggerating. To Valyn's eyes the room was dim, shadowy, but perfectly navigable. The others, however, were staring as though lost in utter darkness. *The slarn,* he realized, a chill passing through him as he thought back to the egg's foul pitch thick in his throat.

"Sure," he said, shoving aside the memory, sliding his tactical lantern from his pack, kindling it, then holding it aloft. The chamber looked even worse in the flickering light. Plaster had crumbled from the walls and ceiling, littering the ground and exposing the rough faces of the stone beneath. A few paces away, a section of floor had collapsed, yawning into the darkness of a cellar beneath. Evidently the builders had dug down as well as burrowing up, and the discovery that he stood atop a warren of rotten rock, the whole thing undermined with tunnels, did nothing to improve Valyn's mood.

It's held together for thousands of years, he told himself. *It'll last another night.*

"There," Tan said, pointing to the stairs on the left.

Valyn glanced at the monk, nodded, slipped one of his short blades from its sheath, and started up.

The stairs climbed gracefully around the perimeter of the entrance hall, and then, as they neared the ceiling, turned away from the room into a high, narrow passage. Valyn slid to the side to let Tan lead, counting the floors as they passed, trying to keep track of which way was *out*. The place reminded him uncomfortably of Hull's Hole, and though he didn't mind the darkness, all the winding back and forth, the rooms opening off to the sides, the branching of the corridors, played tricks with his mind. After a while he lost any sense of which doors led outward and which plunged deeper into the earth. When they reached an open chamber from which new passageways branched in all directions, he paused.

"I hope you know where you're going, monk," he said.

Kaden pointed. "Out is that way."

"How do you know?"

His brother shrugged. "Old monk trick."

"Tricks make me nervous," Valyn replied, but Tan had already started down the corridor.

"He is right," the man said over his shoulder. "And we are close to the *kenta.*"

As it turned out, the trick worked. After forty paces or so, they emerged from the tunnel onto a huge ledge. Fifty paces above them the cliff wall swept up and out in a smooth wave, a towering natural roof that would keep off the worst of the weather while allowing light and air to fill the space. After the cramped darkness inside the cliff, even the watery moonlight seemed bright, too bright. Valyn crossed to the lip, where the remains of a low wall protected against a fall of sixty or seventy paces. They had climbed above the blackpines, high enough to see out over the entire valley. Valyn watched the moonlight flicker like bright silver coins on the surface of the river below. A gust of wind snatched at him, but he didn't step back.

"There were benches," Talal said. The leach had broken off from the group to check the darker corners. "And fountains pouring straight out of the cliff. The masonry is mostly worn away, but the water still flows."

"They carved channels," Triste pointed out, "and a pool."

"Someone had a nice place here," Laith said, gesturing to a large building that stood at the far end of the ledge.

Unlike the tunnels and rooms through which they had climbed, the structure was built rather than carved, a man-made fortress right on the cliff's edge. *No,* Valyn realized, examining the tall windows, the wide, empty door, *not a fortress. More like a palace.* The building filled half the ledge, stretching up four or five stories to where the roof almost touched the sweeping expanse of granite above.

"Huge house," the flier added, "and a private garden halfway up the cliff."

"Where's the *kenta*?" Valyn asked, turning in a slow circle, uncertain what he was looking for.

"Inside," Tan said.

Valyn nodded. "Suits me. Let's get inside."

"I thought you wanted a view," the flier grumbled.

"I want to look," Valyn said, "not get looked at. The palace has windows. The *kenta* is there. We set up shop in there."

Even dilapidated, even crumbling, the inside of the structure lived up to the promise of its setting. Unlike the hoarded warren of low halls and tunnels below, the palace was high-ceilinged, the gracious windows admitting pools of moonlight along with the cool night air. It wasn't built for fortification, but then, there wasn't much need for fortification when you were seventy paces up a sheer cliff.

"Up," Tan said, gesturing to the wide central staircase with its crumbling balustrade.

"I thought we *were* up," Laith griped. "There's such a thing as *too* much elevation, you know."

"And this from the Wing's flier," Gwenna said.

"What do you suppose this was?" Kaden asked, running a hand along the stone.

Valyn shrugged. "King's palace. Temple, maybe. Guild hall, if merchants ran the city."

To his surprise, Triste shook her head. "An orphanage," she said quietly, so quietly he wasn't sure he'd heard correctly.

"An orphanage?" Pyrre asked. Ever since landing, the assassin had seemed curious rather than concerned, but her hands didn't stray far from the pommels of her knives. "I wish the people where I grew up took such good care of their orphans."

Tan ignored the assassin, turning instead to Triste, his stare boring into her. "How do you know that?"

She glanced at Kaden for support, then pointed back the way they had come, to the doorway opening out onto the ledge. "Above the door. It's carved there. No one else saw?"

Valyn shook his head. He really didn't give a shit if the place was a warehouse or a whorehouse as long as it had good sight lines, redundant exits, and enough life left not to collapse abruptly on their heads. Rampuri Tan, however, had fixed the girl with that empty, unreadable stare of his.

"Show me," he said.

"We're going up," Valyn said. "I want our perimeter established before full dark."

Tan turned to him. "Then establish it. The girl is coming with me."

Valyn bit off a sharp retort. The monk wasn't a part of his Wing, not under his command. He could press the issue, but Rampuri Tan didn't seem the type to respond to pressure, and every minute spent arguing was a minute of further vulnerability. Besides, there was something about the monk, something dangerous in the way he held that strange spear of his, in the flat calm of his stare. Valyn thought he could kill him if it came to blows, but he didn't see any reason to test the theory.

"All right," he snapped. "I'll cover you. Let's get this done quickly."

They found the inscription just where Triste said, the words pitted and worn, half obscured by lichen. Valyn squinted at it, trying to make out the lettering before realizing the language was unfamiliar. Linguistic training on the Islands was extensive, but even the characters were alien—sharp and angular, no loops or curves, a script designed to be gouged rather than brushed. He glanced over at Triste, eyebrows raised. "You can read that?"

She was standing in the deep shadow, staring up at the lintel, shivering with the sudden night chill. "I don't . . ." She shook her head, then abruptly nodded instead. "I guess."

"What does it say?" Tan demanded.

She frowned, and for a moment Valyn thought she would admit that the words were foreign after all. Then, haltingly at first, she spoke, her voice oddly lilting and musical. *"Ientain, na si-ientanin. Na si-andrellin, eiran."*

The phrases weren't any more familiar than the shapes graven into the stone, and Valyn glanced over at Tan. The monk's face, as always, was blank. Spending time around the Shin, Valyn was starting to realize how much he relied on subtle emotional cues. Narrowed eyes, whitened knuckles, tense shoulders—it was all a text he could read, one that signaled belligerence or submission, rage or calm. The monks, however, and Tan in particular, were blank pages, palimpsests scraped and scraped until they were utterly empty, utterly clean.

"What does it mean?" Valyn asked, as much to break the brittle silence as anything else.

Triste frowned, then translated, faltering only briefly. "A home for those who have no home. For those who have no family, love."

Pyrre had joined them as Triste spoke, and the assassin glanced up at the words with pursed lips. "Would have saved some carving to just write *Orphanage*. Better yet, *Kids*."

"What language is it?" Valyn asked.

Triste hesitated, then shook her head.

"It is Csestriim," Tan said finally. "More specifically, a dialect of the Csestriim speech used by the early humans."

Valyn raised an eyebrow. "The priestesses of Ciena learn Csestriim?"

Triste bit her lip. "I'm not . . . I suppose I did. There were a lot of languages. The men . . . they come from all over. All over the world."

"You mean you studied up in case you were called upon to pleasure a Csestriim?" Pyrre asked. "I'm impressed."

"I wasn't a *leina*," Triste replied. "I wasn't initiated. . . ." She trailed off, still staring at the words as though they were vipers.

"All right then," Valyn said finally, "the language lesson has been fun." He glanced over the broad swath of stone, and the hair on his arms rose.

Across the ledge, a hundred paces from where he stood, inside the black yawning doorway through which they had first emerged from the cliff: a flicker of motion. No light, no noise, just a silent shape sliding across the darkness, gone so fast he couldn't even be certain it was real. It could have been anything, a leaf caught in the night breeze, a fragment of cloth flapping. *But there is no cloth here,* he reminded himself. Gwenna and Annick had said as much. Only the hard things. Only the bones.

There were animals in the Bone Mountains, crag cats, bears, plenty of smaller, less dangerous creatures. Something might have found a convenient lair inside the cliff. Something might have followed them in. In either case, they were vulnerable standing in the entrance to the orphanage, silhouetted by the light of their lantern. Jumping at shadows was a good way to make mistakes, but so was standing around out in the open.

"Upstairs," he said. "Laith and Gwenna, check the first floors. Talal, Annick, those above. Gwenna, rig the whole place."

He glanced over his shoulder once more, to where he'd seen the motion. Nothing. The night was still, silent. Valyn turned back to the group. *"Now."*

5

Adare spent the better part of the morning hunched beneath a bridge, pressed up against the stone pilings, teeth chattering in the brisk spring breeze, limbs trembling beneath her sodden wool robe, hair damp and cold on her nape, despite having wrung it out a dozen times over. She would have dried more quickly in the sun, but she couldn't leave the shadows until she was dry. A drenched woman wandering the streets would draw attention, and when Fulton and Birch came looking, she didn't want anyone to remember her passage.

Worse than the cold was the waiting. Every minute she waited was another minute during which the Aedolians could organize their pursuit, pursuit she was ill equipped to handle. How long did wool take to dry? She had no idea. Every morning of her life, a slave had arrived with freshly laundered clothes, and every evening that same slave had removed the dirty garments. For all Adare knew, she could be crouched beneath the bridge all day, shivering, waiting.

She bit her lip. That wasn't an option. By the time night fell, Aedolians would be scouring both banks of the Chute, searching for exit points, hunting beneath bridges. She needed to be well away by nightfall, by *noon,* and yet there was no way to wish the cloth dry. Instead, as she trembled and crouched, she tried to think through the next few hours, to anticipate the difficulties in her plan, the flaws.

Difficulties weren't hard to come by. First, she had to find a route to the Godsway that wouldn't get her beaten, robbed, or raped. She risked a glimpse out from beneath the bridge. It was impossible to say how far the current had carried her or where, exactly, she'd finally managed to claw her way out of the water, but the leaning tenements, the narrow streets, the stench of offal and rotten food, suggested one of the city's slums, maybe even the Perfumed Quarter. Somewhere in the near distance she could hear a woman and man shouting at each other, one voice high and biting, the other a ponderous growl of rage. Something heavy smashed into a wall, shattering into pieces, and the voices fell silent. Nearer at hand a dog barked over and over and over.

With numb fingers, Adare slipped the damp blindfold from the pocket of her dress. She tied it in place. In the deep shadow of the bridge she couldn't see much—her own hand when she waved it in front of her face, sunlight reflecting off the water of the canal before it slid beneath the stone arch, the vague shapes of rotted pilings. She'd known the cloth would hinder her ability to see, but she hadn't remembered it being quite so bad when she'd practiced in the privacy of her chamber. After fiddling with it for a while, twisting it this way and that, she pulled it off entirely, untied it, then started the whole process over again.

If the blindfold slipped down, she was dead. If it came untied, she was dead. While the shadows of the tenements retreated across the canal she toyed with the cloth over and over until there was nothing left to adjust. It wasn't great, but she could live with it. Would have to live with it. She tested the wool of her dress with a tentative hand. It was still damp, but not sopping wet. There was a tenuous line between prudence and cowardice, and Adare felt herself edging toward it.

"Get up," she muttered at herself. "Get out. It's time."

The bridge was empty when she emerged from beneath it, and Adare let out a sigh of relief when she realized that the only people in sight were two women twenty paces down the road, one hauling a large bucket, the other bent beneath the weight of a shapeless sack tossed across one shoulder. Even better, in the full light of the sun, she could actually see that they *were* women through the cloth, though the details were hazy. The Chute had carried her west, which meant the Temple of Light lay somewhere to the north. Adare glanced behind her once more, hesitated, then stepped down from the bridge.

All the streets around the Dawn Palace were paved. Some, like the Godsway, were built of massive limestone flags, each the size of a wagon, every single one replaced every twenty years as wheels and weather pitted the surface. Others were cobbled more simply, with brick or uneven stone, open gutters running on either side. Never, though, had Adare walked a street without any paving at all, without gutters or culverts to siphon away the runoff, and she froze as her foot plunged up past the ankle in mud.

She hoped it was only mud, though the stench suggested something more foul.

She yanked her foot free. Then, gritting her teeth, she set out again, stepping gingerly, trying to choose the firmest, highest ground, to avoid the troughs and ruts. It was slow going, but she'd managed to keep her boots on, to make her way steadily in the direction she desperately hoped was north, when laughter from behind made her turn.

"Y'aren't gettin' yer boots dirty, are ya?"

While she'd been picking and choosing her steps, hitching her dress up to keep it clear of the mire, two young men had come up behind her, plodding through the muck. They were barefoot, she realized when they drew close enough to see, indifferent to the splashing and splattering along the ragged hems of their pants. One carried a canal hook casually over his shoulder, the other a rough basket. *Canal rats,* Adare realized.

There was a living to be made—a meager one—loitering on Annur's bridges, plucking from the current whatever detritus floated beneath. Adare had grown up on children's tales of Emmiel the Beggar Lord, who dredged a chest of gems from the waters and found himself the richest man in Annur. These two seemed not to have had Emmiel's luck. The basket was empty, and judging from their gaunt cheeks, it had been empty for a while.

The youth with the hook gestured at her. He had short hair and a pointed weasel's face. A sly smile. Adare felt her stomach clench.

"I *said,* y'aren't gettin' yer boots dirty, are ya?" He paused, noticing her blindfold for the first time. "What's wrong with yer eyes?"

Had Adare not rehearsed the response a hundred times she would have stood there stupidly, her mouth hanging open. Instead, she managed to mutter, "River blindness."

"River blindness?" The hook-holder glanced at his companion, a short, pimpled youth with a gourd for a head. Gourd studied her a moment, then spat into the mud.

"River blindness?" the first young man said, turning back to her.

Adare nodded.

He swung the canal hook down from his shoulder, waving it back and forth before her eyes. "Can ya see that?" he demanded. "Whatta ya see?"

"I can see," Adare replied, "but the light hurts."

She turned away, hoping they would leave it at that, managed five steps before she felt the hook snag her dress, pulling her up short.

"Hold on, hold on!" the one with the hook said, tugging her back, forcing her to turn. "What kinda boys would we be if we let a nice lady like you get 'er boots dirty? A poor *blind* lady?"

"I'm not really blind," Adare said, trying to disentangle the hook from the cloth. "I'm all right."

"Please," he insisted, waving his compatriot over. "We've no employment t'trouble us for the moment. Let us help you at least as far as Dellen's Square. The road gets better there."

"I couldn't."

"The basket," he pressed, gesturing toward the wicker basket. It was wide as her circled arms, large enough to hold almost anything they might haul from the canal, and fitted with heavy wooden handles. "Sit yer ass right there and let Orren and me carry ya."

Adare hesitated. The two youths frightened her, but then, she was quickly discovering that everything outside the confines of the red walls frightened her: the canal, the narrow streets, the shouts and slamming doors, the people with their hard, defiant eyes. The whole 'Kent-kissing world was turning out to be terrifying, but every Annurian citizen couldn't be a robber or a rapist. The rich, she reminded herself, did not have a monopoly on decency. She tried to think about the picture she presented: a mud-smeared young woman suffering from a strange sort of blindness, navigating a particularly treacherous street. Maybe they just wanted to help.

"C'mon," the youth pressed. "Skinny thing like you can't weigh but a few pounds."

He gestured to the basket again.

Adare took a deep breath and nodded. Maybe they wanted to help her out of simple kindness, but more likely they were hoping for a few copper suns when they reached the square, something to mitigate their failure at the canals. Palanquins were ubiquitous in the city, and what was the basket but a poor-man's palanquin? She felt surreptitiously for the purse secreted inside the dress. If they expected coin, she had enough to pay them a thousand times over. Besides, her legs were trembling after the effort of fleeing her guard, swimming the river, then crouching cold beneath the bridge. It would feel good to be carried again, if only a short distance.

"All right," she said. "Just as far as the square. I appreciate your kindness."

The youth with the hook winked, gesturing toward the basket once more.

Adare took two steps toward it when a new voice brought her up short.

"Unless I've forgotten my geography, this isn't your turf, Willet. Last time I checked, you worked the streets south of Fink's Crossing."

She looked up to find the speaker watching her from the intersection a few paces distant. She couldn't be sure through the blindfold, but he looked older than the canal rats, maybe ten years older than Adare herself, tall, rangy, and handsome in a rough sort of way. She squinted, eyes adjusting to the shadow. The man's deep-set eyes, the lines stamped into his forehead beneath his short-cropped hair, made him look worried, even severe. He had a large soldier's pack on his back, though he wore no obvious uniform, just leather and wool. It was the sword hanging from his hip that drew Adare's eye.

The youth with the hook paused, then spread his hands. "Lehav. Been a while. We was just doin' the lady a good turn, carryin' her to Dellen's Square. . . ."

"A good turn," Lehav replied. "Is that what you call it now?"

Adare hesitated, then backed away from the basket and the soldier both. She had no idea where Fink's Crossing was, but she understood the talk of geography and turf well enough. She was somewhere she didn't belong, and the arrival of the soldier, this coded exchange, the way that he looked at her with those hooded eyes, put her even more on edge.

"Just helping," Willet said, nodding. "Nothing to do with you, Lehav."

The soldier eyed her for a long moment, looked her up and down as though she were a slave for sale on the blocks, then shrugged again.

"I suppose it's not," he said, then turned to the rats. "But remember: if Old Jake finds you working his streets, someone will be using that hook to fish your corpses out of the canal."

He started to turn, but Adare flung out a hand.

"Wait!"

The soldier paused, glanced back over his shoulder.

She scrambled to think of something to say. "They're going to rob me."

He nodded. "That's correct."

His indifference took her aback. "You have to help me."

"No," he said, shaking his head evenly, "I don't. You'll be all right—these two will take your coin, but they'll leave everything else intact." He glanced over at the rats. "You haven't turned rapists in the last few years, have you?"

Orren spat into the mud, then spoke for the first time. "No business of yours if we did."

"No," Willet said, cutting off his companion, raising his hands in a conciliatory gesture. " 'Course not, Lehav. We got sisters. Just gonna take the nice lady's purse and see 'er on 'er way."

Lehav nodded, turned back to Adare. "You're lucky. If it were Old Jake's men found you . . ." He raised an eyebrow. "Safe to say the result wouldn't be pretty."

Adare was shaking now, her breath hot and ragged in her lungs. She felt suddenly trapped, vulnerable, her feet sunk in the mud, dress hitched up around her thighs. Annur had thousands of guardsmen responsible for keeping the peace, for stopping just this sort of thing. The Dawn Palace spent tens of thousands of suns on them each year. You couldn't stroll fifty paces through the Graves or the High Bluffs without seeing them walking in pairs, armor shining, keeping the Emperor's peace. But then, this wasn't the Graves.

"Wait," she said, glancing desperately at Lehav's sword. "You're a soldier. You're a *soldier*. From the legions. You swore an oath to protect the citizens of Annur."

Lehav's expression hardened. "I'd advise you not to instruct me in the matter of my own oaths. I left the legions years ago. Found a purer cause."

Adare glanced over her shoulder. Willet had his eyes fixed on Lehav, but Orren was looking straight at her, the gash of his mouth twisted in a cruel smile. The soldier and his callous indifference frightened her, but he, at least, had shown no desire to do her harm. There were no guardsmen on the narrow street, no saviors. If she couldn't convince Lehav to help her, there would be no help. The man knew the canal rats, but he wasn't friends with them, that much was clear. If she could only figure out where to drive the wedge. Her mind scrambled, her thoughts numb and clumsy with fear.

"That's right, Lehav," Willet was saying. "You don't wanna be wastin' your time down here jawin' with the likes of us. You got outta this shit trap, remember?"

The soldier shook his head. "Sometimes I'm not sure." He pursed his lips, glanced at the muddy road, the rotting boards facing the buildings, the thin strip of sky. "This whole city is rotten," he said, more to himself than anyone else. "This whole empire." After a long pause he shook his head again and turned away. "So long, Willet. Orren."

Adare's heart seized. Her tongue felt like leather in her mouth.

Willet smiled a wide grin, obviously relieved. "See ya someday, Lehav."

"No, you won't," the soldier replied.

And then, as when a scattering of individual stones on the *ko* board resolved themselves into a pattern, Adare understood: a soldier, a "purer cause," someone who got out, who wasn't coming back, a man with a sword on his hip but a large pack on his back.

"Please," she blurted desperately, "in Intarra's name, I'm begging you."

Once again Lehav stopped, turned, fixed her with an unreadable stare. "What is the goddess to you?"

Yes, Adare thought inwardly, relief and triumph flooding her. It wasn't done yet, but she could see the path.

"She is the light that guides me," she began, intoning an old prayer, "the fire that warms my face, a spark in the darkness."

"Is she." The soldier's voice was flat.

"I'm a pilgrim," Adare insisted. "I'm going now, to the Temple of Light, to join the pilgrimage. I'm leaving Annur for Olon."

Willet shifted uncomfortably at her side. "Don't worry about it, Lehav."

The soldier frowned. "I think I might worry about it, in fact." He turned to Adare once more. "You don't wear a pilgrim's robes."

"Neither do you," she pointed out. "I'm going to buy them. Today. On the Godsway."

"She's lyin'," Orren snarled. "The bitch is lyin'. She's got nuthin'. No pack. Nuthin'."

Now that Adare was into the lie the words tumbled from her lips.

"I *couldn't* bring anything, not without my family knowing. I had to sneak out in the night."

"What are you doing here?" Lehav asked. "In this part of town?"

"I got *lost,*" Adare sobbed. She didn't need to simulate the tears. "I was trying to get to the Godsway by dawn, but got lost in the night."

"Just let 'er go," Orren growled. "Just keep walkin'."

The soldier looked up at the narrow strip of sky between the dilapidated buildings as though weary with the whole scene, the rats, the mud, the stench.

Please, Adare begged silently. Her legs shook beneath her as though palsied. She wanted to run, but knew she wouldn't make it a dozen paces in the mud. *Please.*

"No," he replied finally. "I don't think I will keep walking." His thumbs remained casually tucked into the straps of his pack. He didn't so much as look at his sword.

"Might be we'll kill you, too, then," Orren said. "Might be we'll kill you both."

"It is certainly your right to try."

Willet's face had gone white and frightened. He tightened his grip on the hook, shifted back and forth uneasily in the mud while his companion sidled forward, a knife held before him, tongue flicking anxiously between his lips. Lehav unclasped his hands and set one palm silently on the pommel of his sword.

Later, when Adare had a chance to think back on the moment, it would occur to her that it was the simplicity of the gesture, the utter lack of bombast, that decided things. Had he taunted the other two, had he threatened them or warned them away, the scene might have ended differently. The absolute stillness of that hand on the well-worn pommel, however, the total economy of movement, suggested an unwillingness to do anything but fight, kill.

A long moment passed, heartbeat after hammering heartbeat. Then Orren spat into the mud, his thick face twisted with anger and fear.

"Ah, *fuck* this," he muttered, shaking his head, turning back toward the bridge.

Willet hesitated a moment, then wheeled to face Adare, shoving her viciously back into the mud.

"Ya miserable cunt," he snarled. Then, with a glance over his shoulder, he fled in the wake of his companion.

Lehav considered her where she lay sprawled in the mud. He made no move to help her up.

"Thank you," Adare said, forcing herself to her knees, then hauling herself out of the filth, wiping her hands ineffectually on her dress. "In the name of the goddess, thank you."

"If you are lying," the soldier replied, "if you are not a pilgrim, if you have used Intarra's sacred name for your own advantage, I will take your coin myself and make a special trip on my way out of the city, a trip right back to this very spot, to leave you for Willet and Orren."

6

The bones spoke clearly enough. Skeletons littered the wide hall-ways and narrow rooms of the orphanage, skeletons of children, hundreds and hundreds, some on the cusp of adulthood, others no more than infants, their ribs narrower than Kaden's fingers. The grinding passage of years had dismembered most, but enough of the tiny forms remained intact—huddled in corners, collapsed in hallways, clutching one another beneath the stairs—to speak of some horror sweeping down upon them, sudden and unimagined.

Kaden had tried to ask Tan about the city, but Valyn was pushing hard for them to get upstairs, and the older monk, after the strange diversion at the entrance, seemed just as determined to reach the topmost floor and the *kenta* that waited there. When Kaden posed a question as they climbed, Tan had turned that implacable glare upon him.

"Focus on the present," he'd said, "or join the past."

Kaden tried to follow the advice as they mounted the stairs, tried to watch for hidden dangers and unexpected threats, to float on the moment like a leaf on a stream, but his eyes kept drifting back to the skeletons.

Half-remembered stories of the Atmani bubbled up in his mind, of the bright empire founded by the leach-lords, then shattered by their insanity and greed. According to the tales, they had razed entire cities as they descended into madness, but if Kaden's childhood memories served, their empire had been almost entirely confined to Eridroa. It hadn't come within a thousand miles of the Bone Mountains, and besides, the Atmani had ruled millennia after the Csestriim. He stepped over another sprawled skeleton, staring at the tiny, grasping hands.

It could have been a sickness, he told himself, *some sort of plague.*

Only, victims of plague did not retreat into closets or try to barricade doors. Victims of plague did not have their small skulls hacked in two. The bones were ancient, but as Kaden stepped over skeleton after skeleton, he could read the story. There had been no attempt to move the bodies, no effort to lay them out for burning and burial as one would expect if anyone had survived the slaughter. Even across the still chasm of time, he could read the shock and panic of the dead.

The memory of Pater filled his mind, of the small boy held aloft in Ut's armored fist, calling out for Kaden to flee even as the Aedolian's broadblade cut the life from him. Kaden's jaw ached, and he realized he was clenching it. He drained the tension into his lungs, breathed it out with his next breath, and replaced the awful image of Pater's death with memories of the boy as he had been in life—darting through the rocks around Ashk'lan's refectory, diving into Umber's Pool and coming up sputtering. He allowed the scenes to play across his memory for a while, then extinguished them, returning his attention to the flickering light of the lantern where it slid across the crumbling walls and brittle bones.

Fortunately, Valyn and Tan agreed on their ultimate destination—the top floor of the orphanage—though they had different reasons for their urgency. Valyn seemed to think it would make for the best defensive position, but it was also, according to the monk, where they would find the *kenta*. Kaden didn't much care why they agreed just so long as he didn't have to pull on his imperial mantle to adjudicate another dispute. He was exhausted—exhausted from running, from fighting, from flying, and something about this dead city weighed on him. He was curious about the *kenta*, curious about whatever history Tan finally decided to provide for the place, but at the moment he was content to stump along behind as they wound their way up the wide staircase.

The four members of Valyn's Wing caught up with them in the central corridor of the topmost story. All had weapons drawn.

"Threats?" Valyn asked, glancing over his shoulder. There was something tight and urgent in his voice.

"Depends what you mean by 'threat,'" the flier replied. Laith reminded Kaden of Akiil—the irreverence, even the grin. "I saw a rat the size of Annick. Not that Annick's very big, but still . . ."

"The whole place is about to fall over," Gwenna said, cutting through Laith's words.

"Tonight?" Valyn asked.

She scowled, though whether at Valyn or the building itself, Kaden couldn't say. "Probably not tonight," she conceded finally.

"Provided no one jumps up and down," Laith added.

"Or descends the stairs," the Wing's leach added.

"What's wrong with the stairs?" Kaden asked.

"I rigged the last flight on the way up," Gwenna replied, smiling grimly. "Two flickwicks and a modified starshatter. Anything tries to come up, we're going to need a broom to sweep up what's left of the bodies."

"Was that wise?" Kaden asked, glancing around at the gaping cracks in the masonry.

"Look . . ." Gwenna began, raising a finger.

"Gwenna," Valyn growled. "You are speaking to the Emperor."

For a moment it seemed as though the girl was going to bull ahead despite the warning, but finally she pulled back the accusatory finger, twisting the gesture into a half salute. "Well, tell the *Emperor,*" she said, turning to Valyn, "that if he'll manage the emperoring, I'll take care of the demolitions."

Valyn tensed, but Kaden put a hand on his shoulder. It was hard to know just how fiercely to assert his new title and authority. Clearly, he would never convince Annur of his legitimacy if a handful of soldiers led by his own brother treated him with contempt. On the other hand, he was, aside from Triste, the least capable member of their small group. The fact galled him, but it was there all the same. Before people saw him as an emperor, he would have to act as an emperor. He had little enough idea how to manage that, but it didn't seem as though pitching a fit in a hallway would be a step in the right direction.

"You have a deal," he said, nodding to Gwenna. "I'll stay out of your way, but maybe when we're settled you could explain something about your munitions; normally I'd stick to emperoring, but there doesn't seem to be all that much here that needs my attention."

The woman narrowed her eyes, as though she suspected a joke, but when Kaden held her gaze she finally snorted something that might have been a laugh.

"I can show you something," she said. "Enough you don't blow us all up. You couldn't be much worse at it than your brother," she added, jerking her head at Valyn.

Kaden smiled.

"Thanks for the confidence, Gwenna," Valyn said. "Anything else to report from down below? Anything moving?"

"Aside from Annick's rat sibling?" Laith replied. "Not a thing."

Valyn's shoulders relaxed fractionally.

"All right. Everyone to the front of the building except Laith. You check all the empty rooms on this floor."

"For more rats?" the flier asked.

"Yes," Valyn replied, voice hardening. "For more rats."

✝

The room fronting the top story was larger than the rest, spanning the full width of the building and opening through several tall windows out onto the night. Wide hearths stood at either end, though they were choked by debris that had fallen from the chimneys above, plaster and chunks of stone spilling out onto the floor. Wind and weather had torn away a corner of the roof—Kaden could make out the great sweep of the cliff a few paces above—and night air gusted through the gap, chill and sharp.

For a moment he stared around in perplexity, searching for the *kenta*. He had formed an image in his head of something massive, grand, like the Godsgate of the Dawn Palace—marble, maybe, or polished bloodstone, or onyx—but nothing massive or magnificent waited in the middle of the room. He squinted in the meager lamplight. Nothing at *all* stood in the middle of the room.

"Talal," Valyn said, gesturing curtly, "center window. I want eyes on the ledge before full dark. Gwenna, see what you can do about rigging a chunk of this floor to drop out."

"I could *kick* a hole in the 'Kent-kissing floor," the woman replied, digging at the crumbling mortar with her boot, "and you want me to rig it? I seem to remember someone back at the Eyrie teaching us something about not sleeping on top of our own explosives."

Valyn turned to face his demolitions master. His jaw was tight, but his voice level when he responded. "And I remember something about having two ways out of any defensive position. You rigged the stairs, which keeps the bad guys out, which is good. It also keeps us *in,* which is less good."

"If they can't get in, why do we need to get out?"

"Gwenna," Valyn said, pointing at the floor, "just do it. If you blow us all up, I'll make sure I don't die until you have a chance to punch me."

"Yes, Oh Light of the Empire," she said, bowing to Valyn as she yanked the charges out of her pack. "At once, My Noble Leader." The words were sharp, but Kaden noticed some of the acid had gone out of her challenge. The whole thing sounded like sparring now, rather than actual fighting.

Valyn shook his head. "You can't pull that shit anymore, Gwenna," he said, jerking a thumb at Kaden. "He's the Light of the Empire. We're just here to make sure no one puts him out. Speaking of which," he went on, turning to Tan and spreading his hands, "where's the gate?"

Tan gestured toward the wall. Kaden squinted, then took a few steps closer. The *kenta* was there, he realized, almost as tall as the ceiling, but built, if built was the right word, flush with the masonry behind it. The arch was surprisingly slender, no more than a hand's width in diameter, and made of something Kaden had never seen, a smooth gray substance that might have been part steel, part stone. The graceful span looked spun rather than carved, and the light came off of it strangely, as though it were illuminated, not by Valyn's lantern, but some other, invisible source.

"What is the point," Valyn asked, "of building a gate right into a wall?"

"The other side is not the wall," Tan replied. "It is not here."

"That clarifies a lot," Valyn said, stooping to pick up a chunk of stone. He bounced it on his hand a few times, then tossed it underhand toward the *kenta*. It flipped lazily end over end and then, just as it passed beneath the arch . . . ceased.

Kaden could think of no other word to describe the passage. There was no splash, no echo, no sudden winking out. He knew what to expect, but some part of his mind, something deeper and older than rational thought, quailed at the sight of something, a hard, real part of the world, becoming nothing.

If Valyn was discomfited, he didn't show it. "Looks like it works."

Tan ignored him. He had acquired a lantern of his own from one of the Kettral, and was holding it aloft, running a finger along the outside of the arch slowly, as though searching for cracks.

"Where did it go?" Valyn asked.

"Nowhere," the older monk replied.

"How useful."

"The Blank God claimed it," Kaden said, shaking his head. "The stone is nothing now, nowhere." *And pretty soon,* he reminded himself silently, a chill spreading through him, *I'm going to be following that stone.*

"What would happen if I jumped in?"

"Nothing."

"Doesn't sound so bad."

"Then you fail to appreciate nothingness," Tan replied, straightening from his examination of the ground in front of the gate. "It is clean on this side."

"Clean?" Kaden asked.

The monk turned to him. "Like all gates, the *kenta* can be blocked or barbed. Since those of us who step through are forced to step through blind, there is a danger."

"Ambush," Valyn said, nodding. "Makes sense. You want to set a trap, you do it at a choke point."

"But who would be setting traps?" Kaden asked. "Only a few people even know they exist."

"Few is not none," Tan replied, turning to the gate. "I will check the other side."

"Is that safe?" Valyn asked, shaking his head.

"No. But it is necessary. If I do not return before the Bear Star rises, the *kenta* is compromised. Abandon this course, and quickly."

Kaden nodded. He wanted to ask more, about the gates, the traps, about the strange city in which they found themselves, a city that appeared on no maps, but Tan's eyes had already emptied, and before Kaden could speak, the older monk was stepping through the *kenta*.

For a few heartbeats after he disappeared no one spoke. Wind whipped through the holes in the ceiling, chasing dust and dirt across the uneven floor. Kaden stared at the gate, forcing his heart to beat slowly, steadily.

Pyrre raised an eyebrow finally. "That was interesting." The Skullsworn had been making a slow circuit of the room, peering up the chimneys, examining the masonry, running her fingers along the window casings. She paused to consider the gate. "I can't imagine my god approves."

"Why not?" Kaden asked. "Dead is dead."

She smiled. "But it makes a difference who does the killing."

Valyn ignored the conversation, gesturing instead to the spot where Tan had disappeared. "We've got some real bastards back on the Islands, but that guy . . ." He shook his head, turning to Kaden. "I've just got to say it one more time: riding a bird sure has its risks, but it seems ten times safer than that thing."

"That thing," Kaden said again, trying to force some confidence into his voice, "is what I trained for." If he couldn't use the *kenta,* then all his years with the Shin had been for nothing. His father had used the gates;

all the Malkeenian emperors used the gates. If he failed here, well, maybe he wasn't cut from the right cloth. "I have few enough advantages as it is," he added. "I can't afford to go tossing them away."

Worry creased Valyn's brow, but after a moment he nodded, then turned to Talal.

"What's happening on the ledge?"

"Night," the leach replied. "Wind."

Valyn crossed to the window, glanced out, then turned back, scanning the room.

"All right, we're not going to be here long—one night for everyone to rest up. The monks leave in the morning. We're gone right after them, hopefully before dawn. In the meantime, let's do what we can to button the place up."

The sniper glanced skeptically at the gaping windows, at the hole in the roof. "Unlikely," she said.

"I don't love it either," Valyn said. "But it's the best defensive position we've got and we do need rest, all of us. I want crossed cord on each window, and while we're at it, a belled horizon line straight across the outside face of the building. . . ."

"That's you, Annick," Gwenna said. "I'm not climbing around on the wall of this wreck."

"How's the cord supposed to protect us?" Kaden asked.

"It doesn't," Valyn replied. "Not really. But if someone climbing trips the bells, we'll know they're here, and the cord on the window will slow them down."

Kaden crossed to the window and leaned out. He couldn't see much in the darkness, but the wall of the orphanage dropped away forty feet or so to the broad ledge below. The masonry was crumbling, leaving gaps between the stones, but it hardly looked like something a human being could climb.

Annick studied Valyn for a heartbeat or two, then nodded, slipping out the window. If she felt uncomfortable hanging from her fingertips while standing on the tiny ledges, she didn't show it. In fact, she moved smoothly and efficiently over the stone, pausing every so often to free a hand and spool out the cord, then moving on. It was a simple solution, almost laughably simple, but when she was finished, Kaden could see how the thin line might tangle a climber or provide some warning.

"If it's other Kettral who are after us," Annick observed, dusting off her hands and reclaiming her bow from where it leaned against the wall, "they'll expect the cord."

Valyn nodded. "They'll expect everything we do. That's no reason to make it easier on them."

"The sturdiest section of floor is over there," Gwenna said, gesturing without looking up from her work stringing charges. "If you're going to hunker down in one spot, that's where I'd do it."

Annick crossed to the area the demolitions master had indicated, then nudged at a pile of debris with the toe of her boot.

"Anything interesting?" Valyn asked.

"More bones," she replied.

He shook his head. "Any sense of what killed these poor bastards?"

The sniper knelt, running a finger along the pitted surfaces.

"Stabbed," she replied after a moment. "Blade nicked the third and fourth ribs in each case, probably ruptured the heart."

She might have been talking about shearing goats, those blue eyes of hers glacially cold in the dim lamplight. Kaden watched as she went about her work, trying to read her curt movements, to see the sniper's mind in the constant sweep of her gaze, in her tendons as they flexed with the motion of her wrists, in the angle of her head as she turned from one rib cage to the next. What did she think, looking at those old, brittle bones? What did she feel?

The monks had taught Kaden to observe—he could paint any member of his brother's Wing with his eyes closed—but to understand, that was another matter. After so many years surrounded by the stone of the mountains and by men who might have been carved from that stone, he had little sense of how to translate words and actions into emotions; no idea, even, if his own attenuated emotions bore any resemblance to those of others.

He still felt fear, and hope, and despair, but the sudden arrival of the Aedolians and Kettral, the arrival of people who were *not* Shin, made him realize just how far he had traveled along the monks' path, how fully, in the course of those long, cold mountain years, he had filed smooth his own feelings. He was Emperor now—or would be if he survived—the ostensible leader of millions, and yet all those millions were animated by feelings he could no longer understand.

"What about down below?" Valyn asked, jerking a thumb back over his shoulder.

"Same," Annick replied. "Most of the bones have gone to dust, but it's clear enough what happened. Quick work, efficient—no cuts to the arms or legs, no doubling up, every strike a kill. Whoever did this, they were good."

She rose to her feet and shrugged as though that settled the matter.

Triste, however, was standing a few paces away, mouth open, staring. She had been silent since reading the script on the lintel, lost in her own thoughts or exhaustion as she followed the rest of the group up the stairs and down the long hallway. Annick's words seemed to jar her back into the present.

"Good?" she asked, her voice cracking as she spoke. "*Good?* What about this is good?" She spread her hands helplessly, gesturing to the small skulls, to the gaping doors leading back the way they had come. "Who would murder children?"

"Someone thorough," Pyrre observed. The assassin was leaning against one of the window frames, arms crossed, tapping her foot idly, as though waiting for the rest of them to quit dithering.

"Thorough?" Triste demanded, aghast. "Someone goes through an orphanage stabbing kids in their sleep and you call it *good*? You call it *thorough*?"

Annick ignored the outburst, but Valyn put a hand on Triste's shoulder. "Annick was just making a professional assessment," he began. "She doesn't mean that it was good. . . ."

"Oh, a professional assessment," Triste spat, shrugging away from Valyn's touch. She was trembling, slender hands clenching and unclenching. "They murdered all these children and you want to make a *professional* assessment."

"It's what we do," Valyn said. His voice was level, but something raw and untrammeled ran beneath those words, something savage kept savagely in check. His irises swallowed the light. "It's how we stay alive."

"But we *could* sing dirges," Pyrre suggested. The assassin held a perfectly straight face, but amusement ghosted around her eyes. "Would you like to sing a dirge, Triste? Or maybe we could all just link hands and cry."

Triste locked eyes with the older woman, and, to Kaden's surprise, managed to hold the gaze.

"You're loathsome," she said finally, casting her glance over Annick,

Valyn, and the rest. "Skullsworn, Kettral, Aedolians, you're all loathsome. You're all killers."

"Well, we can't all be whores," Gwenna snapped, glancing up from her charges.

Despite the size of the room, despite the gaping windows and shattered roof open to the sky, the space was suddenly too small, too full, bursting with the heat of raised voices and the blind straining of untrammeled emotion. Kaden struggled to watch it all without letting it overwhelm him. Was this how people lived? How they spoke? How could they see anything clearly in the midst of that raging torrent?

Triste opened her mouth, but no words came out. After a mute moment, she shoved her way past Annick, out into the hallway, back the way they had come.

"Watch out for the stairs," Pyrre called after her cheerfully.

✝

Triste returned sooner than Kaden expected, tears dry, one hand hugging herself around the waist, the other holding a sword. Kaden remembered impressive weapons from his childhood—jewel-crusted ceremonial swords; the long, wide blades of the Aedolians; businesslike sabers carried by the palace guard—but nothing like this. This sword was made from steel so clear it might not have been steel at all but some sliver of winter sky hammered into a perfect shallow arc, then polished to a silent gloss. It was *right*.

"What," Valyn asked, turning from the darkness beyond the window as Triste's too-large boots scuffed the stone, "is that?"

"Sweet 'Shael, Val," Laith said. He and Talal had returned to the front chamber after checking the whole floor. "I think you're a good Wing leader and all, but it worries me when you don't recognize a sword."

Valyn ignored the flier. "Where did you find it?" he asked, crossing to Triste.

She waved a vague hand toward the hallway. "In one of the rooms. It was covered up with rubble, but I saw the glint off it. It looks new. Is it one of ours?"

Valyn shook his head grimly.

"So we're not the only ones flying around the ass end of nowhere," Laith observed. The words were casual, but Kaden noticed that the flier drifted away from the open doorway, eyes flitting to the shadows in the corners.

Valyn put a hand in front of Kaden, drawing him away from the sword, as though even unwielded the weapon could cut, could kill.

"Annick," he said, "back on the window. Gwenna and Talal, when we're finished here, I want another sweep of this floor."

"They just swept the floor," the demolitions master observed.

"Sweep it again," Valyn said, "eyes out for rigged falls and double binds."

"What about bad men hiding in the corners?" Laith asked.

Valyn ignored him.

None of it meant anything to Kaden, and after a moment he turned back to the sword. "Does that style of blade look familiar?" He asked. There might be a clue in the provenance of the sword, but he didn't know enough about weapons to say.

"I've seen things similar," Valyn replied, frowning. "Some of the Manjari use a single-sided blade."

"It's not Manjari," Pyrre said. She hadn't moved, but she had stopped sharpening.

"Maybe something from somewhere in Menkiddoc?" Talal suggested. "We know practically nothing about the entire continent."

"We're in the Bone Mountains," Valyn pointed out. "Menkiddoc is thousands of miles to the south."

"It's not from Menkiddoc," Pyrre added.

"Anthera is close," Kaden pointed out.

"Antherans like broadblades," Valyn replied, shaking his head curtly. "And clubs, for some inexplicable reason."

"It is not Antheran." This time, however, it was not Pyrre who spoke.

Kaden turned to find Tan in front of the *kenta,* a robed shadow against the darker shadows beyond, the *naczal* glinting in his right hand. For all his size, the monk moved silently, and none of them had heard him as he reentered the room. He stepped forward. "It is Csestriim."

For what seemed like a long time a tight, cold silence filled the room.

"I guess you didn't die on the other side of the gate," Gwenna observed finally.

"No," Tan replied. "I did not."

"Want to tell us what you found?"

"No. I do not. Where did you find the blade?"

Valyn gestured down the hall as Kaden tried to put the pieces together in his mind.

Tan had said earlier that the script above the door was human, but ancient. This was a human building, a human city, but the Csestriim had created the *kenta,* created one here, in the center of a city filled with bones. The sword looked new, but then, so did Tan's *naczal.* It could be thousands of years old, one of the weapons used when . . .

"The Csestriim killed them," Kaden said slowly. "They opened a gate right here in the middle of the city, bypassing the walls, bypassing all the defenses." His thought leapt outside of itself, into the emotionless minds of the attackers. Through the *beshra'an* it was all so clear, so rational.

"They came through, probably at night, killing the children first because the children were humanity's best weapon against them. They started here, at the top. . . ." The memory of the small skeletons on the stairs flared up in his mind. "Or some of them did," he amended. "The Csestriim set the trap first, then drove the children down, stabbing them as they fled, cutting them down on the stairs or in the hallways, then doubling back to kill those who had hidden behind doors or under beds." He slipped from the mind of the hunters into the fear of the hunted. "Most of the children would have been too terrified to do anything, but even those who tried to escape . . ." He gestured helplessly. "Where would they go? We're halfway up the cliff." He glanced to the window, living the screaming, the slaughter. "Some would have jumped," he said, his heart hammering at the thought. "It was hopeless, but some would have jumped anyway."

Trembling with the borrowed terror of children millennia dead, he slipped out of the *beshra'an* to find half a dozen pairs of eyes fixed upon him.

"What is this place?" Talal asked finally, gazing about the room.

"I told you earlier," Tan replied. "It is Assare."

Valyn shook his head. "Why haven't we heard of it?"

"Rivers have changed their course since people last drew breath here."

"Why is it *here*?" Kaden asked. He tried to dredge up what little he'd overheard about urban development during his childhood in the Dawn Palace. "There's no port, no road."

"That was the point," Tan replied, seating himself cross-legged beside the sword. The monk considered it for several heartbeats, but made no move to reach out. Kaden waited for him to continue, but after a moment the monk closed his eyes.

Laith stared at Tan, looked over to Kaden, then back again before spreading his hands. "That's the end of the story? Csestriim came. They killed everyone. Dropped a sword . . . time for a nice rest?"

If the gibe bothered Tan, he didn't show it. His eyes remained closed. His chest rose and fell in even, steady breaths.

To Kaden's surprise, it was Triste who broke the silence.

"Assare," she said, the word leaving her tongue with a slightly different lilt than Tan had given it. She, too, had sunk to the floor beside the blade, her eyes wide in the lamplight, as though staring at a vision none of them could see. " 'Refuge.' "

"More *leina* training?" Pyrre asked.

Triste didn't respond, didn't even glance over at the woman. "Assare," she said again. Then, *"Ni kokhomelunen, tandria. Na sviata, laema. Na kiena-ekkodomidrion, aksh."*

Tan's eyes slammed silently open. His body didn't so much as twitch, but there was something different about it, something . . . Kaden searched for the right word. Wary. Ready.

Triste just stared at the blade, those perfect eyes wide and abstracted. She didn't seem to realize she had spoken.

"Where," Tan said finally, "did you hear that?"

Triste shuddered, then turned to the monk. "I don't . . . probably at the temple, as part of my studies."

"What does it mean?" Kaden asked. Something about the phrase had set Tan on edge, and he wasn't accustomed to seeing the older monk on edge.

"No," Tan said, ignoring Kaden's question. "You didn't learn it in a temple. Not any temple still standing."

"She knew the language down below," Valyn pointed out.

"She *read* the words down below," Tan corrected him, rising smoothly to his feet. "It was unlikely, but possible. There are plenty of scholars who read Csestriim texts."

"So what's the problem?" Valyn pressed.

"She didn't read this. She pulled it from memory."

Laith shrugged. "Good for her. Jaw-dropping beauty *and* a brain to go with it."

"Where," Tan pressed, eyes boring into the girl, "did you come across that phrase?"

She shook her head. "Probably in a book."

"It is not in the books."

"This is all very dramatic," Pyrre interjected from her post by the window, "but I could probably get more invested in the drama if I knew what the secret words *meant.*"

Triste bit her lip. "In growing . . ." she began uncertainly. "In a flooding black . . ." She grimaced, shook her head in frustration, then started once more, this time shifting into the somber cadence of prayer or invocation: "A light in the gathering darkness. A roof for the weary. A forge for the blade of vengeance."

7

The blessing of the pilgrims felt more like a death sentence than a celebration.

For one thing, Lehav had practically marched Adare to the Temple of Light, allowing only brief stops at the stalls along the Godsway for her to buy a small pack, a change of clothes, some dried fruit and salted meat, and, of course, the golden robes of one of Intarra's pilgrims. It was all part of her plan, but she had expected more freedom in executing the design, less scrutiny, the chance to pause and go over each step before taking it. Instead, she felt as though she had fallen into the Chute all over again, swept along by a force beyond her control, a force that, if she faltered once, would kill her.

Not that Lehav had been rough or ill-mannered. After his first threat, he had contented himself with small talk during their long, muddy trek to the Temple of Light, asking the sort of questions Adare had prepared for, while she responded with answers she had rehearsed a hundred times over. Her name was Dorellin. She was the daughter of a prosperous merchant. The blindfold? A consequence of the river blindness that had struck a year earlier. Yes, she could see, but her sight was failing month by month. At first it was only the sun that pained her, but more recently she had to shield her eyes from fires, even candles. No, her parents didn't know where she was. They insisted she was foolish, but Adare had faith in the goddess, was certain that if she made the pilgrimage to Olon, to Intarra's most sacred shrine, the Lady of Light would restore her sight. No, she hadn't fully considered the difficulties of the journey. Yes, she was prepared to walk for weeks. No, she hadn't planned farther than Olon itself, had no idea whether or not she would return to Annur, had thought no further than this one terrifying act of devotion.

The soldier only nodded at each response, but she caught him looking at her from time to time, judging her answers, weighing them. She wasn't sure if she wished she could see more of his expression through the blindfold, or less. It was a relief when they finally arrived in the massive square before the Temple of Light.

The temple itself was one of the wonders of the empire—a huge, glittering structure, more glass than stone, like a great cut gem set into the earth beside the Godsway, panes flashing in the midmorning light. The Godsway itself stretched out to the east and west, wide enough that fifty horsemen could ride abreast without brushing the shops and stalls to the north or south, the avenue cleaving the city like a sword stroke. Both the temple and the Godsway, however, shrank to insignificance beneath Intarra's Spear. Even a mile distant, it loomed overhead, a terrible, impossible splinter. The priests of Intarra had tried to build their temple outside of its shadow, but nothing in Annur was beyond that shadow, and Adare found herself staring at it, trying to make sense of the scale. It was hard to appreciate the Spear's height from inside the Dawn Palace, but standing in the center of the Godsway, gazing up at the tower's top, she felt dizzy, as though she might lose her footing and fall upward into the open sky. With an effort, she looked down, finding the flagstones, then over at Lehav, who was studying her intently.

"I don't know how to thank you," Adare said, extending a hand.

"Thank the goddess instead."

Adare nodded piously. "No doubt it was Intarra herself who sent you. I will be forever grateful, Lehav."

He didn't smile or take her hand. "You speak as though we were parting ways."

"No," she replied, hastily shaking her head. "We will be sharing the path together." She gestured to the pilgrims thronging in front of the temple. "I hope to come to know you much better in the days to come."

"And I," he replied, narrowing his eyes in a way that made her shiver, "will hope to know you better as well. Dorellin."

†

Hundreds had gathered for the long trek, some young and alone, carrying no more than a light pack over the shoulder, some in families of four or eight, wagons piled high with rickety wooden furniture and food, crates full of clothing, everything necessary to start a new life in Olon, hundreds

of miles to the south. Farmers had tethered pigs to their carts, filled cages
with squawking ducks, yoked teams of two or four water buffalo to haul
the whole mess. Lean dogs threaded through the crowd, sniffing and
growling, snapping at one another, ignoring the calls and commands of
their owners in the chaos. The group—those leaving and those come to
bid them farewell—had snarled traffic on the Godsway for hundreds of
paces east and west, blocking porters and horses alike.

And this happens every week, Adare thought to herself.

Uinian's death had occasioned the largest migration inside the empire
in decades, and yet, though she'd been following the reports, she hadn't
really *understood* the numbers until she approached the assembled crowd.
The gathering was intended as a celebration, a joyous valediction for those
following their faith to a fertile land beyond persecution. It was intended as
a bold gesture of defiance, and yet, even through the thick cloth of her
blindfold, Adare saw desperation everywhere: in the men joking too loudly,
the neighbors slapping shoulders too often and too vigorously, the couples
trying to drown their fear and foreboding in mindless, jocular patter.

"When you're freezing your nuts up here next winter, I'll be lazing by
Lake Sia," a young man called over the noise, while immediately to his
right a youth that could have been his brother buried his face in an old
man's shoulder, body shuddering with sobs. Not everyone could make the
trip, of course: the old or infirm, those too poor to start over in a strange
new city, or too frightened. In an hour or so, just after the priest's blessing,
parents would leave their grown children, brothers would bid sisters farewell, friends of two score years would part.

It was a sobering spectacle. One old man cursed at his horse when the
beast refused the halter, struck it across the nose, then buried his tear-
filled face in his hands. Two young children, a pale-faced, saucer-eyed boy
and girl, stood silently in the midst of the chaos, holding hands tightly,
obviously torn between excitement and fear. Olon wasn't *that* far. Merchant caravans could make the trip in a few weeks, canal boats even more
quickly, and yet these people were not merchants, not canal captains.
Most would never set foot in the capital again.

Because of me, Adare thought, feeling awed and sick at the same time.

Uinian's disgrace had seemed like a perfect opportunity to geld the
Church of Intarra, to seize back the rights and allowances so foolishly
granted hundreds of years earlier by Santun III, to recapture decades of
lost revenue, and perhaps most importantly, to cripple the power of the

Sons of Flame. With il Tornja's backing, she had moved quickly, drafting up the Accords of Union over the course of two days and two sleepless nights, then shoving them through the various ministries.

On the surface it looked like a fair deal, even a magnanimous one on the part of the Unhewn Throne; after all, the Chief Priest of Intarra had *murdered* the Emperor—or so everyone believed. The Accords offered a gracious reconciliation between Intarra's faithful and the larger empire of which they were a part, including a seemingly massive gift to the Church, ten thousand golden suns, "to greater glorify the goddess and her servants." Il Tornja, in his role as regent, had placed the golden amice on the stooped shoulders of the new Chief Priest himself.

It was all a sham, of course. To be sure, ten thousand suns would widen the eyes of most merchants, but the figure was less than a rounding error for the Ministry of Finance, a meager pittance compared with the amount the throne would claw back every year by reinstating taxation on Church rents and tithes. The glorification of the main temple on the Godsway was only a distraction from the forced shuttering of the smaller temples spread throughout the city. And the Imperial Blessing, that newly instituted ritual in which the Emperor would give his formal sanction to the Chief Priest, required the priest to kneel in supplication before the entire court. The rankest scribe in the Dawn Palace saw the Accords for what they were, but then, Adare hadn't written the measures to mollify the throne's scribes; if she could convince the common folk of Annur, the petty merchants and laborers, the fishermen and farmers, that the Unhewn Throne continued to support the Church of Intarra, then she could have her triumph while avoiding a backlash from those eager to scream religious persecution.

It almost worked. The new Chief Priest, Cherrel, third of that name, was a weak, watery-eyed, bookish man. Devout, but utterly lacking in the sort of political savvy and ambition that had made Uinian so dangerous. He had caviled momentarily at one or two of Adare's demands before caving utterly, obviously relieved that his Church was not to be scrubbed from the streets. According to the observers Adare had placed inside the temple, Cherrel counseled his flock on personal purity and political obedience, counsel they may well have heeded had Adare herself not overreached.

The problem, as always, was the Church's private army. As long as the Chief Priest, *any* Chief Priest, was permitted to keep thousands of men—soldiers both well trained and well paid—under arms within the borders

of the empire, within the borders of the 'Kent-kissing *capital,* all the genu-
flection in the world wouldn't lead to true submission. The Sons of Flame
needed to be disbanded, and so Adare had drafted the edict disbanding
them, allowing only one hundred for "the immediate protection of the
temple and the greater glory of Intarra." It had seemed a prudent step, a
necessary step, and yet she had not considered the consequences.

Many soldiers found difficulty in returning to civilian life, and the
Sons of Flame were no different. In fact, they were worse, their martial
experience compounded by single-minded religious fervor. In drafting
the Accords, Adare had hoped the Sons would simply melt away—join the
bakers' guild, or ship out with a fishing fleet. It was idiocy, in retrospect.
Her father would have recognized the problem, would have avoided it,
but her father was dead, and if she didn't clean up her own mess, it would
soon start to stink.

There was no outright rebellion. In fact, it seemed at first that the Sons
of Flame *had* simply drifted off, dissipated, like smoke before a stiff
breeze. Then Adare received the first reports from her tax collectors on
the road to Olon: the soldiers were headed south. Not in a single group, to
be sure. Not marching down the road in rank and column. Had they been
so bold, she could have sent the legions after them for defying the terms of
the Accords.

No, the Sons of Flame were moving south in a nebulous body—half a
dozen here, two or three there, retaining their armor and weapons while
discarding the banners and uniforms. Hundreds and hundreds of men
like Lehav, leaving Annur. Evidently one of the bastards, a man she'd never
heard of, named Vestan Ameredad, was behind it all, urging the men to
regroup quietly in Olon, the ancient seat of Intarra and the site of her first
temple, to leave Annur for a holier city farther from the grasping claws of
the Malkeenians. The exodus of soldiers seemed to have kindled similar
sentiment in the more devout civilians as well. Hence the weekly caravans
to the south.

It was a disaster, Adare thought, staring at the crowd pressed around
her, a disaster for those leaving their homes and for the empire itself. She
had incited something perilously close to open rebellion in the very streets
of the capital.

And the irony, she thought grimly, *is that without this 'Kent-kissing rebellion I'd have no stones left to play against Ran.*

What she was planning felt like madness, a desperate gambit to leverage the instability of the empire itself in order to reclaim the Unhewn Throne for her family, and yet it wasn't really the end of the Malkeenian line that worried her. Despite her own eyes, Adare had no illusions about Malkeenian sanctity. Over the centuries, her family had furnished dozens of emperors, some capable, some less so. The idea of leaving the empire to il Tornja, however . . . that seemed both a dangerous and cowardly course.

The sedition of the Church of Intarra, dangerous as it might prove, was predictable, comprehensible. The Intarrans, like dozens of religious sects before them, wanted power. They resented the encroachment of secular government into those spheres of life they deemed holy, and they deemed everything holy. It was an old story and a familiar one, almost comforting beside the mysteries of il Tornja's coup.

Adare had no idea why the *kenarang* had murdered her father, no idea what he intended toward her, no idea if he had already killed her brothers, no idea what he planned for the empire. She'd been over and over the matter, coming at it from every conceivable angle, but there just wasn't enough information. It was possible that il Tornja was some sort of foreign spy, that he had been suborned by Anthera or Freeport or the Manjari Empire. Maybe he was acting alone. Perhaps he wanted to destroy the empire or maybe he just wanted to milk it for his own material gain. There was just no way to know.

Her ignorance was infuriating, but as her father had said many times over, *Often there is no good path. That does not mean we should not walk.*

In the end, Adare kept circling back to the same basic point: the Church of Intarra, so recently her deadly foe, could well prove the salvation, not just of the Malkeenians, but of Annur itself. Only the Sons of Flame had the training and the numbers to pose a plausible threat to il Tornja. If she could bring them under her aegis, if she could incite them to turn against the regent, she would have a ready-made army of her own. *If.* The word was like a knife pressed against her throat.

This, however, was not the time to flinch. She was committed now, had been since she fled her own guardsmen, which meant going south, meeting with Vestan Ameredad, humbling herself, admitting her error with Uinian, then trying to piece back together an army she had done everything in her power to destroy. The only good thing about the situation was that the outflow of pilgrims to Olon gave her the cover necessary to hide her flight from the city.

It had seemed simple enough to join the group—a matter of good boots, a pilgrim's robe, and the muslin cloth to cover her eyes. Now that she was a part of the throng, however, her stomach knotted inside her. The odds of being recognized were low, especially with the blindfold; nearly a million people lived in and around Annur, and those emigrating to Olon were not likely to have spent any time in the Dawn Palace. On the other hand, Adare had ridden in dozens of imperial processions over the years, spent countless days sitting before the court. Just months earlier, thousands upon thousands of citizens had seen her at Sanlitun's funeral. Her newly cut hair and pilgrim's robes felt like a meager disguise in the midst of so many eyes.

She wondered what would happen if she were discovered. It would be insanity for them to kill a princess, certain treason, but then, no one in the Dawn Palace had any idea where she was. Her fellow pilgrims could beat her bloody, slit her throat, and toss her in the canal without anyone the wiser. Bodies washed up in the Basin all the time. She imagined her corpse, bloated and rotting, face disfigured. One of the canal tenders would fish her out with a long iron hook, toss her body on a cart, and dispose of it in some shallow pit outside the city, all without a second glance. The missing princess would remain missing. Ran il Tornja would remain on the throne.

She set her jaw, shoved the thought from her mind, pushed into the crowd, searching for a wagon that wasn't too overloaded. She'd bought only a few changes of clothes, a decent-sized water skin, a wool bedroll, and a supply of fruit and nuts in the event that the caravan didn't pass through a town for a day or two. It didn't look like much—plenty of the men and women clustered on the Godsway were laden with three or four times that weight—and yet Adare could already feel the leather straps of the pack biting into her shoulders, the muscles of her neck and back clenching beneath the unfamiliar load.

She had no idea how long it would take her body to adjust. It was tempting to simply grit her teeth and carry the pack herself, but the thought of walking fifteen miles a day already had her nervous. The group of pilgrims provided both her shield from il Tornja and her protection from bandits along the road. An injury that forced her to leave the caravan partway could well prove disastrous. Better to be cautious. For a few copper flames, one of the families would be willing to toss her small pack on the back of a wagon each day.

Most of the carts were piled so high she didn't even bother to approach. A converted carriage seemed a likely choice until she drew close enough to see the way the boards bowed at the sides, the warp of the wheels. She didn't know much about transport, but the thing didn't look as though it would make it past the Annurian walls, let alone all the way to Olon. She was sizing up a low farmer's cart when a vicious cursing cut through the conversation around her.

"Ya've cross-lashed it, ya shriveled nutsack! Straight-lashed, I said. It's t'be *straight*-lashed."

Adare turned to find a tiny, wizened woman, well into her eighth decade judging from the bone-white hair pinned up on the back of her head and the wrinkles etched into her weathered skin. She was cursing at a crabbed, gray man in a voice so loud it seemed impossible such an instrument could issue from such a tiny form. Despite her stoop, the cane in her right hand appeared superfluous: rather than leaning on it, she used the worn length of wood to stab at the provocative lashings.

"I swear," she continued, spitting as she spoke, "if our mother hadn't'a squoze us out'a the same fuckin' cunt, I'd knock ya on that fool fucking head of yours, take the cart my own self, and have done with ya."

"Please, Nira," the man replied, muddling with the straps. "We are part of a religious pilgrimage now. This is no way to speak among these devout folk." His language was more precise than hers and a good deal more polite, but there was a vagueness to his voice when he spoke, an emptiness in the eyes, as though he had just woken up, or were immensely weary.

"Pilgrimage my withered, bony arse!" the woman replied. "It's a bunch'a fucking cretins never spliced a yoke or mended an axle in their lives."

The words produced an eddy of discontent in the crowd. People paused in their work or their farewells, turning toward her angrily. Several appeared on the verge of speech, but the woman's advanced age seemed to earn her a reprieve. The old man had not so much as glanced at the other pilgrims or looked at his sister. He continued to tug with obvious futility at the wrong knot. His mind was going, Adare decided, irritated at the woman for so abusing him in his dotage.

"I will fix the lashing, sister," he said quietly, "if you will cease prodding it for a moment."

The old woman snorted, but she lowered her cane and turned from the wagon as though searching for another target. Her eyes lit on Adare.

"And what in the fine fuck is wrong with *you*?" she demanded, squinting beneath her wrinkled brow.

Adare froze, uncertain how to respond.

"Ya blind?" the woman pressed. "Dumb?" She took a step closer, waving her cane in the air before Adare's nose in the way a horse breaker might show a beast the halter. "Sweet 'Shael, ya ain't sluggish in the head, are ya?"

"No," Adare managed finally, trying to keep her voice low. The old woman had drawn too much attention already.

"Good," she snapped, " 'cause I got more than plenty a' crazy with this brain-buggered arsehole." She jerked a thumb at her brother, shook her head in irritation, and half turned back to the wagon. Adare started to blow out a sigh of relief, but the woman hesitated, cursed under her breath—something about *letting the fool girl wander*—then, with obvious reluctance, rounded on her once more, stepping in close this time. "What's with the cloth on your eyes?"

"Nira," the man interjected, shaking his head and peering suddenly up into the sky, "the young woman's attire is really none of our business. The clouds," he waved a vague hand, "*they* are our business. The clouds and the sky and the rain . . ." He trailed off, staring blankly into the distance.

"Oh bugger off with your business, Oshi," the woman snapped. "Child's standing 'ere like a poleaxed steer, baffled as a bitch in heat, and you're on about business. What about fixing the fucking lashing while you're at it, eh? What about that business?"

She turned back to Adare, waving her over imperiously.

"Quit standin' there like a silly slut and let me have a look at the problem. River blindness, is it? I've seen plenty river blindness, and a strip a' cloth is no way to handle it. . . ."

Adare tried to back away, but the knot of people had tightened around her as more pressed in from the periphery. She could try to force her way free, but that seemed likely to draw more attention than the old woman herself.

"It's not river blindness," she muttered. She knew as soon as the words were out that the lie was foolish. She'd already told Lehav that she *did* have river blindness, but this woman seemed intent on checking the injury for herself. Adare raised a nervous hand to the blindfold. "I don't think it's river blindness," she said again, a little more loudly. "I don't have the bleeding or the lesions."

"Let me have a look," the old woman said, stretching up and frowning. "No good hiding from the truth."

Adare jerked back. "I'm not hiding," she snapped, more loudly than she had intended. More heads turned and she cursed herself silently. "It's a normal case of dimming," she went on more quietly. "My physician said binding them, shielding them from the light, would slow the damage."

The old woman spat on the broad flags. "Physician, is it? How many pretty gold suns ya toss his way for that fine piece of fuckery?"

"He knows his work," Adare countered.

"Bilkin' the rich, ya mean?" The woman shook her head dismissively. Something that might have been the shadow of pity flashed in her shrewd eyes. "No way ta stop the dimming," she said. "Sorry, girl, but the light's going, pretty cloth on your eyes or no."

Adare nodded slowly. "I know that. It's why I'm joining the pilgrimage, to show my devotion to Intarra. Perhaps the goddess will hear my prayers and restore my light."

It had seemed an elegant solution—her disguise was also her motivation. With one story she could explain the blindfold and the journey both. Nira, however, seemed less than convinced. She cocked her head to one side, fixing Adare with one unwavering dark eye, a stare that seemed to stretch on half the morning.

"That's what *he* thinks," she said finally, waving the cane at her brother. "Hopes the goddess might unscramble his egg. I told 'im she's just as likely ta hoist up m'tired old tits, and I ain't countin' on that, either."

"Sister," Oshi said, turning from the lashings. "Leave the girl her hope. Intarra is ancient and her ways are inscrutable. . . ."

"*I'm* ancient," Nira snapped, "and I've screwed on a *few* tables, and I'll tell ya this for free: better to 'ave a pig than a goddess." She waved her cane at one of the black-bellied beasts nosing for scraps around the wheels of the wagon. "A pig's real. You can hit a pig," she said, thwacking the beast across the flank and earning an outraged squeal in response. "You can kick a pig. If you're lonely and not particular, you can fuck a pig, and then, in the mornin', butcher it up for bacon. A pig's *real*," she said again. "Realer than your flim-flammy bitch of a goddess."

Oshi shook his head. "I have explained to you, sister, the importance of faith in these matters."

"Yes," Adare said, nodding eagerly. "I, too, have faith in the goddess. With her divine care, all will be well in the end." It sounded like the sort of mindless patter a naïve young pilgrim might well believe.

Nira rolled her eyes. "Better a limp fuck than a whole bucket a' faith. Faith gets ya killed, and you," she continued, stabbing a finger at Adare, "oughta pay attention ta that little lesson. As for all bein' well in the end, th'end's gonna come sooner rather than later for you, ya don't smarten up."

Adare nodded hesitantly.

Nira waited for her to respond, then grimaced, glancing around at the milling crowd. "C'm'ere," she muttered, lowering her voice, gesturing to the far side of the wagon where a crush of squealing black pigs had forced away the pilgrims. Adare didn't move.

"Come *over* here, ya willful little slut," she pressed, glaring. " 'Less ya want me saying what I got to say right out here in the open, which I'm thinking ya don't."

Adare hesitated. What she *wanted* was to slip away from the woman as quickly as possible, but slipping away didn't seem to be an option. Worse, there was something knowing in Nira's tone, something almost accusatory, that pricked up the hairs on the back of her neck. After a moment more Adare nodded, then followed, clutching at her dress, trying to keep it clear of the press of muddy pigs. When they had stepped far enough around the wagon that the sideboard obscured the closest pilgrims, Nira rounded on her.

"Listen," she hissed, voice low, eyes shifting vigilantly over Adare's shoulder. "You want to leave your palace and play poor little blind girl, I'm sure you have your reasons."

Fear took Adare by the throat. "I'm not—" she began.

Nira waved down the objection. "Quit it. I'm not in the secret-trading trade and I'm not looking to join it now. A girl's got a right to her lies— 'Shael knows I've learned that lesson a few dozen times over—but," she continued, stabbing Adare squarely in the chest with a bony fingertip, driving her back against the rough wood of the wagon, "you look likely to step squarely in the shit without any pushing on my part." She shook her head, jabbed at the mud with her cane, and muttered angrily under her breath. "I've got enough to do keeping Oshi's cracked nut in one piece, and now I've got you, too."

"You don't have—" Adare began, heart slamming against her ribs.

"Oh, 'Shael's shit I don't," the woman snapped, raising her voice once more. "Without me, you'd be fucked up the arse with a thick, crooked dick before we slipped past the city walls. Now toss your sack on the wagon and move outta my way before I get cross."

8

Valyn stood by the window, cold wind scouring his face, staring out into the night. He had insisted on taking first watch, and the rest of his Wing, accustomed to catching fragments of rest whenever, wherever, converted their coats and packs into makeshift blankets and pillows, arranged weapons for easy access, then dropped abruptly into sleep. The others weren't far behind, and by the time the first stars were glittering overhead only Kaden remained awake. He sat cross-legged just a pace away, gazing out over the low lintel of the same window. For a long while neither said a word.

"What's the point in standing watch," Kaden asked finally, "when you can't see anything?" He gestured toward the window. "I feel like I'm looking into the bottom of an iron pot."

Valyn hesitated. He hadn't told Kaden about his experience in Hull's Hole, hadn't told him about the slarn egg or the strange abilities it had conferred, hadn't told him . . . anything really.

"Why are *you* still awake?" he countered. "The plan was to get some sleep before you have to step through that thing."

Kaden glanced toward the *kenta* and nodded, but made no move to lie down. "I don't think a little more sleep is going to tip the balance one way or the other."

"Those gates are really all over the empire?"

"And beyond it, evidently. They're many thousands of years older than Annur. The boundaries of the empire weren't even imagined when the Csestriim built them."

"But Father knew about them," Valyn pressed. "He used them?"

Kaden spread his hands. "That's what the Shin told me."

"Where is it?" Valyn asked. "The gate in Annur?"

"I don't know. I never saw anything like this. Never *heard* of it before the abbot explained it all to me."

"How do people not know?" Valyn wondered, staring at the gracile arch. "How could Father cross half the world in a heartbeat without anyone *suspecting*?"

"I've thought about that a lot," Kaden said. "It wouldn't be as obvious as you think. Say the Emperor steps through a gate from Annur to . . . oh . . . Ludgven. The people in Ludgven don't know that he was in Annur. All they know is that the Emperor arrived unexpectedly. One of the chroniclers could piece it all together later, someone who kept detailed notes and a careful calendar, but it would have been difficult to keep good notes about Father's coming and going. Half the time even *we* didn't know where he was, and we lived in the palace."

Valyn nodded slowly. Sanlitun had disappeared for days at a time when they were children. "Meditating," their mother told them. "Praying to Intarra for guidance." Valyn had never understood the need for all that prayer and contemplation. As he pondered the use of the gates, however, Sanlitun's self-imposed austerity began to look far less arbitrary. As Hendran wrote: *Be a rumor. Be a ghost. Your foes should not believe in your existence.* The Emperor of Annur couldn't afford to recede entirely into rumor, but their father had kept himself so aloof from the day-to-day business of the empire that he could well have disappeared for days without anyone noticing.

"All those years," Valyn said, shaking his head. "All those years, and we had no idea."

"We were children."

"We were children." Valyn exhaled slowly, watching his breath mist in the cold night air. "There was a lot I wanted to ask him."

Kaden remained silent such a long time that Valyn thought he had faded off to sleep. When he glanced over, however, he found his brother's eyes still open, still burning, twin embers in the darkness.

"What does it feel like?" Kaden asked finally. "The grief, I mean."

Valyn tried to make sense of the question. "For Father?"

"For anyone."

Valyn shook his head. "You tell me. You just saw your entire monastery destroyed."

"I did," Kaden replied, not taking his eyes from the darkness. "I did. There was a little boy, Pater . . . I watched as Ut stabbed him through the chest."

"So why are you asking me about grief? Seems like there's plenty to go around."

"I'm asking because the monks train it out of you. I felt it when Pater died, felt like my legs might just give way beneath me, but now . . ." He shook his head slowly. "You learn to set it aside, to move past it."

"Sounds like a 'Kent-kissing blessing to me," Valyn replied, more bitterly than he'd intended. Just the memory of Ha Lin's limp body as he carried her from the Hole, of the wounds running down her arms, of her hair brushing his skin, made his breath stick in his chest. "Sometimes, when I think about it too much, I feel like my muscles have torn clean off the bones, like someone snapped all the tendons and ligaments holding me together. I *wish* I could move past it."

"Maybe," Kaden replied. "And maybe it's not real if you can toss it aside like a cracked cup."

"*Fuck* real," Valyn spat. Blood throbbed at his temples. His knuckles ached. Memories flooded over him: of Balendin laughing as he recounted Lin's torment on the West Bluffs, of blood gushing from the knife in Salia's neck, of Yurl groveling in front of him in the darkness, hands lopped from his arms. He would have yanked the bastard back from death, out of Ananshael's iron grip, just so he could stab him again and again, a thousand times over, so he could split his skull open. . . .

Breath rasped in his lungs. Sweat streamed down his back, cold in the cold night air. Kaden was staring at him, he realized, eyes wide with confusion or concern.

"Are you all right?" he asked. "Valyn?"

Valyn focused on his brother's eyes, on his voice, vision and sound braided into a cord that was drawing him up, up from the bottom of a deep well where he had been drowning.

"I'm all right," he said finally, voice ragged, wiping his brow with a sleeve.

"You don't look it."

Valyn chuckled grimly. " 'All right' is relative."

He started to say something more, a few more words to ease the tension, when something, the faintest sound at the very edge of hearing, brought him up short. Kaden stared at him.

"What is—"

Valyn cut him off with a raised hand. He could hear the various members of his Wing sleeping—Talal's light snore, Gwenna's constant shifting—he could hear the lisp of the wind over the stone, even the rumble and hiss of the waterfall as it plunged off the cliff a few hundred paces to the north. But there was something more, something else. He closed his eyes, straining for the sound. It was hard to hear past his own pulse thudding in his ears, and for a moment he thought he'd imagined it. Then it came again—a soft scuff of fabric over stone. Someone outside the window, someone climbing, quieter than the wind.

Without thinking, Valyn took Kaden by the shoulder, hauling him back into the room while putting his own body between his brother and the gaping windows. Climbing meant Kettral, and though he had no idea how they'd managed to track him through the mountains, a part of him had been prepared for this moment. He slid a blade from the sheath over his shoulder as he pushed Kaden deeper into the room, offering up a brief thanks to Hull that his brother had the good sense to move with him, to remain silent.

The scuffing was gone, but there was a strange smell on the air, the faintest hint of smoke. Not woodsmoke, not a hearth or campfire. Woodsmoke didn't taste like that, didn't sting the nasal passage in quite the same way. This was a different smell, more dangerous, one familiar from a thousand training missions. . . .

"Cover up," Valyn shouted, shattering the night's quiet. "Explosives incoming."

Even as he said the words, he was dragging Kaden to the floor, then throwing his own body on top as he covered his ears with his hands. He couldn't know what sort of munitions their attackers were lighting, but if the explosion didn't kill them all, the first moments after would prove crucial. He wanted to be able to hear, to see. Kaden went completely still beneath him, and Valyn shifted to shield as much of his brother as possible. Something clattered to the floor behind them. He squeezed his eyes shut just before the world went white, opening them only when the initial elemental fury had passed, subsiding into a more prosaic mess of shouts and screams.

They were alive. He'd felt the blast, but no shrapnel had ripped through his flesh. He wasn't on fire. That meant they were using smokers. Smokers and flashbangs. *So they're not trying to kill us, at least not yet.* On the other hand, it wasn't looking much like a diplomatic mission. The whole point of smokers and flashbangs was to force the foe into panic and error. Which meant the first step was not to panic, not to rush. There was time. Not much, but time.

Slowly, Valyn told himself silently. *Slowly.*

If he raised his head more than a foot above the floor the smoke blinded and choked him, but there was still a hand's breadth of relatively clean air beneath the pall, and Valyn dropped back down into it. He could see his Wing's tactical lanterns—both still lit—and the shapes of the rest of the group moving in the fickle illumination. It was hard to be sure who was who, but Valyn could pick apart the voices now—Triste screaming, Gwenna and Laith cursing, Talal and Annick nearly silent as they moved over the floor. Of their attackers, Valyn could hear nothing.

"That other Kettral Wing?" Kaden asked, shifting beside him. "The Flea?"

"Might be," Valyn said, working the problem through from a dozen angles at the same time. The attackers hadn't simply blown up the building, which would have been easy enough. Either they wanted prisoners or, better yet, they had seen the carnage in the mountains, had sorted through the bodies and realized what it meant.

Be on our side, Valyn prayed silently. *Please, Hull, let them be on our side.*

"What should—" Kaden began.

"Stay quiet," Valyn hissed, "and get down below the smoke."

He glanced over the room once more, counted bodies. Pyrre was missing, he realized, although where the assassin had gone, Valyn had no idea. His Wing was handling the attack as they'd been trained, staying low, crawling toward the walls in order to follow them to doors, windows, cleaner air. The problem was that whoever tossed the smokers was probably waiting at those very doors and windows, and rigging the stairs had cut off their own most obvious escape route.

The most obvious escape route, Valyn thought, checking the distance to Gwenna's charges, *but not the only one.*

He patted his belt pouch for the Kettral whistles. There was no way of knowing if their birds were still in the air, but if he and his Wing could win free of the building, the ledge was large enough for a grab.

If, he reminded himself. *You're not on the 'Kent-kissing ledge, and you've got four people who've never even contemplated a grab-and-go.*

It was a grim fucking position, no doubt about it, and likely to get a whole lot grimmer.

A few feet away, Triste had risen to her hands and knees. Blind with the smoke and her own confusion, she was crawling frantically but aimlessly, trying to shout but choking each time she drew a breath. It wouldn't be long before she passed out. Worse, she might remain conscious long enough to stand and stumble out one of the low windows. Valyn started toward her, then checked himself. *Prioritize.* Kaden was the Emperor, which meant Valyn needed to get Kaden to safety first, even if Triste fell to her death.

He scanned the narrow space between the floor and the roiling smoke. His Wing had taken up defensive positions around the perimeter of the room—or the best positions they could manage while staying below the smoke—then drawn their blades and bows and waited. Rampuri Tan, however, was standing, moving, his feet and ankles visible. The monk was taking careful, deliberate steps toward Valyn and Kaden, the end of his strange spear sweeping the floor in front of him. The movements had none of Triste's spasmodic terror. Valyn turned back to his Wing. Talal was waving at him silently, his face against the stone floor. When he saw Valyn looking, the leach shifted over to hand sign: *No injuries. Weapons intact. Orders?*

Valyn allowed himself a small smile. The initial attack had wrought plenty of chaos, but it hadn't broken them. He still had command of his Wing and contact with Kaden. Better yet, only a few dozen heartbeats had passed since the initial assault, and they were already starting to recover. *If surprise doesn't work in four heartbeats, it's not surprise anymore.* Even better, the fact that the attackers clearly wanted someone alive—for whatever reason—severely constrained their options: no hail of arrows, no barrage of starshatters. It might be possible to talk. Worth a try, at least, though Valyn didn't intend to count on it.

Stand by to blow charges, he signed back, indicating the section of floor that Gwenna had rigged earlier. *Wait for my signal.*

Talal nodded, and Gwenna crawled forward on her elbows, striking stick in her teeth.

Finally the attacker spoke.

"Valyn." It was the Flea's voice, gravelly and dry, pitched to carry, but with no hint of urgency or anxiety. He was on the roof, near the corner that had been torn away by the weather.

Half draw, Valyn signed to Annick. *Hold fire.*

She nodded and rolled into place. It was a ridiculous position to shoot from, lying on her back, head cocked to the side to breathe the clean air, bow drawn across her body, but the sniper made it look natural, easy.

"Valyn," the Flea said again, his voice almost weary, "I just want to talk."

Valyn held his silence. Talking was all well and good, it was what he'd hoped for, but he didn't intend to give away his position just to have a conversation. A part of him was relieved to hear the Flea's voice. Back on the Islands, the man had always seemed hard but fair. On the other hand, if the Wing leader *was* a part of the conspiracy . . . Valyn didn't like to think about the possibility.

His own Wing was good enough to squeeze out of a tight place, but then, this wasn't your garden-variety, all-fucked-up, odds-stacked-against-the-good-guys tight place. Up on that roof, no more than a dozen paces away, was the best small-team tactical commander in the world, the man who literally wrote the book on inverted rose-and-thorn scenarios, who, in his early twenties, avenged the deaths of two older Kettral Wings by assassinating Casimir Damek, who went down into Hull's Hole *every year* to haul out slarn for the Trial. After Hendran himself, there was no more revered Kettral commander, and now he had the high ground and the drop on them.

So you'd best think quick, Valyn growled silently, *and skip the fuckups.*

"Look," the Flea continued after a moment, "I understand that you can't talk because you don't want to give away your position. You're doing everything right. Better than right, actually. I have no idea how you managed to move before we threw the smokers. You're young, but you're smart, and I'll stop insulting you with stuff from the old Kettral bag of tricks and traps. We trained you not to talk, so don't talk. Just listen.

"No one's run screaming out the window, and aside from the girl, who stopped hacking up her own lung about a minute ago, everyone's quiet, which means you're belly-down, sucking up the good air." He paused. "Speaking of that girl, you might want to move her toward a window."

Valyn glanced over at Triste's limp form. In the chaos he hadn't noticed her slump to the ground. Her face was ashen, her hands curled into claws, and for the second time Valyn started to move toward her. For the second time, he stopped himself. Fainting had dropped her out of the smoke. She was breathing clean air now. There was no need to move her anywhere.

"Suit yourself," the Flea continued after a moment, and Valyn realized that the man hadn't dropped the tricks at all. They'd spent three whole months on this back on the Islands, learning to exploit civilian casualties, to use an adversary's own feelings of guilt or heroism against him. He could hear Nhean Pitch's voice twanging in his ear: *If you're going to shoot some bastard, shoot him in the stomach. Stomach wounds hurt and they kill slow. Odds are, you'll get one of the other bastards to look after him, and that's one less bastard you've got to fight.* The Flea was testing him, Valyn realized, probing, systematically searching for a weakness. The trouble was, there were too many civilians to protect.

Valyn scanned the floor again, then turned to Kaden.

"Can you get out through that gate?" he hissed. "You and the monk?"

Kaden hesitated, then nodded.

"And they can't follow you, right?"

"No."

Valyn grinned. That was one trick the Flea wouldn't be expecting. Even better, it meant that however things played out, Kaden would be free and clear. If Valyn could hold off the attack for just a little while longer, the Emperor would be safe. *Then* he could see what the Flea had to say. If the man was telling the truth, maybe they could work something out, and if not . . . well, at least his brother wouldn't find himself caught in the middle of a bloodbath.

"Let's go," Valyn whispered, bellying forward. "We'll grab your monk on the way."

The Flea started in again just as they began to move.

"You can tell Annick to put the bow down," he said. "She's not going to hit anything from that position. The game's up, kid. We've got the windows covered and the stairs, too, although Gwenna did such a nice job laying those charges that you wouldn't be able to get down them anyway. Newt says the girl's got real talent."

A pause. How Rampuri Tan was still moving toward them through the smoke, Valyn had no idea, but they were fast converging on the monk's sweeping spear. Valyn hesitated. Tan couldn't see them through the smoke, couldn't know that it *was* them, and surprising him seemed like a good way to get that blade in the belly. Valyn considered a quick takedown, but Tan didn't seem like the sort to go down quickly. That meant talking, which meant giving away their position, but there was nothing to do but get on with it.

"Tan," he hissed, as loudly as he dared. "I'm with Kaden. Drop down below the smoke."

The sweeping spear paused, then the monk's hands and face appeared a few feet away. Tan let out a long, slow breath, glanced at Kaden, then Valyn, then nodded. He'd been holding his breath, Valyn realized, probably since the smokers first dropped. It was possible, though the presence of mind involved rivaled that of Valyn's own Wing, and they'd actually trained for this kind of shit.

"The gate," Valyn whispered, gesturing toward the wall where it stood. "You and Kaden get through and you'll be safe."

The monk nodded as though that had been his plan all along.

"We'll cover you until you're clear," Valyn said.

"What about you?" Kaden asked.

"Don't worry about us. We'll be fine."

Or captured, or dead, he amended silently before glancing over his shoulder. His people were still in position, still awaiting orders. It was the Flea who had told him, what seemed like a lifetime ago, that it seemed like they'd make a good Wing. They'd held together; now it was his job to get them out alive.

First, Kaden, Valyn reminded himself, bellying forward once more. Then talk. If the talk didn't work, Gwenna could blow the floor. Then they'd see who was surprised.

"Valyn," the Flea continued after a moment. "I'll be straight with you. I saw what happened at Ashk'lan, the slaughtered monks. We found what's left of Yurl's Wing and the other Aedolians spread over half the mountainside. Back on the Islands they're naming you a traitor, but I'm not so sure. You never struck me as the traitorous type, and now that I've seen what I've seen . . ." He let the suggestion hang in the air a moment. "Come on out, let's discuss this, before you do something dumb and Finn has to put an arrow through you."

Valyn tried to weigh his response.

"Besides," the Flea added, "you might as well talk to me now. I can hear you muttering down there."

Valyn took a deep breath. He'd given away his position, but maybe a little conversation would buy time for Kaden. "The thing is," he replied loudly, thinking back to the mountain pass days earlier, to the way he'd naïvely ordered his people to surrender their weapons, "trust hasn't been working out too well for me recently."

The Flea chuckled. "Looked like it worked out even less well for the men you were trusting."

"Yeah, well, we got lucky."

"Why don't you put down your weapons, and you can tell me about it."

Valyn tensed. He wanted to believe the man, but he'd be shipped to 'Shael before he willingly disarmed again. Right now they could still maneuver, bargain, fight. Without weapons . . . well, he didn't intend to throw the dice more than he had to.

When they reached the gate, Tan started talking to Kaden.

"Picture the bird," he began slowly.

"What?" Valyn demanded.

"It's a mental exercise," Kaden said quietly.

Valyn shook his head. "Fuck the fucking bird," he spat, "and get out of here. The Flea's all sweetness and small talk now, but he's not going to keep talking forever."

The older monk turned that stony gaze on Valyn. "If Kaden steps through the gate without the necessary preparation, he will cease. It cannot be rushed."

Valyn flexed and unflexed his sword hand. He could feel his luck flexing, straining, starting to splinter with each hammering heartbeat. "How long?"

"More time, the more you talk."

Valyn bit back a retort. He couldn't help Kaden, but he could use the time to prepare for the coming storm. Pivoting on his stomach, he scanned the room. Pyrre's disappearance worried him. The woman seemed to be on his side, but according to Kaden she'd already murdered one monk just for slowing things down. With any luck, the flashbangs had knocked her out a window, but luck didn't seem to be in much supply, and Valyn didn't like the idea of the Skullsworn prowling around where he couldn't keep an eye on her.

But then, what's to like?

Gwenna was gesturing toward him furiously, evidently confused by the delay. Annick held her position like a statue while Talal and Laith had split up, moving to opposite walls. *Stand by. . . .* Valyn signed. Blowing the floor was a way out, but a risky one. As long as the Flea was still trying to negotiate, there was still a chance they'd all walk away without violence. As long as he stayed on the 'Kent-kissing roof.

"I'm not ordering my people to disarm," Valyn said. "That's something else you taught me. But I don't mind talking. You keep your people up there. I'll keep my people down here. Very civilized."

"Works for me," the Flea replied.

"Now," Tan murmured to Kaden, "when the bird has flown from sight, fill your mind with the sky and step through the gate."

Valyn risked a glance over his shoulder to see Kaden's eyes, only a foot away but somehow impossibly distant, bright as coals from the forge, cold as the stars. His brother nodded once, then rose to his feet, disappearing into the smoke. It was only a step to the wall and then he was gone.

"Did it work?" Valyn hissed at the other monk. "Did he make it?"

"I will know when I reach the other side," Tan replied, then closed his own eyes, evidently in preparation.

Across the room Triste was stirring. Valyn still hadn't figured out how to handle her. He tried to run through the options. She was small, light enough to carry, but that would slow him down considerably. They could leave her to the Flea, use her as a diversion. She raised her head slowly, eyes baffled and full of fear. Valyn was about to motion to her to stay low, to keep quiet, when a pair of black boots hit the floor behind her.

"Company!" Laith shouted. "North window!"

Triste turned, screamed, then lunged to her feet, plunging through the smoke directly toward Valyn and Tan. She passed by coughing, flailing, close enough that Valyn was able to put out a hand, to feel the cloth of her borrowed uniform pass between his fingers. Then, suddenly, she was gone.

The gate, Valyn realized, ice in his stomach. She went through the gate, and with none of Kaden's preparation.

"She's gone," Tan said. If he felt at all sorry for the girl's annihilation, he didn't show it. "See to your own."

Then the monk rose into the smoke, stepped forward, and vanished.

Gone. The two monks *and* Triste. The Emperor was safe.

Valyn spun back to face the attacker. So all the Flea's offers of talk had been bullshit, a ruse. Valyn drew his second blade, ready to hurl himself at the attacker, then paused. There was something about those boots; Pyrre's boots.

"Wait, Gwenna," he shouted, rolling away from the gate. "They're not . . ."

Too late. The charges were already exploding, sharp cracks followed by the deafening rumble of stone folding in on itself. Valyn took a bearing on the location of the hole, cursing to himself as he slid into a crouch, readying himself to jump as soon as the rumbling ceased. If they'd had any hope of talking their way free, it was over now, or as good as. The only thing now was to get out, to get clear.

Only, the rumbling didn't stop. The whole building was shuddering beneath him now, stone falling from the ceiling at the same time as the floor dropped away. He couldn't see a 'Kent-kissing thing, shrouded as he was in smoke, but he could hear the structure protesting. He took a tentative step backward, away from the source of the explosion, and then, with a sickening lurch, the stone beneath his feet gave way.

9

"Go over it again," Nira said, prodding Adare in the gut with her cane.

Adare tried to swat it away, but the old woman was too fast, swinging the stick clear in a wide arc, then swatting her across the backside. The treatment was infuriating, humiliating, and terrifying all at once, but somehow Nira had ferreted out her identity, which meant that, until Adare found a solution to the problem, she had no choice but to endure the endless cursing and the welts crisscrossing her ass.

"Again," Nira insisted.

The second morning of the pilgrimage should have been pleasant—the air was cool and damp, the sun warm overhead, the reek of the city giving way to the smell of grass and dirt and growing things. The buildings were gone, replaced by wide fields, open sky, and the green-brown thread of the canal flowing out of the south, bearing colorful, narrow boats loaded high and bound for Annur. Adare couldn't see all the far-off details through her blindfold, but she could make out the colors, the generous contours of the countryside, the space.

It was tempting to believe she had escaped, had eluded il Tornja's reach when she slipped the boundaries of the city, but whenever she glanced over her shoulder she could still see Intarra's Spear, surface dazzling with refracted sunlight, a glass needle bisecting the northern sky. It had been her home for twenty years. Now the sight of the tower made her hands sweat. She tried not to look back.

Oshi rode atop the wagon, wrists protruding like sticks from his golden pilgrim's robe, eyes fixed on a pear he had been holding, uneaten, for hours. He chewed at the inside of his slack cheek and hummed tunelessly as he considered his fruit. Nira walked alongside, occasionally clucking her tongue at the team of water buffalo. They had fallen into a wide gap between the pilgrims ahead and those following behind, a space large enough that Adare could almost forget that in order to flee from one foe, she had surrounded herself with a group of others. It would have been nice to forget. Unfortunately, Nira was having none of it.

"Get going, girl," she said, thumping her cane against the side of the wagon.

"My name is Dorellin," Adare said wearily. "My father is a merchant. . . ."

"What does he sell?"

"Cloth."

"What kinda cloth?"

"Si'ite silk, primarily, although he supplements his trade with double-dyed wool from up north."

Nira blew out an exasperated breath. "Meshkent's great buggering cock, but you're a thickheaded bitch."

Adare colored with confusion and anger.

"What, exactly, is the problem with importing wool and silk?" she demanded, her irritation getting the better of her fear.

"*Primarily,*" Nira replied, ticking the word off on a gnarled finger. "*Supplements. Importing.*"

"They're hardly obscure words," Adare replied.

"Not if you spent your life pampered and petted in a palace."

Nira's accent and idiom seemed to shift as she spoke. In general the woman's speech was crude, crass, piled high with colorful expletives, but some times, as now, she slipped into a more polished idiom, as though she knew deep down how a woman ought to speak, but couldn't be bothered most of the time.

"According to the story, my father is rich. It's plausible that he educated me."

"Oh, it's *plausible,* all right, but we ain't shootin' for fuckin' *plausible*—which, by the way, is another bright, shiny word you ought not let slip past those pouty lips. We're shootin' for utterly *forgettable*. These cretins"—she waved a gnarled hand at the golden-robed faithful before and behind—"are near as thick as you, but they're not utterly without brains. You want 'em sayin' to each other, 'That Dorellin certainly is a bright young woman. She speaks so eloquently, so insightfully.'" She raised an eyebrow. "You want that?"

"The empire is filled with eloquent, insightful young women."

Nira snorted. "*Is* it? Where'd ya learn that? In the years ya spent down by the docks? Maybe it was all the time ya wasted loiterin' around the Greymarket, talkin' to other merchants' daughters." She furrowed her brow. "Well? How 'bout it? How many merchants' daughters ya meet sitting on your little princess throne?"

"Look," Adare said, seeing the point but refusing to concede it, "I appreciate your trying to help me, but I don't think it's working out. I'll be just fine on my own. I think it's best if we keep to ourselves, keep our own counsel from here on. People are more likely to notice us talking than they are to remark on a young woman walking quietly by herself."

"More idiocy," Nira snapped. "You got enough stupid to fill up a bucket."

Anger abruptly boiling over, Adare turned on the woman, stepping directly into her path, forcing her to stop. She stood more than a head higher, and she used every inch of her height, leaning in close, the words tangling in her throat before spilling out.

"I am an Annurian princess," she hissed. "I am a Malkeenian, and, until I fled the palace, I served as the Minister of Finance. I have no idea who you are, or how you decided that I was your responsibility, but, while I appreciate your aid, I will not tolerate either your treatment or your tone any longer."

She realized, when she finished speaking, that she was panting, the breath hot in her throat. The brief tirade had taken only a moment, and she had kept her voice quiet enough that none of the other pilgrims seemed to have noticed, but the cart following them was rapidly approaching, and Adare turned abruptly, striding ahead, not looking to see if the other woman was following. A band of fear tightened around her chest. It was one thing to resent Nira's ministrations, quite another to snap at the woman openly, almost publicly. So far, she'd been trying to help, but if she turned on Adare, she could end the whole façade with just a few words.

Stupid, Adare muttered at herself. *Rash and stupid.*

After a few worried paces, she heard the woman approaching, cane tapping on the stone flags. She was wheezing with the effort. No, Adare realized, not wheezing. Nira was laughing at her. Relief welled up, followed closely by a new surge of anger.

"You're a stupid slut, all right, but at least ya got some spirit to ya. Now go over it again, or I'll tell this whole lot who y'are."

Adare took a deep breath, quelling her temper, vowing not to let the woman's gibes get the better of her again. Merchants' daughters might be proud, but they weren't as proud as princesses, and Nira's insults weren't likely to be the last that Adare faced. She couldn't afford to explode every time she felt slighted, not if she wanted to survive the pilgrimage. Not if she wanted to reach Olon, Vestan Ameredad, and the disbanded Sons of Flame.

Adare opened her mouth to rehearse her story once more when Oshi, from his perch atop the wagon, abruptly began to weep. He sobbed with his whole body, skinny frame convulsing, hands still clutching the pear just inches from his face.

"No," he moaned. "No, no, *no . . .*"

Nira grimaced and turned to the wagon, Adare forgotten. With surprising nimbleness, the old woman climbed onto the loaded bed and seated herself next to her brother.

"Knock off with that pissin' and moanin'," she snapped. "No one wants ta hear a cracked old man sobbin' over some 'Kent-kissing fruit."

The words were hard, but Nira slid a hand in gentle circles over her brother's back as he wept. Oshi's tears dampened his robe where they fell. Seen from behind the blindfold, those wet patches on the golden cloth might have been stains rather than tears, or burns in the fabric.

"It's dead, Nira," he sobbed, holding up the pear. "I killed it."

"You didn't kill it, ya old fuck," she snapped, rooting in the wagon bed as she spoke. "Whoever picked it killed it, and besides, it's gotta be dead if ya want to eat it, don't it?"

Oshi just shook his head helplessly, then pressed his furrowed brow against the pear, as though trying to commune with the fruit. After a little more rummaging about, Nira came up with a rough clay bottle, unstoppered it, moved the pear aside, and held the vessel to her brother's lips.

"Here," she said. "Have some of this. It'll make ya feel better."

Adare caught a whiff of some unfamiliar liquor, both potent and acrid. Even at a distance, it made her eyes water, and yet Oshi slurped at it eagerly, taking the bottle in his own hands and tilting it backward until Nira stopped him.

"That's plenty now. Bad enough listening to all your groanin' without having ya piss all over the wagon."

Oshi relinquished the vessel reluctantly, and Nira recorked it, then set it down inside the wagon's bed out of the sun.

"Now eat your pear, ya crazy old bastard," she said, handing back the fruit.

The man took a small bite, tested the soft white flesh on his tongue, then chewed it slowly.

"It's sweet," he said, as though marveling at the discovery.

"Of course it's sweet, ya idiot," Nira replied, draping an arm across his shoulders. "Of course it's fuckin' sweet."

Suddenly embarrassed, Adare turned away. There was nothing remarkable about the sight, just an old man and an old woman sitting side by side, one munching through a pear, the other watching him with a blend of fondness and irritation, the whole thing transpiring in the open, beneath the warm gaze of the sun. And yet, for some reason she couldn't place, Adare felt as though she were spying, witnessing a moment that should have been private. Confused and chagrined, she stopped, looking out over the canal as the wagon jolted on down the road.

It was impossible to imagine sharing such a scene with Kaden or Valyn. Even as children, before they were sent away, there had been a distance between Adare and her brothers, a gap of years and gender that proved impossible to bridge. The boys' invented adventures in the Dawn Palace seemed so pointless, so childish, next to the very real politics and maneuvering unfolding all around them.

"You should stay with your brothers," Sanlitun told her once, when she demanded to accompany him to yet another imperial audience. "You should try to know them."

"There's nothing to know!" Adare had complained. She was eight years old at the time, which meant Kaden was five and Valyn even younger. "They're babies. They play like babies and they cry like babies. I want to go with *you,* to do something important."

"They will not be babies forever, Adare," Sanlitun replied, putting his arm around her shoulder. "A day will come when they need you, especially Kaden."

And yet, despite the admonishment, he had allowed her to accompany him, to sit silent and still on an upholstered cushion to the right of the Unhewn Throne as he went about the business of the empire. And then, one day, her brothers were gone, shipped away to opposite ends of the earth.

For years she had barely noticed their absence. Her studies consumed her at first. Then, as she grew older, Sanlitun gave her more and more responsibility: the greeting of foreign delegations, year-long apprenticeships in the various ministries, short journeys beyond the city walls, always heavily guarded, to observe the local estates and industries. When she reached her fifteenth year, Sanlitun even had a second desk moved into his study, a smaller version of his own, where she was allowed to work with him late into the night, the two companionably silent as he reviewed the endless ephemera of government and she studied whatever stack of maps or papers he set in front of her.

She knew it wouldn't last forever, that one day Kaden would return, that one day her father would die. The knowledge had done nothing to prepare her for the event. Now, with both her parents gone and her only home vanished down the long road behind her, with nothing ahead but fear and uncertainty, she wondered how it might feel to have a brother, two brothers, siblings who understood something of what it meant to grow up in the Dawn Palace, whom she could talk to about her father and mother, whom she could trust. *We wouldn't even need to talk,* she thought, stealing a glance at Nira and Oshi, *if they were just* here.

She felt her eyes filling, and, forgetting about the cloth for a moment, tried to scrub the unshed tears away with an angry swipe of her sleeve. There was no telling where Kaden and Valyn were, no way to know if they were still alive, and no promise she could rely on them even if they were. Wishing was all well and good, but if her brothers were still alive clearly they were in no position to do anything to help either her or the empire. They were strangers, absent strangers. Despite the hundreds of pilgrims walking the road before her and behind, despite Nira and Oshi sitting on the wagon a few paces distant, she was alone.

10

The smoke was gone, and the shouting, and the rough stone beneath his feet. Kaden had walked from darkness and chaos into daylight, the sun shining hot overhead, warming his face, his hands. But the sun was wrong. At Ashk'lan it never rose so high in the sky, not even during the summer solstice. And the wind: warm and wet as a cloth drawn steaming from the wash and heavy with salt. The sounds, too, wrong: a keen skirling of seabirds; a scrape like rough steel across stone that Kaden recognized, after a moment, as waves. Gone, the spice of juniper. Vanished, the chill stillness of the granite peaks.

In the emptiness of the *vaniate* he registered the impressions one after another but felt no alarm, no surprise. These were facts, nothing more, details of the world to be noted, tallied. This is the earth. This is the sky. No fear attended the strangeness of the sight, no excitement its novelty. Here are the small, fork-tailed birds darting into the waves. Here is the sea.

Kaden glanced back through the empty gate, half expecting to see smoke and madness, to hear the shouted orders and cries of dismay from which he had just fled. But there was no darkness. There were no shouts or cries. All he could see beneath the arch of the *kenta* was a long line of unbroken swells, swift and silent as they rode the ocean's back. Altogether elsewhere—a thousand miles off . . . two thousand . . . a few steps through the *kenta*—Valyn was fighting for his life, fighting or captured, dying or dead. It was real, but it didn't feel real. It might have been a dream, all of it. It might never have happened. The sun, the sea, the sky, all of it seemed too much, too present, and suddenly Kaden felt like he was falling, unmoored from the ground below, the sky above, cut free from his own self, and he turned, searching for something more steady than the gray sea's sway.

He stood on a grassy sward a few paces from the edge of a large bluff where the ground plunged straight down—a hundred paces or more—into the gnawing surf. Waves battered the rock, flinging spray into the air. The too-high sun cast a crisp, foreshortened shadow of the *kenta* on the earth before him, and after a moment, Kaden realized he was on an island, the whole thing no more than a quarter mile around, edged with cliff on every side. Beyond, the ocean stretched unbroken to the horizon, where heat blurred the line between heavy air and the heavier water below.

Before he could take in more, a figure stumbled through the gate, lurching into him, knocking him to the grass, shattering the *vaniate* like crockery. Not Tan. Too small to be Tan. Fear flooded in, knife-bright and sudden. Someone had followed him through the gate. It should have been impossible, but the gate itself was already impossible. Someone was on top of him, fingernails scratching at his eyes, hands groping for his neck, searching for some purchase as he twisted beneath the weight. Confusion and anger followed the fear, and he twisted out from beneath his assailant, struggling to protect his face and throat, to bring his emotion under control once again, to wrest sense from the chaos.

Long hair. Skin like silk. A scream like an animal makes when the jaws of the trap snap shut. The smell of sandalwood.

"Triste!" he shouted, pivoting to bring his weight to bear. During his time with the Shin he had wrestled plenty of panicked goats to stillness beneath the shears, but the girl, lithe though she was, weighed more than a goat, and the strength in her slender limbs surprised him.

"*Triste,*" he said again, bringing his voice under control, stilling his own emotion and willing a similar stillness upon her. "You're safe. Safe. You're through the *kenta*. They can't pass . . ."

The words melted away as the girl relaxed against his grip, staring up at him with those eyes of hers. Her nearness hit him like a slap, the press of her hips as she shifted beneath him, the rise of her chest as she struggled for breath. She was steady now, her panic drained away, and yet for the moment he did not release her wrists.

"How are you here?" he asked. The last he'd seen of her she'd been collapsed on the crumbling floor of the orphanage, overcome by smoke. Even awake, she shouldn't have been able to pass through the gates. That, after all, was the whole point of his years of training. He heard Scial Nin's words once more in his mind: *Men, whole legions, stepped through the* kenta *and simply vanished.* But then, here she was, skin warm as sunlight against his skin, full lips parted slightly as her panting slowed.

"Kaden," she said finally, releasing a long, shuddering sigh. His name sounded strange on her lips, foreign, like an old dialect spoken only in prayer.

"How did you pass the *kenta*?" he asked again. Then, even more urgently, "Is Valyn all right?"

She shook her head. "I don't know. I woke up coughing. It was dark. Someone tried to grab me and I ran . . . I fell . . . here." She glanced around, awe and fear warring in her expression. "Where are we?"

Kaden shook his head. "Far away from where we were."

Triste's eyes widened, but before she could respond, Tan stepped through the gate. Where the girl had stumbled, desperate, panicked, as though flung from the violence of the far side, Tan moved quickly but deliberately. His eyes were cold as water dredged from a winter well, reptilian in their indifference, their distance. The vaniate, Kaden realized, wondering if his own eyes had looked like that.

The monk scanned the island, glancing over the ring of impossible gates as though they were so many withered junipers. He ignored both the wide sky and the encircling sea, but when he turned his attention to Kaden and Triste, something moved in those eyes, like the flicker of a great fish glimpsed through winter's thickest ice. His pupils dilated a hair and then he swung the *naczal* spear around in a curt arc, bringing the blade to rest against the fluttering pulse at Triste's throat.

"What are you doing?" Kaden demanded, shock jarring the words from his throat.

"Get off her," Tan said quietly. "Move back."

"What's wrong?"

"Move back."

"All right," Kaden said, half disentangling himself from the girl's limbs. He reached toward the spear, to block it or push it back, then hesitated. The smallest nick of the blade could kill Triste. "All right," he said again, standing, raising his hands. Emperor he may have become, but even the harrowing events of the preceding week had not completely effaced the old obedience of an acolyte. Besides, there was something new in the monk's voice, something sharp and dangerous. In all the months of Kaden's excruciating tutelage, he had heard indifference and disdain daily, but never this deadly focus, not even when Tan had faced the *ak'hanath*. He studied the monk's face, but couldn't tell if he remained in the *vaniate*. That frigid stare of his pinned Triste to the grass where she lay sprawled, the Aedolian uniform clutched about her. The bright tip of the *naczal* pressed at her throat.

"What are you?" Tan asked, each syllable distinct.

She glanced from Kaden to the surrounding sea, then shook her head.

"I don't know what you're asking. . . ."

Tan flexed his wrist and the blade slid a finger's width, smooth steel over smoother skin. A moment later, blood welled in its wake: three drops, hot beneath the hot sun.

"Stop," Kaden said, stepping forward, his mind scrambling to make sense of the scene. Moments before, they'd been struggling to escape the trap that was the orphanage, all focus on the *kenta* and *vaniate,* and suddenly, when Kaden wanted nothing more than to ask about Valyn, about the unfolding fight, about whether his brother was still *alive,* Tan had decided to turn on Triste. It made no sense. Triste was on their side. She had helped them to escape, had fled alongside him from the Aedolians through the vertiginous passes of the Bone Mountains, had, when the time came, played her part perfectly in the ruse that allowed them to defeat Ut and Adiv. The livid slice Pyrre had taken out of her cheek was proof enough of that. Kaden shifted toward her, but Tan brought him up short.

"Don't."

"I'm not going to let you kill her," Kaden said. His heart slammed against his chest. He struggled to bridle it, to bring it under control, along with his breath.

"It is not your choice," Tan replied. "Even you can see that."

Kaden hesitated. Triste's blood stained the tip of the *naczal.*

"All right," he said, stepping back a stride. "I can't stop you, but I can urge you to wait. To think."

"It is you," Tan replied, "who would do well to think. You might think about how she came here. About how she passed the gate. Before you are so quick to defend her, think about what it means."

Triste, for her part, hadn't so much as twitched when the blade cut. Her panic from a minute before had vanished.

"What are you doing, monk?" she asked carefully. Tan had caught her in an awkward position, half lying, half seated, but her body showed no strain. Her voice, frayed with panic a moment earlier, didn't waver. She might have been reclining on a divan in the Dawn Palace.

"What are you?" Tan asked again.

"I'm Triste," she replied, though she did not sound like Triste. She sounded older, braver, more certain. Kaden stared, studying her face as she spoke. "We escaped from Ashk'lan together. We went to Assare. Someone was attacking us just before I fell through"—she gestured with the barest nod of her head—"your gate."

"I know your story, but it crumbles here. The Blank God is exacting. He does not permit emotion, and yet you fell through thrashing and screaming."

"Your theories are wrong and so you put a blade to my throat?" Triste asked, arching an eyebrow. "It's somehow my fault that you don't understand the *kenta*?"

It was wrong, Kaden thought. All wrong. He studied her face. Where was the girlish innocence, the terror, the utter confusion that had poured off her moments earlier? Why did Kaden himself feel a shudder of fear when he met her gaze?

"I understand the *kenta*," Tan replied, voice flat as a file. "It is you I do not understand."

"Tan," Kaden began carefully, "maybe the gates have . . . weakened somehow over thousands of years. Maybe anyone can pass now. It's possible they don't work the way we think."

The monk paused. Behind and below them, the waves continued to gnaw at the cliffs. Sweat had begun to soak Kaden's robe.

"They have not weakened," Tan said finally. "My order tests for such things. Only Shin can pass the gates, and Ishien. And Csestriim."

"No," Triste said, shaking her head despite the blade at her throat. The fear was suddenly back in her voice, blood-raw and rank, as though she was just now awakening to her predicament. "I'm not Csestriim."

Kaden tried to sort and assemble the new information—Tan's accusation, Triste's confusion, her lightning-quick shifts from terror to steely defiance back to terror, the sheer impossible fact of the gates themselves. For the second time since stepping through the *kenta,* he felt he had come unmoored from reality, lost on this fragment of land adrift in the sloshing sea with a monk who was not a monk and a girl who might not be a girl locking eyes over the haft of a spear left behind by a long-extinguished race.

"Tan," he began, "what we need to do is—"

"Be clear on one thing," the monk cut in, his low voice driving through Kaden's own like a chisel through clean wood. "You are Emperor of Annur, but we are not in Annur. The fact that you have entered the *vaniate* means no more than that: you have entered the *vaniate*. You still cannot see clearly, nor think carefully, nor kill quickly, and all three may be required, and soon. Your feelings still blind you to the facts of the world. You are not yet what you need to be."

"Here is a fact," Kaden said. "She helped me."

"A single fir is not the forest."

"Meaning what?"

"Meaning there is more to her tale than helping you. Much more." Tan kept the *naczal* at Triste's throat at he glanced over at Kaden. "Destroy what you believe."

Destroy what you believe. Another Shin aphorism. Another monastic exercise on which Kaden had spent years.

You believe the sky is blue? What about night? Storm? What about clouds?

You think you are awake? How quaint. Perhaps you are dreaming. Perhaps you are dead.

Grimly, Kaden set to work. According to the story, Triste was meant as a distraction, a lure to hold Kaden's attention while the Aedolians went about surrounding his tent and butchering the monks. If so, she had proven utterly superfluous. He tried to imagine the scene without her— the arrival of the imperial delegation, the feast, the vast pavilion . . . Triste wasn't necessary for any of it.

And then there was her endurance through the high peaks, endurance to match a Skullsworn assassin and two monks who had spent their lives running in the mountains. Where would a girl raised on the velvet cushions of Ciena's temple learn to run like that? Where did she learn the ancient script of Assare? How did she know *anything* about the ravaged city? And the *kenta* . . . how had she passed unscathed through a gate that should have annihilated her?

Kaden forced himself to consider Tan's claim. According to Sami Yurl, the Kettral leader Valyn had slaughtered, the Csestriim were involved in the conspiracy against his family, a claim buoyed up by the presence of the *ak'hanath*. Would immortal creatures, creatures of godlike intellect and perfect reason, give their plot wholly over into the hands of men, flawed men like Tarik Adiv and Micijah Ut? Kaden stared at Triste, trying to see past his own initial conception, to shatter the lens of belief. She looked like a young woman, but the Csestriim were immortal; age did not touch them. And then there was the stony calm she had showed just a moment before, as though her mask had dropped. . . .

"Hundreds of years ago," Tan said, speaking as though they were all seated around a table back in the Ashk'lan refectory, as though his spear wasn't leveled at Triste's neck, as though she wasn't bleeding, the delicate red stream staining the collar of her tunic. She watched him with wary, animal eyes, body tensed to flee. "During the final years of Atmani rule, when the leach-lords and their massive armies clashed, turning farmland to mud, blood, and ash, obliterating entire cities, two Ghannans from the hills north of Chubolo risked their lives to save the local children."

It wasn't like Tan to linger over stories, but as long as the monk was talking, he wasn't killing Triste, which meant Kaden could pause, could try to order his thoughts.

"The Ghannans," Tan continued, "a man and woman, went from city to city, town to town, sometimes arriving even as the dust kicked up by the encroaching armies darkened the sky behind them. From their own fortune, they were able to supply wagons and food. They were able to promise ships waiting in Sarai Pol, ships that would take the children to Basc, where the fighting had not yet reached. Parents thrust infants into their arms, lifted sobbing toddlers into the beds of wagons, instructed the older children to care for the younger, then watched as the caravan departed, pushing east just ahead of the coming violence.

"As promised, the ships were waiting. And as promised, the children were whisked away before Roshin's armies swept across eastern Ghan. As promised, they arrived in Ganaboa. They were saved. Then they disappeared."

"What does this have to do with me?" Triste asked, eyes wide. "With anything?"

Kaden glanced at her, then turned back to the older monk. "Where did they go?"

"For a long time," Tan replied, "no one knew. The wars of the Atmani threw the world into chaos for decades. Uncounted thousands died, first in battle, then of famine, of disease. People weren't able to protect their own homes, to harvest their crops. Basc might have been on the far side of the world. Parents prayed for their children, a few scraped together the coin to go looking, but none found them.

"That took the Ishien. More than thirty years after the two strangers led the children away, fifteen Ishien finally managed to follow the trail to the southern coast of Basc. It is all jungle. Almost no one lives there, but tucked away in the hills they found a small cabin, and beneath the cabin, a warren of limestone caves, and in the caves, a prison, a vast prison."

"The children?" Kaden asked.

Tan shrugged. "Were adults. Or dead. Or crippled. The Ghannans, on the other hand, the man and woman who had saved them all—those two had not aged a day."

"Csestriim."

Tan nodded.

Triste stared, aghast. "What did they want with the children?"

"To experiment," the monk replied grimly. "To prod and to test. They want to know how we work, how we are put together, why we differ from them. They nearly destroyed us thousands of years ago, and while we have almost forgotten, those Csestriim that survive have never given up the fight, not for a single day." He turned from Triste to Kaden, stare hard as a hammer. "Consider the patience, to wait decades, centuries for the upheaval necessary to lead away so many children. Consider the planning, to have the coin stockpiled, the ships waiting at anchor, the caves and the cells prepared. The Csestriim do not think in days and weeks. They work in centuries, eons. Those who survived did so because they are brilliant, and hard, and patient, and yet they look like you or me." He nodded toward Triste. "Or her."

"No," Triste said, shaking her head once more. "I would never do something like that. I'm *not one of them*."

The monk ignored her, fixing his attention on Kaden.

"This is not something separate, some idle vendetta of my own that will distract you from the answers you hunt. If she is Csestriim, she is a part of the plot against your family and your empire. Erase Adiv and Ut from your mind. This creature is the one carrying the truth."

Kaden stared, first at the monk, then at Triste, trying to make sense of it. She didn't look like an immortal, inhuman monster, but then, according to Tan, neither had the Ghannans who stole the children. Parents had entrusted their families to the Csestriim. . . . *Destroy what you believe*. It all came back to that.

"You can't kill her," he said finally.

"Of course not," the monk replied. "We need to know more. But this changes things."

"What things?"

"The Ishien," Tan replied. "I was wary of this course of action to begin. I am doubly so now."

Kaden considered the response. In all the time he had known the older monk, Tan had never seemed really wary of anything: not Scial Nin, not Micijah Ut or Tarik Adiv, not even the *ak'hanath*.

"You're concerned," he said slowly, "about what the Ishien will think of Triste. About the fact that she passed through the *kenta*."

"We don't need to go," she protested. "We can walk back through the gate."

"When I want you to talk," Tan said, pressing the blade against her neck firmly, "I will tell you."

Triste opened her mouth to protest, then thought better of it, sagging back onto the grass, exhausted and defeated. Kaden wanted to comfort her somehow, to assure her that everything would be all right, but, when he searched for the words, found he had no comfort to offer. If she was what Tan claimed, his comfort would mean less than nothing.

"What will the Ishien do if they decide she is Csestriim?" Kaden asked.

The monk frowned. "The Ishien are unpredictable. In their long fight against the Csestriim, they have carved away much that made them human, not least of which is their own ability to trust. The Ishien believe the Ishien. Everyone else is a fool or a threat."

"But you were one of them," Kaden said. "Will they listen to *you*?"

"It will depend almost entirely on who leads them."

"Who does lead them?"

Tan frowned. "A northerner named Bloody Horm, but he has been gone from the Heart for decades."

"Gone?" Kaden asked, shaking his head.

"Hunting Csestriim," Tan replied, "among the Urghul or the Eddish. What matters is who leads the Ishien now, in his stead."

He paused, considering Triste. She watched him with frightened eyes, the way a hare watches the hunter when he comes to pluck it from the trap. "Regardless, bringing her may purchase a measure of respect. Fewer Csestriim walk the world than in the past. The Ishien find them very rarely."

"She's not some sort of token for us to barter," Kaden said.

"No. She is far more dangerous than that."

"I'm not what you think," Triste said quietly, hopelessly. "I don't know how I walked through that gate, but I'm not what you think."

Tan watched her for a while. "Perhaps," he said finally, then turned to Kaden. "You should remain here. It will be safer. I will bring the girl and speak with the Ishien."

Kaden stared at the windswept island. "Safer?" he asked, raising his brows. "Any one of your Ishien could walk through these gates at any time. If they will distrust me arriving with you, they might *murder* me if they find me here unexpectedly." He shook his head. "No. I started this. I will see it through. Besides, I need the Ishien. You might learn what I need to know, but *I* need to talk to them, to forge some sort of relationship."

He had no idea how Triste had passed the *kenta,* no idea how Tan's former brothers would respond to her sudden arrival or his own, no idea what he would do if it turned out Triste was lying, but the old fact remained: the Csestriim were involved in the plot against his family, they had killed his father, which made Kaden Emperor. He didn't rule Annur—not yet—but he could do this.

"I'm going," he said quietly.

Tan studied him for half a dozen heartbeats, then nodded. "There is no safe path."

"Please," Triste begged quietly. "Before I came through the gate, you were trying to convince Kaden *not* to go."

"It is because you passed the *kenta* that I changed my mind."

"Why?" she whispered.

"There is no other place where I am more likely to learn the truth about you."

Triste turned to Kaden, eyes wide and frightened.

"Kaden . . ."

He shook his head. "I need to know, Triste. If it's not true, I'll see you free, I'll take you away myself. I swear. But for my father, for my family, I need to know."

The girl turned away, body sagging in defeat.

Tan gestured to Kaden. "Take the belt from your robe. Bind her. Use the slaughter knot."

"And her feet?"

"A short hobble. We are not going far."

Kaden glanced around himself once again. The *kenta* through which he had entered was not the only one on the island. Dozens of the slender, delicate gates ringed the periphery, as though the entire block of land had once supported an enormous tower. He imagined some awful storm toppling the structure—buttresses and corbels, ramparts and flutings, all of it—into the sea, leaving only the doors, dozens of stone arches open as silent mouths.

"These are the gates," he said, shaking his head even as he slipped the belt from his robe. "This is what Nin described: the gates kept by the Malkeenian kings." For the first time, he started to understand the power such gates could bring. To move from one end of the empire to the other in a few strides . . . it was little wonder Annur had remained stable over the centuries while other kingdoms fragmented and fell. An emperor who could cross from northern Vash to western Eridroa in a handful of steps would be almost a god. He half expected to see his father emerge from one of the *kenta,* chin bent toward his chest in that way he had when he was thinking. But no . . . Sanlitun was dead. The gates were Kaden's responsibility now.

"Work," Tan said, gesturing toward Triste.

Kaden knelt beside her, knees pressing into the damp earth. She met his gaze, even as he rolled her onto her stomach, his hands rougher than he had intended. He was used to trussing up sheep and goats, not men or women, and his belt dug deep into her soft flesh as he pulled it tight.

"Leave a loop," the older monk said. "To guide her."

"You're enjoying this," she said, disgust thick in her voice.

"No," Kaden said quietly. "I'm not."

She clenched her jaw as he pulled the rope tight, but refused to look away. "I didn't spend my whole life in Ciena's temple without learning something about men. Ministers or monks—you're all the same. Makes you feel good, doesn't it? Strong." Kaden couldn't tell if she was about to sob or snarl.

He started to respond, to insist that the whole thing was just a precaution, but Tan cut him off.

"Do not attempt to argue with her. Finish the work and have done."

Kaden hesitated. Triste glared at him, tears standing in her eyes, then looked away. Not, however, before he had carved a *saama'an* of the rage and fear, the betrayal etched in her expression. He took a deep breath, then twisted the cloth once more before finishing the knot. A goat could slip free of such a loose knot, but Triste was not a goat, and he refused to cinch the rope any tighter. Still, the whole thing felt wrong. *I'm not hurting her,* he reminded himself. *And if Tan's right, all this is crucial.* The thinking was sound, but he could feel what the Shin called the "beast brain" prowling, agitated, inside the steel cage of reason.

He straightened from his task, then, at the monk's direction, pulled her to her feet. She swayed unsteadily. Tan's *naczal* never left her neck.

"That way," he said, gesturing with his head toward a gate on the far side of the island. "The girl first."

"You don't need to do this," Triste began. She ignored Kaden, spoke through him to the older monk as though he didn't exist. *And for all the good I'm doing her, I suppose I don't.* He was surprised to realize the thought stung, and he went to work on the emotion, grinding it out as one would grind a stray ember from the hearth beneath a heel. Tan did not respond, just pressed slightly with that spear of his until Triste stumbled forward.

"Which one leads to the Dawn Palace?" Kaden asked carefully.

Maybe the older monk was right, maybe Triste was Csestriim, and evil, and bent on some nefarious purpose; in that case, Kaden would do what was necessary. Could he bring himself to kill her? He tried to imagine it, like butchering a goat, a quick pull on the knife, blood urgent as breath, a final spasm, and it would be done. If it turned out that Triste was in some way responsible for the slaughter at the monastery, for the deaths of Akiil and Nin, for Pater, for his father, he thought he could do it. But if she was *not*, if it were Tan whose vision was clouded, well then, the time might come when acquiring his own knowledge of the network of gates would prove crucial. "Are they marked in some way?"

"None leads to the Dawn Palace," Tan replied. "Nin spoke the truth about the Malkeenians and the *kenta*, but the Csestriim built more than one network. Your lineage knows nothing of this island, these gates. Nor do the Shin."

Kaden frowned. "Then how do you . . ."

"The knowledge of the Ishien is older than that of the Shin, more complete."

The monk stopped them in front of one arch identical to the rest. Up close, Kaden could see the script carved into the keystone, a word or words; it was hard to be certain how many. Evidently there were scholars back in Annur who could read those sharp angles as though they'd been raised on the language, but Kaden, of course, had been afforded no opportunity to study with the scholars of Annur.

He eyed the arch, curiosity and caution warring within him, but it was Triste who spoke.

"Where does it lead?"

"You cannot read it?" Tan asked.

The girl bit her lip but refused to respond.

"You choose a strange time to begin your deception," the monk observed. "You read a similar language in Assare."

"I'm not Csestriim," Triste insisted. "Even if I *can* read it."

"What does it say?" Tan pressed.

"Tal Amen?" Triste said finally. "No. *Tal Amein."*

Kaden shook his head.

"The Still . . . Self?" she translated, squinting as she did so. "The Missing Heart?"

"The Dead Heart," Tan said finally.

Fear slicked a chill finger along Kaden's spine. The arch looked like the rest of the arches: slender, still, almost inviting. Through the open space he could see the black-tailed seabirds darting into the waves, sunlight shattering off the broken panes of the sea. There was no telling what lay on the other side, but Tan's translation promised something less inviting than this lost island.

"The Dead Heart," Kaden said, trying out the words. "What is it?"

"It is dark," Tan said. "And cold. Hold your breath as you step through the *kenta.*"

"Who goes first?"

"She does." The monk nudged Triste forward with his *naczal.* "If the guards decide to loose their shafts, better her chest for the broadheads."

11

The Flea was waiting.

Even as Valyn rolled to his feet, shielding his head with one hand from the rubble still raining down from above, retrieving with the other the blade he had tossed away from himself while falling, even as he scanned the room for his Wing through the kicked-up haze of smoke and stone dust, even as he tried to slow the hammering in his chest, to see the scene clearly, to fucking *think*, he knew something was wrong.

It's too bright, he realized, squinting about him, flexing his left elbow, which felt badly bruised but not broken. *It's lit.*

The realization punched him in the gut. He had fallen from near total darkness into a chamber hung with lanterns. Even in the smoke, he could see Talal lurching to his feet across the room, see Laith pressing a hand against the side of his head. The flier's twin blades lay on the ground just a pace away, but a pace, in a tight spot like this, might as well have been a mile. Gwenna had made the jump, too, and Annick, all according to plan, and yet, as Valyn's eyes adjusted to the light, his stomach soured further. The light came from Kettral lanterns, tactical lanterns almost identical to his own, three spread around the perimeter of the room.

He squinted.

His Wing was not alone. There were other figures in Kettral black, figures Valyn recognized all too well from his long years on the Islands, men and women with blades out and bows drawn, arrows trained on his chest.

"Just stop, Valyn, before someone gets hurt."

The Flea's voice, again, although this time it was coming, not from above, but from one of the exterior windows. A moment later, the Wing leader stepped through, down into the room, nodding as he surveyed the rubble.

"Rigging the floor was smart," he said. "Risky, but smart."

"A man who takes no risk will rot," the Aphorist observed.

The Flea's demolitions master, a short, ugly man with a long, ugly beard and bright eyes, slouched against a doorway on the far side of the room, flatbow pointed at Gwenna. "Valyn was right to trust the girl. She knows her work."

"Fuck off, Newt," Gwenna snarled at him. She had sheathed her swords before blowing the floor, and crouched empty-handed, eyes fixed on the Aphorist. "I'll bugger your ugly ass with a starshatter before this is over."

A few paces away Sigrid sa'Karnya made a harsh rattling noise deep in her throat. Despite her pale skin, the Flea's leach was the most beautiful soldier on the Islands, a stunning blond woman from the northern coast of Vash, but the priests of Meshkent had cut out her tongue years earlier, and aside from hand sign, the only language remaining to her was a set of guttural hacks and scrapings.

"My gorgeous friend here," the Aphorist translated affably, "takes issue with your language."

"Tell your gorgeous friend that I'll go to work on her next," Gwenna spat.

Sigrid didn't respond. She just fixed the younger woman with those bright blue eyes and dragged the tip of her belt knife—the only weapon she had bothered to draw—along the inside of her own arm. A line of dark blood welled up behind the steel. She pointed the blade, still dripping, at Gwenna's throat. Gwenna wasn't afraid of much, but Valyn saw her swallow heavily. Back at the Eyrie, Sigrid's reputation for beauty was matched only by the stories of her cruelty, and though the Flea had been a fair, if demanding trainer, the rumors surrounding his Wing were much darker.

"How did you know?" Valyn coughed. His head throbbed, and he could taste blood, hot and bitter on the back of his tongue. He felt the dark anger rising inside him, anger at Gwenna for blowing the floor before his order. Anger at himself for failing to outthink the Flea. Jaw clenched, he waited for the wave of fury to pass. No one was dead. That was the important part. Despite the explosion, despite all the drawn steel, no one was dead. There was still time to talk, to negotiate. It was still possible the Flea wasn't trying to kill them at all, that they could work something out. Valyn just needed to keep the arrows from flying a little bit longer. "How'd you know we were going to blow the floor?"

The Flea shook his head. "We've been doing this a long time, Valyn."

He sounded weary rather than triumphant. "You did well, with the camp and the escape. Against a lot of other Wings, you'd be free now, and we'd be cursing as we dusted off our blacks."

Valyn smiled bleakly. "But we're not up against the other Wings."

The Flea shrugged. "Like I said, we've been doing this a long time." He gestured toward Annick. "Now tell your sniper to put down her bow. Then we can talk."

Aside from Valyn's own drawn blade, Annick was the only one who had managed to bring a weapon to bear: her string was drawn, the arrow's point fixed on the Flea. If it bothered the other Wing's commander to stand a finger's twitch from death, he didn't show it. His lined face didn't show much of anything.

There were plenty of vets back on the Islands who looked like Kettral from their boots to their brains, all muscle and jaw. Not the Flea. Short and dark, middle-aged and pockmarked, with gray hair hazing his scalp, he'd always looked to Valyn more like a farmer stomping in after a long day in the fields than the most successful Wing commander in the history of the Eyrie.

"We shouldn't disarm," Annick said. "Not after last time."

"I wasn't there last time," Blackfeather Finn interjected in his deep, urbane baritone, "but a precise observer would be obliged to note that you're not exactly *armed* in this situation." The Flea's sniper sat reclining against the doorframe, flatbow cradled in the crook of his arm. He might have been the Flea's opposite—tall, olive-skinned, clean somehow despite the rigors of the mission, and almost preposterously handsome. He smiled apologetically, teeth white in the lamplight. "Annick and Valyn are the only ones actually holding weapons—for which I commend them—and even Valyn is missing one of his blades."

"Who else is here?" Valyn asked, ignoring the sniper, trying to see the whole picture, to formulate some kind of plan. "What other Wings?"

"There's a few looking," the Flea acknowledged, "but this is a big range of mountains. Guess we're the only ones that found you."

So it was five against five if it came to a fight. The sudden brightness of the lanterns dazzled, and Valyn squinted, trying to make sense of the room. No sign of Chi Hoai Mi, the Flea's flier. So five on four, maybe, giving Valyn's Wing the numbers, not that the numbers were worth a steaming pile of shit, not when you were pinned down and exposed. Not when you were fighting other Kettral.

Slow down, Valyn reminded himself. *No one's fighting yet.*

The Flea sucked something out of his teeth and nodded toward Annick again. "So. About putting down that bow . . ."

"You understand," Valyn said, studying the other Wing leader for any hint of his intentions, "that it's a risk. You've got the drop on us as it is. If you're lying . . ." He shook his head. "You're asking me to take an awful chance. To put my Wing in danger."

The Flea pursed his lips as though considering this. "Thing is," he replied finally, "there are the chances you take because you want to, and those you take because you have to."

The Aphorist nodded. "Seeing a door is not the same as unlocking it."

"And please," the Flea went on, "tell Talal not to do anything dumb. Usually, we'd knock out a leach right away, but I've left him conscious as a courtesy. A gesture of good faith. We all know what he's capable of, and if he gets twitchy, someone's going to have to shoot him."

Talal met Valyn's eyes. Sweat glistened on his bare scalp. Though the night was cool, Valyn's own blacks were likewise drenched, and his heart battered at his ribs. Kettral lore was filled with stories of Wing commanders in similar situations—outmaneuvered, overmatched, caught wrong-footed—who somehow managed to string together a series of desperate gambits to save their Wing. Only, Valyn was all out of gambits.

Any action, any attack, could only end in defeat and death. Even Annick's arrow, so carefully trained on the Flea, would probably be swatted down by Sigrid's strange powers before it left the bow. Valyn hated disarming, but, as the Flea said, you took some chances because you had no other choice. His elbow throbbed and his head ached. His throat felt too dry to speak, but the words came out clearly enough.

"Stand down. Talal, Annick, everyone just stand down."

Annick hesitated a moment, then lowered her bow. Talal looked relieved.

"Sometimes," Newt said, nodding in approval, "it is the fool who fights, and the fighter who folds."

The Flea ignored him.

"Where's the other one?" the Wing leader asked, "the woman with the knives?"

Valyn shook his head. "I'm not sure." He hadn't seen the Skullsworn since her boots had sent Triste running panicked through the gate and caused Gwenna to blow the floor. She should have fallen, just the same as everyone else, but Valyn could see no sign of her.

" 'Not sure' makes me nervous," the Flea said, flicking a sign toward Blackfeather Finn.

"She makes me nervous, too," Valyn replied. "She's not with us."

"Sure looks like she's with you. Don't lie to me, Valyn. We've been watching. We know about the monks, about the girl. Where are they, all of them?"

Valyn hesitated, unsure how much to reveal. According to Tan, no one else could pass through the gate. Kaden was free. Safe. At least, that was the theory. Valyn couldn't see any reason to put it to the test before he had to.

"I'm not sure where they are," he said again.

The Flea's lips tightened. His fingers darted through another two or three signs. Valyn didn't recognize them.

"You're playing games, Valyn," the Flea said, "and there's too much steel out for games."

Sigrid and the Aphorist shifted to cover Finn's position as the sniper rose to his feet. Flatbow leveled, he stepped into the dark hallway beyond the doorframe, paused, then groaned.

"What?" the Flea asked.

Finn turned back, his mouth open, gestured with one hand—a graceful, florid little motion, as though he were getting ready to take a bow—to the hilt of a knife plunged in his chest. He stood there a moment, blood flecking his lips, then fell. The Flea was shouting orders before the body hit the floor.

"*Burn* it, Sig. Newt—get hunting!"

For half a heartbeat Valyn just stared at the body. Two things were clear: Pyrre had killed Finn, and no one had killed Valyn himself. Before he could think it through further, a series of detonations rocked the hallway. The empty doorframe, murky black a moment earlier, erupted in a fog of blue flame. Sigrid's work, Valyn realized, a leach's kenning rather than munitions. If Pyrre was out there, she was dead now, but Newt darted through the fire anyway, blades drawn, while Sigrid flicked a dismissive hand at Annick and Talal. They reeled as though struck, the sniper's arrow careening off through an open window as she struggled to keep hold of her bow.

The Flea's Wing was fully in motion, and Valyn hadn't moved. None of his Wing had. He shifted his weight, stepping backward to create space just as the Flea attacked. Valyn knocked aside the first blow, parried the second, slid under the third, the man's double blades raining down in a series of forms too fast for Valyn's mind to follow. He abandoned thought, letting his body do the work it had been trained for, that the Flea had trained him for, parrying and slicing, stabbing and riposting, lunging and countering . . . and then it was over, fast as it had begun, his own sword forced wide by one of the Flea's blades, the soldier's other steel pressed against his neck.

"I didn't know . . ." Valyn said.

The Flea shook his head, eyes hard. "You killed Finn."

Valyn glanced over his shoulder toward the sniper's crumpled form. "Pyrre—" he began.

"Save it," the Flea cut in. "We're done talking."

Valyn stared. It was a hopeless position. Beyond hopeless. The Flea could slice his throat with the barest twitch of his wrist. The fight was over; it had been over from the beginning, really. Only . . . Valyn's mind scrambled for purchase on the situation. The Flea hadn't killed him. *No* one had killed him. Despite the madness unfolding all around, his entire Wing was still shouting, fighting. Which meant the Flea wanted to take them alive. It was a slender thread to hang his own life from, but Valyn had nothing else. He took a deep breath, raised his hands as though in surrender, then, with a roar, half fear, half fury, he lunged forward, directly into the sword's bright point, tipping his head back to bare his neck more fully.

For half a blink he thought he'd fucked up and badly, killed himself on the other man's blade, but the Flea was as fast as Valyn had hoped. The Wing leader cursed, yanking his weapon awkwardly aside, and Valyn seized the advantage, bulling directly ahead, knocking the man hard into the wall, gaining just enough space to pull free and bring his own weapon to bear once more.

"That was stupid," the Flea said, shaking his head.

"Look—" Valyn said, raising a hand.

Before he could finish the sentence, something whistled past his ear, a soft, almost timid flutter, and the Flea jerked back. One of Pyrre's knives sprouted from his shoulder. Not a bad wound, but had the man not moved it would have taken him straight through the neck. Without pausing, the Flea shifted stance, putting his good arm forward, letting the hurt one drop into a low guard. If the pain bothered him, he didn't show it, but the distraction had put a space between them, and Valyn used it to glance over his shoulder.

The Lord of all Chaos had unleashed his full fury upon the room.

The advantage, so skewed toward the Flea at the start, had changed dramatically with Pyrre's appearance and the death of Blackfeather Finn. There was still no sign of Chi Hoai, which meant that Valyn had the numbers, six to three, and Newt had gone after the Skullsworn, ineffectually, it seemed, which made five to two inside the room itself.

Unfortunately, the advantage didn't seem to be doing them much good. Sigrid's attack had snapped Annick's bowstring, and Gwenna's demolitions would be suicidal in the tiny space. That left the four members of Valyn's Wing facing Sigrid. It should have been good odds, but the blond leach had managed to hold her ground, twin blades naked, one of the two dripping blood. As Valyn watched, Gwenna went down cursing, clutching at her knee, and Laith reeled backward, battered by another invisible attack.

Valyn turned back to the Flea barely in time to knock aside the flat of the other man's blade. The *flat.* Valyn stared. Even now, even bleeding from the shoulder, the Flea wasn't trying to kill him. That the two Wings were fighting at all looked more and more like a horrible mistake.

Valyn parried two more attacks, stepping back to buy space, time. If he and the Flea were alone in a room, they could talk things out, but they were not alone. Behind Valyn, steel rang viciously against steel, Laith and Gwenna were cursing, and Sigrid's unnatural fire continued to rake the chamber. The Flea might be pulling his punches, but the rest of his Wing was not, not anymore. Valyn couldn't blame them. Somewhere back there crumpled on the crumbling stone floor lay Blackfeather Finn, the man who had taught them all to shoot. He was fucking *dead.*

Valyn stared at the Flea, trying to think of something to say, some way to stop the madness. There were no words. Some things you just couldn't take back. The only goal now was to get clear, get free, before more people started dying.

He beat away the Flea's weapons with a vicious fury of blows, then spun. "The doorway," he bellowed to his Wing, slashing a sword behind him to cover his retreat. "Get the doorway."

As though summoned by the words, Newt crashed back into the room, reeling unsteadily, blood sheeting down his face from a vicious gash across his scalp. Valyn smashed him out of the way with the flats of his blades. The Flea was closing again, and from across the room, Laith was shouting and waving. He'd taken the doorway, he and Talal. Valyn lunged toward it, but halfway there a sharp, hot punch in the back of the shoulder slammed him forward into the floor. A flatbow bolt, he realized, as the pain erupted through his back, straight through the muscle, and lodged against the bone. He tried to push himself up, but his wounded shoulder buckled beneath his weight, and his chin smashed against the floor. Were they trying to kill him finally, or just slow him? There was no way to be sure.

Pain and confusion clamped a dark hand over his eyes, and Valyn fought against the beckoning oblivion. The bolt hadn't killed him, but the sharp head ground against the bone every time he moved, each hot swell of agony threatening to drown him.

"Get up, you bastard!" Someone was shouting in his ear, hauling him forward by the armpits. Gwenna, he realized. "Get *up!*"

Valyn bit into the side of his cheek hard enough to draw blood, the bright new pain somehow balancing the old, holding it at bay. His arm should have been useless below the shoulder, but he could feel a knotted strength even in the mangled tissue, some sort of animal endurance. *You can move,* he growled to himself, *or you can die.*

He moved.

Annick and Talal were in the doorway, the leach grimacing with concentration. Both were bleeding from half a dozen minor wounds, but Valyn himself seemed to have the worst of it, and even with one arm, he could still fight. Annick had managed to get her shortbow restrung in the madness—he had no idea how—and she was laying down covering fire, hands moving so fast Valyn couldn't track the motion. He shoved Gwenna through the doorway in front of him, then followed, crashing to the floor as another arrow whispered overhead.

"How the fuck did they get in?" Laith demanded, panting hard.

"I would be tempted to place more emphasis," Pyrre said, stepping from the shadows, "on how *we* are going to get *out.*" The assassin held a slender knife loosely in each hand. A constellation of fresh blood—evidently not her own—flecked her face, but other than that she looked calm, relaxed, as though she'd just come from chopping carrots for the evening meal. With the back of her hand, she brushed a few stray strands of hair from her forehead.

"We're not going anywhere," Gwenna snapped. She was hunched over, fingers busy with some munitions Valyn couldn't make out. "We're fucking *winning.*"

"I *do* like winning," Pyrre mused. Then her arm flicked out, one of the two knives streaking end over end through the doorway. "But your old friends are quite good, and I think it might prove a disappointment were we not to *continue* winning."

Valyn rounded on her, rage taking him by the throat, blotting out everything but the assassin's face. He brought his sword level with her neck in a single smooth motion, and despite the new blades in her hands, blades that she seemed to keep drawing from some inexhaustible supply, she made no move to resist. If anything, she looked amused by his sudden fury.

"Are you planning to kill me?" she asked, raising an eyebrow. "Before you do, I'd like to observe, in my defense, that I seem to be the only one here capable of actually beating your talented colleagues."

Something coiled and furious, some beast buried deep in Valyn's brain, was snarling at him to kill her, kill her, *kill her*. It would be simple enough, a single gesture and it would be done. With an effort, he held the sword steady, forced down the voice, dragged a few jagged words from the depths of his chest.

"Killing them is what *started* all this. . . ."

Pyrre waved a knife dismissively. "They started it," she said, "when they crept up on us in the night with weapons drawn."

"I could have talked them down," Valyn spat.

"Really?" she asked. An arrow whistled past Valyn's head, then another as he threw himself against the wall. "They don't seem like the conversational type," Pyrre continued.

Two more arrows. They were shooting blind with all the smoke. Evidently, the Flea had given up on taking people alive.

"What's the play?" Laith called. He'd taken up point a dozen paces away at the head of the stairs while Annick and Talal continued to hold the door.

"Kill her or don't kill her," Gwenna said, her fingers a blur as she rigged the charges, "but quit fucking talking."

"Don't kill her," Annick said. "We need her."

"Valyn," Talal groaned. "Please hurry."

Valyn locked eyes with the Skullsworn, his blade hovering at her throat. "No more deaths," he ground out.

Pyrre pointed down the hallway with a knife. "Why don't you tell that to them?"

"No more killing," he said again.

"I like you, Valyn," Pyrre said. "You're a nice young man with a strong sense of civic virtue. But I don't work for you."

Valyn took a breath, pressed his blade against her throat until it just drew blood. The assassin didn't pull back. She didn't even flinch.

"Are you willing to die for this?" he demanded.

She smiled. "I don't think you understand. Skullsworn are always willing to die. It's what makes us different, you and me. It's what makes me better."

"*Valyn!*" Laith snapped.

One more heartbeat, then Valyn let the blade drop. He hated the woman, hated her for what she was, for the fight she'd so casually caused, but now the fight was on, and Annick was right, they needed her. The exchange had taken only a few moments, but moments were everything when the arrows were flying.

"Stay close," he told the assassin. "If you fall behind, I'll leave you for the Flea."

He didn't wait for her to reply, turning instead to the open doorway, running the options. The Flea was bottled in the room, but he wouldn't stay bottled for long. Chi Hoai was still out there somewhere, but that was just tough shit; there was no time to go inching down the hallway looking in every room.

"They're regrouping," Annick called, ducking back behind the doorframe as a flatbow bolt skittered off the stone where her head had been.

There would be no more chances, that much was clear. Not with Blackfeather Finn's blood smeared all over the floor. There were only three possibilities now: they could run, they could kill, or they could die.

"Gwenna," he said, grabbing the woman by the front of her blacks. "Two starshatters in the doorway."

She shook her head. "They'll bring down the whole 'Kent-kissing place."

"Do it!" he bellowed, digging in his belt pouch for the Kettral whistles. There was no way to know if the birds were still circling, if they were still *alive,* even, but sometimes you had to roll the dice. If they could win free of the building, if they could get out on the ledge, they'd have a chance. Blind grabs were risky; a bird without a flier was less precise, less predictable. A blind grab from a cliff ledge in the darkness was near madness, but even madness seemed preferable to going toe-to-toe with the Flea's Wing now that they'd had a chance to regroup.

"Talal," he said, glancing over, "can you screen the door?"

The leach was panting, and sweat poured off his forehead. For a moment Valyn thought he hadn't heard the question; then he nodded.

"All right," Valyn said. "Gwenna—smokers in the room. Talal, throw the shield. Gwenna, starshatters here. Then we go. I'm going to bring the bird in hard. It's gonna be a goat fuck, but we're getting out of here."

He took a ragged breath. The flatbow bolt tore at his shoulder with each movement, a bright bar of pain through his flesh, but it was only two levels down to the ledge. He'd lived through Hull's Trial; he could make it down a couple flights of stairs.

"Bringing the bird in hard sounds very exciting," Pyrre said, "but I worry it might pose problems for those of us who are . . . less experienced."

Valyn cursed. The maneuver was going to be difficult enough for his own Wing, and they had thousands of hours of training. There was nothing to be done for it now, though. If they waited for 'Ra to settle, they were all dead.

"Just stay by me," he said, "and you'll be fine."

Pyrre raised an eyebrow, ran a finger along the tiny slice Valyn left on her neck. "How reassuring."

Valyn started to say something more, something about cueing in early on the trace strap and the importance of flexing with the takeoff, but an explosion ripped the words away, seemed to tear the very air itself in half, knocking the wind from his lungs and leaving him breathless. A moment later Gwenna staggered from the smoke, head gushing blood, one arm clutched at her side. Valyn seized her with his good arm, and a moment later Talal appeared on her other side.

"I'm fine," she screamed, but he could feel her sagging against his grip.

"Let's go," he shouted, hauling on Gwenna, bulling his way down the hall. "Go!"

Pyrre glanced back toward the explosion, threw another knife, although Valyn couldn't see that there was anyone to throw at, slipped two more from somewhere in her coat, and followed.

They burst from the building onto the broad ledge. After the dimness and smoke inside the orphanage, the pale rock seemed to positively glow in the moonlight, and Valyn sucked in the fresh air, feeling, for the first time, that they might just survive. He put the silver whistle to his lips, then blew a few short bursts, hoping to Hull he was thinking clearly through the chaos and the pain. His plan, which had seemed so sound before the Flea attacked, now looked like the most ludicrous fantasy. Not that there was any time to change it.

He looked up, scanning the windows above. Smoke poured out of them in great, gray billows. That, at least, would give them a little cover as they fled across the ledge. It was impossible to say just where the Flea's Wing was, whether or not Gwenna's starshatters had killed anyone, but once Valyn's Wing ventured farther out onto that ledge they would be ducks for anyone with a bow and a clear shot.

"Where's 'Ra?" Laith hissed at Valyn.

"It's a whistle, not a 'Kent-kissing leash," Valyn snapped, scanning the darkness for some sign of the bird. "And I'm not calling 'Ra."

The flier stared. "Are you insane? How do you expect to get out of here?"

Valyn ignored the question.

"There," he said after a moment. The bird was little more than a silent smudge on the darkness. She was coming in at a low angle—standard blind-grab posture—that would put her right over the center of the ledge.

"I'm waiting for the next instruction," Pyrre said.

Talal stared at her, evidently realizing the problem for the first time.

"Tell me it's just like mounting a horse," the assassin went on, then frowned, "although I was never much good with horses."

"There'll be two straps," Valyn said, heart hammering as the bird approached. "Get a hold of the lower of the two." He turned to the group. "We're all underneath, which means three to a talon. Talal and Laith, you're with Gwenna. . . ."

"I can make the grab myself," she growled, but her face was as pale as the stone, and it looked as though simply standing was an effort.

"Just make sure she gets on the bird. Annick and Pyrre with me on the far talon. Remember we're on the edge of a fucking cliff, so blowing the grab's not an option, dropping is not an option. Get on and stay on, I don't care if your shoulder rips out of the socket. You fall"—he waved a hand toward the darkness—"you're gone."

"It's all well and good to talk about it," Laith said, gesturing furiously, "but we've got to *move* if we're going to make it."

Valyn laid a hand on his flier's arm. "Not yet."

"What in Hull's name are you waiting for?"

Valyn stared at the bird until his eyes hurt. Had he misgauged the situation? There were so many variables, so many things that could go wrong. If he'd made the wrong assumption about one of them, then the rest . . .

Then the second bird appeared, above and behind the first.

"Oh," Laith said, staring.

"Tell me it's Chi Hoai," Valyn said, voice tight. The flier could recognize the various kettral far better than Valyn ever would. "Tell me that second one is the Flea's bird."

"It is." Laith sucked a worried breath between his teeth. "She's going to tear Yurl's bird out of the air."

Valyn blew the second whistle just as Chi Hoai struck. She had the height and the angle both, and her own kettral seized Yurl's by the back of the neck. The lower bird shrieked as claws sank into her neck and shoulders, as the hooked beak plunged again and again, savaging her eyes. A kettral could slice through a horse with those talons. Valyn had watched them hunt back on the Islands, watched them snap the heads off of sheep and carry off whole cows in their claws. Yurl's bird twisted in midair, screaming as she tried to fight, but the fight was over, or as good as. Chi Hoai was already pulling her own mount back.

Then Suant'ra hit.

She smashed down from above like a ton of falling rock, silhouette blocking the stars, stabbing at the other kettral with her beak, raking the wings with her talons. Chi Hoai's bird shrieked, her own prey forgotten, and rolled in the air, trying to come to grips with her assailant. The two tumbled from view, tearing furiously at each other. For a moment Valyn could only stare. The whole thing had worked as he'd planned—the bait, the attack, the counter—until 'Ra disappeared. If all the birds were gone, they were stranded. The Flea's kettral might be dead, but the Flea himself was very much alive.

"Into the tunnels," Valyn shouted, pointing with his blade. It wasn't what he'd hoped, but hoping too hard was a good way to get dead. Once inside the actual cliff, they could disappear. They could figure out later how in 'Shael's sweet name they were going to get out of the mountains without 'Ra. If they lived that long.

Laith, however, was shaking his head. "No!" he shouted. "We have to wait for the grab!"

" 'Ra's *gone!*" Valyn said, taking him by the blacks and shoving him toward the cliff.

The flier shoved back. "She's not gone. She had the speed and the elevation. She's just tangled up! We have to wait for the extract!"

A flatbow bolt struck just at Valyn's feet, raising a line of sparks as it skittered away across the ledge.

"They have the range," Pyrre observed, shifting to put Valyn between herself and the orphanage.

"I know my bird, Val," Laith said, lips drawn back in a snarl. "I know her. You gave her every chance and *she will win.* We just need to hold for a few more heartbeats."

"There's no cover," Talal said. "We can't hold here."

"The tunnels," Valyn said, grabbing Gwenna under the arm. *"Now."*

As he said the last word, however, a great winged shape rose up over the ledge, screamed once at the stars, and came to rest on the very lip.

"That's 'Ra!" Laith yelled, surging forward.

Even in the moonlight, Valyn couldn't be sure, but Laith was already running. As Hendran wrote: *Sometimes the good leader has to quit leading and trust his men.*

Valyn swallowed a curse, hauled Gwenna around, almost passed out as the bolt in his shoulder grated against the bone, and then, with a brief prayer that everyone else was doing the same thing, ran as hard as he fucking could.

12

Cold like a fist to the heart. Sudden, frigid darkness pressing against his chest, on his face, in his unseeing eyes. The *vaniate* shivered a moment, then sloughed away like a violently molted skin, and when Kaden opened his mouth to shout, icy brine forced its way down his throat, into his lungs, strangling him. *Underwater,* he realized. Too late to call back his squandered breath.

He started to grope for the gate, to try to haul himself back through into the light and the air, then realized that to enter the *kenta* in such a state of agitation invited an annihilation even swifter than that offered by the sea. He forced his body to stillness, willing his mind to follow. Dim lights flickered around the edges of his vision, but whether they were real or the product of a mind starved for air he couldn't be certain. His body convulsed while his lungs tried to heave a breath where there was no breath to be had. Panic prowled the edge of thought, hungry, circling closer as the cold clamped down.

Breathe, he told himself, *and then follow the breath.* He raised a hand to his mouth, feeling for the bubbles as they trickled through his fingers, forcing himself to wait a moment to be sure. Then, with legs like lead, he kicked for the surface.

He broke from the relative silence of the water into chaos. Someone was thrashing a few feet away, and men were bellowing—two or three voices piled on one another: *Stop . . . Kill them now . . . Put the bow down.* The air was almost as frigid as the water and only slightly brighter. A few torches gave off more smoke than light, illuminating what seemed to be a stone chamber, a small grotto carved out by the sea. Kaden twisted in the water, mind desperately sifting the various shadows, searching for the source of the voices, for a place to haul himself to safety. A quick, hard blow caught him on the lip, driving his face back under the surface. He came up, the lights spinning across his eyes, mouth filled with blood and brine. Triste was still tied, he realized, tied and drowning.

He caught her beneath the arms.

"Still," he gasped, trying to hold her up. "Be still."

A moment later Rampuri Tan's shaven head breached the water and with it, his voice:

"Memory," he ground out, as though intoning the opening passage to some lost ritual, "is the heart of vengeance."

Triste finally stopped her flailing elbows, and Kaden took a moment to seize a full breath. The passage through the *kenta* had practically drowned him, but the older monk spoke with his normal implacable force.

The other voices fell silent. Someone cursed. Then:

"And vengeance is the balm of memory."

"I am Rampuri Tan."

"I am Loral Hellelen."

"Keep your bows on the girl," Tan said, hoisting himself from the water onto a small stone shelf, ignoring the sodden weight of his robe as he stood. "She is more than dangerous."

"And the other?"

Kaden still couldn't see the speaker, but he stroked weakly toward the rim where Tan had emerged, dragging Triste behind him.

"He is with me," Tan replied. He had not relinquished his *naczal* when he stepped through the *kenta,* and the blade glinted in the dusky light. "Watch the girl."

By the time Kaden reached the low shelf, his muscles had gone rigid with cold. It was all he could do to hold on to the stone with one hand while keeping Triste's head above the water. He could feel her trembling beside him, shivering uncontrollably. Wet hair plastered her skin, and her lips had gone a blue so dark they looked black in the smoky light.

"Kaden," she whispered between chattering teeth.

Before he could respond, two men lunged from the shadows, seized her by the elbows, and lifted her, shaking, from the water.

"Careful," he said. "She is tied. You could hurt her."

The guards ignored Kaden, dragging Triste roughly onto the stone shelf while he hauled himself, sodden and shivering, into the cold air.

Only after he had coughed the last salt water from his lungs, then straightened, could he finally take in his surroundings. When he first

passed through the gate he thought himself submerged in the ocean somewhere, but now he could see that they had surfaced inside a large chamber, perhaps fifteen paces across, walls and ceiling cut from the same
undressed stone. In the center, the black waters of a pool glistened in
the torchlight. The place reminded him faintly of Umber's, back in the
Bone Mountains, but where Umber's Pool was open to the wide arc of the
sky, this room was dark and cold, cut off from everything by the cave's roof.

The Ishien, too, were nothing like the monks he remembered. Despite
Tan's warning, Kaden had expected them to look vaguely familiar. Instead
of robes, however, the three men in the chamber, two of whom pinned
Triste roughly against a wall, wore greasy leather jerkins and sealskin. None
had shaved their heads, and though only one had a proper beard, a week's
worth of stubble obscured the jawlines of the others. Most striking, the
Ishien were clearly warriors; each wore a short sword at the hip and carried a loaded crossbow. The speaker had leveled one of those crossbows
directly at Tan.

"Rampuri," he said, the word ringing like a curse.

"Point your weapon at the girl, Hellelen," Tan responded.

"I will point my weapon where I please."

Kaden stilled his shivering and tried to read the scene. Loral Hellelen
looked to be around Tan's age, a tall, wiry Edishman with a rough blond
braid running halfway down his back. He might have been handsome
once, but a cadaverous hollowness had gouged away his cheeks and sunk
his eyes in pits so dark they looked bruised. Kaden watched those eyes
carefully. They glittered in the torchlight, bright, almost feverish. Hellel-
en's finger stroked the trigger to the crossbow.

"It was a foolish gamble, stepping through that gate after twenty years."

Kaden glanced over at Tan. No one at Ashk'lan had ever called Rampuri Tan a fool, but if the older monk was nonplussed, it didn't show.

"Only a gamble if the old ways have slipped."

"Don't speak to me of slipping," the blond man shot back. "It was you
who left your post."

"And I have returned." Tan gestured toward Triste with his *naczal*.
"Perhaps with one of the Csestriim. She passed through the gates. Untrained.
Unprepared."

Confusion registered in Hellelen's eyes, then shock. After a moment's
hesitation, he shifted his crossbow from Tan, pointing it instead at the
young woman pinned against the wall. "She is too young to be Csestriim."

Tan shook his head. "She is a woman grown, though the clothes obscure the fact."

"And she passed the *kenta*."

Tan nodded.

"We don't know what it means," Kaden added quietly, careful to keep his voice level, reasonable. "She might be Csestriim, or she might be . . . something else."

Hellelen glanced in his direction, narrowed his eyes at the sight of Kaden's own blazing irises, then snorted. "Ah. The princeling."

"He is the Emperor now," Tan observed.

"Not here, he's not," Hellelen spat. "This isn't your palace," he said, "and we're not your monks. If I have a question for you, I will ask it. If I do not ask, keep your imperial mouth shut or, however short your sojourn in the Dead Heart might be, you will spend it inside a cell."

Kaden glanced over at Triste where she stood trembling against the cold stone wall, arms trussed behind her, crossbow bolts leveled at her heart and head.

"This doesn't make sense," he said. "Triste has *helped* me, has helped *us,* at every step. We'd be dead without her. Even if she is Csestriim, I want her to be treated well."

Hellelen sucked air between his teeth. "You think you know the Csestriim?" he demanded, voice like a file running over steel.

Kaden shook his head.

"You think you understand how they think? You want to walk in here and start *lecturing* us, lecturing *me* on what does and does not make sense?" He took a step toward Kaden, sudden fury scribbled across his eyes, the crossbow swinging around to point at Kaden's heart. "I will show you—"

The words cut off as Tan slid the haft of his spear between them, blocking the Ishien's approach.

"Hellelen," he said quietly, "you would do better to focus on this creature," indicating Triste, "rather than lecturing the Emperor of Annur. If she is Csestriim, she is involved in a plot to destroy the Malkeenian line."

"The Malkeenian line," Hellelen snorted, "long ago abandoned its post." He stared at Kaden. "Do you even know what those gates are for?"

"I do," Kaden replied. "They are a tool. One that can be used to hold together an empire and to fight the Csestriim both."

"Let me guess which one you're more concerned with." Hellelen shook his head in disgust. "I heard how someone gutted your father. What happened? The same men come after you?"

"It may be more than men," Kaden replied. "As you say, we face the same foe."

He glanced over to where Triste shivered against the wall. Guilt stabbed at him, sharp and jagged as a stone caught in a sandal. He set the pain aside. It was already clear the Ishien cared nothing for pain, Triste's or his own.

"The girl is at the center of it," Tan said. "At the center of your fight, and Kaden's. You may find you have more in common with the Emperor than you think."

Hellelen watched her awhile, then spat onto the stone. "I knew the Shin were weak, but you, Rampuri? I didn't realize you were so eager to scrape before a throne."

Tan ignored the gibe, and after a few heartbeats Hellelen turned back to Triste, staring at her awhile, then blowing out a long, slow breath between his teeth. "A female, is it?" He prodded her cheek with the tip of the crossbow bolt. "We could learn much from a female." His voice had gone tight with something that sounded like anger or hunger. "You're certain she is Csestriim?"

"You listen poorly," Tan replied. "Nothing is certain, but the signs are there. We can discuss them in more detail once she is secure. Take her to a cell."

Hellelen narrowed his eyes. "You're not in charge here, monk." He spat the last word. "You were never in charge."

Kaden recognized the disgust in Tan's gaze from moments in his own training. "I will tend to her myself, then, while the rest of you bicker. Stand well back. She is faster and stronger than she appears."

"What about your beloved sovereign?" Hellelen demanded. "He is to simply wander free through the Heart?"

Kaden wanted to object. He never expected to command the Ishien, but as the Emperor of Annur, he shared with them a common task: the guarding of the gates. He had hoped for civility at least, for mutual respect. He had hoped that he would have some say in Triste's treatment. But, as the Shin were fond of saying, *You cannot drink hope. You cannot breathe it or eat it. It can only choke you.*

Coming to the Ishien was starting to look like a mistake, and a grave one at that, but there was little he could do to correct his decision while standing unarmed and heavily guarded beside the frigid pool. Maybe Triste was Csestriim, and maybe she was not. Either way, she deserved to be treated decently, gently, until she proved herself a threat. He wanted to say that one more time, but it was pointless. He had no traction in the situation, no leverage. With an effort, he stifled his fear and anger, slid all expression from his face, then stepped back.

Tan fixed Hellelen with a stare. "Kaden is my pupil," he said, "not my sovereign. I would tell you to leave him free, but, like a child, you dislike being told."

†

The Ishien didn't shut Kaden in a cell, but they didn't trust him, either. Trant's presence was evidence enough of that. Hellelen had ordered the other man to "escort and guide" Kaden while the rest of them, Tan included, bustled off down a different corridor, dragging Triste roughly behind.

"Escort and guide" sounded welcoming enough, but when Kaden asked to follow the others, Trant refused. When he asked where Triste had been taken, Trant said he didn't know. When he asked to see the commander of the fortress, Trant muttered that the commander was busy. Kaden chafed to know what was going on, to begin unraveling even a part of the tangled conspiracy that had killed his father, but Trant didn't know the answers, and he wouldn't let Kaden near anyone who did. There was little to do aside from follow, and so Kaden followed, misgivings mounting.

The Dead Heart was unlike any fortress Kaden had ever encountered: no curtain walls or gates, no crenellations or arrow loops. The twisting passages and low ceilings, the utter lack of windows, suggested that the whole thing was underground, hacked out of the stone itself, lit by smoky lanterns and smokier torches, the air cold and damp, freighted with salt and sea. At junctures in the passageway, Kaden could sometimes make out the dull susurrus and slosh of the waves. When that faded, there was nothing but the scrape of boots, the irregular drip of water into cold pools, and everywhere the sensation of weight, of thousands of tons of rock pressing down from above, silent and invisible.

Only when they finally reached a narrow hall filled with long tables and reeking of salt and stale smoke did Trant finally stop, gesturing Kaden to a bench while he filled two battered trenchers with steaming white fish, then seated himself across the table. For a while Kaden thought the man intended to eat in silence, sucking soft flesh from the bones, prodding at his meal with filthy fingers as though it displeased him.

If Trant had a family name, it had not surfaced. Like the rest of the Ishien, he wore a heavy sealskin cloak over oiled leather over wool, and like the rest of the Ishien, a short blade hung at his hip. Matted, tangled hair hung halfway to his shoulders, and he had a habit of sweeping it from his eyes when he spoke. If he had bathed in the past week, the water had had little effect on the grime caked beneath his fingernails and into the wrinkles of his knuckles and wrists.

Back at Ashk'lan, Kaden would have been whipped for such slovenliness. Another reminder, if one were needed, that the Ishien were not the Shin. Where the monks were cold as winter granite, solid as a hard frost, these soldiers, Trant very much included, struck him as less . . . hale. Not that they were weak or enfeebled, but the reek of smoke and sea on their clothing, the hooded shadow in each gaze, the feral intensity to all speech and movement struck him as wrong, somehow. Unnatural.

Finally Trant looked up, found Kaden's gaze upon him, and frowned.

"It's an island," he said, gesturing vaguely around by way of illustration. "The whole thing."

Kaden blinked. "An island? Where?"

"No," Trant replied, eyes sly above a mirthless smile. "No, no, no. *Secrecy is survival.* Do you know Kangeswarin? Of course you don't. That's something he said. Wrote. *Secrecy is survival.*" He intoned the words as though they were scripture. "The Order hasn't kept its freedom this long just to come under the thumb of some upstart emperor now."

"I have no interest in bringing you 'under my thumb,'" Kaden responded, careful to keep his voice level. He had hoped for deference and prepared for defiance. Trant's casual dismissal, however, the apparent indifference of everyone in the Heart, was not a response he had reckoned on. His whole purpose in visiting the Ishien was to learn what they knew, perhaps to forge an alliance, and here he was defending himself to a filthy, low-ranking soldier in the mess hall. "I am hardly an upstart," he continued. "My father was Sanlitun hui'Malkeenian. I trained with the Shin, as have all those of my line. I have the eyes."

Trant narrowed his own eyes, sucked at a morsel of fish stuck between crooked teeth. "The eyes," he mused, as though he had not considered that. "You do. That's true. You do have some eyes. Long time ago there were men could tell the Enemy by the eyes."

"The Enemy?"

"Childkillers. Builders. Graveless. Call them what you want. The fucking Csestriim. Long time ago, there were some could tell the Csestriim by the eyes."

Trant stared at a blank space of wall, as though expecting the Csestriim to materialize from it. Like a goat in the early stages of brainworm, his eyes twitched erratically. He seemed unable to still his hands. Kaden shifted uneasily in his seat.

"The Csestriim didn't have burning eyes—" he began, but Trant cut him off, waving a hand.

"Yes, yes. I know. The Malkeenians. Intarra. The Emperor. I know." He squinted. "Or it could be a trick. A kenning."

"A trick?" Kaden asked, trying to find his balance in the conversation. "I'm not a leach. And why would I play a trick?"

Trant raised his eyebrows in surprise. "A thousand reasons. Ten thousand. Man might fake the burning eyes to milk coin out of fools. To seduce a noble lady. To seduce just about any silly-minded slut, at that. To stir up war. To avoid war. Just to lie. To *lie*. For the unbridled joy of *deceit*." He paused, shaking his head, then bulled ahead. "A man might lie about his eyes," he continued, voice rising, "to unseat an entire dynasty. To drive an empire to wreck and ruin."

Kaden shook his head. "It is my empire. I have no desire to see it ruined. That is why I am *here*."

"So you say," Trant muttered, turning back to his fish. "So you *say*."

"Are you so distrustful of everyone?"

Trant leaned back in his chair abruptly, dark eyes glittering in the lantern light. He seemed unable to hold a position for more than a few heartbeats. "*More*. I'm giving you the benefit of the doubt because you came in with Tan." He paused, waggled a finger across the table. "But you also brought the Childkilling whore."

Kaden leaned back, caught off guard by the sudden hatred in the man's voice, the sheer red boiling fury of it.

"Triste hasn't killed any children," Kaden replied, shaking his head.

"That you *know* of. That *you* know of. Tan said she was Csestriim."

Kaden started to argue the point, then checked himself, remembering Tan's tale of the Ghannans and their ships filled with orphans. Trant didn't seem the type to be convinced through rational argument, and Kaden was no longer quite sure that the rational argument was on his side anyway. "Are you going to hurt her?" he asked instead.

"Me?" Trant asked, raising his eyebrows and poking himself in the chest as though to be sure of the question. "Am *I* going to hurt her? Oh no. No, no, no. I don't hurt the prisoners. I'm not *allowed* to hurt the prisoners. That's for the Hunters."

"The Hunters?" Kaden asked, worry prickling the back of his neck.

Trant rapped a fist against the side of his head. "Trouble hearing? The Hunters, I said. The ones in charge. When there's hurting to do, they do it. Been that way since before your empire. Since before the Atmani, even." He nodded sagely, as though pleased with the order of things.

Kaden shook his head, trying to follow the baffling account. "What are you? What's your role?"

"I'm a Soldier," Trant said, pounding his chest with a fist. "Soldier, seventh rank."

"How many ranks are there?"

Trant grinned, revealing a row of brown teeth. "Seven."

"Will you ever be promoted?" Kaden asked. "To Hunter?"

The Ishien stared at him as though he'd gone mad. "It's not a rank," he said, shaking his head. "Hunter's not a fucking *rank*."

"What is it?" Kaden asked, taken aback.

"I'll tell you what it is," Trant said, leaning far over the table, eyes wide. He waved Kaden closer with his knife, close enough that Kaden could smell the reek of his rotting teeth. "It's a blessing, is what it is. A *blessing*."

Kaden hesitated. All the talk of Hunters and Soldiers seemed to be making Trant more and more agitated. He rocked front and back, as though seated atop a lame horse, and watched Kaden with febrile intensity. Suddenly, the wisest course seemed to be finishing the meal in silence, saying and doing as little as possible to disturb Trant further. But then, if Kaden was going to forge any kind of trust with the Ishien, if he was going to convince them to work with him, to share what they knew, he needed to understand them, and at the moment, the only person who could explain the workings of the Dead Heart was Trant.

"What makes the Hunters Hunters?" Kaden asked finally, carefully. "How do you decide?"

"Decide?" Trant laughed bleakly, scratching suddenly at a vicious scar on his forearm. "We don't *decide* any more than you decided to have those eyes. Some men have it inside them. *It.* The blessing. Some don't. Just . . . don't." He paused, eyes darting off toward the roof, as though reliving something. "Learned that clearly enough in the purging." He seemed, abruptly, to be talking about himself.

"The purging?"

Trant sucked in a great breath, then bared his teeth. "The purging. The passage, we call it, sometimes. Sometimes just the *pain.*" He shivered, his whole body trembling. "The 'Kent-kissing *pain.* It's how they sort the Hunters from the Soldiers, how they see who has the gift."

"What is it? The purging or passage?"

"What? *What?* It's what it fucking *sounds* like, is what. Pain on top of pain piled on pain. Weeks of cutting and burning," he continued, almost shouting as he pulled open his jerkin. A web of scars stretched across his chest, old, brutal wounds that had healed poorly. Kaden jerked back, but Trant was too absorbed in his account to notice. "Cutting," he said again, drawing the word out as though tasting it, "and burning, and breaking. The fucking *breaking.* Drowning. And cold. Again and again, over and over until you shatter," he said, stabbing at his own skull with a finger. "Until you break *up here.*" He shivered himself still, then turned his eyes on Kaden. "The pain," he said again, more quietly, as though that explained anything.

Kaden stared for a moment, corralling the horror stampeding through his chest, taming it. "Why?" he asked finally.

Trant shrugged, abruptly and utterly indifferent to the torture he had just relived so vividly. "Sometimes what breaks off," he said, "is the feelings." He snapped a bone off the fish carcass, sucked at it. "You know— love, fear, fucking *hope.* Sometimes the pain chips them right off. At least, it does for the ones with the gift. The ones who can use the gates. Those are the ones in charge, the Hunters."

For a while Kaden just watched the man eat. When Tan warned him, when he explained that the Ishien were nothing like the Shin, Kaden had thought he was talking about differences in culture and outlook, changes in the methods and modes of training. Even after arriving in the Dead Heart, after seeing Loral Hellelen and the others, after having a loaded crossbow pointed at his chest, the gap had seemed wide, but bridgeable. Now . . .

Kaden tried to make sense of what Trant had just described. Clearly the Ishien had their own way of achieving the *vaniate*—if it even *was* the *vaniate*—a way that had nothing to do with meditation and discipline, silence and persistence. It sounded as though they were tortured, all of them, brutally tortured, and those few who went numb as a result became the leaders, while the rest . . . Kaden watched Trant suck broth from his wooden bowl. The man hummed a tuneless song, the same few notes over and over.

Then another thought struck Kaden like a blow across the face.

"And Tan . . ." he said.

Trant looked up from his bowl, nodding eagerly as broth dripped off his unshaven chin.

"Um-hmm," he said. "Yes. *Yes.* Rampuri Tan was a Hunter. Almost as tough as Bloody Horm, least in some ways. A *Hunter.*"

Kaden exhaled slowly, measuring his pulse. "Will you talk to them for me?" he asked. There didn't seem to be more than a few score men in the entire fortress. Kaden had heard enough to understand that Trant didn't make the decisions, but he would have access to the people who did. "Your commander needs to know that Triste helped me to escape. She deserves some decency."

"Oh. Decency. *Oh.* The Emperor wants to talk about decency." Trant dropped his voice and his eyes both, muttering to himself, but no sooner did Kaden lean in than he started upright, slashing a rigid hand through the air between them. "Do you know . . . Do you *know* what the Enemy did to us?"

For a moment he just snarled wordlessly, lost in his rage. "You hear about the Atmani all the time—Roshin, Dirik, Rishinira, the other three. . . . Everyone tells stories about the fucking leach-lords, about how they killed people and shattered the fucking world, but let me tell you this . . . the Atmani were *nothing* next to the Csestriim. They were leaches, sure. Somehow they were immortal, at least till someone put a knife in them. But at least they were *human.* Everyone talks about the Atmani and *no one's warning anyone* about the Csestriim. It's like everyone just *forgot.*

"With the Csestriim it wasn't just killing, it was *slaughter.* You know, *murder.* Kids. Thousands of kids."

He leaned across the table, eyes bulging from their sockets. "They. Tried. To. End. Us.

"So when you talk to me about decency, you know, about treating that bitch you brought with decency, what I say is *fuck* decency."

"Triste might not be Csestriim," Kaden said, trying to keep his compass in the maelstrom of emotion. "She has feelings. Fears and hopes."

"No," Trant said, body suddenly still, voice quiet. "That's what she wants you to think. They *know* how all this works." Grinding a finger into his temple. "They know how to use it against us. You understand? You understand what I'm telling you?"

Kaden started to protest, then stopped himself. Worry about Triste nagged at him like a cracked rib, but for the moment there was nothing he could do. He didn't know where she was, didn't even really know where *he* was, and, though the Dead Heart appeared surprisingly empty, there were still enough men with bows and blades to keep him neatly penned wherever they wished.

Learn first, he told himself, *then act.*

"Scial Nin told me about the Ishien," he said, trying to change the subject. "You were the first monks, the predecessors of the Shin."

Trant snorted. "Not monks." He frowned, turning back to his fish. "Not ever monks."

"Then what?"

"Prisoners. *Slaves.* Beasts to be prodded, and poisoned, and gutted." He punctuated each word by stabbing the fish with his knife. Abruptly, he pulled the blade from the bones and waved it around him. "This place, this fucking *place,* was our pen."

Once more Kaden considered the heavy stone walls. "The Csestriim built this."

Trant nodded. "Builders. Oh, the bastards were builders, all right."

Kaden frowned. "Why? I thought they just wanted to destroy us. Why build prisons?"

"Ever see a cat?" Trant asked, then snapped his teeth at Kaden, clawed at the air. "They don't just kill, no. Nope. Cats—they tease, they toy, they taunt. Same thing with the Enemy . . . they wanted to see what we'd do. It's all *here,*" he insisted, waving his hand toward the walls. "All here. Scrolls, codices, all of it. They filleted some of us like fish, cut the eyelids off others. What's *wrong* with us—that's what they wanted to know. What's *wrong*?" His lips twisted into a grimace. "It's all here," he muttered. "Bastards wrote it all down. It's *all* here."

Trant was staring at him wolfishly, and after a moment Kaden turned away to look at the chamber once more. The weight of the place had grown more oppressive, as though too much blood had soaked into the stone, as though history had its own stench that no amount of salt water could ever fully expunge. The Dead Heart wasn't a fortress at all, it wasn't even a prison; it was a grave, and the Ishien who stalked the halls were like the ghosts of men, still fighting a war they refused to let die. This was the place to which Kaden had insisted they come, the place to which he had unwittingly brought Triste. This charnel pit was Tan's home. The chill of the air settled deeper into Kaden's flesh, pricking at his clammy skin. He wasn't a prisoner, not exactly, but it wasn't at all clear that he could leave.

13

Night saved them, night and the heavy clouds that obscured their flight as they clutched the bird's talons, rising free of the shattered city, then from the canyon itself, rising, rising, with what felt like agonizing slowness, until they were clear of the highest peaks, buried in darkness and cloud. Valyn had no idea whether Suant'ra had killed the Flea's bird, no idea if Chi Hoai Mi was alive, or if the Flea himself was following. That fear kept him awake through the first part of the escape. The fear and the pain.

As the night wore on, however, as 'Ra winged unevenly westward through the achingly cold night, it was all he could do to stay conscious in his harness, to brace himself against the buffeting gusts of the bird's massive wings, to keep his numb fingers wrapped around the strap overhead. He couldn't draw a bow, not with the quarrel buried in his shoulder, could barely even hold himself upright, and yet he was faring better than both Gwenna and Talal.

Gwenna slumped unconscious in her harness, having succumbed to her vicious head wound as soon as they were in the air. Annick had lashed her to 'Ra's talon with a length of rope, which kept her from spinning free in the wind, but the slackness of her jaw and the way her eyes rolled back in her head had Valyn worried.

Talal was faring a bit better. An arrow had punched into his leg during the chaos of the grab, and though he was managing to stand on the far talon, Valyn could tell from the angle of the shaft that the steel head was buried close to the bone. Getting it out would prove both dangerous and time-consuming, and, in a best case, the wound would slow the leach.

Most worrisome of all, at least at the moment, was the fact that 'Ra herself was struggling, the normally effortless beating of her wings irregular and labored, her great body listing to port. Valyn had read about fights between wild kettral, but, aside from a few harmless skirmishes between hatchlings, he'd never witnessed one. How 'Ra could fly at all after trading blows with the Flea's bird Valyn had no idea, but fly she did, albeit weakly. He couldn't even guess where Sami Yurl's bird had ended up in the chaos.

We're alive, Valyn reminded himself. *We got out.*

At least, he hoped they had. There had been no sign of the Flea's Wing since Assare. It was possible, more than possible, that Chi Hoai was dead, her kettral was crippled, and the rest of the Wing was stranded. On the other hand, the two birds hadn't been out of sight for that long, not long enough to be certain of anything, and trusting to someone else's failure made for shit strategy. And so, for hour after hour he stared east, vision blurred by his wind-whipped tears, searching in the stacked columns of cloud for some sign of pursuit. His eyes ached, but at least the effort took his mind off his own pain. Nerve-fraying as it was, staring into the empty darkness was better than looking at Gwenna's limp form.

He'd managed to do his job—Kaden was clear, Valyn's own Wing was alive—and yet all he felt, aside from the wracking pain in his shoulder, was a sick slosh of guilt and anger. Guilt for the injuries to Gwenna and Talal; anger at Pyrre for starting the fight and at himself for not stopping it; and yet more guilt for Blackfeather Finn.

They might be part of the plot, he reminded himself. *They could have been keeping us alive for questioning, for torture.* It was possible, but the possibility didn't change the fact that a man Valyn had liked and admired was dead.

An hour out, he called a short stop. He hated to do it. Landing turned them into a grounded, stationary target, but they needed Laith on top of the bird, not strapped in beneath, they needed to regain something like a fighting configuration, and Valyn wanted at least a few moments to look over Talal's wound and Gwenna's.

"I'm fine," the leach said, grimacing as he straightened his knee. "I'm not going to die of a leg wound."

In fact, there were plenty of ways to die of a leg wound—the Eyrie medical archives were packed with them—but Valyn wasn't going to press the point. If the leach could stand, he could fly, and for the moment, flight was imperative.

Gwenna's case was more troubling. Valyn refused to light a lantern, but her normally pale skin looked even paler, ashen to his night eyes, and though she winced and cried out when he searched through the tangled mess of her hair for the wound, she didn't wake up. Blood had soaked into her curls, then frozen, and after a moment he hacked away several handfuls with his belt knife. She'd probably curse him for the decision when she woke, but waking was a prerequisite to the cursing. Her skull felt intact, though his fingers were too numb to be certain, and regardless, it was easy enough to wreck the brain without damaging the skull. In the end, all he could do was wrap her in a heavy blanket to keep off the worst of the chill, then strap her to the talon once more.

The rest of the flight was cold, long, and miserable. Laith hugged the valleys and passes, trying to keep them low enough that the ridgelines would hide them from pursuit, but not so low that they all got dead. The flier knew his business, but it was dark and they were belly-to-the-dirt. Valyn could see the cracks in the boulders, the small caches of snow secreted beneath the stones. A single mistake from Laith would leave them all smeared across the side of some granite cliff.

By the time they crested the final ridgeline, Valyn was nauseated from the pain in his shoulder, from peering endlessly into the darkness, from feeling his muscles clench every time they scraped over some jagged escarpment. It didn't help that light was starting to soak the eastern sky. In an hour the sun would be up, and then they would *really* have problems. The Kettral worshipped Hull for good reason: even wounded, even fleeing, Valyn's Wing had a chance as long as it stayed dark. With the arrival of dawn, however, they'd be visible from the ground and the air both. If the Flea could fly, if he had guessed their direction of travel, if he, too, had been pushing west through the night, he'd be able to spot them from twenty miles off. Farther, if he used a long lens. It was a lot of "ifs," but then, the Flea had made a career out of turning "ifs" into "whens."

Valyn scanned the grasslands unfolding below. Though the Kettral had flown plenty of missions north of the White River, especially in recent years, striking at various Urghul bands, most of the action happened nearly a thousand miles to the west, in the Blood Steppe and the Golden Steppe, where the nomadic tribes butted up against the boundary of the Annurian Empire. The vast, undifferentiated swath of land below, empty grasslands flowing into the jutting teeth of the Bone Mountains, was marked "Far Steppe" on the Eyrie maps, but Valyn couldn't remember much more about it. There were tribes this far east, but the Kettral trainers dismissed them as irrelevant—an omission Valyn regretted now. He was going to have to land—that much was clear. Gwenna and Talal required serious attention, and the bolt in his own shoulder would have to come out. Just as crucially, 'Ra needed to rest before she dropped out of the sky.

Pyrre prodded him in the shoulder, breaking his concentration.

He turned to face the woman. That she had survived the fight in Assare, the fight *she* had started, seemed grossly unfair, but then, there were no judges in battle, no one to adjudicate the dispute and keep everyone between the lines. Valyn had no idea what to do with her when they were finally clear of the mountains. He was tempted to simply leave her on the 'Kent-kissing steppe, but that was a decision that could wait.

She prodded him again, and he swallowed a curse.

"What?" he shouted, leaning so close to the assassin that her hair whipped at his face. If she was frightened to be flying a wounded bird above dangerous territory while pursued by a Kettral Wing, she didn't show it, didn't smell it. Valyn had yet to see the woman really scared.

"Fire," she mouthed, pointing off to the northwest.

He followed her finger. They were still too far off to make out more than a dull orange smudge, but the flame wasn't large, probably a cook fire kindled in the predawn. Which meant Urghul. Valyn tightened his grip on the strap, leaning out into the dark for a better view. His trainers might have skipped an analysis of the eastern tribes, but he'd learned enough about the nomadic horsemen to be wary.

Unlike the other polities surrounding Annur—the Manjari Empire, Anthera, Freeport, and the Federated Cities—the Urghul had no government, which meant no law, no significant trade, and no respite from the constant blood feuds, vicious intertribal vendettas lasting dozens of years at a time. Evidently, it was all a part of their worship of the Lord of Pain. The Annurians knew the god as Meshkent, but the Urghul had a different name, one in their own language: Kwihna, they called him, the Hardener. There were no cities on the steppe, but over the millennia the Urghul had erected hundreds of altars to their god, some massive stone tablets, others little more than piled cairns where they carried out their savage worship of pain and blood sacrifice.

Valyn tried to remember the occasions for such sacrifice: the full moon, the new moon, solstices and storms, floods and famines, all requiring breathing bodies to offer up to the god. Gent had demanded to know how there were any of the bastards left after so much blood and burnt offering, but according to Daveen Shaleel, there were more Urghul than most people realized—maybe a million in small tribes, *taamu,* they called them, scattered across the enormous grasslands. Valyn always found that number unsettling. Although the population of the empire itself ran into the tens of millions, the legions rarely fielded more than half a million soldiers, and those were spread all over the border. The Urghul, on the other hand, had no dedicated military; every man, woman, and child was a fighter. Consummate horsemen, physically and mentally toughened by a hard life in a hard place, well-blooded through constant conflict, they could pose a serious threat to Annur, if they ever stopped fighting amongst themselves.

More to the point, they posed a serious threat to Valyn's Wing. Cadets weren't kept formally apprised of Kettral missions, but there was always buzz in the training yard and the mess hall, enough that Valyn knew the Eyrie had been flying missions over the steppe nearly every month for the past several years. Who the target was, or why an empty chunk of grassland without cities or towns was so important, he had no idea, but it hardly mattered now. The Urghul immediately below might not have encountered Kettral, but they would have heard tales of great birds dropping out of the sky bearing men and women dressed in black. The odds of a welcome parade were not high.

But still, he thought as he stared out over the land, all shifting grays and blacks beneath a cloud-wracked anvil of sky, *We might have to go down there.*

He considered the campfire once more. Gwenna's head wound required rest. They *all* needed rest. The rations they'd stolen in their flight from the Eyrie were nearly gone. Both Talal's injury and Valyn's own needed to be cleaned and cauterized, which meant fire and yet more rest. It was possible to make their own camp, to go without food, to tend their own wounds and steer clear of the people below, but that choice presented its own risks. In the end 'Ra's deteriorating wingbeat decided him.

The bird couldn't stay in the air much longer. She was gliding in long sweeps, losing hundreds of feet of altitude as she rested, then struggling mightily to regain the lost elevation. The stutter in her wingbeat had grown worse, and she was flying head-down. Laith would have to look her over on the ground to discover what was wrong. Worse, a battered kettral could take days or weeks to recover. That campfire meant Urghul, and Urghul meant horses. Valyn hated riding, but it beat walking, if Gwenna even *could* walk.

He reached for the signaling strap, tugging out the relevant code: *Circle target.*

For a moment nothing happened, then he felt the bird bank slightly to the north, aiming directly at the campfire.

He leaned over to Talal, cupping a hand to his mouth. "How's your Urghul?"

The leach grimaced, though whether at the question or the pain in his leg, Valyn couldn't say. "Awful," he replied.

"Can you tell them we don't want a fight?"

"I don't think *Don't want a fight* is an Urghul concept."

"How about, *If you move, the bird will rip your throat out?*"

Talal frowned. "*Bird kill you* is about the best I can do."

"*Bird kill you* it is."

"Are you certain about this, Valyn?" the leach asked.

"No." It had been a very long time since Valyn felt certain about anything.

He turned back to the flame. As they grew closer, his spirits rose. There was only a single fire with a few small figures gathered around it. Two *api*, the collapsible hide tents favored by the Urghul, stood a little way off, with a line of hobbled horses between them. The camp probably contained about ten people. No more than a dozen. Even injured, a Kettral Wing would be equal to ten or twelve nomadic savages.

"I've got no 'Kent-kissing certainty whatsoever," he went on. "But we need food and fire, rest and horses—and they're all right there."

✝

All in all, the drop went better than Valyn had dared to hope. The Urghul tending the campfire were just kids—the oldest maybe ten years old—preparing the morning meal while their elders enjoyed a few final moments of sleep and warmth inside the *api*. The oldest girl, a pale, blond child of nine or ten, hurled herself at them, screaming imprecations in her strange language and stabbing with her cooking knife until Laith knocked her unconscious with a carefully calibrated blow of his sword hilt. The two younger children glanced uncertainly from the massive bird to the *api* and back, but, aside from shouting a few vicious-sounding threats, they made no move to interfere.

The adults were a different story. As soon as the children stopped shrieking, a man barreled out of the entrance flap of the nearest tent, stark naked save for the spear in his hand, face twisted with confusion and rage. The sight of Suant'ra looming over his cook fire slowed him for a moment, but if he was frightened by six well-armed, black-clad figures materializing out of the predawn murk, he didn't show it. With a bellow, he hurled the spear directly at Valyn. Valyn slid aside, letting the shaft glide harmlessly into the night, but then, before he could take a step forward, a knife sprouted from his assailant's throat.

Valyn glanced over his shoulder at Pyrre.

The Skullsworn smiled at him, then winked.

"We're not here to kill them," he spat.

"Please stop using the first-person plural," she replied, bouncing another knife on her palm. "I'm not a part of your Wing."

"I *am* on the Wing," Laith interjected, "and I'm all right with killing them. I remember those lectures on blood sacrifice and pain ritual, and I'm not all that eager—"

He broke off as a woman burst from the *api,* naked as the first man, a shorthorn bow in her hand. Her skin, like that of all the Urghul, was onion-pale, almost lambent in the firelight, and her hair, too, a great blond mane, might have been spun from white-hot fire. She took a step forward, then paused, eyeing the assembled Kettral. A chill, vicious wind sliced through the camp. She didn't shiver.

"Go ahead and say it," Pyrre remarked. "She's a woman. And *we* don't kill women. I don't mind. Tell me how helpless she is."

Valyn stared at the Urghul. Scars puckered the skin of her belly and legs—lance wounds and arrow punctures. Her hair whipped at her face, but she paid it no mind, focusing instead on Valyn. She hadn't yet drawn the bow, but an arrow was nocked to the string, and, from the easy way she held it, he imagined she was familiar with the weapon.

"If she moves," he said slowly, "kill her."

"How *barbaric*," Pyrre replied, amusement bright in her voice. "Triste would never have approved, poor girl."

Valyn ignored her. "Talal, start talking. Quick."

The leach hesitated a moment, then began haltingly: *"Wasape ebibitu—"*

"You killed my *wasape,*" the woman said, cutting him off, indicating the sprawled corpse with her chin. "Do not savage my language."

That she spoke the Annurian tongue was something of a surprise, but it meant Valyn could handle the negotiation himself. As the woman spoke, other figures had emerged from the two *api,* some wearing leather riding breeches and rough tunics, others bare-chested. As Valyn had hoped, they numbered just half a dozen. Ten with the kids and the dead man.

"He attacked us," Valyn said, indicating the corpse. "We killed him only in defense."

The woman considered the body for a moment, then shrugged. "There are other warriors to warm my nights."

To her right, a young man growled something incomprehensible. He had a knife in each hand, and from the way he was crouched forward, looked eager to try his luck.

"Annick . . ." Valyn began.

"I've got him," she replied.

The Urghul woman looked at the sniper, then turned to her companion, uttering a few curt words.

He snapped something angry in response, waved a knife at the Kettral, then spit full in her face.

Without blinking, the naked woman pivoted, slamming her arrowhead through his throat. She held it there firmly as the dying man dropped his knives, clutched at the wooden shaft, then released it as he crumpled. She considered the body for a moment, then turned to the other Urghul. Valyn caught the words for *chief, dead,* and *challenge.* She spread her arms wide as if inviting attack from her own people, evidently indifferent to her own nakedness, the biting wind, and the Kettral Wing a few paces away. Only when the other Urghul had nodded did she turn back to Valyn.

"I am Huutsuu," she said. "*Wohkowi* of this family. Do we fight or do we eat?"

"I think I'm in love," Pyrre said appreciatively. "I hope I don't have to kill her."

Valyn stared at the Urghul. If the lack of guards, the motley weapons, or the two newly dead men on the grass were anything to go by, they were hardly masters of military tactics. On the other hand, the woman showed no fear of her own death, nor any remorse over the bodies before her. She waited, arms spread, for his response.

"We eat," Valyn said finally. "I regret your . . . men."

Huutsuu shrugged. "*Men* would have killed you. These two . . ." She waved the bow in their direction. "Fools."

"Nonetheless," Valyn said, uncertain how to proceed in the absence of any sort of grief or anger, "we would avoid fighting."

"Then we eat." She turned to the children, both of whom were still glaring at Valyn. "Peekwi. Sari. Slap your sister awake and put the pot on the fire. I need my furs." She turned, ducking back into the *api* without a word, and abruptly Valyn found himself standing in the center of an Urghul camp in which people went about their early morning routine—pissing behind the *api,* checking horses, rubbing chilled hands by the fire—as though nothing amiss had occurred, as though half a dozen soldiers hadn't just dropped out of the sky on a giant bird to murder one of their number. Even the pair disposing of the bodies appeared indifferent to the manner of their death, bickering incomprehensibly as they stripped the few ornaments, tossed aside the weapons, and hauled the corpses into the high grass.

"This makes me nervous," Talal murmured.

Valyn nodded. "Annick, keep your bow handy."

"Maybe we got lucky," Laith said, vaulting off the back of the bird. "Nothing wrong with a little good luck every now and then."

Valyn allowed himself a moment of hope, then crushed it. *"Optimism kills soldiers,"* he replied, quoting Hendran.

"Steel in the guts kills soldiers," the flier countered. "Or steel in the leg," he added, glancing significantly at Talal. "Or the shoulder."

"We're getting there," Valyn growled. He hardly needed to be reminded of the searing pain of the flatbow bolt grating against his scapula. "Talal, Laith—gather their weapons."

"I need to look over 'Ra," Laith said. "Something is really wrong with her."

"The Urghul first," Valyn said. "Then we patch up our people. Then the bird. Annick, cover them. Pyrre . . ."

"Just a gentle but firm reminder," she replied, "that I am not on your Wing."

"How unfortunate. Do you think I could prevail upon you to watch a hostage or two?"

"I don't know—I might kill them."

"That," Valyn replied, gritting his teeth, "would miss the point of taking hostages." He scanned the group, picking two Urghul at random. "Him and her." He turned to Talal. "Can you tell them—"

"I'll tell them," Huutsuu replied, stepping out through the flap to her *api,* a massive bison hide draped over her shoulders and belted around her waist. The thing made her look larger, but slower. Had Valyn not witnessed her stabbing a man in the neck moments ago, had he not seen the sinew shifting beneath her bare skin, he would have underestimated this woman. It was a good lesson.

Huutsuu gestured to the two Urghul Valyn had selected, barking something rough as she gestured to a patch of ground a little space off from the fire. They hesitated, anger and doubt scrawled across their faces, but they went.

"Tie them if you want," she said, crossing to the fire without a second glance, prodding with her finger at something in the large pot.

Valyn took a deep breath, surveying the scene. Everything appeared under control. Talal and Laith had made a large pile of bows, knives, and spears; Annick stood a short way off, scanning the camp, bow in hand.

Pyrre caught him watching her and smiled a wide, open smile. "Don't worry," she said. "My god accepts all sacrifice, but I've always felt that the unarmed make for meager offerings."

She knelt behind the two hostages, trussing them quickly with the length of cord Talal had tossed her. It looked safe. If the Urghul were going to fight, they would have done it already, when they still had their weapons and full numbers.

"I apologize for this measure," Valyn said, gesturing toward the tied Urghul.

Huutsuu shrugged once more. "It is a while since we were Hardened. Kwihna will be pleased."

Valyn shook his head. "Hardened?"

She nodded. "Through pain."

"No," Valyn said. "We're not here to harden you."

"Less ethnography, Val," Laith cut in. "More medicine."

Valyn waved him down. "We're here because we have wounds that need cleaning and cauterizing. We need food, and maybe horses as well."

Something dangerous flashed in Huutsuu's eyes. "No horses."

Valyn started to point out that the woman wasn't in a position to contest the point, then thought better of it. For all their success thus far, the situation had him edgy. Between his own pain, worry for his soldiers, wariness regarding the Urghul, and fear that the Flea would drop out of the sky, he felt like a flatbow cranked a turn too far, the whole apparatus so tight that a touch could snap the string or shatter the bow's arc.

The injured first, he reminded himself. *Then the bird. Then food.*

Talal's wound was straightforward enough, or it would have been if the clouds hadn't opened up, pelting them with a vicious rain while lightning lashed the steppe a dozen miles distant. Valyn considered moving his Wing into the *api,* but that would leave them blind to what was going on outside. He could split the group, but splitting a small force was a piss-poor idea, no matter how complacent the enemy appeared. Which left them all out in the rain, close enough to the hissing fire that the heat taunted without doing anything to warm him. At least the sudden squall would limit the Flea's visibility, if the bastard was even up there.

Valyn tried to force aside his worries and focus on Talal's injury. He wiped his forehead, blinking past the sheeting rain, then took hold of the arrow while Laith held the leach's leg. The wet wood was slick in his hands, and each time he lost his grip he felt Talal's body spasm beneath him, heard him groan through clenched teeth. Finally, his hands mired in blood, and rain, and mud, Valyn forced the arrow through, twisting it as best he could to avoid scraping the bone, bearing down viciously to get it out and over as quickly as possible. Talal growled low in his chest, straining against Laith's grip, then went slack as the arrowhead burst out. He was panting, eyes wide, rain streaming down his face.

"You all right?" Valyn asked.

The leach expelled a long, shuddering breath between his teeth, then nodded. "Finish it."

Valyn broke the shaft with one quick motion, then yanked the remainder of the arrow free as Talal bit off a curse.

Behind him, Huutsuu snorted. If the rain bothered her, she didn't show it, leaning over the fire to get a better view of the injury. "You are warriors?" she asked.

Valyn nodded curtly, taking the heated knife from Laith's hand, then pressing the glowing metal to the exit wound. Talal twisted sharply, then passed out. Valyn breathed out slowly. Unconsciousness would spare the leach the pain of the second cauterization and keep him still while Valyn attended to the entry point.

Huutsuu snorted again. "A warrior should face his pain."

"He faced it well enough," Valyn snapped. "We've been flying all night."

"He fled," the woman replied, waving a finger at the flier's limp body. "Fled into the Softness."

Valyn pressed the knife to the entry wound, counting to eight silently, then rounded on Huutsuu.

"We don't want a fight," he snapped, "but keep talking, and you'll find out something about pain."

The woman regarded the glowing knife with scorn. "This is a small thing," she replied, "for one who is *tsaani* three times over."

"What in 'Shael's name is she talking about?" Valyn demanded of no one in particular.

"Children," Talal murmured, rousing from his stupor. "She's had three children."

Valyn shook his head. He had no idea why that mattered. Between the driving rain and the pounding agony in his shoulder, all piled on the fatigue of a long night spent in the harness, he felt ready to snap.

"I don't give a *shit* how many kids she's got." He pointed at Huutsuu with the blade, then gestured toward the tied Urghul. "Over there. With them. Now."

She looked him up and down a long moment, then shook her head and stalked away.

The sky had gone from black to a grudging gray. The serrated line of the eastern peaks still hid the sun, but the clouds were starting to clear. They'd be hard-pressed to finish tending wounds before full daylight, and Valyn still wasn't sure what he planned to do then.

"Laith," he said, voice rough with urgency and weariness, "get this fucking thing out of my shoulder."

The bolt came out more easily than Talal's arrow, although Laith needed to make a pair of slices in the surrounding skin in order to free the small barbs on the quarrel's tip. Aware of Huutsuu's eyes upon him, Valyn clamped down on his pain, refusing to cry out even as he felt the muscles of his shoulder pull, then tear. The searing agony of the hot knife threatened to plunge him into unconsciousness, but he clenched his jaw and forced back the fog on the fringes of his vision.

"I'm good," he said, when he trusted himself to open his mouth again. "I'm good. Go check on 'Ra. I can take care of Gwenna."

The demolitions master was by far the most worrisome case. She still had not regained consciousness, and in the meager dawn light her face looked even worse than it had in the dark, pale and waxen, her red hair plastered flat to the skin by the rain. The wool blanket was rapidly soaking through, and she was shivering, lips dark in her pallid face. Valyn ran a finger along the inside of her hand, but there was no response, no grip or reflex. There wasn't much to do with head wounds but wait and hope, which meant they were going to have to get her warm. Which meant going in the *api*. Sometimes there just wasn't a good option on offer.

"Talal?" he asked, glancing over at the leach. "Any thoughts?"

Talal frowned.

"We've already moved her too much. It was a rough night, and with the two drops . . ." He trailed off, shaking his head. "I don't know."

"*Valyn,*" Laith cut in, all trace of levity vanished from his voice.

Valyn turned, hand on his blade, half expecting to find the Flea facing him down. There was only Laith, though, Laith and the bird. Suant'ra had half extended her enormous wing for him, and Laith stood beneath it, hands above him, prodding the joint with both hands. His face was grim.

"What?" Valyn asked.

"Not good." The flier took a deep breath, then blew it out. "There's serious damage to her shoulder—probably a patagial tear."

"Meaning what?"

Valyn had sat through the lectures on kettral anatomy, they all had, but it was the flier's responsibility to care for the birds in the field, and some of the more specific terminology had slipped.

"Meaning she can't fucking fly."

"She flew us here," he pointed out. "She flew all night long."

"Which tells you something about how tough she is," Laith snapped. "Most birds would have fallen out of the air. The damage is bad, and the long flight made it worse. The joint is swelling. By noon she probably won't be able to get in the air at all."

Valyn glanced up at the kettral's head. She was watching Laith, her huge, dark eye swiveling in its socket to follow him as he ran his hands beneath her feathers. He'd often wondered about the kettral, about what they thought and understood. Did 'Ra know she was injured? Was she frightened? It was impossible to read anything in those dark eyes.

"How long for it to heal?" Valyn asked.

Laith shook his head. "Weeks. Months. Maybe never."

"We don't have weeks, let alone months," Valyn said. "How many miles can she make each day like this?"

"You're not *listening* to me, Valyn," Laith said. "She can't fly at all, certainly not with us hanging off of her."

Valyn stared, the implications sinking in. Kettral training was all well and good, but it was the birds that made the warriors legendary. Without 'Ra they lost their mobility, the element of surprise, and a vicious fighter in the bargain. Without 'Ra, they were stranded on the ass end of the steppe with no good way to get back to Annur, or anywhere else, for that matter.

"We have to stay," Laith was saying, "set up a camp here while we tend her, pray she gets better."

"Bad idea," Annick said. The sniper hadn't taken her eyes off the Urghul prisoners, but she'd clearly been listening to the conversation. "Suant'ra is too easy to spot from the land or air. The Flea will come, or more Urghul."

Valyn nodded slowly. "We can't hide her, and we can't fight them all."

Laith stared, aghast. "So . . . what? You just want to *leave* her?"

Valyn glanced east. The sun was just topping the peaks, etching the snow and ice with fire.

"No," he said finally. "I want her to leave us."

Laith started to object, but he held up a hand. "You said she could still fly before the swelling gets too bad, at least a little bit. Send her south, back toward the Islands. All the birds know how to get home, right?"

"She won't *make* it to the Islands," Laith replied, fury and fear roughening his voice.

"She doesn't have to," Valyn said. "She just needs to get away from us. Fifty miles. Even twenty. Far enough that anyone who finds her doesn't find us, too."

"And what happens," Laith demanded, "when someone finds her? When she can't fly?"

Valyn took a deep breath. "She's not a pet, Laith. She's a soldier. The same as you. The same as me. She'll do what we'd do: fight until she has to retreat, retreat until she can't, then fight one more time." He tried to soften his voice. "She saved us, Laith, but she can't help us anymore. Not now. All she can do is get us caught or killed, and I'm not going to let that happen."

Laith glared at him, mouth open but silent. To Valyn's shock, there were tears in the flier's eyes. For a few heartbeats, it seemed like he was going to keep arguing, to refuse, but finally he nodded, a quick jerk, like he hadn't meant to make the motion.

"All right," he said, voice hoarse. "All right. I just need to strip the harnesses. Give her the best chance I can."

Valyn nodded. "I'll help."

"No," Laith barked. Then, more quietly, "No. I'll do it."

It didn't take long for him to remove 'Ra's rigging—just a matter of a few knots and buckles, and she was clean. Even then, though, Laith didn't let her fly, running his hands instead through the feathers over her throat, murmuring to her in syllables Valyn couldn't understand. The bird remained statue-still, her head cocked at an angle as though listening to the flier. When Laith finally stepped back, she watched him for a moment, then lowered her head slowly, until it was level with the flier's own. He put a hand on her beak, a curiously gentle gesture that covered the bloodstains from the earlier attack, smiled, then stepped back, gesturing to the sky.

"Get out of here," he said. "You fought well, now get out of here."

'Ra bowed her head once, then launched herself into the air with a shriek, great wings moving raggedly as she struggled to gain height. Valyn watched, stomach in a knot, as she turned south, disappearing over a low line of hills.

He turned back to Laith. "I'm sorry."

The flier met his eyes, gaze hard beneath the tears. "I hope you've got a fucking plan."

The plan, for the moment, was simple: rest. Gwenna still wasn't awake, Talal looked like he might fall over at any moment, and Valyn himself felt like he'd been beaten with boards for the better part of a week. He felt vulnerable without the bird, stranded, almost naked, but he couldn't see any other way. Without 'Ra they could wear bison hides over their blacks, and aside from their dark hair, dark skin—easy enough to cover with hats and hides—blend in with the horsemen. They wouldn't fool other Urghul, of course, but no one looking from the air would see anything amiss. Even if the Flea wasn't following, he'd been clear enough back in Assare that the Eyrie had sent multiple Wings after Valyn.

And so, along with Laith and Talal, Valyn spent the better part of the morning erasing all signs of Suant'ra and the predawn fight. They mounded stone over the bodies of the two Urghul, raked out the bird's claw marks from the soft earth, and moved the prisoners into the larger of the two *api*. The movement kept Valyn's muscles from knotting too badly, and helped him to avoid thinking, at least for the moment, about the challenges ahead.

They'd just about finished carrying Gwenna into the smaller tent when Annick spoke from the other side of the fire, her voice level as usual.

"Keep working. Don't look up."

Valyn suppressed the natural reaction, bending instead to throw a couple more logs on the cook fire.

"What is it?" he asked.

"Bird," she said. "Approaching high and from the east."

It took an effort of will for Valyn to keep his hands away from his knives and blades, to squat down by the fire to prod at the contents of the rough kettle, but Annick had the better angle. Of course, the Kettral on the bird would probably *expect* a small group of Urghul to look up as they passed, but anyone scanning with a long lens would see his face, his features. Better to keep his eyes down and pretend he didn't notice.

"They're past," Annick said finally.

Valyn glanced up, shielding his face with his hand, following the shape of the retreating bird.

"They were too high for me to make out," the sniper continued.

Valyn squinted. The bird *was* high, but he could see the pinions, the shading of the wings and tailfeathers, his eyes keen even in the full daylight. He let out a long, slow breath.

"The Flea," he said. "It was the Flea."

14

Adare returned from the evening's sermon both weary and wary. The days were long enough—waking before dawn, walking half a dozen miles, a brief stop for lunch, then another five or six miles— without having to listen to some petty priest for the first half of the night. When the caravan finally halted, Adare wanted nothing more than to roll into her blankets and pass out. Nira, however, had pointed out that Adare was dumber than a dead ox for skipping sermons while posing as a pilgrim, and so, night after night, she went, stumbling over the uneven ground in the gathering gloom, squinting to see through the blindfold, trying to avoid the dark shapes of the wagons, all to sit on the fringes of the fire, juggling the contradictory hopes that the others would note her attendance without paying her any special attention.

It hardly made for easy listening. One night the young priest lectured on the sinful excesses of the Malkeenians. Another on the ideal of an Intarran state, free from secular meddling. The most recent harangue—an extended eulogy for Uinian IV—struck even closer to home. It was impossible to read the faces of her fellow pilgrims in the flickering firelight, but the mood was clear enough. She thought she had managed to kill both the priest and his reputation when she revealed him to be a leach, but while the man stayed dead, his good name was proving frighteningly resilient. Most people hadn't been at the temple on the day Uinian burst into flame, the day his own congregation tore his burning body apart. They knew what they believed, and regarding the Malkeenians in general and Adare more particularly, they were willing to believe the worst. By the time the tirade was over, Adare had worried a gash in the side of her thumb with a nervous fingernail.

She picked her way back slowly through the wagons and cook fires, wanting nothing more than a few bites of Nira's fish, a few moments warming herself over the flames, then sleep. As soon as she returned to the cook fire, however, she realized something was wrong. The old woman had spent every night for the past two weeks over an iron pan, grilling up carp from the canal with pepper and rice purchased along the road, muttering over her cooking as though the words were spice. Now, however, she stood atop the wagon, peering into the darkness. Her hair, a white haze around her head, had broken free from her bun. The cane trembled in her hands.

"Oshi," she shouted, voice twisting up at the end, then cracking. "Oshi!"

As Adare approached the wagon, the old woman turned to her.

"He's gone," she said. "I came back to the fire, and he was gone."

Adare hesitated. Oshi's mind was far more feeble than she had initially realized, but the madness was easy to overlook. It usually manifested quietly, in endless, absorbed silences, or bouts of soft weeping. When he ranted, he ranted gently, muttering over and over again in his scratched voice to the birds or the wagon or his own fingernails. Whenever he grew particularly distressed, Nira was always there with a hand on his shoulder and sip from her crockery jar, the combination of which calmed the lost old man. Evidently something had gone amiss.

"We'll find him," Adare said. She squinted, trying to make out the scope of the pilgrims' camp. It was large, but not impossibly so. Maybe forty or fifty fires and as many wagons spread over a couple of acres. "He can't have gone far," she said, gesturing. "We'll split up. Check the camp—"

"I've checked the camp," Nira snarled. "Twice. He's gone, and no one saw him go."

Adare drew back at the woman's tone. She had grown accustomed to the harsh language, but this was something new, something harder and sharper.

"How long were you away from him?" she asked carefully.

Nira took a deep, shuddering breath. "I left just before dark. Needed to pick up some fish. I told him to stay by the fire, which he generally does."

Since sunset, then. A fit man could have run a couple of miles, but Oshi was not a fit man. The canal bounded them a few hundred paces to the west, which meant he could go north or south along the road, or east into the fields.

"Has he done this before?" Adare asked.

"Not for a long, long time."

Before Adare could reply, Lehav stepped around the wagon, a hand on the pommel of his sword. She couldn't make out his eyes, but there was something alert in his posture, something ready. Two pilgrims flanked him, both obviously fighters, one still carrying a shank of dripping meat.

Lehav glanced from Adare to Nira, then back.

"I heard shouting," he said.

Adare nodded. She wanted Lehav's attention even less than she wanted to sit through the nightly sermons, but shying away now would look odd. Besides, if he could assist in finding Oshi, so much the better.

"We need your help," she said, hesitated, then wrung her hands, hoping the gesture might look suitably pathetic.

One of the men—a short, heavily muscled brute with a frog's mouth—leered at her, then turned to Lehav.

"Lady needs your help, Captain. Pretty little thing, all flushed and outta breath. Reckon you oughta give her some . . . help." Adare could see his tongue in the firelight flicking between his lips like a pink, feral creature.

"I'm not a captain, Lodge," Lehav said absently, glancing over the wagon. "Left the legions a long time ago."

"Sure thing, Captain," the frog replied, grinning.

"Knock it off, jackass," said the soldier to Lodge's right, slapping him across the back of the head roughly. "The young woman's a pilgrim, like us. Not some silly, savage slut from the frontier."

Lodge frowned, but fell silent.

Lehav ignored the exchange entirely. If he felt any desire to spring to Adare's defense, he didn't show it. The fact that he'd saved her back in Annur sometimes tempted Adare to think of him as an ally. It was a dangerous temptation.

"What do you need?" he asked, fixing her with a stare.

"Oshi's wandered off," she said, trying to keep her voice high and frightened. "You know the old man? Nira's worried about him."

Lehav shifted his gaze from Adare to Nira. "I've heard you talking," he said, the mildness of his voice belying the edge in his words. "I've heard your heresies." He shook his head. "I don't know why you joined this pilgrimage, but if you're worried about your brother, you can find him yourself."

Adare started to protest, but Lehav cut her off with a quick chop of his hand.

"It's bad company you keep, Dorellin. Sinful company. River blindness is one thing; make sure you aren't blinded to Intarra's light at the same time."

Before she could respond, the soldier turned on his heel and stalked off into the night, his two companions following.

It was a measure of Nira's fear that she didn't curse him, didn't even seem to register his departure.

"It's all right," Adare said. "We don't need him. The two of us can check the road, one north and one south. We'll be faster than your brother."

"Ya can't even see at night, not beyond the fires, not with that thing wrapped over your eyes."

"I'll move slowly. I'll call out."

Nira hesitated, then nodded curtly, anger and confusion yielding to something like her customary stony resolve. "I'll go south."

"We'll find him, Nira," Adare said, laying a hand on the older woman's arm. She was surprised to find her trembling. "He hasn't been gone that long, and out here it's just fields and the canal—he can't get into too much trouble."

She turned and hitched up her robe, but Nira stopped her.

"Wait," she said, voice low. Adare turned back, and the woman grasped her wrist with one clawlike hand, skewering her with a level gaze. "If you find him . . . be careful."

"I'll make sure he doesn't hurt himself," Adare assured her.

Nira shook her head. "Don't be careful *for* him, you fool. Be careful *of* him."

Oshi's arms were twigs. His neck didn't look capable of holding up his bald head. And yet the old woman's voice burned with a fierce urgency, and she refused to release Adare's wrist.

"When you find him," she pressed, "bring him directly to me. *To me.* And try to keep him calm."

"It'll be all right," Adare said, pulling away gingerly, suddenly worried. "It will be all right."

†

Adare waited until she was beyond the ambit of the fires, then pulled off her blindfold. It was a risk, probably a foolish one, but something in Nira's tone, in the old woman's trembling arm, made her want to hurry, and she couldn't hurry with the muslin wrapped over her eyes. She kept the knot in the cloth, ready to pull it back on if someone approached. Then she started running.

It was hard to gauge distance in the darkness, but from the ache in her calves and the turning of the stars in the sky, Adare figured she must have backtracked on the road at least two miles, calling out Oshi's name occasionally, alternately scanning the open ground sloping down to the canal and peering into the growing stalks to the east. Night and moonlight had leached away the green fecundity of the fields, leaving only gray stems and the shadows between them. If Oshi had wandered even a little way from the road, if he had fallen among the ripening crops, Adare might pass within a few paces without noticing him. She told herself, when she finally turned back, that the old man had gone a different direction, that Nira had already found him, but when she returned to the sprawling camp she found Nira standing by the side of the road, alone.

"Anything?" Adare asked, though the answer was clear enough.

Nira shook her head. Her jaw was tight, the skin stretched taut across her knuckles where she gripped her cane.

"We must find him."

"It'll be easier when the sun rises," Adare pointed out.

"It will be too *late* when the sun rises," Nira snapped.

"Too late for what?"

"To help him," the woman replied quietly.

Adare looked over the camp. Searching for one man in the darkness was a fool's errand, especially if he was too mad to hear his own name when they called it. Especially if he didn't want to be found. It was clear, however, that Nira intended to keep looking until she collapsed from exhaustion, and in the world outside the walls of the Dawn Palace, she was the closest thing Adare had to an ally.

"We haven't searched down by the canal," Adare pointed out.

"I can see clear ta the water from here."

"He could be just over the bank. Could have fallen in."

Nira hesitated, then nodded. "You go north along the bank. I'll go south."

Halfway to the canal, Adare started to lose hope. Though the ground was uneven, riddled with divots and small depressions, it offered no place a grown man might disappear. She pressed on anyway, partly out of stubbornness and partly just to see the thing through. There was no telling if there might be a thin sandbar where the current had undercut the shore. It seemed unlikely, but there was no way to rule it out without looking.

She was almost to the water when she heard the sound. At first she thought it came from the deckhands on one of the canal vessels, a few men up late drinking plum wine and singing at the moon. When the breeze dropped, however, she realized it wasn't singing at all, but a high, thin keening, a human voice, ragged and tremulous as a harp string tightened to the breaking point. The language was unfamiliar, if it was a language at all and not simply the raw expression of grief and confusion. The voice sounded close by, but Adare couldn't see anyone, nor any trees or bushes that might obscure a person. Shoulders tightening, she moved down the bank.

She almost walked directly into the pit. No, she realized, pausing on the rim, peering down into the shadow below, not a pit, a foundation. It was small, maybe fifteen paces across, and the large stones at the lip had mostly tumbled inward. The few that remained teetered precariously, cracked and covered with moss, hidden by the tall grass and uneven ground. Down at the bottom, a few paces below her, Oshi crouched in the corner, golden robes ripped and begrimed, palms pressed to his ears as though to drown out the sound of his own voice.

"Nira," Adare called, looking over her shoulder for the old woman. She was searching the canal bank a little way to the south, and Adare had to call once again, more loudly, to get her attention. "He's here!" she said, gesturing toward the yawning hole in the earth. She turned back to find Oshi staring at her. He had fallen silent, worrying his upper lip with his teeth, and begun rocking back and forth in a quick, convulsive rhythm.

"Oshi," Adare called down to him. Nira's warning flitted through her mind, but the man was clearly lost, helpless, maybe even injured. "Oshi, why don't you come back to the wagons?"

His eyes darted from her, to the ragged clouds above, to his own palms, which he held before his face as though they were ancient and inexplicable artifacts. Adare took a deep breath, picked out a collapsed section of wall where she could scramble down into the pit and, awkwardly clutching the lantern, slid down into the foundation, landing off-balance, but managing to keep her feet. She turned to find Oshi glaring at her.

"What happened to my tower?" he breathed, gouging at the dirt between the stones. His voice rose, "Who wrecked my tower?"

Adare considered the foundation. It may have once supported a slender tower, but farmers had long ago carted off the stone for their own walls and houses. How Oshi found it in the first place she had no idea, or how he had clambered down the uneven walls without hurting himself.

"*Who destroyed my tower?*" he demanded once more, louder this time, rocking more violently. "Shihjahin? Dirik? *Who?*"

Adare took a step back.

The man was mad. Ranting. Shihjahin and Dirik were two of the Atmani, both a millennium and more in the ground. Oshi must have been paying close attention to the ancient structures fronting the canal, absorbing the long arguments between the pilgrims over the leach-lords who had built them. He'd come untethered from reality, from his own time, drifting back centuries upon centuries to an era of war and horror.

He had stopped rocking, stopped moving entirely. He sat straight up, still as a statue.

"Are you all right?" she asked hesitantly.

His eyes shifted to her, picked her over, then shifted away. Adare was about to step closer, to wrap an arm around his shoulders as she'd seen Nira do so many times, when he slapped his hands together, an imperious gesture, part summons, part warning, then spread his palms slowly. Adare realized to her horror that the air between them had caught fire, the squirming blaze a dozen times brighter than the meager light of her lantern. An icy sliver of fear pricked the back of her neck.

A leach. Nira's brother was a leach, and one descended partway into madness.

"Did Dirik send you?" he asked, voice gelid.

He flexed his fingers as he spoke, and the fire coalesced into a bright, burning web, malevolent red filaments pulsing. A leach. There was a whole ministry in the Dawn Palace—Purification—given over to the rooting out and hunting down of leaches, and each year dozens of young ministers were killed confronting their quarry. Adare's stomach squirmed inside her like a fish. She had faced down Uinian, but that was with il Tornja by her side and a trained assassin backing her play, all in the full light of day.

This . . . this was something else.

"Oshi," she began, trying to speak slowly, quietly, the way she'd heard the kennel masters talk to their wounded dogs. "Oshi, it's just me. Dorellin."

He frowned, flicked a finger, and a small web of flame broke off from the great ball spinning slowly between his hands.

"Your name doesn't matter," he said, shaking his head. "It doesn't matter. Doesn't matter. You are Dirik's knife. Or Ky's. Or Shihjahin's . . ." He trailed off as the scrap of flame rose and spread, stretching out like a net, floating, Adare realized, for her. She felt bile rise in the back of her throat, opened her mouth to scream, and vomited instead, her whole body trembling and weak. She glanced at the walls, but they looked higher, steeper than they had from above. She might have been standing at the bottom of a well.

"I will cut away the layers," Oshi rasped, showing his teeth, "strip the skin from your face, flay the muscle from your bone, deeper and deeper, until I find out whose creature you are."

The great web stretched wide just a pace in front of Adare, swaying like a snake, the strands shifting and flexing. Oshi started to ball his hands into fists. Adare sobbed once, paralyzed, and then Nira was there at the rim of the pit, cane brandished before her as though to beat back the horrible, writhing kenning.

"Roshin," she snapped, voice laden with anger and grief, but hard, determined. "*Roshin!* Stop this at once."

Roshin, Adare thought, a tiny part of her brain still calm, curious, a stone unmoved by the buffeting terror. The fifth of the Atmani, the brother of . . . "Rishinira," she breathed, turning to the small woman behind her. It was impossible. The Atmani were ancient history, practically myth, destroyed by their own madness and paranoia. The Deaths of the Undying were familiar tales, a favorite subject of painters for more than a thousand years: Dirik and Ky, wrapped in a fatal embrace, a desperate clutch that might have been love, save for his hand on her throat and her fingers gouging at his eyes. Chirug-ad-Dobar impaled on Shihjahin's lance, and Shihjahin's own stand, the lone leach atop his rocky hill, land boiling about him as his own armies closed in. They were dead, dead and gone.

Not all of them, Adare reminded herself.

The fates of the youngest of the Atmani—Roshin and Rishinira—were unknown. Some historians claimed that they perished early in the civil wars that rent both the empire and the land itself. Others argued that they fell in the final siege of Hrazadin, their bodies broken and lost beneath the rubble. There were, naturally, a few dissenting voices, stubborn writers who insisted that the last of the Atmani had somehow escaped the violence and destruction engulfing half of Eridroa. Lian Ki's most famous painting, *Flight of the Immortals,* depicted two cloaked figures, tiny inside a frame filled with fire and destruction, picking their way across the blasted landscape toward the inky darkness of the horizon. Lian had cloaked their faces in shadow, and Adare stared at the woman behind her, then at the man.

"Roshin," Nira said again, gesturing to the web. "Put it away. At *once!*"

"Rishi?" he said, confusion blooming in his dark eyes as he peered up at her. He gestured to the crumbling stone around him. "They destroyed it, Rishi. They destroyed everything."

Nira grimaced. The web still hung before Adare, but it had withered, the fire fraying, fading to the sullen red of old coals.

"It is long over, Roshin," the woman replied, eyes fixed on her brother. "They are gone now. They cannot hurt us anymore."

"What about *her?*" Oshi wailed, stabbing a finger at Adare.

"She is a friend," Nira replied.

"A friend," the old man said quietly, as though testing an unfamiliar word. "Our friend?"

"Yes," she replied. After a moment, the unnatural fire died, leaving its writhing lines seared on Adare's vision. The cellar hole fell into shadow as Oshi dropped his hands. With surprising agility, Nira clambered down the rough stone walls, dropping the last few feet to land beside her brother. "Here," she said gently, sliding a bottle from somewhere in her robes, uncorking it with a thumb, then holding it to his lips. "Drink, Oshi. You will feel better."

"Better?" he asked, baffled, peering into the darkness. "Will it ever be better?"

"Yes," Nira said, tipping back the vessel. Some of the pungent liquid spilled down his chin, but he slurped at it greedily. "It will get better," she murmured.

When he'd emptied the bottle, he settled slowly to the ground, then lapsed into sleep, leaning half against his sister, half against the rough wall behind him, lips twitching as though trying to form words.

Nira considered the foundation, then shook her head wearily. "I had forgotten this was here," she said, partly to herself, partly to her sleeping brother. "After all these years, brother," she went on softly, "and you were the one to remember."

"What is it?" Adare breathed.

The woman turned to her, as though realizing for the first time that she was still there, eyes narrowing, hand closing protectively over Oshi's shoulder.

"A place that was pleasant for him, once," she replied.

Adare just shook her head, uncertain how to respond.

"He was going to kill me," she said finally.

"Yes," Nira said. "He was."

"Why?"

"His mind is gone. They destroyed it. They destroyed all of us."

"Who?" Adare asked, trying to make sense of the elliptical statements. "Who destroyed you?"

"The ones who made us. Who made us what we were." She grimaced. "What we are."

"Atmani," Adare breathed quietly.

For a long time, Nira didn't respond, not even to nod. She turned from Adare to gaze on her brother's sleeping face, on his chest, slowly rising and falling.

"You have trusted me with your secret, girl," she said finally, not looking up, "and now you have mine. Betray it, and I will tear out your heart."

15

It proved nearly impossible to track the passage of days inside the cold chambers of the Dead Heart. There was no sun or moon. There were no stars to follow in their circuit through the sky, nothing but smoke, and damp, and the constant stench of salted fish. Kaden was given his own small cell in which to sleep, but whenever he opened the door he found a guard outside—sometimes Trant, sometimes another of the Ishien. Each time, he demanded information about Tan or Triste, neither of whom he'd seen since arriving, and each time he was refused. His own impotence in the face of the armed soldiers was galling, but he couldn't think of any way around it. The Ishien had blades and bows; he did not. The Ishien had military training; he did not. He briefly considered trying to wrest a weapon from one of his guards, but could dream up no scenario in which such defiance ended in anything other than his own death or imprisonment.

While the guards allowed him to move freely between his cell and the mess hall, the rest of the fortress was off-limits. At first, Kaden tried spending more time at the long tables where the men ate, hoping he might learn something about Triste or the Csestriim. The Ishien, however, proved guarded to the point of paranoia. Some glared at him, clutching to their silence like a shield. Some screamed in his face. Most simply ignored him, moving around him as though he were no more than another wooden chair.

It was maddening not to know what was going on, either inside the Dead Heart or beyond. For all Kaden knew, Annur had fallen into the grip of some Csestriim tyrant while he wandered the subterranean halls. His frustration, however, was solving nothing, and so he crushed it out, gave up talking to the Ishien altogether, and started spending the majority of his time in his cell instead, cross-legged on the stone floor, practicing the *vaniate.*

The trance didn't seem important, not compared to Triste's imprisonment, or the uncertainty of Valyn's fate, or the murder of the Emperor of Annur. But Kaden couldn't do anything about Triste, or Valyn, or his own dead father. What he *could* do was practice the *vaniate.* He could make sure that if the time came when he needed it, he would be ready.

Despite having entered the trance several times in the Bone Mountains, he still found it surprisingly fickle and elusive. Some days he could fall into the emptiness after only a few breaths; others, the whole exercise proved impossible, like trying to grasp an air bubble under the water. He could see it, but not feel it. Touch it, but not hold on to it. When he closed his mind's fist around its shimmering absence, it slipped away.

With nothing else to occupy his hours he set about the task grimly, pausing each day only to eat a little fish, to use the crude latrine carved into the stone a few doors down, to sleep in brief stretches. There was no way to tell time in the sunless, starless dark of the Heart. He pushed himself until sleep claimed him where he sat, slept as long as his body allowed, and then when he woke to sharp stone against his cheek, or a pressure in his bladder, or the unremitting chill of the place, he would rise, blink away the exhaustion, square himself once more in the center of his cell, and close his eyes. It was a grim study, but it gave a shape to his shapeless days, and after a time he found he could slide in and out of the emptiness almost at will.

At least while motionless. With his eyes closed.

When he'd mastered that, he set about entering the trance with his eyes open. It was far more difficult, as though the world itself blocked him from the blankness, but he kept doggedly at it, determined to wrest some value from the long, dark days. He was in the middle of just such an effort, staring at the flame of his lone candle, willing away his self, when Tan pulled open the heavy wooden door, stepping into the space before Kaden could register surprise or alarm.

The older monk took in the scene at a glance, then nodded. "The emptiness comes more easily now."

It was not a question, but Kaden nodded, grinding away his confusion, surprise, and irritation at Tan's unexpected arrival.

"You should be able to reach it running," the monk said. "Fighting."

"I'm still working on just keeping my eyes open."

Tan shook his head. "Not anymore. Not now. Come with me."

Kaden stared. "Where are we going? Where have you *been*?"

"With the Ishien. Trying to learn something about the girl."

"While I've been a prisoner."

"I warned you that we took a risk in coming here."

"We?" Kaden asked. "It looks like you have the run of the place."

"Does it?" Tan asked, fixing him with a stare. "Is that what you have decided after observing me so closely?"

"You're not locked in a cell."

"Neither are you," Tan said, turning to the door behind them, pulling it firmly shut. When he turned back to Kaden, he lowered his voice. "The Ishien distrust me for leaving, and they distrust me for returning. My position here is almost as tenuous as yours. Any support I offer you will weigh against me in their scales."

He fell silent, but the rest was clear: Tan was the only link between Kaden and the outside world. If the Ishien turned on the older monk, *really* turned on him, they were all finished.

"All right," Kaden said slowly, "I understand. How is Triste? What are they doing to her?"

Tan considered the question, gaze weighing, measuring. "They do not understand what she is." Another pause. "Neither do I."

"What do you mean?"

"What we've observed is inconsistent. We need more information."

Kaden frowned. "And that's why you're here," he said after a moment. "That's why you've come to me. Why they *sent* you to me."

Tan nodded. "Triste knows you. She appears to trust you. The Ishien believe, as I do, that she might reveal something to you."

"Has she said anything about my father? About Annur or the plot against my family?"

"No. As I said, we need more information."

Kaden stared. "The Ishien have kept me penned in here for what . . . weeks? A month? And now they want help?"

"Yes."

"Why would I help them? Why would I conspire with my jailers against Triste, who has done nothing but help me from the first night we met?"

"You will help," Tan said, voice blunt as an ax, "because if you do not, you may never leave this cave."

Kaden took a deep breath. Two. The monk had only said what Kaden himself had been thinking since the day he stepped through the *kenta*. And yet, hearing someone else speak the words made them real.

"The girl is not what you think," Tan continued, "and even if she were, you cannot afford loyalty. Not here. Not among these men. You help no one, Triste included, if you die in an Ishien cell."

Beneath his ribs, Kaden's heart bucked. He haltered it, soothed the animal part of him that wanted to kick, to bite, to flee, then nodded.

"Where do we go?"

"To the cells."

The cells. Which meant he'd be leaving this section of the Heart, that he'd be seeing new territory. It wasn't much, but it was more than he had now. Greater knowledge of the prison's layout might suggest the location of the exits, and it looked more and more likely that a time might come when he needed one of those exits.

"All right," he said quietly, "I'll go."

Tan held up a hand. "There is more."

Kaden shook his head. "More?"

"The Ishien are bringing up another prisoner at the same time. They want to surprise the girl, to overwhelm her, to shock her into revealing something."

"What prisoner?" Kaden asked, confused. "Why would Triste reveal anything to some poor soul the Ishien have locked up in their dungeons?"

"Because he is Csestriim," Tan said after a long pause. "And he is dangerous."

Kaden stilled his pulse, controlled his face. "They have a Csestriim. Is there anything else I should know?"

Tan nodded slowly. "The current leader of the Ishien is a man named Matol. Be careful of him. In his own way, he is as dangerous as the prisoner."

✝

"The bitch of it is," Ekhard Matol explained, spitting onto the damp floor to emphasize his irritation, "that the Csestriim don't respond to torture the way we do."

Though Tan claimed that Matol was the commander of the Dead Heart, he wore no uniform or mark of rank, dressing in the standard wool and leather, the garments moth-eaten and battered. He was short and thick, with fists like hammers, a nose like a chisel, and a badly pockmarked face. Physically he looked nothing like Trant—he must have been at least ten years older, for one thing—but the same air of unwholesome dampness clung to him, the same feral intensity burned in his eyes. And, like Trant and Tan, like all the Ishien Kaden had encountered, scars webbed his flesh.

Tan had led the way wordlessly through winding corridors, past two banded doors, past a trio of guards, then into the cramped antechamber beyond, a small room furnished with a low wooden table and a single chair, in which Matol sat. Kaden hadn't expected an apology for his earlier treatment, but the man didn't so much as acknowledge it. Kaden might have been a menial or slave, an insignificant underling who had been called upon to perform a task. That Matol spoke to him at all seemed an indulgence.

"What have you done to her?" Kaden asked, trying to keep his voice level, the question objective.

"The usual," Matol replied with a shrug, gesturing to the door behind him, presumably the entrance to Triste's cell. "Slivers of glass under the fingernails. Thumbscrews. First-round stuff. We've left her alone for quite a while now, to give her a chance to heal up, to get her nice and complacent before we start again."

Kaden's stomach twisted inside him, but he kept his expression even, his face calm.

"I don't want her hurt any further," he said, trying to project something like his father's imperial authority.

Matol furrowed his brow, got slowly to his feet, then walked around the small table, pausing when his face was inches from Kaden's own. He smiled, the expression sharp as a blade, then whispered, "Maybe Rampuri didn't tell you. Maybe he forgot how we do things in the years he's been away, so let me fill you in. . . ." He took a deep breath, then screamed, *"WE ARE NOT YOUR FUCKING SUBJECTS!"*

Kaden was accustomed to monastic disapproval, to the slow shaking of heads, and even to the brutal penance that often followed. This sudden explosion, however, was something else altogether, and he rocked back on his heels as though he'd been struck.

"Maybe not," he replied finally, trying to steady himself. It wouldn't do to show he could be cowed by a fit of shouting. "But we are on the same side in a very old fight."

Matol shrugged, his momentary fury utterly vanished. "Used to be, but the Ishien remembered their charge, held to their post, while you and your family abandoned it long ago." He paused, as though waiting for Kaden to object, then pressed ahead. "When we're finished with this bitch, which might take some time, I'll have questions for you. I want to know about this plot against your family." He waved a dismissive hand. "Not because I would care if the people of Annur rose up and gutted every living Malkeenian, but because this is how they *work,* the Csestriim. They find a structure, an order at the heart of our world, something *we* created, and then they go to work on it, chipping at the walls, undermining the foundation, until it crashes down, until we're crushed by the very thing we built." He stared at Kaden, eyes wide and furious. Then, abruptly, he laughed. "Which is why I might need to keep you here for a year or ten. After all, if *we're* using you, then *they're* not."

A chill ran up Kaden's spine.

He glanced over at Tan for some sign of tacit support, but the older monk's face betrayed nothing, and he made no move to speak. Kaden swallowed the insult and the fear both. Pride and fear were illusions—dangerous illusions, in this case. Here, hidden beneath tons of stone and sea, cut away from the cloth of society, a man like Matol could do whatever he wished. Kaden wasn't going to help Triste or Annur by insisting on his own honor.

This is why we have courts and laws, he thought to himself. *This is why we have an emperor.*

When Kaden first learned of the Ishien, their mandate had sounded like a noble cause, like something pure. That single-minded purpose, however, stripped of the aegis of law and tradition, religion and the order religion brought, began to look very much like madness. For the Ishien, anything was justified if it might lead to the Csestriim. Any lie. Any torture. Any murder.

"Is there anything new from the girl?" Tan asked.

Matol snorted. "Same shit. Sobs, begs, whimpers, tells us she hasn't done anything wrong. Problem is, she doesn't squirm *right.*" He turned to Kaden, brows raised as though waiting for the obvious question. When Kaden held his peace, the man blew out an irritated breath and explained.

"The enemy *look* human, but they're not. They're not right," he tapped his head with a grimy finger, "in *here.* When it comes to torture, they feel the pain—Meshkent has his bloody hooks in them, same way he does in the rest of us—but they don't feel the *fear.* They're older than the young gods. Kaveraa can't touch them."

Kaden turned the claim over in his mind, trying to imagine what it might be like to encounter pain without the fear of pain. Like experiencing starvation without hunger.

"So what's the point?" he asked finally. "If you think Triste is Csestriim and Csestriim don't respond to torture, why are you driving shards of glass under her fingernails?"

Matol grinned. "Well, we weren't *sure* she was Csestriim, were we? And I didn't say they don't respond. I said they don't respond *right*. The old archives point out that you can usually tell a Csestriim spy from the *lack* of terror."

"But Triste's terrified. You just said that. She begs and pleads."

"Sometimes," Matol acknowledged, then leaned in so close that Kaden could smell the fish on his breath as he hissed, "but she doesn't beg *right*."

"You still haven't said what that means."

The man paused, staring at some unseen point in the air as he marshaled his memories of pain and pleading. "There's a certain . . . shape to terror. A kind of writhing of the body, a rhythm to the screams. Everyone responds differently to fear and pain, but beneath the difference there's something human trying to shove its way out. If you know what to look for, you can recognize that thing, that *human* thing."

Kaden shook his head. "How can you recognize it?"

Matol smiled, a wide vulpine smile. "Because I've been through it." He raised his hands, and Kaden noticed for the first time that scars marred the ends of his fingers where the nails should have been.

"The pain," Kaden said quietly.

The man nodded. "So someone *has* bothered to educate you about our ways."

"It seems," Kaden began slowly, "that what you do to yourselves is worse than what the Csestriim might do."

Matol stared, teeth bright in the lamplight. "It seems that way, does it? It fucking *seems* that way?"

He looked away suddenly, studying the scars as though he'd never seen them before, as though they were something utterly alien and unknowable, then turned his glare back on Kaden.

"This, all of this, everything we know about pain—we *learned* it from the Csestriim, from their manuals, their books, from the hundreds of years of meticulous history in which they tortured and killed us. You think this is bad?" He shoved his scarred hands in Kaden's face. "You think this is *worse* than what the Csestriim might do? This is the fucking *mild* shit. This would have been a *relief* for our ancestors."

Kaden forced himself to look at the scars for three heartbeats, forced himself to keep his face calm, impassive. That the Ishien were sick, broken, was growing clearer and clearer, but he could feel a hard truth in Matol's words, and unbidden, the memory of the skeletons in Assare filled his mind, the small, clutching hands, the skulls. If the Ishien were broken, it was the Csestriim who had shattered them.

"Enough talk," Tan said, gesturing to the door.

Matol shook his head. "We're waiting for someone. Someone I want her to see." He narrowed his lids, looking slyly from Tan to Kaden, then back. "I told Rampuri not to mention it, but I suspect he told you something about our other prisoner." He stabbed Kaden roughly in the chest with an extended finger. "Didn't he? *Didn't* he?"

Kaden held his breathing steady. Inhale. Exhale. In and out.

"What other prisoner?"

⸶

At first glance, the other prisoner appeared neither deadly nor immortal.

The Shin warned their acolytes about the dangers of expectation, the power of anticipation to distort both sight and memory. Kaden had, accordingly, avoided putting a face to the Csestriim menace. *They don't look like monsters,* he reminded himself as he waited for the prisoner to be hauled up from the deeper dungeons. *They were able to pass as human.* Even the man's name was unremarkable: Kiel. It might have been the name of a baker, a fisherman.

He'd been shocked to discover that the Ishien already *had* a prisoner, one of the immortal beings they had hunted for so long, but once he accepted the notion, he thought he was prepared for anything. When the guards kicked open the door, however, and shoved their charge through, hands bound before him with a stout length of rope, Kaden realized he'd been expecting something after all, something harder, more formidable.

Kiel was an old man, stooped and hesitant, a faint limp marring his already uncertain gait. Scars puckered his face and hands—a delicate tracery of white lines punctuated by blunt, ugly weals, the result, Kaden surmised queasily, of heated steel. The Csestriim looked dark-skinned, but when he put a hand to his face to scrub the tangled hair from his eyes, Kaden realized that most of the darkness resulted from layers of filth and grime. The man's apparent age, too, was an illusion—cleaned and healthy he might look only halfway into his fourth decade. Even so, he was a far cry from the formidable monster Kaden had unknowingly expected.

Then he raised his eyes.

It was hard for Kaden to articulate, even to himself, what he saw there. Kiel's eyes were certainly less striking than his own blazing irises, less arresting than Valyn's blackened gaze. They were ordinary eyes, and yet, Kaden realized as the man studied him, they did not match the body. That body had been rent and battered by years of unrelenting questioning, and when the prisoner moved, it was clear that things had been torn and shattered inside. The eyes, however, were unbroken.

Kiel glanced briefly at Matol, considered Kaden for half a heartbeat, then turned to Tan.

"Rampuri," he said, his voice quiet and lean, like smoke in the air after the fire has been doused. Kaden had to resist the urge to lean forward. "I have not seen you in a very long time."

Tan nodded, though the monk did not speak.

"I thought you had forgotten me down in my quiet cell. I almost came to miss the company afforded by torture."

"We did not bring you up for further torture," Tan said.

Kiel pursed his lips. "Is it time, finally, to die?"

"It's time," Matol cut in, shards of impatience edging his voice, "to do what you're told."

The prisoner glanced down at his bound hands, over his shoulder at the armed guard standing behind him.

"It would seem you've given me very little choice. Perhaps you could tell me how long I've been in my cell?"

"Not long enough," Matol replied. "But you'll have plenty more time to stare at the darkness once we've finished here."

Kiel considered his interlocutor for a long moment, seemed about to say something more, then turned his attention unexpectedly to Kaden.

"Rampuri and Ekhard I know, but you and I have not met, though I knew your father well. . . ."

Matol's fist took Kiel in the gut before he could finish speaking, doubling him over.

"Keep your mouth shut and your lies to yourself, or I'll see you spend the next twenty years in a box instead of a cell."

After a long fit of coughing, the prisoner straightened slowly, then caught Kaden's eye for the barest fraction of a heartbeat.

I knew your father well.

Kaden struggled to make sense of the claim. It seemed unlikely, beyond unlikely, but then, what did Kaden really know about his father? Growing up, he had admired Sanlitun with a child's mindless admiration, worshipped him absolutely but ignorantly. Only after he was sent away, years after, did he begin to realize how slenderly he had known the man, how little he understood what drove him, what he wanted or feared.

Kaden had taken strength, through the most dire of his monastic trials, in thinking that his suffering at the hands of the Shin was the same suffering his father had experienced decades before, that the running and digging, carrying and fasting, were actually bringing him closer to Sanlitun, despite the gulf of miles between them, that one day, when Kaden returned to Annur, they would sit down together, one man with another, not just to learn the necessary apparatus of government, but to really talk for the first time.

That possibility had shattered like old crockery when Adiv's treacherous delegation arrived in Ashk'lan. There would be no reunion. No discussion. No meeting as men. Sanlitun hui'Malkeenian remained remote as the graven statue of him that looked down sternly on the Godsway. Kaden had no idea if his father had preferred water or wine, let alone whether or not he would have conferred with the Csestriim. He considered the prisoner once more, the begrimed face, the unwavering eyes. Would Sanlitun hui'Malkeenian have broken bread with such a creature? There was just no way to know.

"May I ask," Kiel said quietly, when he'd straightened up, "why I am here?" He gestured to the doors leading into the torture cells. "Are you certain it's not for more pain?"

"There is another prisoner," Tan replied. "One we want you to see."

A look that might have been curiosity crossed Kiel's haggard face. "One of my kind? Who?"

"That," Tan said, "is what you are here to tell us."

✝

It was almost possible, in the dim light of the low-ceilinged cell, to believe that Triste was just resting, that the heavy wooden chair to which she'd been chained was just another chair, that the lanterns had been turned low to accommodate an easier sleep. As Kaden's eyes adjusted, however, he could make out the steel manacles binding her wrists and ankles, the streaks of tears on her grimy face, thin lacerations running the length of her arms. Clearly she had been flogged or whipped.

"Couldn't you give her a cloak?" he asked.

Matol snorted. "Are all you Shin so tenderhearted?" Then, as though to a small child, "This is how torture works. You start on the mind well before you begin with the body."

Kaden couldn't pull his eyes from that body, from the angry strips of red where the flesh had broken. Horror welled up inside him. The Shin had taught him to deal with emotion, but never in the face of such savagery. When he finally managed to look away from the wounds, he found that Triste had opened her own eyes, that she was staring at him silently in the flickering light.

"Kaden," she said quietly. His name in her mouth sounded like a plea and an accusation both, and he realized that she had been watching him stare.

He opened his mouth to respond, but no response came. He had no comfort to offer, no promise of reprieve. He still wasn't entirely sure why he had been summoned. "I'm here," he said finally, the words weak on his tongue. "I'm here."

"How touching," Matol observed. "He's here, which means we can get started again. But first . . ." He motioned curtly, and the two guards holding Kiel shoved him forward as Matol himself reached out, seized Triste by the hair, and twisted her head viciously around.

"Look," he demanded, shaking her roughly by the hair. *"Look."*

Silent convulsions racked her body. Kaden still wasn't sure what the older men hoped to achieve. It seemed to him that even if Triste and Kiel *were* both Csestriim, even if they did know each other, they would have the good sense to conceal the fact. On the other hand, the shock of recognition after what might be thousands of years was something you would notice, at least in a human. Did the Csestriim feel surprise? It was too late to ask Tan now. He considered Kiel's face, carving the moving image for later scrutiny.

The Csestriim, for his part, showed nothing more than a bland curiosity, raising an eyebrow.

"A beautiful young woman," he observed quietly.

"Are you with them?" Triste asked, hope and fear tangled in her voice. "What do you want?"

"No," Kiel replied, "I am not with them. And I imagine you and I want similar things: freedom, light."

"Help me," Triste begged.

"I wish I could," he said, raising his tied hands, "but as you see, I am powerless to help myself."

"Why?" she asked.

"This is what they do," he replied. "But you can take solace in this: Ananshael is stronger than Meshkent; in the end, death will release you from the pain."

Triste's voice, so lost and baffled just a heartbeat before, went suddenly hard as steel. "Do not presume to lecture me on the ministrations of Meshkent." She set the words before her like knives, sharp and precise.

Kiel's eyes widened. He tilted his head to one side, evidently interested for the first time in his fellow prisoner. Triste stared defiantly back at him, turned her gaze to Matol, then back to Kiel. She had barely moved, but everything had changed. The terrified girl of moments before had molted away like a dead skin.

"Tell me," Kiel said quietly. "Tell me about your pain."

Triste repeated the word slowly. "Pain." She might have been savoring a bloody cut of meat.

"Yes," Kiel said again. "When did you first encounter pain?"

Triste laughed, a full-throated, opulent, predatory laugh that made something deep inside Kaden quail. The sound went on and on, filling the tiny room, pressing back against the walls, battering at the stone itself until, abruptly, it was not laughing, but sobbing once again.

"Please let me go," she whispered, voice ragged. "Please just let me go."

Matol glanced at Tan. "Anything?"

Tan paused, then shook his head. "Only more of what we have already seen."

"What about you?" the Ishien commander asked, turning to Kaden. "What do you make of that luscious burst of defiance?"

Kaden took a deep breath, looked inward at the *saama'an* of the preceding moments, trying to make sense of what he had just witnessed. That shift in Triste's tone, the sudden strangeness in her eyes, the careening between poise and panic . . . He'd seen something like it back in Ashk'lan, in goats with brain rot. A creature in the advanced stages would stand placidly for hours, empty, angular pupils fixed on the horizon, unresponsive to gentle stroke or vicious strike, to food or speech. Then, with no provocation at all, with no warning, that strange, animal gaze would focus abruptly and the goat would attack anything that moved, charging, thrashing with its hooves, hooking the horns over and over. The diseased creatures had always discomfited Kaden, something about their lack of consistency, of continuity. He had felt the same queasiness in his stomach during Triste's transformation, but he couldn't say that to Matol, not if he ever hoped to convince the man to set Triste free.

"I think she's exhausted," he said finally, keeping his voice level, matter-of-fact. "I think she's terrified. You want to see a Csestriim, and so that's what you find. All I see is a frightened young woman who has done nothing to deserve this. I see you breaking a friend of mine."

It was several leagues wide of the truth, but the Ishien commander didn't seem to notice. He just spat onto the stone floor.

"What in 'Shael's name have the Shin been teaching you?"

"To observe," Kaden replied.

"Obviously not."

He turned abruptly from Kaden, gestured to the guards to pull Kiel back into the shadows, then focused once more on Triste.

"Too bad for you," he said, addressing the woman. "I thought we'd try something new, but it looks like we're back to doing things the old-fashioned way."

He waved a hand, and another guard, one who had been standing in the shadows, stepped forward. Smirking, he handed over a wooden box. It clanked ominously when Matol set it on the rough table next to the slab. He flipped the lid, and paused for a moment, looking from Triste to the tools and back again.

"Do you have any requests?" he asked, arching an eyebrow. "I'll tell you what—you can pick the body part, and I'll pick the tool."

Triste shook her head weakly in protest. "No," she pleaded. "Please, no."

"No?" He pursed his lips. "You want to pick the tool and I pick the body part? We can do it that way if you want, but I don't recommend it. Better for you to pick the body part."

"Kaden," Triste panted, twisting in the chair, pulling against her restraints until blood trickled, black and thick, down the flesh of her wrists.

"Yes," Matol agreed amiably. "That's Kaden. Although it'll be harder to recognize him after we go to work on your eyes."

Kaden turned to Tan. "You have to stop this."

The monk shook his head. "What Matol does is necessary. The girl is not what you think."

"It doesn't matter what I think—" Kaden began, but Matol's scream cut him off.

"One more *fucking WORD* about stopping and I will chain you to the wall behind her and burn off your sad little cock just for the fucking *FUN* of it. *DO YOU UNDERSTAND ME?*"

"No," Kaden said, forcing himself to stand straight, to meet the man's eye. "I do not understand. I don't understand either your obsession, which looks like blindness, or your methods, which don't work."

"Kaden," Tan cut in, voice sharp with warning. "You are not here to judge."

Kaden shook his head. "What *am* I here for?"

"You were here," Matol said, voice rising, neck bulging, "to tell us something fucking useful. *AND YOU FAILED!*"

"I told you what I saw, but you are unable to listen."

Matol looked ready to seize him by the throat, to hurl him to the ground and choke the life out of him. And then, with horrifying suddenness, the snarl vanished. The tendons in his neck and hands loosened. He was smiling, a wide, toothy smile. The emotional swings were almost more frightening than the rage itself. It seemed as though something had come loose inside the man, unlatched, like a stable door blasted open by a storm, hung on a single, rusted hinge, slamming open and shut, open and shut, over and over and over.

"You could help," Matol suggested finally, waving a long serrated blade in Kaden's direction. He frowned at the blade, then seemed to think better of it. "Now that I think about it, never mind. You'd probably just fuck it up. Take off a whole leg or a tit or something and have her bleed out."

"Observe," Tan murmured to Kaden. "Enter the *vaniate* if you must."

Kaden tried to still his pulse enough to find the trance, but the sick twist in his gut nagged at him until he thought he would be ill. Matol hemmed and hawed for a while, fiddled with a vicious variety of blades, hooks, and small vises, before tossing everything back in the box and selecting a lamp from its hook on the wall instead.

"Fire," he grinned. "Sometimes I get so carried away with the tools that I forget about fire."

With a practiced motion he unscrewed the base from the glass shield until the naked flame, hissing and reeking of low-grade oil, licked at the air. Triste's eyes widened. She started to moan.

"Please," she begged. "I've *told* you everything."

"You have not," Matol replied, testing the flame with his finger, then wincing at the heat.

"What do you *want?*"

"I want to know where you learned to read Csestriim script."

Triste's eyes took on a desperate, hunted look. "In the temple," she managed. "They taught me everything, everything but the high mysteries. Every *leina* learns languages, sometimes more than a dozen." She was babbling, terrified. "Men come from all over Eridroa and Vash, all over the world. . . ."

Matol shook his head. "You told me earlier that you didn't know where you learned it."

"I forgot! There was so much I learned—music, dancing, language. They taught me a little. I remember now, a few words when I was very young!"

She twisted against her bonds as she spoke. *Observe,* Kaden told himself, *Just observe.* He threw himself into the Carved Mind, etching the strokes of the *saama'an* as the scene unfolded, using the discipline as a shield against what was taking place.

"You're claiming that the whores of Ciena taught you 'just a few words' of the Csestriim tongue in case . . . what? In case a creature everyone else in the world believes was destroyed thousands of years ago wanders in hankering for a *fuck?*" He laughed a long mirthless laugh at the absurdity of the notion. "Manderseen," he said at last, gesturing toward the smirking guard, "hold the lamp here while I take this young lady's hand."

The Ishien guard stepped forward, smirk broadening into a grin. Matol took Triste's wrist almost gently in his larger, scarred hard, then pulled it toward the flame. The girl let out a low wail as the fire lapped at her skin, her fingers scrabbling like the legs of some tormented creature. "Please," she moaned, body convulsing, legs thrashing, as though the movement could carry her hand from the fire. *"Please!"* Her voice rose and rose into a high, horrible keening.

Observe, Kaden told himself, forcing his hands to his side. There was nothing he could do, and besides, he'd burned himself more severely on several occasions working in the kitchens back at Ashk'lan. Of course, this was only the beginning.

Matol released her hand finally. Two of the fingers were red and blistered, the kind of burn that would only heal after a night in an ice bucket and a week in wrappings. Triste tried to pull it to her chest, but the shackle would not permit her. Her eyes were still open, but she wasn't focused on anything beyond the looming horror of her own pain.

"It looks like real fright," Kaden murmured to Tan. "She's not faking it."

To his surprise, the monk actually seemed to consider his words, then shook his head. "Keep watching."

"How did you use the *kenta*?" Matol asked, passing his own hand back and forth through the flame idly, quickly enough to avoid a burn.

"I don't know," she panted. "I'd never seen a *kenta*." There was something strange about the way she said the word, and Kaden filed it away for further consideration. "I'd never even *heard* of one before a couple of days ago. I just . . . I fell and I came out the other side."

"You see," Matol said, turning to the other two Ishien. "The girl is perfectly innocent. She simply fell."

The one named Manderseen chuckled. "Maybe we should let her go."

"Maybe," Matol replied, pretending to consider the notion. Then he shook his head. "Nah. Let's hurt her some more."

What happened next took place too quickly to comprehend. Kaden was focused on the scene as Matol reached for her wrist, his mind sketching the *saama'an*. It wasn't until later, however, when he had a chance to fully scrutinize the vision, that he really *saw* what had happened. Even then it didn't make sense.

Triste, practically gibbering with terror a moment before, twisted as Matol reached for her. The manacle didn't afford much freedom, but as his hand started to close, she lashed out and caught *his* wrist instead. The movement was precise, almost too quick to see, like a serpent darting from a bush. Matol didn't have a chance to register surprise before she pulled, a savage tug somehow strong enough to yank the man off his balance, tumbling him half on top of her, forcing Manderseen to drop the lantern with a curse and fall backward. Triste leaned close to the Ishien commander, her lips by his ear.

"A time will come," she hissed in a voice every bit as cold and dark as the surrounding stone, a voice utterly devoid of fear, "when the pain you visit on me here will seem a dream of pleasure, when blades and fire seem tender ministrations to you. I will, then, watch you beg, but stoppered to your cries will be my ears, and dried to dust the wide lake of my mercy."

She was twisting, Kaden realized, her slender fingers twisting Matol's broad hand with a savage strength until something snapped, the man's face contorted, and, his balance regained at last, he lurched toward the wall, cradling the broken hand and cursing.

The whole thing lasted several breaths, but Rampuri Tan made no move to intervene, neither to stop Triste nor to help Manderseen or Matol. His eyes remained on the girl the entire time, measuring, parsing.

"Did you see?" he murmured when it was done.

Kaden nodded dumbly. He could only stare. For a moment Triste locked eyes with him, and her gaze was . . . what? He groped for the word. Feral? Regal? Language failed. Then, like water slipping through a sieve, the look drained away.

"Kaden?" she whispered, voice small and shattered, filled with fear once more. "Kaden, *please*. Please help me."

For a moment, no one moved. Shock had scrubbed the smirk from Manderseen's face, and he stared at Triste, baffled. Tan also watched the girl, though with none of the Ishien's confusion, as did Kiel, his eyes still as pools, tied arms relaxed before him, supported by the frozen guards at his side. Triste looked from one face to the next, evidently reading the confusion and slow-gathering fury scribbled through the expressions of the Ishien.

"No," she said, shaking her head. "No."

The words seemed to jar Matol from a waking dream. He raised his broken hand, staring at it a moment as though it were some small creature broken in a trap, then turned his gaze on Triste.

"Oh yes," he said, stepping toward her once again. The pain from his mangled hand must have been excruciating, but he ignored it, gesturing instead to Manderseen. "Oh yes, indeed. Bring me something hot, or hard, or sharp," he barked. "Better yet, all three. I'm through lavishing this bitch in gentle caresses. It's time to cut her deep, to see what's really inside."

"No," Kaden said, surprised to hear the syllable slip from his own throat. It was madness to intervene, suicide, especially now, especially with Matol caught in the grip of this new, cold rage. And yet, he found himself stepping forward. "This isn't working," he said. "Your whole approach isn't working."

"Stand aside, Kaden," Tan said. His voice was quiet, but the syllables were built of stone.

Kaden shook his head. "I've stood aside for days. Longer." He could feel the blood racing in his veins, started to slow it, then let it run. He could kill the emotion, but he needed it now, needed his own anger if he was going to hold his ground against Matol and the rest, if he was going to do anything for Triste.

"I understand that she's not what she seems," he said. "I see it now. I understand that she may even be Csestriim, but this"—he gestured to the hard, bloody tools—"is not the way. It is not *working.*"

Matol turned from Triste to stare at him. When he spoke, his voice was barely more than a whisper. "You come here, to *my* fortress, into *my* Heart, you bring this inhuman *whore* into this sanctuary, and then you defend her? Hmm?"

"I'm not defending her—" Kaden began.

Matol cut him off. "You think you're going to tell me, tell *me* how to fight this fight when your own family just up and quit? Is that it?"

"Enough," Tan said.

"Oh, I quite agree," Matol replied, still quiet, still sharp. "It *is* enough. It is well *past* enough."

"Take him," he said, gesturing to Kaden. "Find him a cell down below along with the other one." A finger flicked at Kiel. "Something with a heavy door."

Manderseen stepped forward, but Kaden twisted away, unsure whether he wanted to put himself between Triste and the Ishien or use the chair to which she was shackled as a shield. She was watching him with huge, frightened eyes. Kiel, too, was watching him, silent and impassive from across the room.

"Tan," Kaden said, trying to find the words.

"Get over here," Manderseen spat.

Slowly, slowly, Rampuri Tan shook his head. "This was your choice. Not mine."

Kaden seized a knife from the table at Triste's side, brandishing it before him. He had no idea how to fight, but he had watched Valyn and the others back in the mountains, had carved the images on his brain for future use, and as the Ishien guard came on he tried to approximate the pose.

Manderseen paused, then unlimbered the sword at his side, the grin coming back to his face. "Kill him?"

Matol didn't answer. Kaden risked a glance behind him just as a fist took him across the face, knocking him clean into the wall. The attack jarred the knife from his hand, and Manderseen was on him in a moment, all steel and strength, shoving Kaden's body against the stone.

"Kill him?" he asked again.

Kaden struggled to turn, to see Matol, but Manderseen had his head shoved over at a brutal angle. The only person he could see was Kiel. The Csestriim had made no move to struggle or intervene, but as Kaden watched, his lips moved silently, mouthing the shape of words. Everyone else was staring at Kaden. Only Kaden was watching Kiel, even as he strained to breathe.

He's talking to me, he realized. That the man expected him to follow, to be able to unfold the shape of the words, seemed unbelievable. Kaden himself was bleeding from the head, blood slick on his face, and the Ishien sword was at his throat. Kiel ignored all of it. If he really *had* known Kaden's father, then he knew something of the monks, and if he knew the monks, knew about the training and discipline, then he knew about the Carved Mind. He knew Kaden would remember the scene later. Remember it perfectly.

"I would not kill him." Tan's voice this time. Distant. Indifferent. "He is the Emperor, and may prove useful still."

"I could take out an eye," Manderseen suggested with a chuckle, shifting a hand to press against Kaden's eyeball. "Maybe crush one of his nuts. What were you saying about cocks?" He groped between Kaden's legs. "We could see how loyal he is to this bitch after we rip his cock off. . . ."

Silence loud as a scream.

"Take him below," Matol snarled finally. "Lock him up with the Csestriim. He may know more than he's told us. We'll take a look at his blood after we get through with hers."

16

"K ill them," Annick said, gesturing to the Urghul. "We can't bring them, and we can't leave them."

Valyn had gathered his Wing a hundred paces off from the camp, leaving Pyrre to guard the tied and kneeling prisoners. In the three days since they sent Suant'ra south, there had been little to do but wait, rest, and worry. To Valyn's great relief, Gwenna had come to by the end of the first day, but she was clearly in no shape to travel; she could barely walk a circuit of the camp without feeling dizzy and nauseated. Talal's leg was healing, healing faster than Valyn would have expected, and Valyn's own wound was already knitted closed. *The slarn eggs,* the leach suggested. *It's possible they made us stronger, more resilient.* Valyn had mulled that possibility with a mixture of hope and unease. Talal was right. A deep puncture wound to the shoulder should have taken at least a week to knit up properly, not days.

On the other hand, they were hardly invincible. Talal still limped, Gwenna still slept more than half the hours of the day, and truth be told, Valyn wasn't sure he was ready for a forced ride across a thousand miles of steppe either. Pain lanced through his shoulder whenever he raised his elbow, which meant fighting with a single blade and forget about the bow.

So, they waited, rested, and worried.

On the second day, another Kettral Wing passed overhead. Valyn hunched down into his bison cloak, shaded his face with his hand, and tried to look Urghul while the bird circled once, then headed south. He let out a long, uneasy breath, feeling like one of the marmots that foraged for food on the grasslands. They, too, kept looking up at the sky, not that it did them much good. Valyn had seen three taken by eagles in a single afternoon.

By the third day, Gwenna was insisting she was ready to ride, and Valyn himself was itching to get moving, pain or no. They were already going to miss the meeting with Kaden back in Annur, miss it by weeks, but that was no reason to sit any longer than necessary. Valyn insisted on one more night of rest, and on the morning of the fourth day he gave the order to set out.

It was easy enough to break down what they wanted from the camp, to put the horses on long lines, and pack a week's worth of extra food, compliments of the Urghul. Then they needed to decide what to do with the Urghul themselves. That was proving a more difficult proposition.

"I don't like it," Laith said, shaking his head. He'd lost his habitual good humor when 'Ra left, and the question of the prisoners had done nothing to lighten his mood. "In fact, I fucking hate it. Three of them are kids, and the rest . . ." He gestured at the kneeling figures. "It's not like we're killing them in a fight." He blew out a long breath. "But we have to do it. We have to kill them."

"We don't have to do anything," Gwenna growled.

Valyn nodded slowly. "Gwenna's right. Whatever Hendran said on the matter, they are *our* prisoners, our responsibility. It's our decision."

"Fine," Laith said, "then I've *decided* that we need to kill them. Is that enough responsibility for you?"

"No," Valyn replied, reining in his own anger, keeping his voice level. "It's not. You said it already. Three of them are kids, Laith. Children."

"Doesn't matter," Annick said. "Taking them with us is too risky, and if we leave them, they could follow."

"On *what*?" Valyn demanded. "We're taking the 'Kent-kissing horses. I don't care how fit these sons of bitches are, by the end of the morning we'll be *gone*."

"And what if they talk?" Laith demanded. "What if another batch of Urghul finds them and asks what happened to their horses?"

"Then we'll fight them," Gwenna said. "We already fought these, and it was a pretty short fucking fight."

Annick shook her head, a curt, dismissive motion. "This is a tiny group. Some of the *taamu* number into the hundreds."

"Then we run," Gwenna insisted. "We retreat."

Laith barked an incredulous laugh. "We outride the 'Kent-kissing Urghul on their own steppe on their own horses? How do you expect *that* to go?"

Valyn took a deep breath, then spoke. "This is beside the point."

"Seems to me it's exactly the point," Laith said. "What are the risks? How do we minimize them? I seem to remember an entire year spent studying this shit back on the Islands."

"We talked about minimizing risks in legitimate fights," Valyn said. "Not about murdering kids who can't hurt us."

"What is a legitimate fight?" Annick asked.

"A mission," Valyn said. "Against the enemy. Not just an uncomfortable situation we crashed into the middle of."

"The Urghul *are* the enemy," Laith pointed out. "They boil people alive. They cut off your eyelids. The Eyrie has been flying missions over the White for *years* now."

"Not to kill kids," Valyn replied. He held up a hand to forestall the flier's objection. "Why did you join the Kettral?"

Laith shook his head. "I don't know. Because they showed up and told me I could fly massive killer birds. Because they're the *Kettral*, for 'Shael's sake."

"And if the Urghul had birds? Would you fly for the Urghul?"

"Of course not."

"Why not?"

"Everything I just got done *telling* you. They're barbarians, Valyn. Do you remember *anything* about their religion, their blood worship? If our fight had gone the other way, they'd be flaying us right now, taking us apart strip by fleshy strip. That's why we have to kill them."

Valyn shook his head. "That's why we can't."

Laith stared. "What the fuck are you talking about?"

It was one question too many, and something inside Valyn, some wall that had been holding back both the anger and the words, gave way, crumbling as though before a great wave. *"We are not them, Laith!"* he shouted. "We are not *her!*" he went on, stabbing a finger at Huutsuu, "or *her!*" at Pyrre. "We can kill people, sure. We spent a whole lot of time learning to kill people, and we're *good* at it. But *lots* of people can kill people. Pyrre has been fucking killing people since the day we found her. The thing that makes us Kettral is something else: we kill the *right* people."

Gwenna was nodding furiously, but Annick brushed aside the tirade with the back of her hand. "Right and wrong. Just a question of which side you're on."

"No," Valyn said, rounding on her. "No, it's not. If that's true, then why did we even come here? Why did we leave the Eyrie and rescue Kaden?

Why do we give a pickled shit who sits on the Unhewn Throne? If it doesn't matter, we could hire out right now as mercenaries to Anthera or the Manjari. We could make a tidy fortune telling them everything we know about the Kettral!" Despite the chill breeze, he was sweating beneath the heavy bison coat. With an effort, he brought his voice back down, unclenched his fists. "We don't do that because it *does* matter what side you fight on. It does matter who sits the Unhewn Throne. People like Sami Yurl and Balendin—they need to be stopped. They are *bad*. So were the Csestriim. So were the Atmani." He shook his head, suddenly weary. The shoulder wound ached. Everything ached. "I joined the Kettral so I could defend Annur, and I wanted to defend Annur because it is *better* than the Blood Cities or Anthera, better than the Manjari or the tribes of the Waist."

"Spare me a lecture on the virtues of our great empire," Laith said. The words were dismissive, but the fire had gone out of his resistance.

"It's a short lecture," Valyn said. "We have laws. Laws that keep the most powerful among us from destroying the weak and the unlucky."

Laith shook his head. "You really did grow up in a palace, didn't you?"

"Am I right?" Valyn asked, ignoring the gibe.

"Annur's great and powerful exploit the weak and poor all the time," the flier snapped. "I *know,* my family is *both*. Your father raised taxes on blacksmiths—did you know that?" He didn't wait for Valyn to answer. "Of course you didn't. The thing is, the Emperor of Annur didn't bother differentiating between the huge city blacksmiths with dozens of apprentices and small shops with one man and a forge. A little oversight that put my father into debt." He shook his head in disgust. "My father went to a moneylender. The bastard was happy enough to supply the coin but at a rate no human being could possibly repay. My father worked eight years at it, eight years without a single day of rest, and he died at his fucking forge, more in debt than when he started."

Valyn stared. In all his years with the Kettral, in all their days of training and nights nursing their wounds, he'd never heard Laith tell the story.

"Look," he began slowly, uncertain how to respond. "The empire isn't a perfect state . . ."

The flier raised his brows. "But this was unusual? The exception?" He jerked a finger at Talal. "What about him? The citizens of our good and noble empire hunt down and kill leaches in huge, gleeful mobs. No trial, no law—just a fire or a rope."

Talal nodded slowly. He hadn't said a word throughout the entire argument, watching silently, arms crossed over his chest. "Annur has flaws," he said quietly. "Deep flaws. There are liars and murderers to go around." He glanced over toward the prisoners. "I do not want to be one of them."

"Well, *fuck*," Laith said, shaking his head. "Neither do I. I just don't want them coming after us."

"That's the chance we take for doing the right thing."

"Fuck," the flier said again.

"Does that mean you agree?"

Laith blew out a long breath, then nodded reluctantly. Valyn turned to Annick.

"What about you?"

"I told you what I think," she said. "You're the Wing leader."

"All right then," Valyn said. "We take the horses, take most of the food, take an *api* so that we look like real Urghul. I'll retie the knots holding the prisoners, something they can wriggle out of in two or three days. We head north. . . ."

"I thought we were going west," Gwenna said. "There's nothing north but steppe, then ice, then icy ocean."

"We head north," Valyn said again, "half a day, in case they decide to follow our tracks. We'll tack west when we find a stream to follow."

He turned on his heel before anyone else could object, leaving his Wing to their preparations. The prisoners were on the other side of the camp, giving Huutsuu plenty of time to stare at Valyn as he approached. Pyrre glanced over when he was close.

"Let me guess, you can't bring yourself to kill them."

"We're tying them up," Valyn said tersely. "Heading north."

The Skullsworn smiled, then patted him on the wounded shoulder. "How did I know?"

"I will find you," Huutsuu said, as Valyn knelt to check the knots binding her wrists and ankles. "You are a fool not to listen to your people."

"If I listened to them," Valyn said, cinching the knot, "you'd be dead."

"You are soft."

"You're the one tied up."

✝

For the better part of two weeks, the Wing made good time, driving westward each day, camping in the low folds between the hills at night. The Urghul horses, though small, were sure-footed and utterly indefatigable.

Valyn had wondered how often he would need to rest the creatures, but discovered, to his dismay, that by the time he called a halt each night it was his own aching legs and back that needed respite. Judging from the groaning and stretching of the rest of his Wing, he wasn't the only one.

He'd charted a course just north of the White River, close enough that they could often see the frothing surface; distant enough that they wouldn't run smack into any Urghul watering their horses. There had been some discussion of going south. The fastest route back to Annur would be to ride hard for the Bend, then take a ship for the capital. It was also the most obvious way. If the Eyrie had any hint that Valyn was still alive, they'd have someone watching the docks, watching the walls, watching the whole 'Kent-kissing city. Riding overland to the west was less risky. Less risky, but much, much longer.

The steppe stretched all the way to the horizon, a great green sea with hills like swells. Aside from the occasional limestone outcrop or stand of stunted trees, there were no landmarks, no mountains or forests, just massive emptiness spread beneath the bowl of the sky. Even the streams looked the same—narrow, low-banked, stony brooks draining south into the White River.

Valyn found the open space unnerving. It offered nowhere to hide, nowhere to make a stand. The low hills rose and fell just enough to obscure the surrounding territory without providing any shelter. They could be riding parallel to an Urghul *taamu* for all Valyn could tell, the horsemen just out of sight over the next fold, and his neck grew sore from constantly pivoting, endlessly scanning the green horizon.

After a few days, Talal pointed to the south. Valyn squinted. A line of golden hills flanked them in the far distance, miles and miles beyond the river. Sand, he realized, the huge, undulating dunes of the Seghir Desert. Entire armies had been swallowed up in the Seghir, foreign and Annurian, bones and armor lost beneath the shifting sand. Even north of the river, where his own Wing rode, the soil began to turn dry and cracked, forcing Valyn to alter course, breaking away from the river for greener grass while still pushing west.

Twice they spotted herds of bison in the distance, thousands of shaggy brown beasts three times the size of the horses they rode. Despite the curving horns, the creatures seemed docile enough, lazily cropping the long grass, pausing occasionally to snuffle at the air. When they broke into a run, the whole mass wheeling and charging away into the distance, Valyn could feel the ground quiver beneath his feet while the air trembled with a sound like thunder.

Near the end of the fourth day, they pulled up atop a low hill just in time to see a much larger band of riders—maybe three or four hundred—also headed west, probably half a day's ride ahead of them. Despite the size of the group, they were hammering hard, even harder than Valyn's Wing, the herd of horses kicking up a haze of dust that hovered over the steppe like a storm cloud, dimming the noon sun. Valyn counted three more *taamu* after that, all headed west, moving fast. It was easy enough to stay clear, to avoid the hilltops and rises, but the sight of so many Urghul on the move made him nervous.

"Where do you think the bastards are going?" Gwenna asked.

"No idea," Valyn replied, shaking his head. "Hopefully not the same place we are."

The lack of cover during the long, sun-baked days made Valyn sweat, but it was the rain, finally, that did them in.

He had called a halt early. Though daylight lingered, the east wind reeked of storm, Gwenna, for all that she refused to complain, looked ready to fall out of the saddle, and Valyn himself didn't feel far behind. As Hendran wrote, *There is speed in slowness.* Much as Valyn chafed to be back in Annur, to find Kaden, to find whoever was behind his father's murder, and the monks', and Ha Lin's, there were miles of steppe and little to be gained by trying to cross it all in one frenetic push.

The rain started just after dark. It would have been nice to set up the *api* or build a fire, but fires meant light and smoke, and the *api* would do nothing but trap half the Wing and limit its visibility. Better to be cold and ready than warm and dead, and so they wrapped themselves in their bison cloaks, the wet hides chilly and reeking, checked weapons, then sat down to gnaw through strips of dried meat and chunks of hard Urghul cheese before falling asleep.

Valyn took the first watch. The wound in his shoulder was healing, but still stabbed at him whenever he moved wrong. The others had settled into a rough circle, as though around the memory of a campfire. Asleep, wrapped in the huge cloaks, they looked younger than they were, more innocent, almost like children. Even Pyrre, with her graying hair, might have been a fishmonger or a merchant rather than a vicious death-priest with her hands steeped in blood. It seemed like weeks since Valyn had had the space and time to really *think* about his Wing, about what they'd given up when they fled the Eyrie, about what they faced in the weeks ahead. The responsibility clamped down on him like a hard fall frost. Then the rain began in earnest.

The heavy drops soaked his hair in a few heartbeats, chilling his face, seeping down the back of his cloak even as they churned the ground to mud, turned the night air to a black, sheeting murk. Valyn sat up straighter, ignoring the cold settling into his bones, a hand on his belt knife. He didn't realize how accustomed he'd grown to his heightened hearing, but now, with the quiet roar of a million raindrops spattering against the earth, he felt deaf, disoriented, vulnerable.

He rose to his feet, slipping a blade from beneath the cloak, and walked to the top of a small rise. Whatever he might have seen beneath a full moon or stars was scrubbed out utterly by the downpour. There was the rain and the earth at his feet, nothing more. After a long pause, he turned back to the camp, unease tickling at his neck, sickening his gut. Gwenna was cursing, trying to get comfortable, and Talal and Pyrre kept shifting, searching for a position that might keep off the worst of the rain.

To 'Shael with it, Valyn thought. *No one's sleeping anyway.*

They could be miserable on the horses just as well as on the ground. They could rest again when the weather cleared. For all that they needed a break, they were Kettral. A long night on horseback wasn't going to kill any of them. Besides, he didn't like sitting still when there was no way to mount an effective guard. They might stumble over someone on horseback, but at least they'd be mounted. At least they'd be ready.

He was just crouching down to rouse Annick when the drumming of the rain resolved, suddenly, horrifyingly, into the drumming of hooves. He spun about, desperately raising his blade as the mounted Urghul, lances leveled, soaked hair streaming behind, screaming and ululating, galloped down the low hill and into the miserable camp.

✝

It was Huutsuu. Of course. But not just Huutsuu.

Laith and Annick had been right. Another *taamu,* much larger, five or six hundred at least, had found her far to the east. Everything Valyn knew about the Urghul suggested that they should have killed her, offered her up to Meshkent in some hideous ceremony, but evidently everything he learned had been worse than useless. Not only did they not kill her and her people, the larger tribe offered horses and help in hunting down the Annurians.

Valyn managed to kill two in the fury of the first assault, and Pyrre, somehow, took down four more with her knives. The rest of the Kettral were taken utterly off guard. Within heartbeats, they found themselves ringed with dozens of spearpoints, a sharp, shifting collar inches from their throats. Even then, they looked ready to fight, hands on knives or blades, Annick clutching her half-drawn bow, death in her eyes until Valyn, the words like stones on his tongue, gave the order to stand down.

†

In another place, captured by another foe, the fact that they were still alive might have been a comfort. Not here. Valyn remembered his training clearly enough: the Urghul took captives only to offer them later, as sacrifice to Kwihna. If half the stories were true, they might well wish they'd been killed instead of captured. There was a simplicity, a finality to a foot of sharp steel in the gut. The same couldn't be said of flaying, disemboweling, or burning, the standard fates that awaited an Urghul captive.

All the more reason, Valyn thought grimly, testing his bonds for the hundredth time, *to get uncaptured.*

Not that he'd arrived at any grand plan for escape. There were no prisons on the steppe, no brigs or dungeons, but the Urghul were thorough enough when it came to restraining their prisoners. Along with the rest of his Wing, Valyn was bound at the wrists and ankles, the rawhide cinched so tight he lost feeling immediately, then tossed over the back of a horse and tied in place. His head dangled down by the beast's belly, so low that the front hooves threatened to strike him when the animal broke into a canter, making it almost impossible to see anything except the dark mud as they rode. With every stride, the horse's spine battered his ribs. His wounded shoulder felt ready to rip from the socket. The Urghul had stripped their cloaks, and the frigid rain soaked him until he trembled uncontrollably.

The pain was constant, staggering, but the pain was the least of it. Over and over again as the horses cantered north through the night and storm, Valyn ran through his decisions: leaving the bird, letting the prisoners live, riding west rather than south. He'd made a mistake, that much was clear as a knife to the eye, but it was hard to know what, exactly, he could have done differently. Even lashed to the horse's back, he couldn't imagine killing the children in Huutsuu's camp. And the bird . . . if they'd tried to fly south, the Flea would have found them, killed them.

It's done, he growled at himself after a while. *You fucked up somewhere. The question is what you do now.*

It was difficult enough just not to pass out, but, with much straining, Valyn managed to twist his head and half raise his torso, the joints of his arms screaming as he stretched up and back, searching for his companions in the driving rain. There were scores of Urghul, a mass of shifting horseflesh and riders, and though the storm had started to abate, he caught only a glimpse of Laith and Gwenna, trussed like sacks of grain over the backs of their own horses.

The Urghul finally called a halt in the chill gray hour just before dawn. When the horse went still, Valyn thought he was dreaming at first, that his mind had lifted clear of the constant stabbing misery of his body. Then someone sliced the cord holding him up, and he tumbled to the ground, unable to bring his dead arms up to block the fall. The Kettral, of course, had trained him for captivity. Though he was still bound at the wrists and ankles, he began flexing his legs, drawing them up to his chest, then lowering them, over and over. Then his arms. He knew how to fight with tied hands, and if the opening presented itself, he intended to be ready. His frozen muscles groaned in protest. The Urghul were laughing, he realized, watching him writhe on the ground like a worm. He ignored the sound, kept moving, though the action ground his face against the stones and wet earth.

Just when he'd gone from shaking to simply trembling, just as he'd managed to stop biting his tongue with chattering teeth, someone seized him by the neck, then wrestled him roughly to his feet. When he managed to straighten up, he found himself staring at Huutsuu. Or, to be more precise, at Huutsuu's horse. The *ksaabe* who had dragged him up stepped back, as though to offer Valyn and his captor a measure of intimacy, but the Urghul woman hadn't bothered to dismount. She sat her horse lazily, short spear balanced in the crook of her arm, the thin line of a smile creasing her face.

"I told you this. I told you I would find you."

Valyn glanced at the spear, then the horse, gauging the distance between himself and the rider. Though his feet were still tied, he could probably grab the weapon, rip it out of her hands or pull her off the horse, maybe even plant it in her chest. He opened and closed his hands. They were still numb, but they seemed to work.

And then what?

He glanced over his shoulder, able, for the first time, to make sense of the milling bodies around him. Huutsuu had brought him to a sprawling Urghul camp many times larger than the one in which he'd found her. Valyn stared. Truth be told, the place was more like a town than a camp, with hundreds of *api* thrown up haphazardly among the cook fires and hobbled horses, men and women riding to and fro, even children darting about between the tents, pale legs and faces spattered with mud. The place reeked of burning horse dung and cooking horseflesh, wet hide and wet mud. Pennants of fur and feather whipped from long lances planted in the earth. Men and women gathered between tents and around fires, tended to their horses or their children, calling to one another in their odd, singsong language. There must have been a thousand Urghul, maybe more.

Valyn turned his attention back to Huutsuu, leaning back slowly on his heels, forcing himself to stay still, to check his own rage. Even if he managed to kill the woman, he'd still be tied up, trussed like a pig for whatever happened next.

This is not the time, he told himself silently, repeating the words in his head as though rehearsing them again and again could keep him from folly. *This is not the time.*

"Where are we?" he asked instead, jerking his head at the surrounding camp.

Huutsuu smiled. "These are my people."

"I thought your people hated large camps. I thought you lived in *ta-amu,* not nations."

The Urghul woman shrugged. "We did. Not anymore."

Before Valyn could make sense of that, other riders pulled up beside them, each Urghul trailing a horse with a sodden human shape lashed across the back. Relief mingled with fury, Valyn watched as, one by one, the other members of his Wing were cut from their horses, then dumped unceremoniously on the ground. The rest of the Urghul, like Huutsuu, refused to dismount, watching impassively as the horses shifted beneath them, their hooves making sucking sounds in the mud.

Annick was the first up, struggling to her knees, then her feet. She moved awkwardly, as though she had strained or torn something during the long ride, but Valyn could see her testing the rawhide at her wrists as she stood, searching for some weakness. Gwenna cursed the Urghul until one of the riders knocked her across the back of the head with the butt of his spear, sending her reeling into the mud once more. Talal got to his feet slowly, silent and intent. Valyn studied the leach, then flicked a sign: *You're well?*

Talal made an almost imperceptible nod.

So, Valyn thought, allowing himself a small smile, *that's something.*

Before he could respond, however, two new Urghul rode up. The taller of them handed a waterskin to Huutsuu without a word, and she, in turn, tossed it to Valyn.

"Drink," she said as he caught it awkwardly.

He eyed the bladder. He knew from experience what a single day without water could do. If he was going to stay sharp, alert, he needed to drink. He locked eyes with Huutsuu, raised the skin to his mouth, then tilted it back.

At first, there was nothing but the delicious wash of cold water as he sucked it down, his body greedy for the drink. Only after a few swallows did he finally taste the adamanth, the root's bitter residue roughening his tongue.

Huutsuu smiled as she watched him pause.

"For the leach," she said, gesturing to the waterskin. "My people, too, have such creatures."

For a moment, Valyn contemplated draining the full skin, draining it or ripping it open on one of the Urghul spears. The adamanth wouldn't do him any harm, of course—it might even ease the ache in his shoulder, in his bruised ribs—but the strong infusion would cut Talal off entirely from his well. The Kettral used an even more concentrated form of the tea, but simply boiling the root would prove more than effective. Clearly, the Urghul didn't know which member of his Wing to be wary of, but it hardly mattered. They would make them all drink.

Valyn hefted the skin in his hands, testing its weight, then discarded the idea of destroying it. Adamanth was common enough—no more than a weed, really—and one could find it in ditches and swamps from the Waist to the steppe. If he threw away one skin, the Urghul would simply produce another. He glanced at Talal. The leach's eyes were wary, grave, but he just shrugged. Valyn turned back to Huutsuu, matching her stare as he drank long and full from the skin. At least he could deny her the sight of his own disappointment.

As the Urghul passed the skin among the prisoners, Valyn considered the camp once more, then his captors.

"What happens next?" he asked.

Huutsuu gestured at the forest of tents. "We pack, then we ride."

"Ride where?"

"West."

"What's west?"

"Long Fist," the woman replied.

"What in Hull's name is Long Fist?"

"You will learn that when you meet him."

So the Urghul weren't planning to sacrifice them right away. Of course, there was no telling how far west they planned to ride. It wasn't much, but it was something.

"Is that where the rest of the *taamu* are going?" Valyn asked. "West? To meet Long Fist?"

"Too many questions," Huutsuu said, waving a hand at three of the younger Urghul. "Take them. Put them with the other one. Watch them close. They are a soft people, but fast."

"The other one?" Valyn demanded, shaking his head, trying to make sense of it. "Who's the other one?"

Huutsuu smiled. "Go. See."

The Annurian prisoner was tied up a dozen paces beyond the last row of *api*. The Urghul had bound his hands to his feet, forcing him into a hunched crouch. It wouldn't have been horrible at first, but a day, even half a day bent double like that would be enough to crack most men and women. Worse, despite the chill drizzle, they'd stripped him of his shirt. The man clearly hadn't eaten anything in days. Valyn could count the knobs of his spine, the ribs, could count the seeping gashes in his skin where he'd been whipped. The prisoner didn't look up as the horses approached. He could have been knocked out. Maybe he thought there was nothing to see.

"Who is it?" Valyn demanded, turning to the young rider, the *taabe,* who guarded him.

"Warrior," the *taabe* sneered. "Great warrior. Like you."

The other Urghul laughed.

"When we get out of here," Laith said, shaking his head, "when we get a bird, I am coming back, and I am going to kill every one of these miserable bastards."

"Might take a long time," Valyn said, glancing over his shoulder. "There are millions."

"I'll help him," Gwenna growled.

"Me, too," the prisoner said, without bothering to raise his head. "I bet we'd make a good team."

Valyn froze, chill rain trickling down the back of his neck, making him shiver. The man's voice was hollow, weak, but there was something there. . . . He took a step back, looking for space, ignoring the sharp spearpoint pressing against his back.

"So you lived after all," he said, trying to keep his voice steady.

Balendin Ainhoa raised his head. A massive bruise purpled the side of his face, half closing one eye. His upper lip was split, and, high on his shoulder, a mirror of Valyn's own wound, the half-healed scar left by Kaden's crossbow bolt leaked pus and blood. If the leach was bothered by his injuries, however, he didn't show it. "Of course I lived. What did Hendran say? *If you haven't seen the body, don't count the kill.*"

"You shit-licking whoreson," Gwenna snarled, lunging forward, her Urghul captors forgotten. One of the horsemen extended a spear and she went down face-first in the mud.

Balendin just raised his brows, his bonds not permitting much else. "I see that you're not getting along with our hosts any better than I am. I guess that means we're on the same side. Again." He started to smile, then grimaced as his lip cracked open, bleeding anew.

"We were never on the same side," Valyn said. Despite the cold, his skin blazed. His skin and his blood. Even the breath in his lungs seemed to burn. Like Gwenna, he'd nearly forgotten the surrounding horsemen. Whatever the Urghul were, whatever they were planning, this was the man who had murdered Amie and Ha Lin, who had come so close to murdering Kaden. Everything—their flight from the Eyrie, the Flea's pursuit and Finn's death, even their current captivity—could be traced right back to Balendin Ainhoa. Had Valyn not been so tightly bound, he would have leapt on the leach, would have wrung the life from his flesh. "We were never on the same side," he said again. "And we never will be."

He tried to collar his anger, to choke it back. Fury so blind and unreasoning was dangerous in any situation; around Balendin it was deadly. Valyn wasn't likely to forget their last fight, that desperate night battle high in the Bone Mountains, Balendin knocking aside Annick's arrows with the tiniest flick of his fingers, Balendin sending stones hurling through the darkness, Balendin chuckling smugly, knowing that as long as Valyn hated him, he would have power. All leaches were strange, unnatural creatures, but there was a world of difference between Talal, who relied on iron for his strength, and Balendin, who fed off the emotions of his foes. Balendin needed the fear and the rage, cultivated them, and while Valyn could, for the most part, master his fear of the leach, the rage was another matter entirely. Clearly the Urghul had drugged Balendin in the same way they had Talal. Had they not, the vicious bastard would already have gutted them all.

Balendin pursed his lips. "You've always had a hard time with compromise, Valyn. It's a shame, particularly now. I could use an ally." He cocked his head to the side. "And from the look of it, so could you."

Before Valyn could reply, one of the *taabe* slammed a spear shaft into the backs of his knees, dropping him into the mud.

"Talk less," the rider said, dismounting with obvious distaste, then tying Valyn in the same uncomfortable manner as Balendin.

Valyn tried to reply, but the Urghul cuffed him across the cheek.

"Talk less."

Balendin smirked as Valyn's Wing was bound. "Well, just think about it, Valyn. I know we've had our differences, but . . ." He shrugged, the movement cut short by his cords, "I think we could get past all that."

17

Over and over, day after day, like the chorus to a desperate song, the words revolved in Adare's mind: *It can't be true. It can't be true. It can't be true.* When the song stopped, however, when the tune fell off, she heard a different voice, cold and rational: *Yes. It can.*

The history of the Atmani was ancient, to be sure, but though the wounds to the cities and land had long healed, the scars remained. Certainly, the accounts were fresh enough. Adare had read dozens of them as a child, tales penned by people who were there, who saw what happened. The chronicles didn't agree on much, but the basics were clear: the Atmani kings and queens, six immortal leach-lords, ruled Eridroa well and justly for close to five hundred years. Then they went mad.

When three decades of civil war were finally over, they had destroyed half the world in fire, famine, and war. It was true that Roshin and Rishinira hadn't been quite as brutal as the others, disappearing entirely before the last spasms of slaughter began, but that didn't mean much. If Nira and Oshi were the last of the leach-lords, they had the blood of thousands on their hands, tens of thousands. It was almost impossible to believe, but Adare had seen the hovering net of flame, had heard Oshi's ranting. He'd been ready to kill her, to murder her for destroying a tower that had collapsed centuries earlier.

Adare glanced over at the old man. He sat on the bank of the canal, on a wide, flat stone where Nira had put him while they ate their lunch, comfortably away from the other pilgrims. Since the terrifying scene in the old tower, he had returned to his quiet, gentle madness, but Nira never let him wander from her sight. She was always there with the bottle when he grew puzzled or distressed, helping him to tip it up while the pungent spirits dribbled down his chin. There were dozens of bottles of the stuff clinking softly in the bottom of the wagon. What it was, Adare still had no idea, but it seemed to work. At the moment Oshi was gazing down the steep bank, singing a soft, incomprehensible song to the rising carp.

And Nira . . . Adare studied her surreptitiously while she ate a small bowl of cold rice. While it was true that the old woman had proven helpful, even kind, in her brusque way, since the scene by the canal she had become more guarded, her eyes more dangerous. She understood as well as Adare that the balance of power had shifted between the two of them, and it was clear she didn't appreciate the shift. Nira had redoubled her lashings, both verbal and physical, as though newly determined to teach the young woman a lesson, any lesson.

"Look," Adare said finally, wiping her chin with the back of her hand. "I appreciate your hiding me these past weeks, but things have changed."

Nira's eyes narrowed.

"Don't seem that different to me."

"They don't?" Adare asked, trying not to raise her voice, shooting a nervous glance at Oshi. "Have you forgotten the other night? Forgotten what I saw?"

"Don't see that it matters."

Adare exhaled slowly. "Yes. Well. I do." She leaned in. "I know who you are. You've kept my secret, and I appreciate that, but traveling with you is an enormous risk. . . ."

"Being a princess disguised as a pilgrim is a risk."

Adare nodded vigorously. "Which is why I don't need any *more*." She took a deep breath, trying to slow herself. "The other pilgrims already distrust you. You heard Lehav the other night. I think it might just be best if we went our separate ways."

Nira frowned, then shook her head. "Don't think so."

Adare stared. "You don't think so?"

"Think we'll keep on as we've been."

"No," Adare said, the fear rising up inside her. "You're not listening. I will find other companions."

"And have me wonderin' every day if you sold us for a bit a' trust from yer newfound friends?"

Adare shook her head. "I wouldn't do that. Never. Besides, if I went to the pilgrims claiming that Roshin and Rishinira are just over there, cooking fish by the wagon, who would believe me? People would think I'd lost my mind."

"They might not believe the Atmani part," Nira said grimly, "but it don't take much talk a' leaches to see a couple old fools strung twitchin' from a tree."

"I wouldn't do that," Adare insisted again.

Nira smiled a toothy smile. "I know. B'cause you'll be right here with us till the long walk's over."

Adare took a deep breath, gathering her nerve. The woman and her brother were leaches, they could kill her with a gesture, but the three of them sat in plain sight of the rest of the pilgrims, barely a hundred paces of untilled field between them. Surely Nira wouldn't be bold enough to attack Adare where the others might see, might notice. Adare tried to believe that as she leaned forward once more.

"This is not a negotiation," she said firmly. "It is a fact."

Nira rounded on her snake-quick, snapping the side of her cane into Adare's temple, knocking her a few paces down the steep embankment. For a few heartbeats Adare fought the throbbing pain and the rising darkness. Finally she was able to struggle to her knees, then her feet. At last, holding her skull, she looked up to find the old woman shaking her head, a quick, curt motion, lips tight.

"I understand you're a princess and all," Nira hissed. "You're bright. You're ambitious. You've won a few petty little battles. . . ."

"Petty battles?" Adare demanded, trying to get her feet beneath her. To show weakness now was to fail, and she could not afford to fail. "I saw the Chief Priest of Intarra destroyed. I gelded his entire Church."

Nira snorted. "A batch of sun-blind fools."

Adare wasn't sure how to respond to that, but the woman was already bulling ahead. "You've been a minister a few months. I ruled this whole fucking continent"—she paused to stab her cane into the soft earth—"for centuries. You had a quarrel with a priest? We," she included Oshi in her gesture, "battled Dirik and Chirug for *decades*. I faced Shihjahin on the black rock for three nights and three days while the earth cracked around us and men died by the thousands."

Her lips were drawn back in a snarl. Adare felt a cold hand close around her heart.

"I saw your family rise from nothing, watched Terial struggle to found his little empire, scraping together our ashes and calling them a civilization. I saw Terial die. And Santun, and Anlatun—*all* of them. Missed your father's funeral tendin' ta Oshi's cough, but make no mistake about it girl, when the time comes, I will see *you* stuck in one a' those caves, bony hands folded on your chest. So if you think, you presumptuous little bitch, that because you are a fucking Malkeenian, a princess, a clever girl in a stupid world, think this: for a thousand years and more I have refrained from using my powers. For a thousand years I have kept my brother from destroying everything he sees. I *hope* to continue doing so until I've done what I intend to do, and if you'd seen what my brother is capable of, my hopes would be your fucking prayers."

She shook her head, and some of the fury had drained from her voice when she spoke again. "Our fight is not with you, girl, but if you cross me, you'll wish it had been you and not that useless priest who burned in Intarra's fire."

When the woman finally fell silent, Adare realized she had taken two or three steps back, as though driven bodily by the force of Nira's fury.

"Sister?" Oshi asked, looking up from the carp, worry and confusion in his cloudy eyes. One hand opened and closed as though attempting a fist. "Is there danger?" He glanced at Adare uncertainly, then at the land around them, eyes fixing on the pilgrims atop the bank. "Must we fight?"

Nira shifted her eyes from Adare to her brother, then back.

"Ask her," she said.

Adare hesitated, fear, humiliation, and awe raging high inside her like a river about to burst its banks. She wanted to lash out, to physically strike the old woman. She wanted to whimper. There wasn't much space left over for rational thought, but it was to that remaining sliver of her mind that her father's voice spoke from the depth of her childhood. *You cannot see clearly, Adare, when your sight is clouded by your own emotions.*

She took an unsteady breath, then another. Rishinira was a leach, an abomination, one of the twisted vipers responsible for the deaths of thousands, but not, at least not necessarily, Adare's enemy. Her mind spun, trying to see the truth. The old woman had helped her, hidden her, protected her, and asked for nothing in return except Adare's complicity.

"No," Adare said slowly, raising her hands. "I don't want a fight."

Nira studied her for a long time, then nodded brusquely. "All right then. When we've got to Olon and done what needs doin' there, ya won't see us again. We'll disappear." She glanced at her brother. "We're good at that, ain't we, ya stupid sack a' shit?"

Adare frowned. She had spent so much time worrying about how to handle Nira and her brother that she never paused to wonder *why* the two

had joined the pilgrimage in the first place. It seemed an unlikely decision. Travel involved unexpected surprises. Joining a large group increased
the chance of awkward questions, prying glances, inadvertent disclosures.
Adare's own nerves were frayed ragged from two weeks maintaining her
disguise, and yet, for some reason, the two Atmani had sought out the
company, willingly attaching themselves to the other pilgrims for the long
march south.

"And what," Adare asked slowly, "are you doing on the road to Olon?"

Nira eyed her warily. "Didn't we just get done pissin' on each other
over the keepin' a' secrets? Now you want ta go sharing more?"

Adare paused. It would be easy to let it go, to leave the conversation on
a note of uneasy détente and turn her attention to the challenges awaiting
her to the south. There were enough dangerous people hoping to see
her dead without adding the 'Kent-kissing Atmani to the list. On the
other hand, Nira's presence in the pilgrimage seemed too strange to be utter coincidence, as though she, too, were swept south on the same unsettled
political tide that carried Adare. It was hard to imagine what an immortal
leach might want with a crumbling city like Olon, but there was a chance
that her unspoken goals coincided in some way with Adare's. Unfortunately,
the trading of secrets involved trading.

Don't give, Adare thought grimly, *don't get.*

"I'm raising an army," Adare said. "That's why I'm going to Olon."

Nira pursed her wrinkled lips. "S'wrong with the four ya already got?"

"They aren't mine," Adare replied.

"Annurian armies. Annurian princess. Sound like yours ta me."

"They belong to il Tornja," Adare said, voice tight. "And he is not my
ally."

"Ah . . ." Nira let the syllable hang in the light breeze. "It's like that,
then." She shook her head. "Civil war, girl. It's nothing ta fuck with."

"I've got no choice," Adare said, more heat than she intended in her
voice. "The *kenarang* murdered my father."

Nira shrugged. "Your father sat on that ugly rock, but he was just one
man. Lot more than that are gonna die, you go startin' a war. Who's gonna
do the dyin' on your side?"

"The Sons of Flame," Adare replied.

Nira raised a bushy eyebrow.

"They hate the empire already," Adare went on, trying to sound like
she believed the words as they left her lips. Trying to believe them. "I just

need to convince Vestan Ameredad that I'm a different type of Malkeenian."

She fell silent, waiting for the old woman to berate her for shortsightedness, stupidity, or both, but Nira just sucked air between her crooked teeth. "Ameredad," she said after a while. "Might be we're not just on the same path, but in the same wagon, too."

Adare frowned. "What do you want with him?"

"Maybe nothing. Can't say till I see the man, till I see his face."

"What's that going to tell you?"

"Whether he's the one did this to us," the old woman replied, voice hardening.

Adare hesitated. A cold wind had picked up, whipping down from the north, churning the canal to a froth of chop and spray, whipping Adare's face with her hair. Oshi turned from the water, shaking his head, tears coursing down his weathered cheeks.

"They're gone," he said, gesturing to the water. "The fish are gone." His voice was lost, plaintive, pitifully weak against the gusts. "Did I kill them, Nira? Did I kill them all?"

"No," she said, keeping her eyes on Adare. "You didn't kill them, Oshi."

"Did *what* to you?" Adare asked.

Nira waved a hand at Oshi. "Made us immortal. Made us kings and queens of half the world. Made us mad."

Adare shivered at the words even as she tried to make sense of them. She'd read dozens of accounts of the origin of the Atmani, but not one, not even Yenten's *History*, claimed any certainty about where the leachlords had acquired their longevity or power.

"Who . . ." Adare began hesitantly, searching for a way to frame the question. "How . . ."

"Csestriim," Nira hissed, then spat onto the dirt. "Didn't realize it then. Didn't learn till later, when we caught and killed two of them. Two of the three."

Adare shook her head at the impossibility of the notion. "Why would the Csestriim want to . . . help you?"

"Help?" Nira choked on a laugh, then stabbed a bony finger at Oshi. "Does that look like helping ta you?"

"But they made you immortal," Adare protested. "They gave you powers."

"The powers were ours before we ever met them. They just . . .

enhanced them. As for immortal . . ." She held out a withered arm. "Looks like they didn't get that quite right either. This body's going ta dirt. It's just takin' a lot longer than it oughta." She grimaced. "The Csestriim didn't give a rotted shit for us, girl—they were trying to make a new breed, or to remake an old one. Thought they'd found a way to bring back their race."

Adare stared. "But you're not Csestriim. You have feelings."

Nira snorted. "You noticed? Like I said, they tried to play at Bedisa's work and they fucked up."

"The beginning of your reign was a golden age," Adare pointed out.

"And then it went straight into the shitter. We weren't meant to live this long, to have this much power. Something up here," she rapped at her skull with a knuckle, "can't take it."

"But *you* aren't . . ."

"That's because I realized it first. Quit dipping into my well. I tried to get Roshin to stop, too, but he was wrapped up in the dream. The dream first, and then the war." Her eyes were dark, bleak. "He catches glimpses, sometimes, of what it's done to him, but if I left him alone for a full day, he'd throw himself right back into it."

"A thousand years," Adare breathed, mind reeling at the thought. "For more than a thousand years you've done nothing but keep him drugged. Keep him in check."

"Not nothing, girl," Nira snapped. "Learned ta knit a few centuries back. Picked up the flute a bit." She shrugged. "Since forgot it."

"Why?" Adare asked quietly. "If you resent the immortality so much, couldn't you . . ." She trailed off.

"Bash his head in?" Nira asked brightly. She turned to her brother. "Whatta ya say, Rosh? How'd ya feel about a quick brick to the brain?"

He turned his rheumy eyes on her, open mouth revealing his yellowing teeth. "If you think so, Nira . . ." he responded hesitantly. "Whatever you think is best."

The old woman let out an exasperated sigh. "Whatever I think is best. What a pathetic pile o' bones you've become." She turned back to Adare. "I'm tempted to kill him almost every day. Seems it'd be a mercy, but then, he's my brother. Bad thing to kill your own brother with a brick. Besides, maybe I can heal him. Maybe I can find the one who knows how."

"The last Csestriim," Adare said.

Nira nodded. "The smart one. The one with the ideas."

"And you think it's Vestan Ameredad?" Adare asked, shaking her head. "Why?"

The old woman frowned. "Nah. Not really. Been looking for a lot of years, and only had a couple of brushes ta show for it."

"But why Vestan?"

Nira nodded, as though considering the question anew. "He's a meddler, this bastard I'm hunting. Meddled with me. Meddled with others. Likes to be near the center of the pile of shit. We weren't the only kings he propped up over the years, and if this Ameredad's fixing to topple your empire . . ." She shrugged. "I've walked across half a continent for less. 'Sides, sounds like he more or less fits the bill—tall, dark, unfunny, smart."

Adare stared. "There must be a hundred men who fit the description. A thousand. If the Csestriim you're looking for cleaves to centers of power, why aren't you in Annur? Why aren't you in the Dawn Palace?"

Nira raised an eyebrow. "Just walk up ta the palace and batter at the door with m' cane? Is that it?" She shook her head. "Ain't as easy ta get in and out a' those nice red walls as ya think. 'Sides—Oshi and I just did a couple decades in Annur. Nothin' but burned rice and shit stink. It's in Olon that the pot's boilin' over, and so Olon's where we're goin'. Like I said, probably ain't Ameredad, but ya sit in one place too long, ya get old."

Adare studied the woman. It seemed like a mad plan, crisscrossing the earth looking for the creature who had given them immortality, but then, the Atmani *were* mad. That was the one thing on which all the historians agreed.

"And if it *is* him? If the man leading the Sons of Flame is the one you're looking for? What then?"

"See if he can fix us." She jerked a thumb over her shoulder at Oshi. "Fix him."

"And if he can't?"

"Kill him."

"I need Ameredad," Adare blurted. "I need the Sons of Light to overthrow il Tornja."

"Well then," Nira said, voice flat, hard, "you'd best hope he's not the one I'm looking for."

18

Olon straddled the blue-brown shallows of the northern end of Lake Baku like a gracile thousand-legged spider of stone, her body an oblong island a few hundred paces offshore, her legs the narrow quays stretching into the shimmering water and the slender stone bridges reaching toward the north bank. Even seen through the blindfold, the narrow towers and shapely domes were far more elegant than Annur's stark angles and rigid lines, but Adare couldn't spare much attention for the architecture, not with two score armed men blocking the bridge on which she stood.

The men weren't uniformed, not that she could make out, anyway, but it was clear enough from the neat ranks, from the well-polished weapons and obvious military discipline that they weren't a band of thugs out to rob pilgrims. They might have been legionaries, only they weren't wearing imperial armor, and besides, none of the armies had a legion stationed in Olon. Which meant the Sons of Flame. Which meant the reports Adare had heard were true. She wasn't sure whether to be relieved or terrified.

She had thought, at first, that the men were just running a routine patrol on the bridge, checking carts and carriages, maybe strong-arming money out of the merchants, some sort of "levy" to support the faithful. As she approached, however, caught up in the knot of pilgrims, she realized they were waiting—forty or fifty of them, well-armed and alert—just waiting. Adare glanced over her shoulder, half expecting to find another army marching on the city, an attacking force that might warrant the presence of so many armed men, but there was no army. Only the stragglers of her own pilgrimage alongside a few local cart drivers lashing ponderous water buffalo.

"Looks as though the light lovers think they own the bridges," Nira groused, spitting onto the flagstones.

Adare nodded nervously. She'd expected the Sons of Flame to be hidden away somewhere, holed up in alleys and cellars, not standing at attention athwart the main bridge into the city. Ameredad was either very bold, very stupid, or both. Such an open display of force risked the full retaliation of Annur, at least once il Tornja heard of it.

On the bright side, she thought bleakly, *at least I don't need to go hunting around for them in the taverns. At least they're* here.

She reached up to adjust her blindfold, squared her shoulders, then moved forward with the mass of gold-robed faithful, just another pilgrim returning to the city where the faith was born. The soldiers, younger men mostly, some with onion-pale skin, others dark as charred wood, watched the throng approach. Adare waited for them to move aside, to allow the devout into the city, but they did not move. Instead, when the first wagons reached the height of the bridge, a broad-shouldered man with a neck like a dock piling stepped forward. He must have been well into his fifth decade, though the years had done nothing to chip away at the heavy muscle of his arms and chest.

"Stop," he said, voice loud enough he didn't bother to raise a hand.

The pilgrimage clattered to a halt in a welter of confused questions, those behind demanding answers from their friends nearer the top of the bridge. Adare's hands were slippery with sweat. She forced herself to leave them at her side, not to wipe them on her robes. She felt light-headed, as though she might pass out. It would be a disaster, of course. If she fell, the pilgrims who came to her aid would remove the blindfold, and then she was dead.

Keep standing, she told herself silently. *Stay on your 'Kent-kissing feet.*

The Sons of Flame hadn't moved, but their commander was running his gaze over the golden-robed men and women at the front of the line, his mouth twisted in a scowl.

"Where is the Malkeenian?" he asked finally.

Ice slid down Adare's spine. She wanted to flee and fight all at the same time. The bridge balustrade was only a few paces off. She couldn't see what lay beneath, but if she hurled herself off of it . . .

"Keep still, ya dumb wench," Nira murmured, voice pitched for Adare's ears alone. "And keep your mouth shut."

Legs trembling beneath her, Adare stood still, heart slamming against her ribs. Suddenly, her blindfold and backstory seemed pathetic, a flimsy shield against so many ideas, so many curious minds. Of *course* someone recognized her, recognized or suspected that the tall young woman traveling alone, the one hiding her eyes, might be more than she seemed. Despite Nira's admonition, Adare was ready to run, to leap into the lake below, when a strong hand took her by the elbow, the fingers like steel.

"What . . ." she cried, breaking off when she twisted to find Lehav holding her.

He smiled grimly. "Let's go."

"I'm not—"

"Of course you're not," he said, shoving her forward. "Let's go."

Adare glanced over at Nira, hoping, praying that the woman might do something, but Nira just watched, eyes like slits in her wizened face, then gave an almost imperceptible shake of the head.

By the time Adare had recovered her wits enough to struggle, she stood in the wide space between the Sons of Flame and the pilgrims, Lehav still at her side, still holding her by the arm, his grip so tight she could feel the bruises forming. The bridge had gone silent. Hundreds of stares bored into her, most of them confused, some already angry. For a fleeting moment she thought she might be able to bluff her way through, then discarded the idea as stupidity, insanity. Somehow Lehav knew her, knew who she was. The only hope was to put a brave face on the thing, to do what she had come to do.

With her free hand she reached up and pulled the blindfold free.

"I am Adare hui'Malkeenian," she said, "daughter of the murdered Emperor, princess of Annur, and the Minister of Finance. I have come here to set right a wrong, and to forge again a bond that has been broken between my family and the Divine Church of Intarra."

The pilgrims stared, shocked. Even the soldiers looked somewhat taken aback. Lehav, however, just snorted.

"Nice speech. Are you finished?"

"No," she said, squaring her shoulders, standing a little straighter. "I am not finished. I came to speak with Vestan Ameredad, not to be manhandled by one of his minions."

The muscled soldier, the one who had first called out her name, laughed at that, a quick, scornful bark.

Adare turned on him, a queasy feeling in her gut. "You are Ameredad?" The man seemed brutish and ill-mannered, a poor combination, given what she hoped to achieve. At her question he just laughed harder.

"That's enough, Kamger," Lehav said.

The man's laughter ended instantly.

Adare turned in horror, realizing her mistake, but the pilgrim she knew as Lehav ignored her, gesturing instead to the men and women he had walked alongside during the march south.

"These people have come a long way. They are tired and hungry. It seems you want to make a show, but they have not come here for a show. They have come here because of their devotion to the goddess, not for some sordid spectacle of a lying bureaucrat brought low."

Adare rounded on the man, anger stiffening her trembling legs. "I am neither lying, nor a bureaucrat."

Lehav studied her a moment, seemed about to say something, then shook his head, turning instead to the assembled crowd.

"My mother named me Lehav, but the goddess gave me a new name: Ameredad. I thank my brothers and sisters of the road for their companionship and piety, their quiet devotion and sacrifice to Intarra. You have given up much to come here—work and family, security—and I will see to it that this new city, this holy city, welcomes you as you deserve.

"As for this . . ." he said, jerking his head toward Adare without bothering to look at her. "You witness here Malkeenian treachery firsthand. Do not forget it."

Most men would have said more, would have waited for the applause and the stamping of feet, but when Lehav had finished speaking he turned, passing Adare to Kamger without a glance over his shoulder.

"See that she's brought to the Geven Cellars. Double guard. I will be along after I have cleaned myself, prayed, and made my offering to the goddess."

Kamger saluted, but Lehav was already striding through his troops and into Olon as though Adare had ceased to exist. That was when the Aedolians struck.

At first she thought the pilgrims behind her were just voicing their confusion and outrage. There were shouts, cries that could have been accusation or anger, the clatter of hooves. Then she saw the faces of the soldiers gathered around her, the sudden surprise and fear in the eyes of the Sons of Flame, followed by the desperate scramble to draw weapons. A scramble ending in failure.

At first, all Adare knew was that two men, both mounted, both swinging swords as long as her arm, were riding straight into the mass of Intarran soldiers, cutting furiously into the men on foot. She saw a head split open and an arm severed at the elbow, watched one man raise his sword only to see the weapon smashed straight into his face. Kamger seemed as confused as the rest, struggling to pull his blade free while keeping his grip on her arm. Adare turned just in time to see Fulton lean over the pommel of his saddle, swinging his broadblade in a great arc that opened the huge soldier from his neck to his chest. Blood, hotter than monsoon rain, splattered Adare's face, and then she was free.

"Quickly, my lady," Fulton said, wheeling his horse to a stop, reaching down with his free hand. "Into the saddle before they regroup."

Adare's mind reeled, but her body took over. She seized the Aedolian's hand, dragging herself up onto the horse even as the Sons of Flame closed around them again. A part of her, the part that wasn't drenched in blood and terror, noted that Fulton looked thinner, older, his eyes and cheeks sunken and haggard. How long had the two men been following her? *Why?* The questions were irrelevant in the midst of the chaos, inane, but her mind had retreated from the blood soaking her robes, from the screaming of the injured, from the shapes of the shattered men splayed on the flagstones. For a moment she thought she might start singing, whether from euphoria or madness, she couldn't be sure.

It looked like they would make it. Birch was holding back the Sons while Fulton spurred his horse to a gallop, charging straight back through the ranks of the pilgrims. *We're going to break free,* Adare thought. The realization tasted like clean air, fresh and cold in her lungs. *We're getting out.*

Then, with no warning, the horse was screaming, tumbling forward, and she was off, flying through the air, flying. Flying, then not.

✝

Ameredad's minions knew their work, bustling her through the ancient city's bafflement of alleyways and side streets with businesslike efficiency. Adare could barely walk, the gash on her head throbbed, and her vision was hazy, blurry. She wanted to ask about Fulton and Birch, to know whether they were still alive, but someone had stuffed a foul-tasting gag in her mouth, and between the stench and the dizziness, it was all she could do not to vomit.

The small party turned and backtracked so often that Adare quickly lost all sense of direction, and after a short while she quit trying to keep track of where she was and paid attention to the city itself, hoping to learn something that might save her life. The reek of whitefish, turmeric, and smoke filled the twisting alleys, and the streets and windows were alive with barter and banter. Still, something about the place seemed moribund, as though it had died years earlier.

The buildings were as graceful as they were venerable, but most had begun to crumble, mortar and stone falling away, marring the sweeping curves with ugly, ragged holes. Those that had not yet submitted to the ultimate indignity of collapse were rough and battered, paint and plaster stripped by decades of storm and neglect. Half the walls in the city looked badly in need of repair. It wasn't quite a ruin—perhaps it never would be, considering the lucrative trade that passed through it—and yet, Olon was a city with a dagger in her heart.

A dagger we put there, Adare realized grimly. *A wound dealt by the Malkeenians.*

Perhaps Terial hui'Malkeenian hadn't intended to gut the capital of the ancient kingdom of Kresh when he founded his nascent empire, but neither had he chosen it as his ruling seat. Money followed power, and after the government shifted to Annur, Olon began to crumble. Canal and lake trade kept her alive, along with the voracious appetite of the capital, but the once-palatial residences along the water had been converted into taverns, brothels, and flophouses for wagon-drivers and sailors weary from the rough passage across Lake Baku. A few stubborn descendants of the old aristocratic houses squatted inside familial manses they could no longer maintain, while thieves and orphans, rats and wind reclaimed the rest.

It looked like a miserable place to live, but a perfect city to defend. As she was dragged through the streets, Adare glimpsed no fewer than ten pairs of Ameredad's guards, hard men with blades and bows lounging in the shadows or blocking the heads of narrow lanes. They wore no insignia or livery, certainly nothing to connect them to the Sons of Flame, and she might have mistaken them for common street toughs had it not been for the silent nods and curt gestures they exchanged with her captors as she passed.

The whole 'Kent-kissing city is this bastard's fortress, Adare thought bleakly as she stumbled over the uneven cobbles, trying to keep her feet. She tried to imagine an Annurian legion taking the place, and failed. Olon's maze of collapsing buildings and piled rubble would render legionary tactics and formations pointless. The Sons of Flame could blend with the local population, hiding in attics and cellars, sniping from open windows before disappearing into their ancient warren.

For the first time Adare realized that Ameredad's choice in coming to this particular city might have been influenced by more than simple religious devotion. Il Tornja might be a brilliant general, but this was no city for generals. A thousand men could die in Olon's alleyways without anyone noticing. A thousand men, or one very stupid princess.

✝

Despite the low ceiling and stone, the ponderous walls and lack of windows, the small room—a basement below a basement beneath a basement, judging by the number of stairs they had descended—looked more like a study than an abattoir. Rolled maps and piles of parchment, letters and supply lists, waited in tidy piles on the wide table. Someone had stacked a few crates neatly in the corner, the topmost of which was stamped *INK*. A tattered, moldy map of Olon was tacked up on the far wall, although Adare couldn't make out much but the bridges and the dark outline of the island itself. The place spoke of caution, deliberation, and resolve. Lehav, Ameredad—whatever his name was—the man seated across from her was clearly more than just some power-hungry, up-jumped soldier.

"You understand," he said, considering Adare bluntly over the rough wooden table, "that many of the faithful, probably most, will want to see you burned."

"I am a Malkeenian princess," Adare replied, trying to keep her voice steady. "Hundreds saw me on the bridge. If you kill me, you will have a brief civil war followed by the annihilation of your faith."

Lehav shrugged. "The faithful would call your death justice, justice for Uinian. As for the rest, we are all in Intarra's hands."

"Intarra didn't take such good care of Uinian."

Lehav frowned, but he didn't respond, his silence leaving Adare to wonder if she had scored a point or sealed her own doom. If the man decided to kill her, the cramped, windowless room was as good a place as any. Aside from the two soldiers who had dragged her in moments before, no one knew that she was there. The heavy stone walls would blot out her screams. Her blood would drain out readily enough through the rough iron grate set into the floor.

He's not going to kill you, she told herself firmly, suppressing a shudder. *Not here, at least.*

"What were you doing in Annur?" Adare asked, trying to seize back some scrap of initiative. "Why did you disguise yourself? Join the pilgrimage?"

Lehav raised an eyebrow. "It would seem that I should be asking the questions, and you should be answering them."

"And yet, so far all you've done is threaten me."

"No. It is you who threaten us," the soldier said, voice quiet, but hard. "You struck at Uinian, at our priest in the heart of our temple—"

"Uinian was a 'Kent-kissing *leach*," Adare cut in, suddenly furious in spite of her fear. "He lied to you, to his entire congregation, and you all *believed* him. You should thank me for unveiling him, for seeing him killed."

Lehav studied her. "That much, perhaps, is true. Unfortunately for both of us, you didn't stop there, did you?"

"The Accords," Adare said, watching him warily.

"Accords." He shook his head. "What a sweet little word. Like calling a knife to the gut a *tickle*."

"The Accords were intended to find a new balance between Intarra's Church and the Unhewn Throne, one that—"

Lehav cut her off without raising his voice. "The Accords were laws, laws *you* made, to humiliate the Church, cut off her revenue, and destroy the force that defended her. The new Chief Priest is your puppet, and this *balance* you describe is the balance of a tyrant with her boot on the throat of a conquered foe." His raised his brows. "Do I have it more or less right?"

Adare hesitated, trying to see past both her anger and her fear. When she planned for this moment, she had imagined Ameredad to be either a religious zealot, ignorant of the serpentine twists of imperial politics, or a shrewd opportunist like Uinian, a man more interested in his own glory and advancement than the fate of the thousands who followed him. Apparently, her imagination had failed her. She could stick with her rehearsed speech, but that speech looked likely to see her burned before a vengeful mob. She took a deep breath, marshaled her thoughts, then nodded.

"You have it right," she said. "The Accords were a play to cut your Church off at the knees."

The man leaned back in his chair, clearly surprised.

"And you've come here now, why?" he asked slowly. "To finish what you started?"

Adare shook her head. "To fix it. To make it right."

"To make it right," Lehav said, looking past Adare to the map on the wall. He frowned, as though the layout of the streets and alleyways displeased him. "It doesn't make sense. You could retract the Accords from the Dawn Palace. Retract or amend them. You didn't need to come here to meet with me. You certainly didn't need to *walk* all this way with a blindfold over your eyes." He turned back to her, fixing her with a hard stare. "You are still lying, and each lie brings you closer to your death."

The words were mild, but then, Adare had never heard the soldier raise his voice. She was reminded of his warning to the canal rats back in the muddy ruts of the Perfumed Quarter, the way he didn't threaten so much as offer alternatives. He'd been willing to leave her then, willing, before learning she shared his faith, to let her be raped and killed without even knowing who she was. How much more readily would he let her go to the fires now?

"I am not lying," she said slowly, "but there is more."

He watched her for a moment, then, in a fluid motion, drew his belt knife. The blade gleamed in the fickle lights of candle and lantern, and for a moment he considered the steel, turning it back and forth, watching the flame and shadow play over it.

Adare stared, still as a cobra in the grip of the wooden flute's soft song. *He's not going to burn me,* she realized. *He's not going to wait that long.* She imagined the wide map with her blood splattered across it.

Lehav, however, just gestured with the point of his knife toward a thick candle on the edge of the table, then flicked his wrist, scoring a line in the wax a finger's width from the top.

"You have until that line to talk," he said, "and then we are finished."

Adare tried to collect her thoughts. There wasn't much wax remaining above the notch, and the case she had to put before the soldier was a complex one. There would be no second chances and there could be no missteps.

"Ran il Tornja murdered my father."

Lehav's eyes narrowed, but he didn't speak. Adare glanced at the candle, then plunged ahead.

"The *kenarang* is at the center of a conspiracy to remove the Malkeenian line from power."

"I serve Intarra," Lehav said, "not the Malkeenian line."

"You might want to rethink that position. My family is not il Tornja's only target. We might not even be his main one. He wants your Church gone, destroyed, scrubbed from the face of the empire."

"Why would the *kenarang* concern himself with domestic matters of religious freedom?"

"Because he wants to be emperor, not *kenarang,* and he understands that there are only two entities with the power to resist him." She held up two fingers. "My family, and your Church." She frowned. "I should say, we *had* the power to resist him, but he has already stripped most of that away. I did not draft the Accords alone, nor was I the sole author of the strike against Uinian. Who do you think brought me to your temple in the first place? Who do you think *told* me that your Chief Priest killed my father?"

Lehav studied her over steepled fingers. "So you allowed yourself to be used. If this is true."

"I was a fool," Adare agreed, shoving down her pride. "I spent years hearing about Uinian's hatred for my family, and when the time came, I believed what I was told."

"And your judgment was further impaired when you made yourself the *kenarang's* whore."

Adare stifled a sharp retort. Though she had hoped word of her romantic liaison would remain in the Dawn Palace, she hadn't really expected as much.

"My personal mistakes are beside the point here. . . ."

"It seems to me that they are exactly the point," Lehav replied. "Even if I accept every article of your tale, look what I am left with: you admit that you were a willing participant in the murder of my priest. . . ."

"A *leach,*" Adare insisted.

Lehav waved the interruption aside. "You admit that you spent time in the bed of the *kenarang,* the man behind both Uinian's murder and your father's, and admit conspiring to ruin Intarra's one true Church with your Accords. Even if you are honest, you have proven yourself a fool and a foe to the faithful. Why would I do anything *but* burn you?"

"Because if you burn me, you will fail," Adare said bleakly. "Il Tornja will have turned his two chief foes against each other, and he will win."

"We will face il Tornja when the time comes," Lehav said. "This city is better defended than you realize."

Adare thought back to the pairs of soldiers blocking the alleyways above, to the warren of streets and ruins. It could well prove the end of an Annurian legion, especially if the local population sided with the Sons of Flame. Il Tornja would have to raze the place to dislodge them, and razing an Annurian city would be insanity for a usurper of the throne. Not since

Terial the Short laid siege to Mo'ir three centuries earlier had an Annurian emperor attacked his own citizens, and that hadn't ended well for Terial.

"I have an army," Lehav continued. "I have a growing stock of weapons and armor. I have a fortified position, and the tactical and strategic experience to properly defend it. You have . . . what? The dress on your back, and a sad story about the murder of one tyrant at the hands of another. You want something and you can give nothing. You are a highborn beggar, nothing more."

Adare smiled. "I have the eyes."

"I am far from convinced," Lehav replied, "of the divinity of those eyes."

"That's a shame. There are three players in this game: my family, your Church, and the *kenarang*. We each have our followings. If you burn me tomorrow, il Tornja will spin an outraged tale of your treachery. He will explain in great detail and with even more righteous anger how you abducted and murdered me. The millions of Annurians loyal to my family, instead of siding with you, will become *his* followers. You might hold Olon, but if you attempt to leave it, you will find yourself awash in a sea of enemies. For every mile you travel, men will lame your horses and burn their fields to deny you food. They will tear up the roads before you and drive away their livestock." Adare shook her head. "Il Tornja won't even *need* his legions. Which means you will stay here, trapped with your few followers on this sad, decaying island until you starve or the *kenarang* destroys you at his leisure."

Lehav frowned. "Well, that's a dire tale. And you offer what, to prevent it?"

"Legitimacy. With me at your side, il Tornja won't be able to brand you traitors. Lovers of Intarra and loyal citizens of the empire alike will unite behind us. It will be the *kenarang,* not the Sons of Flame, who finds himself trapped behind the walls of his city."

"Loyal citizens of the empire," the soldier said, scorn in his voice as he repeated the words.

Adare stared. "My father was a capable Emperor and a just man. For every disgruntled priest during his reign, there were fifty farmers and merchants, nobles and soldiers, all grateful for the peace and prosperity he brought. What is it about Annur that makes you hate it?"

The soldier studied her from across the table. Adare tried to remain still, to keep her face calm, but now that her words were spent, fear flowed in to fill the space left behind, and she realized she was clutching at the fabric of her dress, wringing it desperately between her fingers. With an effort she loosed the cloth, then smoothed it, running her hands over the wrinkles again and again.

"I grew up in the Quarter," Lehav said finally. "Not too far from where I found you. Didn't know my father, barely knew my mother—the swelling pox killed her when I was six—raised my younger brother myself for three years, until someone put a rusty chisel through his eye and tossed him into the canal. . . ."

Adare opened her mouth to say something, but no words came, and the soldier waved her to silence.

"A kid in the Quarter . . ." he went on, voice flat. "You learn early on to kill, to steal, to fuck, or to hide. Hopefully all four, if you want to stay alive. Even those skills won't save you if you don't know when to do what. My brother could steal and hide, he could fuck and kill, but he made a mistake somewhere. I never learned what it was, but he read someone wrong, stole when he should have killed, killed when he should have fucked. The point is, back in the Quarter we didn't see so much of your father's fine justice.

"I was lucky. Smarter and stronger than most of the others, but mostly lucky. The day I joined up with the legions, I thought I'd finally made it, got out for good. Three meals a day, free clothes, nice bright spear, and a *cause* to fight for. I held on to that spear and that cause all the way down to the Waist, where I spent six years killing jungle tribesmen who had even less than the poor bastards back in the Quarter." He shrugged, the indifference of the gesture belying the words. "I was good at it, kept moving up the ranks until I commanded an entire legion."

He shook his head. "I never regretted killing the men and women. They're beasts down there, worse than beasts. A wolf will kill you, gnaw the marrow from your bones, but the jungle tribes? They'll take the skin off a man one strip at a time. They'll pull every tooth in your mouth while you choke on your own blood. They need to be put down, and I was good at putting them down. When we started burning villages, though, when we started putting spears in children . . ." He broke off, staring at nothing.

"That's when you quit."

"That's when I found a purer cause," he said finally, staring at her.

Adare watched him for a long time, trying to find a shape for her thoughts. "Intarra's light burns bright," she said finally, "but we live here, on the earth, in the mud."

"That's no reason not to reach for her flame."

"And in this world," Adare replied quietly, "there is no fire without fuel. No flame without ash." She shook her head. "I am not a goddess, but I am a princess of Annur, and Annur is real. It is here. My hands are bloody, but unlike those of the goddess we both serve, I can do real work with them. I can hold a sword or a scepter. I can help people, real people right now, but not without the Sons."

Lehav watched her awhile, then looked over at the candle. The soft wax had folded over his notch and the flame wavered in the cool draft.

"All right," he said finally.

Adare let out a long, unsteady breath. "All right."

He turned back to her. "I can save you, but your men, those Aedolians . . . they killed eleven of the Sons."

"No," Adare said, jarred from her tiny moment of relief. "They were only trying to help me. They were doing what they swore to do."

Lehav laughed grimly. "We've all sworn to do something. They killed my men. If I am to have any credibility before my people . . . if *we* are to have any credibility, they have to burn."

Adare felt as though a stone were blocking her throat.

"They are good men," she managed finally.

"As you said," Lehav replied slowly, "there is no flame without ash."

19

I know a way out.

In the long undifferentiated darkness of his imprisonment, Kaden revolved the words in his mind, listening to them as though they were a faint strain of music in the silence, studying them as he might a glimmer of light in the endless shadow. Again and again he went back to the *saama'an,* the perfectly carved memory of those final moments in Triste's cell when the Csestriim had met his eyes, then mouthed those five words.

I know a way out.

It was a baffling claim, horrible in the hope it offered, maddening because Kaden could make no sense of it. When the Ishien slammed shut the door of his cell, turned the key in the lock, Kaden had waited for a thousand heartbeats before standing, before exploring with fingers and palms the rough stone extent of his prison. His burning eyes offered a pathetic measure of light, enough to avoid walking into a wall if he moved slowly, and so he shuffled painstakingly around the tiny chamber. There was little to learn. The walls were damp. The wooden door felt heavy. In the corner, a small hole no larger than Kaden's hand opened into unmeasured darkness below.

It was a meager consolation, but the cell did not offer any other, and as the sound of retreating boots echoed to silence, he began to realize just what he had risked in trying to defend Triste. What he had risked, and how badly he had failed. Panic prowled his mind on velvet feet, and for a while it was all he could do to keep from hurling himself at the door, from screaming into the darkness. Instead, he found the middle of the room as well as he could, sat cross-legged on the stone floor, and closed his eyes, replacing the darkness of the world with his own inner darkness, the emptiness of the cell with a greater emptiness. When he finally emerged from the *vaniate,* the fear remained, but it was a small thing, a distant scream like far-off smoke against a vast, silent sky.

Methodically, he set about exploring his cell again, running his hands systematically over the stone, testing the privy hole, reaching up for the invisible ceiling. He went to the door last, hoping it would offer some recourse that the rest of the stone had refused. Steel or iron banded the thick wooden slab, metal cold and pitted beneath his fingers. A small slot opened at the very bottom, barely the height of his hand—for food perhaps. He found a keyhole narrower than his finger halfway up, briefly allowed himself to imagine that he might pick the lock and break free, then squashed the hope. He had no tools, nothing but his robe, and even if he had, he knew nothing about locks, nothing about escape.

Only when he had exhausted the other possibilities did he finally speak.

"Hello?" he asked, voice little more than a whisper. Even that was enough to crack the brittle shell of the *vaniate.* "Triste? Are you there?" He hesitated. "Kiel?"

The darkness lisped his own syllables back to him, but there was no response. He tried again, raising his voice, then again and again, over and over until he was bellowing, pounding his fists on the door's indifferent steel. When he gave up, the silence clamped down once more, closing on the cell like a vise.

It might have been a day before the first meal arrived—maybe two— there was no way to tell, no mechanism to divide the time, to part one chill, invisible day from the next. There was silence, then bootheels on the stone beyond the door, a wooden trencher shoved beneath, bootheels retreating, then silence once more. Kaden felt sick, dizzy, but he forced himself to eat.

After each meal, he returned to the center of the floor, emptied himself, and entered the *vaniate.* If he could do nothing else, he could continue his training. After moving in and out of the trance scores of times, he changed position, lowering himself into a flat plank, toes and palms on the floor, body rigid, then reached for the emptiness once more. It eluded him, but he held the pose, held it until his shoulders shook and the muscles of his stomach rebelled, dumping him onto his face. He lay still for a few exhausted breaths, then, without moving, took hold of the trance. When he found it, he let it go, then raised himself into the plank once more. Tried, as his body trembled, to find that space beyond the body.

Each time the slot in the door opened, he spoke to the person beyond, always to no avail. Somewhere beyond the Dead Heart the great wheels of the world turned, seas sloshed in their basins, green shoots pushed up through the earth, men and women struggled, laughed, and died, and yet Kaden's cell might have been the throne room of the Blank God, a shrine to emptiness, blackness, and silence.

Then Tan came.

A rattle in the lock preceded the monk, then a lamp, the dim light so bright to Kaden's atrophied sight that it seemed someone had bored a hole in the nothingness. Bored a hole, or set it ablaze. When he could see, finally, he found his *umial* standing before him, Shin robe gone, exchanged for the boiled leather and sealskin of the Ishien.

"How long?" Kaden asked, voice rusted.

"Long enough," Tan replied. "I could not come sooner."

"What is happening?"

The monk shook his head. "Idiocy. Idiocy and fanaticism."

Kaden glanced at the closed door. "Are you here alone?"

"There are three guards in the corridor beyond. I persuaded them to stay behind. I said you would be more tractable if I came in alone."

"Tractable," Kaden said, the word bitter in his mouth.

"Matol wants to use you against Triste," he said. "He wants you to go to her alone. To see what she will reveal to you."

"Where is she now? Is she all right?"

"She is alive," Tan replied, as though that were the same thing. "After the last interrogation, the Ishien moved her here, to give her time to recuperate before they start again. That was five days ago."

Kaden shook his head helplessly. "She won't tell me anything more than she's told them."

The monk nodded tersely. "I agree. I am not here to do Matol's work."

"So," Kaden replied, studying the monk carefully, "why are you here?"

Tan glanced over his shoulder, then beckoned Kaden farther into the small cell. When his spoke, his voice was low as the scuff of leather over stone.

"It was a mistake to come to the Heart. The Ishien know nothing about the plot against your family. They have learned nothing from Triste. They follow a pointless path while the empire reels."

Kaden stared. "You've had word of the empire? Of my brother?"

"Nothing of Valyn, but Ishien returning through the *kenta* say that your sister has disappeared."

"Disappeared?" Kaden asked, suddenly sick.

"She may be dead. She may be imprisoned. The Ishien do not know, nor do they appear to care."

"And you do?" Kaden asked. After so long locked in the seamless darkness, the sudden wash of light and words threatened to overwhelm him. "I thought you were indifferent to politics."

"I am," Tan replied. "This goes beyond politics. The Csestriim have struck at the heart of Annur. I cannot fathom their reasons, but one thing is clear: they will use the chaos, they will exploit the disorder, and I will not give them that advantage. You need to return to Annur. You need to take your place on the Unhewn Throne."

Hope bloomed inside Kaden, flowered a moment before he crushed it out. He gestured to the slick stone walls, the weight of rock above their heads, to the massive iron door. "The Ishien seem to have other ideas."

"I am finished," Tan said, "with the ideas of the Ishien. They are not the order I left more than a decade ago."

"So . . . what? We just walk out?"

Tan shook his head. "You listen poorly. Three men wait beyond this door. They trust me little more than they do you. You will leave when they aren't watching you."

"How?"

The monk reached inside his jerkin, sliding free first an old, rusted key, then a short knife, the blade no longer than Kaden's finger. It wasn't a weapon—he could imagine someone using it to cut the heads off fish— but it looked sharp.

"Where did you get the key?"

"Perhaps you forget," Tan replied, "that I lived here a long time before I left for the mountains."

"All right," Kaden said, measuring his breathing, stilling the sudden excitement moving inside. "You leave, then I take the key—"

"Listen," Tan said, cutting him off, "before you talk." He waited, silent and unmoving, until Kaden nodded. Then he extended his arm. "Find my pulse."

Confused, Kaden reached out, taking the older monk's wrist in his hand. After a few moments he found the vein, then the steady beat of the blood pent up inside. The pulse was slower than his own, regular as the drip in the back of his cell, as though it had beaten out the same silent rhythm for months, for years.

"Match it," Tan said.

Kaden nodded once more, closed his eyes, then slowed his own heart, parsing each beat until it mapped perfectly onto the low, slow tidal thrum of his *umial*'s heart.

"Done," he said finally.

"You can hold it there?" Tan asked, pinning him with a stare.

Kaden hesitated. Shin training was filled with exercises of pulse and breathing. Once, when he had barely turned eleven, he counted every heartbeat for two days. Still, there were limits. "Not if I have to run."

"There will be no running, not if all goes as I plan."

"And what, exactly, is the plan?"

"At eighty-six thousand beats, use the key to leave your cell."

"Eighty-six thousand?"

"A day. You will leave the cell and walk to a small alcove just outside. Wait there until the guard comes, then step from the alcove and kill him."

Kaden's heart jumped for two beats, and with an effort he slowed it to the same steady pulse.

"How?" he asked.

"Just as you would kill a goat," Tan replied. "A single cut across the neck."

Kaden shook his head, fear and confusion clawing at his calm.

"The Ishien are warriors," he protested.

"The Ishien will expect you to be in your cell, unarmed and helpless. They know that I am dangerous, and so they have sent extra guards. You . . ." He shook his head, a single curt gesture. "They do not fear you."

"Then what?" Kaden asked, putting from his mind for the moment the vision of the knife clasped tight in his grip, of warm flesh folding back beneath the blade.

"The guard who brings your food is also the one who watches the door to this branch of the prison. When he is dead, the way will be clear. You will wait for another four thousand heartbeats, then go."

"Go *where?*"

Tan slid the knife along the inside of his own arm, raising a slender trail of blood. It was black in the lamplight, like pitch or shadow. He dipped a finger into the blood, then turned to the wall, sketching a map over the rough stone. As Kaden watched, the monk inked a tree of corridors and stairwells, the branches ramifying across the wall.

"Here," he said finally, pointing to a small room off a long, straight hall, "is your cell. And here"—another, much larger room—"the harbor."

"The harbor?" Kaden asked, shaking his head.

"The Ishien need supplies, and not everything can be transported through the *kenta*. There is an underground harbor carved by the sea. You will go there."

"Won't it be guarded?"

"At the mouth, yes," Tan replied. "But they will not expect anyone to be leaving. You will climb aboard the vessel tied up to the stone wharf, hide among the barrels, and wait. I will join you. When the tide turns, the ship will sail, and we will be gone."

"What about the body?" Kaden asked, sweat dampening his palms. "The guard I'm supposed to kill?"

"The guards' shifts do not match the tides," Tan replied. "By the time his relief arrives, we will have sailed. At the moment, there are no other boats moored in which they might follow."

Kaden frowned. It seemed a tenuous plan—sneaking through the halls of the Dead Heart, finding the hidden harbor, climbing aboard a ship and staying out of sight until they were well beyond reach of the fortress.

"What about the *kenta*?" Kaden asked. "Why don't we use that?"

"Do not be a fool. The Ishien guard the *kenta* chamber more carefully than any other place in the Heart." He gestured to the bloody map. "Do you have it?"

Kaden considered the lines and curves for a moment, the boxes and branches, then nodded. Tan scrubbed at the lines with the heel of his hand until nothing remained on the stone but a ruddy stain. When he was finished, he handed the knife and key to Kaden.

"What about the pause?" Kaden asked. "Why do I have to wait between killing the guard and moving to the harbor?"

"To allow the men changing shifts above to reach their posts. The Ishien follow predictable patterns. Waiting four thousand heartbeats will give you the best chance of finding the halls above empty."

Kaden digested this. "Doesn't sound like a sure thing."

"It is not. If you encounter anyone, keep your head down and your eyes hidden."

"What about Triste? Where is she? How do we get her out?"

"We do not."

Kaden took a long, slow breath. "They will kill her."

"Most likely."

"We can bring her with us. If the ship can hold two, it can hold three."

Tan shook his head. "No. The risk is too great. The girl is not what she seems, you witnessed enough to understand that, and you have not witnessed the tenth part of it. She is dangerous and she is unpredictable."

"What about trying to learn something from her?" Kaden demanded. "Something about the Csestriim? About the conspiracy?"

"Slow your heart," Tan growled. "The timing is crucial."

Kaden checked his pulse, slowed it a fraction, then continued, his voice little more than a hiss. "She has answers."

"She does," Tan replied, "but none she will reveal to us. Matol has pushed her hard, even harder than I would have." He shook his head. "She cannot help us."

Kaden started to protest, but Tan raised a hand.

"The corridors above should be empty if you keep to the timing, but as you have observed, *should be* is not *will be*. Alone, dressed in the Ishien garb, you have every chance of passing unremarked. With Triste in tow, you would be noticed instantly. The risk is too great and it offers scant reward."

He turned before Kaden could object further, opened the door and stepped through.

"You have the count?" he asked, without looking back over his shoulder.

Kaden listened to the slow tattoo inside his chest. "I have it," he replied.

"Do not make a mistake. There will not be another chance."

╋

It wasn't a mistake. Mistakes were errors of ignorance or neglect, ineptitude or poor planning. Mistakes were miscalculations or errors in judgment. This was something else altogether, something worse.

More like a fully flowered act of madness, Kaden thought as he felt his way down the long corridor, knife held before him as though it could keep back the limitless dark.

He had counted off ten thousand heartbeats, forcing himself to silence and stillness in the center of his cell, before moving. As Tan had promised, the key turned in the lock, though the steel protested with a scream that raised the hairs on the back of his neck. By the vague light in his eyes, he could make out the outlines of the wall, the shallow standing pools. He moved slowly, carefully, but the quieter he forced himself to be, the more the halls around him seemed to stir. Air lisped uneasily through the passages, drafts rasping over the uneven stone. The plinking of water seemed to come from everywhere at once. Behind it, or below it, a sound that might have been the wash of waves and tides thrummed through the rock, so low it was impossible to be sure if the sound was real or only in his mind.

The doors lining the hall were heavy wood banded with iron, some locked, some hanging open, all of them identical—wood and iron, wood and iron.

Take him below, Matol had snarled. *Lock him up with the Csestriim.*

Which meant Kiel was locked up somewhere along the endless corridor. Kiel, who knew a way out. Perhaps it was folly, stupidity, to insist on trying to see Triste freed, but of all Annur's uncounted millions, she was the only one in the Dead Heart, the only one he could help. As Tan claimed, she was dangerous—that much was clear—but she had helped Kaden, and he would be ill-fit to govern an empire if his first act was to abandon her to the unending torture of the Ishien. If Kiel was here, if he knew another way out, maybe he could free Triste, too.

After a hundred paces or so, Kaden came to a different sort of door. The original framing had been chiseled away, the banded wood replaced with a great slab of steel hung on hinges as thick as Kaden's wrists. Five wide steel bars set into metal brackets held the thing shut—enough weight to pen an enraged bull. Dripping salt water had left long, weeping stains on the metal, gnawing the surface to pits and long flakes of rust, and though the door itself looked ready to crumble, when Kaden pushed a tentative hand against it, he might have pressed on the stone wall itself. There was no telling how thick the metal was, but clearly the rust had done nothing to compromise its strength.

He took a long, slow breath, turning his focus from the hallway to his own mind. Fear clung there, spiked and recalcitrant as a mountain burr lodged in the cloth of a new robe, though whether that fear was for Matol and Ishien, who could come looking for him at any moment, or for the man beyond the door, Kaden couldn't say. He worked at the emotion, prying it looser and looser with each breath. He needed clarity when he heard what the prisoner had to say. He needed calm.

Here is the floor, he told himself, feeling the rough stone, cold and slick beneath his bare soles.

Here is the light from my eyes.

The future held perils, but he did not live in the future.

Here is the latch, he said, moving the metal catch to open the small, barred window set into the steel door. *Here is the window into the darkness.*

Through the narrow open slot, he heard the rustle of cloth against cloth, then a wet, unhealthy cough, the noise growing closer as the prisoner approached.

"Another visit?"

Kaden heard the voice first, the same spare articulation he remembered from his encounter with Kiel days earlier. Then the man's begrimed face appeared in the narrow slot, squinting as his eyes moved from utter darkness to the meager light of Kaden's own eyes. Kiel glanced at him, then past, into the hallway beyond.

"Where are Rampuri and Ekhard?"

Kaden shook his head. "I am alone."

"Good," Kiel murmured after a moment. "You understood. You trusted me."

"No," Kaden cut in. "I do not trust you."

Kiel paused. "And yet you are here. . . ."

"Because I was taught to look before judging. To listen."

The prisoner made a sound that Kaden recognized, after a moment, as a chuckle. "I'm glad to learn that the Shin are still so rigorous. And Scial Nin? Is he still the abbot?"

"Scial Nin . . ." Kaden began, then paused. The fact that Kaden needed him, that they shared the same foe, didn't make the Csestriim any less dangerous. Kaden needed answers to his questions, not to spend time spinning yarns about a life long left behind.

"You know a way out?" Kaden asked.

Kiel nodded.

"How? Where?"

The Csestriim shook his head slowly. "Opening this door would be a generous gesture."

"I'm not here to be generous," Kaden said.

"Then perhaps you should not be here at all," the man said. "The Malkeenians I knew understood the value of generosity. Of trust. Of mutual support."

Kaden stared, dazed. "What Malkeenians?" He forced his heart to keep the same steady time, his lungs to rise and fall in deep, measured breaths.

"Your father, for one."

Kaden shook his head. "Tan told me you would lie."

Kiel raised an eyebrow. "As with all zealots, Rampuri Tan's zeal distorts his vision of the world. I have given him no reason to distrust me."

"I've *seen* the reason," Kaden said. "I've been to Assare, to the orphanage where the bones are piled up like wood."

"Ah, Assare," Kiel said, blowing out a long, slow breath. "What a mistake that was."

"A *mistake*?" Kaden asked. "You murdered hundreds of children, an entire city of people, and it was a mistake?"

"I was not there," Kiel replied, "but yes, I call it a mistake. How would you term it?"

Kaden searched for the word. "A massacre." He shook his head. "An abomination."

"Abomination," Kiel said slowly, as though tasting the sounds. "It seems as though Scial Nin and his monks did not succeed with you. Not completely. Although," he said, spreading his hands, "you passed the *kenta* to come here."

Kaden nodded, realizing only as he did so that the statement was a trap, a trick. Kiel hadn't known how he arrived until Kaden himself nodded. Irritation pricked at him like a bluethorn.

"You said you knew my father," Kaden said, trying to return the conversation to safer ground.

The Csestriim nodded. "We were . . . not friends, but something analogous."

"Prove it."

Kiel considered him awhile. "That will be difficult. You've been with the Shin since you were a child."

"I remember him well enough," Kaden said, suddenly resentful of the idea that this inhuman creature claimed to know Sanlitun better than he had himself.

"All right then," Kiel said. "Do you remember what he used to say about ruling his empire? *The strongest leader is the one who does least.*"

Kaden had heard his father voice that idea or something similar dozens of times, but, after a moment, he shook his head. "All that shows is that you were in the Dawn Palace. Or that you knew someone who knew someone in the Dawn Palace."

Kiel cocked his head to the side. "Fair enough. How about the formation that he kept on the *ko* board in his study whenever he wasn't playing. The Fool's Fortress."

Kaden's mind filled with the tiny cluster of stones.

"He kept it there," Kiel went on, "to remind him of the weakness built into any perception of strength, to remind him that confidence sows the seeds of its own destruction."

"I never heard him say that," Kaden said.

"You never heard him say a lot of things," Kiel replied. "You couldn't have been more than ten when he sent you away."

"It still doesn't prove anything, doesn't prove that he knew you, that he trusted you."

For a long time the prisoner remained silent, staring out through the bars of the cage at a life Kaden could neither see nor comprehend. Finally, he focused on Kaden once more, a smile tugging the corners of his mouth.

"Your leg," he said, "there is a small mark shaped like a crescent moon on the inside of your right thigh."

Kaden resisted the urge to reach down and touch the small, dark spot. "How do you know that?"

"I was there," the prisoner replied. "At your birth. You burst from between your mother's thighs with plenty of vigor, but for a long time you were silent—you didn't cry, didn't scream, just stared at the world around you with those burning eyes." He shook his head at the memory. "The midwives were terrified that you were going to die, but your father calmed them. 'This child understands the road he must travel. He is already practicing silence.' And, in time, you began to cry in the way of all human children."

Kaden stared, dumbfounded. He had never heard the story, not from his parents or his sister. Certainly not from the Shin. He had no way of knowing if it were true, but he did bear the crescent mark on his thigh. All his life it had been there.

"Why were you at the birth?"

"As historian," Kiel replied. "It is what I do, what I am for. It is how I came to know your father in the first place."

Kaden tried to make sense of the claim. All he had heard of the Csestriim involved war and slaughter, with a few vague references to their cities. "You were a historian?" he asked. "A Csestriim historian?"

Kiel nodded. "Your language is imprecise, but I believe you would say *The* Historian. I chronicled my people's age-long war with the Nevariim, then the war with your kind. I was there for the reign of the Atmani—both the brilliant beginning and the tragic end. And I've been there for the centuries during which your own family has ruled."

For a while Kaden just stared, then shook his head. "Still not good enough. There must have been half a dozen people at my birth."

"There were eight," Kiel said.

"Any one of them could have spread the story of the mark on my leg."

The prisoner shook his head quietly. "At some point, Kaden, you must trust. It is this ability that the Ishien have lost. You must have realized already that they are nothing like the monks among whom you were raised. They found a different path to the blankness, one that has broken them. We showed them how, of course, inadvertently, when this was still a prison and we were still testing your people. We showed them how, but they perfected the technique."

Kaden's memory filled with Trant's account, the tale of men gouging eyes, cutting off fingers, ripping out teeth, all in the awful cold and darkness, all to achieve their twisted version of the *vaniate*. This was the place to which he had dragged Triste. The horror of it settled on him like ice while a distant part of his mind, one untouched by either Kiel or the Ishien, continued to count, measuring out the heartbeats, cataloging them, keeping the dark passage of time.

"Your way out," Kaden said. "Can we take Triste?"

Kiel hesitated, then nodded. "If you can break her free. And me."

Kaden took a deep breath and ordered his thoughts while the Csestriim watched, silent, through the thin slot in the door.

"And how do I do that?" Kaden asked finally.

"The guard has the key. You start by killing him."

20

The heavy cloud shoved up out of the south, blackening the sky over the lake, hazing the horizon. A few small, broad-beamed lake boats raced in front of it, heeled over, sails filled with the wind, canvas bright with the lingering light. Fishermen, probably, trying to get back to port before the rain. Trying and failing. One by one, the storm overtook them.

Adare watched it from the deck of the crumbling building, the remnants of a once-proud palace, the cellar of which housed Lehav's war room. She stood in the full light of the sun, watching the storm come on like a wall, blackening the waves, stippling the dark waters. The morning sun shone on her face and shoulders, so warm she felt like she was looking at the painting of a storm, distant wind and fury a matter of clever brushstrokes and perspective. As she stared, though, it drew closer, closer, and then, in a moment, it was upon her, raindrops heavy as coins beating against her scalp, her shoulders, hammering the slate roof behind her. The air went limp and sodden. A wool blanket of muggy cloud blotted out the sun.

It drenched her clothes, whipped Adare's sodden hair against her cheeks, but the storm was still easier to face than what waited inside. She watched the lightning lance down, forking out in jagged inverted trunks to strike the waves, wondering for the hundredth time if there was a way out. Cloth clung to her skin. She started to shiver. If there was a way to avoid the killing to come, she couldn't see it.

They might be guilty, she told herself, trying out the tired line once more. *They might be in league with il Tornja.* The words, words she'd been repeating all night long like a fragment of prayer, failed to convince. With a sick slosh in her stomach, she turned from the roiling darkness of the storm to the still, vacant darkness inside the building.

Her captured Aedolians were in the same building, although the Sons of Flame had them chained and locked in a deep basement. For two days, Adare had been forbidden to speak with them. She had railed against the restriction, but the horrible secret truth was that beneath the fury and indignation, she was relieved at the enforced separation. If she wasn't allowed to see the Aedolians, she wouldn't have to witness her own deceit in their eyes, wouldn't have to tell them what her allegiance with the Sons of Flame had cost. Wouldn't have to tell them that they would be the ones to pay. In the end, however, her own objections caught up with her. Just that morning, Lehav had agreed to let her see the two men. Adare wanted to vomit.

The commander of the Sons of Flame met her on the rain-soaked balcony, glanced out at the storm, then gestured her inside.

"It's time," he said, when she stepped through the door. "Ivar will show you to their cell."

She nodded, voiceless.

Lehav considered her for a moment. "A piece of advice," he said finally.

Adare nodded uncertainly. She was shivering uncontrollably, the water from her soaked robes puddling on the floor.

"The less you talk," Lehav said, "the easier it will be for everyone."

"I owe them . . ."

"What?" He raised an eyebrow. "An explanation?"

"Yes."

"You can explain a lot of things to a man. His own death is not one of them."

✝

Each Aedolian was wrapped in enough chain to hold a small bull, bound at the ankles, wrists, and throat, then locked to iron rings set into the stone. They looked as though they hadn't slept or changed clothes since the day Adare fled. Their long traveling cloaks, usually so immaculate, had turned brown with kicked-up dust and mud. Weeks of hard travel had scraped away any spare flesh, leaving their cheeks hollow, eyes sunken in their sockets. Birch's golden mane had gone brown and stringy, and Fulton must have lost twenty pounds. The room stank of spoiled food and rot. A small puddle that might have been groundwater or urine had collected in a lower corner of the chamber.

Birch blinked at the sudden light, then twisted against his chains to get a better look.

He managed an awkward nod.

"My lady," he said after a moment, voice a weak rasp. "The yellow robe suits you. Brings out your eyes."

And all at once, the grief and confusion that had stalked her for days on silent feet took her by the throat. She stood helplessly as the door swung shut behind her, staring at the two men who had watched over her since she was a child, horrified by what Lehav had done to them. *No,* a grim voice reminded her, *what* you *did to them.* Whatever role the Sons of Flame had played, it was Adare herself that had brought the two men to Olon. Tears mixed with rain on her cheeks.

"My lady," Fulton began, then broke off with a hacking cough, body shuddering. When the fit passed, he spat onto the floor: phlegm or blood, it was hard to tell in the lamplight. "Pardon, my lady," he said, "but just what in the sweet name of Intarra is going on?"

She had hoped, even prayed—though she was not given to prayer— that the two Aedolians were in league with il Tornja; it would be so much easier to see traitors fed to the flames. Facing them, however, the notion seemed ludicrous, petty, stupid. They weren't the *kenarang*'s men, they were *her* men. Her guards. A part of her had known that even when she fled from them in the plaza by the Basin.

"You're not part of it," she said, shaking her head hopelessly, voice little more than a whisper.

"Part of *what,* my lady?" Fulton demanded. "Are you in danger?"

It all spilled out then, il Tornja's treachery, Adare's terrified flight, her need for an alliance with the Sons of Light. She crossed to them as she spoke, tugging futilely at the chains in an effort to make them more comfortable.

"You should have told us," Fulton said, when it was all finished, shaking his head.

"I know," Adare said, slumping to the ground, the life vanished from her legs. "I know. I wasn't sure who to trust."

"Although," Birch said, raising his eyebrows weakly, "I've always wanted to visit Olon in the summer."

"What now?" Fulton asked.

Adare trembled. The truth was a rusted dagger, but she owed them the truth. "Lehav, Ameredad—it's the same guy—he wants you dead. Justice for the Sons you killed trying to rescue me."

Fulton's lips tightened, but he didn't speak.

"Well, for a religious man, that's just downright inhospitable," Birch said. The joke was typical, but the words came out weak, as though rusted, corroded.

"I've tried to get him to relent," Adare said, speaking fast, trying to drown out the guilt and shame with the sound of her own voice, "but he won't. His people, the Sons of Flame and all the rest, they want you burned, and he won't refuse them." She fell silent. The words were useless. Worse than useless. Insulting.

"Without the Sons, I've got nothing. Il Tornja wins. Even if I refused Lehav—"

"No," Fulton said, voice still as a stone. "You will not refuse him."

"Ah, fuck," Birch said, glancing away.

"This is what we are *for,* Alin," the older guardsman said, turning to his companion. Adare had never heard anyone use Birch's first name. She hadn't even known it herself. "Our lives for hers. If she refuses this, there's no saying what the zealots will do to her."

"There's no saying what the zealots will do if she *agrees,*" Birch pointed out. "We can't save her if we're *dead.*"

"That is a risk that the princess will have to assess for herself. Our duty is to serve."

"I thought service meant fighting," Birch protested, but the anger had gone out of him. Resignation thinned his voice.

"Sometimes, Alin," Fulton replied, nodding. "And sometimes it means dying."

Adare had Intarra's irises, but the guardsman's gaze burned. Adare could argue, fight to save them both, but she knew already that she was not going to argue. She had known, even as she spoke of confronting Lehav, that Fulton would refuse her offer, known that his duty would weigh heavier in the scales than her guilt, known that her suggestion was empty as air even as she spoke it. She had watched it all coming from a long way off, watched it just as she'd watched the black storm move in. She'd seen it all coming except for the sick pit of self-hatred that gaped inside her, that ate at her guts, that would never, ever heal.

✝

For just a moment, the sight of the Everburning Well distracted Adare from the killing that had to happen there.

Over the last few nights of the pilgrimage she had stared at the column of light bisecting the horizon, white and pale as a thousand moons, blotting out the meager pinpricks of the stars to either side. For sixteen centuries, the Everburning Well had been a beacon for the faithful and a warning to unbelievers both, an eternal symbol of Olon's sanctity, the origin of the faith, and the reason Annur's pilgrims had chosen this crumbling city over a dozen others.

Despite Adare's flaming irises and the alleged ancestry of her own family, she had always been skeptical of the gods. Divine favor was too easy to claim, too difficult to disprove. Anything could be the work of the gods—a fallen sparrow, an unexpected flood, a single tree flowering earlier or later than the rest. The stories were all too old, the evidence too scant.

It had to be admitted, though, that the Everburning Well was no fallen sparrow. It was an actual hole in the earth, maybe a dozen feet across, and the light gushing forth from it, light so bright that to stare directly into the depth for any length of time would blind the observer, could not be denied. Even the surrounding stone bent to the brute fact of the Well, having sagged and crumbled in a circular crater, as though the earth itself were trying to funnel all that came near into that astounding brightness. Adare had heard tales of Intarra's devout hurling themselves in, hoping to unite with her prophet. There were the other stories, too, of men and women shoved into the blazing depths as punishment for their heresies.

Even from just inside the round wall ringing the site, with the Well still a good thirty paces off, Adare had to squint, half raising a hand to block the heat radiating from the column of light. Then, realizing how such a gesture might look to the assembled mob, she lowered the hand and straightened her back, her neck, forcing herself to stare directly into the brilliance. Driving rain streaked through the light, a thousand falling stars. The stabbing lightning over the water looked wan, weak, beside that inexorable radiance.

According to the tales, the light had burned day and night for over a thousand years, fueled by the piety of Intarra's first prophet. There were variations to the myth, but all agreed on the basic facts. When a virgin named Maayala appeared in the city—then the capital of an independent Kresh—Odam the Blind had her seized for peddling a new faith. The Kreshkan kings, Odam very much among them, worshipped Achiet—their name for the lord of war—while Maayala insisted on the primacy of the Lady of Light, arguing on the streets and in private homes that all light, that of the hearth, of the stars, of the sun, was one, and that one given by Intarra. She claimed that Intarra's light animated all human souls, giving blood its heat, bodies their warmth. According to Maayala, mortals need not fear death, since the dissolution of the body frees the fragment of the divine hidden within, allowing it to join with the greater lights of earth and the heavens. Maayala absolved the Kreshkans of their martial duty, claiming that everyone, even the weak, even the crippled, so long as their skin remained warm to the touch, carried the divine spark inside. No fighting was necessary. No heroic feats in battle.

Odam declared the woman a liar, a heretic, and an impostor. He had her dragged to the courtyard of his fortress, tied to a stake, and, in mockery of her unflagging worship of light, he had her burned.

"If the Lady of Light loves her," he famously said, "the Lady of Light can take her."

And take her Intarra did.

Maayala burned, fitfully at first, with a great deal of smoke, then more readily as the fire below her truly caught. Her flesh turned to flame and that flame burned brighter and still brighter, red, then yellow, then purest white. The fire consumed the wood, then the stake itself, and yet Maayala still stood, incandescent, bright as the noonday sun, so bright that Odam and his soldiers were forced to look away, and when they looked away, they realized the flagstones of the courtyard were glowing, too, first red, then yellow, then white, burning, melting to slag, the entire ground sagging around Maayala the Undarkened as she bored into the earth, her heat and light creating the Everburning Well.

It destroyed Odam's fortress, and, according to the chronicles, nearly destroyed Odam himself. The king barely managed to escape through a sally port as his walls folded inward, malleable as softened butter. The rock didn't cool for a month, and when it did, the terrified and curious began to come, tentatively, to stare at the amphitheater of melted rock, at the column of light issuing from the Well at its center. Odam himself walked to the very edge of the pit as penance for his sin, staring down into the light until it blinded him.

"Ill-served I have been by these eyes," he said when he returned. "Without them I can see at last."

Adare envied the long-dead king his blindness and his clarity both.

She could make out little more than shapes through the torrential rain, but she could see enough to know that the walls around the Well were filled to bursting. The Sons of Flame stood closest, but the faithful of Olon pressed up behind their ranks, faces fearfully bright but smeared by the rain to a nightmare of open mouths and eager eyes, all fixed on her, waiting for the promised justice. A justice that was starting to look terrifyingly like sacrifice.

Fulton and Birch were bound at the wrist but able to walk. Behind them half a dozen grim-faced Sons with long spears stood at attention. Before the prisoners, a cleared pathway ran straight into the Everburning Well.

"When the march begins," Lehav said to the two men, "I suggest you move. One way or the other, you will be fed to the flame. Better not to have a spear in your side when you die."

"We will walk," Fulton said, fixing the man with his sunken-eyed stare, "without being prodded like pigs."

Lehav shrugged. "Bold words are easy at this distance. You might feel more reluctant as you approach the Well."

"With this rain?" Birch quipped. He seemed to have passed through his anger and reluctance and emerged once more into his customary jocularity. "I'll *jump* in your 'Kent-kissing hole just to dry off."

The crowd was growing restive, a few of the bolder members hurling insults into the driving rain. Thunder rumbled just overhead, drowning out the voices while the flash illuminated faces twisted with fury.

"It is time," Lehav said, gesturing.

"Let's get this over with," Fulton growled. "I grow tired of listening to the bleating of these sheep."

Get it over with. As though he were talking about a tedious imperial audience rather than his own life. Adare nodded, trying to steady herself, trying to see straight in the rain.

"Wait," she said, raising her voice just high enough that they could hear over the rain. "I'm sorry."

Worse than useless, those words, a threadbare cloak to cover her own horror.

"Do one thing for me," Fulton said.

Adare nodded eagerly, pathetically. Even at this distance she could feel the heat from the Well. Her robes were steaming, her hair, her hands. The crowd had taken up some sort of martial hymn. "Anything," she said.

"Win," he replied grimly.

"I'll second that," said Birch.

Adare stifled a sob. She tried to speak, but found her throat closed as a fist.

Sweet Intarra, she prayed, *forgive me. Forgive me. Forgive me.*

Fulton watched her for three or four heartbeats, until Birch nudged him with his elbow.

"Come on, old man," he said, face slick with mingled rain and sweat. "You getting tired right here at the end?"

Forgive me, Intarra. Forgive me.

And then the two men, the guards who had watched her door since she was a child, who had flanked her when she left the palace and stood behind her chair at state dinners, who brought her soup when she was ill, and listened to her complain about her brothers, her parents, the two men who, in some ways, knew her better than anyone alive, began their march toward the flame. Despite the heat of the Well and the fury of the crowd, they held their heads high, and even when the mob started hurling stones and dung, they refused to flinch.

Forgive me, Intarra, Adare begged, but the whole miserable bit of theater was not Intarra's idea, not Intarra's fault, and when the two soldiers had marched into their grave, it would not be Intarra who bore the awful weight in her chest day in and day out. It was all well and good to pray to the goddess, but Adare was the one with the hands, with the voice, and suddenly she realized she was screaming, lurching forward toward the Sons of Flame. With clumsy hands, she seized a spear from the nearest of the soldiers, the long shaft heavy and wet, unwieldy in her grip.

"No!" she bellowed, charging down the open path in the wake of the Aedolians. It was a foolish gesture, beyond foolish. She couldn't save the men, and the simple act of defiance would see her burned as well, but, suddenly, it didn't matter. She would die here, in the miserable fucking miracle of a well, but she would not be part of the murder of these men who had watched over her so long.

It's on you now, Kaden, she thought grimly, brandishing the steel pointlessly above her head. *On you, Valyn. And as for you, Intarra, you can fuck yourself, you miserable bitch.*

And then, as if in response, Intarra spoke back.

Blinding light. Perfect black. Ringing like a million mouths, screaming, singing. Body instantly and utterly gone. Gone the rain. Gone the mob.

Gone her own mind and will. Gone everything but a single voice, Fulton's and then not Fulton's, deeper, higher, fuller, broader, broad as the wide sky, broad as the stars, a woman's voice but greater than any woman, as great as creation itself, uttering a single, ungainsayable syllable: *Win*.

21

Eight.

Or nine.

Valyn had lost track of how many times he, Pyrre, and his Wing tried to escape during the endless ride west.

Which made them zero for eight.

Or zero for nine.

In the last attempt, Valyn had dislocated his left shoulder in order to win free of his restraints, Pyrre had strangled two Urghul with her belt, and the rest of the Wing managed to steal half a dozen horses. Valyn had refused to include Balendin in the planning, but the leach was tied up right next to the rest of them, and when the time came to fight, he managed to rip out the throat of a *ksaabe* with his teeth and kick another one half to death. A reminder, if Valyn needed a reminder, that even drugged, even half starved, the leach was as dangerous as the rest of them. Not that it mattered.

There were thousands of Urghul, more joining the group every day. Even if the Kettral managed to break out of the constantly moving horde, which they hadn't, there was nowhere to run but empty steppe. It was a bleak situation, no doubt, and their defiance earned them little more than busted faces and bruised ribs, but it was fight or die, and while Valyn had no illusions about the odds, he didn't intend to be led to his slaughter like a sheep. When the ninth attempt to break free failed, he was already plotting the tenth.

Huutsuu, however, had other ideas. The woman rode up, surveyed the carnage, barked a few orders, and in a matter of moments the prisoners were separated, each dragged off by his or her own *taabe* or *ksaabe*. Old knots were retied and new restraints added at the elbows and knees, which meant an end to all walking and stretching. From that moment on, numbness alternated with screaming pain in Valyn's legs and shoulders. He had to beg his *taabe* to pull down his pants whenever he needed to take a shit.

The ensuing days proved a repetitive itinerary of agony and endurance: struggling not to cry out each morning in the predawn dark as his nameless captor kicked him awake; refusing to wince as he was lashed across the back of the horse, tight cords biting into his bloody wrists and raw ankles; shivering in the icy rain or sweating beneath a brutal sun while the horse's relentless gait bruised his ribs and battered the organs beneath; tucking his chin and holding his tongue whenever he was whipped across the back or shoulders; ignoring the famished ache that seemed to be boring a hole through his stomach. . . . And the days were the fucking good part. Every night, bound hand and foot and tethered to a stake, he shivered on the cold, broken earth, watching the flames of the surrounding campfires lap at the sky, listening to the strange cadences of chanting and song.

Valyn had his own chant and his own fire. His fire was the crackling rage inside him, a heat he fed with his hopes and vows, his shame and resolve, stoking it until it seared, even on the coldest nights. His chant was simple: *Don't quit. Don't quit, you fuck. Don't ever quit.* He managed to break his captor's nose one morning; to bite off a good portion of thumb on another, but, lashed tight as he was, there was no way to follow up the small victories, and each petty revolt ended with him curled on the ground, kicks and punches raining down. The struggle was pointless, but it was all he had, so he kept at it, looking for the openings, the little chances when he could get in his useless licks.

In between, the Urghul set an astounding pace, hammering westward from well before dawn until hours past dark, stopping only to switch horses, an excruciating process during which Valyn was untied, shoved to the ground, then, before he could do anything to stretch his legs, hurled onto another horse and lashed down once more. He tried to keep track of the days. There'd been at least ten when he was still with his Wing, and probably double that since they were separated. He had no idea where they were going, but there couldn't be much steppe left.

Occasionally—when they crested a hill or rode along a ridgeline—he caught a glimpse of the entire Urghul strength. Each time, the sight of it staggered him like a fist to the face. The Eyrie trainers had described tribes of fifty or a hundred, little more than extended families, really, nothing like the group in which he rode. There must have been tens, maybe hundreds of thousands, the herd of horses stretching out over the steppe as far as he could see. There was no column, no order of march, just a pounding, thundering mass of horseflesh and riders flowing over the hills like a shifting blanket. No one set up tents, not anymore—the Urghul were in too much of a rush—and some nights, when Valyn could see out over the black hills, he felt as though he were adrift on the night sea, that each of the campfires was a star reflected in the chilly water, that, bound hand and foot as he was, he might sink beneath the surface and drown.

He tried to gauge numbers, to count fires or horses, but there was no way to keep track. Not that it mattered. Even when he was lashed to the horse's back, even when he could see nothing but clods of dirt, sweaty flanks, and streaming tails, he could hear the sound clearly enough, a thunder louder and deeper than thunder, the very ground trembling with the Urghul passage. It was not a *taamu* that he rode with, not a tribe, but a whole people.

Old Fleck back on the Islands had insisted that the Urghul could manage fifty miles a day, riding hard. The figure had always struck Valyn as inflated, but he was starting to understand how it could be possible. The riders ate on their horses, pissed from their horses, slipped a knee through the crude girths and slept on their horses when necessary, yellow-white hair streaming behind them. Valyn had even seen some of the younger *taabe* and *ksaabe* leaping from the back of one cantering beast to another, as though the ground itself were anathema. At one point he caught sight of an enormous herd of bison darkening the plains to the north. The nearest beasts swung their stupid, noble heads ponderously toward the passing horses, and a few score riders peeled off, lances held high, voices eager in the morning air. The rest of the mass continued west, hammering relentlessly across the steppe.

Just when he thought they would never stop, they did. One moment he was jolting along, rehearsing yet another possible escape attempt, the next his horse slowed to a walk. He half raised his head, realizing they were on the outskirts of an enormous camp, the *api* packed as closely as trees in a forest. His *taabe* led the horses through the tents, pausing occasionally to trade words with the other Urghul, to banter or ask a question. People seemed curious about the prisoner tied up and slung across the horse, and more than once Valyn felt his ribs prodded by the butt of a spear.

When they finally stopped, he was cut free with the same lack of ceremony as always. Legs numb, arms numb, shoulders screaming in their sockets, he rose slowly to his knees, then staggered to his feet. When he finally raised his head, he stared.

On every hill in every direction, the Urghul were shouting to one another as they hobbled horses and unloaded the poles and hides for their *api*. This was new. Valyn spat a bolus of blood, crouched, then stood once more, trying to work some feeling back into dead legs. He expected his *taabe* to punch him in the gut or sweep his legs with a contemptuous kick. Instead, the youth seized him by the hair and dragged him through the throng of people and horses. Valyn staggered behind, refusing to fall, trying to see through the haze of his exhaustion and pain, to understand what was happening. For weeks he'd been waiting for a break in the routine, a new sort of opportunity, and now it had come.

When they'd traversed half of the unfolding camp, the *taabe* finally shoved him to the earth with a grunt, kicked him in the head one final time, then turned and stalked off without a word. Valyn hauled himself to his knees to find Huutsuu leaning on a long lance, head cocked to one side, blue eyes fixed on him. She smiled a slow, vulpine smile.

"Still alive," she observed.

Valyn nodded silently.

She lowered the lance in a fluid motion, leveling the shining tip at his midsection. With a casual motion she prodded lightly at his ribs, his shoulders, his stomach, his crotch, drawing blood with each contact, lifting his blacks from his emaciated frame.

"We have Hardened you," she said. "Kwihna will be pleased."

"Kwihna can fuck himself," Valyn replied wearily. "Where's my Wing?"

"They, also, we have Hardened."

Valyn debated seizing the lance as it loitered around his chest, using it to pull the woman off-balance, then wrapping his bound hands around her throat. Huutsuu was fast—he remembered that from the first night in the rain—but he was faster. Or he had been, before spending the better part of a month lashed to a horse. Now, he wasn't sure. He'd managed to stand, but his legs wavered beneath him and his fingers felt weak and stupid when he tried to clench them into fists. His belly might have been made of mud. The weakness and helplessness were infuriating—years of training scrubbed out in a few weeks—but they were real. He'd managed to stay alive this long. Little point in getting himself skewered now. Besides, Huutsuu had said the others were hardened. Hardened wasn't killed.

"Where are they?" he demanded.

She nodded past his shoulder, and he turned to find a young *ksaabe* prodding Gwenna forward, a bared knife at her back. For the first time in what felt like years, Valyn smiled. Gwenna was filthy and battered. Both eyes were swollen half closed, the sockets fading from purple to brown, one cheek crusted with blood. She was battered but awake. She was walking. Valyn glanced at the *ksaabe* behind her, and his smile widened. The Urghul woman had a fresh bite mark on her own cheek, a gash closing above her eye, and fury in her eyes. When they reached Valyn, she smacked Gwenna across the head with the pommel of her knife, then kicked her legs out from beneath her. Gwenna twisted as she hit the ground, lashing out with her own foot, but the *ksaabe* danced back, spit in her face, then snapped something angry at Huutsuu.

"I am going to slaughter that little Urghul bitch," Gwenna snarled, rolling to her stomach, then shoving herself to her knees. "I'm going to kill her, then eat her."

"Looks like you already made some headway," Valyn observed.

Huutsuu just laughed and flicked a dismissive hand at the younger warrior.

"You look like shit," Gwenna said, turning her attention to Valyn with a frown.

"You're no princess," Valyn replied. "You seen any of the others?"

The others, as it turned out, were in similar condition—beaten, battered, but alive. One by one they appeared out of the turmoil, each escorted by an Urghul. Talal seemed the most hale, which made sense—he would have offered the fewest insults. Laith's captor, on the other hand, had leashed him with a length of rawhide, the cord leaving angry welts ringing his neck. Despite his wounds, the flier still managed a fierce grin.

"This is my liaison, Amaaru," he said, gesturing to the iron-jawed *taabe* behind him. He turned to the warrior. "Am I pronouncing your name correctly?" The youth took a swing, but Laith ducked. "He tells me that his name means 'Horse Anus' in the proud tongue of his people, and he has been a most gracious host."

Annick showed up with a rough sack over her head, which spoke eloquently to her level of resistance, but Pyrre, evidently, had rattled the Urghul worse than any of them. She arrived last, arms lashed to her sides, preventing all movement save the slightest twitching of her fingertips. Instead of one guard, she had four, two men, two women, all older than those assigned to Valyn and his Wing, ringing her with daggers drawn.

"All right," Laith said, raising an eyebrow at the woman. "It galls me to say this, but clearly you win."

"What did you do to earn them?" Valyn asked, gesturing to the warriors.

She tried to shrug, but her bonds truncated the gesture. "I introduced a number of our newfound friends to the god."

"Which god is that?" Valyn asked. "I've had about enough of Kwihna."

Pyrre's face hardened. "So has Ananshael."

"Five," Huutsuu interjected with something that might have been admiration. "Three *taabe,* two *ksaabe.* She killed five."

"It's not as though you're going to run out," Laith said, nodding to the thousands of Urghul milling around them.

"And yet, one must draw a line somewhere," Huutsuu replied, eyeing Pyrre. "Five," she said again, shaking her head. "I could grow to like this woman."

"And you haven't seen the half of my talents," the Skullsworn replied, raising a coquettish eyebrow. "You've been wasting your time dallying with these . . . boys of yours."

Huutsuu laughed, a rich, full sound. "If I took you to my *api,* I might never come out."

"You could tie me," Pyrre suggested.

"Tying you has failed several times already."

"Enough of this horseshit," Valyn cut in. Guilt throbbed in his bones, guilt for allowing his Wing to be captured on his watch, for failing to do anything to break them free, and meanwhile Huutsuu and Pyrre were trading smiles and innuendo as though they were browsing the Lowmarket on a lazy summer afternoon. The Skullsworn, for all her sleek urbanity, was no better than the Urghul savages. They were blood-drunk killers, all of them.

"Pyrre, let me handle this," he continued. "Why are we stopping? Where are we?"

Pyrre frowned at Huutsuu apologetically. "Valyn forgets from time to time that I am not a part of his Wing. He takes his work very seriously."

"*I* haven't forgotten that you're not on the Wing," Gwenna said, "and if you don't stop talking, I will stop you."

Huutsuu looked from Pyrre to Gwenna, considered the amused quirk of the Skullsworn's lip, then the open fury in Gwenna's eyes. "This," she said, shaking her head, "seems unlikely."

Before Valyn could cut in, two more Urghul shoved their way out of the crowd, dragging Balendin between them. The leach didn't resist, not even when they tossed him to the ground at Huutsuu's feet, but Valyn saw the way the *taabe* watched him, eyes wary, almost frightened.

"Ah. Valyn," the leach said, elbowing his way to his knees. "I've missed your playful banter each evening." The words were light, but Balendin smelled weary, wary.

"I'm glad the Urghul didn't kill you," Valyn replied.

Balendin raised an eyebrow. "Reconsidering my offer of cooperation?"

"Not at all. It's just that I'm planning to put the blade in you myself."

"An easy thing to say when there are no blades around."

"Just wait," Valyn replied. "Just wait."

Huutsuu was shaking her head. "Civilized people. This is how you speak to one another?"

Valyn turned back to the woman. "Where are we?" he asked again. "What is this?"

The Urghul woman gazed over the encampment, as though considering the question herself. Thousands of fires smudged the sky with their smoke. Valyn could smell burning dung and burning meat, horse shit and human, turned-up earth and wet hides. Thousands of voices murmured in his ears, so many he could never hope to untangle them. He hadn't been around so many people for years, not since leaving Annur.

He turned back to the Urghul woman. "What are you planning?"

"I will let Long Fist explain," she replied. "He is eager to look upon you."

"And just who in Hull's sweet dark is Long Fist?"

Huutsuu remained silent a moment, as though there were no easy answer to the question. "A priest. A shaman. The one who binds us together," she replied finally.

"And what does he want with me?"

"He is curious about the Kettral, about the Skullsworn, and about you, Valyn hui'Malkeenian. It is not often the son of an Annurian emperor comes among us. Long Fist would witness this for himself."

22

Adare woke on a lumpy bed in a chilly room. At first she thought it was night, then realized the darkness in the sky was storm. Someone had tried to pull a scrap of oilcloth over the window, but the wind had torn it free at two corners, and it thrashed madly against the sill while rain spattered on the floor with each gust.

The room was unfamiliar. When she tried to probe her memory, she found a wide, bright blank. The last thing she recalled was arriving on the bridge at Olon, pilgrims at her back, and even that memory felt blurry and inchoate, like something she had dreamed rather than lived. Thought came slowly, reluctantly, and when she tried to think about what happened *after* the bridge, about how she had come to the small, stone room, she could hear only a voice, the echo of immensity, singing in her ear.

Win.

Her heart pumped unstoppably, as though held in a great warm hand.

Shivering took her, and she tried to pull up the thin, itchy blanket, then realized that she was naked. Alarmed, she started to sit up, then subsided against the mattress, as though she were a puppet and someone had silently, almost tenderly, snipped all her strings.

"We had to cut off your clothes," a voice said, gravelly and indifferent.

Adare turned her head to find a man—dark skin, close-cropped hair— seated on a wooden chair in the shadows. *Lehav,* she thought idly. His name was Lehav.

"They were burned, singed to your skin in places."

Her skin burned, a bright sensation, clean, not entirely unpleasant.

"What . . ." She trailed off, raising a hand, then letting it drop.

"Lightning," Lehav replied. "At the Everburning Well."

The Well. Memory leaked in: faces, light, endless rain. A cool long spear heavy in her hand. Why was the Well on fire? What was she doing there?

"You're lucky," Lehav continued. "I saw lightning hit three of my men down in the Waist—storms down there make this look like a clear day— saw it from thirty paces off. One minute they were standing on a small rise, the next . . ." He stared out the window. "Burned them black, all three of them. They were dead before they hit the ground. When I tried to pick them up, to carry them back to camp, the skin just sloughed off."

Lightning. Adare lifted the blanket to look at her own body. She felt as though she'd been hurled from a great height, as though she were still fall- ing, or else not falling at all, but at the very moment of striking the earth, the terrible impact infinitely extended. Fire laced her flesh. Angry red lines, thin as hairs, graceful as lace, swooped and whorled over the curves of her skin, a delicate, indelible brand left by the lightning. The lines looked like seams, felt like seams, as though she was nothing but heat trapped inside skin, a burning light ready to burst free.

Adare dropped the blanket, and Lehav's words swam back into focus. The vision of his dead soldiers tugged at her, mixed with her own reluc- tant fragments of memory. The story seemed impossibly sad, tragic. She wondered how he handled the guilt, then realized there was no guilt. Lightning came from the sky. Lehav couldn't stop it. It wasn't as though he'd killed the soldiers himself. Why was she crying? It wasn't as though she'd served in the Waist. She hadn't seen her men—

The full memory lashed across her mind like a whip, so vicious that she cried out.

Lehav was out of his chair and across the space in an instant, his cool dry hands on her forehead, then checking her pulse.

"What's wrong?" he demanded, sliding back the blanket, searching for the source of the pain. Adare's breath was gone. She had no words to tell him that it was not her body that ached.

"Fulton," she managed finally, too horrified by the memory of the Well, of what had happened there, to care about Lehav's hands running over her skin. "Birch. What happened? Did they . . ." She couldn't bring her- self to say it.

He paused, looked her in the eye, then, evidently satisfied that she wasn't dying, tossed the cloth back up over her shoulders. He did not, however, retake his seat. Instead, he stood at the window, staring out into the storm, ignoring the gusting rain.

"What happened?" He shrugged. "Well, that very much depends on who you ask."

"Are they *alive*?" Adare demanded. The words hurt as they left her, as though they were barbed hooks pulling free, ripping out ragged pieces of pink flesh.

He nodded. "Both of them. The lightning that hit you dead-on knocked them both out of the way—knocked a few dozen people out of the way—but those two landed far clear of the Well. A little stunned, but fine."

"And you didn't insist on . . . going through with it? Going through with the execution?"

Lehav frowned. "I've seen plenty of lightning," he said finally. "Down in the Waist. Up north." He shook his head. "There was something different about this. It was . . . brighter. Sharper. More than natural, somehow."

Adare stared.

"And then people started to talk," he went on. "About the lightning—*Intarra's* lightning. About the fact that you were hit but not harmed. About those lines on your skin." He shook his head once more. "Never seen lightning leave marks like that."

It took a few moments for Adare to understand.

"A miracle," she breathed finally.

"Their word," he said. "Not mine." Again he shrugged, but he'd turned away from the window, and there was something new in his eyes when he looked at her, something she couldn't quite name. "I'm stubborn," he went on after a pause, "but not stupid. It wasn't the right moment to go throwing heretics into the Well."

"They weren't heretics," Adare said, relief flooding her like liquor, sweet and sickening all at the same time.

"Maybe."

Adare raised her head. She felt stronger now, though her skin still burned. "Where are they?" she asked.

He snorted. "Just because I'm not killing your friends doesn't mean I'm letting them wander around. They're alive. They're well. That's what you want to know, right? Congratulations."

The last word raked her with shame. *She* had done nothing to save her Aedolians, nothing effective anyway. It was the lightning that did it. Lightning and luck. Her skin burned, and she slipped an arm from beneath the blanket, studying the ruddy pattern, a sharp, bright sensation that might have been fear blooming in her mind.

"They're alive," she murmured. Tears streaked her face.

"Normally it's a good thing when your men make it," Lehav said, cocking his head to the side. "Doesn't always happen that way."

Adare stared at him. "How do you do it?" she asked, voice little louder than a whisper.

"It?"

"Decide. Who lives and who dies. You've led men, both in the legions and for the Sons of Flame. Some of them must have died on your orders. As a commander, how do you make the decision?"

Lehav glowered at the storm. "You don't think about the dying. You decide what needs to be done, you pick the best men to do it, and you send them out. The dying, that's Ananshael's business."

Adare looked at the soldier. "And the things that need to be done," she asked. "You ever wonder if they really need to be done?"

He met her gaze squarely. "All the time."

†

When Adare woke again, it was night, the storm had settled to a quiet patter of raindrops, someone had lit a lantern beside her bed, and Lehav was gone. For a while she lay still, feeling the burns lacing her skin, the bright ache like a spike of light in the meat of her mind. Unlike her earlier awakening, this time she remembered everything.

"Sweet Intarra's light," she breathed.

"You've been a 'Kent-kissing prophet half a fuckin' day and you've already started with the holy horseshit."

Adare started up, yanking the blanket around her. Nira sat in the chair by the head of her bed, tapping impatiently at the cane laid across her lap. Adare swung her legs off the bed, letting the blanket drop, then realized that Oshi stood in the far corner, inspecting a section of chipping plaster, and hastily pulled it up again.

"What are you doing here?" she demanded. "How did you get in?"

Nira raised her brows at the tone. "You've only got the three guards, girl. Two of 'em are still try'n'a walk straight after almost getting tossed in a burning well, then skewered by fire, and the third seems t've had a change of heart after your show down there in the city." The woman raised her bushy brows. "Ya *do* know what them dumb fool fucks in the street are sayin'? What they're callin' ya? Intarra's second prophet. That's what."

Adare put a hand to her forehead. The fierce, clean fire was gone, re-

placed by a throbbing ache. The guilt over Fulton and Birch, submerged
for a while in her exhaustion, had settled on her like a leaden coat. She
couldn't face Nira and her questions, not right now, but she had no idea
how to get her to go away.

"What do you want?" she asked.

The woman raised an eyebrow. "Wanted ta gaze on the prophet in all
her burned, skinny glory. Seen a lot of things in my life, but never a prophet."

"I'm not a prophet," Adare said, shaking her head. "I just got lucky." It
was the rational way to look at the situation, but the words felt wrong,
somehow, ungrateful. Disrespectful. "I prayed and the goddess answered
my prayer."

Nira raised her brows. "Ya don't have ta play the pious fool for me, girl."

"I'm not playing," Adare replied quietly. "Fulton and Birch are alive
because of that lightning. Intarra's lightning."

"And there are black pines burned to char in the Romsdals, also hit by
lightning. Ya think your goddess has got something against tall trees?"

Adare took a deep breath, then let it leak out slowly between her lips.
She had no response, largely because it was exactly the kind of crack she
might have made herself a month earlier. Lightning struck all the time,
blasting barren mountaintops, stabbing down into the wide oceans, burning through the solitary oak in the field, most of it, probably, in places
where there was no one to pray in the first place. Embracing a goddess
because of a bolt of lightning was stupid; but then, it wasn't just the lightning. Adare closed her eyes and felt the deep, cool relief bathing her heart,
the gratitude flowing like blood through her veins. The lightning she
could write off, but not the answer to her desperate prayer.

"Intarra came," she said, feeling defiant and foolish all at once. "She
was there."

Nira stared at her a moment longer, then shrugged. "Well, this was a
disappointment. Guess one revelation looks pretty much like another."
She got to her feet, leaning on the cane. "Good luck rulin' your empire,
girl. C'mon, Oshi, ya demented ape."

Adare blinked. "You're leaving?"

Nira nodded. "Your man—Ameredad, Lehav—he wasn't our man.
Didn't expect he would be, really, but there were enough pieces that fit.
Not the first time we've crossed a quarter continent for a dead end. Won't
be the last. *Oshi!*" she said again, jabbing her cane at the door. "Time to
leave Our Lady the Princess Prophet Minister to her great and noble tasks."

The old man raised his head from the plaster, looked over at Adare as though seeing her for the first time, then abruptly lost interest.

"Don't go," Adare blurted. "Come north with us."

Nira frowned. "And why, in the name of Meshkent's buggering cock, would I want ta do a shit-witted thing like that?"

"I need you," Adare said, shocked at her own words, but recognizing the truth in them even as they left her lips. "I need a councillor."

"Seems ta me you're well on your way to being over-counseled as it is."

Adare shook her head. "No. Lehav will use me, but doesn't trust me. Fulton and Birch will guard me, but they won't talk to me. . . ." She trailed off, staring at her hands. "I'm in charge of an army now, Nira. I'm starting a civil war against maybe the best general in the history of Annur, and I have no idea what I'm doing."

Nira's lips tightened. "I'm sorry, girl, but I can't help. You might'a forgot," she lowered her voice, "but things didn't work out all that well when we were in charge, Oshi and me. 'Sides—ya got Intarra now ta guide your every dainty step."

"Just because she saved me once, doesn't mean she'll do it every time," Adare protested. She realized she was pleading, and found she didn't care. "I need someone who knows about power, who's been there before."

Nira glanced at her brother, then shook her head. "No. I got my own work ta see to."

"Yes!" Adare said, seizing on to the idea. "You walked all the way here looking for your Csestriim. Why? What was it you said? *He's always at the heart of important things.* Well, there's nothing closer to the heart of things than the Dawn Palace. The palace you were telling me weeks ago you couldn't get inside."

"This," the woman said, casting a skeptical look around the crumbling room, "doesn't look much like the Dawn Palace."

Adare ignored the crack, pressing ahead. "I'm going to Annur. I'm going to destroy il Tornja, and take back the Unhewn Throne."

"Last time I checked, it was your brother supposed to be sittin' on that ugly hunk a' stone, not you."

"I have no idea where Kaden is," Adare snapped, "and I can't afford to wait for him. None of us can. If you come with me, you'll see every important player in this empire. If your Csestriim is there, we'll find him."

Nira narrowed her eyes, clicked her teeth together. "And if I come with ya, if I'm your councillor, the *kenarang* might put both of our heads on a sharp stick."

"Sometimes in order to get what you want you have to take a risk."

Nira laughed at that, a quick, brittle sound like sticks snapping. "Seems to me it's *you* ought'a be worrying about risk, girl. Ya just pestered two of the most hated people in the long history of this rotten world to join your cause." She laughed again. "Two leaches. Two *crazy* leaches."

Adare shot a glance at Oshi, lowering her voice. "Only one of you is crazy."

Nira grinned a wide, yellow-toothed grin. "Call it one and a half."

23

Long Fist—priest and shaman, the only chief to unite the Urghul tribes in a land and history littered with ambitious, bellicose chiefs—was the tallest man Valyn had ever seen: at least a couple inches taller than Jack Pole back on the Islands, who was a head taller than Valyn himself. Unlike most extremely tall men, however, who tended to move in a series of gangly lurches, as though all their ligaments had gone slack, Long Fist carried himself with the languid grace of a cat, every motion of his approach a coiling or uncoiling, as though the deliberation with which he moved were a soft pelt sliding over sinew.

Valyn had yet to see a chair among the Urghul. Instead, the chief seated himself upon a modified travois, thick buffalo hide stretched between a wooden frame, each end of the thing borne on the bare backs of two kneeling Urghul, a man and a woman, their elbows and palms planted in the earth, faces inches from the dirt. They seemed, at first glance, to be balancing it; then Valyn noticed the blood on their backs, weeping from beneath the travois, and realized with a sick lurch that the frame was barbed, held in place by the steel hooks driven into their pale flesh. The shaman was not a small man, and the pain of those hooks must have been excruciating, but neither the man nor the woman moved. Valyn could not see their downturned faces.

For all the attention Long Fist paid his bearers, he might have been perched on a ledge of stone or a wooden stool. Instead, he was speaking in a voice too low for Valyn to make out, addressing a knot of older warriors, gesturing with a carefully extended finger toward something in the sprawling camp and shaking his head in the slow, menacing cadence of displeasure. Only after those warriors had been dismissed, jogging down the low slope toward whatever errand awaited, did the chieftain turn his eyes to Valyn. They were predatory, those eyes, deep bleak blue and patient as the sky. Valyn felt himself being measured, weighed, and judged, and he tried to meet Long Fist's scrutiny with his own.

Despite the chill on the afternoon air, the shaman wore a sleeveless tunic of bison hide. Dozens of necklaces ringed his neck, leather thongs threaded through bone, some short, some long. They shifted and clacked whenever he changed position. He wore his blond hair long, but instead of tying it back, in the fashion of the Urghul warriors, he let it hang free in a pale cascade reaching halfway to his waist. A poor tactical decision if it came to a fight, but Long Fist didn't appear worried about a fight. He nodded as Valyn and the others approached, not a greeting, but a gesture of satisfaction, the smile revealing a perfect row of white teeth, the upper canines of which looked to have been sharpened.

"So," he said, spreading his hands wide, as though inviting Valyn to sit at a bountiful feast. Only there was no feast. Nowhere to sit.

"What did they do?" Valyn asked, jerking his chin toward the bearers of the makeshift throne.

Long Fist raised an eyebrow. "They were brave," he replied.

Valyn shook his head. "And for some reason you didn't like that?"

"Quite to the contrary," the chief replied, running a finger along the ribs of the kneeling man, "their bravery pleased me greatly, and so I have extended them this honor."

Valyn blew out a long, ragged breath. "Remind me not to please you."

Long Fist shrugged. "You are a soft man from a soft world. You would not understand."

"Oh, I think I get it well enough. It makes you feel strong to hurt others. People like you aren't so uncommon."

"On the contrary," the shaman replied, showing his teeth in a predatory smile. "People like me are extremely uncommon, and this," he said, gesturing to the bent and bloody bearers of his seat, "is not for me. It is for them."

"What horseshit."

Long Fist turned to Huutsuu. "Perhaps you would attempt to enlighten our guest."

She nodded. "You worship weak gods, and so you are weak. All peoples have the gods they deserve." As though that clarified anything.

"We worship civilized gods," Valyn replied. "I've studied your history, your worship. It is bloody and savage. Bestial."

"Civilized," Long Fist said, holding a hand before him, palm up, as

though weighing the word, feeling its heft. "*Savage*. Like a horse with blinders, you see only what your language allows you to see. This is the danger of relying too heavily on words."

"The words represent things," Valyn replied. "Law. Prosperity. Peace."

The chief shook his head, bemused. "More words. More confusion. Consider your law—what is it except a shield for the weak?"

"That's the point. We protect those who need protection."

"Infants need protection," Long Fist replied patiently, "but men and women grown? To protect them, to force your protection upon them, to assume that they need or desire that protection, is to strip them of their own nobility. You call us savage. You say we are like beasts. I say it is you with your law and your prosperity that makes swine of men, makes cattle of women, reduces them to cowed conformity. Kwihna would raise their eyes once more, would ennoble their hearts."

"I see how Kwihna *ennobles*," Valyn said, gesturing to the kneeling figures, trying to hold on to his side of the argument. For all the chieftain's scorn for words, he wielded them deftly as weapons, twisting meaning and changing context until Valyn found himself utterly wrong-footed, defending rather than attacking. "It looks great—as long as you're the one sitting on the litter and not the one holding it up."

"Surely," the man replied, pulling open his tunic slowly to reveal his chest, "you do not believe that I would allow others to claim an honor that I myself refused."

Valyn suppressed a shudder. Someone had carved a tangled web of jagged, puckered slashes into his white skin, scores of lines, hundreds of them, a cloak of glabrous, glistening scar laid over his flesh. On either side of his chest, toward the pits of his arms, large healed punctures, like old spear wounds, gouged the muscle. Following Valyn's gaze, the shaman nodded. "It was here," he said, pressing a fingertip into one of the shallow divots, "and here that they put the hooks. For one full moon I hung suspended by the steel while every morning the tribe gathered, every man and woman, even the children, gathered to drag their knives across my flesh, to participate in my sacrifice."

Valyn tried to gauge the claim. It seemed almost physically impossible. Almost. If none of those knives had severed an artery, if someone had provided the shaman with water, if the wounds were smeared periodically with coagulant, a man could survive. *Something* had left the scars. Valyn imagined hanging from those hooks like a beast after a botched slaughter, skin peeling away in strips, flies in the wounds, tongue swollen so fat beneath the steppe sun that every breath was a struggle against strangulation.

"You didn't die," he pointed out.

"Of course not," Long Fist replied, shrugging his tunic shut. "I made my sacrifice to Kwihna, not to Wakarii."

"Wakarii?"

"The Coward's God. The Lord of the Grave."

It was the first time Valyn had heard Ananshael referred to as a god for cowards, but he wasn't interested in debating theology. "What do you want?" he asked. "Why did your people tie us up and drag us halfway across the steppe?"

Long Fist gazed up at the shifting clouds, as though the answer to the question was scrawled across the wind. "What do I want?" he mused. "I suppose that what I want is to know whom to help, and whom to destroy."

"I volunteer for the former," Balendin said, stepping forward, managing an awkward bow over his bound hands.

Long Fist considered the leach for a moment. "I recognize Valyn from his eyes and from his father's description." Valyn stared at the mention of his father, but Long Fist pressed ahead as though he'd said nothing surprising. "Huutsuu informs me that these others are the prince's warriors. . . ."

"Not all of us," Pyrre said.

The chieftain raised an eyebrow, studied the assassin for a moment, then turned back to Balendin as though she had not spoken. "You, however. You were captured separately."

The leach shrugged. "Different Wing. We're all Kettral."

"You fickle, traitorous fuck," Gwenna spat, shouldering her way forward. She glared at Balendin for a heartbeat, as though deciding whether or not to tackle him, then turned to Long Fist. "You should kill him. You can't keep him drugged forever, and whatever he tells you now, when he comes undrugged you'll wish to Hull he was dead."

"I do not wish," Long Fist replied, "I pray. And I do not pray to Hull. More, I do not kill men until I know what use they might have."

Balendin smiled. "Oh, I'm useful. I can promise you that."

Long Fist merely nodded, considering the leach once more, then gesturing to someone behind them with one extended finger. A young *ksaabe*, barely older than Valyn, came running with a wooden pipe. She set it in the shaman's outstretched hand, then retreated. Long Fist took a long drag, held it a moment, then exhaled slowly, the smoke wreathing his face.

"I have questions," he said finally.

"You can bugger yourself with your questions," Laith replied, spitting at the shaman's feet.

Long Fist took another long puff on his pipe, staring at the flier from behind the cloud of smoke.

"If you speak to me like that again, I will cut out your tongue." The words were level, matter-of-fact, as though he were discussing a new bowstring or the morning rain.

Laith looked ready to snap, but Valyn spoke into the ensuing silence before the flier could respond.

"What are your questions?"

"First," the shaman raised a finger, "what are you doing on my steppe?"

Valyn had expected the question, but he responded carefully. Balendin might know nothing about the Flea, about Assare and the *kenta,* and Valyn didn't intend to give him any extra information. "My Wing was forced down after a fight in the mountains."

Long Fist glanced at Huutsuu, and she nodded.

"A fight," he mused. "You killed the monks?"

Valyn blinked. He hadn't expected the shaman to know anything about Ashk'lan, but then, the Shin had traded with *someone.* For all he knew, the eastern Urghul tribes had frequented the monastery before its destruction. The real question was how Long Fist felt about the monks. The fact that Ashk'lan, perched above the eastern steppe, had never been destroyed spoke volumes. Valyn took a deep breath, then plunged.

"No. We killed the men who killed the monks." He nodded contemptuously toward Balendin. "His Wing. And others."

Long Fist raised an eyebrow. "Your own men. You killed other Annurians."

"Traitors," Valyn amended, anger at the memory shoving aside fear and caution both.

"And your brother? He is dead?"

Valyn hesitated. "No."

"My comrades," Balendin said, shrugging as he spoke, "were more zealous than skilled. As you can see, I'm no friend of Valyn, his family, or his empire." He smiled slowly. "Which could make me very useful to you."

The leach wasn't even trying to disguise his treachery, which, Valyn had to admit, might well prove the shrewd decision, given the frayed relations between Annur and the Urghul. The horsemen might respect the monks, but they loathed the empire. If Long Fist were looking for an ally, who better than a Kettral-trained leach, one with an intimate knowledge of Annur's military?

"As I recall," Valyn said, turning to face Balendin, "it was you yourself who underestimated my brother, who nearly died at his hands." He nodded toward the leach's shoulder. "How's that bolt puncture?"

"Healing nicely, thank you for asking," Balendin replied. "As for your brother, I'm looking forward to cutting out those fancy eyes of his the next time we meet."

Long Fist seemed half bored, half amused by the exchange.

Gwenna, however, rounded on Valyn, eyes ablaze. "Are we going to keep talking?" she demanded. "Or do you want me to kill him?"

It was an implausible threat. Balendin snorted, but he took half a step back all the same. *He's nervous,* Valyn realized, tasting the fear on the air. Normally, the leach would have been feasting off Gwenna's rage, bathing in the power that came from her emotion, but drugged as he was with adamanth root, her fury brought him no strength.

"Stand down, Gwenna," Valyn said. He wanted Balendin cut to pieces as much as she did, probably more, but he didn't intend to make a spectacle of his Wing in front of the Urghul chieftain.

"Why?" she demanded, glaring at him, then jerking her head at Long Fist. "So we can please this bloody son of a bitch? When we finish Balendin, we ought to start on him."

Valyn tensed, ready for some sort of retribution, but Long Fist just raised his brows.

"Such hatred," he said. "Before you kill a man, you should be sure he is not your brother."

"My brothers are all in the legions," Gwenna spat. "On the frontier. Keeping you bastards out."

"You see?" Long Fist said, looking past Gwenna to Huutsuu. "This is what most Annurians believe."

"What?" Valyn demanded. "What do we believe?"

The shaman spread his hands. "That my people are trying to invade your empire."

Valyn frowned, then nodded to the sprawling camp. "What's all this then? We've got to be all the way into the Blood Steppe, probably just a few days from the White, and you've put together a 'Kent-kissing army."

"A defensive army," Long Fist replied. "Protection against your preda-tory war chief."

Valyn shook his head. "War chief?"

"Ran il Tornja," Talal said quietly. They were the first words the leach had spoken, and the Urghul chief turned an appraising eye on him, then nodded.

"This is his name. My army, as you call it, is no more than a shield against his depredations."

"There's a guy back on the Islands," Laith observed, "Great Gray Balt. He loves his shield—beaten twenty men to death with it."

Long Fist nodded. "More than twenty will die if Ran il Tornja comes across the White. But I have no longing for this fight." He pointed at Va-lyn with the stem of his pipe. "Your father understood this. I wonder . . . do you?"

"What do you know of my father?" Valyn demanded, the chieftain's earlier words coming back to him.

"More than you. We met yearly to reestablish our common border, to discuss our common goals. I sparred with him just ten moons past."

Valyn felt the ground shift beneath him. Sanlitun hui'Malkeenian had less than nothing in common with this savage. The ideals of the empire were diametrically opposed to those of the Urghul. And yet . . . Valyn's father *had* tried to exercise restraint regarding the steppe nomads. Until the last few years, imperial policy had called for a hard border at the White River, no intervention to the north.

"Met him? Where?"

"East of here. A place sacred to the Urghul."

Valyn shook his head. "A lie. It would have taken him months to make the trip and months to return. The whole court would have noted his ab-sence."

Long Fist smiled. "Such certainty."

Even as he spoke Valyn realized his error: the *kenta*. He had never heard of the gates before fleeing the Islands, but according to Kaden, the whole point of the Shin training was to allow the Emperor access to the *kenta*, to provide him with the keys necessary to oversee all Annur. If there was a gate buried in the Bone Mountains, there could be a gate stuck in the middle of the steppe, a lone arch somewhere on a wind-beaten hill, an indestructible span of something that was neither stone nor steel. A primitive people like the Urghul would likely hold such a place sacred.

For the hundredth time, Valyn wished he had known his own father better. Would Sanlitun have traveled alone across half the length of a continent to parley with some blood-soaked barbarian chief? He tried to dredge up his childhood memories, but could snag only fragments and shards: Sanlitun sitting the Unhewn Throne, a finger extended in judgment; Sanlitun teaching him to hold a blade, rapping Valyn on the knuckles again and again, insisting on a looser grip; Sanlitun seated cross-legged on the roof of Intarra's Spear, gazing out over the ocean, indifferent to the wind tearing at his hair or the vast city sprawled below him, focused on something Valyn could neither see nor comprehend, something terribly distant. All of Valyn's memories were like this: he could make out the lines of his father's face, the burning eyes, the set of his shoulders, while the thought and emotion beneath remained opaque, unknowable.

"Your father had no desire for war with the Urghul. We are different peoples with different ways. He was content to leave it so. But there are factions within your empire who think differently." He nodded toward Balendin. "Obviously."

The leach shifted uncomfortably, opened his mouth to respond, but Valyn spoke into the pause.

"So, if you and my father were such great friends, if you've got such respect for the empire, why am I tied up? Why have your people been beating my Wing for the better part of a month?"

Long Fist tilted his head to the side.

"Huutsuu has given me to understand that it is you who surprised her, that *you* have killed many of my warriors during the long ride west."

"We killed them," Valyn spat, "because—"

The chieftain waved his objection aside with a languid hand.

"I understand. You are warriors. It is forgiven."

He gestured, and Huutsuu stepped forward, knife in hand.

Despite the word *forgiven,* Valyn half expected the woman to plunge the steel into his stomach, and he shifted to put space between them, raising his hands in defense. She snorted in disgust.

"Stop moving. I am freeing you."

Valyn stared as she sliced the rawhide cord binding his wrists, his elbows, trying to make sense of his sudden liberty. Before he could rub the blood back into his hands, the rest of his Wing was likewise free. Even Pyrre seemed subject to Long Fist's sudden, shocking amnesty. The assassin smiled at Huutsuu as the Urghul woman cut her free, then sketched a curtsy, as though they were nobles at a ball.

"I can't help but notice," Balendin said, when all the cords but his had been cut, "that I'm still tied up. I hope it is an oversight."

Long Fist turned those cat-calm eyes on the leach.

"By all means, feel hope if it gives you strength. I will remind you, however, that you have already admitted to your part in this plot to kill your Emperor."

Balendin licked his lips, a quick, furtive motion. He glanced over at Valyn, as if for support, but Valyn just smiled. He had no idea what was going on, no idea what game Long Fist was playing, but he was free for the first time in weeks, free when he'd expected to be tortured or killed, while Balendin remained bound, stinking of fear and desperation. Valyn allowed himself a moment to bask in the feeling.

"Why don't you say a little more," he suggested, "about how you tried to kill my brother?"

Long Fist nodded. "Yes. Say more."

Balendin shook his head warily. "What do you want to know?"

The chieftain spread his hands, almost an invitation. "Who sent you to kill the Emperor?"

The leach shook his head again. "That would be telling."

"You can tell now," Long Fist replied casually, "or when I hold your still-beating heart in my fist."

"Go on," Valyn said. "You already turned on your empire and your order. One more betrayal shouldn't be a huge weight on your conscience."

"It's not a matter of conscience," Balendin said, responding to Valyn, but keeping his eyes warily on Long Fist. "It's a matter of practicality. While I've got secrets, I stay alive."

"You may not find living such a blessing," Long Fist mused, "when the life lived is one of pain. You know something of my people, yes? Have you learned that we can cut out the heart without slicing the veins that feed it? Twice yearly, we hold a march in Kwihna's honor; the tributes carry their own hearts in their hands. I can offer you pain without death's escape." He gestured to Huutsuu with a single finger. "Show him."

The woman stepped forward, smiling, the knife she had used to free Valyn still ready in her hand.

"Begin with his small finger," the shaman said.

Balendin backed up a step, but the *taabe* and *ksaabe* behind seized him by the shoulders and elbows, holding him in place as Huutsuu took his hand firmly in her fist, then set the blade to the knuckle. Valyn had slaughtered chickens and pigs on the Eyrie—all part of the training in anatomy—and he remembered how easily the tendons parted when he found the gap between the bone. Huutsuu didn't bother hunting for that gap. It took the Urghul woman a few moments to pry Balendin's little finger loose from his desperately clenched fist, and then she went to work, hacking through the flesh as the leach cursed and writhed, then sawing away at the bone itself for what seemed like an age before the blade, as if of its own accord, finally sliced through the tendon.

Balendin slumped against his captors while she held up the finger, inspecting it in the sunlight as though it were some sort of dubious vegetable.

"I'll kill you," he panted. "I'll fucking kill you."

Huutsuu frowned, then turned to Long Fist.

"Another finger?"

The shaman shook his head.

"Not yet, I think." He turned to Balendin. "I am quite willing to take your body apart joint by joint. It would be a great sacrifice to Kwihna. If I leave you whole, it will be because there are things you can tell me whole that you cannot tell me in pieces. And so I will ask again, in the hope that this time you will tell me: Who sent you to kill the Emperor?"

Balendin hesitated, glanced down at the blood spurting from his severed finger, then spat.

"Ran il Tornja," he said.

Valyn stared, uncertain that he'd heard the words correctly. "Il Tornja is the *kenarang*," he said finally. "He was *appointed* by my father. It was the Chief Priest of Intarra, Uinian, who assassinated the Emperor."

Balendin shot him a scornful glance. "Il Tornja pinned Sanlitun's murder on the priest, you fool. Or did you really think a 'Kent-kissing *cleric* could get past the Aedolian Guard?"

"The Aedolian Guard isn't living up to its reputation these days," Valyn replied, trying to make sense of the leach's claim. "Or maybe you don't remember our meeting with Micijah Ut out in the Bone Mountains."

"They were *in* the Bone Mountains because they were the ones il Tornja could *trust*. He couldn't send anyone loyal to your brother because they wouldn't *kill* your fucking brother. That's another clue for you, if you needed more clues. Uinian didn't control the Aedolian Guard. He couldn't have sent Ut anywhere."

"And you," Valyn said slowly, the magnitude of the betrayal sinking in. "Il Tornja commands the Kettral."

"It still doesn't make sense," Talal said, frowning. "Why send Yurl and Balendin when he could send Fane or Shaleel? Why not send the Flea?"

The leach shook his head, as though incredulous that they could be so stupid. His rictus of pain did nothing to hide the scorn. "Because the Flea and Shaleel serve the Emperor. Il Tornja needed new blood, a young Wing, loyal to him and only him."

"Loyal," Valyn spat, "is a sick word to hear on your lips."

"You're the one asking the questions," Balendin snarled. "You and your newfound Urghul ally."

Long Fist raised a finger and they all fell still.

"Why did your war chief kill your emperor? What does he want?"

"The usual," Balendin said, voice tight. "To rule. Rule everything. The Emperor is dead. Everyone thinks the priest murdered him. . . ."

"And now the priest, too, is dead," Long Fist concluded.

Valyn frowned. "The trial is finished?" The last he'd heard, Uinian was still in captivity. Of course, that news was more than a month out of date now.

Long Fist nodded. "The princess," he said. "Your sister. She burned him."

"No," Valyn replied, shaking his head. The shaman clearly had a tenuous grasp of imperial justice. "Adare didn't burn anyone. Even traitors live under the rule of law in Annur. If Uinian was executed, he was convicted by a jury of the Seven."

The shaman shrugged. "The priest is dead. Burned alive."

"And you know this how?"

"I have watchers in your city."

Valyn paused. It was unlike the Urghul to use spies. As far as the Kettral knew, the nomads were too disorganized, too indifferent to strategy and politics to manage much more than the occasional raiding party. Long Fist, however, was unexpected. He had managed to unify the Urghul, which meant he saw further or deeper than his fellow chiefs. Perhaps here, too, he was pressing the boundaries of tradition and custom. In any case, Valyn hadn't heard a word regarding the situation in Annur, not since quitting the Islands. Even the shaman's garbled intelligence was better than nothing.

"Where is Adare now?"

"Gone," Long Fist said. "Disappeared."

"Starting to see the pattern?" Balendin growled. "You don't have to take my word for it. Il Tornja killed your father, then your sister. He ordered me to kill you, and he sent Ut and Adiv to take care of Kaden."

"If il Tornja's behind all this," Valyn asked, trying to work it through, "why hasn't he claimed the throne for himself yet? Why hasn't he named himself Emperor?"

"Because he's not fucking stupid." The leach was cradling his maimed hand in his good one, but blood dripped from between his fingers. Valyn could smell it the same way that he could smell the leach's mounting fear.

"Emperor," Long Fist said quietly, exhaling the syllables in a slow wash of smoke. "It is, as you say, a name. A word. Nothing more. On the steppe we do not worship names, but your people are different. Perhaps il Tornja hides behind another word—*regent*—until his foes forget their opposition. On the steppe"—he made a curt, slashing motion with his hand—"it would not work, but among a soft folk obsessed with words, choosing the right word is nearly as important as doing the right thing."

The shaman turned his attention back to Balendin, sucking slowly through the stem of his pipe as he watched the leach, then breathing out a slow cloud of smoke.

"And what," he asked finally, "does Ran il Tornja want with my people? Why does he order these attacks against us?"

"I'm not his 'Kent-kissing confidant," Balendin hissed, "but it seems pretty obvious."

"Make it clear to me."

"Legitimacy."

Valyn stared at the leach, the pieces falling into place. Sanlitun's political foes had often termed his policy with the Urghul appeasement. Since il Tornja's elevation to *kenarang,* however, Annur had begun to take a harder position, fortifying the northern border, building new forts, even allowing strategic incursions over the White River.

It was hard to say precisely why il Tornja would want to antagonize the Urghul, but history furnished a few examples. Maybe he was angling for more coin in the coffers of the Ministry of War. Maybe he was looking to expand the upper ranks of the army, to justify the promotion of a few confederates. Or maybe he wanted an open war. Valyn forced himself to consider that last option. It made a certain mad sense, especially if the *kenarang* aspired to the Unhewn Throne itself. A sufficiently violent conflict would terrify the people of Annur, maybe terrify them enough that they would accept a seasoned warrior on the throne and overlook the fact that il Tornja lacked Intarra's burning eyes.

Valyn hesitated, Sami Yurl's final words echoing in his ears. "What about Csestriim?" he asked slowly. "Yurl claimed that the Csestriim were involved."

Balendin stared at him, incredulous. "I understand that growing up in a palace could give you an inflated sense of your own importance, but I didn't realize it went this far." He shook his head. "Csestriim."

Valyn frowned. There was something . . . strange in the leach's words. Something missing. Before he could put his finger on it, however, Long Fist was putting down his pipe. He looked first at Balendin, then at Valyn.

"What, precisely, did this person—Yurl—say?" For the first time he looked truly invested, leaning forward slightly, hand on his knee.

Valyn shook his head. "He said the Csestriim were involved somehow. That they were behind it."

"And there were those creatures, too," Talal added. "The *ak'hanath*."

Balendin shook his head. His face had gone ashen, but he kept his feet. Whatever else was true about him, the leach had spent half his life with the Kettral, and the Kettral trained you to deal with pain. "Yurl was an idiot. He fought well, but he was an idiot. We knew about the *ak'hanath*. Adiv told us they had something to do with the Csestriim originally, not that the Csestriim were still alive, still involved."

He was lying. Valyn knew all at once, without understanding how he knew. Something about the smell of him, an oily scent that was not a scent at all, a sweet intangible reek of the raw nerves that accompanied deceit.

"Another finger?" Huutsuu asked, looking to the chieftain.

Long Fist nodded.

"No," Balendin protested. "You fucking fools . . ."

But the Urghul woman was already on him, peeling back the small finger on the other hand, then driving the knife into the joint, twisting and sawing, blood spattering her face as the leach thrashed. When it was all finished, Balendin slumped against the warriors who restrained him.

Long Fist looked at him for a long time. "The Csestriim?" he asked again.

"There were no Csestriim," Balendin spat. "Unless you think il Tornja is Csestriim."

Valyn inhaled slowly, but whatever he'd smelled or thought he'd smelled was gone. There was only the ragged, rusted edge of the leach's fear, fear he held firmly in check.

The shaman frowned, but did not respond.

"More?" Huutsuu asked.

He shook his head. "He has told us what he knows." After a long pause, Long Fist turned to Valyn.

"I trusted Sanlitun," the Urghul leader said quietly. "Although he led a soft people, he understood something of hardness. Now . . ." He held a hand toward Valyn, palm up, as though offering something precious but invisible. "Your father is dead, murdered, and I believe we share a common foe."

"Meaning what?" Valyn asked, his legs suddenly unsteady beneath him.

"Meaning that together we can avoid a war."

Despite Long Fist's words, the sounds of martial readiness shivered the air: the drumming of hooves, shouts of men and women, cold clatter of steel on steel. *Just a shield,* the shaman claimed, but thousands of mounted warriors were never just a shield. Full-scale war had not come to Annur in generations, and now, according to Long Fist, the decision to halt it lay in Valyn's hands.

"And how do we avoid war," he asked carefully, "when il Tornja, the *kenarang* and regent both, is bent on it?"

The shaman smiled, revealing those bright, sharpened canines. "You kill him."

24

The burn was not a burn. Not, at least, like any burn Adare had ever seen. The intricate tracery of red scar looked more like the swirls of henna that brides from Rabi and Aragat inked onto their skin, a thousand ramifying twists and whorls snaking around her arms and torso, down her legs and up her neck like tiny red vines spreading into her hair. Unlike vines, however, unlike ink, the burn was a part of her. When she flexed her arms or fingers, those burns shifted with the flesh, the scar-smooth skin catching the light until it seemed to shine, to glow. The wounds throbbed, but the pain was cold and bright rather than chafing. Still, when Adare tried to get out of bed, she felt her legs turn to water and her mind fade, all thought blotted out in a great wash of light.

It was a day before she could cross to the window and another before she could reach the door, but on the third morning, despite the wobble in her gait, the brightness stamped on her sight, she insisted on seeing her Aedolians. Lehav and Nira had assured her over and over that both men had survived the ordeal, but Adare needed to witness it herself, to stand in the same room with them, to touch them and hear them speak.

The room was dark, blinds drawn over the windows, the single lamp unlit on a bedside table. At first Adare thought they were sleeping, then Birch raised his head weakly from the pillow, and she stifled a gasp. The lightning had burned him, too, but there was nothing delicate or graceful about the bright red weal smeared across half of his once-handsome face. Of the wounded eye, she could see nothing. It was either lost or the lid had burned shut. Any expression must have been excruciating for him, but he raised his brows.

"Come to finish us off, my lady?" He tried a grin, but his voice was thin as smoke.

Adare shook her head. "I wanted . . . I came to see that you were all right."

"We're fine," Fulton cut in, although when he pushed himself up in his cot he looked anything but fine. The lightning had spared his face, but a rogue branch of the bolt had torn down his chest like a talon, ripping the skin apart. The bandages over the wound were heavy with seeping blood and pus, and he was even thinner than before the botched execution.

"Are they feeding you?" she demanded.

Fulton nodded. "Broth, at the moment. Neither of us can hold down much more."

He narrowed his eyes, studying her. "Your face, your neck. You are well?"

"Well enough," she said, nodding.

"Thanks be to Intarra," the man murmured.

"For what?" Birch asked. "Grilling us like fish on a skewer?"

"For sparing the princess," the older man replied.

"I thought it was prophet now," Birch said. "Didn't I hear something about a prophet?"

Adare nodded weakly. "That's what some of the people are saying."

"And what about us?" he asked, gesturing to his face. "Are we prophets, too?"

"We are soldiers," Fulton ground out, warning heavy in his tone. "The same as we have always been."

"The same?" Birch demanded. "I don't think so."

For a moment the two men seemed to forget that she was there, glares locked like the horns of rutting bulls. Adare could only watch, her legs too weak to carry her forward, her mouth too dry to speak. At last Birch turned his head away, shoved the blinds aside, and stared out the window into the rain.

"I'm sorry," she said finally, the words flimsy as wet paper, tearing apart even as she spoke them. "I'm so sorry."

"There's no need to apologize, my lady," Fulton said. "You did what you had to, and so did we. Everyone's alive. In another day or two, we'll be able to resume our duties."

Birch kept his eyes on the window, and his voice was so low when he spoke that Adare wasn't sure she heard him clearly.

"Speak for yourself, Fulton."

"Forgive him, my lady," Fulton said. "The lightning has—"

"The lightning woke me up," Birch snapped, turning back and half rising in his bed to glare at Adare.

"Mind your tone before the princess, soldier," Fulton growled.

"Princess? She's a prophet now, or didn't you hear? The thing is, I didn't sign on to serve a prophet." His eyes were wide, almost wild, accusatory and pleading both. "I would have taken a blade for you, Adare. A bolt in the belly. I would have run into a burning tower to haul you out."

"You might still have the chance," Fulton growled.

"No," Birch said, voice suddenly horribly weary. "I will not. I'm done. I always knew I might be killed for you, Adare. I just never figured I'd be killed *by* you. By a deal *you* made." He dropped his head back to the pillow, turned his gaze to the window, and fell silent.

Jaw tight, Fulton started to pull himself upright in bed, but Adare crossed to him, put a hand on his shoulder. He was feverish, skin aflame, and weak as a child when she pushed him back against the pillow.

"It's all right," she murmured. "Leave him be. I already owe him more than I can repay."

Birch didn't turn his head. From where Adare stood, she could see only the unburned side of his face, the handsome side, the side she recognized. Tears sheeted his cheek, but he refused to look over, didn't meet her eye. He was alive, saved, either by the grace of Intarra or Adare's own mad folly, and yet she had lost him all the same.

He is the first to see through me, Adare told herself, staring at the man, trying to remember his casual laugh, his grin. *But he will not be the last. Or the worst.*

†

"I'm not a prophet," Adare said, shaking her head, meeting Nira's glare from across the table. "I'm *not,* regardless of what they say."

"The fuck does that have ta do with anything?" the woman snapped.

"I won't drape myself in a lie and call it *glory.*"

"Oh for 'Shael's sweet sake, girl, you think you can rule an empire without lying? You think your father didn't lie? Or his father? Or any of your goldy-eyed great-great-founders of Annur? It's built into the *job.* Bakers have flour, fishermen have nets, and leaders have lies."

Adare ground her teeth and looked away. They sat just inside the wide glass doors of the old palace where Lehav had made his headquarters. To the south, the lake stretched away farther than she could see, all waves and gray, like a great chipped slate. On the far side of the water, well out of sight, sat Sia, a twin city to Olon, but richer, and more beautiful. Past Sia lay the trellised vineyards of central Eridroa, then the jade hills, green as emeralds, if the paintings were to be believed, sparkling with ten thousand terraces. Adare had seen the vibrant scrolls hung in the Dawn Palace, but she had never been farther from Annur than Olon, and the sudden mad urge seized her to set out south on a lake boat, to slip out of the city when no one was watching and just disappear.

It was a childish fantasy, of course, the opposite of what she had come to do, but then, despite her success, what she had come to do was looking harder each day. According to Nira, she should have been grateful that the devout were calling her Intarra's second prophet, that the scene at the Well was being hailed as a miracle. In a single day, she'd won the loyalty of Intarra's most faithful, and besides, it wasn't as though she'd never had a title before.

Princess. Malkeenian. Minister of Finance. She'd grown accustomed to the big names, but this newest honorific—prophet—hung on her heavily as an ill-fitting coat. She still couldn't explain what had happened at the Well, couldn't be sure why she had walked away unscathed from the lightning. That Intarra had answered her prayer, Adare was just willing to believe, especially when her mind filled, as it still did several times each day, with that boundless, brilliant light, a wash of peace and power so burning hot it felt cool as balm. She'd come to the city a skeptic, and was leaving with a reverence kindled in her heart—fine. But none of that made her a *prophet*.

"It's not even your lie," Nira went on, stabbing a bony finger into the tabletop. "It's the *people* saying it. All ya have to do is nod your dumb head and smile."

Adare sucked a long breath between her teeth. The old woman was right enough. Word of Adare's miraculous survival was already spreading, of a Malkeenian princess who had forsaken her palace and throne to join a sacred band of pilgrims, to make her own sacrifice at the Well, who had been marked twice over by Intarra, once with the burning eyes, and a second time, to reaffirm her holiness, by a sacred web of bright scar laid into her skin. Most hagiography, of course, was bullshit. In some of the tales, people had Adare stepping into the Well itself, then borne up on a fountain of light. And yet, she had few enough advantages in the fight against il Tornja as it was.

"Listen, ya priggish idiot," Nira said, spreading her hands. "People don't *want* men and women for leaders—they want saviors."

"And what if I don't want to be a savior?"

"Then you're dumber than I took ya for. Which was pretty fuckin' dumb." She shook her head in frustration. "Let me lay it out, plain as cloth: a fisherman tells his own story—where he fished, whether his nets came back full or no. A tailor tells his own story. Even a whore tells her story, though there are plenty a' crooked cocks who'll try ta take it from her.

"But a queen? An emperor?" She shook her head. "You can sit on the throne and talk till you're outta air, but it's them," she said, stabbing her cane at the wall, at the Sons of Flame drilling in the courtyard beyond, at the citizens of Olon, at the entire empire. "It's them who tell your story. And listen to this bit, girl, listen good: there aren't but two tales to tell. You're a savior, or a curse. An answered prayer or a 'Kent-kissing monster. So when people go tellin' tales with the words *blessed,* and *goddess,* and *prophet,* ya thank your bright shiny goddess and ya nod and ya fuckin' smile. It's you who made me councillor, so I'm counselin'—take the worship and be glad for it."

Adare stared, taken aback by the tirade. "All right," she said finally, "but they believe all this, all this business about prophets, because they haven't *met* me. The people who know me know the truth." In her mind she watched again as Birch met her eyes, shook his head, and turned away, one man, at least, who wanted nothing to do with her divinity. "When they come to know me, they will come to know it."

Nira nodded as though she'd been making that precise point all along. "Which is why ya don't let people know you. Why ya can't."

Adare shook her head wearily, staring out at the waves. The best wines in the world came from Sia, reds and whites both. She could go south, take a room in a tiny whitewashed house overlooking the lake, spend her days baking and fishing. . . . And then il Tornja would win. He would destroy her empire as he had murdered her father. She tore her eyes from the water, turning back to Nira.

"All right," she said. "Prophet. As long as I don't have to push the story myself. As long as that's it."

"It?" Nira asked, brows rising. *"It?"*

"Yes. It. I'm doing this to see il Tornja captured, tried, and killed. Not so I can follow in the footsteps of Maayala."

"And if ya succeed?" the woman demanded. "What then?"

"Then Kaden will take his place on the Unhewn Throne—"

"Kaden!" Nira hooted. "Your poor bastard of a brother's feeding the crows by now. Ya think the 'Kent-kissing *kenarang* went t'all the trouble ta gut your father just so Kaden could dance back home and plant his bony, ignorant ass on the throne?"

Adare held up a hand. "I realize he may have gone after Kaden. The delegation sent north, the one with Adiv and Ut, they *could* have been part of the plot." She shook her head at the magnitude of the suggestion. "But could il Tornja *really* win over both the Mizran Councillor *and* the First Shield of the Aedolian Guard? And if he wants Kaden dead so badly, why didn't he kill me? I would have been the easiest target of all."

Nira looked her up and down, then snorted. "You were worth more to him bedded than dead. And there was no threat that you'd take the throne." She pursed her withered lips. "Is there?"

Adare let out a long, slow breath. "Annur would never accept me on the throne. And Kaden . . ."

The old woman waved the name aside. "I've heard about enough a' Kaden. He's dead, girl. Dead as meat."

Adare glanced down at her hands and realized she'd torn a nail right down to the quick. Blood pooled in the nail bed, then, when she tried to wipe it away, smeared across her hand. In all the long march south, she hadn't allowed herself to think beyond the need to win over the Sons, and now that she had them, all she could consider was il Tornja's destruction. Nira was right, though. If they *did* succeed, if the *kenarang* didn't plant all of their heads on spikes over the Godsgate, someone would need to rule Annur.

"I could do it," she said slowly.

Nira smiled, a tight, grim expression. "You're a thickheaded bitch, Adare, but when you're in the shit deep enough, at least ya know ta start swimmin'."

✝

Despite her reservations, after several more days, Adare was forced to admit that the events at the Everburning Well, divinely ordained or not, had worked a small miracle for her cause. Not only were the Sons of Flame flocking to Lehav's call, but the common people of Olon, sons and daughters both, came in scores, then hundreds, then thousands, some begging to join the holy army, others bearing baskets of food, or even, in one strange case, a dozen iron rakes.

Can strip the skin from some legionary bastard with a rake as well as a sword, the giver proudly proclaimed.

The words made Adare sick. She needed to see il Tornja unseated—that much she had never doubted—but now that her own army was gathering, she was starting to tally up the true cost for the first time. She wasn't just preparing to fight a war, she was putting together a military force that would kill Annurians, loyal soldiers doing their best to hold their posts and defend the empire. It was a grim thought, one that refused to leave her as she worked with Lehav to make the force ready to march.

As it turned out, rallying an army wasn't simply a matter of running a flag up the pole, making a few stirring speeches, and passing out swords. Not even for a princess. Not even for a prophet. Adare had thought she understood something of military logistics from her reading, but the books made everything seem tidy, manageable, as though the main work were lining up wagons and procuring rations, meting out rank and enforcing discipline. Whoever wrote the books, however, had evidently authored them from a comfortable chair far from the mess of actual mobilization.

It took Lehav almost a full week just to assemble a respectable force out of the disbanded Sons of Flame. Most of the soldiers had quit Annur, traveling south partly to escape the capital, partly to chase the whispers they'd heard of a force coalescing secretly in Olon. Coalesce it certainly had—there were thousands upon thousands of Sons in and around the city—but the secret part meant that, for all but a few hundred, Lehav's innermost circle, there was no clear hierarchy, no established muster point, no protocol for the dissemination and verification of orders, nothing beyond a shared desire to defend Intarra with the force of their arms and a tenacious hatred of the Malkeenians.

The miracle at the Well had rehabilitated Adare in the eyes of many, but Lehav had been laying on anti-imperial propaganda with a trowel for a long time—it was the chief reason so many citizens were so ready to take up arms in the first place—and it took a concerted effort to reverse the message, to explain to scores, then hundreds, then thousands, that Adare was, in fact, a victim of the same vile treachery that had taken down the Intarran Church. Every morning and every night Lehav and Adare appeared in a small plaza before a new group of hardened faces, explaining that the conflict between them had been a misunderstanding, that both longed fervently for a strong empire in which the worship of Intarra would play a central part, that Ran il Tornja, *kenarang* turned regent, was their common foe.

"He knows we're coming," Lehav said one night, as the two of them sat picking over the bones of a fried carp. Despite his burns, Fulton had resumed his duties, but he waited just outside the door, leaving Adare and the soldier alone for the meal. "The palace has spies here, same as everywhere else, and there's no way to disguise what we're doing."

Adare nodded wearily. "Not that we have much of a choice."

"There are always choices."

She looked up from the fish, studying the man. Despite their common cause, despite Fulton's pardon and Adare's own sudden rise in stature among the Sons of Flame, Lehav still made her uneasy. He accepted her, worked with her, but she had no feeling at all for how he *felt* about her, and she had not forgotten that day in the Perfumed Quarter when he almost left her to the canal rats. She didn't question his devotion to the goddess, and Adare hoped that devotion might be enough to keep their paths running parallel, but there was no way to be sure. Unlike the others, Lehav referred to her as a princess still, not a prophet.

"Are you having doubts?" Adare asked.

Intarra knew she was having plenty of her own, but that didn't mean she was ready to lose the Sons of Flame. Without them, her defiance was dead, as she would be, when il Tornja finally caught up with her.

"I have questions," he said, setting his knife down, the blade disappearing into the thick sauce in the bottom of the platter.

"All right then," Adare said. "Ask them."

For a moment, he remained silent, studying the carcass of the fish. After a few heartbeats, he pulled off one of the ribs, sucked on it a moment, then tossed it back onto the tray.

"What is he like?" he asked finally. "The *kenarang*? What kind of man is he? What kind of soldier?"

"Why don't you tell me? You're the one who served under him."

"I was in the south, in the jungles. At that point, il Tornja was still a regional commander all the way up in Raalte. I've never even met the man."

Adare frowned, then shook her head. "I've read all the classic treatises, but I don't know the first thing about soldiering. Men say he's brilliant, that he wins battles no one else could win. His soldiers would follow him around the earth if he asked it, which I suppose makes him dangerous enough."

She paused. Her memories of il Tornja were like knives; bright and sharp, cutting.

"As for the man," she went on, trying to find the right words, "he seems flippant, dashing, insouciant . . . but it's not real. Not all of it, at least. I thought I was smart, but he used me, used me like a fine tool that he had chosen and polished for his purpose, used me without my even knowing it."

Lehav watched her, the reflected flame of the candle alive in his narrowed eyes. "You escaped," he pointed out.

She nodded bleakly. "And now we're going back."

Over the following days, the fear and uncertainty gnawed at her like a rat trapped in her guts. Still, speech by speech, day by day, the force grew. Men polished their armor, honed their blades, and joined the growing camp just north of the city. Just as importantly, the citizens of Olon and her hinterland gathered as well, some to gawk at the unexpected force, some from genuine devotion to either Adare or Intarra, some because they had something to sell—wagons, horses, grain. Offerings to Intarra's prophet were all well and good, but people needed to make a living, and there was good money to be made outfitting an army.

Where the money came from was a different question and one that, to Adare's surprise and satisfaction, she proved uniquely able to answer. Olon, for all its poverty and dilapidation, still acted as a funnel for most of the trade between central Eridroa and the capital itself. Significant trade meant significant taxes, and Adare, leveraging her twin roles as Malkeenian princess and the Minister of Finance, insisted on access to the imperial coffers, coffers packed with coin. Enough coin, as it turned out, to back an army.

A week after the lightning at the Well, the Sons of Flame had most of the supplies necessary to reach Annur. On the following day, they marched, leaving the city while a baffled population looked on, some cheering, some wary, wondering what effect that war would have on them, on their homes and families.

Only when Adare finally saw the army moving, marching, rank upon rank of men headed north, did she realize just how crucial the Sons of Flame were to her goals. She had known it in her head, of course—it was her whole reason for coming—but she could see it now, hear it, feel it in the trembling dirt beneath her boots. Despite their dislocation and the partial collapse of their Church, most of the Sons had served their order for years, and found little difficulty falling back into the old structures of command, the lifelong habits of discipline that distinguished a professional fighting force from a rabble of angry men with steel in their hands. Adare could have seized the Olonian treasury and tried to raise her own army, but the men would have had no cohesion, no training, no experience working in units, probably no idea how to walk in a line without stepping on one another's heels. As she marched north with the Sons, however, recapitulating in reverse her long miles along the canal, things went so smoothly that it was easy to forget that at the end of it, they would have to fight a battle. That at the end of it, prophets or not, they might all be dead.

25

K aden could remember slaughtering his first goat, sliding his carefully honed knife along the neck as he held the warm, trembling creature beneath one arm. He remembered the way the hair parted, then the skin beneath, the pink flesh fresh and unblemished for half a heartbeat before the blood welled in a hot, wet gush and the legs went abruptly slack.

He was only ten years old at the time, but he remembered Chalmer Oleki standing at his shoulder, instructing him to lay down the knife, to take up the large crock for the blood, to hold it beneath the wound. *"Blood and meat,"* Oleki had pointed out. *"A little bone. A little hair. But no soul."* He chuckled gently at the notion, a soft sound, like a stream running over smoothed rocks. He had shown Kaden how to gut the animal, lifting each organ in turn: *"The heart. The brain. The belly. A creature is no more than this.* You *are no more than this."*

So, too, this man that Kaden was readying himself to kill.

It was surprising how easy it had been to create the opportunity. He stood in the darkness of the door across from his own cell, knife at the ready, and waited, counting down the final heartbeats, until the man came, carrying the trencher in one hand, the storm lantern in the other. When Kaden heard the door at the end of the hallway open, he closed his lids over his flaming irises and waited, listening, until the footfalls paused. When he opened his eyes, the guard was setting down the lantern, back turned to him.

It was a simple thing. One cut across the throat and it was done: brutal, but simple. As Kaden stood in the darkness, however, parsing the guard's breaths, trying to measure the empty space between knife and neck, the most basic elements of the action suddenly seemed implausible, impossible. How would he cross the corridor? How would he pivot to bring that knife to bear? Should he move slowly, to avoid suspicion, or lash out all at once, murdering the man in one quick slice?

No, he reminded himself. *Not murdering.* "Murder" was a sloppy term, imprecise, laden with judgment and emotion. *Killing.* Killing described the action, nothing more. *I've killed goats,* Kaden reminded himself. *I thought I'd killed that leach back at the saddle.* Still, it was one thing to discharge a flatbow at Balendin from the still depths of the *vaniate*: a twitch of the finger, the reverberation of the spent bow, the brief whistle of the bolt in the air, and the man was gone, vanished off the side of the cliff. It hadn't felt like killing. It hadn't felt like anything. Cutting the guard's throat would be harder, messier.

He considered the exposed flesh below the jaw. *Here is the knife. Here is the neck.*

In the end, it was a simple matter of three steps followed by an extension of the arm. The blade bit immediately, snagged for a moment on the tough cartilage of the trachea, then pulled through, slick and hot and wet. The guard managed to half turn, reaching a hand toward Kaden's shoulder as if in friendship. Then the life fled his limbs and his head caved forward into the wreckage of his neck. Blood drenched Kaden's face and chest, slicking the hand that held the knife, pumping in stubborn dark sheets down the front of the dead man's sealskin cloak to puddle in the pits of the floor. The body slumped forward, then fell.

For a moment, Kaden didn't move. He stood, gory knife at his side, blood soaking his fetid clothes. Some feeling, delicate-pawed and silent as a mouse, prowled the edges of his brain, slipping away each time he tried to look at it directly. Guilt? Kaden glanced at the slumped form, the mound of bone and flesh that had, until moments before, been a man, then closed his eyes, trying to corner the elusive sensation. Regret? Doubt? It glared at him a moment, tiny, feral, then darted farther into darkness.

He'd lost track of his pulse in the attack, but it didn't matter now. Kiel's route out didn't involve the corridors above. The schedule of the Ishien no longer mattered.

Kaden picked up the storm lantern, slid open the shutters, allowed his eyes a few moments to adjust to the light, then rifled through the guard's tunic for the keys. At first he thought he'd gambled wrong, that the man wasn't carrying what he needed, but then, when he pulled aside the blood-soaked neck of the tunic, he found them, hanging on a chain around the neck.

Freeing Kiel was simple, a matter of lifting aside the heavy steel bars, fitting the key into the lock, then hauling the door open. Kaden winced as the hinges screamed in protest, his pulse rising for a moment, then settling.

"The guard is dead?" Kiel asked, stepping from the shadows.

Kaden nodded.

"Then there should be no one to hear us." He glanced past Kaden, as though searching for someone else. "Where is the girl?"

"This way," Kaden said, gesturing.

Kaden had found Triste's cell nearly a day earlier. Their captors had separated their three prisoners in widely spaced cells, making sure they couldn't communicate, and Kaden had spent almost a thousand heartbeats finding a locked door that showed signs of recent use. He'd considered freeing Triste then, explaining the whole plan to her, even enlisting her to help in the killing of the guard. It was tempting to have a companion, another conspirator, but he decided against it at the last minute. There was no telling what Matol and the Ishien intended, no telling when they might arrive to drag her back up to the chambers above. It seemed safer to leave her ignorant and in darkness until the time for escape had come. As he shoved open her door, however, he wondered if he'd misjudged the situation.

All he could see, by the meager light of his own eyes, was a slumped form crouched against the rear wall of the cell. Even in the cramped space, Triste looked small, huddled in the farthest corner, a clenched ball of fear and pain. She cried out at the sudden light, shielded her eyes with a hand, and turned toward the stone as though she could burrow into it. There were cuts on that hand, Kaden realized, burns and lacerations. *This is why I killed the guard,* he reminded himself. *This is why I defied Tan.* He took a few steps forward, approaching the shivering girl as though she were a frightened, wounded beast slipped from the fold and lost in the mountains.

"No," she moaned. "Please . . ."

"Triste," he said, the word brittle in the chilly air. He tried again, forcing more warmth into the syllables. "*Triste.* It's Kaden. We're leaving. We're *leaving.*"

She half raised her head, blinking at him from between tangled threads of hair, still blind from the light. Blood and grime ran in streaks down her arms and face. Someone had hacked off most of her hair. The Aedolian uniform she had been wearing since the Bone Mountains was nearly shredded. She ran her fingers over the wet stone, caressing it as though it were the cheek of a sleeping child. Her fingernails, Kaden realized, were ragged, bloody.

"Leaving?" she asked quietly.

"Fleeing. We have to move fast, before the next guard comes. Before Matol sends someone else."

She shivered at the name, then pushed herself unsteadily to her feet. "What do we do?"

"Go with Kiel."

"Who's Kiel?"

"Someone who can get us out."

✝

The still, black pool seemed to drink the lamplight, as though it were pitch or oil rather than salt water, as though anything dipped into it would slide instantly into utter darkness. It was barely more than a pace across, the diameter of a small well, but Kaden could imagine it plunging down endlessly to the very center of the earth.

"This is it," Kiel said.

Kaden glanced over at Triste. She was trembling, staring at the pool as though into the maw of some great stone beast.

"There's no other way?" she asked, her voice tiny, terrified. "What about the ship that Kaden mentioned? The one Tan suggested?"

Kaden hesitated. Staring into the dark water, it was tempting to double back, to break out through the main door of the prison, to hope they could hide Triste during the long walk to the underground harbor. It was tempting, and foolish. Triste's tattered Aedolian uniform did nothing to conceal her identity, less than nothing. Even in shadows, even at a glance, it was obvious that she was a woman, and there were no other women in the Dark Heart. They could sneak into the corridors above hoping for the best, but Kaden was through hoping.

"Too much risk if we go the other way. This will take us straight to the *kenta* chamber."

"But the men," Triste said. "The ones with the bows . . ."

"Will never see us," Kiel said. "They're outside the pool, waiting on the ledge above it. We'll never break the surface."

"And they don't guard this?" Kaden asked, gesturing to the pool.

Kiel raised an eyebrow. "Would you?"

"What's down there?" Triste asked.

"Tunnels. Rooms. Old halls. When the Ishien flooded the *kenta,* they flooded dozens of the lower passages, too. It was a reasonable decision. No one's likely to navigate that maze after stepping through the gate, not underwater, not before their air runs out."

Kaden stared bleakly at the still surface of the pool. "No one except us," he said.

"Well." Kiel spread his hands. "We're going to try."

"How far?" Triste asked.

The Csestriim paused, eyes going distant and unfocused for a moment, then nodded. "One hundred and eighty-seven paces. Give or take."

Kaden stared. "Did you measure it?"

"In my mind. It's been thousands of years. I could be off."

"Two hundred paces," Triste groaned, shaking her head. "I'm not sure I could swim that far *above* water."

"You don't have to swim," Kiel replied. "Not much. I'll guide you, pull you."

"And what about you?" Kaden asked, shaking his head. "It seems almost impossible, even without the extra effort."

"There are techniques," the Csestriim replied, "to slow the heart, to use the muscles more judiciously. . . ."

Kaden paused, realizing all over again that the man beside him was not a man at all. The Shin, with their training and their discipline, could manage amazing feats, could sit nearly naked in the winter snow or stay awake for a week, but compared to Kiel, the Shin were children, fools, tiny creatures exploring the first rooms of a vast city, the scope of which they could barely apprehend.

"And me?" Kaden asked.

"You will enter the *vaniate* here," Kiel replied. "That will do something to slow your pulse and keep you from panic. If you are judicious with your breath, it will be enough."

"If," Kaden said, shaking his head. "*If* you remember the distance correctly, *if* I can follow you down there, *if* I can hold on to the *vaniate* . . . It's all *ifs.* I'm starting to wonder if we shouldn't risk the ship."

Kiel cocked his head to the side. "Nothing is certain. If we travel the tunnels above, you trust to luck. If we take this route, you have only yourself to rely on."

"And you," Triste said, rounding on him, her voice high, close to hysteria. "You're *Csestriim*. Now that Kaden's broken you out, you could take us down there and leave us. We don't even know the tunnel leads to the *kenta*!"

Kiel nodded. "I could. And you don't. What you do know, however," he went on, indicating the lacerations around Triste's wrists, the blistered fingers of her right hand, "is what will happen to you if they capture you again. The water may kill you, but not like this."

Triste blanched, glanced down the corridor the way they had come. Kaden followed her gaze.

"I don't like leaving Tan," he said, shaking his head. "The Ishien don't trust him any more than they do me. When we disappear, they will put the pieces together. They'll know what happened."

"So will he," Kiel said. "Rampuri Tan is more dangerous and resourceful than you know. He will find his own way."

"And if he does not?"

The Csestriim met his eyes. "Then he does not. There is no easy path, Kaden. You can save Triste, or you can save Tan, not both."

Kaden looked over at the girl. She was hugging herself, shivering in the chill dark.

"All right," he said slowly. "The *vaniate*."

"I don't know the *vaniate*," Triste said, voice crumbling. "I don't know how to slow my breath."

Kiel nodded. "I'm not sure you'll survive to the *kenta,* but the choice is yours."

She turned to Kaden, eyes wide, pleading. "What do we do?"

He hesitated. He didn't want the decision, didn't want the responsibility that came with it, but wanting, as the Shin had told him hundreds of times, was just another way to suffer.

He set aside the fear and emotion both, tried to see the situation clearly, coldly. If they escaped, if he retook his throne, he could come back for Tan. More, if Triste *was* Csestriim, he needed her, needed what she knew, to understand the plot against his family. It was a hard choice, but Rampuri Tan had taught him something about hardness.

"There is a strength inside you, Triste," he said. "Something even you don't understand. It's why they imprisoned you in the first place. You ran through the mountains. You passed the *kenta* twice already—"

Furious shouts split straight through his words, cleaving the calm he had so carefully guarded. He tried to count the voices. There were three, no . . . five, and loudest among them, Matol, bellowing his fury.

". . . want them found, and I want them found *now*. Two men in each cell, take this fucking place *apart*. And someone find Rampuri Tan, that treacherous bastard."

Boots clattered on the stone. Steel hinges screamed. Men barked commands back and forth.

"It's too soon," Kaden said, staring down the corridor. "They shouldn't be here."

"There is no *should*," Kiel said quietly. "Only *is*. Prepare yourself."

Kaden measured a long breath, holding it in his lungs, but before he could exhale, the first Ishien rounded the corner, blades bright with the light of their lanterns. For a moment, no one moved. Then the leader— Hellelen, Kaden realized, the same man who had first challenged them at the *kenta*—smiled.

"Here!" he shouted over his shoulder. "They're here, cowering in a corner."

"Quickly," Kiel murmured.

Kaden reached for the *vaniate*, but it was like clawing at cloud. His mind passed through the emptiness, but failed to enter it. The gong of his heart tolled in his ears.

"I can't," he said, shaking his head.

Triste had turned to face the men, teeth bared, hands twisted into claws as though she intended to rend the skin from their faces.

"They cannot follow us," Kiel said. There was no fear in his voice, no urgency. "Find the trance."

"I'm *trying*," Kaden replied, but the Ishien were already advancing, moving slowly down the hallway, obviously enjoying the sight of their trapped quarry. And there were more behind, more than enough to kill them all a dozen times over. Even as Kaden stared, another figure rounded the corner at a full run, sword spinning in his hands.

No, he realized, shock blazing over his skin before he managed to snuff it out. *Not a sword, a spear.*

A *naczal*.

The first two men went down without a sound, one with a slit throat, the other stabbed through the chest. The third Rampuri Tan hamstrung. The Ishien fell, trying to bring his sword to bear as Tan shattered his skull. Hellelen stood a moment longer, lips pulled back in a snarl. He feinted right, danced left, but Tan ignored both motions, lashing out with one end of his spear, then spinning it in a great, vicious arc that hacked halfway through Hellelen's neck. The monk didn't even watch the body slump to the floor, turning instead to Kaden.

"You are a fool," he said.

"There's a way out," Kaden insisted, stabbing a finger at the pool behind them.

It was less than no explanation. It didn't explain Kiel or Triste, didn't begin to tell how the motionless water could lead to safety, but after a glance at the dark surface, Tan seemed to understand.

"You are trusting your life to a Csestriim," he said grimly.

"There was no other choice," Kaden spat. "I'm not leaving Triste."

"We are not all what you fear," Kiel said quietly. "I am not Tan'is. Not Asherah."

The monk locked gazes with the prisoner, then shook his head curtly. "It hardly matters now. The dice are already thrown."

"Stay close to us," Kaden said. "In the tunnels."

"No," Tan replied. "There is no time. I will cover your retreat."

"You don't have to—" Kaden began, but even as the words left his lips, Matol charged around the corner, a dozen Ishien flanking him, then skidded to a stop at the sight of his quarry. He paused, flexed his free hand, then smiled.

"I will flay the skin from each of you piece by dripping piece."

"You are welcome to try," Tan said, turning toward him, the *naczal* light in his hands. "Go, Kaden."

"I don't—"

"Go."

The *vaniate* came grudgingly, but it came at last. While Tan held back the Ishien, his spear bright and faster than thought, Kaden found the trance, dropped into it as though into a deep well while Matol roared, bodies crumpled, and blood ran over the stone.

"Follow closely," Kiel said, then stepped into the pool.

The last thing Kaden saw before the water folded over him was Rampuri Tan, his teacher and tormentor, the last and hardest of the Shin monks, fighting desperately, viciously, trying to hold back the Ishien for another heartbeat, and another, and another, fighting to buy Kaden time to escape. In the blankness of the *vaniate*, Kaden watched as the monk fought and staggered, watched, but could not care.

┼

The darkness of the flooded levels of the Dead Heart was cold, absolute, and crushing. Even deep inside the *vaniate,* Kaden could feel fear prowling the edges of his mind like a winter-starved wolf, could feel his muscles wanting to buck, kick, thrash. Normally he would have taken deep, long breaths to quell the faint agitation, but there was no breath to be had in the watery maze, and so he counted the beats of his heart instead, feeling the muscle contract and relax, contract and relax, and he moved forward with careful strokes of his arm, measured kicks of his legs below the knee, keeping one hand fixed firmly on Triste's ankle.

Her flesh was so cold beneath his touch that she might have been dead already, drowned beneath the great weight of water and stone, save for the occasional jerk or spasm when Kiel bumped her up against some hard, invisible corner. Kaden tried to envisage the darkness around them as halls and rooms, corridors and entryways, the normal architecture of human habitation, but it was no good. There was only the darkness, and the cold, and the salt, and the stone. It didn't feel like the world at all, but like the weightless, shapeless dreamscape of nightmare.

For all his recent training with the *vaniate,* the trance felt tenuous, as though a sharp jolt might shatter it. He tried not to think what would happen if he slipped from the calm into the relative clamor of his own mind. The *vaniate* was keeping him alive during the slow, creeping passage, but more important, it would allow him to pass the *kenta* at the end. Without it, the gate would annihilate him.

Feel the water on your face, he reminded himself. *Feel the wet cold on your skin. This is the world. The future is a dream.*

Around his eight hundredth heartbeat, Triste began to twist and jerk. At first the motions were just spasms, like the twitch of a leg from one on the edge of slumber. Within a few dozen heartbeats, however, she had begun to thrash and flail, kicking her legs madly as the panic seized her, heel striking Kaden in the head, the eyes, over and over as he struggled grimly to hold on to her ankle and the *vaniate* both.

Kaden's own chest felt tight and his lungs burned. Triste couldn't have much longer. Her body was rebelling, the instinct to tear her way free of danger crushing whatever part of her reason that tried to resist. It was making Kiel's work harder, although the Csestriim labored on, hauling her down the invisible corridor, moving, if anything, even faster than he had, although it was difficult to gauge speed in the darkness. There was only the water, the cold, Triste's terror, the rough stone, and the awful empty airlessness searing Kaden's own chest, the sluggish weight of muscles barely able to move.

They were going to die down there, all three of them, their bodies vanished inside a fortress that had, itself, vanished from the world. Sadness beckoned, like faint sunlight seen from beneath deep water. Kaden turned away from it. If he followed that light long enough, he would burst from the *vaniate,* and he had no desire to face his own slow suffocation outside the trance.

The pain is just pain. The pressure of the water is just pressure. Listen to the movement of your heart. It is only a muscle. It is only meat.

He repeated the words until his mind swam in the darkness with his body. It was a good place to die, a peaceful place. He let the darkness pour into him, fill him, flood him, until there was no line between his own flesh and the surrounding sea, until the ocean thrummed in him like his own heart, until, with an awful wrenching jerk, gravity seized him, hauling him, dazed and baffled, into the wide awful air and the blinding light of the sun.

Alive, Kaden thought. *I'm alive.*

Deep inside the *vaniate,* the thought brought him no joy. No sorrow. It was a fact, nothing more.

26

Hundreds of years earlier the walls of Annur had actually ringed the city; torches had blazed in the guard towers punctuating their length while armed men walked the parapets, spears in hand. It had been generations, however, since any foe posed a plausible threat to the capital, and Annur had long ago burst its seams. The houses and warehouses, stables and temples spilled out into the countryside, eating up the open fields and burying the walls behind entire neighborhoods—Newquarter, Canal, Fieldstreets—all of them utterly exposed. From the fields, Adare stared at the city's outermost buildings—a motley collection of stone granaries and stilted teak houses built over the canals and streams—dread gnawing at her guts.

Water buffalo cropped the early summer grass, ducks scrabbled for scraps in the dusty roads, two cranes balanced in the shallows of a trash-choked canal, beaks darting for fish, but there were no people. There should have been wagons on the roads and farmers in the surrounding fields, the chatter and hum of men and women going about their lives. Instead, there was stillness, silence, a hot sun stuck in the sky as though nailed there. The citizens of these outlying quarters of Annur were gone, or hiding, neither of which did anything to alleviate Adare's fear.

No army had met them on the long march north. At first, Adare had felt relieved by that, then surprised, then worried. Lehav had set a brutal pace, and the Sons had outdistanced all the wagons on the road. Still, dozens of canal boats had slipped past them, gliding effortlessly on the current, all packed with deckhands gaping at the army, all headed for Annur. For all their haste, there was no way they had stolen a march on il Tornja, and their approach—a straight shot up the canal road—left him with a number of ways to respond.

Each day, Adare expected her own scouts to return with news of an Annurian army camped athwart the road. Mostly, she had dreaded the word, but at least a battle on the road might take place well clear of the city. The armies would churn the fields to mud, ruining the season's crop, but if a crop was all that came to ruin as a result of her revolution, Adare would count herself lucky. The fact that the *kenarang* had not already opposed them terrified her. If he chose to make his stand in the cramped streets of the capital itself, houses would burn, shops and businesses. Men and women, Annurians, would die.

What's your plan, you bastard? she wondered, standing in her stirrups, trying to peer into the shadowed gaps between the buildings. *What's your angle?*

"Looks like he's aiming to meet us at the walls," Lehav said, squinting through his long lens. "Good."

Adare stared. *"Good?"*

He nodded. "The old walls are at least ten blocks back, packed between houses and shops. We'll see what the scouts have to say about the fortification of the streets, but city fighting should give us the advantage. The legions train to fight on open ground, but the Sons have been drilling street warfare since before Uinian's death."

"To fight us," Adare said, studying him. "To fight the throne."

"This fight's been a long time coming," he said, meeting her gaze.

Adare clenched her hands around the reins of her horse. Her old general had murdered her father, her new general had been scheming for years to fight her empire, and her only councillor was a half-crazed leach. The fact that she was still alive seemed nothing short of miraculous, and the odds of remaining so loomed longer by the moment.

"If we go to the streets," she said, "people will die. I've read about siege warfare. Houses will burn. Businesses. Whole quarters of the city could be destroyed."

Lehav fixed her with a hard stare. "You came here to start a war. Or did you forget?"

Before Adare could respond, two riders cantered out of the city, hooves of their horses raising a nervous tattoo on the earth. Lehav raised the long lens again, watched for a moment, then grunted. "Ours."

The men reined up before them, bowing in their saddles to Adare, then turning to Lehav.

"Defenses?" he asked.

The older of the two—a short man with a lopsided mouth and ears that looked nailed to the side of his broad head—frowned, then jerked a thumb back over his shoulder.

"Nothin', Commander. No folks in the streets, but no soldiers either."

Lehav frowned, then glanced over at the other scout. "And you?"

"Same. No army. No sign of an army. There's no one at all on these streets here, but you get five or six blocks in and it's packed with folks, same as any other day, like they don't even know that we're here."

"An ambush," Fulton said. The guardsman had remained still as stone throughout the conversation, mounted on his own gray gelding just behind Adare's left shoulder, but he nudged the beast forward now. "Ran il Tornja will have his men inside the shops and houses. Once you commit your force to the streets, they'll close in behind you, cut your own army into pieces. Take you apart one block at a time."

Lehav nodded. If he was irritated by the Aedolian's comment, he didn't show it. "They can't block every street," he said. "We'll march west, come in through the Stranger's Gate—"

Fulton raised a hand, cutting him off, then pointed past them all, toward the city. "You may be spared the march."

Adare pivoted in her saddle to find another knot of riders emerging from the buildings, maybe a dozen men on horses gleaming with silk and bronze. Unlike the scouts, the new party rode at a stately walk, pennons snapping at the breeze above, pennons stitched with the rising sun of Annur.

"Who is it?" Adare asked.

Lehav trained the long lens on the group. "Palace guards, squared up in a standard protective knot."

"Who are they protecting?"

He shook his head. "I don't know him. He has long hair and . . ." He paused, squinting. "Looks like a blindfold over his eyes."

Adare took a deep breath, held it a moment, then let it out, trying to order her thoughts.

"The Mizran Councillor," Fulton ground out. "Tarik Adiv. Part of the delegation to retrieve Kaden."

She nodded grimly. "Looks like he's back."

Fulton and Lehav positioned themselves between Adare and the approaching horsemen. She glanced over her shoulder, reminding herself that an army stood at her back, then tried to keep her back straight and her hands steady on the reins as she watched the men approach.

When Adiv was still ten paces distant, he dismounted. Then, to her shock, he bowed low, lower than he ever had when she was merely a princess. It was hard to interpret that bow—something short of the obeisance owed to an emperor, and yet more than her own collection of titles warranted, certainly more than Adare had expected. Adiv was il Tornja's man. He had no reason to bow to her.

"Keep your distance," Fulton said, stepping in front of Adare, broadblade naked in the morning light.

Adiv simply smiled. "Your loyalty does you credit, Aedolian, but I have no desire to harm the princess. Quite the opposite, actually." He cocked his head to the side in that way he had, as though he were studying her through that heavy blindfold. "The regent has asked that I escort you to the Dawn Palace with all due respect."

Fulton shook his head. "Not a chance."

Adare put her hand on the Aedolian's arm, moving the sword from her path.

"I'm sure the regent is clever enough to know," she said, careful to keep her voice low, level, "that I am here, *we* are here because of him. Where is Kaden? The last I saw you, you were bound north to retrieve him."

Adiv winced. "I beg you, my lady, let us discuss these matters in the privacy of the palace. There is much you do not know. Events have outpaced you during your sojourn in the south."

"Is my father still dead?" Adare demanded. "Has Kaden claimed his throne? Does Ran il Tornja still make a mockery of the Dawn Palace?"

Adiv shook his head gravely. "The Emperor, bright were the days of his life, is dead, of course. Kaden has not returned. The regent himself is gone."

"Gone where?"

"Raalte. Marching hard with the Army of the North."

"Raalte?" Adare frowned. It all made less than no sense. "To what end? Against whom?"

Adiv's lips tightened, and he took a step forward, approaching until the point of Fulton's sword lay against his chest. "We should not speak of this here, my lady," he said, lowering his voice. "While you were away, the Urghul moved, attacking in force against our northern border. Il Tornja goes to turn them back."

"An opportunity," Lehav observed quietly. "If it is true."

The Mizran Councillor turned his unseeing gaze on the soldier. "An opportunity to see Annur destroyed."

"I don't serve Annur. I serve the goddess."

"You may find that more difficult," Adiv said pointedly, "if the Urghul take over. The only prayer will be a prayer of blood."

"You understand," Adare hissed, "that I know the truth. All of it. I came here to destroy the regent."

Adiv grimaced. "A fact the Ministry of Truth has labored late into the night to obscure. Now, of all times, Annur needs unity, in appearance as well as fact."

Adare stared. "How do you obscure an army of thousands marching up the canal road?"

She gestured over her shoulder to where the Sons of Flame waited, butts of their spears bedded in the earth, the shafts a forest of stark trees, denuded in the summer heat, as though struck by some awful blight. Sun flashed from the bronze of shields and breastplates, bright enough to blind.

Adiv followed her gaze, as though, despite his blindness, he could sense the weight of that army, the sheer mass of flesh and sharpened steel. "We told the citizens of Annur," he said quietly, "that you were coming to help. That you went to Olon to reconcile the throne with the Church of Intarra. Which it seems you have." He paused, then beggared his hands, imploring. "Annur needs you, my lady."

"We're all well fuckin' aware of that," Nira spat, kicking her horse forward. "Seems ta me, the question is whether it needs *you*."

Adiv turned to face the old woman, brows rising behind his blindfold. "I don't believe I've had the pleasure. . . ."

Nira snorted. "Save it. The princess isn't goin' ta the palace."

Fulton nodded. "I agree."

"I can offer myself as surety," Adiv said. "My life hostage against her safety."

"The life a' one overdressed blind bastard against a princess?" Nira said. "Against a prophet? I don't think so."

"Nira . . ." Adare said, putting up a hand.

"You made me councillor," she snapped, "so I'm counselin'."

"I'm going," Adare said.

"My lady," Fulton burst out.

Adare cut him off. "If the Mizran Councillor wanted me dead, he would hardly be offering himself as surety. I don't understand what's happening here, but if there is an opportunity to avoid open war in the streets of Annur, I will not be the one to turn it down. This is my city, these are my people." She looked up, past Adiv, past the jumbled riot of houses and stables, to the great ironglass needle bisecting the sky, its impossible height bright with the sun's own light. "It is my palace. My empire."

✝

The outer neighborhoods of Annur may have been quiet, the people frightened inside their homes by the sight of an approaching army, but the streets of the city center were awash with the usual hum and clatter. Wagon-drivers goaded along their oxen and buffalo; shopkeepers hawked their wares from windows and doorways; porters shoved their way forward through the throng, some bent nearly double beneath bolts of cloth, baskets of firefruit or coal, loads of fresh-cut lumber still smelling of sap. Alone, Adare would have found it nearly impossible to move through the press, but then, she was hardly alone.

Adiv's guards ringed her in a loose net, along with Fulton, Nira, and Oshi, who rode at her side. Adiv himself rode in front of the procession, trusting to the crowd to part before the pennons flapping behind and above him. Lehav had remained behind with the Sons of Flame, the implicit threat of the army one more blade to hold at the Mizran's neck. By the time they reached the Godsway, word of her entry to the city had spread. Men and women had halted their conversation and commerce to stare, then bow their heads at her passage. If the Mizran Councillor intended to murder her, he had certainly picked a strange way to go about it, and as they progressed farther and farther into the city, Adare's confidence rose.

Nira, however, was less sanguine.

"He's a leach," she hissed, leaning over in her saddle to speak almost directly in Adare's ear.

Adare stared. "Adiv?"

The old woman nodded. "Strong, too. Dangerous."

"My father appointed him Mizran Councillor," Adare said, shaking her head.

"Then your father appointed a leach."

Adare studied Adiv's back, the knot in his blindfold. "How do you know?"

"Live a few hundred years, you pick up a few things."

The revelation was a shock. Leaches were perversions, twisted creatures, and Nira's own identity, the awful powers she held in check, still chafed at Adare like a sharp stone in a shoe. For all that she had begged the woman to be her councillor, she still found herself stealing glances at her several times a day, found herself wondering if she had made an awful mistake, had invited a serpent into her home. In a way, Nira's identity made Adiv's less shocking, and yet the thought that a leach sat near the very top of the ziggurat of Annurian power, that he served the *kenarang*, that he, of all people, had been dispatched to the Bone Mountains to recover Kaden, set her heart hammering.

Nothing for it now, she said, trying to sit straight in her saddle, to look unworried, imperial. Thousands of eyes were on her, and though she intended to see il Tornja's head parted violently from his shoulders, it would do no good to let the citizens of the capital read her fury on her face.

After a circuitous route through Annur's southern streets, they reached the Godsway. After Olon, where even the largest thoroughfares twisted unpredictably between towers and falling palaces, where to leave the main streets was to step into a labyrinth of alleyways so narrow that Adare could almost touch both walls with her hands, the Godsway felt more like a geological feature, a massive, sword-straight rift bisecting the city, than it did a road built by men. Storefronts lined both sides of the street, merchants and craftsmen selling everything from firefruit, to bright-plumed birds, to small, intricate altars of wood and stone. Down the center of the avenue, set on stone plinths twice her own height, huge statues of the young gods and the old watched over the city—Intarra and Hull, Pta and Astar'ren, Ciena and Meshkent and their children set one after the other. The people of Annur used the statues as they might any other landmark— "Go to the butcher just north of Eira." "I'll meet you by Heqet's feet"— but Adare felt the stone gazes of the monuments as she rode beneath them, hard and unforgiving, and after glancing up a couple of times, she kept her eyes forward.

After the congestion of the city and the stares of the gods, it was a relief to finally approach the red walls of the Dawn Palace. Intarra's Spear loomed over it all, slate gray in the fading light, the top of the tower lost in cloud. Adare resisted the urge to crane her neck to peer up at the thing. It was her palace, after all, her home. It would not do to be seen gawking.

The huge cedar doors of the Godsgate remained closed, of course. No one, not even emperors, presumed to use the gateway ordained for the passage of the divine. The Great Gate beside it, however, was flung open wide, flanked by what must have been a hundred palace guards at stiff attention. She had fled the palace in the drab wool of a servant, but was returning in all the splendor of a Malkeenian princess. Somehow, it seemed too easy.

Adiv's men escorted them beneath the massive walls—thick as a house and banded with red iron—through the Jade Court and the Jasmine, passing along the Serpentine in the shadow of Yvonne's and the Crane, then through the shattered refraction cast by Intarra's Spear. They bypassed the Hall of a Thousand Trees, and the hanging staircase leading to the Floating Hall, ending, finally, in the Chamber of Scribes. It was an old name, and an inaccurate one. The scribes who once used the small complex of pavilions had been displaced centuries earlier by the upper echelon of an expanding bureaucracy, and the chamber itself was decorated like an atrep's palace rather than an austere scriptorium. Delicate Liran ivories stood in the wall niches, Rabin carpets splayed across the floor, and carved cedars from the Ancaz stood sentry in the corners.

When the slaves had set cool water and Si'ite wine in iced decanters on the table, Adiv sent them away with a negligent flick of his hand, shutting the door behind them.

"So," Adare said, tongue dry in her mouth, palms slick, "what in 'Shael's name is going on?"

Adiv hesitated, then gestured to Nira and Oshi, to Fulton where he stood by the doors. "What I have to say is known only to a small circle. Do you really wish to enlarge it?"

"Yes," Adare said stiffly, glancing at Oshi, hoping she wasn't making a mistake.

"As you wish, my lady," the councillor replied, spreading his hands. "Wine?"

Adare shook her head curtly. "Answers."

Adiv bowed his acquiescence. "As you say, my lady."

"Where is Kaden?"

"Your brother is dead." He shook his head slowly. "We arrived too late. The monks were slaughtered—"

"Horseshit," Adare snapped, cutting through his words. "You expect me to believe that he just *happened* to die at the very same time as my father, that you crossed half of Vash with a contingent of soldiers and had nothing to do with his death? You expect me to believe that?"

Adiv pursed his lips. "No," he said slowly. "In fact, I do not, nor do I blame you for your distrust. Nonetheless, it is the truth."

"Who would kill a batch a' monks?" Nira demanded.

"The Urghul," Adiv replied. "As you may know, Ashk'lan sits in the mountains overlooking the steppe. It is a remote place, and one vulnerable to the depredations of those blood-hungry savages."

Adare shook her head. "You've ignored your history, Councillor. Ashk'lan has stood for at least five hundred years. Perhaps much, much longer. Not once, in all that time, have the Urghul attacked."

"And not once," he replied evenly, "in all that time, have the Urghul united under a single leader. Not once have they ridden, all together, against the empire itself."

"Unified?" Fulton asked, brow furrowed. "Doesn't sound like the Urghul."

"It is not."

"Under whom?" Adare demanded.

"A chieftain named Long Fist. Or a shaman. It's not entirely clear. Our scouts rarely return, and though il Tornja has dispatched several Kettral Wings against the man, they have failed to find him, let alone eliminate him."

"But why would they attack a group of monks?"

"Presumably," Adiv replied, "they were not after the monks. I would suspect this is all a part of Long Fist's plan. He aims to destabilize the empire by killing Sanlitun's heir, then to strike in the ensuing confusion." He hesitated, clasped his hands before him.

"What?" Adare demanded.

"There is more."

"I got that. What *is* it?"

"Your brother," Adiv replied after a pause. "Valyn. It looks as though he may have been involved."

Adare stared. *Valyn.* He would be a man grown by now, a Kettral in his own right, but all she remembered was the wiry, dark child who had raced about the Dawn Palace brandishing wooden swords. He'd been loud and reckless, irritating when there was work to be done, but never cruel.

"Say more," she growled quietly.

Adiv spread his hands. "We can't be certain, but he disappeared from the Islands in direct violation of orders. Ashk'lan was burned by the time we got there—clearly Urghul work, as I said. But . . . there were signs of Kettral presence as well. A smoke steel blade lost in the rubble." He shook his head. "We can't be certain, of course. No one actually *saw* your brother, but he is still missing. It would not be the first time siblings killed over the Unhewn Throne."

"No," Adare said abruptly, the blood mounting to her face, fingers curling into claws. "*No.* The *kenarang* murdered my father. Murdered him and then made me his tool to cover the murder. I *know,* you fucking bastard. *I know all of it.*"

Nira put a withered hand on her arm, but Adare shrugged it off. She was shouting, she realized, and though a faint voice in her mind told her she should keep her voice down, that no one was served by her strident accusations, the return to the palace had torn open the memory of her father's death, of his body laid in the tomb, and she wanted nothing more than to find il Tornja and everyone else responsible, to slit their throats and tumble them, graveless, into some stagnant canal.

If Adiv was taken aback by her rage, he didn't show it. Instead, he nodded and reached forward, plucking a small scroll from the neck of a slender green vase at the center of the table.

"The *kenarang* told me that you would say as much. He instructed me to give you this."

Adare took the scroll—fine vellum stamped with the rising sun of Annur—and turned it over warily in her hands.

"What new lie is here?" she asked, running a finger over the wax impression.

Adiv shook his head. "I am ignorant of its contents. It is for your eyes alone."

Frowning, Adare flicked open the wax seal with her nail, then scanned the contents, blood ablaze in her veins.

Adare,
   You fled the palace believing I killed your father, and I can't blame you. I did.

The blunt admission was like a cold claw gripping her heart, and for a moment she couldn't breathe, couldn't even see. Her father's note was one thing, but this, the brutal, ineluctable truth of it . . . Breath burning in her lungs, she forced herself to read on.

Please believe me when I tell you I didn't want to do it. In almost every way, Sanlitun was an ideal emperor: pragmatic, honest, clever. His only real flaw was his relationship with the Urghul. For reasons I still cannot fathom, he trusted Long Fist, believed there could be an accord with the man. I fought the Urghul chief for years. I know him far better than your father ever did, and I assure you, Long Fist intends to see Annur destroyed.

Again and again I tried to explain this to Sanlitun, but something blinded him to the urgency. In the end, my choice was between your family and the empire itself. Believe me when I say it was not a choice I wanted.

You will distrust this note, as you should, but I ask only one thing. March north, in the tracks of my own army. When you catch us on the frontier, you can judge for yourself whether I have lied to you about the Urghul threat. If I have, better to have our battle there, where no citizens will die. If you decide that I have told the truth, however, you can join your army to mine. I promise you, when the contest comes, every spear will matter, every sword, every 'Kent-kissing fist.

I am sorry for your father's death. I liked the Emperor and I respected him, but he was only one man. Annur is millions.

If, as my people tell me, you have Intarra's favor, pray for us all. The darkness rides.

Your Kenarang,
Ran il Tornja

When she'd finished reading, it was all she could do to keep her feet. She stared at the vellum, the lines and angles of the words shifting before her eyes. Only when the first tear hit the ink, blurring it, did she realize she was crying.

"My lady?" Fulton asked, taking a step from his post by the door. "What does it say?"

Adare took a deep, shuddering breath. "It says we march north."

Nira stared. "For what?"

"To fight," Adare replied.

"Fight who?"

"I haven't decided yet," Adare said grimly.

Adiv nodded his support. "The *kenarang* said you would understand the urgency, that you would make the wise decision. He has instructed me to aid you in any way I can, to support you in every particular." He spread his hands. "You need only speak."

For a long time, Adare said nothing. She studied the note in her hands, then the hands themselves. *They should be trembling,* she thought. She felt as though her whole body were trembling, caught in the grip of loss, and grief, and anger. Her hands, however, were still. She might have been testing a bolt of fine silk between her fingers rather than holding a message from the man who had murdered her father. She had come to Annur to start a war, only to be welcomed into her own palace. She had come home, returned to her place, but it was not hers, not fully, not yet.

"You have heard," Adare said, raising her eyes to the Mizran Councillor, "of the events at the Everburning Well?"

Adiv nodded slowly. "I hear, in the murmurs from the south, the same word again and again: prophet. Would that I had eyes to see Intarra's markings on your flesh."

Adare ran an absent finger along the burns on her wrist, tracing the ramifying swirls.

"You will repeat the murmurs," she said. "You will confirm them, here in the capital."

The man hesitated, then nodded. "Of course, my lady. Of course. Intarra has ever smiled upon your family, and if anyone deserves this title, it is you—"

"That is not all," Adare said, cutting him short.

Adiv paused, pursing his lips.

Now, Adare thought. The burns on her skin flamed, as though traced with a glowing knife. She could hear her heart in her ears, and wondered in brief amazement that the others couldn't hear it, too. *It has to be now.*

"I will march north," she said, "and I will do what needs to be done, with the Urghul and il Tornja both. I will do this because there is no one else to see it through. My father is murdered, Kaden is murdered, and though Valyn may survive somewhere, I have the eyes. I will sit the Unhewn Throne. I will see Intarra's justice done."

27

*C*ollateral.

Even back on the Islands, Gwenna had hated the word. For one thing, the two meanings were always getting tangled up. She'd eavesdrop on veteran Wings in the mess hall just after they touched down, and collateral seemed to come up a lot. Trouble was, you couldn't always tell whether they were talking about collateral as in *hostage,* or collateral as in *some poor, miserable idiot who had nothing to do with anything and ended up dead anyway.*

'Course, it didn't help, the way that the former seemed to have a habit of becoming the latter. As far as Gwenna was concerned, the word was just a way to weasel around a hard truth. Instead of, "I had to grab the guy's kid and put a knife to her throat to get him to cooperate," you were encouraged to say, "We had collateral when we hit the target." Instead of saying, "The kid got burned down with the building," it was just "some collateral damage."

As much as she hated the word on the Islands, however, she was discovering that she liked it even less now that she—she, and Annick, and Pyrre—had become the 'Kent-kissing collateral.

"Are we just going to sit here?" she demanded. It was a stupid question, but it felt good to say something. Talking wasn't doing, but it was a long sight better than waiting with your thumb up your ass to see if the bloodthirsty, savage chief in whose care you got dumped intended to play nice, which, as far as Gwenna could tell, was exactly what they'd been doing for the past day.

"Certainly not," Pyrre said, raising her head from the far side of the fire. "I intend to drink heavily."

The assassin was making the most of the comforts of the *api* Long Fist had provided. Sprawled out on a mound of bison hides, half reclined, one hand playing idly with her hair, she might have been waiting on a servant to bring another pitcher of chilled juice. Only she wasn't drinking juice. Gwenna had tried one gulp of the clear liquor in the skin and nearly spat out her own tongue. Pyrre just tipped back her head and shot a long stream into her mouth.

"You shouldn't be drinking," Annick said, looking up from the bloody shank of bison she was cutting into strips, then drying over the fire. "We should be planning."

"I *do* love a good plan," Pyrre agreed. "Why don't you girls whip something up and let me know the details?" She frowned. "Hold on. A plan for what, now?"

"Oh, for 'Shael's sake . . ." Gwenna spat.

The Skullsworn stopped her with an elegantly raised finger. "Have a care about how you invoke my god."

"A plan," Annick said, ignoring the exchange, "for how to get out of here."

"And why," Pyrre asked, raising her eyebrows, "do we want to get out of here?" She gestured to the fire, the sizzling meat, the bulging skin of liquor in her hands, then to the clean hides stretched over the poles above them, keeping in the heat, the light. "Admittedly, we got off to a rough start, but Long Fist is turning into a gracious host. Maybe it was just those boys of yours he didn't like. . . ."

If Long Fist didn't like the men on the Wing, he was well rid of them. Valyn, Talal, and Laith had ridden out the day before, strapped with arms and laden with provisions, packs filled with anything that might kill— poisons, arrows, even a blowgun. It was an insane mission—going to kill the Annurian *kenarang*—but the shaman had made sure they had everything they might need to get it done. Everything, that was, except for half of the fucking Wing.

"You will remain here, my honored guests," he had said to the women— almost an afterthought. When Gwenna told him how she felt about that, told him that she intended to make her own decisions, he had only spread his arms in invitation: "Certainly you must decide your own fate: honored guest, captive, or corpse."

Valyn tried to step in then, but the ugly fact of the matter was that they had no leverage. They were free only because Long Fist had set them free, and for all the tall bastard's talk of cooperation and mutual understanding, he wasn't suffering from an overabundance of trust. Valyn's word was all well and good, but Long Fist wanted something more substantial, more persuasive, and so Annick, Gwenna, and Pyrre had graduated from *captives* to *honored guests*.

Honored guests. It was worse than *collateral*.

"You should relax," the assassin continued. "Life is an eyeblink. Try to enjoy some of the largesse spread before us."

"You're so busy guzzling the rotgut," Gwenna snapped, "that you might not have realized Long Fist's *largesse* doesn't include a single weapon. We've got one pathetic belt knife between us," she said, gesturing to the slender blade Annick was using to saw at the meat. "A *dull* belt knife."

"Probably," Pyrre said, "because the last time we had weapons, we tended to leave the sharp parts of them inside his soldiers. Besides," she went on, eyeing Annick's belt knife, "it's simple enough to kill men with a belt knife. *If* we decide there's a pressing reason to trade the meat, drink, and fire for an unwinnable fight."

"You were fighting hard enough when they had you tied up," Gwenna snapped. "And the fight was even *less* winnable then."

The truth was, Pyrre made her all sorts of uncomfortable, and being uncomfortable made Gwenna mad. It wasn't just that the Skullsworn was good at killing—everyone on the Islands was good at killing. The thing that really set Gwenna's teeth on edge was Pyrre's indifference, her obvious failure to give half a shit about all of the things Gwenna herself was ready to die for. Squaring off against an entire Urghul army was daunting enough without having the Skullsworn mocking her the whole way.

"When I was tied up," the assassin said with a shrug, "I was tied up. Now that we have—"

Before she could finish her thought, the door to the tent flapped open and a man stepped inside. He was tall, bent nearly double to get through the opening. At first Gwenna thought it was Long Fist, but when he straightened, his smirk took her in the gut like a fist.

Balendin Ainhoa.

Just discovering the leach was alive had made her furious. In fact, one of the tricks she had for staying sane during the unbearable drive west had been to remind herself that Balendin was still out there, that she needed to stay alive herself, stay sharp, so that one day she could kill him. When Long Fist started taking fingers, it had looked as though he might assume that responsibility himself. It didn't look that way anymore.

The leach was no longer tied, no longer wearing the same stinking blacks in which he'd been captured, and though no one could put back his missing fingers, someone had provided him with clean cloth for bandages. He wore a dark bison cloak in the Urghul fashion over leather breeches and a tunic, a new set of necklaces draping his neck, a new array of rings on his fingers. The reversal was as terrifying as it was abrupt, and for a moment Gwenna sat speechless, trying to understand how things could have gone so wrong so quickly.

As if reading her thoughts, Balendin smiled. "Happy to see me, Gwenna?" When she didn't respond, he shrugged. "I've certainly missed you. I've had a lot of favorites over the years, but there's never been anyone quite like the volatile Gwenna Sharpe for sheer, unbridled, uncooked, untamed, brute-stupid *passion*."

He paused, licked his lips. Annick had stopped cutting, one hand still on the haunch, the other holding the bloody knife loose between two fingers. Gwenna realized with horror that not only was the leach free and walking around, not only was he obviously the recipient of Long Fist's sudden favor, he was undrugged. All trace of the adamanth was gone from his eyes, and the cocksure, predatory gleam was back.

Gwenna fought down the urge to go after him. He was only a few paces off, standing with his arms crossed just inside the door to the *api,* but she'd seen enough of the leach's power to know she wouldn't make it even halfway.

"You're a sack of last week's festering shit, Balendin," she said instead. The words were a lousy substitute for a knife, but they were all she had. "Brave though, to come in here alone after the reaming we gave you in the mountains. Shame about the rest of your Wing—the bloody pieces are probably spread over a few square miles of mountainside by now. Shame about your fingers."

The leach frowned. He was thinner than he had been on the Islands, Gwenna realized. He'd always been lean, a whip rather than a club, sinew and muscle twisted around a slender frame, the fine, elegant bones of his face clear under sun-darkened skin. Now, though, by the shifting light of the fire, she could see that his cheeks had gone from gaunt to cadaverous. The dark braids draping his shoulders looked thinner and oilier than she remembered, while the tattoos snaking his arms had crumpled slightly as the skin slackened with the shrinking muscle beneath. None of that made him any less dangerous if he had access to his well once more.

"Gwenna, Gwenna, Gwenna," he said, shaking his head. "I've just walked back into your life, free and whole. . . ." He glanced at his hands ruefully. "Well, almost whole. In any case, you've spoken five sentences to me, and already you've made three mistakes." He held up a finger. "First, it takes no bravery to face you; I could pin you to the dirt and burn this tent down without blinking. Second, *you* didn't have anything to do with my very temporary setbacks; the fire-eyed fuck got the drop on me the first time, and the Urghul found me the second. Finally, while the bones bleaching in the mountains were, technically, my Wing, you're wrong in thinking I care that they're dead. I was always so much better than them, my goals were so much more . . . capacious. Are you familiar with the word *capacious*?" He smiled. "It means large."

From across the tent, Pyrre raised a hand. She was looking at the leach with frank interest.

"Excuse me," she said. "I'm so sorry to interrupt. We've met several times, but under such unfortunate circumstances that we've never been properly introduced. My name is Pyrre Lakatur."

Balendin raised his eyebrows and sketched a small bow. "And I am—"

"He's the miserable fuck who murdered Lin and tried to kill Valyn," Gwenna cut in. She knew she should have held her peace, waited for Balendin to play his hand, but she couldn't just sit by while the leach and the Skullsworn traded pleasantries as though they were sizing each other up in some tavern. She had no idea where Balendin came by his clothes and rings, no idea why he was free, no idea why he seemed so fucking smug, but the whole situation frightened her, and she hated being frightened. "He was with those Aedolians," Gwenna said, trying to make Pyrre understand the danger. "He's a 'Kent-kissing *traitor*."

Pyrre ignored Gwenna entirely. Instead, she smiled at Balendin, rolled languorously onto her stomach, then stretched upward like a waking cat. The top buttons of her shirt hung open, and the pose left little to the imagination.

"I remember Valyn going on about that at some length," she said. "The thing is, I also have a somewhat flexible notion of political loyalty. I certainly wouldn't want to let something so petty as 'treason' come between me and a kindred spirit." She trailed a few fingers along her arm, then nodded to Balendin's tattooed biceps and wrists. "I like your art. Is there more under that shirt?"

Gwenna felt like her head was going to explode, but before she could say anything, Annick cut into the conversation, her voice clipped, professional.

"Why are you here, Balendin? Why did Long Fist free you?"

The leach allowed his eyes to linger on Pyrre for a moment. Then he let out a long sigh as he turned to the sniper.

"Annick, just because I had to string up your little slut doesn't mean you should be so sour about everyone else's fun." He spread his arms. "The world is wide, and there are plenty more whores in it."

The sniper barely twitched, the motion so quick and curt that Gwenna could have missed it, save for the small knife whipping through the air toward Balendin's throat . . . then knocked aside by some invisible shield. The leach smiled indulgently.

"Long Fist has requested that I leave you unharmed, so I'll make believe that you just slipped while cutting your meat."

Annick's lips tightened, her hand flexed, as though wanting another weapon, but she refused to take the bait.

"Now," he said after a long pause, "where should I begin the story of my miraculous survival and sudden rehabilitation? In the mountains, perhaps . . ."

"It's not a fucking mystery," Gwenna spat. "You staggered out of the Bones, and the Urghul picked you up the same way they did us. You want us to be impressed that you got caught by a bunch of horse-fucking savages?"

Balendin's eyes narrowed. "I would point out," he said slowly, "that you, also, were captured by those same horse-fucking savages."

"I didn't say I was proud of it. I certainly wouldn't *flaunt* the fact. You're stuck here, same as us."

"Oh, Gwenna," the leach replied slowly, smiling once more. "I understand your frustration, but unlike you poor ladies, I am hardly stuck here." He shook his head slowly, watching her expression through the smoke, his eyes bright. "You're right, of course, that we were both captives of our nomadic friends, and for a time, Long Fist trusted me no more than he did you. Since then"—he shrugged—"our stories have diverged. While you wait here, tacit prisoners, Long Fist has invited me to join him. He has . . . elevated me. To a position of some importance. The man is a savage, but even a savage understands the value of someone with my talents, with my knowledge."

Gwenna suppressed a shudder. Despite Long Fist's claims about his friendship with Sanlitun, about the purely defensive nature of his army, she didn't trust him, didn't like his collection of scars or the satisfaction he obviously derived from the suffering of his people. She had, however, considered him a relatively objective threat, a foe of the empire, perhaps, but not a particularly unusual one. For Long Fist to ally with Balendin, however, for him to join forces with a leach who had tried his best to murder two members of the Malkeenian line—that suggested something far darker.

"What does Long Fist want with you?" she asked.

Pyrre groaned ostentatiously. "Why," she asked, arching her neck to get a better look at Balendin over the fire, "do we have to waste time on something so dull? Gwenna," she added, flicking a dismissive hand. "Annick. Why don't you two walk around the camp a few hundred times. Make some nice new friends."

Gwenna stared. "Why don't you fuck yourself, you Skullsworn bitch? You know he's a leach, right? You know he tried to kill Kaden, who you were *hired* to *protect*."

Pyrre made a silent, coquettish O with her mouth. "A leach. How exotic." She didn't take her eyes from Balendin. "As for fucking myself, Gwenna, it is sometimes a necessary expedient. Not, however, when there are promising alternatives."

Balendin tossed the woman a vulpine, toothy smile in response, but then, to Gwenna's surprise, shook his head.

"Unfortunately, those alternatives will have to wait. The Kwihna Saapi is about to begin."

"What is that?" Annick asked.

"A ceremony," Balendin replied. "Long Fist requests your presence."

"And by *requests*," Gwenna said, "you mean *demands*."

Balendin grinned. "Yes. I mean demands."

†

The Kwihna Saapi, whatever the fuck it turned out to be, was to take place in a narrow gully between low hills where a meager trickle of water had, over the centuries, worn through the gentle flesh of the earth to reveal the bones of the limestone beneath. Wind and rain had corrugated the rock, gouging out runnels and pockets in which generations of Urghul had set the bones of their slaughtered foes—a femur shattered just below the joint, a cracked skull, a pile of small bones that might once have been fingers or toes spilling from a low shelf—as though the pockmarked earth were disgorging its hoard, vomiting up shards so old it was difficult to tell if the bleached and pitted shapes were rock or bone.

More worrisome than the stony gorge were the tens of thousands of Urghul waiting on the slopes above it. Most crouched flat-footed, clustered in knots of five or six, but those along the gully's edge stood, the points of their long lances angled down, as though to keep anything from escaping. Long Fist had taken a place of honor at the very lip of the gully, where he lounged on a travois supported by his own bloody warriors.

Balendin led Gwenna, Annick, and Pyrre to the lip of the stony defile.

"A holy place," he said, then, with no warning, shoved Gwenna over the lip.

The fall was only half a dozen feet, and she landed on her feet, curses tumbling from her lips. She spun to find the leach smiling down at her.

"Don't worry," he said. "I'll see that your friends have an outstanding view."

Both women were watching her. Pyrre looked curious. Annick looked like Annick. Balendin waited a moment, then led them to Long Fist's travois.

The limestone walls were low, no taller than Gwenna herself. Climbing free would be a trivial matter were it not for the Urghul with their lances lowered at her chest. Gwenna considered seizing one of the weapons, then discarded the idea. She still wasn't sure what was to happen here, and she didn't intend to die in a heroic last stand if she didn't have to. Instead, she took a moment to look around.

The low stone walls blocked her escape to the east and west, while at either end of the short gully, maybe twenty paces apart, roared massive twin fires, though the sun had not yet set. Someone had dug two narrow holes about five feet apart, similar to long-campaign shit-pits, although what they were for, Gwenna couldn't say. The mounds of excavated earth stood piled neatly and silently beside the holes.

A holy place, Balendin had said just before shoving her off the low stone wall into the makeshift arena.

A killing place, Gwenna thought grimly.

In a strange way, she was almost relieved. She had no idea what game Long Fist was playing, no clue why he would lavish her with food and li-quor all day only to hurl her into a pit in front of what looked to be his entire 'Kent-kissing army, but one thing was clear: *something* was happening, and that was better than sitting on her hands in a tent arguing with Pyrre and being ignored by Annick.

Just too bad that it looked like the *something* was likely to kill her.

At either end of the gully, men and women beyond the flames continued to heap fuel on the crackling monsters. Even paces away, even in the stiff breeze, Gwenna could feel the heat on her face. She tried to dredge up something from her training, some little fact that might save her life. She knew plenty about Urghul mounted fighting tactics and weapons use, but her eyes had tended to glaze over when the trainers droned on about the dull theological details. Balendin had called whatever was coming the Kwihna Saapi. Gwenna had never heard the second word, but Kwihna meant Meshkent, and Meshkent meant pain.

The whole thing had the feel of a ring or arena—the bounded enclosure, the circle of expectant faces, and, oh yeah, the piles of fucking bones strewn everywhere. The place stunk of a fight, and, just as she was scanning the ground, the Urghul shoved someone else into the narrow gully.

Gwenna rocked back and forth, testing her legs. Weeks tied to the horse hadn't done her any good, but it was no use worrying about that now. *The hay,* as the Kettral liked to say, *was in the barn,* and Gwenna offered up a silent thanks to all the bastards back on the Islands—Adaman Fane and Daveen Shaleel, Plenchen Zee and even the Flea—for the long years of brutality, the relentless insistence on perfection. She might not know shit about the 'Kent-kissing Kwihna Saapi, but this was looking like a fight, and she knew a lot about fighting.

Then the young man straightened, and Gwenna's eagerness drained away. She had expected an Urghul, one of the young *taabe* or *ksaabe*. It was an Annurian, however, who faced her, a young man maybe a year or two older than Gwenna, still dressed in the filthy rags of his legionary uniform. Another prisoner. Gwenna had assumed they were the only ones, but the camp was enormous. Long Fist could have a whole legion of Annurians tied up and staked out on the steppe and she never would have noticed. The young soldier looked both baffled and terrified, gaping first at the roaring fires, then at the crowd of Urghul, only turning to Gwenna when the other sights seemed ready to drive him to his knees.

"What's going on?" he breathed.

Gwenna's lips tightened, but before she could reply, Long Fist, draped in a huge bison cloak, rose from his seat and stepped to the edge of the gully. He held two stout sticks in one hand, each no wider around than Gwenna's thumb. He gestured with them to the holes.

"Step in."

"Go fuck yourself," Gwenna replied.

She had no idea what the holes were for, but you didn't fight from a hole.

"Step in," Long Fist said, unperturbed, "or I will have your arm removed." He gestured to the young warriors with their long spears. "I give you this choice."

"What happened to being an honored guest?" she demanded.

He smiled. "The Kwihna Saapi is an honor."

"Well aren't I just tickled," she muttered, stepping into the hole.

The earth came to the middle of her thighs and, as she looked up toward the Urghul chief for some further sign, a pair of young riders leapt down from the stone wall, crude shovels in hand, and began filling in the earth around her.

Gwenna forced herself to remain still, to think. The Annurian in the other hole had already surrendered to panic. He was trying to hoist himself from the small pit, half screaming, half begging, thrashing with both hands at the shovel and the youth wielding it, trying ineffectually to knock aside the dirt. He managed to get one leg out when three more Urghul jumped down from the stone wall and, to the ululation and cheering of the crowd, shoved him into the hole once more and held him there, writhing and biting, while the dirt piled up around him. When the work was done, Gwenna found herself immobilized in the earth facing the terrified young man across from her.

He was all forehead and ear and wide, baffled eyes set in a pimply face.

"Quit thrashing," she said. She couldn't think with him carrying on, and besides, the Urghul were clearly enjoying the show.

"What are they going to do?" he moaned. "What's happening? What are they going to do?"

"Do I look like a scholar of obscure Urghul ass-fuckery?" she snapped. His panic was starting to dig at her, to creep, cold and lizardlike up her neck, over her skin, to bore into her belly. "What are you doing here?" she asked, more to distract herself from the fear than anything else. "How did these bastards get you?"

He stared, as though he himself didn't know the answer to the question.

"Were you scouting?" Gwenna pressed. "Some mission north of the White?"

"I'm not a scout," he protested. "I'm a 'Kent-kissing *infantryman,* barely even that. I been in the legion only four months. The Urghul hit us at the L-fort three nights back." He stared back up at the ring of faces and started scrabbling at the earth again. "What're they gonna *do* to us?"

"The L-fort?" Gwenna demanded, ignoring the last question. "They came *south*?"

"Yes," he wailed. " 'Bout a million of them. The whole fort's gone."

Gwenna took a deep breath, then another, trying to still her rising panic. Long Fist had shattered one of the forts south of the river, one of the forts intended to keep the Urghul out of Annur. He hadn't just turned on the Kettral; he had turned on the whole 'Kent-kissing *empire.* So much for his defensive army. . . . Gwenna would have worried about Valyn and the others—they'd left the camp more or less convinced by Long Fist's promises of allegiance—but whatever miserable shitpile Valyn found himself in, her own predicament was looking quite a bit worse.

The soldier's jaw was quivering. "They're gonna hurt us, ain't they?" His eyes locked on Gwenna's, then flickered down to her blacks. "You're not in the legion," he breathed, comprehension hitting him like a hammer. "You're *Kettral.*"

The words were horrible with hope.

"Can you break us free?"

Gwenna shook her head, furious at that hope, powerless to explain that the legends extended only so far.

"But you'll do somethin', right? *Right?* I mean . . . the *Kettral*!"

"What I'll do," Gwenna said, "is keep my eyes open and my mouth shut."

It came out more harshly than she'd intended, but she couldn't bear the desperate trust in the young man's eyes, the irrational faith. She wanted to shout that the Kettral weren't gods, that they couldn't work miracles, and even if they could, she herself was a pretty shit Kettral. She didn't have Annick's discipline or Talal's cool or anything, really, other than an ability to blow shit up. *If I could save you,* she wanted to scream, *I'd be saving you.*

"Just shut up," she snapped instead, although she'd just gotten done saying it. "Just be ready."

Whatever that meant. Half buried in the earth they could neither flee nor fight. It was like being bound to a dock piling waiting for the tide to come in. The Urghul who packed the earth around them had retreated, climbing back up the low stone walls to leave Gwenna and the soldier alone at the bottom of the gully. The sun had slipped behind the hills to the west, and though a smear of red and orange still lit the sky, most of the light came from the enormous fires, a fickle, inconstant illumination that sketched the shards of bone one moment and plunged them into shadow the next. Above them the Urghul had risen to their feet, shaking weapons and jeering something incomprehensible in their strange melodic tongue, an entire bloody nation gathered to watch her suffer, men and women thick as wheat on the surrounding slopes. Gwenna wished she understood the words, then thought better of it.

Just blood, probably, and death, and doom, and blah, blah, blah.

The cacophony rose and rose, an unholy and discordant chant, until Long Fist swept his sticks down in a curt motion. The screaming stopped at once, the sound severed as though with a sharp knife. Firelight danced in the thousands of eager eyes.

The shaman spoke briefly in Urghul. Gwenna caught a few references to Kwihna, and maybe the words for "fight" and "die." She pivoted at the waist, testing her range of motion, wondering what direction the attack would come from. Maybe it would be warriors. Maybe dogs. There was no way to guess.

"Now," Long Fist said, addressing them, "you will fight. One wins. One dies." He smiled a slow, easy smile.

Gwenna stared, first at the Urghul, then at the other prisoner, whose face was streaked with sweat and blanched with panic. No dogs, then.

The two sticks clattered to the ground between them.

"Swords," the Urghul said, gesturing magnanimously.

But they were not swords. They weren't even weapons—too blunt for effective stabbing, too light for a swift killing blow. Given enough time you could maybe beat someone to death with them, striking over and over, aiming for the throat, the eyes, but it would be a nasty process, slow and messy. Which, Gwenna realized, was the whole 'Kent-kissing point. The Urghul hadn't assembled for a fight. This wasn't a test of bravery or martial prowess, it was a sacrifice, the whole thing—buried legs, spindly sticks—designed to draw out the struggle, to prolong the pain.

A sacrifice to Meshkent.

"No," Gwenna said. She crossed her arms over her chest and locked eyes with the Urghul chieftain. "I'm not taking part in your bloody bullshit."

Long Fist smiled. "Yes, you are. The other Annurians"—he waved a hand over his shoulder, the gesture suggesting scores of unseen prisoners—"I will cut out their beating hearts, but you are a fighter. You will fight."

The legionary was trembling, his breath coming in quick gasps, as though some unseen hand were frantically working the bellows of his lungs. He'd probably never seen battle or blood before the horsemen swept down on his fort.

"What happened to wanting to avoid war?" she demanded.

Long Fist just smiled.

The crowd was growing restless. A knot of men barely older than Gwenna were leaning over the edge of the stone wall, shouting at the prisoners and brandishing spears. Another small group seemed to be taunting the chief himself, although it was hard to be sure. The noise rolled over her, jeers and chanting like autumn breakers dashing themselves on the rocks. Gwenna met Annick's eyes for a moment, hoping to see some encouragement or solidarity there, but the sniper's face might have been chiseled from stone.

The first blow landed just above Gwenna's ear, a flash of bright red pain. She turned, shocked, thinking that one of the Urghul had leapt into the gully, only to discover the young legionary staring at her, a stick in each hand, knuckles white.

"I'm sorry," he cried. A splash of vomit soiled the front of his tunic and stained the rough dirt before him. Tears, whether of remorse or terror, slicked his cheeks. "I'm *sorry*," he sobbed again, and then, with a mindless fury, started raining down the blows.

It took Gwenna a moment to adjust, and the sticks connected twice more, once just above the eye, the other a glancing blow to the shoulder. The pain was sharp but shallow, the sort of pain she'd felt a thousand times before when smashing a finger between an anchor and the gunwale, or ripping free a blackened toenail, or taking a stunner to the shoulder. Gwenna herself would be hard-pressed to kill someone quickly with those sticks, and the panicked young legionary was striking out madly in his terror, blindly. She raised her hands, blocked two blows in quick succession, timed the third, caught the stick before it could connect, twisted out and away, breaking the man's grip, and then she had a weapon of her own.

The soldier paused, stunned, staring at his empty hand in mute incomprehension. He raised his eyes to Gwenna and moaned, a pitiful, helpless sound, before redoubling his attack. With one weapon already in hand it was a trivial matter to defend against the fresh assault. She swatted aside a blow aimed for her chest, inclined her head to slip beneath a high swing, leaned back as far as the earth would allow, inviting the youth to overextend, and then she had the second stick as well. It was easy, so pathetically easy.

The Urghul were shrieking like seabirds, a high keening sharp as a point driving straight through Gwenna's ears and into her brain. The twin fires had grown even larger, the one in front scorching her face, the one behind burning through her blacks. The unarmed soldier spread his hands wide in supplication.

"I'm sorry," he cried. "I didn't want to hit you. Please. *Please.* You're Kettral. I'm just a legionary. You're the 'Kent-kissing *Kettral*! *Please.*"

Gwenna held her attack for a moment. She had slipped into a high Elendrian guard without even thinking about it—an absurd gesture. The idiot buried across from her had probably never even *heard* of the Elendrian guard. He was just an Annurian soldier captured while serving his empire, while trying to do his job. His only preparation for the Urghul would have been lurid tales told in the mess hall and barracks. No one had trained him for this.

Gwenna glanced up at their captors, at the uncountable flashing blue eyes, the pale faces glistening with sweat. Firelight lurched over the bones of the dead and the flesh of the living alike, plunging some figures into shadow, garishly illuminating others. Blood throbbed in her ears, flame on her face. There was no way out, no escape.

"Ah, fuck," she muttered.

"No," the soldier said, shaking his head slowly, seeing the decision in her eyes.

Gwenna gritted her teeth, then lashed out high and right. The feint worked, drawing the legionary's guard wide, and she took the opening. The Urghul wanted pain, an agony built from a thousand punishing blows, to feed their sick god.

Well, she thought as she plunged the tip of the stick through the soldier's eye, driving it deep, deeper, twisting the weapon as the youth spasmed, jerked, then slumped forward, utterly still, *the fuckers will have to settle for death.*

Her throat was raw as she wrenched the stick free. She was screaming, she realized, but the sound was lost in the awful sheet of Urghul screams. She was sobbing, but the heat of the fire had seared away her tears.

28

Kaden crashed out of the *kenta* soaked and gasping for breath, lungs heaving in great desperate gulps of clean air, limbs leaden and useless. His mind registered only that he had moved from a frigid wet darkness into a warm day brilliant as the sun, and for a few heartbeats he allowed himself to simply lie on the soft grass, still swaddled in the *vaniate,* drinking in the sweet sea breeze. A few feet away he could hear Triste retching onto the ground, her body struggling to force out the salt water at the same time as she was trying to breathe. Kiel's own breaths were quieter, more measured, and after a moment Kaden could hear the Csestriim rising to his feet.

"Quickly," he said, keeping his voice low. "This is only the hub linking the gates, and Rampuri Tan will not kill all of them."

"They can't follow," Triste gasped. "Not the way we came."

"They will not have to. When they have dealt with Tan, they will realize where we went, and they will come through the gate after us. We have to be well gone from here when that happens."

Kaden nodded, rising unsteadily to his feet. He recognized the island, the ring of slender arches around the perimeter, although it felt like years since he had last stood upon it. Since then . . . He shook his head, cutting off the thought. Best not to think on the past, on what it would mean for the Ishien to deal with Tan. The *vaniate* wavered. Best to move forward.

He glanced around the green sward. The gate from Assare, he knew, but the writing above the others meant nothing.

"Which way?"

"Annur?" Kiel asked.

Kaden nodded.

The Csestriim indicated an arch a dozen paces distant. Kaden helped

Triste to her feet, helped her stumble across the rough ground, watched her vanish as she stepped once more into the *kenta,* then followed her through, moving from bright light into a dry, dusty darkness. For a moment he just stood, waiting for his eyes to adjust. When they did not, he let the *vaniate* slough away. His limbs were still weak from the lack of air, still trembling. His burning irises illuminated little more than his hand before his face.

"Where are we?"

"Underground," Kiel replied. "In a section of Annur long forgotten. The Ishien know of this place, but no one else."

"Let's go," Triste said, her voice tight as a bowstring. "Let's get out of here."

"Follow precisely in my footsteps," Kiel replied. "The Ishien have set traps around this gate, and there are other dangers in the forgotten tunnels beneath the city."

The three of them spent the next hour winding their way through nearly absolute darkness. At several junctures, Kaden caught sight of stacks of bones—femurs, skulls, heaps of fingers dry and brittle as kindling—stretching back into the cavernous black. Triste kept a hand on Kaden's shoulder. He could feel her trembling, though whether with cold or fear or the lingering pain of the wounds the Ishien had inflicted he wasn't sure. Kiel showed no hesitation as he moved through the darkness.

"How can you see?" Triste asked at one point.

"I don't need to see," the Csestriim replied. "I have the map in my head."

"That's impossible," she replied.

"Ask Kaden."

Kaden tried to imagine the vast network of tunnels, discovering to his surprise that he'd been making a map of his own since they left the *kenta,* some diligent portion of his mind toiling away marking each branch, each fork, each cavern through which they passed.

"Memory," Kiel said, "is a skill like anything else. It can be honed."

The words were true enough, but when they finally shoved aside a slab of stone and stepped blinking from the darkness into blinding light, Kaden discovered anew the limits of his memory. They stood in a green leafy cemetery wedged between walls and buildings atop a low hill. While Kiel muscled the stone slab back into place, Kaden just stared. That the Ishien were behind them, he had no doubt. They needed to be away from the graveyard, and fast, but for the space of a few heartbeats, he found himself unable to move, nailed to the spot as he breathed in the sea salt and smoky air of Annur.

His memories of the city, sketched in his young mind before he'd ever heard of the Shin or the *saama'an,* were bright but static: the looming red walls of the Dawn Palace, the crystalline spike of Intarra's Spear, the pale green of the copper roofs and the dark green of the canals, the white of the statues along the Godsway, and the bottomless blue of the Broken Bay, stretching away to the east. The shapes, too, he remembered, a jum bled geometry of warehouses and palaces, straight streets and crooked alleyways. Everything else, he had forgotten: the noise, the smell, the press of bodies. The heat.

Even in the relative tranquillity of the graveyard, he could feel the city moving around him like some great, feverish beast, and when they slipped through the gate and into the streets, he felt as though Annur had swallowed him whole. The clatter of carts over the flagstones, the clop of hooves, the shouting of drivers and pedestrians jostling for space on the surrounding streets all but obliterated the rustle of the wind-tossed leaves.

Kaden half-expected everyone they passed to stop, stare, exclaim. After all, the three of them, though mostly dry, were still wearing the same mismatched, tattered garb in which they'd fled the Ishien. In Ashk'lan, someone would have noticed instantly, but Annur was not Ashk'lan. This city of a million souls threw her own cloak over them, an anonymity thicker than any wool, while she veiled the eyes of the passers-by in their own busy indifference.

Eyes safely hidden inside the hood of his cloak, Kaden walked through the streets as though in a dream, a stranger exploring the maze of his own memories. After the vast, cool emptiness of Ashk'lan, where half the world was sky, the city felt almost unbearably present. The reek of sizzling oil, of garlic, of peppers and frying fish made him feel as though he was half choking, while the constant tolling of gongs and bells made it hard to sort his thoughts into any type of order.

For a while he just followed Kiel, keeping his eyes down to hide his gaze and to limit the riot of color and motion battering at his mind. Outside the *vaniate,* he could feel for the first time what had happened back in those final awful moments in the Dead Heart. That Rampuri Tan was dead or a prisoner of the Ishien there could be no doubt, and yet questions and doubts, like so many carrion crows, circled and circled. Had

Kaden himself, through some idiotic slipup, caused the attack? He went over the events again and again, studying in his mind the scenes in his cell, in the corridors beyond. Had he made too much noise? Had he botched the timing? There was no way to know. There was only the fact: Tan was gone while he, Kaden, was free, walking the streets of Annur.

He risked a quick glance up at the chaos of those streets, then ducked his head, questioning once more the wisdom of sending him away to Ashk'lan for training. What he had in common with the impatient, reckless people jostling him he had no idea, no idea how he would talk to them, or make sense of their answers. They were Annurians, and he the Emperor of Annur, but they might have been exotic birds, or apes for all Kaden understood them.

Finally, Kiel pulled Kaden and Triste into a narrow alleyway off the main street. It stank of rotted food and urine, but Kaden welcomed the shadows, the relative quiet, the respite.

"We should be safe," the Csestriim said. "We're a mile from the graveyard, and we've left no trail to follow."

Kaden looked up. People—dozens, hundreds—swarmed past the narrow entrance to the alleyway, but no one so much as glanced in their direction. They could have been invisible.

"Where are we?" Kaden asked.

"Old Sticks," Kiel replied. "A small quarter wedged between the Silk Canal and the Fourth. There used to be some small-scale banking and a market for fresh flowers." He shrugged. "That was fifteen years ago."

Kaden grimaced. He'd never heard of Old Sticks, never known that there *was* such a thing as a market for fresh flowers. He'd returned, finally, to his city, to the center of his empire, to discover that he was a stranger in his own land.

"The monk," Triste said, glancing toward the head of the alley. The bruising on her face, the burns on her hands, looked worse, much worse outside of the Dead Heart, in the full light of day. "Do you think he followed us? Do you think he made it out?" Kaden thought of Tan's *naczal* pressed against Triste's throat, of Tan ordering her tied up like livestock, and he wondered if she hoped he had escaped the Ishien or not.

"He couldn't follow," Kaden said. "Not the way we went."

"Rampuri Tan is a formidable hand with his spear," Kiel said, "but not that formidable."

"So he is dead," Triste said dully.

"He is beyond our reach," Kaden replied, trying to move past his own tumult of emotion, to focus on the dirt beneath his feet, the stench of the air.

Triste studied him for a moment, then nodded. "All right," she said. "Where do we go now?"

Kiel shook his head. "I kept a few rooms near here," he said. "I thought perhaps they would still be empty, but we passed them four streets back. It looks as though someone new is living there."

"In your rooms?" Kaden asked. "How could they just move in?"

Kiel shrugged. "Fifteen years is a long time to be gone."

Kaden shook his head, trying to imagine fifteen years among the Ishien, fifteen years locked in the darkness, the only thing waiting beyond the steel door, pain. It could drive a man mad, but then, Kiel was not a man. Kaden turned to face the Csestriim.

"What now?"

Kiel met the stare. "You are the Emperor."

"For you, I mean. We were tied together during the escape, but we are not any longer. Why are you still with us? With me?"

The Csestriim looked past Kaden to the mouth of the alley, where men and women, oxen and children, jostled in the bright light of the sun. "Your history," he said finally.

Kaden raised his brows. "My history?"

"Not just yours. That of your whole race." He paused, frowned, then went on. "As I told you, I was the historian of my people. I have spent a very long life in the study of cities and nations, wars and brief periods of fitful peace."

"You said you knew my father," Kaden insisted. "That you worked with him."

Kiel nodded. "I chronicled his life, or a part of it—his time on the Unhewn Throne."

"But *why*?" Kaden demanded, coming back to his original question. Clearly the historian had no part in his father's death—he had been imprisoned in the Dead Heart for almost two decades—and yet he was Csestriim, built from the same flesh, his mind patterned on the same alien thoughts as the creatures who had burst into Assare millennia earlier to murder the children. "Why would you chronicle *us*? Humans? Why would you help me?"

To his surprise, Kiel smiled. "You are interesting. Your race is interesting, even more so than my own. Humans are unpredictable, self-contradictory. Where our history was a long account of reasoned debate, yours is ablaze with error and ambition, regret and hope, love and loathing, all the things we cannot feel, all animating your every decision. Most of my kind wanted to see you crushed from the start, but I . . . I was curious. I remain curious." He shrugged. "As for why I would help *you,* in particular: as I said, you are the Emperor of Annur. I can come no closer to the unfolding of history."

Kaden watched the man a moment, then nodded slowly. It made a strange sort of sense. More, he realized he *wanted* to trust the historian, wanted another person on his side, someone who understood something of the empire he was supposed to rule.

"Thank you," he said. "For helping us break free."

Kiel frowned. "We are free, but not secure. We still have not decided our next step."

"The chapterhouse," Kaden said. "The Shin branch where we agreed to meet Valyn. We've missed the meeting by weeks, but he could be waiting there. He could have left a message, instructions, a warning."

The Csestriim nodded. "I know the place. It's near here, but the Ishien know it, too."

"The Ishien don't know where we are," Kaden said.

"By now they know we've escaped."

Triste shook her head. "There were at least twenty gates back on that island. We could have gone through any of them."

Kaden blew out a long breath. "But we did nothing to cover our tracks. Matol will be able to follow us."

"And Tan knows where we planned to meet Valyn," Triste said reluctantly, picking at a nasty crescent scab on the back of her wrist. "If he told Matol, the bastard doesn't *need* to track us."

Kaden hesitated, staring out the end of the alley, watching the wagons and water buffalo, the men and women flowing by like a current.

"We have to go," he said, "now. The Ishien, if they even know where we're going, will take time to follow us here, time to get to the chapterhouse. I just need a few minutes to find out if Valyn's been there."

"It's a risk," Kiel observed.

"Everything's a risk," Kaden said. "Waiting will only make it worse."

The Shin chapterhouse didn't look like much: a narrow brick face—maybe ten paces wide and three stories high—crammed between two larger buildings at the border of a small cobbled square in one of Annur's quieter quarters. Nothing marked it as a chapterhouse, which wasn't surprising; the monks Kaden knew had never been much for crests or sigils. There was just the blank brick, the blank wooden door, and several windows on the upper floor, all firmly shuttered.

The rest of the elm-fringed square hummed with quiet activity—people hanging laundry out of windows, men and women bartering in the rough wooden stalls of a market, two water buffalo with noses buried in a stone trough—but around the chapterhouse there was nothing, no one, no ornament, not even flowers in the bare gravel fronting the structure. The place might have been abandoned, save for the tenuous line of smoke rising silently into the sky. There was no sign of Valyn, but then, Kaden's brother would hardly be lounging in the shade in front of the temple with his kettral leashed to a tree. A score of other buildings fronted the square—houses and shops, a wine store with bottles racked high in front of it, a stately old mansion that had seen better days, windowpanes broken, front yard unkempt, utterly uninhabited by the look of it. There was no way to search them all hoping to find Valyn. The only way to know if he had visited the Shin was to knock.

"Stay here," Kaden said. "I'll be fast."

"What should we do if the Ishien come?" Triste asked. She looked as though she were trying to watch every direction at once, trying to study every stranger.

Kaden shook his head. "I don't know."

"There is a way out," Kiel said, "from inside."

"A back door?"

"A *kenta*," the Csestriim replied.

Triste blanched. "Matol and Tan could be in there already! They could be waiting for him!"

"No," Kiel said. "It's a different network. My people built more than one, in case the first were destroyed or compromised."

"And the island we just came from . . ." Kaden asked, absorbing the new information, trying to work through the implications.

"That is one hub, a hub controlled by the Ishien. The gates lead various places—Assare, the Dead Heart, the catacombs from which we just emerged. . . ."

"And what about this?" Kaden asked, nodding toward the chapter-house.

"This is your network," Kiel replied. "The imperial network. The one entrusted to your family. The Ishien know of it, but they do not patrol it. It does not connect directly to the Dead Heart. If you hear any struggle or violence, you can escape through the *kenta*. It's in the deepest base-ment."

Kaden frowned. "Where does it lead?"

"To another hub, an island much like the one we just left."

"And once I'm on the island?"

"Take the second gate to your right. It will bring you to a flooded area beneath the docks of Olon. Once in the city, you should be able to lose yourself in the crowd."

Kaden stared, trying to imagine the escape. He could point to Olon on a map, but that was about it. He had no sense of the climate or culture, the manners of the local people.

"If I flee to Olon," he said, "I'll be hundreds of miles from Annur, with no way to get back."

"Which, I assume, is preferable to the Dead Heart," Kiel said. "It is only a precaution."

Kaden took a deep breath, then nodded.

"Remember, the *second* gate to your right. Not the first one."

"Where does that lead?"

"The Dawn Palace," Kiel replied. "If you burst through there, you'll be filled with arrows before you hit the ground."

✝

The monk who greeted Kaden at the door, a dark-skinned man with dark eyes, graying hair, and a slight limp, glanced once at his eyes, once at his clothes, then nodded as though in response to some interior question, ges-turing him inside with a slight motion of his hand. Kaden was ready with a bushel of explanations—who he was, where he had come from, what he wanted—but the monk said nothing, escorting him to a small chamber with a wooden stool, an earthenware ewer, and a single cup on a low table. He filled the cup with clear water, passed it to Kaden, then straightened.

"Wait here, brother, while I bring Iaapa."

Without another word, the monk slipped out the door on bare, silent feet, leaving Kaden alone holding the rough cup. Urgency pressed down on him like the air before a storm, heavy and pregnant. It was possible Matol and his men were outside even as he waited, watching the chapterhouse, preparing to enter, possible they had already captured Kiel and Triste. . . .

Calm, Kaden told himself, lifting the cup to his lips, taking a small sip, holding the water on his tongue, moving it around the inside of the mouth, then feeling it snake down his throat, cool against the heat that burned inside him. He waited three heartbeats, took another sip, and the anxiety retreated. A moment later Iaapa stepped into the room.

"A visitor from Ashk'lan," he said, round face creasing into a smile. "It is more than a year since we have welcomed a brother from the Bone Mountains."

Aside from Phirum Prumm, Iaapa was the only fat monk Kaden had ever seen, a short man with skin pale as milk and ears that stuck out as though tacked to the sides of his spherical head. He shared no physical resemblance with Scial Nin, the abbot of Ashk'lan, but there was a similar distance in the gaze, a stillness of the body, that suggested many years spent in the discipline of the Blank God.

"What is the word from the other end of the world?"

Kaden hesitated, the pushed ahead. "The word is bleak. Ashk'lan is destroyed and the monks are dead."

Another man might have reeled at the account, raged against it, demanded evidence or explanation. Iaapa simply pursed his lips, waiting silently for Kaden to continue.

"I can't tell you the whole thing," Kaden said. "There's no time. Soldiers came for me, Aedolian guardsmen commanded by Tarik Adiv, my father's Mizran Councillor. It seems to have been part of a plot to destroy my entire family."

"And the monks?" Iaapa asked finally. "We take no part in the politics of the empire."

"Adiv was thorough," Kaden replied bleakly.

"Then we will need to send others to Ashk'lan to rebuild."

There was no mention of mourning, but then, the Shin did not mourn. A part of Kaden felt as though he had abandoned the bodies of the monks at Ashk'lan, but the monks themselves did little more for their dead, carrying them up the trail to the high places where the wind, weather, and ravens could break apart the final illusion of the self. After just a few weeks with people who held their selves and their survival sacrosanct, Kaden had forgotten how lightly the monks who raised him regarded the powers of Ananshael.

"How have you returned here?" Iaapa asked.

"I don't have time to explain. Men may be coming for me even now." Kaden glanced around the small room. "My brother, Valyn. Has he come here? It would have been weeks ago, most likely."

Iaapa shook his head slowly. "We have had no visitors for months."

Kaden's stomach dropped. It was the news he had feared. There were a few possible ways to read Valyn's failure to return, but by far the most plausible was the bleakest: the Flea had killed him. Killed him or taken him prisoner. Kaden thought back to the madness inside the ancient orphanage of Assare, to the smoke and the screaming, the confusion and desperation. Kaden himself had barely escaped, and he'd had the *kenta*. . . .

Grief welled within him, but he quelled it, let it drain away with his breath. Whether Valyn was alive or dead, grief would not help him, and there was no time for it.

"What do you know of the Ishien?" Kaden asked.

Iaapa raised his brows. "A little."

"They will come here," Kaden said. Even if Tan had told them nothing, they would look for Kaden among the monks that had raised him. "You can't tell them I'm in the city."

The fat monk raised two hands, as though to hold the treachery and scheming at bay.

"As you know, brother, the Shin do not deal in politics or secrets."

"But we deal in silences," Kaden replied, "and I am begging for your silence. They are not like us, not really, and they are dangerous."

Iaapa frowned. "I have heard . . . stories."

"They're probably true," Kaden said, glancing over his shoulder toward the door. "In fact, it might be best for you, for all of you, to leave here for a month, several months. To go somewhere more remote. Somewhere safe."

"Safety," Iaapa replied quietly, poking at his head with a wide finger, "is here."

Kaden sucked an irritated breath between his teeth. He didn't have time to argue with the man, to explain just how thoroughly the Aedolians had gutted Ashk'lan, how the Shin had burned just like other men when their buildings blazed around them. Even if he had the time, there was no reason to believe his argument would sway the monk. Fleeing harm, for the Shin, was as foolish as hoarding pleasure; both were paths leading only to disappointment.

He hesitated, then rose to his feet, bowing his head in respect.

"I thank you for your time," he said quietly.

Iaapa remained seated, but he nodded in return.

That seemed to conclude the audience, but just as Kaden reached the door, the monk spoke once again.

"Your father came here often," Iaapa said, "through the gate. Sometimes for just an hour, sometimes for a night, when he wanted rest from the weight of his other duties."

Kaden stared as the monk smiled. "You are welcome, too, whenever you have need of rest."

✝

Despite Iaapa's offer, there was no possibility of remaining at the chapterhouse. The whole meeting had taken less time than the boiling of a pot of water, and even that felt like a risk. Matol would come looking, most likely sooner than later, and it would be safer for everyone if Kaden was nowhere near the monks when he did.

"Valyn hasn't been here," he said, looking from Kiel to Triste, careful to keep his voice down and his hood pulled forward. "And they haven't seen Valyn."

"They killed him," Triste said quietly, staring at him. "The other Kettral killed him."

"It's just speculation," Kaden said, then bowed his head. "But it's likely. In either case, we're on our own. We have no idea what's going on in the city, no sense of who's in charge, who killed my father, who sent Ut and Adiv after me. We need a place to stay while we ask the questions."

Triste frowned. "A hostel," she suggested finally. "Or an inn."

"Better than sleeping in the streets," Kiel agreed.

"But we don't have any money," Triste said.

The Csestriim shook his head. "Actually, I have a great deal of money."

Kaden stared.

"Compounded interest is a powerful force for someone with my longevity."

Kaden shook his head. "Compounded interest?"

"A bank," Kiel explained. "They pay you for the use of your money. The longer they use it, the more they pay."

Kaden glanced over at Triste, but her face was as blank as his own. Again he felt the jarring shock of his return, the futility of the task before him. He'd heard of banks as a child, of course. He'd imagined them to be great stone palaces piled with bricks of silver and gold. The Shin had taught him nothing of compounded interest.

"Which bank?" Triste asked. "The sooner we have the coin, the sooner we can get off the street." She hadn't stopped looking furtively toward the entrance to the alleyway, as though expecting Matol to step out of the sunlight any moment.

"No," Kaden said, shaking his head slowly. "It's too risky."

Triste turned on him. "What's the risk?"

"The Ishien. They captured Kiel fifteen years ago. They might know about the bank. Might look there."

"It's unlikely," the Csestriim replied. "They don't know the name I used."

"Unlikely is not impossible. The Shin had an exercise, a technique, the *beshra'an*. . . ."

"The Thrown Mind," Kiel said. "It was our skill before it became yours."

"Then you know that Matol can use it. It's possible they *have* used it. They may have found your bank. For all we know, the people in those rooms of yours are Ishien, living there, waiting, just on the off chance that another Csestriim shows up looking for you."

Kiel looked out at the street a moment, face blank as a page, unreadable. Finally he nodded. "All right. We'll avoid the rooms and the bank. But that leaves us with no coin and no safe place to lodge."

"Do you know anyone in the city?" Kaden asked.

Kiel started to respond, but Triste spoke first. "I do."

Her eyes were wide with something that might have been fear or hope or both, and she had clutched her hands together so tightly the knuckles had gone white.

"Your mother," Kaden said, the realization settling into place like the last stone in a carefully built wall.

She nodded.

"Did you tell Matol who she was?"

She hesitated, then nodded once more.

"Then they'll know to look there."

"He won't be able to," Triste replied, seized with a sudden vehemence. "The temple is enormous, and it's built for discretion. There are dozens of entrances, most of them hidden, so that the patrons can come and go without attracting notice. If we can get inside, my mother will hide us. I know she will."

Kiel held his hands up, trying to slow the conversation. "What temple? Who is your mother?"

"She is a *leina*," Triste replied, her voice hard and defiant, inviting him to mock her.

He just raised his eyebrows. "A priestess of Ciena."

She nodded. "It's perfect: Annur's richest, most powerful men and women patronize the *leinas*, and my mother used to tell me 'Lust loosens the tongue.' If there's something worth knowing in Annur, we can learn it there."

†

For a sacred structure dedicated to all the pleasures of mankind, Ciena's temple didn't look like much from the outside. It was huge, no doubt, sprawling over more than a city block, but all Kaden could see from the street was a blank stone wall six or seven times his height, the whole thing crawling with flowering vines but otherwise unadorned. Aside from the size, it wouldn't have been so out of place in Ashk'lan.

"I expected more . . ." He searched for the right word. ". . . extravagance."

"It's all on the inside," Triste replied. "Like true pleasure."

Kaden stared at the nondescript stone. "All right. How do we get inside?"

The cobbler's shop was small, but the shoes perched behind the glass windows—shoes in every color and shape, from delicate sandals to boots that would stretch halfway up the thigh, shoes made of soft leather and snakeskin and dark exotic wood—looked as though each pair cost at least a golden sun. Reinforcing the impression, two men stood flanking the door, hands on the pommels of their swords. Both were immaculately groomed and armored, but they had the hard eyes and scarred faces of seasoned fighters.

The closest one ran his gaze skeptically over Kaden and Kiel, then raised a palm.

"Nothing your size here, I'm afraid."

Triste pressed forward, and the guard hesitated, looking her up and down. She murmured something Kaden couldn't make out, and the man glanced at his companion.

"You know her?"

The other frowned, shook his head.

Triste glanced up and down the crowded street, then tugged down the collar of her shirt to reveal the delicate necklace inked around her neck. The guard's eyes rose. She hissed something else, and, to Kaden's relief, he nodded, stepped back, then gestured to the interior of the shop.

"Now that I think of it, I believe there may be something that fits you after all."

The inside of the shop smelled of cedar and fine leather. Mirrors worth more than Ashk'lan's entire flock stood against the wall, angled to provide the best possible view of the feet and ankles. Kaden found himself staring at his rough boots, but before he could think to scrape away some of the grime, the shopkeeper, a wide woman in a dress of very fine silk, bustled into the room. She took one look at Triste's tattoo, then waved them back through a curtain blocking off the end of the shop. She studiously avoided looking at either Kaden or Kiel as she led them down a long hallway to a heavy wooden door, then slipped a key on a chain from between her breasts. The lock opened with a heavy click. She lifted a lantern from a hook inside the door, lit it, then handed it to Triste. Eyes still downcast, she gestured them down a flight of stairs.

"Be welcome to the home of the goddess," she murmured as they passed. "May you find inside the pleasure you seek."

Only after they'd descended the stairs and walked fifty paces through a tunnel floored with burnished black stone and paneled with shining maple did Kaden venture to speak.

"What did you tell them back there?"

"I told them my mother's name, that the two of you were her patrons. That you were wearing a hood because you didn't want to be recognized and that if they left us standing in the street for another moment, I would see that they were flogged and their employment terminated."

Kiel frowned. "You bullied your way past the guards? That would seem to be weak security."

"Not really," she replied. "It was the tattoo that got me through. That and the fact that I . . ." She hesitated, coloring. "I look the part."

"Really?" Kaden asked, raising his brows. He gestured to her burns, to the lacerations cut into her skin. Even without the obvious wounds, Triste was filthy, hardly the image of a pampered priestess.

She bit her lip. "Not all of Ciena's gifts are made of silk and fine wine.

There are . . . rougher pleasures. This will not be the first time the guards have seen a priest or priestess return to the temple looking . . . less than pure."

Kaden grappled with the notion for a moment, then shook his head. "Now what?" he asked. "What happens when we get inside?"

"Now what?" Kaden asked. "What happens when we get inside?"

"We find my mother."

After walking another hundred paces and climbing a spiral staircase, Kaden followed Triste through a second wooden door, this one unlocked, into a small pavilion of cedar and sandalwood. Instead of walls, intricately carved screens shielded them from sight while allowing glimpses of leaves and tree trunks beyond. The noise and chaos of Annur's streets was gone, replaced by the music of birdsong, the soft gurgling of running water, and from somewhere in the distance, two overlapping melodies picked out on great harps. Green vines spilling over with tiny red flowers twisted through the woodwork, their soft scent twining with that of the cedar and sandalwood. Twin divans upholstered with dark silk and piled with artfully arranged pillows flanked the walls of the pavilion, while between them a small stone fountain trickled water into a clear pool.

A quiet chime sounded as soon as Triste shut the door behind her, and moments later a young man in a simple white robe stepped into the space. Like the shopkeeper, he kept his eyes downcast, a humble posture that did nothing to obscure the perfection of his features. He gestured to the divan.

"Please, make yourselves comfortable," he said, setting three filled glasses on a wooden table. "May I ask which of the *leina* you seek?"

"Louette Morjeta," Triste replied.

Her voice trembled, and Kaden glanced over to see her biting her lip.

"So," he said, when the man in white had gone, "this is your home."

He tried to put a name to the feeling that had been tugging at him since they entered the temple, to trace the various strands of emotion, to follow the weave. There was nervousness, and doubt, despair and hope twisted together, even a thin thread of anger. He watched the feeling snare his body in its net, listening as his pulse quickened and sweat beaded his palms. *What is this?* Not resentment. Not fear. He considered the silk hangings, the sweat beaded on the blown crystal filled with wine and crushed mint. He watched himself watching the things of the temple, studied his responses.

Embarrassment, he realized finally. It was an unfamiliar emotion, one he'd not experienced with the Shin for many years. It was surprising to encounter it here, now. After all, he'd grown up in the opulence of the Dawn Palace, surrounded by servants and slaves, grown accustomed early to the genuflections of even the highest ministers. It was, he supposed, a testament to the thoroughness of the monks, to their ability to scrub away all such habits, that he felt so out of place now, among the luxury of the temple. The priestesses and priests, even their servants seemed like queens and kings, all poise and perfection, while he felt acutely the dirt beneath his nails, the oiliness of the beaten wool tunic, the rough stubble hazing his chin.

"You didn't tell me your home was so beautiful," he said, gesturing vaguely.

She frowned, glanced around as though really seeing the place for the first time, then shrugged. "Your monastery was beautiful."

Kaden compared the rough stone buildings of his memory with the sweeping curves and sumptuous fabrics surrounding them. "A different kind of beauty."

"A clean beauty," Triste said. She lowered her voice. "This place . . . it's all wine and silk on the surface, but beneath . . ." She trailed off, shaking her head. "Even in the Temple of Ciena, there are things that are not pretty. And people."

Before she could say more, however, the screen to the pavilion swung open and a woman surged inside. Kaden had expected the poised reserve he'd seen from everyone else associated with the temple, but she utterly ignored him and Kiel, throwing her arms around Triste in a desperate embrace, sobbing her name over and over. After a long time, she pulled back, staring in horror at her daughter's wounds.

"Who did this to you?" she demanded.

Triste opened her mouth to reply, then closed it, shaking her head. Morjeta studied her for a few heartbeats, then gathered her daughter in her own arms once again. Kaden couldn't see Triste's face, buried as it was in her mother's shoulder, but her hands closed convulsively around the fabric of the older woman's gown, and, from the shuddering of her shoulders, it seemed that she, too, was crying.

After a moment he turned away, uncomfortable and unsure where to put his eyes. For eight years the only people to lay their hands on him had been his *umials,* and then only to administer penance. He tried to imagine how it might feel to be wrapped up in an embrace like that. Imagination failed him. He had envisioned his own homecoming hundreds of times over, especially during the early years with the monks, but neither of his parents, if he remembered them correctly, would have wept, and now both were dead. There was no one in Annur who would throw their arms around him. No one anywhere. Kaden tried to make sense of the subtle tug of feelings the thought aroused in him, but Morjeta, finally, was turning away from Triste, rubbing the tears from her cheeks with the heels of her hands, and greeting them.

"A thousand apologies, sirs," she said. "My daughter has returned after a long absence." She cocked her head to the side, curiosity shouldering aside the initial welter of emotion, then glanced back at Triste. She shared her daughter's sleek black hair and delicate features, although Morjeta was taller by several inches, and when she wrapped a protective arm around Triste's shoulders once more, she made her daughter look younger than her years. "*How* have you returned? Who are these gentlemen?"

Triste shook her head furtively, gesturing to the wooden screens around them.

Morjeta's lips tightened, but she nodded, a tiny inclination of the head.

"Once again, you must forgive me. Please, follow me. Once you've bathed and dined, it would be my honor to entertain you in more privacy."

29

Three days' hard ride south of the Urghul camp they hit the White River. Valyn reined in his horse as they topped the rise, gazing down into the shallow, winding valley below. Back at the base of the Bone Mountains the White was shallow enough in some places to swim a horse across, frothing over the jumbled boulders in a spray of foam that gave the river its name. Here, however, a thousand miles to the west, it ran deep and dark, a sinuous snake a quarter-mile wide, draining all the vast pasturage of the steppe.

"Careful," Valyn said, backing his horse down the northern side of the hill.

The chances of being spotted by an Annurian patrol were thin. The river still lay a few miles off, and along this section the border forts were spread at least twenty miles apart. Still, there was no point perching atop the hill, offering a stark silhouette to whoever might be riding in the valley below. The evening sun already smudged the western sky, and in another hour they'd be able to ride the final miles safely.

Laith sighed audibly. "We're swimming, aren't we? At night."

"We are," Valyn replied absently, scanning the far bank for rising smoke or some other sign of one of the forts. After years flying on the back of a kettral, it was frustrating to be tethered to the horizon. Five minutes in the air, and he'd know everything he needed to know, but he didn't have five minutes in the air. He spared a thought for Suant'ra, hoping that she had returned to the Eyrie somehow. That would be the best thing for her, and it would play into his own plans as well. A bird returning empty usually meant the Wing was dead, and if people thought he was dead, maybe they'd stop hunting him for a while, long enough, at least, for him to get close to il Tornja and find out what was going on. To kill the man if necessary.

He was still grappling with Balendin's revelation. He had known, of course, that the plot to destroy his family extended into the highest strata of Annurian society, into the Dawn Palace itself—there was no other way to explain the involvement of both the Mizran Councillor and a large portion of the Aedolian Guard. Still, it felt different to have a name. *The* name. If Balendin was to be believed, il Tornja had devised the entire plot. He had pulled Yurl's strings and Balendin's, Ut's and Adiv's. Every death could be laid at his feet.

Something dark and bestial coiled around Valyn's heart, squeezing, squeezing, until the air burned in his lungs. His knuckles ached, and he realized he was clutching his belt knife, that he'd drawn the blade halfway from its sheath as though the *kenarang* stood before him. He stared at the hand. The knuckles were pale, tendons rigid beneath the skin of the wrist.

"Leave the horses here?" Talal asked, breaking into his thoughts.

Valyn hesitated, shuddered away the rage, slid the knife back into the sheath before anyone could notice, then nodded. Even the indefatigable Urghul beasts couldn't swim the massive flow. It would mean running on the far side, but running was nothing new. Once they hit settled territory it wouldn't be difficult to steal new horses.

"No bird," Laith grumbled as they dismounted, then turned their mounts free. "No horses. We might as well be slogging around in the 'Kent-kissing legions."

"Makes you feel for the common soldier, doesn't it?" Talal asked.

Laith stared at the leach as though he were mad. "Hull can *have* the common soldier. I joined up with the Kettral to avoid this kind of shit."

"Luckily," Valyn cut in, "you know how to swim. At least you're not stuck back in the Urghul camp."

"Are you kidding? Gwenna and Annick have their own tent, a kid to bring them food twice a day, and skins and skins of that horse-piss fire liquor they drink up there. We, on the other hand, just lost our horses and are about to dive into a river that originates with glacial snowpack. I'll take the Urghul side of the equation any day."

The water was cold, far colder than the sea around the Islands, cold enough that Valyn insisted the three of them run the bank until they were sweaty and hot before starting across. All Kettral could swim more or less indefinitely, given the right conditions, but the seeping cold of that black running water would sap the strength from the strongest swimmer in minutes.

Cadets learned about cold water the hard way. Each year the trainers sent a group up to the Ice Sea where they were dumped in the drink and told to paddle for the shore a half-mile distant. It was a trivial distance, but no one ever made it. Valyn remembered swimming until his lips turned blue, his limbs went to lead, and his mind filled with hazy fog. The trainers were there to fish him out once he started to sink, but he still remembered the sensation, first the shock, then the gradual creeping weight in his chest, then indifference swaddling him like a soft blanket.

Halfway across the White River he found the same heavy lassitude pressing him gently beneath the surface. Laith's head and Talal's were barely visible in the moonlight, dark splotches a few paces from him on either side. The flier's stroke was visibly weakening, and when Valyn glanced over at Talal he realized that all of them were struggling.

He rolled onto his side for a moment, lifting his head above the water as he swam.

"Faster," he said. His mouth felt stiff and awkward around the word, as though the syllables were cold stones on his tongue, and for a moment he thought neither of the two had heard. When Laith turned his head for his next breath, however, he cursed briefly but eloquently, then picked up the tempo. Talal, too, seemed to get the message. Valyn was hauling the inflated bag with their weapons, and the other two started to draw away from him. Grimly he rolled back onto his stomach and redoubled his effort. He couldn't maintain the new pace for long, but the choice was stark: swim or die.

When he finally hit the far shore, Talal and Laith were already out, but they stepped back into the current to drag him the last few steps. Valyn's legs had gone stiff and stupid with the cold, and as he emerged from the water into the slicing blade of the evening air it was all he could do to stay on his feet. All three of them were naked, clothes tied tight in the inflated bladder along with their weapons. His jaw chattered uncontrollably, and his throat had gone tight, as though the muscles inside it had frozen.

"Blacks . . ." Laith managed. "Need . . . our blacks . . ."

Valyn shook his head. The light wool was perfect for retaining heat, but they had already shed their heat during the long swim. They needed a fire, but a fire would take too long, and the light would draw Annurian troops. Besides, the south bank of the White was as barren as the north, all broken ground and no trees. Work would have to warm them.

"Run," he said, pointing a trembling arm.

Talal met his eyes, nodded, then set out south at a jerky trot.

Laith growled something that might have been a protest or a curse, but when Valyn started, the flier fell in behind, both of them stumbling over the uneven ground beneath the swaying stars.

They'd been moving for at least an hour before the warmth started to seep back into Valyn's flesh. With the warmth came feeling, and with the feeling came itching, then pain. His soles were rugged from running the Island trails, but fleeing through the darkness over rough earth on feet like clubs had resulted in several bruises, a nasty gash across the arch of his right foot, and the loss of the toenail on his left large toe.

"How are we doing?" he asked, slowing to a walk.

"I hope you don't take it as insubordination," Laith replied, "if I tell you exactly where you can stuff that particular question."

Talal chuckled quietly. "I wouldn't want to do it all over again."

Valyn smiled. "And here I just realized I forgot our gear on the far bank."

"I will drown you," Laith said.

"How about our blacks?" Talal asked. "And the swords, too. I'd feel better with some clothes on my body and a blade close to hand."

"Why?" Laith asked, shaking his head. "I was just going to club anyone who came close with my cock." He glanced down. "Unfortunately, after that dip in the river it's no longer the fearsome, crushing weapon I remember."

Valyn tossed the pack down on the grass and sorted through the weapons and clothes. The dry wool felt good on his skin, and the soft leather boots gave some cushion to his battered feet. The run had both dried and warmed him, and he flexed his hands and fingers, working out the last stubborn patches of stiffness, then rolled his shoulders in their sockets. Already the memory of the desperate cold had started to fade.

"All right," he said finally. "We travel by night for two days, until we're well clear of the border. Il Tornja has no idea where we are, no idea that we're still alive, no idea that we're coming for him, but he's sure to sit up and take notice if one of his patrols picks up the remnants of a Kettral Wing wandering around just south of the White."

"We still don't know if the *kenarang* is responsible for your father's death," Talal pointed out. "Balendin might have been lying."

Valyn nodded. "He might have been lying, but I doubt it. Balendin was frightened when Long Fist questioned him, almost terrified. You both saw him." He hesitated, then decided to leave out the fact that he had also smelled the leach's fear, had tasted it, like a thick, bilious skim over spoiled milk. "Either way, there's no reason to take chances. We stay out of sight until we have some 'Kent-kissing idea what's going on."

"I liked it better when we had 'Ra," Laith said, shaking his head. "I hope she made it clear of the steppe. No telling what those Urghul bastards might do with her if they took her down."

"I'm sure she's—" Talal began, but Valyn cut him off with a curt chop of the hand.

Somewhere behind them, off to the north but hammering closer in a dull tattoo, Valyn could make out the sound of horses.

Laith cocked an ear, then half spread his hands. "What?"

"Riders," Valyn said, "pushing hard."

The flier glanced at Talal. "You hear anything?"

"Just the wind," Talal replied.

"They're coming," Valyn said, crouching down to set an ear to the earth. He listened a moment more, then nodded. "About a mile off. Riding at a canter."

"A canter at night over this ground?" Talal shook his head. "Dangerous."

Laith pressed his own ear to the dirt, waited a long time, then stood. "I have no idea how you heard that, but I hear them now. Sounds like they're on some sort of path. The earth is packed."

Talal had cocked his head to one side, twisting the iron bracelet on his wrist absently as he did so. "I think they're going to pass us to the west. We should be all right."

"You using some kind of secret leach trick?" Laith asked.

"Yes, very secret. Very tricky. It's called listening."

Valyn figured the angles in his head. Four horses pushing south hard in the middle of the night weren't a routine patrol. Even on a path, they were taking a risk with their horses, which meant urgency. Urgency meant information, and the only information this far north was information about the Urghul. Valyn gritted his teeth.

He'd intended to stay out of view, to slink into Annur—past the border first, then into the capital itself—and locate il Tornja without anyone the wiser. Maybe he could meet up with Kaden before choosing his course, maybe not, but waiting for Kaden to tell him what was going on hardly made for a complete plan. Sooner or later he was going to need to decide whether or not to actually kill the *kenarang,* and to do that he'd need to decide whether Long Fist was telling him the truth. The Urghul chief had insisted that his massive camp of horsemen was a purely defensive measure, but tens of thousands of mounted warriors could turn aggressive in the time it took them to mount up. For all Valyn knew, Long Fist was playing him. Either way, this was a chance to get some unfiltered, unblemished, unprepared intelligence. Not only that, but they'd have horses.

"Modified dead-man ambush," he decided abruptly, turning toward the hill and breaking into a jog.

Laith didn't budge. "What about sneaking *past* the patrols?"

"We need the intel and we can use the horses," Valyn called over his shoulder.

"And the soldiers?" Talal asked. The leach had fallen in beside him immediately, but when Valyn glanced over he could see the concern written on his face. "They're Annurians. . . ."

"I'm aware that they're Annurians," Valyn replied, trying to think through the attack. It was hard to say just how far off the horses were, but they only had a few minutes. "We're not going to kill them."

"Captives," Laith observed as he caught up to them, "are complicated."

"We take them," Valyn replied. "Tie their legs. Drop them five miles off the path. Should take them a few days to wriggle back, by which time we'll be well south. With any luck, they won't even know we're Kettral."

"Luck," Laith said, shaking his head. "I'd like to start needing it less or having it more."

As he spoke, they crested a gentle rise, and Valyn paused, scanning the land below. It was almost as bare as the steppe, but there were a few withered pines, a couple patches of twisted alder, limbs silver in the moonlight— enough cover for a dead-man. And there, the only straight line in a landscape of slopes and curves, the hammered earth of the Annurian track, striking south toward the horizon.

"I'm the deader," Valyn said, considering the contours a moment more, then pointing, "right there. Four horses most likely means two riders, with two remounts."

Laith nodded. "You want to go with a V or a half-hatch?" Once the flier got his griping and theatrics out of the way, he actually liked to fight. Not as much as he liked to fly, but then, there wasn't much flying to be had without a bird.

"Half-hatch," Valyn said, indicating a gnarled trunk and a waist-high line of scrub on the far side of the road.

"It's going to be tight," Talal said, turning an ear toward the drumming hooves.

Valyn nodded.

"What's the play?" Laith asked.

"After the halt," Valyn said, spinning out the possibilities as he spoke, "I'll take the dismount. . . ."

"*If* there's a dismount," Talal said.

"No dismount, and we ditch it," Valyn said. "We let them ride."

"You take the dismount," Laith urged, waving a hand impatiently, "then—"

"Spark and bang," Valyn replied. He glanced at Talal.

"Yeah," the leach replied. "I can manage it."

"All right then. Standard. One moves for the bridle. The other takes him down. Don't worry about sound. We've got to be five miles from the river by now. Just make sure he doesn't bolt."

"And if there are more?" Talal asked.

Valyn paused to listen to the drumming hooves. It was tricky to un-thread the different gaits, but the horses were close now. He was all but certain there were only four beasts. "Four men means no remounts," he said, "and that pace without remounts would be idiocy."

Laith nodded, then turned to jog into position.

Talal hesitated.

"Say it or stow it," Valyn said. "They're almost on us."

"Seems right," the leach said after a moment. "Standard protocol. Four horses. Two men." He turned to follow Laith.

✝

Valyn realized the approaching soldiers had buggered the 'Kent-kissing protocol the moment the horses hammered into view.

Four horses. Four men.

Either they had a remount not far to the south or they were utter fools. It hardly mattered. Valyn lay just to the side of the road. Had there been even a little cover, his blacks might have concealed him—the men were riding hard, and couldn't expect a body here, near the very fringe of the empire—but then, Valyn had chosen his spot precisely for the *lack* of cover. A dead-man ambush wasn't much good if the mark rode by without noticing the deader. Cursing under his breath, he rolled toward the low gully a few paces distant, but the soldiers were on him before he was halfway there, the leader calling out to his companions over the clatter of hooves, all of them hauling up short, horses blowing.

"Stand and show yourself," one of the soldiers called out. The command was followed by the uneasy scrape of steel over leather as the men freed their swords.

Valyn rolled slightly onto his side, slipping his belt knife from its sheath as he tried to recalibrate tactics. Three on four made perfectly acceptable odds for the Kettral, especially in an ambush, but you had to be willing to cut some throats.

"It's an Urghul, Kidder," another soldier said, voice high and tight. "A 'Kent-kissing scout."

"What's he doing here then?" A third voice. "Where's his horse?"

Valyn risked a glance at the riders. As he suspected, they wore the light leather armor of legionary messengers. The leader's horse was out in front, but the other three were clustered tight together. Laith and Talal were on the far side of the road, which meant two of the four men were partially shielded from attack. If the first man dismounted, if Valyn could take him down quickly enough, he might be able to hamstring the nearer horse, which would solve one of the problems. . . .

"Stand," the closest rider said again, "in the name of the regent, or I will ride you down."

"No," Valyn moaned, raising a hand, "please. No. I'm wounded. I'm Annurian. Legion."

"Sound like an Urghul to you, Arin?"

"They don't all talk nonsense," Arin replied stubbornly. "Maybe this one's a spy."

"All the legion up this way is tied to the forts," the leader, Kidder, said carefully, turning back to Valyn. "Are you with the Thirty-second?"

Valyn hesitated. Legionary deployments were constantly shifting—generals didn't want their men to get too comfortable in a single place—and the Kettral rarely bothered studying the latest configuration. There was nothing to do but throw the dice.

"Tenth," he groaned. "Please. I'm hurt."

Kidder reined in his horse. "Tenth's way west in the Romsdals," he said guardedly. "What're you doing here?"

Valyn paused. The longer they talked, the more time Talal and Laith had to shift position and rethink tactics, but a large part of the success of the ambush relied on surprise. Even as they spoke, the other riders were spreading out, staring worriedly into the surrounding terrain.

"Messenger," he moaned. Paused. "The Urghul hit me. My partner's dead."

His mention of the Urghul caused some consternation, the other men circling warily. It seemed, however, to earn him some trust with the leader, who dismounted after a moment, then approached slowly, sword drawn. He stopped a couple of paces from Valyn, blade leveled between them.

"What's your message?" he asked.

Valyn shook his head weakly. "For the garrison commander . . ."

"Where's your horse?"

"South," Valyn moaned. "Maybe a mile. I crawled. . . . *Please.*"

The man glanced over his shoulder, and in the short moment his head was turned, Valyn rolled to his feet, knocked the sword aside by the flat, then struck out at the soldier's neck with the heel of his hand. It wasn't a killing blow, wasn't intended to do much more than stagger the man for a few heartbeats, but Valyn felt something crunch, and the Annurian sagged, gagging. There was no time to think about what he'd done, not while the other riders were in play, and Valyn stepped forward, twisted the long blade free of the soldier's grip, then spun away, slashing through the neck of the nearest horse. He needed three mounts, not four.

The beast recoiled, then, before its rider could leap free, collapsed thrashing. The soldier screamed as his leg broke, and then Valyn was on him, knocking him unconscious with the sword's pommel.

That made two down. He turned to find that Laith had already knocked a third clear of his saddle. The fourth, however, the one farthest from the center of their attack, had broken free, and was hammering up the road to the north, his companions forgotten. Valyn cursed and cast about for one of the two remaining horses. The beasts were panicked, rolling their eyes and snorting, and when Valyn edged close to the nearer of the two, it reared up, lashing out with a hoof. He sidestepped the blow, trying to come in close, but the animal pivoted, keeping him at bay.

"Talal!" he called. The whole thing was a goat fuck already, but if the last rider got away they'd have half a legion on them by the time the sun rose.

The leach stood a dozen paces off, chin lifted, eyes fixed on the rapidly retreating figure. As Valyn watched, Talal made a slight gesture with his left hand, like swatting a fly away from his fingers, and, with a scream, the horse collapsed, front legs buckling abruptly. The rider, suddenly free of the saddle, soared through the air, arms scrabbling at nothingness, then hit headfirst with a vicious crunch. Talal went after him, but it was already over. Though the horse thrashed furiously, lost in pain and panic, the slumped shape of the man beneath remained horribly still.

Valyn took a deep breath, then turned back to the scene at hand. The first soldier was bent double, straining to haul breath through his shattered windpipe as he clawed at the dirt with one hand. The man trapped beneath the horse lay still, but it was clear from the awkward angle of his body that his leg was broken. A heavy horrible stone settled in Valyn's gut. In just heartbeats his neat ambush had spiraled utterly out of control. The men down weren't traitors or barbarians; they were Annurians, soldiers of his own empire, loyal troops following orders as best as they were able, and for that loyalty Valyn had attacked them, crippled at least one for life, and possibly killed another.

"Is he alert?" Valyn asked roughly, turning to Laith. The flier had the fourth soldier pinned to the earth, a knee in the small of his back.

"For now," he replied, lacing the man's wrists with a length of light cord. He glanced over his shoulder at the surrounding violence. His eyes showed bleak in the moonlight. "Holy Hull. What did we do?"

"We did what we had to," Valyn replied, trying to shackle his own nausea and horror.

"Had to?" Laith demanded, gesturing at the bodies with a hand. "How did we have to do this?"

"It's done, Laith," Talal said quietly, rejoining the two of them. "It went wrong, but we all did it, and we can't take it back."

"What about him?" Valyn asked, nodding toward the soldier up the road. Talal had slit the horse's throat, and both beast and man lay still.

The leach shook his head. "The fall snapped his neck."

Valyn stared at the shadowy forms of man and horse, then turned his back on them, crossing instead to the soldier with the injured windpipe. The Annurian knelt on his hands and knees, hacking out a shattered sound, half cough, half retch, his body quivering in the still air. For a moment, Valyn could do nothing but watch. Between the moon's light and his own eyes, he could see everything, even the details—the small tattoo of a mouse behind the soldier's ear, the scarring across his right knuckles, the uneven patch where someone had hacked away too much hair with a belt knife. The man had managed to crawl maybe a dozen paces, no goal beyond escaping his own terror.

"Crushed," Talal said, joining him.

"Maybe not," Valyn replied.

"It's crushed," the leach said again, quietly but firmly.

"Someone could treat it. Remember Vellik back on the Islands? He busted his throat in a botched barrel drop, and it healed up all right."

"They got Vellik into the infirmary in less than an hour, and even still, he can barely talk now. I know how to patch up a lot of things, but this . . ." He spread his hands. "It's just a question of fast or slow."

The man finally turned his head at the sound of their voices. He was young, maybe a year or two older than Valyn. He raised a weak hand in a gesture that might have been pleading or accusation, his jaw working around the mangled wreckage of his words.

Valyn blew out a long, uneven breath. Talal was right. The only kindness now was the knife's kindness, and yet Valyn hesitated, feeling for the first time what it meant to command the Wing. With all the swimming and language study, flight training and demolitions work back on the Islands, it was easy sometimes to forget that *this* was what he had trained his whole life to do. *Kettral* was just a polite word for *killer*. Of course, he wasn't supposed to be killing Annurian soldiers, but then, killing was killing. No one wanted to die.

Valyn forced himself to look at the wounded soldier; the least he could do was meet his eyes. The legionary held the stare. What did he see, looking into the darkness of Valyn's vacant irises? Valyn read fear and pain, smelled the hot burn of terror on the air. Maybe the messenger had been following their conversation, maybe not, but one way or another, he knew that his death had arrived.

Which makes every heartbeat a cruelty, Valyn thought bleakly.

Then, before he could think further, he buried his knife in the soldier's neck, ripping furiously through the windpipe and arteries, then tearing up through the muscle until the blade snagged on bone. Hot blood soaked his blacks, and Valyn's own breath came hot and ragged in his throat. The soldier sagged against him, head canting off at an obscene angle, eyes blank, mouth hanging open.

"Holy Hull, Val," Laith muttered. "You didn't need to take his whole head off."

Valyn stared at the body for a moment, then jerked his knife free. The corpse collapsed.

"He's fucking dead, isn't he?" he demanded, knuckles white with clutching the blade. "Let's see what the other two have to say. Let's see if all this was worth anything."

30

Morjeta's personal chambers comprised a suite of breezy, high-ceilinged marble rooms with tall narrow windows three times Kaden's height, where gossamer curtains fluttered with the breeze. After gesturing them in, the *leina* shut the heavy wooden door behind her, turned a key in the lock, then crossed to the windows, brushing aside the curtains, leaning far enough out to see the stonework on either side.

"Can we—" Triste began, but her mother cut her off with a tense shake of the head, waving them ahead into yet another room, this one away from the windows. A wide bed draped with fine silk stood against one wall. A pair of long, upholstered divans faced it across a rich, thickly piled rug. The *leina* shut the door behind them, slid a pair of locks into place, put her ear to the wood for several heartbeats, then finally turned.

"Please," she said, gesturing to the divans, "be seated. I apologize for my haste in leading you here, but sometimes it seems Ciena loves secrets as much as she loves pleasure."

"Can we talk in this room?" Triste asked.

Morjeta nodded. "There are listening holes in the other chambers, but I've found them here. Plugged them."

She turned from her daughter to Kaden and Kiel, her gaze more forthright than it had been in the garden pavilion. If that look were calibrated to put Kaden at his ease, it failed. He felt like a goat sized up before the slaughter, and had to keep himself from tugging his hood even farther over his head.

"Of course," Morjeta continued, "there are already at least a dozen people who know you're here." She ticked them off on a manicured finger. "The guards outside Relli's shop, Relli herself, Yamara, who greeted you, and any of the other women or men we passed on the way here. How crucial is your secrecy? Like the scent of lilac on the spring air, word is already wafting through the temple halls."

Kaden hesitated, then pushed back his hood. "Important," he said.

The *leina*'s eyes widened as she saw his burning irises, and her lips pursed. "Oh," she said, staring for a moment before rising from her seat and dropping into a low curtsy. "Be welcome in Ciena's innermost heart, Your Radiance."

"Rise," Kaden replied, gesturing, "rise." Again he felt the weight of that single syllable, one he'd be forced to utter the rest of his life. *Provided,* he amended silently, *that I have a life ahead of me.* "I hope, someday, to sit the throne of my ancestors, but I expect someone else has beaten me to it. For now, please call me Kaden. Any further ceremony is only likely to get us all killed."

Morjeta paused, then nodded as she rose. "As you say, Kaden." She hesitated. "If I may ask, how—"

"It was a trap," Triste burst out. "Tarik Adiv took me to Ashk'lan. . . ."

"As a gift," her mother said, grief clouding her eyes. "I have not forgiven myself."

Triste waved aside the objection. "Please, Mother. Anything you could have done would have ended in more misery for us both. The point is not that Adiv took me, but *why* he took me. He was laying a trap for Kaden."

"Why?" Morjeta demanded. "Why did he need you?"

"He needed me," Triste replied grimly, "for bait."

Kaden watched the girl, studying her face for some hint that she was lying, for an echo of the fierceness she had shown in the dark chambers of the Dead Heart. There was nothing. Just a young woman, frightened and angry.

Morjeta let out a long, slow whistle, then turned to a silver tray and the ewer perched upon it, poured out four crystal goblets of chilled wine. She passed them to the men first, then to Triste. Kaden noticed the trembling of her hand when she raised her own, the depth of her first sip.

"What is happening?" she asked, shaking her head, then tipping the cup to her lips once more.

"We had hoped," Kaden replied, "that you might be able to tell us."

"I explained to Kaden," Triste said, "how the *leinas* hear everything, everything to do with Annur's powerful and wealthy."

Morjeta grimaced slightly, though the expression looked like something she had practiced in a mirror, calculated to express coquettish displeasure rather than genuine irritation. "Not everything," she said, "but it's true enough. Lust is a great loosener of tongues, and men and women both tend to spill their secrets in the strong grip of the goddess." She blew out a breath and spread her hands. "Tarik Adiv returned to the Dawn Palace weeks ago."

Kaden stared. The timing suggested that the leach could also use the *kenta,* although that would mean . . . He stopped himself, Tan's voice in his mind: *Speculation.*

"How?" he asked.

"The Kettral," Morjeta replied. "He arrived at night, and landed atop the Spear, but people saw the bird." She looked down, smoothing the fabric of her gown against her legs as she turned to Triste, bright tears pricking the corners of her eyes. "I've tried to see him," she said. "Tried to find out where you were. I've gone in person half a dozen times, humbling myself in the Jasmine Court. I've sent letters. . . ." She shook her head. "Nothing. From what the other *leinas* tell me, he's been cloistered almost constantly with the *kenarang.*"

"Ran il Tornja," Kaden said. He'd suspected as much. Micijah Ut had praised the general to the stars, and if anyone was in a position to suborn Kettral and Aedolians both, to murder an emperor in his own capital, it would be Annur's military commander.

Morjeta nodded. "He's been serving as regent since your father's death."

"It fits," Kiel said, nodding. "He can act as regent for a while, then move onto the throne itself."

"Why not just seize the throne right away?" Triste asked.

"He couldn't," Kaden said. "Not until news of my death or disappearance had time to make it back to the capital. He doesn't want it to look like a power grab."

"And it doesn't," Morjeta said. "At least, it didn't until your sister disappeared."

"Disappeared?" Kaden asked, stomach tightening. If il Tornja had attacked Sanlitun, Kaden, and Valyn, it only made sense that he'd go after Adare as well. "When? Does anyone know where she is?"

Morjeta raised her eyebrows. "Everyone knows where she is—marching north to join forces with the *kenarang.*"

Kiel frowned. "We have been, all three of us . . . removed from society for quite some time. It might be helpful if you could begin with Sanlitun's death."

It didn't take long for the *leina* to outline the main points in the story, a story that, to Kaden's surprise and dismay, implicated Adare nearly as much as it did il Tornja. Morjeta explained how his sister had worked hand in hand with il Tornja to bring down Uinian, the Chief Priest of Intarra, how the two of them had crafted Accords that crippled the Church, how the princess had begun sharing the *kenarang*'s bed.

Kaden stopped her there, demanding to know if she was sure.

Morjeta just smiled. "Regarding political gossip, my fellow priestesses and priests are well informed. Regarding romantic follies, the quality of our information approaches perfection. Besides, your sister made no effort to hide the liaison."

Kaden shook his head. "Maybe il Tornja lied to her, manipulated her."

"Maybe," Morjeta agreed. "We weren't certain *what* happened, because not long after, the princess . . . disappeared. For weeks no one seemed to know where she was, not even il Tornja, who was trying to keep the whole matter quiet while simultaneously sending out scores of soldiers to search for her. The next anyone heard, your sister was in Olon. The reports were confusing, but it sounded as though she'd had some sort of religious conversion, fully embraced the worship of Intarra, and, most shockingly, declared the regent a traitor and raised her own army."

"That makes sense," Kaden said, hope like a soft green seed sprouting inside him. "She learned the truth, raised an army, and fought back."

Morjeta shook her head. There was something in her eyes Kaden didn't recognize. Sorrow, perhaps? Pity?

"She didn't fight back," the *leina* said. "She marched her army all the way to Annur, but then she was welcomed into the city, into the Dawn Palace itself, by Adiv. It was not a long meeting, but it appears whatever differences they have were plastered over." She shook her head. "When your sister marched north, her men were calling her a saint, and his men . . ." She hesitated, then spread her hands. "She's claimed the Unhewn Throne, Kaden. Or all but claimed it. She intends to be Emperor."

The words landed like a blow. Not that he felt any particular attachment to a massive chunk of rock he hadn't seen since his childhood. If the Shin had taught him one lesson, it was the futility of coveting such things. Adare, though, had been his one connection to his family, to his father.

While Kaden and Valyn had been struggling through their training at the ends of the earth, Adare had stayed, had lived inside the red walls, had made Annur her home. She was his link to the city, to the father and mother he'd lost, and now, it seemed, that link was severed.

"*All but* claimed the throne?" Kiel asked.

"There wasn't time," Morjeta said. "They're marching north now, the princess and the *kenarang,* to meet some sort of Urghul threat in the north."

Ut and Adiv had mentioned the Urghul back in Ashk'lan. Kaden pulled the memory to the forefront of his mind. Some shaman had united the tribes for the first time, using his collected force to test the Annurian border.

"Il Tornja won victories against the Urghul," Kaden said. "Before my father died."

"It was those victories," Morjeta replied, "at least in part, that won him the role of *kenarang.*"

Kiel nodded. "A familiar strategy in military insurrections."

"What strategy?" Kaden asked, trying to keep pace with the leaps in the conversation.

"Provoke a foe, then use the newfound threat to convince your own people they need a military rather than a civilian ruler."

"It doesn't sound like he's trying to convince anyone," Triste said. "He murdered Kaden's father in secret. He covered it up!"

"But the Urghul threat helps his cause."

"Except," Kaden said, "it's not his cause anymore. Adare's claimed the throne, not il Tornja."

"And," Morjeta said, "all reports are that he's supporting her claim."

Kaden met Morjeta's eyes a moment, then turned away. The *leina's* bedchamber was not small—back at Ashk'lan, half a dozen monks could have shared the room with space to spare, and yet back at Ashk'lan he could have stepped through the door into open air, into a world of sky and snow and stone bordered only by high cliffs and the horizon. Here, one room led to another. He could leave Morjeta's bedchamber, leave her suite of rooms altogether, only to find himself in another room, hemmed in by other walls. Suddenly it seemed he had returned not to a city but to a labyrinth, one he had faint hope of escaping.

"An alliance then," Kiel said finally.

Kaden hauled his mind back to the present.

"Adare gives il Tornja legitimacy," the historian continued, "while the *kenarang* provides her with military power and expertise, the imprimatur of victory in battle. And if they are sharing a bed once more . . ."

"Heirs," Kaden concluded, shaking his head. He hadn't expected to recognize Annur, had expected the city to seem strange, confusing, indifferent to his return. He had not anticipated, though, finding it so fully turned against him, had not thought to find the conspiracy that led to his father's death so deeply rooted and flourishing.

Emotions buzzed inside him like wasps: anger, sadness, confusion. But he'd spent eight years learning to set aside his emotions, and he did so. He tried to remember what he knew of Adare from his childhood. She'd been an impetuous girl, impatient with the dresses and decorum that came with her station, impatient, it seemed to him now, with childhood itself. The one time he could remember his sister paying any actual attention to him was on the day he left for Ashk'lan. She had stood on the imperial docks, lips tight, eyes burning.

"Bid farewell to your brother, Adare," their mother had said. "He is a child now, but when he returns, he will be a man, and ready to take the reins of the empire."

"I know," was all Adare had said before kissing him coolly on both cheeks. She never said farewell.

Kiel's eyes were fixed intently on the air between them, as though scrutinizing some shape or pattern no one else could see. After a long time, his gaze focused and he turned to Morjeta.

"Can you paint?" he asked.

She nodded. "Not as well as some of my fellow *leinas,* but it is one of Ciena's arts."

"Ran il Tornja," he said. "Tarik Adiv. I'd like to see what they look like."

Kaden glanced at the man, suddenly grasping his intent. "You're wondering . . ."

Kiel nodded. "As you told me back in the Dead Heart, there were *ak'hanath* at your monastery, which means my people are involved."

Morjeta frowned, then nodded. "I can make a passable likeness of both men, but it will take some time."

"I'll paint Adiv," Kaden said.

He volunteered as much for the excuse to plunge into something familiar as to expedite the process, and for a few heartbeats after Morjeta produced the necessary materials he did nothing but sit, brush in hand, staring at the fine blank vellum. It seemed a lifetime since he had contemplated something as clean, as straightforward as an empty page, more than a lifetime, as though he'd dreamed the endless hours seated on the rock ledges of Ashk'lan. Finally he dipped the brush into the porcelain saucer of ink.

As the bristles moved over the fine parchment, he felt the knots of his mind loosen. For the first time since fleeing the Bone Mountains, he settled into a rhythm he actually understood, the wetting and clearing of the brush, the faint pressure of the bristles on the page, the easy, fluent movements of the wrist and fingers. He let all thought of Adare and Annur drain from his mind, all worry about the Unhewn Throne, all the faint tangles of grief for his father. Instead, he filled his head with the image of the Mizran Councillor, his blindfold, the shock of hair, the angle of his chin. After the first strokes, even the sense of the man *as* a man faded. There was only light and shadow, hollow and form, teased out in dark ink on a light page. He found himself adding details, unnecessary details, as the painting neared its conclusion—the stiff collar, the mountains behind—until there was nothing left to draw and he reluctantly laid down his brush.

Kiel rose to consider the painting.

"No," he said after just a moment. "I don't know him."

"I'm almost finished," Morjeta said, eyeing Kaden above her own canvas. "Where did you learn to paint?"

Kaden shook his head. The effort of explanation seemed too massive, like trying to unearth a buried stone for which he couldn't even find the edges.

The *leina* studied him a moment longer, dark eyes abrim with curiosity, then gave an eloquent shrug. "There," she said, turning back to her own portrait, rotating it so that everyone could see. "It's finished."

She had painted a bold figure with a strong chin and high cheekbones, lips open in a partial smile revealing a row of perfect teeth. Kaden had expected a stern, severe face, on the order of Micijah Ut or Ekhard Matol, a military man with a mind for tactics and blood. Morjeta's il Tornja, however, looked sly, almost jocular, as though he were on the verge of breaking into laughter.

Kaden frowned. "He doesn't look like Csestriim."

"Csestriim?" the *leina* asked, blanching, eyes going wide. "Are you mad?" Then she met Kaden's gaze and dropped her eyes, bowing until her face almost touched the table. "A thousand apologies, Your Radiance . . ." she began.

Kaden raised a hand to cut her off, but at his side Kiel had gone utterly still.

"The expression is deceiving," he said, voice low but certain. "Over the thousands of years, he has learned to smile."

Kaden turned, feeling his heart kick in his chest. "You know him?"

The Csestriim nodded, but didn't speak. For a few heartbeats, everyone just stared, first at Kiel, then at the page, then back.

"*And?*" Triste said finally.

"Like me, he has worn many names. The first was Tan'is."

"Why did he kill my father?" Kaden demanded. "Why does he hate the Malkeenians?"

Kiel turned to him, eyes like wells. "Hate is a creature of the human heart. Those of us who gave birth to you are strangers to Maat's embrace. The general you call Ran il Tornja does not hate you any more than you would hate a stone, the sky."

"So what does he want?"

"He wants," the Csestriim said, measuring the words as he spoke them, "what he has always wanted. Victory."

"Victory over *whom?*"

"Your race."

"Well, he's getting pretty close," Kaden said. "From the sound of it, he already more or less controls Annur."

Kiel pursed his lips, then shook his head slowly, almost ruefully. "You do not understand. Victory, to il Tornja, is not a momentary matter of draping himself in garlands or sitting atop a throne."

"It's not just any throne," Kaden pointed out. "Annur is the most powerful empire in the world."

"Annur is an eyeblink."

"Hundreds of years of uninterrupted rule are an eyeblink?"

Kiel smiled. "Yes. Il Tornja's goals are deeper. Older. He is still fighting the war that we entrusted to him thousands of years ago."

"When will he stop?"

"When you are gone."

Kaden spread his hands in protest. "Why me?"

The historian frowned. "Your language is imprecise. Not just *you,* Kaden. All of you."

Kaden stared. "All of Annur?"

"All of humanity."

31

The day after the first Kwihna Saapi, as the Urghul folded their *api* and began to break camp, Gwenna knew she had been right. The blood-drenched spectacle wasn't just some arbitrary ritual carried out in accordance with the chieftain's whim or the phases of the moon: it was a particular sacrifice begging Meshkent's favor as the Urghul rode to war.

Long Fist's army had since crossed the White River north of the confluence, avoiding the Annurian forts to the east. The rafts ferrying the horses and their riders were ridiculous, precarious craft, crudely lashed and awkwardly balanced, but there were hundreds of them, hundreds upon hundreds, the numbers alone betraying months of preparation; Gwenna felt sick to her stomach when she saw them lined up along the shore. Long Fist didn't need rafts to defend his land. He needed them to attack.

By the time they'd crossed the river, the shaman had dropped all pretense of their "honored guest" status. Their tent was ringed with guards each night, and they weren't allowed out except in the evening, when they were forced to take part in the bloody nighttime rituals.

It had taken hours for Gwenna's hands to stop shaking after killing the first young soldier. After three more nights of blood and murder, she'd managed to bring her hands under control, but something inside her, something invisible, still trembled as though diseased. She felt like a fool; eight years she'd trained for this, trained to kill with blades and explosives, bows and bare hands, trained until she could choke someone twice her size with one arm or poison an entire legion. She had felt prepared, more than prepared, but when it came time, she found that while her hands could kill, nothing had prepared her mind for the horror. She couldn't shake the memory of the sick, soft give of the stick driving home, the weight of the first young man as he slumped forward, his slick, warm blood on her hands.

And the killing didn't end when Gwenna stopped. Each night, Annick had her turn between the fires, and Pyrre. There seemed to be no end to Long Fist's prisoners: Annurian legionaries, Urghul thieves, and, since they'd crossed the river, a handful of thick-fisted loggers, Annurian citizens living beyond the edge of the empire itself. None were any match for the Kettral or Skullsworn, a fact that filled Gwenna with both relief and disgust. After a while, the Urghul started trying to delay the killing, to draw out the pain, depriving the women of any weapons whatsoever. It didn't work. Annick always went straight for the eyes, accomplishing with her fingers what Gwenna had done with the stick, while Pyrre crushed the windpipe of every adversary with a single, casual blow of her stiffened fingers.

The fights were bad enough, but they were nothing next to the cutting and screaming that followed. Long Fist himself, arms drenched past the elbows in gore, had personally hacked the hearts from a dozen young soldiers staked into the earth. The shaman had a way with his knife, managing to avoid all the major arteries, to keep the victims alive even as he lifted the still-beating heart clear of the ribs, squeezing it in his fist. Unsurprisingly, Balendin had also taken to the work, eyes bright as he drank in the terror of his captives, hands horribly slow and sure as he flayed them, thin strips of skin pliant beneath his knife. It was one thing to hear about the worship of Meshkent in some lecture hall back on the Islands, something else to witness it. Something else to take part.

Worse, the horror of the nightly sacrifices was only a prelude to what would happen on a much broader scale during any actual invasion. If the Urghul broke across the frontier, there'd be a lot more screaming on a lot more altars all across northern Annur. The nightmares woke Gwenna at night, her blacks drenched in a heavy sweat. She'd wanted to try to break free as soon as she realized the army was moving, but Pyrre had talked her down. The assassin's attitude toward her captivity had soured significantly after the Kwihna Saapi began—evidently she preferred to murder on her own schedule—but she pointed out, to Gwenna's frustration, that any escape on the steppe would be short-lived. No trees meant no cover, and no cover meant that the Urghul could ride them down like dogs. Now that they were past the river and starting to move south, however, Gwenna was about finished waiting.

"That," she said, stabbing a finger past the tent wall, past the Urghul camp beyond, over the wet broken ground and the dark trees fringing the horizon to the west, "is the start of the Thousand Lakes. Annur."

"It's not Annur," Pyrre corrected her, picking flakes of dried blood off her hands and flicking them into the fire. The evening's sacrifices had only just ended, and while Gwenna wished she could swim herself clean in the ocean, the assassin treated the human blood on her hands the same way she might a little honest mud. "It's not Annur until south of the Black. This is just . . ." She frowned with distaste. ". . . buggy. *But,*" she continued, raising her hands to forestall Gwenna's boiling objection, "we finally have some trees. I'd say that some point in the next few days would be a good time to bid our farewells, before we outlast our welcome and Long Fist decides to dispose of us more thoroughly."

The Skullsworn's words made Gwenna queasy. They *were* prisoners inside the *api,* inside the camp, but for some reason, Long Fist and Balendin continued to allow them their own tent, to speak to them with mock solicitude. The whole thing seemed like a trap, but Gwenna couldn't see any point to it, not when the Urghul already had them trapped.

"Why hasn't he done it already?" she demanded, grinding her knuckles into her palm. "We're the most dangerous prisoners he has. Why aren't we tied up like the rest?" She gestured vaguely to the comforts of the *api.* "Why aren't we *dead?*"

"A hedge," Annick suggested, not looking up from the bison haunch she was busy butchering. "In case Valyn comes back. Or in case he decides we might be useful."

"Maybe," Pyrre said, picking at the dirt on her pants with a fingernail. She'd been forced to kill three men just an hour earlier, but she seemed most concerned about the damage to her clothing. "But I suspect it's simpler than that."

"Meaning?"

"Meaning we're not dead because Long Fist needs us alive."

"For what?" Gwenna spat. "Fun?"

Pyrre looked up, lips pursed as though ready to make some crack, then paused. "How does a man become a chief?" she asked finally. "A chief of *anything,* let alone a million Urghul?"

"Kills the people who want to kill him," Gwenna said. "That's what I'm *saying.* Long Fist's a fool to leave us alive."

Pyrre shook her head. "If he tried to kill everyone dangerous, he'd never get done killing. There's always someone who wants to murder a chief. Long Fist can't protect against them all. His position isn't fully secure."

"The bastard looks pretty secure when he's hacking out hearts."

"That's because," Pyrre said, "no one can imagine him dead."

"I've been imagining it since I met him," Gwenna snapped, irritated with the assassin's roundabout platitudes. "In fact, I'm about to do some more imagining right now."

"*You* can imagine it," Pyrre said, "but *they* can't. When the Urghul look at him, they don't see a man; they see a legend. All you need is a blade to kill a man." She snorted. "All you need is fingernails, as you so ably demonstrated this evening. But a legend—a legend is unkillable, and he wears his own legend—uniter of the tribes, the man who made his own sacrifice to Meshkent, the one who plans to destroy Annur—just the same way he wears that bison skin. It's a symbol of his power, his strength."

"You're saying he lets us wander around free because he believes his own bullshit?" Gwenna demanded, shaking her head. "That's even stupider than I thought."

"I'm saying that we are *part* of his legend: two Kettral and a Skullsworn tamed by the great chief to fight before his fires."

"Tamed," Gwenna spat. "Speak for yourself."

The assassin raised an eyebrow, and Gwenna colored, the memory of the pleading soldier bleeding into her memory, the feel of his flesh as he died. "At least I haven't quit yet," she muttered.

Pyrre shrugged. "I don't suppose you've ever spent time in the Bend?"

Gwenna shook her head, confused.

"A pity. It's a marvelously barbaric place. I watched a man in the killing pits there once. I studied him all afternoon. He fought animals—bears, bulls, wolves—and always just near the end, before he put them down, he'd turn his back, lay down his blade, and wave to the crowd."

"Pointless," Annick said.

"Maybe," Pyrre replied, "but the crowd loved it. It made him seem fearless. Invincible. You couldn't imagine him losing."

"And we're Long Fist's wolves," Gwenna said grimly.

"Funny thing about that guy, though," Pyrre said. "Just before I left the city, he turned his back on a bear. He had to do it. It was part of the show, remember."

"And . . ."

Pyrre smiled. "And the bear took off his head."

✝

Of course, talking about breaking free and actually doing it were two different things. As the night stretched on and the sun set, the three of them were still in the *api*. Whatever Pyrre said about wolves, Gwenna felt more like a 'Kent-kissing sheep—one waiting for the slaughter, at that.

"It has to be tonight," she said, stabbing at the fire with a long stick. "We've waited too long already. The entire Urghul nation is riding on the frontier, riding to *war,* and *nobody* knows. Annur doesn't. Valyn doesn't."

"I would imagine that," Pyrre said, arching an eyebrow, "is exactly the point. I believe it's referred to among militarily-minded folk as 'stealing a march.' "

"I know what it's called," Gwenna snapped.

"Tonight," Annick said abruptly, as though she'd made a decision, stuffing her cured meat into a pack. "It's time to leave."

Time to leave. As though they weren't surrounded by the largest Urghul army in history.

Pyrre chuckled. "I like it, Annick. Focus on the big picture. Don't get bogged down with the details."

"I've considered what I can," the sniper replied, cinching the pack shut, "but we don't have time for anything elaborate. Every hour counts."

"But they tend to count less," the assassin observed, "if we spend the hours dead."

"It's a risk," Annick said, nodding.

"And are you going to tell us," Gwenna asked, burning with frustration, "what your risky plan is, Annick? Or are you just going to walk out of the tent and start killing people?"

"There's something to be said for simplicity," Pyrre pointed out.

Gwenna rounded on her. "And what the fuck do *you* want with it? Just a few days ago you were happy to drink Long Fist's booze and lounge by his fires. Now suddenly you want to go charging off after Annick? I didn't know you were such a 'Kent-kissing lover of the Annurian empire."

Pyrre's eyes hardened. "Annur can stand or burn. I have my own reasons for wanting to see Long Fist thwarted."

"I don't suppose you'd care to share them?"

"Not particularly."

Gwenna suppressed a growl. This was why Wings had leaders. Between the three of them they had enough experience to come up with something resembling the ass end of a plan, but Annick was about as communicative as a brick, and there was no telling what was going on in Pyrre's murderous brain. This was the kind of shit Valyn had been dealing with since the Wing was established, but where Valyn was good at it, quick to find the strings that would draw the group together, Gwenna just wanted to hit someone.

She muscled down the urge.

"All right," she said slowly. "We agree that we need to get out."

"Consensus," Pyrre said. "I love consensus." She frowned. "Although I distrust it."

Gwenna ignored her. "Annick, what's your thinking?"

The sniper pointed up, through the smoke hole of the *api*. "Climb the poles and out."

"Out *where?*" Gwenna demanded.

Perching on top of the hide tent seemed about as useful as lying down in the 'Kent-kissing fire and hoping the smoke would carry her away.

"You know that Long Fist has people watching this tent, right?"

"I'm going to shoot them," Annick said.

Gwenna stared. "With what?"

The sniper slid aside one of the skins to reveal a rough wooden bow and half a dozen arrows, the tips hardened in the fire.

Pyrre nodded appreciatively. "And the string?" she asked.

Annick gestured to the haunch she'd been butchering. "I used the tendon."

Gwenna eyed the crude thing warily. She didn't doubt Annick's knowledge when it came to archery. The sniper had been making her own bows since before she arrived on the Islands, but she hardly had the required tools or the necessary time to do the job justice. "Can you hit anything with it?"

The sniper nodded. "At close range."

"Define close range," Pyrre said.

"Forty paces," Annick said. "Fifty at the outside."

Gwenna shook her head. At fifty paces, she herself wouldn't be able to hit a house with the thing. On the other hand, she'd long ago learned to believe Annick when it came to sticking anything full of arrows.

"And you were going to tell us about the bow . . . when?"

All this time, the sniper had been working on her weapon and she hadn't said a thing.

"When it was time," Annick replied, meeting Gwenna's glare with a flat, level look. "The fewer people who know about a thing, the safer."

"We're not just people," Gwenna spat. "We're your 'Kent-kissing *Wing*."

Pyrre tsked from across the fire. "Just like Valyn," she said. "Why is everyone so eager to recruit me for the Kettral?"

"Never mind," Gwenna said. "The point is, we're on the same side now, and if we don't start acting like it, this is going to be the shortest breakout in the annals of the Eyrie, bow or no bow."

She glared at each of them in turn, trying to slow down her breathing, to stay calm. Trying and failing.

Pyrre narrowed her eyes. "A *lot* like Valyn," she said again. "Same conviction. Same intensity." She turned to Annick. "Do you see it?" The sniper ignored the question, testing the sinew of her bow instead. The assassin smiled slyly. "You and Valyn would make a sweet pair, Gwenna. Well, maybe *sweet*'s not quite the right word, but . . ."

"Leave it," Gwenna growled.

The Skullsworn raised her hands. "Didn't mean to touch a nerve. All right," she said, sitting up, "enough gossip. We're planning. We're working together. Annick shoots a whole boatload of people, lays down a veritable plague of destruction. Good. Then what?"

"Horses," the sniper said. "We get to the horses. Then the trees."

Gwenna grimaced. It was madness, the whole thing. Unfortunately, she couldn't come up with anything better. They needed to warn Annur. Which meant escaping. There was just no way around it. Unfortunately, escaping probably meant dying in the attempt. "And when someone notices three non-Urghul women strolling through the camp?"

Pyrre smiled. "Then we begin our offering to the god."

Gwenna shook her head again. "You know we're going to die," she said. "This is a shit plan, and it's going to kill us all."

Annick eyed her with that icy stare. "Do you have another suggestion?"

"No," Gwenna replied helplessly.

"Be comforted," Pyrre said, her smile sharp as a knife. "Ananshael is not particular. Our lives, or theirs, the god will be pleased."

┼

The Lord of the Grave must be pretty fucking pleased, Gwenna thought, wiping blood from her face with the back of her hand, trying to see through the cloud-shrouded murk, hoping to Hull that she'd dragged the last body far enough behind the tent that no one would notice it right away. Ananshael. Hull. Meshkent. She was starting to think she'd picked the wrong bloody lot of gods, but, with gore smeared across her blacks and half a million Urghul spread around her, there was no going back now.

They'd waited until just after midnight, long enough that many of the horsemen had taken to their blankets, enjoying one last night in the *api.* The tents would stay, Gwenna figured, judging from the fact that no one had bothered to take them down. Maybe a few score of the old, young, and infirm would stay with them, looking after the temporary city while the rest of the nation pushed hard for the border. That push had Gwenna worried. She'd seen the pace Long Fist's riders set when crossing the steppe, when they'd been burdened with supplies and prisoners. Gwenna would have preferred to wait until more of the Urghul were asleep, but hours wasted now might prove crucial later, and so she found herself moving through the camp, stolen sword held flat against her leg, trying to look everywhere at once without moving her head.

As promised, Annick had managed to kill the young warriors guarding their tent. As hoped, they'd managed to slip unnoticed into the night. And as feared, they had to traverse a camp that spanned the better part of a mile before they could even think about stealing horses. Gwenna's instinct was to hug the shadows, darting from tent to tent, using the darkness and her own slarn-sharpened vision to avoid as many people as possible. Annick shared the impulse, and for a while they crept forward, a few paces here, a few paces there, until Pyrre shook her head in irritation.

"I'm not sure what they teach you on your secret island hideaway, but this isn't going to cut it."

"We haven't been seen yet," Gwenna hissed.

"It's not us I'm worried about them seeing," Pyrre said. "It's the four deceased Urghul with arrows in their necks we left stuffed behind the *api.* Once they're found, our nighttime stroll is going to get a lot less leisurely."

"If *we're* seen—" Annick began, but Pyrre was already stepping brashly out of the darker shadows into the center of the muddy lane running between the tents. Without a glance over her shoulder, she tossed her hair, shrugged her shoulders, then set out at a brisk walk.

"Fuck," Gwenna said, glancing over at Annick.

The sniper's lips tightened. "Fuck," she agreed tersely, then followed the older woman into the lane.

The Skullsworn's approach worked surprisingly well; they didn't have to kill anyone for at least a hundred paces. Between the darkness and the chaos of a military camp getting ready to move out, most people were so intent on their own business that they didn't look twice at three figures moving purposefully through the greater gloom. Pyrre had slipped into something like the Urghul saunter, and she made no effort to hide her face, or shy away from the Urghul they passed. No one challenged them. No one bothered with a second glance.

Then they ran into the young men with the spears. Gwenna was just starting to think they might walk straight out of the camp when the three *taabe* stepped out from the darkness between two tents. The idiots were lugging twelve-foot spears—useful on horseback but potentially deadly in the confusion of a night camp—and they tangled up with Gwenna and Pyrre, wooden hafts and steel heads clattering, blocking the lane.

The youth in the lead shouted angrily in Urghul, a quick barrage of words Gwenna didn't recognize, then yanked on the haft of his spear. The head ripped through her blacks, slicing into her arm. The wound wasn't deep, but it took Gwenna by surprise, pulling her off-balance, and she cursed as the metal bit, then slid free. It was that curse that did it.

The head of the closest *taabe* snapped around at the unfamiliar language, his dark eyes locked on hers, and then, after a baffled heartbeat, his lips drew back into a snarl. He opened his mouth to shout, but Pyrre was already there, sliding a small blade across his neck, a subtle motion, almost gentle. Instead of a roar, a bloody lisp slipped from his lips as he folded to the earth.

The two others were still trying to free their spears, oblivious to the silent death of their comrade. Gwenna hacked one across the face, while Annick killed the other with an arrow shaft in the eye. The fight was over in less than two blinks, but the bodies lay hopelessly tangled with the long shafts of the spears, and Gwenna could see movement in both directions down the narrow lane. There was no time to hide corpses. No time to do anything but put distance between themselves and the bodies.

"This way," Pyrre said, stepping from the path, sliding between the tents. Her voice was low, relaxed, but held none of her habitual mockery. For once, the assassin sounded as though she was taking things seriously. "Quickly, ladies."

Gwenna didn't care for the idea of taking orders from a Skullsworn, but the center of a hostile army didn't seem like the time to contest the issue. She grimaced, slid into close-guard, and followed the woman into the tents. A dozen paces farther they emerged onto another muddy track running parallel to the first. Gwenna's stomach clenched. The Urghul were everywhere, and worse, lit torches lined the path, flames snagging and ripping with the wind. Pyrre didn't hesitate, striding straight across, aiming for the cluster of tents on the far side. She made it halfway before one of the Urghul—a tall bastard with a long yellow braid—noticed her and barked a question.

Pyrre turned to the man, a smile on her face, and opened her arms as if for an embrace. "Kwihna!" she said brightly. The word was nonsensical, but the language was familiar, and the warrior paused, confusion flitting across his face. Pyrre stepped into the pause, wrapped her arms around his neck, and pulled him close for a long, passionate kiss. When she let him go, the man toppled. Gwenna never even saw the knife.

They made it a few more streets before the alarm went up—shouting and bellowing followed by long blasts on a horn. The angry, accusatory note sounded again and again, chasing them through the night, drilling into Gwenna's ears until she half wondered if she'd lost her mind. There was no telling which of the eight or nine corpses they'd left behind had finally done them in. It hardly mattered. The camp—shivering with screams and ululations—knew they were loose. The whole Urghul army knew.

"So much for discretion," Pyrre said.

The next few minutes were all jolting flight, hot breath between the teeth, scrabbling to keep footing in the treacherous mud, Urghul faces stretched tight with fury, and killing. Lots and lots of killing. Pyrre cut down the warriors without breaking stride, slipping her small knives into throats and stomachs, skewering eyes and slitting tendons, each motion delicate, birdlike, and precise. Gwenna was anything but delicate. The Urghul swords she'd picked up off the dead guards were longer and heavier than the smoke steel with which she'd trained, and trying to keep pace with Pyrre it was all she could do just to hack at the bodies as she passed, huge sweeping motions that jarred her shoulder whenever the sharp edge bit.

"Less screaming," Pyrre called back.

"What?" Gwenna shouted, burying her blade in some woman's gut, twisting it, then wrenching it free. Blood ran hot over her hands. Hopefully someone else's.

"You don't need to scream each time you hit someone," Pyrre said. "Try being more circumspect. They'll still die."

Gwenna started to snarl that she wasn't screaming, then realized that her throat was raw, her ears ringing. Not that it made any difference, really. The whole camp vibrated with violence. The part of her that wasn't screaming and hacking, running and panting, tried to tally up the odds. It seemed incredible that they were still alive, but here the fury of the Urghul actually worked in their favor. If all the horsemen had fallen silent and stood still, it would have been impossible to escape. The chaos and confusion covered their flight even better than the darkness. They were just three more bodies in a thrashing sea of flesh, three women among tens of thousands. Better yet, the camp was thinning as they approached the perimeter.

Keep your eyes on the 'Kent-kissing fight, Gwenna, she snapped at herself. *Quit looking ahead.*

Still, it was hard not to feel a hot, bright ember of hope. They'd fought clear of the last knot of Urghul, ducked through some more tents, and suddenly they were alone, free, with room to run. Annick pointed toward a picket of horses a hundred paces distant, but before they'd even begun to cross the space, the riders caught up with them, at least a score of horsemen, spears leveled even as they jumped the tent lines, voices raised in triumph.

"Not ideal," Pyrre said, slowing, shaking her head.

"We can break through," Gwenna said, waving to a gap. Even as she waved, it closed.

Annick was shooting. Where she'd picked up the arrows Gwenna had no idea—probably plucked from the dead. The crude bow still looked ridiculous in her hands, but it was proving deadly enough, and the sniper didn't hesitate as she loosed into the attacking Urghul. A few riders fell, but more arrived to take their place. The sniper's shafts were soon gone, and the horsemen were closing.

"Now what?" Gwenna asked, turning to put her back to Annick and Pyrre, shifting her feet, searching for the best footing.

"Now," Pyrre said, "it is time to greet the god." She sounded ready. Eager, even.

"You're giving up?" Gwenna spat. Not that she could see any way free, but the assassin's calm conviction baffled her. Worried her. If she let go of her own fury, she wasn't sure anything waited beneath but mindless, gibbering fear, and so she clung to her rage, stoked it, heaped it with fuel. "Fuck that," she shouted, then turned to the Urghul. "Who's first?" She gestured with her high blade. "Which one of you bloody shits is *first*?"

Sorry, Valyn, she said silently. *We made a go of it. . . .*

The lead rider—Huutsuu, Gwenna realized—shook her head, lowered her spear, and nudged her horse forward. The scars on her face and arms glistened with sweat in the torchlight. Her lips curled back in a smile or snarl. She had wonderful teeth, Gwenna thought pointlessly. A savage with perfect teeth was going to kill her. . . .

The scream came first, a sky-shattering, blood-boiling scream. The Urghul closing for the kill suddenly struggled to rein their rearing horses, but that scream drove straight into the beasts' brains, triggering something ancient and undeniable in their hearts, a terror that would not be soothed. Again it came, and again, like steel shrieking through ice. The scream, then the wind, then the great shadow of outstretched wings, a perfect dark against the greater darkness of the night, and then the figures in black alighting silently as shadows.

"Valyn," Gwenna called, shock and relief raging through her. "It's Valyn!"

She had no idea where he found 'Ra, no idea how he knew to come back, no clue about any of it, and she didn't care. Somehow, impossibly, the Wing was whole again. She'd been about to die, and now the bird had dropped straight out of the night to lift them clear.

The kettral tore into the closest riders with her talons, disemboweling one man and the horse beneath him. Huutsuu hurled herself clear at the last moment, just before her horse bucked then buckled beneath the slicing claws. The riders on the flanks tried to close, but someone was shooting arrows, the feathered shafts sprouting from necks and shoulders. When a huge *taabe* with a crooked nose bellowed, spurring his terrified horse forward, his skull just . . . folded. Gwenna could think of no other word. She hadn't even seen the blow, but the flesh crumpled in on itself like a rotten gourd dropped from a height.

A kenning.

It had to be a kenning, but when Gwenna whirled about, instead of Talal, she found herself staring at Sigrid sa'Karnya. Not Valyn, she realized, horrified. The Flea's Wing. Sigrid's lips were drawn back in an expression that might have been ecstasy or rage. Blond hair whipped at her face, while blood ran in runnels down her milk-pale skin. The Flea stood just in front of her, shortbow loose in his hand, while a few steps to the side Newt was lighting a . . .

"Starshatter!" Gwenna bellowed, hauling Annick back with one hand, seeing the lit charge spin end over end into the mass of horsemen, bracing herself for the bone-jarring shock that lit half the sky and left her ears ringing. The air concussed. Blue-white flame sheeted up and out, slicing the night sky into shards. Gwenna closed her eyes at the last moment, blocking out the worst of the glare, reeled backward still holding Annick, then found her footing. She was amazed to still be standing after such a close detonation, but then, Newt knew his business, had figured in the mass of horses and men, using his target to shield them all from the back-blow. A dozen of the beasts were down, some still, others thrashing desperately, kicking, screaming as their riders—one missing a leg, another with her face flayed to the bone—tried to claw their way free.

Someone seized her by the arm, and Gwenna pivoted, hacking down with her stolen sword. The Flea blocked the attack casually, sliding it off to the side as he locked eyes with her.

"Where are the rest?" he shouted. "Where's Valyn?"

Gwenna hesitated. She had no idea if the Flea had come to save her or kill her. The attack on the Urghul argued for saving, but then, the last time the two Wings had met, they'd blown up the better part of a large building trying to murder each other.

"Gwenna!" he said, leaning close. She realized that, while their two swords remained locked together, he had brought a small knife to her throat. "If I wanted to kill you, you would be dead. I'm here to help." He lowered the knife. "Now where's Valyn?"

"Gone," she said, waving her hand. "South. It's just us."

The Flea nodded, focused on something over her shoulder, threw the knife, then gestured to the bird with the empty hand. "Load up."

Somewhere to Gwenna's right another starshatter ripped into the Urghul. The camp was a madness of flame, screaming horses, brandished steel, and blood, all of it held at bay, impossibly, by the Flea and his Wing.

"Delay," Newt called over his shoulder, "is the mother of defeat."

"Meaning get on the bird," the Flea said again. "Now."

He tilted his head to the side, as though stretching his neck, and a spear shaft sailed past, embedding itself in the dirt. Gwenna stared at it for a moment, watching it quiver. Then she ran for the bird.

32

Tan'is was among the youngest of us, one of the last Csestriim born without the rot," Kiel said.

Two of the three lanterns in Morjeta's bedchamber had spluttered out during their conversation, and the remaining lamp was burning low, tossing the corners of the room into fitful darkness. No one made a move to refill them. Morjeta herself had subsided against the pillows of the divan, a stunned look on her face. Kaden could sympathize. His own introduction to the Csestriim had been a shock, and the notion that they still stalked the earth had been introduced to him in gradual stages. To learn all at once that the immortal foes of humanity still lived, that one had all but seized control of Annur, that another sat several feet from her, dark stare as wide and deep and inscrutable as the sea, was clearly more than the woman could absorb all at once. There was no time, however, to ease her gently into the truth.

"Why was he appointed your general in the wars against humanity?" Kaden asked. "Why not someone older? Someone with more experience?"

"Because he was the best," Kiel replied simply. "Not the best fighter. There were twenty-two Csestriim more skilled than Tan'is with both *naczal* and sword, at least at the start of the wars. In fact, he wasn't even the greatest pure strategist. Asherah and a handful of others could defeat him at the stones board. In battle, however—" Kiel's eyes went suddenly far, as though he were studying some furious fight thousands and thousands of years past. "—none of my people shared his gift for command.

"A part of it was simply native genius. His mind moves more quickly, more unexpectedly than most. More than that, however, Tan'is understood your race in a way that most of us, especially the older Csestriim, did not. He studied you. . . ."

"You mean he tortured and killed us," Kaden said, thinking back to the lightless corridors of the Dark Heart.

Kiel nodded. "That was a part of his study, although not the entirety of it. The war lasted several human generations, and Tan'is spent that entire time, whenever he wasn't actually leading the armies, in study, learning your peculiar use of the language, your physiology and limitations, your emerging social structures, your weapons and weaknesses, and most of all, your minds. He spent decades trying to discover what had broken inside you, trying to understand whether it had anything to do with the new gods."

"What do you mean, the new gods?" Triste asked. Unlike her mother, she wasn't as jolted by the sudden revelation. After all, they'd been discussing the Csestriim for weeks. Triste had suffered in a Csestriim prison and passed through the Csestriim gates. Somehow, she knew their language. As Kiel spoke, she leaned forward on her cushion, eyes bright, sweat sheening her brow.

"You call them the young gods," Kiel said. "The children of Meshkent and Ciena."

"Heqet and Kaveraa," Kaden said, reciting the names as he had heard them recited a thousand times before leaving for the Bone Mountains. "Eira and Maat; Orella and Orilon."

"And Akalla," Kiel added slowly. "And Korin."

Kaden frowned. "No. There are only six of them. Six children of Pleasure and Pain."

"That is because we killed the other two."

For several heartbeats no one spoke. Morjeta had retreated behind the stillness of her painted face. Triste's mouth hung open, as though in midgasp. Kaden realized that he, too, was leaning forward on his cushion, legs tense, breath lodged in his lungs. He exhaled slowly.

"You're saying you killed two of the gods."

"Tan'is killed them," Kiel said. "He captured them after the battle of Nimir Point. Captured them, studied them, then killed them. I was there as historian. It is how we learned, learned conclusively, of the connection between our children—between you—and the new gods."

Suddenly, Kaden was sitting once more in Scial Nin's study, looking across the rough wooden desk at the abbot, listening to him explain about the *kenta* and the Shin, about the purpose of Kaden's time among the monks. The abbot was dead, one of the hundreds of robed bodies left on the ledges to feed the ravens, and yet Kaden could still hear his patient explanation: *It could have been the birth of the young gods that led to human emotion.*

"They changed you somehow," Kaden said quietly. "The young gods changed the Csestriim into . . . us."

Kiel nodded. "It was only a suspicion at first. The facts fit. We had theory and evidence, but no proof. Then they came down. Here. They breathed their own immortal forms into human bodies, all to help you in your fight against my people."

"And you killed them?" Triste demanded, utterly aghast.

"Only two," Kiel said. If he was taken aback by the girl's horror, he didn't show it. "Like you, they were a threat. A foe."

"Akalla," Kaden said, tasting the strange syllables. "Korin."

Kiel nodded. "Those were the names they took. I do not know their provenance."

"And so they're just . . . what? Gone?"

Kiel pursed his lips as though considering a thorny question of translation. "Perhaps not fully or forever. Gods are not Bedisa's creation. Ananshael cannot unknit them. Even the young gods are . . . larger than us, more complete than this creation." He shook his head. "Really, the language does not serve in discussing them."

"So you *didn't* kill them," Kaden said, frustration fraying the fabric of his calm.

Kiel met his gaze for a moment, then held up a hand, studying it in the lamplight. "Tan'is destroyed the flesh while they were trapped inside, before they could be released. The gods may be eternal, without end or limit, but their touch on this world is not. That is what Tan'is killed—their hold on and influence over those born into their thrall."

"But," Kaden said, "if what we are, if the makeup of our minds and hearts comes from the touch of the young gods, there must have been an effect. . . ." He trailed off, trying to understand what such an effect might be, trying to hold the notion in his head.

"There was."

The historian paused, so long this time that Kaden wondered if he had given up trying to explain.

"Imagine you are blind," he said finally. "That you were born blind. That all your life you have lived in darkness among others like you. If you were suddenly and momentarily shown color, how would you explain it to your sightless race? What words would you use? What formulations of logic or reason? Analogy fails. Induction and deduction fail. This is the best I can do—

"Your ancestors, the first among you, felt differently about the world. Not just differently, but more. It was as though the stones and rivers, the sea and sky, the physical world and the transcendent notions that emanate from it were as crucial to those first, broken Csestriim children as their own human families, their own selves. They would die to avoid unnecessary destruction. They acted and spoke as though the earth itself were a part of them, woven into the fabric of their minds. This world of cities and roads—" He gestured to the walls of the chamber and beyond. "Your ancestors would not have recognized it. They would have loathed it."

"And after you killed the gods?" Kaden asked, voice thin as the last smoke from a spent fire.

"You changed.

"The bodies of the gods died as all bodies die: a hole hacked in the flesh, a break in Bedisa's perfection where the life drained out. I would have expected their deaths to be different from our own in some way. Greater or louder. They were gods, after all. But they were bound and drugged, both of them, and Tan'is killed them with a knife no longer than my hand.

"It took me a century to be sure of the effect, decades upon decades walking among your kind, posing as one of you, asking the same questions over and over:

" *What is this? What is this?'*

"I always met with the same reply, *'It is rock. It is water. It is air.'*

" *'And what do you feel about the rock and the water? What do you feel about the air?'*

" *'Nothing. Nothing. Nothing.'* "

For a long time Kaden could not bring himself to speak. He struggled to conceive the magnitude of Kiel's claim, of the loss. The Shin trained a lifetime to scrub out human emotion, and none ever succeeded, not completely, not perfectly. If Kiel was right, however, Ran il Tornja had managed just that, at least a portion of it, with two cuts of the knife. What would happen if everyone in the empire—everyone in the *world*—all at once lost hope and courage, fear and love? It was like looking down to find the once-solid ground nothing but an illusion. A dream.

Kiel watched him, eyes blank as shells. Only when Kaden finally nodded did he continue.

"Tan'is resolved to destroy the rest of the new gods, to capture and kill them individually, or to strike directly at Ciena and Meshkent. He believed—not without warrant—that the elimination of those two would cripple the others, that the new gods were in some way dependent on or emergent from their parents."

Kaden stared. "Was he right?"

"We don't know," Kiel replied evenly. "We began to lose the war then, and when it was clear that your kind would defeat us, those gods who had taken your side . . . departed. They slipped clear of their adopted flesh. Their influence remains, but they are gone."

"Holy Hull," Triste breathed quietly.

"Yes," Kiel agreed. "Like Hull. The god himself remains remote, unmanifest, but we know his darkness."

"I should have left you in the Dead Heart," Kaden said finally, the words loose before he could call them back. "I should have left you to rot."

"You would not have escaped without me," Kiel replied. "Even if you had won free somehow, you are not prepared to face il Tornja. He will destroy you without my help. He may destroy you in spite of it." He shook his head. "I was accounted a good mind among my people, but Tan'is was always the better strategist, the better tactician."

Kaden stared. "You killed two of our gods, and now you're talking about *helping* me?"

Kiel nodded. "As I said, my goals are not those of Tan'is. He seeks a return to the past. I am more interested in chronicling the present."

The Csestriim fell silent. Kaden stared at him a moment, then turned to Triste. She met his eyes with her own wide, wild gaze, then shook her head helplessly.

"I don't know, Kaden," she said. "He helped us. He keeps helping us. He's *here,* right?"

Kaden blew out a long, unsteady breath. "All right. If you want to help, help. What about Ran il Tornja? What is he doing?"

"As I told you before," Kiel replied, "he has not abandoned his charge. The gods are gone, beyond his reach, but he seeks another way to destroy you. Has sought one for many thousands of years."

"And the fact that he's taking action now . . ." Kaden began, trailing off as the horror hit him.

Kiel nodded. "It is impossible to be certain of the movings of another mind, but it would seem that our lost general has finally found what he seeks."

33

N o, no, no, you're missin' the point, ya ox's ass," Nira said, smacking her cane against her palm, causing her horse to start. "Ya don't *need* ta sign the papers, and swear the oaths, and have yer tits anointed with the holy oils, and whatever all other little bits a' theater yer family's been parading around the last few hundred years. Ya just *do* it."

Adare took a firm rein on her temper. She was exhausted. Exhausted from riding from dawn until well past dusk every day since Annur. Exhausted from trying to anticipate il Tornja's next deception. Exhausted from second-guessing herself. Exhausted from wondering if she had overstepped in claiming the throne, a throne never intended for her, a throne for which she might be killed, or even worse, forced to kill good people, Annurian citizens who would rise up against her, refusing to accept a female Emperor. Exhausted from telling Fulton over and over to back off, to give her space to talk in private, to think. Exhausted from sitting appropriately upright in her saddle when she wanted to collapse over the cantle. Exhausted from the sickness that twisted in her gut every morning, a result, no doubt, of the miserable camp food. Exhausted from worrying about the scars laid into her skin, from trying to wring some sense from the events at the Everburning Well. And exhausted from Nira's endless tirade of acerbic counsel, Nira, who, despite her advanced age, seemed the only person in the long muddy ranks with any energy left.

The road north had given Adare plenty of occasions to doubt whether elevating the old woman to Mizran Councillor had been the wisest decision. On the one hand, Nira *had* ruled an empire of her own for centuries, which gave her hundreds of years more experience ruling an empire than anyone else Adare knew. On the other, that empire had ended in a morass of war, grief, and ruin. So, maybe not such a good model after all.

It had been nine days since Annur, nine days of forced march through terrain that had shifted from open farmland, to low hills, to thick pine forests, dotted with bogs and streams. Without the imperial road—a mind-boggling feat of engineering comprised of stone bridges, wide flagstones, and ditches on either side to channel away the runoff—the army would have been helplessly mired days earlier, as soon as they entered the Thousand Lakes. As it was, the Sons could travel only so fast on a road built more for commerce than military transport. Adare found herself simultaneously exhausted by their pace and chafing at the lack of progress, worried about what might be transpiring ahead of her in the darkness of the primeval forest, and behind, in the capital she had so hastily abandoned. In fact, the farther she marched from Annur, the more she doubted her decision. Facing il Tornja and meeting the Urghul threat—if there even *was* an Urghul threat—had seemed crucial back in the capital, but what had she sacrificed in order to march north? What opportunities had she destroyed?

"If I'm going to sit the Unhewn Throne," she said, trying to keep her voice level, "there are forms to be observed, rituals. And I can't observe them here, stuck in the middle of a 'Kent-kissing forest."

Nira blew out her cheeks. "Sometimes, girl, I'd swear you were denser than my brick-headed brother." She waved a hand at Oshi, who was staring at the palms of his hands as though they were intricate maps, oblivious to the movement of his horse beneath him. "You get a throne by taking it, not by asking for it."

"I can't just take it," Adare protested. "Allegedly, I have il Tornja's support, and that means I've got the army, too, but leaving aside the fact that the bastard murdered my father, that I intend to see him executed the moment we catch up with him, it is the historical precedent that makes a person Emperor."

"A historical precedent," Nira replied, "that is just going to bugger you right up your pretty puckered arse. Yer history is all about *men,* your ritual is about *men.* Unless you're plannin' to strap on a terra-cotta cock and go back to Annur thwackin' people in the face with it—which I don't recommend—ya need to tip the whole board full of history directly into the piss bucket and start over. You need people to see *you,* not the man you're not."

Adare shifted to try to relieve the chafing in her thighs, the ache in her lower back. "But the authenticity," she said, "*comes* from those rituals. It comes from history. Otherwise, what makes the Emperor the Emperor?"

Oshi turned, something about the question having snared his attention. "Ants," he said, "have an empress." He smiled broadly, encouragingly. "The little soldiers—they all serve her."

"Unhelpful, you dolt," Nira snapped. "Ants do what they do because it's built into 'em. They can't *not* follow the empress." She turned back to Adare. "*People,* though . . . people'll follow anyone, anything. I wandered through a village once, a long while back, where the folk were led by a 'Kent-kissing *tree;* asked it questions, thought they heard answers in the creaking branches and the rustling leaves."

"Annurians aren't savages . . ." Adare began, but Nira cut her off with a hoot.

"Savages, is it? That tree was one a' the best kings I ever saw." She gestured to the dark boughs of the pines. "A tree doesn't start wars. Tree doesn't raise taxes to build palaces. A tree doesn't kill the people who refuse to bow down." A sad note had crept into her voice, and her eyes had slipped away from Adare, first to the woods, then to Oshi where he swayed in his saddle, light as a bundle of old cloth. "Could do a lot worse than a tree," she concluded quietly.

"Well, I'm not a tree," Adare said. "And I need the people to accept me as Emperor. I didn't have time for a coronation before leaving Annur, didn't have time for the hundred little ceremonies before and after, which means that right now I'm . . . nothing. I'm not even the Minister of Finance anymore; il Tornja filled the role with someone else after I disappeared for Olon. The Sons of Flame think I'm Intarra's prophet, or her saint, but a saint's a far cry from an emperor. A saint doesn't actually rule."

Nira fixed her with that shrewd gaze once more, all traces of her previous melancholy gone. "Ya know how ya get to run an empire, girl?"

Adare shook her head in frustration. "That's what I've been asking."

The old woman poked her in the chest with the stick. "You run it."

"Meaning what?"

"You see what needs doing, and ya do it. Everything else follows: the throne, the taxes, the title. I've watched a lot of folk try ta rule a lot of land. I've watched men cling ta their fancy titles while their people and their realms just . . . slipped away, and I've watched men who couldn't give a watery shit for the names and the titles rule half a continent. Ya just do what needs doing, and the people will figure out all on their own that you're the 'Kent-kissing Emperor."

Before Adare could respond, Fulton kicked his horse forward, forcing his way between her and a small group of men and women rounding a bend in the road, emerging from the trees a hundred paces or so ahead of them. Two other Aedolians, part of the full guard Fulton had recruited back in Annur, nudged their horses forward until they were flanking her.

"Keep well back, my lady," Fulton said grimly, limbering his sword in its sheath.

Adare hesitated a moment, then shook her head.

"It's a family," she said.

There were two men, one old, one young, both bearded, both carrying axes in their hands. Behind them, a group of barefoot children slogged doggedly ahead, chivvied along by three women dressed all in leather and fur. The children, obviously weary and bedraggled, perked up at the sight of the approaching army, shouting and pointing. The oldest, a girl of ten or so, attempted to dart forward, but her father caught her by the elbow, dragging her off the road along with the rest of the family.

When Adare reined in alongside them, she realized that the younger of the two men was wounded, his arm slashed viciously from the elbow to the wrist. Someone had made a feeble attempt to bind the cut, but the dirty cloth had soaked through with blood and pus.

"Best hurry," he said, jerking his head to the north.

"Why?" Lehav demanded, pulling in his horse beside Adare.

The soldier had initially been reluctant to march north, pointing out that while il Tornja was gone, they could occupy Annur itself, install Adare on the Unhewn Throne, rehabilitate Intarra's Church, and spread word of the *kenarang*'s treachery, word that would make it all but impossible for him to return. It was a tempting vision, but a false one. As Nira pointed out, "Ya ain't gonna last long running an empire if the first thing ya do is ta sit still while the Urghul take a shit all over it."

The words rankled, but the woman was right. If the Urghul posed a legitimate threat, Adare needed to be a part of the solution, regardless of the *kenarang*'s treachery. More, as she pointed out to Lehav, if the Sons of Flame were to win the trust of the empire's population, they, too, would need to march north.

The logger spat into the mud. "Urghul," he said curtly. The smallest child began sobbing. "Burned our house, field, and half our forest. Killed anyone couldn't run."

Adare stared. "This far south?"

"Nah, we're from up north. Way up past the north end of Scar Lake.

Thought about stopping in Aats-Kyl, but the army camped there ain't gonna stop what's comin'—I'll tell you that for free." He glanced down the ranks of the Sons of Flame. "Hope you got more where these came from."

"What is the army doing?" Adare asked. "The one in Aats-Kyl?"

"Didn't stop to ask," he replied. "Been talkin' to you too long as it is."

The logger started to move, but Lehav brought him up short.

"One more question, friend. The army in Aats-Kyl: which way is it facing?"

The logger shook his head. "Not facing any 'Kent-kissing way at all."

"They're not dug in for an attack from the south?"

"What would they do that for? Just got done tellin' you—the Urghul are comin' down from the *north*."

Adare waited until the loggers were well behind them to turn to Nira and Lehav.

"Sounds like the Urghul really are coming."

As she said the words she realized that she'd been praying ever since leaving Annur that the whole thing was a trick, a hoax. If il Tornja had lied about the threat, it would just be one more crime to hang around his neck when the time came. She could fight him, hopefully kill him, and have done with it. The handful of filthy farmers, however, that gash across the arm, changed everything.

"The family could have been trumped up," Lehav observed, jaw tight. "A few coins in their pocket to play a part, to make us complacent."

Nira chuckled. "It'd be a good trick."

"I'd prefer to be the one playing the tricks," Adare said, trying not to glare at the woman.

"And I'd prefer to have a brother who wasn't busted in the head," Nira replied. "Turns out, though, that preferrin' don't have much to do with things."

Lehav, as was his habit, ignored the old woman entirely. "We'll know more when the scouts return."

The scouts, as it turned out, confirmed the logger's account, at least the latter part of it. The men had come across no sign of the Urghul, but they insisted that the Army of the North was peacefully encamped just to the east of Aats-Kyl and that more refugees were headed south, some on the main road, some on the crooked forest tracks.

"The *kenarang* hasn't barricaded the road?" Lehav pressed. "No earth walls?"

The lead scout shook his head. "There's just the normal palisade around the camp itself, the kind of thing every army on the march puts up. There are a few score men working on the dam, but the rest are just encamped."

"The dam?" Adare said, shaking her head. "Why would they be working on the dam?"

"No idea," Lehav replied grimly. "And I don't like not having an idea." He turned back to the scouts. "You swept the forest? It's dense on either side of the road. . . ."

The scout nodded wearily. "Went up on the east, came back on the west. Nothing. No ambush, no snipers. Nothing but hemlock and deer shit. Up near the village we got close enough to listen to a couple men chopping wood at the edge of camp. They know we're coming, know we're close, but they think we're coming to *help* them."

Lehav frowned. "Maybe we are."

It was late afternoon when they finally broke from the damp shadows of the pines into ruddy sunlight. For the first time in days, Adare could see more than a few dozen paces, although the world was so bright that for a moment she wasn't sure just what she was looking at. She blinked, shaded her eyes with her hand. They'd reached a lake, she realized, a wide lake stretching north so far she couldn't see the opposite shore. Sun shimmered like golden coins on the surface.

"Scar Lake," Nira said, "and Aats-Kyl."

A good-sized town of log homes with roofs of turf and shingle had forced back the forest at the south end of the lake. A tall palisade of rough logs ringed the town, wooden towers at the corners. Outside the wall, a rugged patchwork of fields held back the forest, wet ground drained by a ragged network of ditches. Even at a distance, Adare could smell the woodsmoke rising from the stone chimneys, could hear the farmers urging their horses and oxen over the broken ground. Farmers around Annur had begun plowing weeks earlier, but here, with the cold wind scudding down over the Romsdals, planting seemed to come late.

"Well," Adare said, considering the town, "no one's tried to kill us yet."

"Give it time," Lehav replied.

"Where does the road go from here?"

"It doesn't," Fulton said grimly. As the day wore on, he had guided his horse closer and closer to her, checked his broadblade more and more often. Now, he kicked the creature forward a few paces, putting himself between her and the settlement below.

"What's past here?" she asked.

"Forest tracks and logging camps. Trees."

And the Urghul, Adare thought, trying to come to grips with the nature of the threat all over again. She'd left Olon expecting to battle il Tornja in the streets of Annur and instead she found herself in a forest on the very edge of the empire preparing to hold off an Urghul attack. Not for the first time she prayed that she was making the right decision, that she wasn't committing some idiotic mistake that would doom them all.

To her marginal relief, there was no sign of the horsemen, no indication that they'd even come close. Just as reassuring, the Army of the North clearly hadn't deployed to meet her own force, either.

A good 'Kent-kissing thing, she thought, *given the size of the army.*

The men were encamped, all of them, across several of the largest fields, tents and cook fires laid out in a grid so neat it might have been carved in the earth with a straightedge. Despite Adiv's urgency back in Annur, despite the harried march north, despite the refugees on the road south, none of the soldiers in the camp looked to be in much of a hurry. No one seemed to be drilling or fortifying. Knots of men clustered outside their tents, some seated, some lying down, heads propped on their helmets. She could smell the smoke of the cook fires and burning grease hazing the air, as though the whole camp were set up for a festival rather than a war.

Anger and confusion rose inside her. She and Lehav had been flogging the Sons northward for days, Adiv's account of a full-scale Urghul invasion ringing in their ears. Every night she'd prayed to Intarra to hold the horsemen back for one more day, just one more day. Meanwhile, il Tornja had his men lolling about in the sun.

She squinted, trying to make the camp out more clearly. Something wasn't right. No one had attacked them. No one looked likely to attack them. Those facts alone should have calmed her nerves, but clearly there was more to the situation than she understood.

"What are they doing?" she asked, jaw tight.

"Looks like they're resting," Nira replied. "Maybe there isn't such a hurry with this Long Fist, after all."

As Adare watched, an Annurian rider emerged from the nearest gate of the town, and came cantering up the road. Fulton drew his sword well in advance of the man's approach, then leveled it at him as he drew near. The messenger, a gaunt, balding soldier with peeling skin on his scalp, pulled up short at the sight of Fulton's sword, took a deep breath, then turned to Adare and bowed low in his saddle, face pressed against the withers of his horse.

"Your Radiance," he began. The imperial title made Adare shift uncomfortably in her saddle. It was no surprise that Adiv had sent ahead word of her demands, but hearing the words spoken by an Annurian legionary was another matter altogether. On the ride north she had begun to grow accustomed to the Sons calling her prophet. Some even went so far as to touch the hem of her robes as she passed, or to pray outside her tent each night. The reverence was both uncomfortable and disconcerting, but at least it was her own. When soldiers used the imperial title, a part of her wanted to look over her shoulder for her father.

"The *kenarang* instructed me to escort you into Aats-Kyl," the messenger was saying. "A pavilion is being erected for you in the camp itself." He nodded toward a bustle of activity close to the center of the Annurian camp. "But the *kenarang* has suggested that you meet in town to discuss your defense of the empire. He has requisitioned the finest tavern, if you would care to follow me."

"I'm not sure she would," Fulton said, voice hard. His sword remained leveled at the man's throat.

The rider swallowed uncomfortably. He was clutching the reins as though they might offer some protection if the Aedolian lunged with his blade. "I'm sorry?"

"I think," Fulton replied, speaking very slowly, "that Her Radiance would prefer to meet on ground of her own choosing."

"But," the man replied, glancing over his shoulder in confusion, "the *kenarang's* orders . . ."

"It's all right," Adare said, pushing past Fulton. "Lower your sword."

It was a risk, going into the town, maybe a foolish one, but then, the whole 'Kent-kissing expedition was a risk. If il Tornja wanted her dead, he wasn't trying very hard. He could have had her killed before she fled the Dawn Palace or after she returned to Annur. He could have set men to ambush her on the forest road. Instead, his own army lounged in the northern sun. None of it made any sense. He had murdered her father, had *admitted* to murdering her father, and yet the man seemed unconcerned that she might come to extract her revenge.

He's in for an unpleasant surprise, she thought grimly.

It was tempting to refuse the offer to parley, to insist that the *kenarang* meet her in a place of her own choosing, as Fulton suggested. And yet, as she squinted down into the camp below, she could already see that scores of soldiers had stopped in their work, shading eyes with their hands as they stared up at her. If the scouts were to be trusted, the Army of the North believed she had come to help, and if the Urghul were really massing to the north, they would need to present some kind of unified front.

Not that a unified front required the *kenarang.* In fact, facing the Urghul would prove trial enough without worrying that her own general might stab her just before the battle. Whatever il Tornja's strange game was, she had no intention of letting him see it through. She would meet him in his tavern, try to glean what useful information she could from him, and then see him killed. It would have to be quiet, of course. She couldn't afford to spread distrust through the very men she might have to send into battle, but armies were filled with sharp steel and soldiers died accidental deaths all the time.

She kicked her horse into motion.

"Your Radiance," Fulton hissed, "I must protest. . . ."

"Less protesting," she growled. "More protecting."

Lehav rode up beside her, studying her askance.

"You're sure about this?"

"Of course not," she snapped.

He hesitated, then nodded, as though the answer made sense.

"I need you to stay with the Sons," Adare said. "In case things go wrong in town. Set up camp, but stay ready. Keep them separate from the legions. I want a full field between the two armies with nothing in it but turnips or radishes or whatever it is they grow up here. I don't want a battle. I don't want a fight. I don't even want an unpleasant look. I don't intend to have Annurians fighting Annurians because some idiot starts quarreling with another idiot over who is flying what flag. Is that understood?"

"It is," Lehav replied.

Adare chewed the inside of her cheek. "But make sure they keep their weapons close," she said finally.

Lehav considered her a moment more, then nodded, wheeling his horse around, back toward the column still halted in the woods.

"What's going on here?" Adare demanded, glancing at il Tornja's messenger, then turning her attention toward the town below. "Why is the army stopped? Are you preparing for a siege?"

"Stopped to destroy the dam, Your Radiance," the soldier replied, gesturing toward the wide berm of earth that loomed at the lower end of the lake. A wide, artificial sluice punctured the berm near the center. Water from above emptied through it and past a series of waterwheels, then into the channel beneath. If Adare remembered her geography, Scar Lake was, in fact, just a place where the Black River paused, widening to fill the huge natural basin, before narrowing again and flowing east to join the White. The people of Aats-Kyl had dammed the southern end of the lake to control the flow and make use of it, work that il Tornja's soldiers were busy destroying with pickax and shovel.

Adare shook her head. "Why?" She was no hydraulic engineer, but it was clear that a major breech in the dam would endanger a quarter of the town below.

"Not my place to say, Your Radiance," the soldier replied. "The *kenarang* gives the orders, and we carry them out. Not to worry, though. The Urghul are crafty, but no one's smarter than the general."

The claim gave Adare scant comfort.

"Where *are* the Urghul?"

"Not quite certain, Your Radiance."

"And il Tornja?"

"Maybe overseeing the work, Your Radiance," the soldier replied, gesturing toward the dam again. "After I escort you to your lodging, I have instructions to find him and bring him to you at once."

Adare had a dozen more questions, but it was clear that her young escort lacked the relevant answers. Instead of pestering him pointlessly, she focused her attention on the dam. Maybe two hundred men were at work there, just a fraction of the Army of the North, but the most that could effectively maneuver in the limited space. At first glance, she couldn't make much sense of the rising and falling shovels and picks, but as she watched, she realized there was an order to the labor. One group was carving a network of wide ditches, while another carted the excess dirt into the town, where still another knot of soldiers was at work on a series of dikes that would protect against the worst of the flooding. It was a complicated operation, and, as the dam grew weaker and weaker, a dangerous one. Sooner or later the earthen wall would give, and the whole weight of the lake above would come thundering down.

Adare's palms sweated just watching it. Partly she worried for the soldiers. Partly she worried because once again il Tornja was hard at work on a project she didn't understand, his men tearing apart the only surety between the tiny log town and the weight of the massive lake that waited, heavy and silent, above.

34

T his is the *time,*" Triste insisted. "Adare and il Tornja are away, off
in the north. It's just Adiv in the Dawn Palace. You've got to strike
now, while they're away with their armies."

"Strike," Kaden said, shaking his head wearily. "I don't even know
what that means. There are only four of us, Triste."

Dusk had stained the sky outside the tall windows indigo. He and
Triste, Morjeta and Kiel, had suspended their conversation while doe-
eyed women in silent slippers lit the dozens of red paper lanterns hanging
in Morjeta's chambers, then again while still more *leinas*-in-training—
graceful young men and women, silent and gorgeous—brought platters
artfully arranged with succulent fruit, thin glass flutes brimming with
wine. Kaden had stopped after the first glass, wanting his mind clear as he
tried to untangle il Tornja's knot. He might as well have drained the carafe
for all the good his thinking did him.

It was one thing to discover that Ran il Tornja, the general who had
murdered Kaden's own father, was one of the Csestriim. The claim was
shocking, but not beyond belief. To learn, however, that il Tornja was not
bent simply on the overthrow of the Annurian line, that he had murdered
gods in the past and aimed now at the murder of others, that his ultimate
purpose was the annihilation of humanity itself—that was a thought almost too large to comprehend. Kaden had tried for a while, and then, over-
whelmed by the effort, by the implications, set it aside. For now, it was
enough to know that il Tornja and Adare were the enemy, that they were to
be defeated. Whatever the unknown details of il Tornja's plan, he clearly
needed control of Annur, which meant Kaden's goal was to deny him that
control. He could effectively consider a problem of that scope, although
considering a problem and solving it were two different things.

Over and over again he had followed the same trails of thought, always arriving back at the same grim starting place: his enemies had the political power, the military might, and the coin, leaving Kaden with two burning eyes and the clothes on his back. It didn't seem like much, but Triste was convinced he could make use of those eyes.

"You're the Emperor," she insisted. "People can see it if they just look at your face. *Everyone* can't be part of the conspiracy."

"Tarik Adiv is part of it," Morjeta said. "You said so yourself. And the *kenarang* left him in control of the Dawn Palace."

"Then you go take it back!" Triste exploded.

Kaden shook his head. "How? What would I do? Walk up and pound on the Godsgate? Throw back my hood and display my burning eyes?"

"Yes!" Triste said. "Exactly!"

"No," Kaden replied. "Adare and Adiv are not stupid. Il Tornja is not stupid. They have considered this possibility. They have prepared for it. I would be admitted, ushered in with as little fuss as possible, escorted somewhere dark and discreet where men with knives would finish the work that Ut and Adiv began. You heard what Kiel told us: this is more than just a coup against my family. It goes beyond politics. Far beyond."

Kiel nodded. "Tan'is has taken a great risk in acting so openly. He would not do so without the possibility of an equal reward."

The thought chilled Kaden, and so he did not allow himself to linger on it. Il Tornja might be immortal, implacable, bent on an almost inconceivable level of destruction, but the problem facing Kaden remained a political one, political and military, almost commonplace in its outlines.

"I can't go back to the Dawn Palace," he said. "I won't."

"So . . . what?" Triste demanded. "You're just going to give up? You're going to let her win?"

"You could collect allies," Morjeta said quietly. "Assemble a force of your own. In secret."

Kaden considered the idea. "Who? What allies?"

"There are factions," she replied, "inside the court. Ministers bitter about Adiv's promotion. Generals vexed at having been passed over . . ."

Kaden looked over at Kiel.

"It could work," the Csestriim said. "Your father was well liked in many quarters. If we could assemble a list of old-guard loyalists . . ."

Morjeta nodded. "I don't have all the names—not everyone seeks solace in our temple—but it would be a start."

"Yes," Triste said, leaning in. "You work fast, force Adiv out before your sister and il Tornja return. When they get back to the city, you're seated on the Unhewn Throne. Killing you then would be open treason!"

"Yes," Kaden said, the word heavy on his tongue, "but they already murdered one emperor, a man girded far better to withstand their attacks than I am. I *might* be able to get past Adiv, but even then, what would I have? The throne and a group of old men who knew my father. Il Tornja controls at least some of the Kettral. I'd probably find poison in my water or a knife in my back just days after entering the palace.

"There's more than one problem. First, even if I get the throne, *especially* if I get the throne, I'm an easy target. Second, Adare and il Tornja are too far ahead. They've been consolidating power for years. As *kenarang,* il Tornja commands the armies. Adare has seized the political reins, *and* people are calling her a prophet. They control the two pillars on which all Malkeenian rule is grounded."

For a long time the four of them fell silent. Triste picked angrily at a scab on her wrist while her mother gazed into her goblet of wine, as though the answers were scrawled on the mint leaf circling the rim. Kiel's gaze went hard and absent again. Finally the Csestriim turned to Kaden.

"You still have the *kenta,*" he pointed out. "You could get to Aragat. The Malkeenian line originated there. Away from the Dawn Palace, you'll be harder to attack. The old aristocracy, from when the atrepy was a kingdom, may rally behind you, shield you. . . ."

"The old aristocracy is here," Morjeta said. "From Aragat and everywhere else. They arrived months ago for the funeral of Sanlitun, and most have remained for the coronation of the new Emperor."

"Why?" Kaden asked, shaking his head. There were dozens of preimperial lineages scattered through Annur, their power blunted by the rise of his own family. Most kept to their estates, living off inherited wealth, reading chronicles of the days before Annur, when their lands were their own and they owed fealty to no one. It seemed unlikely that they would travel all the way to Annur to pay homage to a murdered emperor or his missing heir. "What do they want?"

Morjeta spread her hands, even that small motion studied, elegant. "To see the new Emperor with their own eyes, to take the measure of the man," she paused, "or woman. To see if they can gain an audience that will lead to some petty advantage. Lower taxation. A favorable trading arrangement. Some of them just enjoy being close to the center of power, like beggars who linger at the gates when a rich man holds a feast, hoping for a few scraps."

"So I have scores of disgruntled nobles to deal with, even if I seize the throne," Kaden said, shaking his head.

"Some of those nobles might back you," Kiel pointed out. "Of course, that will alienate others."

Kaden tried to imagine it, walking the streets of Annur with his hood pulled up, pounding on door after door, showing his eyes to the guards, demanding to be admitted. What would he say? How would he convince *anyone* to join the cause of a dispossessed Emperor with no coin or army, no experience running a state? *Hello, my name is Kaden hui'Malkeenian. Will you help me reclaim my throne from the greatest general in Annurian history? I'd be grateful, but have nothing to offer in return.*

"It's not enough," he said finally, shaking his head. "It's like Adare and il Tornja have been playing their stones for *years* and I've just now sat down at the board."

"They don't control everything," Kiel said. "They can't."

"They control what matters. The army. The capital. The Ministry of Finance. I could *maybe* raise a small rebellion with two or three nobles desperate enough to ride my miserable coattails, but it won't work. My enemies already have me encircled."

"Well, you have to do *something*," Triste exploded.

Kaden almost laughed. *Do something.* The mildest Shin *umial* would have whipped him for the notion. Eight years they'd tried to grind it out of him, this thought that he could be something, do something, have something. Their mantras still whispered in his ears like the sound of his own breath: *Emptiness is freedom. Absence is truth.* Eight years of cutting away, of carving out, of clearing, of emptying, and, right at the end, just as he was starting to master the letting go, to see the true power in the nothingness, here he was, needing to claw it all back.

Himself, first. Then his allies. His throne. His empire.

He felt as though he'd been climbing all his life, working his way up a punishing and vertiginous trail, only to find, as he neared the summit, that he had chosen the wrong mountain. Worse, if he started back down now, even if he abandoned the truth of the Shin, there was nothing to take its place, no knowledge of politics or military tactics, no network of personal ties, no wealth, no worldly wisdom, nothing. The board was filled with Adare's white stones and he had nothing to play in response.

"I won't take part in their game," he said quietly. "I can't."

"So . . . what?" Triste demanded, eyes wide with anger and fright. "You just walk away? You just give up?"

Kaden shook his head, turning to Morjeta. "How many of these nobles come here, to your temple?"

She spread her hands. "The ones who can. The ones worth knowing."

Kaden took a deep breath. "I'm losing the game, which means I have three choices: cede, fight back . . ." He hesitated, wondering if he was seeing the options clearly.

"Or?" Triste pressed.

Then, for the first time since arriving in Annur, Kaden smiled. "Or break the board."

35

The sun-splashed clearing was, Gwenna supposed, as good a spot as any to die. The farm on which she'd been raised had backed up to woods like this, a mix of hemlock, pine, and fir, dark green needles shoved aside by the odd birch shouldering its way up through the gloom. Wood-peas chirruped in the high branches, while blackbirds hunted over the mossy ground, heads stabbing down for the bugs and seeds. It was a peaceful spot, but the Flea wasn't paying much attention to the birds or the trees. After Sigrid and Newt had dragged Pyrre and Annick down to the other end of the small meadow, he turned his dark eyes on Gwenna.

"Here's how it's going to work." His voice was quiet, almost weary. "I'm going to ask questions. You answer them. If you lie, I'll kill you. Start fucking around, I'll kill you. Leave out anything important, I'll kill you. When we're done, I'll talk with my Wing, see what your friends said to them, and if your stories don't match, I'll kill you." He didn't sound like he wanted to do it, but he didn't sound like he was bluffing, either.

"And if they do match?" Gwenna asked.

"Then maybe we can talk about something other than killing."

Gwenna wanted to make some sort of quick, cutting remark, the kind of crack the Kettral were famous for, but she felt anything but quick and cutting. Blood stained her hands, her arms, her face. It had soaked into her blacks, then dried, stiffening the cloth. Her hair was matted with it. Most belonged to the Urghul, but she had a dozen small wounds of her own, and her muscles were watery after fighting halfway through the camp, then clinging to the talon straps for the rest of the night. And then there was the noose around her neck. That didn't help either.

The Flea might have rescued them, but it became clear as soon as they were in the air that he didn't trust them. While his own Wing all wore belt harnesses that allowed them to fly hands-free, Gwenna, Annick, and Pyrre were left clinging to the high loops, smacked about by the wind and the bird's steep, banking turns, one slip away from a long fall followed by a sick crunch. Smart thinking on the Flea's part—if the rescuees proved less than grateful, well, there wasn't much they could do, clutching to the straps and trying not to fall. The other Wing still had weapons drawn—not that they really needed them—and as the bird flew west, the Flea's soldiers stripped Pyrre of her knives, dropped Annick's bow and Gwenna's swords into the hungry night, then fitted each of the three women with the one-way noose the Kettral referred to as a kill-collar.

"Go ahead," Gwenna said, her voice a pathetic croak. Maybe the Flea was a part of the whole 'Kent-kissing conspiracy and maybe he wasn't. Either way, she couldn't see that it mattered all that much what she told him. Wasn't as though *she* had any idea what the fuck was going on, and if you didn't know what was going on, you weren't likely to give away anything all that vital. "Ask your questions," she said wearily.

The questions were repetitive but straightforward. Why did they flee the Islands? How many men died in the mountains? What happened to the monks? On and on and on, while the noose around her neck chafed with each breath, each movement. The Flea didn't do much talking of his own, and his face didn't give much away. He frowned at the possible implication of Daveen Shaleel in the plot, and again when Gwenna told him what she knew about the connection between Balendin and il Tornja. There were dozens of questions that didn't seem relevant at all—What color was Adiv's blindfold? What had the Urghul fed them? Gwenna answered those, too. It was a strange sort of relief, after so many weeks of confusion, not to have to figure anything out, to let someone else do the thinking, to tell what she knew without trying to fit the broken pieces together.

"So," she said, when the Flea fell silent at last, "you going to kill me?"

He considered her for a while before responding. "I hope not, Gwenna." He looked tired. "I hope not."

†

Evidently, the stories squared. At least, that was how Gwenna interpreted her sudden freedom. After spending the better part of an hour tied to the tree, trying pointlessly to slip out of the Flea's knots, she had watched helplessly as the Wing leader returned, nodded, then slit the ropes with a few quick cuts. Annick was similarly freed, although things didn't look as rosy for Pyrre. Gwenna had no love for the woman, but it came as a shock to see her hauled into the small clearing trussed tighter than a pig for the slaughter, Newt's knife at her throat. The Kettral had treated her more roughly than they had Gwenna or Annick. Bruises purpled her face, her nose looked broken, and her left eye had swollen shut. Despite the injuries, she managed a wink at Gwenna when Newt deposited her on the uneven ground.

Sigrid hacked up something that might have been a laugh or a cough. Even after the fight in the Urghul camp, even after spending the end of the night strapped in to the bird's talons, the woman looked as though she had stepped directly into the forest from some aristocrat's ball. Gwenna's blacks were mud-caked, blood-soaked, and torn ragged. The other Kettral looked just about the same, even the Flea. Sigrid's clothes, on the other hand, might have come straight from the laundress, cloth so immaculately dark it looked like velvet. Only her arms, crisscrossed with dried blood and scar, suggested the violence she had just seen and wrought. She opened her mouth again in a guttural stutter, then pointed at Pyrre.

Newt nodded thoughtfully as he picked at some scab beneath his scraggly beard.

"What?" the Flea asked.

"My lovely and esteemed companion suggests," Newt replied, "that we plant a knife in the Skullsworn's eye for what she did to Finn."

The Flea studied Pyrre for a moment, face unreadable, then turned back to Newt. "And you?"

The Aphorist shrugged. "Killing is easier than unkilling."

"Does that mean kill her, or don't kill her?" the Wing leader asked patiently.

"It means what it means," Newt replied. "I have no vote."

"I will abstain from voting as well," Pyrre said, twisting her head around to face the Flea. "Though I appreciate the democratic process, I am ready to meet my god." Her voice was as battered as her body, the words little more than dried husks.

"You can't kill her," Gwenna blurted, amazed to hear herself speak.

The Flea turned to her, eyebrow raised, but Sigrid coughed up another series of broken sounds before he could respond.

"Sigrid also suggests," Newt interpreted, "taking Gwenna's tongue. As a cautionary measure. My companion observes that the girl can do her work without a tongue and will prove considerably less trying."

It sounded like a joke. Gwenna *hoped* it was a 'Kent-kissing joke, but Sigrid's smile held all the mirth of a bloody knife.

"I'm not taking tongues," the Flea said flatly, as though he had to deal with the suggestion weekly. "I'm deciding what to do with the Skullsworn, then we're getting in the air. I'll remind everyone that there's an Urghul army riding for Annur right now, and, unless il Tornja has better intelligence than I'd realized, it's going to hit him like a hammer to the back of the head."

"That's justice," Annick said curtly. "Il Tornja killed the Emperor. He's a traitor."

"Sounds like he is," the Flea agreed, "but he's also the *kenarang*. We all have jobs, and it's his job to stop the Urghul. If Long Fist's army gets past the frontier, it'll be all over except for the screaming, at least in Raalte and the northern atrepies. Doesn't matter who's loyal and who's not when everyone's dead."

"But Valyn's gone to kill il Tornja," Gwenna said, shaking her head.

The Flea grimaced, wiped a hand down over his forehead. "Let's hope he fails."

"So," Gwenna said, shaking her head, "you believe us, but you want to let il Tornja live?"

"Until he defeats Long Fist, yes."

Gwenna's head throbbed. She'd been up all night fighting, running, flying, feeling, most of the time, half a heartbeat away from a knife in the neck. It was a relief to be free, finally. A relief not to be dead. She was ready to fly some more, or ride some more, or even to fight some more, but the thing she just couldn't take was *talking* anymore, especially when all the talk led nowhere, twisting back on itself until she wasn't even sure which end was up.

"Valyn can kill il Tornja," she said, sick with frustration, "and someone *else* can fucking defeat Long Fist. Doesn't Annur have five 'Kent-kissing generals?"

"Ten," the Flea replied, "if you include their seconds, but they're children next to il Tornja. I swear, that bastard is smarter than Hendran and twice as ruthless. If Long Fist breaks past the border, we'll need il Tornja if we ever hope to bottle him up again. As Newt says, 'Killing is easier than unkilling.'"

"So what's the play?" Annick asked. She was staring into the trees to the northeast, as though she could see all the way to the approaching mass of Urghul. If her recent captivity bothered her, she didn't show it. Always the mission, with Annick, and to Hull with normal human things like emotions. "What do we do?"

The Flea spread his hands. "Not a whole great pile of choices that I can see. Long Fist's already crossed north of the confluence, which means he just needs to get across the Black. There are no garrisons out here because even if he gets across it, he's still on the wrong side of the Thousand Lakes."

"So he's screwed, right?" Gwenna asked. "Even without the garrisons, given the terrain, he's totally buggered."

Sigrid made a disgusted sound and walked off across the meadow toward the bird.

Newt watched her for a while, whistling tunelessly between his crooked teeth, then turned back to Gwenna. "A net," he said, "is not a wall."

"What he means," the Flea said, "is that the lakes are just lakes. Lakes and bogs. There's a lot of them, and it'd be a bitch trying to move an army through, especially an army on horseback, but that's not to say it can't be done if you have the right maps and a few dozen good scouts."

Gwenna stared. "So why aren't there any garrisons there?"

The Flea shrugged. "Lot of frontier. Not so many soldiers. The Urghul never had a chief like Long Fist, so we never bothered worrying about one."

"This is edifying," Pyrre said, "but I can't help feeling as though we've strayed from the original—"

The Flea's backhand caught her square in the jaw. It didn't look like much of a blow, but it knocked the woman clean off the log and into a patch of thorns beyond. The Wing leader didn't so much as glance over. "I don't like many people," he said, gazing into the cool shadows beneath the trees, talking quietly, as though to himself, "but I liked Finn. We were in the same group of cadets. Went through the Trial together."

He looked over at Pyrre finally. "It'd feel good to kill you."

The Skullsworn, unable to break her fall, had landed awkwardly, face half in the moss, half pressed against a rotting stump. With an effort, she hauled herself up, then rose to her knees to meet his eyes. The fall had tightened the noose around her throat, and Gwenna could hear her laboring to breathe.

"You know what the difference is between the Kettral and the priests of Ananshael?" she rasped.

The Flea watched her, but didn't respond.

"We're all fighters," Pyrre continued after a pause. "We're all killers. The difference is that you kill in order to keep something else alive: your empire, your Wing, yourself. The death is incidental to the life."

"And you?" the Flea asked.

Pyrre smiled. "For the priests, death is the point, the ultimate justice. You hold the knife, but death belongs to Ananshael, and I will never fear my god."

The Flea watched her awhile longer, his head tilted to the side, then ran a hand over the graying stubble of his scalp.

"Well," he said, "you're going to have to wait awhile longer to meet him."

The Skullsworn raised her eyebrows.

"My god is patient, but I'm surprised that you are."

"I'm not patient," the Flea said. "I'm practical. I can use you."

Pyrre shook her head, the motion limited by the rope around her neck. "What is it with the Kettral? Why does every Wing leader think I'm a part of their Wing?"

"You're not coming with my Wing," the Flea said. "I need you to stay with Gwenna and Annick. To help them."

"Stay with us *where*?" Gwenna demanded. It sounded suspiciously as though they'd been rescued only to be questioned and abandoned. She might not understand a 'Kent-kissing thing about what was going on, but there was a fight coming, that was clear enough, and she'd be shipped to 'Shael before she was left out of it.

"Andt-Kyl," the Flea said, turning to her.

"What's Andt-Kyl?"

"Small town," Annick said, "near the center of the Thousand Lakes."

"A little to the north of center, actually," the Flea replied.

"And what are we doing in Andt-Kyl?"

"Getting ready."

"For the summer fishing season?" Gwenna demanded, incredulous.

"For the Urghul," the Flea replied. "If Long Fist manages to cross the river, there are half a dozen ways south through the Lakes for an army the size of his, but they all pass through Andt-Kyl. We'll drop you there. We can hope the Urghul won't show up, but if they do, it'll be in three days, maybe four."

"Andt-Kyl is a town," Annick observed. "Not a garrison. Not a fort."

"Your job is to fortify it."

Gwenna was shaking her head. "And if the Urghul show up?"

"Hold them. Until il Tornja arrives."

"Il Tornja doesn't even know they're coming," Gwenna said, worry mounting inside her. The Kettral trained to be knives in the night, not to fight pitched battles against entire armies. It was hard to even imagine what they could do. Even with Pyrre, there were only three of them against the assembled Urghul might.

"I'm going to tell him."

"What do you want us to do with the town?" Annick asked. Her voice was cold and measured as ever, but it was clear she felt no more comfortable with the strange orders than Gwenna.

"It's vaguely defensible already. Make it more so. Rally the people." He shrugged. "We spent most of a decade training you. Do what needs doing. The assassin will help."

"And why," Pyrre asked, "would the assassin do that?"

"Three reasons," the Flea replied. "You're stubborn and you don't want Long Fist spreading his pain-worship over half the earth."

Pyrre frowned. "Where did you get that idea?"

"You're not the first Skullsworn I've come across. I know how Ananshael's priests feel about Meshkent."

The Skullsworn's eyes went wide with surprise, then she pursed her lips appraisingly.

"All right," she said, nodding, "and the third reason?"

The Flea met her gaze. "If things go wrong, there'll be dead piled high as the eaves."

"Indeed," Pyrre replied, nodding slowly, then smiling. "One could make a great prayer to the god."

"What about you?" Gwenna demanded, staring at the Wing leader. "Once you've warned il Tornja, you're coming back? Why are *we* holding the choke point? I mean, I want to do it, to help, but you're the fucking vets. . . ."

"And because we're the fucking vets," the Flea replied, "we're going to do the hard work."

"Meaning what?" Annick asked.

"Meaning killing Long Fist and his ex-Kettral traitor of a pet leach before they get to you."

36

The finest quarters in Aats-Kyl were not, as it turned out, particularly fine. The soldiers who had prepared for her arrival had done their best—scrubbing the wooden floors, hanging lanterns from the log walls, kindling a roaring fire in the wide hearth—but the two-story building at the center of the town was little more than a lodge, and the central hall, though cavernous, was gloomy. Adare could feel the cool northern breeze moving through the unchinked gaps in the logs. The antlered heads of moose and deer seemed to watch her with their stone eyes as she stalked across the floorboards.

As soon as the young soldier went in search of il Tornja, Fulton scoured the room, looking behind every door, checking beneath the rustic tables and chairs, even sticking his head into the flaming hearth, as though someone might be hiding behind the roaring fire, ready to leap out. When he had satisfied himself that the room was secure, he took up a position just inside the front door, blade drawn.

"Shall I kill him as he enters, Your Radiance?" he asked.

Adare hesitated. Sweat slicked her palms, and she could feel it cold on her spine beneath her robe. Her heart pounded under her ribs. She could end it all as soon as the *kenarang* entered. And yet . . . slowly she shook her head. "There's too much going on here that I don't understand. I need to talk to him first."

The Aedolian's jaw tightened. His wounds from the Everburning Well had mostly healed, and he had regained some of the weight he lost searching for her after her escape from the Dawn Palace, and yet something had changed about the man. He had always been hard, even severe. The severity, however, had been leavened by Birch, by Fulton's obvious affection for the younger man. With Birch gone, there was nothing left but duty.

"I would ask that you keep the table between you and the *kenarang* at all times, Your Radiance," he said, gesturing to a wide pine table stained with grease and circles of ale. "I will be at your side, but added distance will serve us well."

"You still think he wants to murder me?" Adare asked.

"I believe everyone wants to murder you, Your Radiance," Fulton replied. "It is my job."

Adare shook her head, suddenly very weary, then turned to Nira and Oshi. The old man, oblivious to the tension in the room, had retired to a dark corner where he was gently patting the mounted head of a black bear. Adare watched him for a moment, wondering what it would feel like to have lived so long and to remember so little. Sometimes her own short life felt filled to bursting, the record of her days crammed with memories she could neither understand nor dismiss.

"He'll be here soon," she said to Nira. "How about some counseling?"

The old woman frowned. "Supposed ta be pretty bright, ain't he?"

"He's supposed to be a 'Kent-kissing genius," Adare replied bitterly. "I know next to nothing about military matters, but he certainly outmaneuvered my father."

"The thing about smart bastards," Nira said, shaking her head, "can't trust 'em, but sometimes ya need 'em."

Adare stared. "You're not telling me to let my father's murderer live?"

The woman raised her brows at the tone. "I'm suggestin', ya willful sow, that ya rule your bright little empire."

"Administering justice," Adare replied stiffly, "is central to rule."

"What is central to rule," Nira snapped, "is doing what needs doing, and if you think that's always the same thing, then you might as well have the big man in the armor there put his blade between your breasts because ya ain't gonna make it long, girl. Ya ain't gonna *survive*."

Adare started to reply when the rear door to the lodge clattered shut. Nira whirled about, cane at the ready, then cursed. Oshi was gone.

"The old fuckin' fool never did know when ta stay put," she muttered, striding toward the rear of the large hall. "I'll be back in a skip. Don't kill anyone till I'm back."

Adare started to protest, but the woman had already followed her brother out the back of the building, cursing beneath her breath and brandishing her cane. Adare turned to find Fulton shaking his head. "I don't know where you found her, Your Radiance, but she is a liability."

"These days," Adare replied bleakly, "you're about the only person who's *not* a liability, Fulton. And I include myself in that accounting."

Before she could say more, the front door clattered open, and il Tornja strode in, his boots, breeches, and coat splattered with mud. Adare's stomach twisted at the sight of him. He approached the table smiling, arms spread in welcome. Even after Fulton laid the broadblade calmly against the *kenarang*'s neck, Adare found herself stepping backward, as though she stood on the shore watching a great wave roll in. She had rehearsed the moment a thousand times on the long march north, first from Olon to Annur, then from Annur to Aats-Kyl, had prepared over and over again what she would say, how she would hold herself. Now, faced with her lover, Annur's *kenarang* and regent, and her father's murderer, it was all she could do to stand, to keep the trembling from her legs, to meet his eyes.

If il Tornja shared any of the same concern, he didn't show it. Despite the mud marring his clothes, he looked just as she remembered: handsome, cavalier, even a little bit louche. Instead of armor, he wore a blue wool coat over a darker blue tunic, the latter tucked into leather riding breeches that flared out above black boots polished smooth as stones. It wasn't a legion uniform, wasn't a uniform at all, and yet the man had a way of carrying the clothes that made them seem wholly appropriate, as though every general in Annur ought to be dressed the same, as though the half-dozen rings he wore, cut gems winking in the firelight, were somehow wholly appropriate to the business of battle and war.

The cold northern wind had riffled his dark hair, but his eyes, those steady, unflinching eyes, studied her with the same amused curiosity Adare remembered so well. She felt like livestock, suddenly, like a horse or cow brought to the block to be picked over before the auction, and the feeling kindled a fury inside her, a red flame of rage. For a moment she almost ordered Fulton to twist his sword and have done with it.

"Nice army you brought," he said, waving a lazy hand toward the wall of the building. "Good marchers. There's no end to the irritation when an army can't march." He shook his head, evidently recalling past frustrations, then shrugged. He didn't so much as glance at Fulton or the blade ready at his throat. "You take up generaling while sojourning in the south?"

"A soldier named Vestan Ameredad has the command," Adare replied stiffly.

"Ameredad?" He raised his brows. "That's what my men told me, but it was a tough tale to swallow. I seem to have missed a verse or two since last we danced. Weren't we trying to pound the dear, pious Sons of Flame straight into the mud not long ago?" He glanced speculatively up into the rafters. "I seem to remember a priest named Uinian—dead. Then there were those Accords you drafted so enthusiastically. . . ."

"Enough," Adare spat. "I know you murdered my father. Adiv gave me your letter, but I didn't need you to tell me. I knew long before that. I intend to see you executed for your crimes, and the only reason I've waited is to try to make some sense of what's happening here in the north, what's going on with the Urghul. If you want to discuss that, fine. If not, I'll be happy to instruct Fulton to take your head from your shoulders."

"Ah." The regent set the single syllable between them, still and inscrutable as a stone on the *ko* board. He didn't move. "How did you learn?" There was no gloating, no guilt. He looked . . . curious.

"My father," Adare said. "He was hunting you even as you murdered him. Your attack triggered his trap."

It wasn't much of an explanation, but il Tornja seemed to accept it, pursing his lips, then nodding. "Makes sense. Sanlitun was clever. Clever and tenacious. Much like his daughter."

It was the casualness of the compliment that shattered her reserve. He said the words as though even after his admission Adare might simply slip back into his arms, wide-eyed and breathless for his approval. As though the Sons of Flame and Fulton's blade at his neck—a blade he had not once deigned to look down at—were insubstantial as her father's ghost, wraiths that might be dismissed with the wave of a hand or a strong gust of wind. As though it didn't fucking *matter* that he had murdered the Emperor and seized the throne for himself.

"If my father was so clever," Adare demanded, voice rising, "if he was so tenacious, then *why did you kill him*?"

"If you read my letter, then you know: he was killing Annur," il Tornja replied evenly. His gaze was level, sober, all trace of insouciance suddenly scrubbed away.

Adare shook her head, blood slamming in her temples.

"My father was a good emperor. One of the best. He oversaw a generation of peace and prosperity."

The *kenarang* nodded. "Unfortunately, good men can make bad decisions, and peace is not always possible." He considered Adare. "You seem to have learned that lesson quickly enough."

"I raised an army because you *forced* me to. . . ."

"I did?" he asked, raising an eyebrow. "Was it my series of brutal atrocities? My callous disregard for the people of Annur? Where are the gibbets dangling with my political foes? Where are the burned-out shells of homes?" He shook his head. "Annur may burn, Adare, but if it does, remember this, *you* brought the fire."

Adare's mouth hung open. The man had put a knife into her father's beating heart, framed a priest, and he expected to lay the guilt at *her* feet?

"You flouted our laws and usurped the Malkeenian line," she said, voice tight as a harp string. "I am defending both."

"More's the pity," he replied. "I had hoped you might be here to defend Annur."

"You want me to believe that 'defending Annur' means sitting idly by while you profane the Unhewn Throne?"

"Your throne is an absurd piece of furniture in which I have less than no interest. I would gladly pass it over to you, although from what I'm told, you've already claimed it for yourself. Your Radiance."

She couldn't tell if he was mocking her or not. Threatening her or not. She had expected him to lie, to twist, to deny the truth in a thousand ways. Despite his earlier letter, she had not expected this, neither the honesty nor the accusation, and she struggled to find her balance, to take control of the conversation once more.

"And you expect me to believe that you won't kill me, too, when I grow inconvenient? The same way you killed my father and Kaden?"

He shook his head. "I had nothing to do with your brother's death."

"Well, it's pretty 'Kent-kissing convenient for you that my father's rightful heir never returned to the capital."

Il Tornja shook his head. "Listen to yourself, Adare. Your father. Your brother. You. The fucking Malkeenians. Even if I murdered your entire family, which I have not and do not intend to, Annur has more pressing worries. Worries that extend beyond the tidy walls of your palace. The Urghul are here." He jerked a thumb back over his shoulder. "*All* of them. I am trying to deal with the threat while you are playing a petty political game."

"Justice for my father is not a game," Adare snarled. "And if the Urghul are here, it is because *you* erred. You are the *kenarang* and regent. Why wasn't the Army of the North in place to stop them?"

"I was forced to recall the Army of the North," he said grimly, "to deal with your religious uprising, to put down the threat of civil war. I thought Long Fist remained at the eastern end of the steppe, but I was wrong. When I pulled the men south to face you, he attacked. Unopposed, he will tear through the northern atrepies like a knife through rotted cloth."

"Then I will oppose him," Adare said. "None of this needs involve you."

"Then kill me," he said, spreading his arms wide. "Kill me if you think it necessary. But then march your Sons and the Army of the North hard. There will be daily messengers updating you on the Urghul movements."

Abruptly, Adare felt that she stood on the verge of a high cliff, staring down into fog. She could kill the man, could appoint Lehav or Fulton to command the Army of the North, and yet, what did Lehav or Fulton understand about the Urghul? Had either of them ever *seen* one? Did they know the first thing about how to fight them?

"And when we encounter the horsemen?" she asked slowly.

Il Tornja smiled then, a wry little twist of the lip. "Hope that Long Fist makes a mistake."

"How likely is that?"

"He hasn't made one yet."

Someone shifted on the floor behind Adare, the wide pine boards creaking with the weight.

"The Urghul might not a' made a mistake," Nira said, her voice a rough file over stone, "but you have, you son of a Csestriim bitch."

Adare spun to find the old woman standing just a few feet inside the back door, her brother hunched in the shadows behind her. She looked the same—stoop-backed, hair a curled halo of gray about her wizened face—but there was something in her eyes, something sharp and bright that Adare had never seen there. For half a heartbeat she just stared at the woman she had made her councillor, and then, behind her, just where il Tornja was standing, she heard the clatter of steel dropping to the wooden floor. She turned once more to find Fulton still holding his sword, or what was left of it.

The blade had been cut cleanly just above the hilt, the steel scar seared smooth. The length of the weapon lay on the pine boards at the *kenarang*'s feet, while around his neck floated a bright collar of flame. The slender line of fire throbbed, as though someone had slashed open the world and beyond it lay another world, one filled to the stars and beyond with unquenchable fire. Fulton took a step back, obviously baffled, but il Tornja didn't move. His eyes, lit by the light of the burning collar, had gone hard as stones.

"What is this?" he asked, raising a hand to the ring, taking care not to touch it.

"You might call it justice," Nira said, stepping forward from the shadows. "Or you might call it vengeance." She smiled a tight smile. "Or you might just call it bad fucking luck. Doesn't much matter, because either way, it's gonna kill you."

The *kenarang* turned his head just a fraction to meet her stare, narrowed his eyes, then, after a brief pause, said simply, "Ah. Rishinira."

"Do I look different," she asked quietly, "after all these years?"

He seemed to study the question. "You look stronger," he said at last.

She barked a laugh, while Adare felt her own stomach shift queasily. The pieces fell abruptly, terrifyingly into place. *Someone close to the center of power. A creature long given to schemes and machinations . . .*

"What are you doing, Nira?" Adare asked slowly.

The old woman didn't take her eyes from il Tornja. "Just finishing up a very tiresome errand."

He was Csestriim. That was the only answer. Ran il Tornja was Csestriim. Her father's killer was Csestriim. Somehow, impossibly, he was the Csestriim Nira had been searching for all these years, the one who made her nearly immortal. The brute fact smashed through everything Adare thought she understood about the world, and her mind refused it, kicked it away, grasped desperately for some other explanation. She felt as though she had looked into the bottom of a deep well and seen the sun.

Il Tornja spread his hands, the sort of invitation a host might make upon opening the door to newly arrived guests. "I see you've made the acquaintance of my old friends, Adare." He nodded toward Nira's brother, who was staring at him with eyes like saucers—"Hello, Roshin"—then turned back to her. "I don't know how you found these two, but I assume you are ignorant of their history."

"No," Adare said, shaking her head, forcing down the confusion and the terror. "I'm *not* ignorant of it, in fact. Nira and Oshi have been completely honest with me."

Il Tornja frowned. "Then you understand that they are leaches. That they helped to destroy half of the continent you call Eridroa. They are the Atmani."

"What I understand," Adare said, forcing herself to say the words, though she could only manage a whisper, "is that if they are the Atmani, then you are the monster who made them."

Il Tornja frowned. "*Monster* is a terribly freighted word. As for making them, only Bedisa can weave a soul. She made them, made them a brother and sister, both leaches. All we did was help to extend their power, to give them the life they still enjoy."

Adare felt like weeping, like screaming, but it was Nira who responded, her voice gravid with rage.

"Enjoy?" she spat. "The life we *enjoy*?" She thrust a finger at her brother. "Your *gifts* broke us."

"A fact that I have regretted since the day I realized it was true."

"You're *Csestriim*," Nira hissed savagely. "You don't *feel* regret."

Something alien passed through il Tornja's gaze, an utter emptiness that made Adare quail. "Your certainties, Rishinira, may prove as illusory as my own have."

Blood filled Adare's mouth, bitter and salty. She realized she had bitten through her cheek, and tried not to gag. "What do you want?" she managed. "Why are you here?"

He turned back to her, pausing for a moment as though considering his answer. "I want what I have long wanted," he replied finally. "To protect Annur from her foes."

"A lie," Nira snarled. "Just another fucking lie."

Il Tornja shook his head. "Since its founding, Annur has been ruled by Malkeenians, but in many ways, it is *my* empire. It is the penance I undertook, the thing I created, to atone for my failure with you, Rishinira, and with Roshin, and the rest."

Adare wanted to scream at Nira to tighten the flaming collar and have done with it. The man had lied to her so many times already, and each time she had allowed herself to be led like a docile beast. Just one more step. Always just one more step.

She almost said it. "Kill him," she almost said, opening her mouth to let the words out, but they would not come.

It was the easiest course, the just course, but it also reeked of confusion and desperation. Revenge was a reaction, and she needed to do more than react. She needed to think, to think deeper and better than she had been thinking all these months. She needed to see further than her foes. That il Tornja was Csestriim she could barely believe, but if it was true, the truth had consequence. It explained things. He was not just a human general risen to his post on the strength of his native genius, but something even more dangerous. More powerful.

Adare eyed the collar of flame around the *kenarang*'s throat, watched it shift and writhe. Il Tornja hadn't tried to move since Nira wove it in place, which meant that he was trapped, at bay. The terror inside her still raged, but emperors were not ruled by their terror. It was foolish to destroy something before she fully understood it, before she knew whether or not she could use it.

"How," she asked, her voice rigid as steel, "is Annur your empire?"

He met her stare. "I have been with her since the start. I told Terial where to build his capital. I commanded the army that put down the Second Secession—"

Adare shook her head curtly. "Raginald Went put down the Second Secession."

He grinned. "Have you ever seen a painting of Raginald Went?"

Adare's mind foundered. Raginald Went had refused to be painted. He had refused a statue on the Godsway in his honor, going so far as to have his soldiers tear down the incomplete work. At the time, everyone had hailed his humility, but what if it had not been humility at all?

It was then that the realization started to penetrate, soaking in like a frigid winter rain, freezing her to the core. Ran il Tornja was immortal. This was not his first post, not his first role in the Annurian chronicles. Nira had said it herself on the road south to Olon: the man was drawn to power like a moth to light. How many names had he worn down through the dusty halls of history? How many parts had he played?

He nodded, as though he could hear her silent question. "I was Mizran to Alial the Great. I fought the Manjari at the Rift in the Western Wars, and the jungle tribes down in the Waist during the Dark Summer. I founded the Aedolian Guard to protect your family."

Adare was shaking her head, but no words would come.

"The Kettral study a book on tactics by Hendran," he continued, speaking slowly now, as though to a child. "I wrote it. I was Hendran for almost three decades. At every step, I have been there, a faithful shepherd to Annur and to the Malkeenians both."

"Why?" Adare demanded quietly. "Why would you do that?"

For the first time he hesitated. "My people are gone," he said at last. "Never to return. There can't be more than a few dozen of us left, scattered here and there. The Csestriim will never come back, but I wanted to create something on this earth like what we lost: a kingdom, an empire, a polity ruled by reason and justice rather than fear, and greed, and passion."

He gestured to Nira and Oshi. "We tried with the Atmani, thought that if we found a way to bring immortality to a small, just group of rulers, that they would, in turn, bring order to the world." He grimaced. "We failed. Bedisa did not build your minds for the long passage of years. Instead of ushering in order and justice, we plunged the world into madness."

He turned to Nira. "Do you remember, Rishinira?" he asked almost gently. "How young you all were, and beautiful? How eager for justice and peace? What we did, we did *with* you, not *to* you. We shared a hope. One that went awfully awry."

Adare glanced at the old woman and discovered tears sheeting down her cheeks. "You knew what would happen," she said, balling her hands into fists. "You're Csestriim. You *must* have known."

"No," he replied. "We did not. Even the gods fail, and we were never gods."

He turned back to Adare. "Where I failed with the Atmani, I have succeeded with Annur, at least to a degree."

"Why didn't you just rule yourself?" Adare demanded. "Why make my family your puppets?"

He smiled ruefully. "The Malkeenians were hardly puppets. You're too quick and stubborn for that. And then," he gestured with a hand to her scars, "there is Intarra's hand upon you as well, a hand more powerful than my own will ever be. No, you were never puppets. We have been . . . collaborators in this great project. Men and women accept the Malkeenians, revere you, where they could never accept one of my kind."

Adare took a deep, shuddering breath, trying to sort the lies from the truth. At the side of the room, Oshi had left his bear to stand beside Nira, their fingers laced together.

"Do we fight, sister?" he asked quietly. He stared at il Tornja, but his eyes held no recognition.

"It's not a matter of fighting," she said, gesturing to the collar of flame with a withered hand. "It is a matter of killing. A thought, and he is dead."

Adare stepped forward, her body moving even as her mind scrambled to keep up, putting herself squarely between the Atmani and il Tornja, raising a hand, as though that would do anything to block Nira's kenning.

"No," she said, shaking her head. "You can't."

"Do not lecture me, child," Nira replied, eyes cold as winter night, "on the handling of my own vengeance."

Adare hesitated, tried to think. If she was going to lead Annur, she needed to be able to reason even as her mind reeled. If half of what the man claimed were true, a quarter of it—if he had fought in all those battles, had counseled the greatest of the Malkeenian emperors—then she could use him. No, she amended silently, she *needed* him. Despite her father's tutelage, despite the hundreds of tomes she'd read on politics and law, finance and governance, she had no idea how to handle the threat posed by Long Fist, no idea how to manage the various borders, no strategy to keep peace down in the Waist. Letting il Tornja live was a danger, a risk, but risk was everywhere. The man was a well-honed tool, one she could turn to her advantage, to Annur's advantage. . . .

"Stand aside, Adare," Nira said.

Slowly, Adare shook her head. "Hear me out. For my sake, *and* for yours." She raised her chin toward Oshi. "For his."

Nira hesitated, then spat on the floor.

"You have a hundred words."

Adare didn't pause. "He can fix you."

"Horseshit," the old woman snarled. She looked past Adare at the *kenarang*. "Go ahead, try to ride her lie."

Il Tornja shook his head slowly. "I will not. I don't know how to cure you."

Adare cursed him silently. Why he had chosen this particular moment, after a lifetime of lies, to cleave to the truth, she had no idea, but she pressed ahead regardless. "You might not know, but you have ideas." If there was one thing she'd learned about Ran il Tornja, it was that the man had ideas. On politics. On war. On love. He might not know what had gone wrong with Oshi and Nira, but he'd had hundreds of years to wonder. "You have theories," she said.

He watched her from beneath hooded eyes, then chuckled. "I do," he replied.

"And now that you have the last two Atmani here," Adare said, gesturing to Nira and Oshi, "it's possible you can help them."

He hesitated. "There is always a possibility."

"*Fuck* possibility," Nira growled. "It was possibility that *broke* us in the first place. I will have my revenge, and see an end to this."

The words were rock hard, sharp as chipped obsidian, but Adare could see something in the old woman's face, the first crumbling of doubt.

Adare tried to speak directly to that doubt, driving her argument into the hesitation like mason's spikes hammered into a stone's seam. "You can make that decision for yourself, Nira, but not for your brother."

"Don't go lecturin' me on what I can and can't do. I've been makin' his decisions since before your fucking empire was born, girl."

Adare nodded, meeting her eyes. "You've protected him all this time—for what? So you could find a man, kill him, then die? Did you keep going all these centuries just for this?"

"Pretty much."

"There is another end to this story," Adare said, praying to Intarra that the woman would see, would understand, that the long years had not burned out of her the capacity for hope.

Nira stared at her, jaw set, then turned her eyes to the *kenarang*. For a long time she just watched him, studying the man's face as though it were a page from a book in some barely remembered language.

"I tried to fix it," he said quietly. "The world we broke"—he gestured toward Adare—"building Annur was an effort to put it right."

"Annur can bugger itself bloody," the old woman replied, lips drawn back from her jagged teeth.

"Do we fight, sister?" Oshi asked again, staring at il Tornja with an almost rabid intensity. "Is it time at last?"

Nira looked over at him, watched as her brother's cheek twitched and his fingers clenched and unclenched around the grip of some unseen weapon. He shook as though palsied, and though he had stopped speaking, his lips continued to shape silent words. Slowly, moving for the first time since Adare met her with a weariness appropriate to her age, Nira raised a hand and set it gently on Oshi's shoulder. "No," she said quietly. "Not yet."

Then, as abruptly as it had bloomed, the collar of flame around the *kenarang*'s neck seemed to . . . twist. The air around it went strange, dark, and then it vanished. Nira sagged against her brother, the strength drained from her legs, but her voice was strong when she spoke, her eyes bright.

"The collar isn't gone," she said. "Just hidden. It will move with you, shift with you, travel with you so readily you don't even know it's there. You'll be the freest slave in the world, but you'll be my slave. At a word from me, at a *thought,* it will tighten and end you."

Il Tornja cocked his head to the side. "Using your power like this, Rishinira . . ."

The woman hacked a jagged laugh out of the air. "Will do what? Make me insane?"

"Indeed."

"Then you'd better figure out a way to make me better again before I lose my mind. A little more encouragement for you to help my brother. Ya don't want a crazy woman holding your leash, I can promise you that." She turned to Adare. "You think you need him? Use him. But when you're not using him to save your little empire, he will be working to fix my brother, bending all his long life's learning to making right what he has broken." She raised her eyebrows. "Isn't that how it will be?"

The *kenarang* nodded, a thoughtful, measured gesture.

"Good," Nira said. "Because the day you stop trying to heal us, the day you forget your leash and turn on us, is the day I cut you into a dozen pieces and leave you for the ravens."

Il Tornja took a step forward, tested the air in front of his throat with a hand, then another step.

"You could be bluffing," he observed.

Nira's smile was like a knife. "Test it."

To Adare's surprise, he chuckled, shaking his head ruefully, as though he'd just lost a few suns in a hand of cards. "I'll take your word for it. Now," he went on, turning to Adare as though the two of them were just wrapping up a somewhat dull bureaucratic function, "there is much to prepare. My men have erected a pavilion for you in the center of the camp. You'll be comfortable there, and more importantly, safe. The first thing—"

"Where," Adare demanded, cutting him off, "are the Urghul?"

He grimaced. "By now? Most likely a day or two from the northern end of the lake."

Adare hesitated. "So, at least three or four days from us, right? Isn't that good news?"

"Hardly. Long Fist crossed north of the confluence, well north of our last garrison. It looks like he's headed around the north end of the lake. He's still got the Black River to get past, which he'll almost certainly do at Andt-Kyl, but Andt-Kyl is far from here and we need to get there first. If he crosses before we arrive, it's over. He won't be able to move quickly through the forest, but he won't have to. There are no more choke points after

Andt-Kyl. He can split his army in ten, send them all in different directions. There'll be bodies hanging from the branches from the Ghost Sea
to the Romsdals."

Adare stared, aghast. "So what are we doing here? Why aren't you marching north?"

He crossed to the fire and held his hands a moment in front of the
blaze before answering. "You see the terrain we've been moving through?"
he asked at last. "Bogs. Swamps. Streams. Firs so tight you can't slide between them?"

Adare nodded.

"North of here, it's all like that, and no good road through it. There's a
forest track up the west coast of the lake, but an army this size would churn
it to mud. We'd be weeks picking our way, and we don't have weeks."

"So you've decided to do a little civil engineering instead?" Adare demanded. "Nine out of every ten men you have are *sleeping* in a 'Kent-
kissing *field* right now! They could at least *try* the western track."

The *kenarang* smiled. "There's a quote from Hendran's *Tactics* that I'm
fond of. Chapter fourteen: '*Never fight,*' I believe it says, '*when you can
rest.*' "

37

K aden prepared, as he approached the high-walled estate of Gabril
the Red, for disbelief or fury, a fist in the face or a knife in the gut.
He tried to run through various scenarios, to anticipate what the
young nobleman might say or do, but the future proved as blank and inscrutable as the limestone walls of Gabril's mansion. Annurian law stipu-
lated that no one, regardless of wealth or rank, could build a fortress
inside the city. Early emperors had learned that lesson the hard way, and
since the empire's second century, private dwellings were required to have
a certain number of windows and a gate in every exterior wall. Moats were
illegal, hoardings atop the walls were illegal, arrow loops were illegal. Gabril the Red's estate complied with the letter of the law. Barely.

The windows fronting the street were tall and graceful, arched at their
peaks, but so slim Kaden would have had to turn sideways to slide through
them. The main gate was open, but guarded by half a dozen men in long
desert robes. More guards patrolled the top of the wall, each one with a
spear or a bow ready to hand. The place wasn't a fort, not exactly, but
Kaden was under no illusions. Inside those walls, Gabril could kill him a
dozen times over and no one would ever know.

Kiel and Triste had tried to join him. He had refused. They argued of
course, Kiel pointing out that, even after a decade and a half in an Ishien
cell, he understood the political realities of the city better than Kaden,
Triste arguing more passionately but less coherently that they had to stick
together, to help each other. Kaden, however, had observed that Gabril
might well greet their impromptu embassy with a blade, and if there was
dying to be done, better one person than three. In the end, they couldn't
force him to bring them along, and so it was Morjeta who slipped him out
of Ciena's temple through another hidden tunnel, who led him through

wide streets lined with stately bloodwoods, who pointed discreetly toward this fortress that was not a fortress, and murmured, "The estate of Gabril the Red."

Kaden nodded, considering the place from inside his hood's shadow.

"He is dangerous," Morjeta continued, laying a delicate hand on Kaden's arm. "Not just because he can fight, but because he can think."

Kaden studied the woman. She was frightened. He could see the tension in her neck, in the rise of her shoulders. She was frightened, but she held that fear in check. The whole thing might have been a Shin exercise, and he took a moment to slow his own heart, to cool his skin.

"Dangerous and smart? That's the point, right? That's why we came here."

Morjeta hesitated, then nodded. "When it is over, return to this place and I will take you back to the temple."

Kaden didn't point out that when it was over, he might not have the ability to go anywhere.

When he stepped through the graceful arch of the palace walls, however, and pushed back his hood to show his eyes, when he stated his name and asked to see the First Speaker of Rabi, the white-robed guard just raised his brows, then nodded, escorting him into a wide interior courtyard. Flowering vines perfumed the breeze, and a large fountain tossed a spray of water ten feet into the air. It was a simple, graciously proportioned space, ideal for the lazy sipping of chilled *ta* on a warm summer day. There was, however, nothing lazy about the fight unfolding on the wide flagstones.

Three soldiers with long spears were attacking a man, if the figure engulfed in the black robe *was* a man, pressing him from different angles, probing with their weapons, testing his defenses. At the sight of Kaden, the sparring stopped, and the servant who had ushered him in crossed to the robed figure, murmuring something to him. The robe turned—Kaden couldn't see the man's face inside the voluminous hood—considered him a moment, then a hand emerged from the dark folds, flicking the servant away.

So, Kaden thought, schooling himself to stillness, *Gabril the Red enjoys making people wait.* He filed the thought away as the fight resumed.

The soldiers with the spears immediately redoubled their attacks, weapons slashing and plunging into the robe at their center. Of the man inside the cloth, there was no sign. His hands, his legs, even his head were lost in the swirl of fabric. *A shadowrobe,* Kaden realized. *Holy Hull, he's a shadowrobe.*

He'd grown up on stories of the desert warriors, enjoying them almost as much as tales of the Kettral. Many people considered the desert warriors to be leaches, but Kaden and Valyn had found an old codex in the palace library once, the pages filled with illustrations and diagrams, showing just how a skilled shadowrobe could use the huge, flapping cloak to hide his movements, to disguise the location of his body.

Kaden and Valyn had spent days using old blankets as robes, trying to perfect the techniques, to mimic hips with their hands, to make elbows look like shoulders, to twist their bodies so that what seemed from the outside to be the center of mass was nothing more than empty air. According to the book, men and women sometimes went mad fighting shadowrobes. Kaden never believed that; for all Valyn's efforts, it was always easy to tell his hands from his head, to see his skinny ankles darting about beneath the cloth. Watching Gabril, however . . . Kaden shook his head. Fighting a shadowrobe looked like trying to attack the wind.

The spears appeared to be tearing the First Speaker apart, stabbing again and again into the great flapping garment, burying themselves in the shifting folds of cloth. Blunted edges or no, those thrusts could kill, and as Kaden stared he saw one of the spear points stab right through the center of the robe, then emerge from the other side, the steel bright in the sunlight. The hooded figure did not fall.

Kaden looked closer. The faces of the three attackers were drawn in concentration, their panting audible even at a distance. Though the men obviously knew how to handle their weapons, though they had the numbers, their faces were grim. Great hacking slices that seemed sure to take off a shoulder thwacked harmlessly into fabric that gave way in soft billows. Suddenly, with no warning he could perceive, a short knife flashed out from beneath the robe, the pommel slamming up into the jaw of the closest soldier. Before the body hit the stone, the hand and knife were both gone, disappearing back into that flowing shadow.

At the sight, one of the remaining men lunged forward with a furious cry. His spear passed through a fold of cloth, punched out the other side, and into the shoulder of one of his comrades. As the wounded man fell behind him, the shadowrobe flowed forward, well inside the reach of the spear, and then that furtive blade was out again, pressing against the soldier's throat. The unrobed man cursed, dropped his spear, and raised his hands in surrender. For a long time, the blade at his throat didn't move. Kaden watched, wondering if he was about to see a man die. Then, with a flicker like a fire-cast shadow darting when the wind rises, the blade was gone.

His foes forgotten, the cloaked figure turned to Kaden, then lowered his hood. Black hair lay plastered against his skull, and his face ran with sweat, but he didn't appear to be breathing hard. For a while, he said nothing, just looked. Then he waved a hand at his servant.

"Take our visitor to the study overlooking the acacia tree. I will decide his fate when I have bathed."

†

"I have come," Kaden said carefully, "to offer my condolences for the death of your father."

Gabril the Red said nothing, studying Kaden from behind steepled fingers the way a hawk perched on a high branch might study a rabbit, his stillness the stillness of a predator poised to strike. He had taken his time in bathing, and with his face scrubbed and sleek black hair knotted behind his head, he bore little resemblance to the sweating shadowrobe from the courtyard. He looked like a young, well-heeled nobleman, not a warrior. Only a long, fine scar, light across his dark cheek, and the bright knives glittering in their red sheaths at his belt, hinted at the earlier violence.

"Murder," Gabril said finally. The word was sharp with the accent of the Western Desert, vowels polished, consonants pitted as though by the scouring sand.

Kaden raised his eyebrows. "I beg your pardon?"

"You should," Gabril replied. "You talk of my father's 'death' as though Gabril the Gray choked on the pit of a date or wandered from the well with no water. This is not the truth of the matter."

"He was executed," Kaden said, "in accordance with Annurian law."

"He was murdered," Gabril replied, "by your father."

Kaden slowed his pulse, loosened the muscles of his shoulders and back. The Shin had trained him in all manner of techniques to control his own fear and rage, but they had said nothing about how to calm others—one more way in which they had left him ill prepared to rule an empire, one more deficit he would have to make up on his own, provided Gabril left him alive long enough.

The First Speaker eyed Kaden appraisingly. "You are not dead, as they

say in the streets, but you are not Emperor. You return months after Sanlitun was set in the earth, and you come here, to me, your eyes hidden in
this hood. Why? You must know what passed between our fathers."

Kaden considered what he knew of the young man seated across the
table, searching for a hook, a handle. As a child, he had grown up with
stories of the desert tribes of Mo'ir, tales filled with vengeance, violence,
and blood. He and Valyn had imagined every man and woman a shadowrobe, every meeting a duel to the death. According to Kiel, however, the
stories were almost all wrong, the figment of an Annurian imagination
obsessed with the exotic. Not that there *weren't* shadowrobes in the west,
not that Mo'ir's history lacked its own share of blood, but if Kiel were
to be believed, the tribes valued eloquence over violence, insisting on
speech before every fight. Kaden had wagered his life on that insistence,
but, face-to-face with Gabril, the words he had prepared seemed inadequate.

"I am not my father," he said quietly. "Just as you are not yours."

Gabril studied him for a long time, then raised a hand. A robed servant stepped silently from behind a wooden screen.

"*Ta*," Gabril said, not bothering to look at the man. "Two cups."

They waited in silence as the servant arranged a clay kettle, steeped the
leaves, then poured the steaming liquid into twin clay cups. Kaden hesitated, eyeing the vessel warily.

"Drink," Gabril said, gesturing. "If I kill you, I will use a knife."

It was a slender reassurance, but Kaden lifted the cup to his lips, sipping gently at the bitter, unsweetened *ta*. Gabril raised his own cup, drank
deeply, then set it gently back on the tabletop.

"The first time I journeyed to your city," he said, "I was eight. I did not
want to come, but my father was in chains, and we do not allow a person—
man or woman—to die without witness."

Kaden nodded, unsure how to respond.

"I went to your palace, inside your red walls, and I watched while seven
of your citizens, men and women unknown to me or my father, men and
women whose only sight of sand was a thin strip along the shores of your
sea, decided his death."

"This is the way of Annurian justice," Kaden said. "All cases are decided by a council of seven."

"This is the way of cowards," Gabril said. "Your father watched this
'trial,' but he did not speak. When my father died, your father watched,

but he did not wield the knife. When they dragged me from the hall, I swore I would see your father dead, and now I have.

"You come to me offering 'condolences' for my father's murder? Then I will tell you this: I rejoice in the murder of yours. I came to see Sanlitun dead, to witness the life drained from his bones. I am only sorry I did not plant the knife in his beating heart myself."

He considered Kaden for several heartbeats, then raised his cup, eyes intent above the rim, waiting.

Kaden said nothing. Anger flared, but he extinguished it, then crushed out the sparks of pride and shame as well. He had not come to trade barbs with the son of a dead traitor. To lose himself in a dispute with Gabril the Red was to forget the greater threat posed by Ran il Tornja and Adare, to abandon his best hope of blocking their attack. Kaden revolved Gabril's story in his mind, searching for a crack, a fracture, a way in.

"You saw my father laid in his tomb months ago," he said finally. "Why have you remained in this city you so clearly loathe?"

Gabril's eyes narrowed. "My comings and goings are mine, and not yours to question."

"Then I take back the question," Kaden said. There was a shape to the verbal dance, but one he could discern only imperfectly. "You offered me a tale, and I will offer you one in return."

Gabril hesitated. "Speak," he said finally, "and I will hear your words."

"Your father," Kaden began, choosing his course carefully, "Gabril the Gray, hated the empire."

The First Speaker nodded curtly. "Bedisa creates all the world's people as equals. To set one man above the rest, to steal from the others their own voices, this is an abomination."

Kaden had expected as much. Kiel had already explained to him the Mo'iran system of tribal rule, in which all men and women, regardless how poor, had a voice and a vote at the council fires. The Csestriim had explained the political processes of the Western Deserts efficiently and clearly, but Kaden wanted to hear Gabril himself say the words. Everything hinged on the Speaker.

"Surely," Kaden pressed, "some people are more capable than others? Some see further and deeper into the heart of important matters."

"And those people," Gabril said, "speak first and last at the fires. But to silence the voices of others is cowardice and injustice both. It turns men and women to beasts."

"The people of Annur are hardly beasts."

"Your empire has made them docile. Compliant. Incurious. Your family turns the people into goats, then you strut among them as though you were lions, preying on the weak, devouring them."

Gabril's voice was tight but controlled, his fury carefully reined. Any doubt Kaden had about the Speaker's hatred of the empire had vanished.

"Your father believed this, too," Kaden replied, "and so he worked in secret to bring down the empire. To set in its place a—"

"Circle of Speakers," Gabril said defiantly. "And he would have succeeded, had he not been betrayed. He was not alone in his desire to hear many voices about the fire."

"As you said, you came to Annur to see my father brought low—"

"To see him dead," Gabril said, cutting him off. "To see the great lion gutted."

Kaden ignored the gibe. "But you have *stayed* to continue your father's work."

Gabril's lips tightened. His hand dropped to one of the blades at his belt. Kaden schooled his body to stillness even as he locked gazes with the Speaker.

"You're still here," he said, pushing ahead with a story based in part on Kiel's description of Mo'iran culture, partly on Morjeta's assessment of Gabril's activities in the city, and partly on pure hunch, "because the other aristocrats are here, all the dispossessed nobility from across the empire, in a single city. What better place to continue the work of your father? What better city in which to labor toward the destruction of Annur?"

Kaden fell silent, spread his hands, and waited.

"I had intended," Gabril said, drawing his knife after a pause, "to allow you to depart unharmed."

"And now?"

"Now, I will not repeat the errors of my father. I will see you dead before you can overturn the great work." He rose to his feet, slipped the other knife from his belt, and set it on the table in front of Kaden. The steel was dark as coal save for the edge, which gleamed in the sunlight. Kaden made no move to reach for it.

"I offer you the choice your father never offered mine," Gabril said, gesturing toward the knife. "To die a man."

"I didn't come here to fight you," Kaden said.

"Then you will die a beast."

"And you are certain that killing me will best serve your work?"

"You are the Emperor," Gabril responded, as though that settled everything.

Kaden raised his eyebrows. "Am I?" He fingered the rough fabric of his coat, then ran his hand over the tabletop between them. "The clothes on my back are my only clothes. This wooden table is worth more than all my possessions."

"When you return to your palace—"

"I cannot return to my palace. When my father died, others took his place."

Gabril hesitated, then shook his head.

"And so one lion has replaced another. You have lost your empire and come to me thinking I will help you regain it. You judged me poorly."

"It is you," Kaden replied evenly, "whose judgment has gone awry."

Gabril narrowed his eyes. "You tell me in my own ears that this is wrong, that others have not killed your father and stolen your empire?"

"So far you are right."

"And yet you would have me believe that you do not want it back?"

"No," Kaden said, taking up the knife before him, turning it back and forth, watching the sunlight play off the honed edge. It felt good in his hand, solid and strong. With an easy, fluid gesture he slammed the point into the table, watched it quiver. "I am not my father," he said, "and I am not my sister. I do not want my empire back. I want it destroyed."

38

After a decade spent studying small-team tactics and training to fight in Wings of five or six, it was easy to forget just how impressive a full Annurian field army really was. As a child, Valyn had seen legions march down the Godsway of the capital, rank after perfect rank, pennants held high, spears precisely angled toward the sky. He remembered the pageantry, but had forgotten the sheer mass of men and metal, the sense that an entire city had taken up arms. As he studied the encamped Army of the North from behind a small copse of trees, however, he found himself struck anew by the sight. None of the individual soldiers could match the rankest Kettral cadet, of course, but that was missing the point; the army was never intended for the precise work of the Kettral. Where the Kettral relied on timing and precision, the army was a creature of mass and momentum, slow to start up but near impossible to stop.

What they were doing here, however, buried in the dense forests of the Thousand Lakes, Valyn still couldn't say. The two Annurian riders had been carrying a message for the *kenarang* all right, but the 'Kent-kissing thing proved to be written in some sort of cipher, a long string of meaningless letters and numbers that neither Valyn, Talal, or Laith had the faintest idea how to unravel. Both Annurians claimed ignorance of the contents, and Valyn believed them—there was little point in encoding a message if the meat of it could be extracted from the bearers at the point of a knife. All the messengers could give him was a destination, Aats-Kyl, a logging town at the southern tip of Scar Lake, and so Valyn and his diminished Wing rode southwest instead of south, following miserable tracks through dense northern forests of balsam and pine to Aats-Kyl. If il Tornja was planning an assault on the steppe, he'd certainly chosen an indirect route, but then, maybe that was the point.

"Looks like the entire Army of the North," Talal observed.

Valyn nodded, running the long lens up and down the arrow-straight rows of tents. The Annurians had pitched their camp a little outside of the town proper, on a series of fields that might have been planted with squash or beans. Whatever the crop, it was destroyed now, the labor of an entire season ground back into the mud by the boots of the army.

He tried to estimate numbers, a task made easier by the fact that the Annurians always laid out camp in a neat grid, rank upon rank of taut white legionary tents divided into four quarters. At the center of each quarter stood a complex of larger pavilions: mess hall, blacksmith, quartermaster, and medical. A quick count of tents suggested twenty thousand men; more, if they were double-bunking to drop their carry weight on the march. It was a huge force, but Valyn couldn't help but compare it to the nomadic encampment north of the White. Where the Urghul army had flowed from one hill to the next, their *api* and campfires sprawling over the steppe nearly as far as the eye could see, the Annurian force fit neatly into a single row of fields.

Valyn paused, squinted through the lens at the far side of the camp. He wasn't high enough to get a good view, but it seemed that the soldiers there were armored differently from the rest. Occasionally, as the men worked in the setting sunlight, he caught a bright flash that looked more like bronze or gold than steel. It hardly made sense. The legions were too practical to spend money on ornamentation, but then, Valyn was quickly discovering that there was a lot he never learned on the Islands. The strange armor could have been one of a hundred things, and Valyn let it go, shifting his long lens to look over the town itself.

It was larger than he'd expected, maybe a thousand houses, almost all of them log-built cabins, stables, and sheds, some with stone chimneys, some with simple holes in the roof where the smoke could escape. That smoke hung over everything, a thick haze that Valyn could feel scratching at his throat, that he could taste on the back of his tongue. He had forgotten the stench of cities and villages in his years on the Islands, where the near-constant salt wind off the ocean scoured the archipelago night and day. The men and women of Aats-Kyl, however—mostly loggers, judging from the mills at the edge of the village—seemed not to notice the reek of dung and rot, smoke and cut pine, that lay on their town like ash.

A few thin dogs scrounged scraps outside the doors, and a single sow, evidently escaped from her pen, rooted at the foot of a small well. The streets were mostly dirt, though recent rain and the passage of men and horses had turned them to mud. Valyn picked out two large buildings that looked like temples—to what god or goddess, he couldn't say—and a proud, three-story structure of chinked logs and fieldstone, half hall, half tower, near the town's center. Even that building, however, was overtopped by the dam, a huge embankment of earth, stone, and wood to the north of the town, at the south end of Scar Lake. Valyn turned his attention to the structure, staring through the long lens.

The sun had already settled into the serrated tops of the firs, but close to two hundred men—Annurian legionaries, judging from their uniforms—were hard at work by torchlight, digging through the earthen dam. Their commanders had them on a quick rotation, each group working no longer than two hours before a second marched in to take its place and the first returned to the camp. Valyn had been studying them since just after noon, and the pace never flagged. They showed all intentions, in fact, of working straight through the night, though with what goal in mind, he couldn't say. There were Kettral who specialized in hydraulic analysis—diverting rivers, destroying aqueducts, poisoning groundwater—but even Valyn could tell that a gap in the dam would flood the river below. The town was high enough that it would probably survive, but he couldn't see why anyone would take the risk.

"Something's put an ember up their asses," Laith observed.

It was the kind of comment the flier would have made a month earlier, but all levity was drained from the words. Instead of glancing over slyly as he spoke, he refused to meet Valyn's eyes, keeping his gaze fixed on the town. It had been that way since their botched attack on the messengers four days earlier. Part of Valyn missed his friend's banter, but an even larger part welcomed the new solemnity; it relieved him of having to joke, to smile, to fake happiness or humor. They had come all this way to kill the man who had killed his father, and as long as he focused on that single fact, as long as he focused on the relevant tactics and dangers, the goal would fill his mind, pushing back the memory of the men he had already murdered. It kept him going, but it didn't leave anything left over for smiling.

"The Urghul," Talal said. "It has to be the Urghul."

Valyn nodded. "Long Fist was massing for something," he agreed. "That was clear as rain."

"Which means," the flier observed acidly, "that our dear friend the shaman has fucked us."

Valyn revolved the idea as he considered the army once more. At the center of the camp flew a massive banner emblazoned with the Annurian sun. Beneath the banner, a dozen soldiers were hard at work erecting a huge pavilion. Something that large could only belong to il Tornja, and Valyn panned back and forth with the lens, searching in vain for some sign of the man.

When he and his Wing rode out from the Urghul camp ten days earlier, Valyn had expected to travel all the way to Annur, to have to find the *kenarang* in his own palace and kill him; even for the Kettral, it had seemed a nearly impossible task. Something, however, had flushed il Tornja into the open. It made for an opportunity, but put Valyn on his guard at the same time. It also meant delaying even further his reunion with Kaden, but Kaden would have to fend for himself awhile. Clearly, events had outpaced Valyn since he quit the Islands. There were new stones on the board, and sticking obstinately to an outdated plan was a quick way to get dead.

"An Annurian army on the move could mean one of several things," he said slowly, passing the long lens to Talal. "It certainly doesn't exonerate il Tornja for my father's death. For *any* of the deaths. In fact, it squares with what Balendin told us."

Laith stared at him. "An Annurian army headed north means that someone to the north is misbehaving, and unless you think the actual thousand lakes have sloshed out of their beds to march south, that means the Urghul."

"But according to Long Fist," Talal observed quietly, "this is all a part of il Tornja's strategy. It's easier to justify a transition to military command if there's a war that needs fighting. He could have murdered Sanlitun *and* provoked the Urghul, all with the ultimate goal of consolidating his own position."

"Which means there'll be more than just one death to lay at his feet," Valyn added. "If the *kenarang*'s forcing a major battle just to keep his seat on the throne, he'll be killing thousands. Tens of thousands, Urghul and Annurian alike."

"I'm not sure I want to start laying deaths at feet," Laith replied. "Not given what we've been up to recently."

"Valyn," Talal began, long lens fixed on one of the gates in the palisade ringing the town, where a dirt road spilled out into the fields beyond. Valyn had studied it earlier. It was an obvious attack point, and though the loggers had built squat towers to either side, an experienced siege team would force it easily. Valyn squinted. Figures on horseback were emerging from between the wooden walls.

"Who is it?" he asked, turning to Talal.

"What does your sister look like?" the leach asked.

Valyn shook his head. "I don't know. Tall. Thin. I haven't seen her in ten years. I was hoping to find a way to talk to her in Annur. . . ."

"You might get the chance a little early," Talal said, passing the lens back to Valyn and gesturing toward the valley. "I can't be certain, but that sure looks like a woman with burning eyes."

Valyn stared at the leach, then reached over for the lens. There were half a dozen riders, followed by a dozen or so men on foot. It took him a moment to find the range and focus, but when he finally managed it, a figure on horseback leapt into view. She sat her horse proudly, back straight as a spear, but it was clear within heartbeats that she wasn't really comfortable on her mount; she rode the poor creature as though it were a palanquin, not swaying at all to accommodate the beast's gait, sitting hard and low in her saddle, as though her legs could no longer hold her up.

Adare.

Despite the long years, he recognized his sister at a glance. Even without Intarra's eyes, he would have known her. She was older, of course, a woman instead of a girl, but she had the same lean build, the same angularity to her features, the same honey-pale skin—shades lighter than either Valyn's or Kaden's, except . . . He squinted through the lens. It was hard to be certain at the distance, but it looked as though a delicate tattoo ran down one side of her face, a few graceful lines that seemed to glow in the sunlight, starting beneath her hair and swirling down her neck into her robes.

He shifted the lens to consider those robes more fully. His sister finally seemed to have shed the dresses she spent her childhood cursing. The golden cloth of her clothing was rich enough for any princess's gown, but cut in the austere style of an imperial minister, trimmed at the collars and shoulders with black. The shifting fashions of the Dawn Palace, the subtle social signaling of wardrobe, had never much interested Valyn, but Adare's clothes spoke of authority, even command. That, and the armed men escorting her.

"What in Ananshael's sweet name," he muttered, lowering the long lens, "is Adare doing with an army on the march?"

"Does it matter?" Laith asked. "This is what we wanted, right? She can tell us what's going on. Forget the old plan. We go to her first, see if Long Fist's been selling us shit and calling it fruit. Then, if it still comes to taking down the regent, it might help to have a little royalty on our side."

"Valyn is royalty as well," Talal pointed out.

Laith snorted. "Valyn's a traitor, same as the two of us."

†

Watching Adare from the tree line through a long lens was one thing; getting close enough to her to talk quite another. A young soldier on horseback met Valyn's sister on the road, bowed, face pressed against the pommel of his saddle, straightened up when she waved a hand, talked with her a moment, then bowed again before leading her forward.

Valyn glanced over at the other riders. Just behind his sister rode two soldiers, one, a young warrior with a bronze helm and a stern face that might have been chipped from marble, the other a grizzled Aedolian, hand on the pommel of his broadblade, eyes scanning the surrounding terrain. At Adare's side rode an old woman and an even older man, both gray-haired and stooped in the shoulders. Valyn didn't recognize any of them, but they were making straight for the tents of the army encampment.

"Bunking with the troops," Talal observed. "Good for morale."

"Not exactly 'with the troops,' " Laith noted after a pause.

Adare was threading her way through the tents, aiming for the large pavilion at the very center. *Her* pavilion, Valyn realized, an uneasiness settling in his gut. Not the *kenarang's*.

"Shit," he muttered. "It would have been easier to get at her in town."

"We're not going to be fighting our way into the middle of an encamped Annurian field army," Talal agreed.

Valyn chewed on the problem as Adare approached her pavilion, pointed at something, then kicked her horse into motion once more. The soldiers bowed as she passed, and Adare nodded back, dismounting before a different tent, one half the size of her own, but still large compared with all the rest. Even in the gathering dark, Valyn could see just fine, but seeing the camp didn't make it any easier to penetrate. He could watch Adare all he wanted; what he needed was to get close enough to talk.

"Who wants to play dress-up?" Laith asked. "I figure a cook could get into her tent. Or a cleaning slave. Or a whore."

Valyn shook his head. "You don't know the Aedolians," he replied. "They won't just wave through anyone with a porcelain platter. Those bastards check everyone who enters. Even if I ditch my swords, I'm not sure I'll pass as a cook. Or a whore."

"If we had a bird," Laith observed tartly, "you could just drop through the 'Kent-kissing roof."

"We don't have a bird," Valyn replied.

"Getting into the camp itself shouldn't be hard," Talal said. "We've got the armor we stripped off that messenger."

Valyn considered the idea for a moment. It was bold, but then, most good plans were bold. He had an Annurian horse, Annurian armor, Annurian accent. On the other hand, his burned-out eyes were immediately recognizable. There was no way to know how much communication had taken place between il Tornja and the Eyrie, no way to know what lies the *kenarang* had fed his sister, no way to know whether or not the guards around Adare's tent even knew what he looked like. There were scores of questions and precious few answers.

"I could get past the other pickets easily enough," Valyn said slowly. "It's dark, and men at those posts are just normal legionaries." He shook his head. "The Aedolians are the problem. If il Tornja is half the strategist everyone says, he'll be guarding against us, which means the Aedolians will be guarding against us. They'll know what I look like, which means they'll know what you look like, too."

"I'll tell you," Laith grumbled, "I'm getting pretty sick of the fucking Aedolian Guard. If they're not off in the 'Shael-spawned mountains trying to murder the Emperor, they're swarming all over the two people on this continent that we need to get close to." He turned to glare at Valyn, as though the whole thing were his fault. "When do they go away? Or do they wipe your ass every time you take a shit?"

Valyn was about to snap out a sharp retort when he paused. "No," he replied after a moment, raising the long lens to his eye once more, "they don't."

"Don't go away?"

"Don't wipe your ass. At least, they didn't when I was a kid. Back in the Dawn Palace they would station themselves outside the privy chamber. They never came in."

Talal pursed his lips. "I see where you're headed with this, but we're not in the Dawn Palace. Whatever latrine Adare uses will be ringed with Aedolians, same as her tent. You'll have as much trouble getting into one as the other."

"The difference is," Valyn said, pointing to the soldiers below who had begun digging a hole a dozen paces from Adare's tent, "that I'm not going to have to get inside. I'm going to *start* inside."

✝

By the time Valyn had threaded his way past the outer sentries, picketed his horse with the other animals, then talked his way through the inner guard, he was sweating, despite the cool night breeze. Fortunately, just about everyone in the camp looked half dead on their feet—they were resting now, but evidently il Tornja had been pushing them even harder than Valyn realized—and the guardsmen waved him through with little more than a glance at his Annurian armor and a few cursory questions. It seemed a crude sort of vigilance, but effective enough in its rough way. Even after being waved through, Valyn had to remind himself to walk slowly, to emulate the weary plodding of the other legionaries, to look at the muddied ground before him instead of glancing over his shoulder.

They're exhausted, he reminded himself, *and you're just one more soldier among thousands. And it's night.*

He offered up a small prayer of thanks to Hull for the darkness. Though he could see quite clearly, the night hid his face and his eyes from the Annurians. Now that he was past the picket, no one was likely to challenge him unless he approached the Aedolians around Adare's pavilion. By the time he reached her tent, he had grown almost accustomed to his near-invisibility, and paused for a moment outside the pools of light cast by the torches to size up her guard.

Had he been optimistic enough to hope that the Aedolians might slacken their vigilance while surrounded by more than twenty legions, he would have been disappointed. A pair of men in full plate flanked the doorway while eight more surrounded the tent, two at each corner, back to back, facing out into the night: a double diamond. The position was simple, but nearly impenetrable—double sight lines, redundant postings, physical contact between pairs. . . . There were ways to break it, and Valyn had studied them, but each required multiple attackers and ranged weapons. With his full Wing he could probably get inside, but the odds of emerging again were pretty long. And il Tornja's pavilion was likely to be the same. The thought made his palms start sweating all over again, and with an effort he shoved it aside.

Do what you came to do, he reminded himself. *The* kenarang's *time will come.*

He stepped away from the torchlight and walked back into the chaos of the camp, stealing glances at the soldiers as he passed. He recognized insignia from the Thirty-third Legion, the Fourth, and the Twelfth, plus a few he couldn't quite recall. The composition of a field army tended to be somewhat fluid. Legions rotated in and out, and the individual men comprising the Army of the North would vary considerably over the course of a decade or so.

He circled around Adare's latrine to approach from the opposite direction. Standard legion procedure placed the long lines of latrines on the camp's perimeter, but then, standard legion procedure didn't account for a princess in the midst of so many military men. Adare's presence had forced the camp commander to improvise on the established pattern, setting aside a small patch of earth for her personal use, surrounding it with a rough tent, and conscripting two weary soldiers from their normal duties to dig a deep hole for his sister's safety and comfort.

It was the weariness of the men that Valyn was counting on as he approached.

"All right, assholes," he said, stepping inside the canvas flap, "go eat your fucking chow."

The nearest legionary, a young man with a wine-stain birthmark across half his face, looked up with a scowl.

"And just who in the fuck are you?"

Valyn snorted. "You need a formal introduction? If you want to keep digging, by all means. . . ." He gestured toward the hole, then turned toward the tent's entrance.

"Hold up, friend," called the other. He was older than the first, and leaned on his shovel. The meager lamplight flickered off his sunburned scalp. "What'ya want?"

Valyn turned back, raised an eyebrow. "What I *want* is a nice sweet girl to suck my cock as I fall into a deep sleep, but what I get is Captain Donavic, may Ananshael bugger him bloody, sending me over here to spell you two lucky horsefuckers."

"Who's Captain Donavic?" demanded the younger man.

"Who fucking cares, Hellem?" said the older, climbing out of the hole and scrubbing ineffectually at the dirt on his clothes with a weary hand. "This fella here's good enough to offer to finish our work. . . ."

"Hardly *our* 'Kent-kissing work," the younger soldier spat. "If the Sons of Fucking Flame are so excited about the new Emperor, why aren't *they* digging her latrine?"

Valyn clamped down on his shock, even as the older man made a shhing motion with his hand.

"She's not *their* Emperor, Hellem. She is *the* Emperor. One of the captains hears you talking like this, you'll be lucky if you spend a week in the stocks."

Hellem shook his head, but lowered his voice. "Ain't right," he spat. "I'd follow the *kenarang* straight up Ananshael's arsehole, but this thing, the way he's going along with her . . . It ain't right."

"I don't recall them asking us," the older soldier said. "We signed on to march and to fight, not to do the figuring about politics and palaces. I'll tell you what we do: we obey. If the general says double-time, we kick it in the ass, and if he says dig a latrine, we dig a latrine." He paused wearily, glancing up at Valyn. "Unless, of course, there's someone else good enough to finish the job for us."

"Good enough?" Valyn demanded, trying to keep up the ruse even as he struggled to make sense of what he'd heard. "I'd let you bastards dig till the sun came up, I had my way, but then fucking Donavic would have me in the stocks all night, which is even worse than pushing a shovel so her royal majesty can shit her royal little shits in her own royal little hole."

The young soldier shrugged, then tossed his shovel onto the earth beside the hole. "You coulda come earlier," he grumbled, then pushed past Valyn and out the tent flap.

"What spiny rodent crawled up his asshole and died?" Valyn asked the remaining legionary as the canvas fell back into place.

"Don't mind him," the man replied, handing Valyn his own shovel. "Hellem just joined up. Thought the legions were all about big swords and doe-eyed girls in every town. . . ." He trailed off as he got a good look at Valyn's eyes for the first time.

Valyn shifted his grip on the shovel. He didn't want to hurt the old soldier, but one shout and the entire camp would be on him. Worse, if he failed here, it would mean all the earlier deaths—Blackfeather Finn, the messengers he'd killed—would be pointless, useless. It was a perverse sort of logic that argued for hurting the living in the name of the dead, but unless he was willing to give himself up, there was no way around it. With the flat of the shovel he could knock the man unconscious without killing him. Valyn planted his feet.

"Something happen to your eyes?" the man asked finally. There was curiosity in the words, but no nervousness. Valyn inhaled slowly; the air inside the tent was close, still, rich with freshly turned earth, but there was no stink of fear.

He relaxed slightly.

"Just the way Bedisa made 'em," he replied, forcing a shrug. "By day they're just brown, but they look darker at night."

The soldier considered him a moment longer, then clapped him on the shoulder. "None of my business. I thank you for the relief in here." He gestured toward the hole. "Truth is, there's not much left to dig—maybe another few feet. After that, it's just a matter of making it pretty."

"Never heard of a pretty latrine," Valyn said, turning toward the hole.

"I never heard of a princess coming along on a forced march," the soldier replied. "Thanks again, friend."

"Don't thank me," Valyn said. "Just save my ass if you see some Urghul trying to stick me with a spear."

The soldier was still chuckling as the canvas flap fell shut behind him.

Emperor, Valyn thought grimly. He'd expected to travel all the way to Annur, to find il Tornja on the Unhewn Throne and Adare shoved to the side, baffled and grief-stricken, provided she was still alive. Clearly he had underestimated his sister. Here she was in the middle of an army on the march, evidently *leading* that army, not to mention an entirely separate contingent of the Sons of Flame. That was one mystery solved, at least, though how Adare had come to command the loyalty of the religious order, he had no idea. According to Long Fist, she had murdered their Chief Priest.

He blew out a long, slow breath. He had hoped to find a willing if frightened ally in Adare. Instead, she had the full support of the Intarrans and Ran il Tornja both. She wasn't weeping for their father; she had replaced him. There was no way to be sure what it all meant, but he'd be shipped to 'Shael if it looked good.

With an effort, Valyn turned his attention to the task before him. The latrine had to look right, or Adare would refuse it, and so for the next hour he dug furiously, tamping down the earth around the hole, piling the stones neatly to the side, then arranging the elaborate wooden seat over the hole. The seat weighed half as much as Valyn himself. It was a ludicrous thing to bring on a campaign, and yet there it was, a concession to the tenderness of Adare's royal behind.

As he settled it in place, it occurred to him just how different their two experiences of the world must have been. While Valyn and Kaden had followed divergent paths, both of them had been trained, tested, and tempered by people and institutions utterly indifferent to their birth. Adare, on the other hand, quite obviously lived the pampered life of Annurian nobility. The thought kindled an unexpected anger inside him—he had seen his friends murdered, been forced, himself, to murder and treachery, all in service of the empire, all to avenge his father and protect his brother. Meanwhile, what had Adare been doing? Lounging in a private pavilion while footsore soldiers dug her privy.

He'd expected her to help change the newly imposed order, and suddenly it turned out that she *was* the newly imposed fucking order. It was even possible, he realized, a chill prickling his skin, that she'd been a part of the original plot. The sister he remembered from growing up hadn't seemed the scheming, murderous sort, but then, change had come for them all.

He shoved aside his suspicions and misgivings. There was no point speculating when he'd have the information that he needed within a few hours. He stowed the shovel at the base of one of the tent walls, then checked over the space a final time. He couldn't be sure exactly how it was supposed to look, but there weren't too many moving pieces to arrange. If he'd missed a detail, the blame would land on the soldiers he had relieved.

He nodded to himself, then stood on the wooden seat, reached up with his belt knife, and cut a slit in the canvas overhead. Careful not to tear the cloth further, he reached through, took hold of the tent's center pole, and slipped out through the roof into the night. The canvas sagged a bit, but it was guyed out tightly, and as long as he distributed his weight it seemed willing to hold him up. He checked over his shoulder. The roof of the tent obscured him from the paths immediately to the sides. He could see soldiers going about their business farther out, but the night was dark, he wore his blacks, and, as he looked over the camp, it began to rain, light at first, then heavy. It would make for cold, miserable waiting, but it knocked visibility down to a few paces at best—a good trade. He tucked his chin in his blacks and waited.

The Aedolians came first, lanterns held before them, the light shining off their wet, gleaming armor. It was the type of error the Kettral were trained to exploit: holding the lantern high meant that the flame would blot any night vision the guardsmen had managed to preserve. In an attempt to illuminate the shadows, they were destroying any ability they had to see what those shadows held. Valyn lay still, watching them approach, then looking down into the tent as they stepped inside, covering the rest of the hole with his body to avoid any leakage.

One guard glanced in the privy while the other prodded the shovel where it lay beneath the canvas walls.

"Left their tools," he observed.

The other shrugged. "Makes no difference to me."

Neither noticed Valyn. *Typical Aedolians,* Valyn thought. They could spend all night standing at attention in the driving rain outside Adare's tent, but when checking the privy neither of them thought to look up. After surveying the tiny space one last time, both men exited, presumably to take up their guard. Valyn was left alone with the drumming of the cold rain on the canvas.

It must have been near midnight when Adare finally stepped into the tent, cursing under her breath as she pushed back the sodden canvas, then wringing the rain from her hair. Valyn himself was soaked to the skin and shivering, but he forced the discomfort out of his mind, focusing instead on his sister.

She was both taller and thinner than she had appeared through the long lens, and up close Valyn could see the exhaustion scrawled across her face. She tried ineffectually to brush off her golden robe, then gave up with an exasperated sigh, letting the rain puddle on the floor as she stripped it off. To Valyn's surprise, she was wearing legion wool and leather beneath— higher quality, to be sure, than what was issued to the soldiers, but far more practical than the dress and jewels he had expected.

"Stubborn, 'Kent-kissing *fools,*" she muttered, shaking her head and fumbling with the button on her breeches as she crossed to the privy, evidently still incensed by an earlier conversation. "We'll have the local population at our throats before we even *get* to the Urghul. . . ."

Valyn shifted on the canvas slowly, sliding his head and shoulders through the hole.

Water sluiced through as he changed position, splattering the inside of the tent. Adare looked up, scowl on her face, and Valyn dropped, flipping in midair to land on his feet. She had just opened her mouth to scream when he clamped an arm across her throat, cutting off the cry and air alike.

She started to thrash, but he buckled her legs with a quick knee and she folded to the damp dirt.

"I'm Valyn," he hissed into her ear. The rain on the canvas roof was loud enough to drown out anything but a shout, but he wasn't taking any chances. "Adare, it's Valyn. Your brother."

She went still. Then, just as he was about to relax his grip, she lunged forward, clawing at his arm with renewed fury. Grimly, he tightened his grip.

"I'll knock you out if I have to," he said. "Stop struggling. I'm not here to hurt you. I need to talk."

Once again her muscles went slack.

"I'm sorry I scared you," he went on. "I needed to talk to you, and this was the only way."

He eased up a little more. This time she didn't try to break free.

"What about riding into the camp and asking for me?" she demanded. Her voice was low, but rough with both fear and anger. "The Kettral teach you how to ask?"

"Not really, no. Besides, il Tornja controls the camp. I wouldn't make it ten paces inside the perimeter before someone clapped me in irons."

"You don't understand," she said.

"No, I don't. Not about this army, or the fact that you're marching at the head of it. That's why I came to you. Now, can I let you go? If I wanted to hurt you, you'd be hurt."

It came out more roughly than he'd intended, but Adare hesitated, then nodded.

Valyn loosed his grip and she yanked free, rounding on him, eyes blazing. He could almost feel the heat. Adare opened her mouth as though to scream, and he tensed, ready to seize her once more. When she spoke, however, her voice was quiet but wire-tight.

"So you really have turned traitor. I didn't want to believe it."

He shook his head wearily. "That's what they told you. It's not true."

"Really?" She cocked her head to one side. "Why don't you tell me the truth?"

Valyn glanced toward the door of the tent. He had no idea how much time Adare habitually spent in the privy, but sooner or later the Aedolians outside would start to wonder. Probably sooner.

"We don't have time," he said. "I escaped the Islands to go after Kaden."

"To kill him."

"To *protect* him. Micijah Ut and Tarik Adiv were already there. They'd murdered the monks and were hours away from doing the same to Kaden."

"And you saved him."

He nodded.

Adare spread her hands. "So where is he?"

"Elsewhere," Valyn replied. "Trying to figure out the same thing I am: who killed our father." He watched her reaction, trying to read her face as she licked her lips, glanced toward the door, then locked eyes with him once more. He could smell her raw nerves, but also something else, something deeper. Defiance? Resolve?

"Ran il Tornja," she said finally. "The *kenarang* killed Father."

His heart lunged in his chest like a dumb beast. Fury ached in his veins. In the days since Balendin first named il Tornja a murderer, Valyn had felt the rage growing like a sick plant inside him, but his doubt had checked that rage, stunted it. It was impossible to trust the leach. Balendin was a liar. Valyn had repeated the words over and over to himself as they crossed the steppe, then the river, then the deep forests around the Thousand Lakes. *Balendin lies. Wait until you know the full truth. Balendin lies.*

And now, like a blade to the face, here was the truth. For a moment he stood motionless, awash in the full flood of his anger, ready, almost, to burst from the tent, cut down the Aedolians, and go hunting for the *kenarang* in the midst of the army itself. Slowly, slowly, he brought himself under control. He would kill Ran il Tornja, but he needed more information to do it right, to be sure.

"So," he said slowly, voice ragged, "Long Fist and Balendin weren't lying after all." He shook his head. "What are you doing here, with him? What is the whole 'Shael-spawned Army of the North doing here? Why are people calling you *Emperor*?"

She ignored the questions. "You were with Long Fist?"

"He's the one that warned me about il Tornja. I had to hear it from the fucking *Urghul*."

"No," Adare said, shaking her head. "No, you've got it wrong. The situation is more complicated than you realize."

"What's to get wrong?" Valyn demanded. "The *kenarang* murdered our father. A military coup. Seems pretty straightforward to me."

"Ran killed him," Adare snapped, "because Sanlitun was killing the empire, or letting it die, at any rate. Your friend Long Fist has been plotting an invasion and now he's invading. That's why the army is here." She glared at him. "Or didn't he tell you that part when you were chatting over a cup of *ta*?"

Valyn opened his mouth to retort, then stopped himself. He had expected Adare to either confirm or dispute Long Fist's claim; the idea that she might do both at the same time had not occurred to him. His mind traveled back to that enormous camp north of the White River, to the tens of thousands of horsemen massed within miles of the Annurian border. The shaman had claimed it was a defensive force, but he could have lied.

"Even if Long Fist is attacking," he said slowly, "how does an Urghul threat justify treason and murder?"

"Sweet Intarra's light, Valyn," Adare spat, "you think I didn't struggle with that question? You think it hasn't been at me like a knife stuck in my ribs every 'Kent-kissing day?" Her body was rigid, almost trembling. She looked like she might lash out at him or start sobbing. Maybe both. "I loved our father, loved him more than you ever did, off playing soldier on your tropical islands. *I'm* the one who talked to him about taxation, military levies, canal rights, the price of a fucking bushel of rice. I'm the one who actually knew him. I'm the one who had to see him put in the 'Kent-kissing *ground,* and now you *presume* to arrive in the middle of the night, a knife to my back, and lecture me about our father, about what we owe to his memory." Her teeth were bare, as though she were going to rip out his throat, but her voice, when she spoke again, was quiet, tight as a bowstring. "Il Tornja tried to convince our father of the danger, but he failed. Father was a good emperor in peacetime. He was a *great* emperor, but he underestimated the military threat."

"It was the *kenarang*'s job to demonstrate that threat, to guard against it."

Adare shook her head. "Father wouldn't let him. He said any troop movement to the north was provocation." She stabbed a finger into his chest. "Look, the murder of the Emperor is treason. I will grieve for him the rest of my life, more than you will ever fucking understand, but our father was only *one man,* Valyn. How many more people will die if Annur falls to the Urghul? Your horse-riding friends are probably across the river right *now,* hammering south through the Lakeland. That territory is basically undefended because our father *left* it undefended."

"It's still a military coup," Valyn replied. "There were other ways to handle the problem. Ways that didn't involve murder and treason. Il Tornja went after me, too, Adare. He went after *Kaden.* It wasn't just about protecting Annur—he's trying to annihilate the entire Malkeenian line." He paused, eyeing her. "Except for you, evidently."

Adare hesitated, face twisted with confusion. For the first time, Valyn smelled doubt on her, heavy as forest rot after a week of rain. "That wasn't him," she said finally. "He told me he didn't go after the two of you."

"Oh, he *told* you. It must be the truth. Somehow the First Shield of the Aedolian Guard and the Mizran Councillor crossed half of Vash with a contingent of soldiers, all with the express purpose of murdering the new emperor, and somehow the *kenarang*-regent, the man who already admitted to murdering the *last* emperor, had nothing to do with it?"

Adare took a deep breath, then straightened her spine. "Even if he did, it doesn't matter."

Valyn gaped. "It doesn't *matter*? Tell me how it doesn't fucking *matter*, Adare! When men come for you in the night, when people paid by the *kenarang* kill people you love to get at you, when they tear apart your entire world, why don't you tell me then how it doesn't matter."

"I didn't mean—"

He cut her off. "I know what you *mean*: it's best for Annur; we need the *kenarang;* sacrifice for the greater good." He spat into the packed dirt. "Fuck that. *Fuck* that. Il Tornja might be telling the truth and he might be lying. I don't give a shit. He murdered our father. He murdered Ha Lin— indirectly, but he killed her all the same—"

"Ha Lin?" she asked.

"Never mind," Valyn said grimly, reining in his rage. "He's guilty. And I'm going to see him dead."

Adare's lips tightened. "You can't."

"Because of what?" Valyn demanded. "Because of this?" He waved a hand at the wide camp beyond the walls of the tent. "I spent ten years, Adare, *ten years* learning to get past this. Here I am, talking to you, right now. I can get to il Tornja. I can get to him, and I can put a knife into his heart."

"I don't mean the army," she said. "Maybe you're right. Maybe he deserves to die, but you can't do it *now*. Maybe you haven't been paying attention, but there is a *battle* coming, and whatever Long Fist tells you, it is *not* a fight Annur went looking for. He is not just another tribal chief, Valyn. For the first time *ever* the Urghul are united, united and right on our border. Long Fist did that. He systematically crushed everyone who opposed him, and a *lot* of Urghul opposed him, at least at first. He is coming, bringing with him his blood worship, his human sacrifice . . . he is *coming* with close to a million warriors, and someone needs to stop him."

She stared at him, panting. Rain hammered at the roof of the tent.

"Whatever il Tornja has done," she continued finally, "the man is a genius, beyond brilliant. The best general in ten generations. The soldiers will follow him anywhere, do anything for him." She shook her head. "You think I'd leave him alive if he was just another power-hungry soldier? He *murdered* our father, Valyn, cut him down in cold blood. When I thought that Uinian was responsible, I saw the bastard burned to char in his own temple, and I would do it again, but we *can't*. The Urghul are here. They have the numbers. They have the horses. They have the jump on us, and all we have is Ran il Tornja. I hate him, Valyn. Only the Lady of Light knows how much I hate him, but we *need* him. If we don't have him, the Urghul *win*."

Valyn stared. Whatever else she had done, Adare clearly believed what she was saying. Unfortunately, people held mistaken beliefs all the time. "There are other generals," he said softly, trying to make her understand.

"Not like him," Adare replied, voice hardening. She gestured beyond the walls of the tent. "Did you see the dam, what he's doing with the dam?"

Valyn shook his head. "I don't give a *shit* what he's doing with the 'Kent-kissing dam. . . ."

"And *that*," she said, "is why we need him. Because people like you and me don't think the way he does. He's been leading men, fighting battles for . . ." She hesitated, something that might have been fear passing across her face. ". . . a long time, Valyn. I can't let you kill him. After we've stopped the Urghul, all right, but not before. Not now."

"You can't *stop* me, Adare."

She nodded. "I can shout."

"I can kill you."

"You're really threatening to murder your own unarmed sister?"

"I'm going to see this through."

Adare blanched at something in his expression, but she held her ground. "If you kill me, you'll fail. The Aedolians will find my body, they'll know it was you, and they'll double the guard around the *kenarang*. Triple it."

Valyn hesitated. She had him there. Despite his bold declarations, getting to il Tornja was already going to be nearly impossible. Without the element of surprise, he'd have no chance.

"Listen," Adare said, setting a hand on his arm for the first time. "Just wait. Let the army get north. Let us fight the battle with il Tornja. Then I'll *help* you take him down."

"Just a few minutes ago," Valyn said, narrowing his eyes, "you were defending the man."

"Just a few minutes ago," Adare replied evenly, "I didn't know the full depth of his treachery, didn't know that he'd come after you and Kaden. I love Annur, but I loved our father, too. We need the *kenarang* now. We can use him. But we won't always need him."

Valyn weighed the words. He hadn't expected his sister to be so ruthless and hardheaded, but her argument made sense, especially if Long Fist really was bringing that army over the Black. Killing the general would destroy morale, and putting an untested commander in charge could mean the difference between victory and defeat. He thought back to Long Fist, to the tracery of scar covering the shaman's flesh, to the predatory look in his eye. Ran il Tornja wasn't the only killer that needed watching, that much was sure. So much the better if the two destroyed each other.

"Where is he hoping to fight them?"

"The north end of the lake," Adare said. "A small town called Andt-Kyl. That's where the Urghul intend to cross the Black. Il Tornja says it's the last chance to bottle them up before they get into the empire."

Valyn shook his head. "You'll never get there in time. It's all bog and balsams out there. Nothing even resembling a road."

"The *kenarang* knows what he's doing, Valyn," Adare said.

Valyn nodded slowly. "All right then. Andt-Kyl. He fights in Andt-Kyl, and when the fighting is over, he dies there."

"You don't need to go north," Adare said. "You could wait here. Kill him when the army comes back south."

Valyn shook his head. "No. Battles are baffling things. Units end up dead or out of place. People get lost. The best chance to take him down will be right after, in all the confusion."

The insane thing was that the plan could actually work. The chaos just following the fight would give him as good a chance as any. Certainly it would be easier than killing him in the center of his own meticulously staked-out camp.

"Just make sure you wait for the *end* of the battle," Adare insisted.

Valyn nodded. A few more days. Just a few more days until he put a blade in the *kenarang*'s back. He could wait a few more days.

He stepped up on the privy, ready to climb back through the canvas, then paused, turning to face Adare. Her eyes blazed.

"One more thing," he said. "Kaden isn't dead. The throne is his. And when this is all over, you're going to give it back."

39

"Black suits or no black suits," declared Trevor Larch, the massive man with a huge brown beard who served as the mayor of Andt-Kyl, "it doesn't matter."

He already towered over the Flea, and, as though to emphasize both his words and his height, he took a step closer, stabbing a finger into the Wing leader's chest. It was the last thing they needed. Long Fist was out there somewhere, driving his blood-mad horsemen across the Black, and here they were, wrangling with the head man of some no-account town on the puckered asshole of the empire. Worse, it seemed as though half the town had turned out in the central square to see the huge bird land and watch the ensuing showdown.

"We're more'n capable of taking care of our own up here"—poke—"so why don't you fly on south"—poke—"back where you came from."

The Flea didn't say anything. Didn't move. " 'Sides," the mayor went on, puffed up with his obvious success, "don't know what shit-eating bureaucrat decided it was a good idea to let women do the fighting, but I'll tell you one thing and I'll say it once so listen hard."

"I'm listening," the Flea said quietly.

Larch frowned at the tone, then raised his voice loud enough that the whole crowd could hear. "I've been running this town twenty-three years, I don't take orders from anyone, and certainly not," he concluded, stabbing a thick finger at Gwenna, "from some wench half my age who thinks carrying a sword makes her a man." He chuckled at the thought. "I'd fuck her maybe," he said, spreading his arms, getting some chuckles from the crowd, "but not follow her." He turned back to the Flea, poked him in the chest again. "You got that?"

The Flea nodded, then stabbed him in the neck.

Larch dropped like a sack of rocks, blood spattering the dirt of the central square. Gwenna could only stare. There had been no warning, no escalation. Just stillness followed by death followed by stillness. Then Pyrre started laughing.

"All right," she said, "maybe we *could* learn to work together."

The people of Andt-Kyl took a few more heartbeats to believe what they saw, and then another man, this one shorter but even broader than Larch, came at the Flea with a long knife and a roar.

The Flea killed him, too.

Gwenna reached over her shoulder for her blades, but Newt stopped her with a firm hand.

"Don't make it a fight," he murmured.

Gwenna stared, first at the Flea, then at the Aphorist. "He's the one doing all the killing," she hissed.

"Killing isn't fighting," Newt replied. "These poor folks, they've never seen anything like this. Don't know what to make of a man on a bird stabbing their mayor. Don't know how to respond. If *we* draw, though . . ." He pursed his lips. "Starts to look like a brawl, and in these log towns, if there's one thing they know, it's brawling."

It went against every instinct Gwenna had, but she lowered her hand. None of the other Kettral had so much as twitched. The Flea glanced down at the corpses at his feet, then over the crowd. When he spoke, the words didn't sound loud, but he pitched his voice to carry.

"The Urghul are coming. You're going to stop them."

That sent an eddy of confusion and discontent through the crowd. Several straggling refugees from the tiny hamlets to the northeast had already stumbled into Andt-Kyl, cradling wounds and bringing stories of burned farms and murdered families. Somehow, though, the townspeople weren't alarmed. They seemed to think it was a matter of raiding parties, rather than an entire army bearing down upon them.

"*You* stop them," someone shouted from the crowd. "You're the fighters. We're just here for the lumber."

"You won't be here at all," the Flea said, "after the horsemen come through. They will kill most of you and keep the rest to sacrifice slowly, with steel and fire, to Meshkent. They will burn your town to ash. People at the south end of Scar Lake, all the way in Aats-Kyl, will hear you screaming." He shrugged. "You could run, but they'd ride you down. They might pass by if you hide in the marsh. It's been a long time since I was in a log town, but I didn't take logmen for a bunch of runners and hiders."

"We're not running," said a young man, thinner than Larch had been, but quite a bit taller than the Flea. He held a hooked peavey in one hand, the tool's steel spike bright in the sunlight, but he leaned on it rather than using it as a weapon. "We're not running, but we've got a way of doing things here, and killing the mayor ain't it."

The Flea eyed the peavey, then the man holding it. "What's your name, son?"

"Bridger," he replied.

The Flea nodded. "Good name." He looked over the people assembled, pointed at an old woman in greasy wool near the front. "What do you think of Bridger, here, mother?"

She frowned at the question, glanced over her shoulder for support, found none, then looked back at the Flea. "Good man."

"He get in fights?"

"Not much. Tends to keep to hisself. Quiet feller."

The Flea nodded. "I like quiet fellers. Bridger, you're the mayor."

Bridger frowned. "You can't just make me mayor."

"Just did. Pursuant to Emergency War Measure Fifty-six."

Gwenna leaned over to Newt. "What in 'Shael's name is War Measure Fifty-six?"

The Aphorist shrugged. "Something about taxation on grain, I think."

"So it doesn't . . ."

"Nope."

Bridger looked confused, but the Flea just patted him gently on the shoulder. "You're in charge of the town, Gwenna's in charge of you. If Gwenna dies, it's Annick, but try not to let Gwenna die."

"What about her?" the young man asked, nodding toward Pyrre.

"That's General Pyrre. Listen to her, too."

"Where are you going?"

The Flea pointed up into the shifting clouds. "Find some help."

"Help?"

"From down south."

"What if they don't come in time?"

The Flea shrugged. "Ask Gwenna. Like I said, she's in charge."

╋

Gwenna was tempted to stay on top of the beacon tower. The square stone structure stood atop a cliff on Andt-Kyl's western island, overlooking the lake. According to Bridger, the loggers lit fires in the wide stone pit at the tower's top to guide ships to the town's docks on stormy days. Gwenna didn't give a shit about the ships, but the tower offered an excellent vantage of the entire area. Just as importantly, it gave her a tiny measure of isolation.

After all the languages and tactics, the demolitions and archery, the conditioning and swordplay, Kettral training hadn't left much time for useful tips on how to lead six hundred rough frontier loggers in the defense of their town. Even on the Islands, Gwenna hadn't made a name for herself in the areas of charm and persuasion, and now that she suddenly found herself in charge of a baffled and restive local population, she almost wished she could just fight the Urghul alone. At least atop the tower, there was only Bridger and Annick to deal with. Pyrre was down below with the townspeople, maybe flirting with them, maybe killing them. Gwenna tried not to think about it, focusing, instead, on the local topography. That, at least, she had trained to understand.

Loggers had built Andt-Kyl at the small delta where the Black dumped into Scar Lake, a rough little town of log houses, log bridges, log temples, and log docks spread over two rocky islands at the river's mouth. It was clear at a glance why the Flea had chosen the spot to bottle up the Urghul. The horsemen would have to cross three separate forks of the river, each running dark and deep. The network of bridges linking the islands to each other and to the shores on either side would be easy to control and, where necessary, to destroy.

"So why in Hull's name is Long Fist crossing *here*?" Gwenna muttered.

"The only spot, sir," Bridger replied. He was handling the arrival of a Kettral Wing, the announcement of an Urghul army, the abrupt deaths of his mayor and constable, and his own elevation to the town's leading position about as well as could be expected, but he kept glancing at Gwenna warily when he thought she wasn't looking, and had settled almost immediately into referring to Gwenna and the others as "sir." She had no idea what to make of that, but she figured they had more pressing business than sorting out the honorifics. "Half a mile north," the young man was saying, "the Black bogs out. You could ride a thousand horses in there and not one of them would see the other side."

"What about a hundred thousand horses?" she asked grimly.

He shook his head. "They can't get across up there, not unless they go all the way into the mountains, and then it's all black flies and balsams packed so close you can't see through 'em. There's a few log camps up there, but that's it."

"Log camps?"

Bridger nodded. "A couple score men and ten thousand logs stacked up on the bank. We're late for the log drive this year. No bridges, though. No way across."

"And south is the lake," she said, looking out over the sheet of water to where it hazed into the sky at the horizon. "How long is it?"

"Not sure, exactly. Maybe fifty miles. Maybe more, with Aats-Kyl at the other end."

"So that's why the Urghul are coming here."

The logger looked at her. "Are there really a hundred thousand of them, sir?"

"Probably more," she spat, then immediately regretted it. For all that Bridger looked like some bruised-knuckled logger—all sun-browned skin and ropy arms, bushy beard, and leather on top of wool on top of more wool—he couldn't have been much older than her. She tried to imagine how she would have responded if she'd never joined up with the Kettral, if she'd stayed home on her father's farm and then one day, out of the blue, discovered that an invading army was a few days out, that she was the first and only line of defense. She was tempted to say something reassuring, but then, the assurance would probably just be a lie. "There's plenty to kill us all a dozen times over, if we fuck up."

His lips tightened, but he nodded. "Then we'd better not fuck up."

The most obvious thing was to destroy the east bridge, the one connecting the larger and flatter of Andt-Kyl's two islands to the eastern bank of the Black. There was nothing on that far shore but half a dozen miserable farms, the owners of which did some bitching and some moaning on the subject until Pyrre explained about the Urghul and their love for pain and blood. That got almost everyone across the bridge, all except for one stubborn old bastard who sat on his porch with a pair of sharpened felling axes and a great crock of whiskey, who spat on Gwenna's blacks when she told him he had to move.

She started to go after the man, but Bridger held her back.

"Leave him be," he murmured. "Pikker John'd rather die on his porch than run."

"I'm here to make sure people don't die," Gwenna said, furious at the old man's idiocy. She knocked Bridger's hand off her shoulder.

"Plenty of folks left to save," the young man replied, gesturing back toward the village. "Lot of work to be done, sir, and if you're right about them horsemen, not much time to do it."

They left Pikker John on his porch, honing his axes and taking the occasional pull on his crock. Gwenna told herself that at least the stubborn old bastard might kill one or two of the Urghul, but it felt like a failure. Long Fist hadn't even arrived and she'd already lost a man.

"We've got to blow this bridge," she said, sizing up the wooden span after they'd crossed back to East Island. The decking didn't look like much, rough-sawn lumber tacked down with crude-cut nails, but the whole thing was held up by a dozen pilings, each as thick as a tree, sunk deep in the silt on either side of the channel.

"Blow it?" Bridger asked.

Gwenna grimaced. Kettral munitions weren't exactly a secret—there were too many stories swirling around the world for that—but the Eyrie tried not to spread word of the explosives any further than necessary.

"Like burning it," Gwenna said, "only a lot faster."

"I'll get it taken care of," Bridger said.

"How?"

He smiled. "Those are logs. We're loggers." He jerked a thumb at one of the half-dozen men who trailed him. "Banders—get a group. Cut it down."

The man nodded, then trotted off.

"What about the pilings in the middle?" Gwenna asked. Most were sunk in the mud flats flanking the channel, but four plunged straight into the swift current of the water.

Bridger frowned. "Sunk those twelve years back," he said, "when winter froze the river hard enough to work. Probably can't get at 'em now, but with the rest chopped and the decking out . . ."

"Good," Gwenna said. "Do it." She turned to Annick. "Think that'll hold them?"

The sniper looked at the river, the wide mud flats on either side, then into the dark trees beyond.

"For a while. They can build a new bridge."

Gwenna frowned. She knew enough about bridge construction to understand how to destroy the things, but the time frame for building was a little murky. She turned to Bridger. "How long would that take? To rebuild?"

"Depends on the conditions, sir. And on how many bridges they've built."

"Not many," Gwenna said. "The Urghul are good at riding, shooting, and killing. Not much on engineering."

"Could take weeks, then."

Gwenna nodded. Il Tornja could march an army almost all the way from Annur in weeks. "And let's make sure that the conditions are particularly unpleasant. You have people in this town that can handle a bow?"

Bridger grinned. "This far north? If you're not logging, you're hunting. Got some women are better shots than the men. Kids can pull a bow, too."

"Good. Bring them to Annick. She'll oversee the defense of the east fork."

The sniper's jaw tightened. "I'm not certain I'm the best—"

"Neither am I," Gwenna snapped, "but we need archers, and you're the fucking sniper, so follow Bridger and figure it out."

†

The *kenarang*'s scouts arrived just a few hours later, a dozen hard-eyed men in light legionary armor who looked as though they'd been on the losing end of a battle with about four hundred feral cats. One of the villagers—Apper? Went?—brought them to Gwenna at the western end of the central bridge, where she was overseeing the building of yet another barricade, a fallback if they lost the east island.

"She's in charge," the logger said, pointing to Gwenna.

The lead scout, a thin man with a hawk's profile, narrowed his eyes, glancing over her blacks.

"Kettral?" he asked, obviously surprised. The men behind him shifted warily at the revelation, as though they expected to keel over or explode just from coming close. A few fingered the hilts of their short swords, despite the fact that they were all supposedly on the same side.

"No wonder someone made you a scout," Gwenna said. "You can recognize the color black."

The scout's lips tightened at the crack, but his voice remained level. "The *kenarang* told us there was no military presence this far north."

"Sounds like the *kenarang* needs to brush up on his intel," Gwenna replied. "He *does* know there's a massive Urghul army headed this way, doesn't he?"

She tried to keep her tone light, but her heart was hammering. It all depended on this. The presence of the scouts was good. It suggested il Tornja had been moving even before the Flea got to him. On the other hand, there was no telling how far ahead of the main body of the army the men were scouting. Even with the bridge destroyed, Gwenna had no illusions that she could hold the town forever. Long Fist was a bloodthirsty savage, but he wasn't an idiot, and he had the numbers. Eventually he would find a way across.

"The Army of the North is pushing hard," the leader replied. "My name is Jeril. I have orders to take control of the town. To prepare it against attack."

Gwenna tensed. She'd known it was coming from the moment the scouts arrived. Sending an advance guard was standard legion procedure: fifty or a hundred men unencumbered by all the apparatus of war, trained to travel light and move fast, men who could scout the necessary terrain, begin preparations for battle, and send back word to the bulk of the army behind. To the general. That was the ticklish bit. For all Gwenna knew, the men were here as much to deal with her and Annick as they were to prepare for the Urghul assault.

"Where are the rest of you?" she asked warily.

Jeril grimaced. "We're it."

"Twelve to hold off the whole Urghul army?" Gwenna asked. "You must be really fucking good."

"You haven't seen the terrain south of here," Jeril replied, shaking his head wearily. "It's a nightmare. The western track is flooded out with the runoff, and everything else is worse. It was tough enough getting a dozen men through, let alone a hundred."

"But somehow il Tornja's going to get a whole army up here?"

The man grinned for the first time. "The *kenarang*'s got his ways."

Gwenna raised an eyebrow. "Care to share?"

Jeril hesitated, then gestured toward the lake. "There's a dam at the south end. He's destroying it, probably has it destroyed by now."

Gwenna looked out over the lapping waves, trying to understand how blowing a dam fifty miles off was going to get the army north. She'd thought maybe the *kenarang* planned to use boats, but draining the lake would only . . . *Oh.* She shifted her eyes from the water to the shoreline.

A glistening width of mud and stone was visible just below the tangled bank. It was hard to be certain, but she didn't think it had been there earlier.

"He's draining the lake," she said, impressed in spite of herself.

Jeril nodded. "Not the whole thing—that would take weeks—but enough to march his army up along the coast."

Gwenna eyed the uncovered shelf of stone, sand, and mud once more. "It's wet," she said. "He'll have to wait at least a day for it to firm up."

Jeril nodded tensely. "It's going to be close."

Despite the genius of the plan, something about it bothered Gwenna, like a stalking shape half glimpsed through the trees. "The Urghul," she said, seeing it at last. "The Urghul will be able to use the same strip of land to press south along the eastern bank. They won't *need* to cross here."

Jeril nodded again. "But there are two things stopping them. First, they don't know the *kenarang*'s plan. As far as they're concerned, this might just be normal fluctuation in the water level. They might ride halfway down the eastern bank and find the lake rising again."

"Pretty fucking thin," Gwenna said, shaking her head. "Long Fist has enough men to spare a few thousand on a hunch."

"He can't," Jeril replied. "Not yet. A man on horseback is almost ten times heavier than one on foot, and the Urghul won't leave their horses. As the fringe of the lake bed starts to harden, the legions will be able to use it days before any cavalry."

Gwenna blew out a long slow whistle. "Holy Hull," she muttered, "he really is a genius."

Jeril smiled wearily. "No one sees his way through a battle like the *kenarang*. Sometimes I almost pity the bastards who have to fight him."

His last words dug at Gwenna like a dull knife. There was no knowing where Valyn was, or whether he'd even managed to intercept the army. It was possible he'd already murdered il Tornja, possible he'd tried and failed, was captive or dead, his head impaled on a pike in the center of camp as a warning to would-be traitors. The thought made her sick to her stomach, and with an effort she shoved it out of her mind, turning instead to the half-finished barricade rising at the end of the bridge.

"Higher," she called to the men lifting a log into place. "Those Urghul horses can clear that."

They looked at her skeptically, then nodded.

"How are you here?" Jeril asked, frowning. "If the *kenarang* didn't send you . . ."

"The legions react to problems," Gwenna bluffed. "It's our job to anticipate them."

The scout narrowed his eyes, then glanced over the work. "Well, you've made my job easier, for which I thank you, but we'll take it from here."

"Actually," Pyrre said, stepping out from behind the barricade, "Gwenna's doing a nice job. I'd recommend letting her keep at it."

Jeril frowned. "Who are you?"

"Pyrre Lakatur," the assassin replied, sweeping into a low bow. "I realize it's customary to add 'at your service,' but you Annurian military folk make the habitual mistake of thinking I work for you already, and I don't want to confuse matters."

Jeril started to respond, then shook his head, turning back to Gwenna. "Doesn't matter. I have orders to take command of the town."

Gwenna was half tempted to let him have it. She'd done her part. The eastern bridge was gone, the villagers were warned, the barricades were mostly built. She could hand the whole defense over and slip away before the *kenarang* arrived, figured out who she was, and put her head on a pole. She hesitated. Problem was, whatever the scout's background, he wasn't Kettral. She knew the training that legionary scouts went through, and, rigorous though it was, it paled beside her own. The Flea had put her in charge because he thought she could hold the town, and she found, to her surprise, that she intended to do just that.

"I have the command here," she said, knowing the words sounded cold, aggressive, but unsure how to warm them.

A grumble passed through the scouts behind Jeril. A few shifted wide, making room to draw swords, to fight.

"I can use you," Gwenna said, wincing inwardly at her own tone. "I'm glad you're here, but the command is mine."

Jeril's jaw tightened. "I have orders to remove—"

"The thing about orders," Pyrre said, stepping forward, arms crossed over her chest, "is that they absolve a woman from the responsibility of thinking her own thoughts." She glanced over at the scouts, then frowned. "Or a man, for that matter." She raised her eyebrows. "Have you fought against the Urghul, Jeril?"

The scout hesitated, then shook his head.

Pyrre shrugged. "Gwenna has. She infiltrated their camp, met with their commander, gauged their strength, then fought her way free."

Gwenna concentrated on keeping her mouth shut. The assassin's claims were barely true, but they seemed to be having an effect.

"Do you know the people of Andt-Kyl?" Pyrre continued, gesturing to the folk building the barricade behind them.

Another shake of the head.

"Gwenna does. She's been working with them for days now. They trust her. Which leads me to my third question: Do you love Annur?"

Jeril nodded tersely.

"Then why don't you do what's best for Annur? When your general gave you your orders, he didn't know that the Kettral were already here. If he had, your orders would have been different. Use that brain that Bedisa gave you. Hm?"

The scout glanced at the men behind him. By the hard set of their faces, they didn't care for either the assassin's tone or her suggestion, but they were military men. They would obey their officer.

"All right," Jeril said, turning to Gwenna. "I need to send two men back each day, one at dawn, one at dusk, to bring a report to the *kenarang*. The rest of us are yours."

┼

Gwenna looked into the predawn mist and steam rising off the bogs and ponds, streams and lakes to the east. It threaded through the balsams and pines like smoke, draped thick over the lake, brightening slowly as the sun rose from a wooly gray, to white, to dull orange, as though the whole forest had caught fire. Each morning for three days, she'd climbed the beacon tower, in part to survey the town's fortifications, in part to hunt for some sign of the Urghul, but mostly because it allowed her to be alone, to step outside of the throng of people for a few minutes, to leave behind the unending questions and requests, demands and complaints and pleas.

The whole thing was less of a shit-show than she'd expected, actually. The East Bridge had been hacked to kindling, save for the four final pilings thrust up from the channel like dead trees. Jeril and his scouts had been useful in overseeing the movement of all food and relevant supplies off East Island. Despite her hesitation, Annick had built up an impressive set of earthworks and barricades on the eastern shore of the island, and even now had half the village making arrows. Andt-Kyl's two forges had been ringing day and night as the blacksmiths pounded every scrap of extra metal—pot iron and scrap steel, barn hinges and old nails—into arrowheads. Some people had griped about that. Annick sent them to Bridger, Bridger sent them to Gwenna, and Gwenna sent them back to their homes with a few choice words and orders to scare up more steel.

It was exhausting trying to think through every aspect of the defense, and infuriating arguing with the loggers over every little point, but the hardest part was the worry, a sick, corrosive acid in her gut, a never-silent humming in her brain that refused to let her sleep more than a few hours each night, that made it hard to keep down anything more than a biscuit and water. Truth be told, she'd been frightened for weeks, ever since quitting the Islands, but that was a different kind of fear, one for herself and her Wing. The trainers had prepared her for that—*When you fight,* went the motto, *sometimes you die.* There had been no motto, though, for people who didn't expect to fight, for the loggers and farmers and fishermen who would end up on Urghul lances if Gwenna failed. The Eyrie had told her all about killing, but there hadn't been much about keeping tiny little villages at the end of the empire alive.

"Sir?" It was Bridger, stepping up through the trap onto the broad platform atop the tower. Above them, the flimsy wooden roof creaked. She glanced at it: the beams were rotted with damp, just about ready to collapse, but she had more pressing worries than the roof on the beacon tower. The battle wasn't shaping up to take place there.

"What?" she asked.

"We've moved the boats from the docks and anchored them just off the western shore of the lake, as you requested."

Gwenna turned. The fog had lifted enough for her to see the hulls bobbing peacefully as the water lapped up against the steep bank. She had no idea what to do with the boats, but it seemed like they might be useful and she didn't want them falling into Urghul hands if she lost East Island. That was strategy in a nutshell—doing things you didn't understand with the hope they might pay off later. And there were so many things she didn't understand. . . .

"You ever been in a fight, Bridger?" she asked.

The man hesitated. "Couple of times, down at the Duck. Had to get firm with some boys from down the south end of the lake."

Gwenna shook her head. Bar brawls. The whole Urghul nation hammering down on them, and she was leading a few hundred people whose best approximation of battle came from bar brawls.

"You ever kill anyone?" she asked.

He shook his head slowly. "I know you're worried, sir, but we're strong folk up here. Logging's hard work. Breeds hard men and harder women. I figure putting an ax in a man can't be that different from putting it in a tree."

They were brave words, given the circumstances, but they filled Gwenna with rage. She wanted to scream at him that felling some mountain pine was *nothing* like killing a man, wanted to tell him how it had felt when she stabbed the young legionary in the eye during the Kwihna Saapi, how he'd sobbed and pleaded before she killed him, and then, worse, sagged against her, slack, limp, like something that had never lived. She wanted to tell him about the Urghul camp, and the blood on her sword, in her eyes, sticky between her fingers. She wanted to tell him that even after eight years on the Islands poring over corpses and beating people bloody in the ring she still wasn't ready for it. He was watching her, dark eyes nervous.

Before she could respond, a shrill horn shivered the air to the east, then another, then another, then a thousand. An enormous flock of birds alighted, dark shapes wheeling in a great, swift circle, then flying west, south, and away. The horns kept on and on, coming and coming, until she thought they would drive her mad. When they finally stopped, however, the silence was even worse.

"Is that . . ." Bridger began.

"The Urghul," Gwenna said. "I guess the Flea didn't get to Long Fist."

It seemed as though she'd always known he wouldn't. Whatever the case, there was no time to worry about the older Wing Leader, not anymore.

"What do we do now?" Bridger asked.

"We fight. Make sure all the very old and young are off East Island and out of the way. Tell Annick to get the archers ready." It was a pointless order. Knowing Annick, the men and women probably had their bows half drawn by the second horn. Still, saying something made Gwenna feel like she was doing something.

Bridger nodded, turned, then Gwenna stopped him.

"It's not that different," she said.

He shook his head. "What's not?"

"Killing a man. Felling a tree. Just hit it with the ax until it goes down. Not that different."

The logger smiled shakily. "Thank you, sir. We know how to hit things with axes, here."

Gwenna turned back to the dark trees lining the eastern bank before he could see the lie in her eyes. Maybe she should have told him the truth, maybe he deserved that, but with Long Fist somewhere back in those dark shadows, the truth didn't look likely to do anyone a 'Kent-kissing bit of good.

40

"N eutral ground" turned out to be a dilapidated wooden ware-house down by the docks, a huge, cavernous place stacked ceiling high with crates and barrels, reeking of salt, and tar, and mold. Pulleys and tackle hung silently from the rafters overhead, ropes as thick as Kaden's wrist ending in great steel hooks. It was only the apparatus necessary to the movement and storage of heavy cargo, but late at night, in the flickering light of their storm lantern, the silent lengths of rope with their rusting tackle seemed morbid, menacing. Gabril had offered to host the secret meeting in his own palace, but the others had refused, insisting on neutral ground. That insistence, too, seemed menacing.

The three of them, Kaden, Kiel, and Gabril, paused just inside the door, allowing their eyes to adjust to the darkness.

"You must remember," Gabril murmured, "that these people hate your empire, but their hatred bubbles up from different wells."

"But you're all in agreement," Kaden replied. "You see eye to eye on the basic issues?"

The First Speaker frowned. "For a long time we hoped to fight the same foe."

"Not the same thing," Kiel observed quietly.

"It is a bond," Gabril said.

Kiel shook his head. "A tenuous one, and delicately balanced. I have seen it plenty of times."

Gabril turned to stare at the Csestriim. They had been working together for days, since Kaden's visit to the First Speaker's palace, and the two had developed a delicate verbal dance, Gabril trying to ferret out Kiel's history while Kiel deftly deflected the questions, always turning the conversation away from himself.

"You claim to have seen a great many things," the First Speaker said.

Kiel shrugged. "I watch carefully. The point here is that a common foe makes for a fragile foundation. A single shift in the balance and alliances crumble."

"A shift?" Kaden asked. "We're about to take a sledge to the whole political edifice."

"And we would do well to hope it doesn't fall upon us," Kiel replied.

Gabril shook his head. "Hope is for fools, but your councillor is right. I have shared *ta* and unleavened bread with these men and women, but there are those here tonight who would stab me in an eyeblink. Or you, if they see an advantage."

"Remind me what keeps us from getting stabbed?" Kaden asked.

"This," Gabril said, tapping his skull with his fingernail. "These," gesturing to his knives.

"And this," Kiel added, patting the leather case at his side.

Kaden took a deep breath and nodded. The work of the last few days felt a flimsy aegis, a few words inked on parchment, but if those words failed, it seemed unlikely that Gabril's smarts or his skills with those knives would keep them safe.

⸸

The three of them were, by design, the last to arrive. *Better to be waited upon,* Gabril insisted, *than to wait.* Such blatant disrespect struck Kaden as an odd way to win a dozen suspicious nobles over to his side, but Kiel had agreed with the First Speaker, and so they had delayed their arrival enough that as they approached the center of the warehouse they found a small open circle from which the barrels and crates had been shoved aside. Someone had lit a few lamps around the perimeter and arranged a few of the lower crates as seats, but, with the towering stacks of merchandise on all sides, the space felt like the ill-lit bottom of a deep well.

The people there, most dressed in nondescript, deep-hooded cloaks like Kaden himself, sat or stood uneasily, as though trying to keep as much space between themselves as possible. A few held muttered conversations, but all conversation stopped when Gabril stepped into the circle of light.

For a moment, no one said anything. Then a wiry gray man, his face badly pitted by some childhood pox, leveled a finger at the First Speaker.

"You endanger us all by calling this meeting. Your notes—"

"—were coded," Gabril said, shaking his head. "As they always are, Tevis."

The man knocked the explanation aside with an impatient hand. "The tyrant could have broken our codes. . . ."

Gabril started to respond, but Kaden stepped forward into the lamp-light. "The tyrant is right here," he said, pushing back his hood, turning his head slowly, allowing everyone a nice long look at his eyes. For one heartbeat, two, three, there was no response. Then Tevis was reaching for the rapier at his side while two or three others broke out in exclamations, part fear, part anger.

"Traitor!" Tevis snarled at Gabril, his slender blade bare.

"You are startled," Gabril said, laying his palms slowly on his knives, "and so I will allow you one chance to unsay what you have said."

Tevis's eyes darted from Gabril to Kaden then back.

"What is he doing here? Where did he come from? Explain this!"

"I would have to imagine, Tevis," a new voice drawled, "that the boy came here to do just that. Unfortunately, you waving your skinny little wand in his face seems to be . . . what is the word you educated folk use? *Impeding* the explanation? Is that it?"

Kaden tilted his head to consider a very fat woman reclining in the shadows. Unlike many of the others, she seemed to have made little effort to disguise her identity. She wore a sumptuous green dress, sparkling rings on every finger, golden bangles around her wrists, and a pendant necklace draped across her enormous bosom. Kaden guessed her to be somewhere in her mid-fifties, but she had the rich, smooth skin and hair of a much younger woman.

From Gabril's description, she could only be Kegellen, the sole person in the room not descended from nobility. According to the First Speaker, she was the Annurian *akaza,* the lord of the criminal underworld, absolute master of everything from smuggled goods to imperial bribery to assassi-nation. She hardly looked the part, but then, Kiel hardly looked like an immortal Csestriim historian. The important thing was that she had power—more power, if Kiel and Gabril were right, than any of the assembled nobles, at least inside the city of Annur. She could be a crucial ally, if they could convince her.

Tevis rounded on the woman, rapier still drawn. "And the fact that you're here, defending him, is an indication of just how low this council has sunk." He spat onto the dry dirt. "I swear to Intarra, Kegellen, if you lived in Nish, I would have seen you hung a dozen years ago."

The fat woman just yawned, holding a puffy hand to her mouth. "A good thing, then," she said as she lowered it, "that I don't live in Nish." She turned her attention back to Kaden. "Now, Gabril, my beautiful boy, why don't you explain to this august assembly where you found our most noble Emperor? I promise Tevis will sit down and listen politely . . ."

"I will do no such—" the man began, but the woman talked right over him.

". . . or I will have my ministers cut off his shriveled testicles and feed them to him in a broth of brandy and ginger."

Tevis's eyes bulged. "You don't frighten me, you fat bitch," he began, but another man, shorter, with a wide face and fleshy nose, hauled him hastily to a seat on one of the crates, whispering something furiously in his ear. Tevis glanced back at the woman, hesitated a moment, then shook off his companion. Rage twisted his face, but Kaden noted that he did not stand, nor did he speak again. The others watched the woman warily.

Kegellen ignored them all. "Now," she said, spreading her hands in invitation, "Gabril, you delicious rock of a man, why don't you explain where you found yourself an emperor?"

Gabril shook his head. "The Malkeenian will speak for himself."

Kaden breathed out a slow, quiet breath, then stepped forward. Gabril and Morjeta had warned him of the difficulties entailed in his plan, warned him dozens of times over, and while Kaden had understood those difficulties intellectually, the true challenge of what he faced was only now setting in. The nobles were already clawing at each other's eyes; there was every chance that the offer he'd come to make would lead to blood on the floor of the warehouse, but there was no going back now.

"My name is Kaden hui'Malkeenian, son of Sanlitun hui'Malkeenian, the Scion of Light, the Long Mind of the World, Holder of the Scales, and Keeper of the Gates. I am the heir to the Unhewn Throne."

"Nice list," said a tall, broad man with a huge, red-gold beard—Vennet, according to Gabril's description. "You come here to rub our faces in your pretty polished titles?"

Kaden fixed the speaker with his burning eyes, waiting until he looked away. "No, Vennet," he said quietly. "I came here to tell you I am done with them."

Glances darted like swallows in the dark silence that followed, men and women sizing up Kaden and then one another, tempted to see their own advantage in his words, but wary and uncertain.

Tevis narrowed his eyes. He had slipped his rapier back into its sheath, but kept one hand on the pommel.

"What do you mean by *done*?"

"Just that," Kaden replied evenly. "I am giving up the titles. Giving up the Unhewn Throne."

Kegellen pursed her lips, flicked absently at one of her dangling earrings with a fingernail. "Giving them," she asked mildly, "to whom?"

Kaden shook his head. "To no one. Perhaps I misspoke. I said I was giving them up. What I meant was that I plan to destroy them."

The air in the room went suddenly taut as the summer sky before a storm. Kaden shifted his eyes from one face to the next, watching the reactions, memorizing them—the twitch of an eyelid here, a jaw clenched, a fingernail picking nervously at a fleshy knuckle. Tevis's lips were drawn back in a half snarl, a cornered animal uncertain whether to attack or flee. Kegellen twisted a golden bangle absently around her wrist again and again, the motion as simple and repetitive as the moving meditations of the Shin.

"Then what?" Vennet asked finally. "No more empire? Back to the good old days when we all ran our own kingdoms?"

"We did not all have kings, Vennet," Gabril said.

Vennet smiled a broad, contemptuous smile. "Of course. You desert dwellers will be overjoyed to return to your savage customs."

"I'm sorry to hear that you consider his customs savage," Kaden said, taking a small step to put himself between Gabril and the bearded man, "as I have drawn heavily upon them in my remaking of the empire."

For several heartbeats no one said anything. Wind gusted through cracks in the warehouse walls, tugging at the lantern flames.

"Making it into what?" Vennet asked finally.

"A republic," Kaden replied. "A government of shared responsibility."

Tevis threw his hands in the air. " 'Shael save us, a *republic*? Meaning every filthy, dirt-grubbing peasant has a say and a stake?"

"It would be inefficient," Kaden said quietly, "to bring every filthy, dirt-grubbing peasant to the capital for the sake of governance. I propose something more limited."

Kegellen narrowed her eyes. "A council," she said, tapping a finger against her fleshy lips. "You want to have a council."

Kaden nodded.

"A council?" Tevis spat, lips drawn back in a sneer. "Of whom?"

"You," Kaden replied. "You will provide the spine. Plus representatives from those atrepies who are not here in the city." He gestured over his shoulder to Kiel, who slipped the rolled parchment into his hand. Kaden held the scroll up to the light, but made no move to unfurl it.

Vennet snorted. "What is that?"

"A document," Kaden replied, "setting out the new laws, prerogatives, and responsibilities. A constitution."

Kaden could never have come up with the thing on his own. After eight years in the Bone Mountains, he knew maybe one Annurian law in a hundred, and had almost no sense of the governing structures of foreign states and nations. He remembered from his childhood that Freeport and the cities north of the Romsdals formed a federation, that the Manjari had an empire like the Annurians, but with an empress instead of an emperor, and that the Blood Cities all insisted on their own independence, alternately fighting and trading with the others. It was an absurdly small base of knowledge for the drafting of a constitution that would govern a polity the size of Annur.

Gabril had proven useful, outlining the traditions of his people, as had Morjeta, whose training in the Temple of Pleasure had afforded her a surprising amount of time for the study of politics. In the end, though, it was Kiel who put it together. The historian seemed to know every detail of every human culture since the fall of the Csestriim. He anticipated the general problems of human governance, the specific problems posed by a transition from empire to republic, and provided plausible solutions to both. Morjeta and Gabril had both stared at the historian with increasing awe as they worked and reworked the document.

"How do you know all of this?" the First Speaker demanded at one point.

Kiel smiled. "It is my work."

His raised his brows. "You memorized every detail, every name and date?"

"Yes," he replied mildly, then gestured them back to the scroll.

Kaden had insisted on one thing only: that the document be simple. It was going to prove difficult enough to convince a score of suspicious, scheming nobles to put aside their historical rifts and grievances without presenting them with a five-hundred-page treatise. Kiel resisted, arguing that any lapses or oversights would lead, eventually, to the fragmentation and dissolution of the government, and the historian saw lapses and oversights everywhere. He wanted to address each possible contingency, outlining solutions to debacles ranging from assassination of council members to double taxation on long-distance merchants.

"I have studied republics, Kaden," he said, shaking his head. "They start with the noblest of intentions, and they tear themselves to shreds."

"How long does that take?" Kaden asked. "The shredding?"

Kiel spread his hands. "There are dozens of scenarios. Decades, sometimes. Maybe a couple of centuries. Not long."

Triste laughed out loud at that. "If we make it through the next few *months,* I think we'll all be happy. Come next summer, Kaden can start worrying about deflation and price-fixing and whatever else it is you've been talking about."

"Come next summer," Kiel replied, "Kaden will not be in charge. Not if we are successful."

"One page," Kaden said, cutting off the conversation. "We're doing this to deny power to Adare and il Tornja, not as some experiment in the founding of a political utopia."

"While we are doing one—" Kiel began.

Kaden shook his head, held up one finger. "One page."

And so, as he stood in the damp warehouse, flanked by piled crates and musty barrels, ringed with hostile, baffled stares, it was one page that he held up.

"This," he said quietly, "is the constitution I propose for Annur, an Annur ruled, not by an emperor, but by representatives from the various atrepies, people familiar with and dedicated to the traditions, history, and interests of their people."

For a moment there was silence, the calculation of possibility and risk.

A slender, ink-skinned woman with red nails and a shaved scalp—Kaden took her for Azurtazine, from the southern island of Basc—shook her head. "How many?" she asked carefully. "How many representatives?"

"Forty-five," Kaden replied. "Three from each atrepy."

Azurtazine pursed her lips. "To be chosen how?"

"By you," he said, "each for his or her own territory."

Kiel had protested endlessly against the method, arguing that the nobles would scheme to promote their family and friends, then use their newfound power to crush both their political and personal foes. The new system, he pointed out, would be hopelessly tied to the interests of the few and the rich.

The point was a good one, but there was no chance that these remnants of an old world order, families who had spent hundreds of years hoarding their grievances and counting their slights, would allow any government in which they were forced to share power over their own restored lands. Doubtless there were better systems, but il Tornja and Adare would not be fighting the Urghul forever, and by the time they returned, the fledgling republic needed to be established firmly enough to deny them power.

"It seems like you're giving up a lot," Triste had said, shaking her head as she studied one of the final drafts.

Kaden almost laughed. "That's the point. I can't match anyone strength for strength, blow for blow. Not Adare. Not il Tornja. Not the assembled nobles."

"Then how do you control them? How do you win?"

The vision of Gabril in his shadowrobe danced through Kaden's mind, of the attacking guardsman lunging forward, of his spear piercing the cloth, missing the body inside, then driving into the flesh of the other soldier. If the Shin had bothered to fight, that was how they would do it.

"There might be more strength," he had said, staring at the drying ink on the parchment, "in simply standing aside."

Faced with the sharp glares of Annur's nobility, he was starting to question that decision. They could well have been a pack of hungry, late-winter wolves stumbling upon a deer carcass, snarling and sizing each other up, wondering who was going to get a bloody haunch, who was going to starve in the blood-soaked snow.

"And what," Kegellen asked, still twisting those bangles as she eyed him, "will your role be in this great enterprise? Or do you long to return to a contemplative life in the mountains?" She smiled brightly, but her dark eyes were shrewd. Kaden forced himself to meet her gaze, to deliver the words as he had practiced them.

"I will be your servant," he said, voice level.

Kegellen laughed, her cheeks and chins jiggling with levity. "How delightful! A strong young thing—with burning eyes, no less!—to rub my aching feet and pour my wine." She glanced about her, false irritation flickering across her face. "And speaking of wine—why did no one think to bring any?"

Kaden ignored the last question. "The council will vote on every law, deciding on the direction of the republic and upon the surest paths to reach our collective goals. I will not be a part of the council. As Servant of the Annurian Republic," he went on carefully, "I will not have a vote, nor will I have a veto over what you decide. My only role will be administrative. I will call the meetings, and I will see to it that the laws you set in place are executed according to the spirit in which you intended them."

Fifteen sets of eyes watched him. Kaden forced himself to breathe easily, steadily.

"Why?" Kegellen asked slowly, lower lip turning out in a frown. "Why would you want this? You could be Emperor."

"I spent most of the last ten years beyond the borders of Annur," Kaden replied. "I saw another way."

"Great," Tevis snorted. "Another way. How enlightened. Or maybe it's that you lost your power already, let your sister seize it, and now you're trying to claw back any pathetic bit that you can."

Tevis's crack struck close to the bone, but Kaden had prepared for it.

"You're right," he replied evenly. "My sister and the *kenarang* have taken power for themselves. They tried to see me killed, and, if we succeed in what we are doing, they will try to kill you, too."

The revelation had the intended effect—shocked faces, indignant exclamations—but Kaden rode right over them.

"You are right about Adare," he continued, "but you are wrong about me. If I wanted power, I would hardly offer myself as your servant.

"Right now, Adare and the *kenarang* are in the north. When they return, they will either find their power kept nicely warm by their minions here in the city while the rest of you keep meeting in damp warehouses by the docks, or they will find a republic, a ruling council led by you, deciding the fate of Annur." He shrugged. "Whatever happens, I have no intention ever to sit the Unhewn Throne."

For a long, tantalizing moment, he thought he had them. Oil hissed in the lamps. Somewhere lost in the darkness above, birds shuffled on the rafters. No one spoke. No one moved. Kaden watched the faces, willing them to see the opening, the chance at power, to *lunge*. Tevis was nodding, licking his lips. Azurtazine studied him appraisingly, breathing out slowly between pursed lips. They all saw the risk, but their conspiracy had always been dogged by risk. They had all dreamed of an opportunity like this, but none had dared hope for it. Kaden waited, his face calm, eyes still, his hand extended with the parchment. He had them. They would take it.

Then Tevis shook his head.

"I want more."

Kaden frowned. "More what?"

"More representatives on the council. Six from Nish. We hold the northern passes through the Romsdals. We keep the Ghost Sea swept of pirates. I want more."

"The council is based on equal representation," Kaden began, but Tevis cut him off.

"We're not all equal." He flicked a contemptuous thumb at a short man with wide-set eyes. "Channary? Hanno? They were added to the empire in the last century. They're barely even atrepies."

Kaden felt his stomach cave even as the chorus of voices rose in fury, smashing the silence into shards. The shouts and recriminations washed over him.

"Si'ite provides the silver . . ."

"The population of Kresh is three times that of . . ."

"Aragat deserves more seats . . ."

". . . more votes . . ."

"More power . . ."

He shut out the words. It was obvious he had already lost, and the protestations, for all their difference, were all the same: a litany, the power of which he had long ago forgotten, a desperate string of syllables stronger than any prayer, the ancient, ineluctable chant of humanity itself: *I want . . . I want . . . I want . . .*

41

It took longer than Valyn had expected to reach Andt-Kyl. The Thousand Lakes, as it turned out, was comprised of a lot more than just lakes; the whole region was a maze of bogs, swamps, streams, and ponds. What solid ground there was seemed crammed with pines and balsams, the dark trunks so close that in most places you couldn't see ten paces through the heavy needles. The western "road"—so named because it ran north vaguely parallel to the west coast of Scar Lake was little more than a network of muddy tracks, crude bridges, and hastily bucked logs laid side by side over the deepest swamps. Even dry, it would have made for rough going, and it was anything but dry.

The land itself had slowed them to an agonizing slog, and the land wasn't the only problem. The Thousand Lakes was dotted with small logging villages, some built on high ground, others on teetering stilts, all of them directly athwart the submerged track. Passing through would be simple enough, except that someone was sure to notice their passage, someone who might talk to il Tornja's scouts, who, in turn, would tell the *kenarang* about three soldiers in Kettral blacks, three young men evidently unattached to any unit, one with coal-dark skin, another with burned-out eyes. . . . It wouldn't take a brilliant military mind to recognize their descriptions.

Valyn's meeting with Adare, far from reassuring him, had been both surprising and unnerving. Her insistence on the *kenarang*'s loyalty to Annur, her willingness to pardon his flagrant murder of the Emperor, and her veneration for the man's military mind all set Valyn's teeth on edge. Worse, the discovery that Long Fist was on the march made it pretty 'Kentkissing clear that he was just using Valyn as a tool in his own war, one in which he aimed to overrun Annur itself. Which meant that Gwenna and

Annick weren't guests at all; they were prisoners. Valyn and Laith and Talal had been over it two dozen times already, but the ugly fact was that, without a bird, there was nothing they could do for the two women. The best hope, in fact, lay in killing il Tornja, in hoping that after the *kenarang* was dead they could find some way to go after their Wing mates, to free them.

The fact that he had left them, abandoned them, gnawed viciously at Valyn, but for all the hours he'd spent rehearsing the decision, he couldn't see a way around it. He'd joined the Kettral expecting to fight on the side of justice and imperial order, but the last few months had disabused him violently of that notion. Instead, he was caught between conflicting evils; any damage he did to one would make him complicit in the crimes of the other.

And yet, standing aside, refusing to take part, was nothing but a coward's course, and so Valyn dug down until he came to something like bedrock: Ran il Tornja had murdered his father and suborned the empire. The agreement Valyn had hammered out with Adare seemed like the best available: he would let the *kenarang* stop the Urghul, but then he would see him dead. All of which meant, of course, that il Tornja couldn't know Valyn was near, was waiting for him. It would be tough enough to kill him unsuspecting, and Valyn had no intention of giving the man an advance warning.

And so, over Laith's strenuous objections, they detoured around every town, wading through frigid, chest-deep bogs, swatting away biting flies that seemed to grow large as birds, holding their blades above their heads in a futile effort to keep them dry, slogging forward straight through the night and all the next day at a pace so slow they'd barely reached the northern end of the lake by dusk. It was a pretty weak showing for three soldiers trained to cover distance quickly and quietly—fifty miles in a full day—but it was enough. No one had seen them pass, which meant, when il Tornja did arrive, he'd have no idea they were waiting.

"Well," Laith said, holding the branches aside with one hand so that he could get a view out over the northern arm of the lake to the small village straddling the Black River, "looks like the Urghul move almost as fast through the forest as they do on the steppe."

Valyn's stomach slipped. "Have they taken the town?" he demanded, peering through the gathering gloom as he slipped the long lens from his pack.

"Doesn't look like it," Talal replied after a moment.

Valyn nodded slowly. Bonfires raged on the far bank, but the town it-self looked unscathed, no burning buildings lighting the sky, no furious ringing of alarms, no smoke, no screaming. He raised the long lens to his eye, focused it. The horsemen on the far bank snapped into view, hundreds of them, thousands, and more in the trees.

"What are the bastards waiting for?" Laith demanded.

Valyn shook his head. "Can't see. If the people in town aren't idiots, they'll have burned the far bridge, but I don't have the angle to be sure." He shifted the long lens back to the town. The eastern sky had already purpled to black, but Valyn could make out the details clearly enough: rough log buildings similar to those in Aats-Kyl, all piled onto two islands nestled in the forking arms of the Black River. Docks stretched out into the lake from the eastern island, and on the southernmost tip of the west-ern one, built directly out of a rocky cliff, stood a tall, stone tower—probably for signaling boats coming up from the south. When the wind dropped, he could hear hammers or axes echoing from the wall of dark firs fronting the eastern shore of the lake.

The villagers were busy running back and forth, some with weapons, others lugging logs, still others carting what must have been food and valuables west over the central bridge, onto the nearer of the two islands, trying to get them as far from the horsemen as possible. Valyn tracked a few figures—mostly loggers in rough leather and wool—then paused, grinding his teeth.

"Il Tornja's scouts are here."

Talal nodded. "Not unexpected."

"But a pain in the ass nonetheless," Laith said.

Valyn frowned. "Means we'll have to take care in setting up shop. If they're sticking to protocol, they'll be sending men back two, three times a day. We can't let the *kenarang* know we're here."

"All right," Talal said. "What's the play?"

"We wait until full dark," he replied, "then move in. We'll take up a position on top of the tower. Should give us a good view of what's going on and, with any luck, a line of sight to il Tornja when he arrives. The bas-tard may be a brilliant tactician, but tactics never blocked an arrow."

"And you still want to do this?" Laith asked. "Kill him? Even after what you learned from your sister? If Long Fist is coming, that means he lied, means he played us. . . ."

Valyn's jaw tightened. Laith had distrusted the Urghul shaman from the start, but the encounter with il Tornja's army, the realization that the horsemen were actually planning to push across the river, made the flier furious. He was right, of course—the shaman's army, his so-called shield, was starting to look a lot like a fucking spear—and yet Laith couldn't see *beyond* that point. It would do them little good to defeat the Urghul only to hand the empire to il Tornja when the fighting was done.

"Long Fist *lied* to us," Laith continued, as though the revelation were a shock.

"It was a smart play," Talal said. "He risks nothing by using us to get at il Tornja. If we succeed, he wins. If we fail," he shrugged, "he was planning to fight the battle anyway."

Laith spat. "And we're just cheerfully going to keep doing what this horsefucker wants?" He stared at Valyn, the challenge hard in his voice. "We've already killed a couple Annurian soldiers for the great and mighty Long Fist—what's a little more Annurian blood? Is that it?"

"There is more than one fight here," Valyn ground out. "The fact that one is evil doesn't make the other good. Long Fist lied to us, but il Tornja murdered the Emperor."

"According to Balendin," Laith said, voice rising in disbelief.

"According to my *sister,*" Valyn replied, trying to keep his voice calm. "Adare confirmed it. The *kenarang* killed my father and seized control of the empire."

"It is your sister," Talal pointed out quietly, "who has taken on the imperial mantle."

"She's il Tornja's puppet," Valyn snapped. "She thinks she's doing the right thing, but she doesn't understand the larger forces at play."

"Seems to me," Laith said archly, "that she *is* one of the larger fucking forces. She's the Malkeenian in charge now, she's declared herself Emperor, she has the *kenarang* jumping to her tune, the Army of the North, and, in case you didn't notice it, the 'Kent-kissing Sons of Flame into the bargain."

"The Army of the North is the *kenarang's* army," Valyn growled. "When we kill the *kenarang* we can bring it back under control. Kaden can appoint a new commander."

"If Kaden is alive," Talal said, meeting Valyn's eye as he spoke. "Adare didn't mention him."

Valyn drew a deep, ragged breath. Worry for his brother had gnawed at him since the two groups were separated back in the Bone Mountains.

Their whole scheme seemed like madness now, a plan with a hundred possible holes. The gate itself could have killed Kaden, or the Ishien on the other side of it. He could have returned to Annur and run afoul of il Tornja's men, could have avoided the conspiracy altogether only to end up dead in a canal with some footpad's blade in his back. The old monk, Rampuri Tan, had seemed capable with that strange spear of his, but there wasn't any telling how far even *he* could be trusted. Looking back on it, Valyn wished he'd done more to stay at Kaden's side. At the time, there hadn't seemed to be any choice.

It had been a long time since he'd felt as though he had a true choice. Abandoning the Islands, losing Kaden, fighting the Flea, landing on the steppe, leaving half his Wing in Long Fist's clutches—each decision looked like the wrong one now, but at the time they hadn't seemed like decisions at all. Instead of contemplating a series of forking paths, Valyn felt as though he'd been racing down a single treacherous track, just a half step ahead of his foes, no time to look either back or forward.

He stared out over the dark water toward the small town. Maybe this was a mistake, too. He could still turn back, try to find that invisible fork, try to take a better path, but the other paths all looked even worse than the one he was on. Leave il Tornja to his triumph? With a crucial military victory tucked tight in his belt, the man would be even more difficult to unseat. Continue north in hope of freeing Gwenna and Annick from the Urghul? The odds of success looked worse than pathetic, and if he died in the rescue attempt, he couldn't kill il Tornja or help Kaden. Return to the Islands and lay the information about the plot before Daveen Shaleel and the rest of Eyrie Command? They reported to il Tornja; for all Valyn knew, they were complicit in the plot.

There were dozens of variables, none of which he could control—Long Fist, the Ishien, Rampuri Tan—but about Ran il Tornja, at least, he could do something. He could *try* to do something.

"Kaden is going to have to look after himself for now," he said. "But we can do our vicious bloody best to make sure that if he's alive, when he does return to Annur, that a backstabbing traitor isn't sitting on his seat." He wasn't sure if he was talking about il Tornja or Adare. Possibly both.

Laith raised his hands in surrender, let out a snort half weariness, half disgust. "The whole thing is above my pay grade. I trained to fly birds, and now we don't even have a 'Kent-kissing bird."

"Speaking of which," Talal said, raising the long lens toward the town once more, "how do you plan to get to that tower? Without 'Ra, it looks a little tricky."

The sun had set, but Valyn could see well enough in the gray-green darkness. Dozens of lanterns and fires blazed on the two islands—the extravagance of wood and oil speaking eloquently to the fear in the streets. The loggers' preparations, though, would face east, toward the approaching Urghul. No one would be looking south over the water, and if they were, well, the Kettral wore blacks and worshipped Hull for a reason.

"We swim," he said. "Exit at the cliff. Climb straight up to the top of the tower."

"A half-mile swim in glacial runoff followed by a seventy-foot climb," Laith grumbled. "Just what I was hoping for."

Valyn fought down a sudden and powerful urge to seize the flier by the neck. There was a time, not so long ago, when Valyn had trusted Laith more than any other member of his Wing, but combat had changed both of them, changed them for the worse. Laith's jocularity had crumbled into a series of snipes and complaints, and Valyn could feel his own tolerance fraying like a worn rope. No one wanted to swim the fucking lake. No one wanted to climb a tall stone tower in the middle of the night with cold hands and wet blacks, but they were *Kettral*.

"This is what we do," Valyn said, leashing his voice, keeping it low, holding back the shouting that snarled and prowled inside. "This is what we are for."

"Come on," Talal said, sensing the tension and stepping between them. "Let's just get it over with."

Over. Valyn almost laughed at the word. Once they swam the lake, they'd have to climb the cliff. Once up the cliff, they'd face the tower. Once on the tower, he'd need to kill il Tornja, and if he managed that, he needed to find a way to free Gwenna and Annick. One fight just led to the next, on and on and on. It wasn't really over, none of it. Not until you were dead.

†

The swim was mercifully shorter than Valyn had expected, but the climb above proved brutal—seventy feet of narrow ledges made even more treacherous by the darkness, their sodden boots, and the crumbling mortar of the old tower itself. Three times Valyn trusted his weight to seemingly solid stone only to have it give when he tried to move up on it, ripping clear of the wall to plummet into the lapping waves below, leaving him to cling desperately with one hand while the other scrabbled for purchase.

It was painstaking, difficult work, but Valyn found it strangely calming. There were few decisions to make—this stone or that, this ledge or that—and the consequences of each choice were immediate: the rock crumbled, or it did not. No lies. No deception. No one to kill. His body warmed with the exertion, and his focus narrowed to the vertical swath of stone immediately above and below him. He was almost disappointed when he reached the roof, pulling up and over onto the rough boards, though his forearms ached and the tips of his fingers bled.

For a moment he just laid on his back, staring at the stars, each one a hole stabbed in the darkness. Then Talal's voice pulled him back to the present.

"Someone's been working hard," he murmured, nodding toward the eastern bank of the Black. "They've got the place locked up tight."

Valyn rolled onto his stomach, then pulled the long lens from his oilskin.

"What've we got?"

Talal nodded into the darkness. "Looks like the bridge is out, destroyed, like you said. Hard to say in the darkness."

Between the fires and the stars, the night was plenty bright to Valyn, and when he raised the lens to his eye, the chopped pilings leapt immediately into view, jagged teeth stabbing up from the mud flats on either side of the central channel, a few stray planks strewn about.

"I wonder who warned them?" he said, scanning the town below.

The place was a hive of activity, men and women pushing and pulling all manner of carts, some filled with tools, others loaded high with tables or logs, while children scurried through the streets, shouting messages to the adults. It was chaotic, but after watching for a few minutes, Valyn could start to see a kind of order imposed on the madness: laden carts headed east, toward what appeared to be some sort of barricade on the far bank of the East Island, then returned filled with food and jugs of water, all manner of provisions. Valyn followed the activity to a knot of figures in the small town square, brought the leader into focus, then almost dropped the lens.

"Holy Hull," he breathed, then found himself laughing, joy and relief washing over him like a cool wave back on the Islands, scrubbing away for just a moment all the doubt and the anger. "Meshkent, Ananshael, and holy black Hull."

"Is there a joke I'm not getting about the fact that this whole miserable town's about to be burned to the dirt?" Laith asked.

For once, even the flier's cynicism couldn't dampen Valyn's spirits. He just smiled and passed the long lens. It took Laith a moment to find Gwenna in the shadows, and then he, too, was laughing.

"That tough, stubborn bitch," he marveled. "Leave it to Gwenna Sharpe to decide she's fed up playing prisoner to an entire army of Urghul." Shaking his head, he handed the lens to Talal.

"Annick's there, too," the leach said after a moment. "And Pyrre."

Valyn's face hurt from smiling. It seemed like forever since he'd had a reason. "I wonder how they got free. . . ."

"Those three?" Laith asked. "Probably just kept clawing eyes and biting throats until there weren't any Urghul left. Here we are wandering all over Raalte killing our own men, and they've busted themselves free, humped it back ahead of an entire mounted army, and started preparing the defense." The bitterness had crept back into his voice. "Starts to make you wonder why we even bothered."

The smile slid from Valyn's face like a shadow. "We bothered," he said, "because it seemed like the right choice at the time."

"Well, we're here now," Laith said, rising to his feet on the crumbling roof. "Let's get down there while there's still work to do."

Valyn hesitated, then shook his head. "No."

For a moment no one moved. No one spoke. The wind whipped spray from the waves, tossing it against the rock. It riffled through the boughs of the pines, scratched at the clouds, whipped the fires below into sparks and ruddy blaze.

The flier turned on him slowly, incredulous. "No?"

"We stay here," Valyn said, keeping his voice low. "The mission is to kill il Tornja. That hasn't changed."

"And what about the fact that our Wing is right down there?" Laith demanded, waving a hand at the small town below. "What about the fact that the 'Kent-kissing Urghul are coming and these people need *help*?"

"Gwenna has it in hand," Valyn said, his own words bitter on his tongue. He wanted to be down there as much as Laith, standing with his Wing and his people, throwing up barricades, thinking through strategy. . . . Three more bodies wouldn't mean much when it came to the actual fight, but three Kettral-trained soldiers could do a lot right now when it came to organizing and leading the townsfolk. It would feel good to lift something, move something, *do* something. It would also jeopardize the mission.

"Il Tornja's going to be here in a day," Valyn said, "and unless you forgot, those men down there, the ones with the nice swords, are his scouts. If we go down, they'll make us in a heartbeat and report back. If il Tornja knows we're here, we've lost the element of surprise, which, right now, is our only 'Kent-kissing advantage."

Laith snorted with disgust. "*Fuck*, Valyn. Half the Wing's already *down* there. You think if il Tornja hears about Gwenna and Annick he's not going to assume you're along, too?"

Valyn grimaced. It *was* an unexpected problem, but a problem didn't mean a disaster. "Gwenna knows the truth about il Tornja, she knows that we're hunting him, and she's smart enough not to piss in the broth."

"There's another reason to stay clear," Talal said, frowning. "It's hard to see how this all ends up, but if, when it's over, il Tornja finds Gwenna and Annick, he's going to realize they survived Yurl's attack, which means he's probably going to assume they know the truth about him. Or at least suspect it. I wouldn't be surprised if he locks them up for questioning—discreetly, of course."

Valyn nodded. He hadn't considered that angle, but, as usual, Talal was right. "Which gives us two reasons to stay out of sight."

Laith shook his head. "Right. Two reasons: *what if . . .* and *just in case . . .* We're a brave new breed of philosopher soldier, keeping our hands clean while other people swing the swords."

Valyn didn't reply. He had a sense that they'd all be swinging swords soon enough, and once they started, there was no telling when they'd stop.

42

Old Pikker John said he'd rather die on his porch than run, and he got his wish. Well, the dying part of it anyway. Gwenna couldn't say how long he'd managed to hold on to his porch, but when the Urghul dragged him out onto the east bank of the Black, he'd lost his axes, his crock of whiskey, and, if the way his head lolled on his shoulders was any indication, the ability and will to fight.

"They got him," Bridger said.

"Of course they got him," Gwenna snapped. "Did you think one old man was going to see off the entire Urghul nation all by himself?"

She bit off the rest of the tirade. She was mad at John, not Bridger, mad at the old man for his stupidity, for his stubbornness, and for making her watch what had to happen next.

From behind Annick's barricades on East Island, Gwenna could see the far bank clearly enough, could make out individual faces of the Urghul as they scouted up the river and down along the drying east shore of the lake, she could see the markings on their horses, the fletching on their arrows. They were close enough to shout to, to shoot, and the only thing holding them back was the narrow strip of mud and water. It seemed a feeble defense.

Gwenna glanced up and down the ranks of townsfolk Annick had arrayed behind the barricades. Men and women crouched behind the stacked logs, some kids, too, whose shortbows lacked the range to get much past the water. If the Urghul got close enough for those bows to hit, the whole island would be almost overrun. Gwenna would have preferred to send the kids somewhere else, but then, if the Urghul broke through, there *wasn't* anywhere else to go. Besides, the place was their home—they had more right to die on it than she did.

As she watched, someone loosed an arrow. It floated up, high over the river, then fell harmlessly into the silt on the far side of the channel.

"Knock it off!" Gwenna shouted. They couldn't afford to waste the shafts. There were already more Urghul than arrows, not that she wanted the loggers dwelling on that fact. "No one looses an arrow until they try to cross!"

She wasn't sure whether to be worried or relieved that none of the horsemen had tried to swim their mounts. It would be utter suicide, obviously, but the Urghul weren't generally known for their sophisticated grasp of tactics. Not before Long Fist, at least.

Strangely, of the shaman himself, there had been no sign. He might have been lurking back in the trees, directing the fight from a safe distance, but his absence made her nervous, as did his choice of lieutenant. If Long Fist was nowhere, Balendin Ainhoa seemed to be everywhere, stalking up and down the bank in his cloak of dark bison hide, pointing and giving orders as though he'd lived among the Urghul all his life. If the horsemen resented him, none showed it, which, Gwenna supposed, was smart, given what she knew about Balendin.

As she watched, he was directing a knot of *taabe* and *ksaabe* to make a space in the open area between the trees and the mud flats. When most of the riders had moved aside, Pikker John was thrust, stumbling, to the ground. Balendin stood above the man for a while, gazing over the river toward the town, as though he felt Gwenna's eyes upon him from behind the barricade. While he waited, other prisoners were dragged forward from the trees—scores of them—then forced facedown in the dirt where they could see the leach and the old logger. Someone stepped forward with a handful of ropes, and Balendin, with a few practiced motions, cinched them around Pikker John's wrists and ankles.

"What are they doing?" Bridger asked.

"I don't know. Something fucking terrible," Gwenna said. She didn't want to watch. It was one thing to kill and see people killed in the middle of a fight. The fear and fury that came with battle didn't leave any time to dwell on the sights and sounds of men becoming meat. Watching from behind the barricade though, as they hitched the four ropes to the saddles of four separate horses, Gwenna felt like she might retch all over her boots. A dismayed muttering spread through the crouching townspeople as they realized what was about to happen, and their fear and nausea quickened her own. She wanted to turn away, but she couldn't, not while she was the leader of the town's miserable defense, and yet her body needed an outlet, needed *something* to distract her from the scene playing out on the far side of the river.

She surged to her feet, drew her sword, and leveled it across the river. "Watch!" she shouted.

The loggers turned to her, but she shook her head angrily. "Don't look at me, you assholes. Look over there, at the man you called your neighbor. Watch what they do to him."

The riders of the horses, two *taabe,* two *ksaabe,* nudged their mounts forward, slowly, slowly. As the ropes drew taut around his wrists and ankles, Pikker John's body rose into the air, and an awful, guttural moan escaped his lips. The Urghul had fallen utterly silent. Balendin, however, began to chant something incomprehensible in Urghul. Where the bastard had learned the words, she had no idea, but the thousands of horsemen seemed mesmerized by the spectacle. Gwenna could hear the horses' hooves striking the ground, the strain of the ropes as they pulled.

"Watch!" she shouted again, her heart slamming away at her ribs. "You want to know who the Urghul are? *This* is who they are."

The chanting on the far bank quickened, then quickened further, keeping pace with Gwenna's pulse. The other Urghul joined in, and it grew louder. Pikker John screamed, an awful, animal sound, and with his scream, the riders lashed their horses, crops rising and falling over and over, the body suspended between them writhing, his mouth a gaping howl lost on the storm of Urghul voices. In the midst of the chaos, Annick stepped up beside Gwenna, leaning in to whisper in her ear.

"I can stop it. One arrow."

Gwenna hesitated, watching the horses strain, watching John's body as it twisted and writhed. "No," she said, swallowing the bile that came with the word. "They need to see this."

The sniper turned those hard blue eyes on her.

"They're not soldiers. It's terrifying them."

"They *need* to be terrified," Gwenna hissed. "If we lose, if the Urghul take the town, this is waiting for all of them, and you won't be there to end it with an arrow." She turned away before Annick could argue with her further, vaulted atop the highest log in the barricade.

"This is what is coming," she shouted at the crouching townsmen. "It is not a raid. It is not a skirmish. It is the entire Urghul nation, and if we don't hold them here, they will offer up everyone you know to Meshkent just like they're doing with Pikker John over there. This is what they do. This is how they worship. This is who they *are*. So pay fucking attention!"

She wasn't sure anyone could hear her over the commotion on the far bank, but the message seemed to get through. One man just at her feet was retching into the mud, but most of the small force straightened up, staring at the horror unfolding in what had, until that morning, been a part of their home.

Pikker John must have been made of gristle and bone. Even after he lost the strength to scream, his body held together. Even when the shoulders popped from their sockets and the joints went horribly loose, the ligaments held. For what seemed like hours, the horses pulled on him, pulled, and pawed at the dirt, and snorted, and pulled some more, until all at once, with an awful lurch, an arm tore away. The Urghul shrieked in a kind of collective ecstasy as the one rider galloped down the bank, pumping his fist in the air as that grisly tail bumped along behind him.

The other riders eased off their horses, allowing what was left of Pikker John to settle back to earth, where, amazingly, he writhed until his life drained out of him with his blood. The Urghul unhitched him, dragged the corpse to the river, and tossed it in. Balendin raised his eyes, looking first at the prisoners cowering behind him, then across the river at Gwenna once more.

It's over, she told herself. *They killed one old man, but they're still on their side of the river.*

But it was more than one old man. As she watched, a woman, probably someone from the outlying hamlets to the northeast, was dragged pleading toward the riverbank. The sacrifices were just getting started, and with each one, the leach's power, sucked from the terror of his captives, would grow.

✝

By the end of the second day, the Urghul had torn apart dozens more people, those poor, miserable souls who lived between Andt-Kyl and the Black, who had had no warning of the approaching army. The far bank was muddy with blood, while the bloated corpses dotted the river mouth, tangling in the roots and rushes where the current slowed. The Urghul killed, and killed, and killed, but they had made no effort to cross.

That made Gwenna nervous.

Around noon on the second day, she'd thought they were starting a push. A few dozen *taabe* and *ksaabe* had tossed some tree trunks into the river, watching them float down toward the old bridge pilings where they tangled between the posts. It wasn't much, four or five logs, enough that some brave, stupid shithead might sneak across, but certainly not enough for a full-fledged attack. The Urghul stared at them for a while, as though expecting the bridge to grow itself, then went back to killing people. It was like they didn't even care about getting to the town.

"What the fuck are they doing?" Gwenna demanded, biting her lip as she looked across the small table at Pyrre and Annick. After a day at the barricades, she'd had Bridger set up a command post inside one of the most easterly of the buildings, where she could still get to the river fast, but where she could discuss strategy with Annick, Pyrre, and Bridger out of earshot of the townspeople. It was good protocol, insulating the troops from the decision-making process, but mostly Gwenna just didn't want the people of Andt-Kyl to hear how little their commanders actually knew.

"Long Fist *has* to be aware that the Army of the North will get here eventually. Every day the bastard waits is a risk."

"We haven't seen Long Fist," Annick pointed out. "We don't know he's with his army."

"Where else would he be?" Gwenna demanded.

Pyrre pursed her lips. "Off in the forest, perhaps. Torturing small woodland creatures."

Gwenna ignored her, rounding on Bridger. "Are you *sure* there's not another way to cross? Somewhere to the north?"

He shook his head. "I've been all through that territory logging. In the winter, when the bogs are frozen, you could *maybe* move across, but now you'd be weeks trying to get through even on foot, let alone with horses. The firs grow so thick on some of the high ground that you have to squeeze between the trunks, and the swamps'll swallow you right up."

"And there are no other towns?" she asked. "No bridges?"

"Nothing but the log camps, and they don't have any need for bridges. Unless those horses can balance on rolling tree trunks floating downriver, there's nothing to help him in the north."

"I wonder what became of your short, bellicose friend and his large bird," Pyrre mused. "Maybe he got to Long Fist after all. Maybe they're all just milling on the far bank because they have no idea what else to do."

It was a tempting explanation, but after a long pause, Gwenna shook her head. "Doesn't make sense," she said. "If the Flea carried out the hit, he'd be back by now. And if Long Fist were really dead, wouldn't the Urghul tear each other apart? Even Balendin wouldn't be able to hold them without the shaman's power backing him."

"Just trying to be optimistic," the assassin said with a shrug. "Bridger, do you have any more beer?" She gestured to the tankard in front of her. "Sitting on one's ass watching men and women get rent limb from limb tends to lead to a thirst."

Gwenna started to respond, but an urgent chorus of shouts from just outside cut her off. She was out the door in three steps, scanning the far bank, the near bank, the lake, hunting for the attack that she'd missed. The townspeople were pointing upriver, but, in the growing gloom, she couldn't make out much. Certainly there was no Urghul assault.

"Oh sweet Ciena," Bridger swore, horror in his voice as he followed her eyes. "The drive."

"The drive?" Gwenna demanded. "What's the drive?"

"The log drive," he said, pointing to the dark shapes bobbing just above the surface of the river, so thick on the water Gwenna hadn't noticed them, a loose raft of shifting logs jostling one another as they floated south with the current.

"They can't cross on those, can they?" Gwenna asked.

"Not there," he said. "Not on horses. But that's not the problem."

Gwenna scanned down the river, then stopped at the old bridge pilings, fear punching her in the chest.

"There," she breathed.

He nodded grimly. "That's why they tossed in the first logs. They're going to make a dam."

"How many of those are there?" Gwenna asked, gesturing upstream.

"Enough to clog the whole north end of the lake. Enough for a dozen bridges, if they get hung up."

"Why would they get hung up? Don't you drive the logs through those pilings every year?"

Bridger nodded bleakly. "But we usually have men and women on the bridge with poles to make sure they don't get stuck. To break up a jam before it starts. Now . . ." He gestured helplessly. "There's no bridge."

"How long?" she asked, but even as she watched it was happening, the logs bumping up against the others the Urghul had floated in place. A few nosed over, forced on by the press behind. Others spun with the current, then ducked beneath the surface, driven down and replaced by still others. There seemed no end to the logs. As far north as Gwenna could see the river was packed with them. And there was no way to stop the river.

"Those," Pyrre said, raising her eyebrows, "are going to be a problem."

"They'll fill the whole river," Gwenna said, the horror mounting inside her. They would fill the river, and then the Urghul would cross. *That* was what they'd been waiting for.

"The other channels," Bridger said. "We've got to divert the logs down the other two channels, the ones that aren't blocked."

Gwenna stared at the mass of logs, the sheer, unstoppable tonnage. "And how in Hull's name do we do that?"

"We have to . . ." He shook his head. "I can't explain. I have to go! Miller!" he bellowed. "Franch!" Two men from the line of archers turned. "Two drive crews. Get 'em up, get 'em going. Now!"

"We need poles and dogs!"

"Then *get* them!" Bridger shouted. "Get them, and get to North Island."

"Well," Pyrre observed as the logger sprinted away, "he certainly seems excited."

It *was* a shocking transformation. Bridger had been nothing but deference since the Flea killed the two head men in the town square, asking questions and jumping to do as he was ordered. Now that he had a task that he understood, however, all hesitation vanished. The problem was, the drive crews were pulling men and women from the line; the toughest men and women, by the look of it, and this while the Urghul were riding out of the trees on the far bank, shrieking and bellowing, horses pawing at the ground as the logs piled up. One *ksaabe,* a good bit bolder than she was smart, kicked her horse into a charge. It was an ill-fated attack; her horse bogged in the mud, buried to her knees in the soft silt. Screaming, the young woman leapt from the beast's back, charged laboriously through the rest of the silt, then tried to run across the logs. Gwenna watched as a trunk shifted beneath her. She teetered for a moment, then disappeared, the weight of wood shifting closed before the splash had even subsided.

"They can't cross yet," Annick observed.

"They will," Gwenna replied grimly. Whatever Bridger managed above the fork, there were enough logs already in the east channel to form a dam once the current packed them in densely enough. It would be a treacherous crossing, to be sure. Logs would shift, and Urghul would die, but they were coming.

The line of archers, so pathetic to begin with, looked like a group of slack-mouthed farmers shown up from the countryside for the village fair, except they were about to be shooting at people instead of straw butts, and if they missed, they died. A few of them were glancing over their shoulders, as though thinking of running. Gwenna had been gnawing the inside of her mouth so viciously that it had started to bleed. She spat the coppery blood out into the mud, and tried to *think*. Great generals could win impossible battles, but she wasn't a great general. She was barely Kettral, and a declared traitor at that.

"Are you contemplating the beauty of the northern forest at dusk?" Pyrre asked.

"I'm *thinking,* you miserable bitch," Gwenna snarled, fury at her own impotence spilling over toward the Skullsworn. The woman had done nothing since they arrived but drink beer and make her mocking little cracks. "Why did you even *come* here?"

Pyrre took a contemplative pull on her tankard before responding. "You may recall that the choice was this or a quick, inglorious death among the pines."

"Well, this goat fuck is shaping up to be pretty quick, inglorious, and deadly, too," Gwenna said. The Flea had left her the command, and now everyone from Andt-Kyl looked likely to die. Worse, instead of figuring out a way to stop it, here she was trading barbs with a woman who actually relished slaughter, who would look with joy on the deaths of children, men, and women, a whole town full of folk who, until two days earlier, couldn't imagine that war's hammer was about to descend upon them. "You should have saved yourself the trip," Gwenna spat. "You and me both."

"On the contrary," Pyrre said. "Here, I have the comforts of human society as I face my god. The bond of a sisterhood in arms."

"Bugger your fucking sisterhood."

Pyrre frowned speculatively. "I was picturing a different type of sister-hood."

She started to raise the tankard to her lips once more, and then Gwenna's knife was out, stabbing toward the Skullsworn's throat in pure, unpremeditated fury. There were plenty of little knife fights back on the Islands, cadets and vets settling scores by squaring off and fighting to the first blood. This wasn't that. Gwenna put her whole weight behind the thrust, pivoting with the blow, twisting her wrist to feather the blade as it sunk into the flesh . . . only there was no flesh to find. The blade clattered against something, and Gwenna's wrist jammed with the impact. She tried to slice sideways, but the Skullsworn had caught the knife inside her tankard. Gwenna yanked it back, trying to pull it free, and Pyrre stepped into the open space, hammering up with the heel of her hand, slamming Gwenna's mouth shut so hard that her teeth throbbed and her neck snapped back as she tumbled to the mud.

The whole thing had taken less than a heartbeat. Most of the loggers hadn't even noticed, and by the time they looked over, Pyrre was extending a hand to Gwenna, her smile broad, her eyes hard.

"Careful, sir," she said, echoing Bridger's deference. "The footing through here is treacherous."

Gwenna glanced over at the curious archers, shackled her pride, and took the woman's hand. Pyrre's grip might have been hammered from steel. When she yanked Gwenna to her feet, she pulled her close enough to murmur in her ear.

"I came here to kill Urghul, which means that, in theory, we are on the same side." She paused, allowed Gwenna to regain her footing and pull back. "Am I wrong?" she asked, voice sickeningly mild.

"No," Gwenna growled. "You're not wrong."

"Excellent!" She smiled. "The thing is, I'm good with the killing, but not all that great when it comes to the tedium of tactics and strategy, so maybe you could"—she waved a hand toward the logs piling up in the river—"think through all that sort of thing. In the meantime," she held the empty tankard aloft, "I seem to have spilled my beer."

Gwenna ground her teeth as the woman turned back toward the houses, tried to ignore the blood hammering at her temples, tried to figure out how to get the fewest people killed. It was tempting to pull everyone back to West Island, maybe as far as the West Bank, and then to destroy the bridges behind them. That would put a little more space between the people of Andt-Kyl and the Urghul, plus two more channels of flowing water. The trouble was, she'd already tried that trick once, and Long Fist had anticipated it. She could give ground, then find herself on the far bank facing the same army without even the semblance of a defensive position. At least here the Urghul would have to pick their way slowly across the shifting and uneven dam, and while they were picking, the loggers could be shooting.

Gwenna looked over the crew, trying to see something different, something that might give her hope. She cursed the Flea again for putting her in charge. She wasn't a general. She was a demo master. She'd trained to blow things up, not to lead people, she—

"Oh, Holy Hull," she breathed, staring at the dam. "Oh fuck."

She tried to run through a dozen calculations at the same time—weight, force, flow, distance, density—and failed. It was impossible to say how deep the dam went, how tangled the logs were, what it would take to dislodge them, but it was suddenly, perfectly clear what she had to do.

"Annick," she said, turning to the sniper. "Hold them here."

The sniper blinked. "Where are you going?"

Gwenna waved at the bridge. "I'm going to blow it."

"They'll fill you with arrows before you get halfway across, and a star-shatter on the surface . . ." She shook her head. "It won't work."

"I'm not going across," Gwenna said. "I'm going under."

She had the faint satisfaction of seeing Annick's eyes widen a fraction. She waited for the sniper to tell her it was insane, impossible, that the water was too cold, the dam too wide, the explosives inadequate to the task. Instead the sniper just nodded. Not that that should have been surprising.

Gwenna took a deep breath, then turned away from the barricades. She was going to die, that much seemed clear, but this kind of mission, at least, she understood.

"If you don't see anything by full dark," she said, "it didn't work."

The sniper nodded again. Then, as Gwenna grabbed her pack of munitions, Annick extended a hand. For just a moment she looked small, girl-like, confused.

"Good luck, Gwenna," she said quietly.

Gwenna wasn't sure whether to cry or shit herself.

✝

By the time she got to North Island, the Urghul were already trying to cross back at the logjam. She couldn't make out much more than the shapes of men, women, and horses in the distance and thickening dark, but it looked as though Annick was holding them, Annick along with the mud flats on either side of the channel and the precarious nature of the dam itself. Still, the Urghul had the numbers. Sooner or later a group would reach the near bank, and then it would be villagers and their wood axes against mounted horsemen with spears. Gwenna tried not to think about that.

To the north, Bridger and his crews had managed to divert the majority of the logs into the central and western channels, but enough still slipped through the east that simply floating with the current would be treacherous. As Gwenna watched, two huge trunks nudged together almost gently, bumping and rolling with the current. A person trapped between them would be crushed.

Well, she muttered to herself, *best not get trapped.*

It took only a moment to ready her starshatters and drop her boots, then three times as long to get up the courage to actually dive into the swirling, black water. The icy cold knocked the wind from her immediately, and she swirled out into the main channel kicking and gasping, trying to get a full breath as her chest constricted with the cold. She'd known it wouldn't be like the ocean around the Islands—the Black was fed directly from the glacial runoff from the Romsdals—but this . . . her teeth were already chattering, and her fingers felt fat and foolish. She'd always found water more frightening in the darkness, as though it were a great pool that went all the way down into the earth, a hungry pit with no bottom, and darkness was falling fast.

There was nothing for it but to stroke hard downstream, to try to conserve the meager heat she'd built running north by swimming south, and so, starshatters tucked into her belt, she kicked hard for the dam. Halfway there, a log almost took her head off. She dove at the last moment, coming up on the far side as it smashed up against a floating raft of trunks. From the water, the mounted Urghul loomed up in silhouette against the gray night sky. She tried to count them, but it was all she could do to stay clear of the shifting logs, to keep her head above water as her limbs turned to lead. Somewhere ahead, a horse screamed, and someone tumbled into the water, clawing for a moment at the dam, then sucked beneath.

And then, all at once, she was almost on top of it, the jagged logs crushed together, looming like teeth from the swirling surface. She caught a glimpse of bodies pressed up against twisted wreckage, riders pinned by the current, drowned, their faces just inches from the good air. It sounded like there was fighting on the island, but she had no way to see it. There was just time to raise the starshatters above the surface, light them with a flick of a hand, to suck in a huge breath, manage half a prayer to Hull, and then dive, kicking down, down, down into the frigid, perfect blackness of the river bottom.

43

The midnight gongs had long since tolled when Kaden, Kiel, and Gabril began the long walk back to the Temple of Pleasure. They walked in silence, partly because they couldn't speak freely on the streets of Annur, partly because there was nothing to say. Kaden had played his gambit, and it had failed. He could still hear the chaos of the warehouse, the various nobles shouting over each other, accusing, condemning, demanding. . . . Such a scene would have been impossible among the Shin, but then, that was the problem; neither Kiel nor Kaden had anticipated the full extent of the aristocrats' irrationality, the strength of the clutching grasp in which their emotions held them.

He kept his hood up and his head down as they moved through the winding streets, eyes fixed on his own feet and those of Gabril and Kiel, who led the way a few paces ahead. For once, he was grateful for the disguise—the hood let him stay silent, let him drift in his own thoughts. Those thoughts—visions of failure and futility—had consumed him so fully that he almost strode directly into Kiel's back when the man stopped short. Kaden started to speak, but Kiel pushed him back, quietly but firmly, down the street from which they had just emerged.

When they finally stopped, Kaden raised his head carefully, glancing from Gabril to the Csestriim.

"What?" he asked quietly.

"The Ishien," Kiel replied. "Two of them, waiting in the shadows just outside the cobbler's shop."

Kaden took a long breath, forcing himself to calm. "Did they see us?"

Kiel shook his head.

"Who," Gabril asked, "are the Ishien?"

Kaden started to explain, then thought better of it. "Enemies," he said curtly. "Do you know another way into the temple?"

Gabril frowned. "Several." He glanced over his shoulder. "These enemies of yours, they can fight?"

Kaden nodded.

"How did they follow you?"

Kaden considered the question. Matol couldn't have tracked them from the *kenta* in the catacombs all the way to the temple. The memory of the *ak'hanath* sprang to mind, of their twisted, unnatural legs, of the red eyes bulging from the joints. But Matol wasn't Csestriim. He didn't have *ak'hanath*. Which meant the *beshra'an*.

"They didn't follow," Kaden said. "They anticipated. There are only a few places in Annur I could go, only a few places to which I have any connection. They've probably got men watching all of them."

"You did not tell me this," Gabril said, jaw tight.

"I didn't know they would pursue me so quickly."

"We can discuss it further," Kiel said, "when we're inside the temple."

Getting inside the temple proved easier said than done. Gabril led them to three more entrances before they found one—a low stable outside a modest palace—that was unwatched. By the time they'd murmured Morjeta's passphrase to the pair of guards, descended through the long tunnel underground, and emerged into one of the small garden pavilions, Kaden wanted nothing more than to sleep. Dawn would be soon enough to fully confront the implications of his failure, both with the council and the Ishien, soon enough to start searching for another path. His mind felt battered by the strange tides of emotion: the hope, fear, anger, and despair. How most people lived with such emotions every day, with feelings a hundred times stronger, he had no idea. Even the residual tug of longing and loss was enough to disorder all hope of rational thought.

Sleep, he reminded himself. *Sleep first, then thought.*

When they stepped through the wooden door into the pavilion, however, the strain on Morjeta's face said immediately that there would be no sleep. He started to ask what was wrong, but she waved him silent, the motion quick and urgent. Behind Kaden, Kiel and Gabril went still. Over the slow wash of water, through the gentle ringing of the wind chimes, Kaden could make out a voice, a man's voice, smooth and urbane, but sharp as oiled steel.

"I have nothing but respect for your temple and for your goddess, but I speak for the Unhewn Throne, and in this matter I will not be denied."

Kaden felt the cold claws of fear prick through the skin of his neck. He had heard that voice only briefly. It had been more than a month since he last saw the man walking out of the Bone Mountains, clothing ripped, face bloody, but he knew the accent and idiom as though they were his own. The Shin had taken from him the luxury of forgetting. While the Ishien were hunting him outside, here, within the very walls of the temple, Tarik Adiv had come, searching for someone.

"It is not a matter of denial, Councillor," said a woman's voice, warm as liquid honey. "The young man you seek is not within our walls."

"How disappointing," Adiv said, voice slick with disbelief. "You won't mind if my men just . . . check. There are so *many* people coming and going, and, in the aftermath of ecstasy, it's easy to forget certain . . . details. . . ."

Kaden crossed silently to the wooden screen separating his pavilion from the lush garden beyond. Adiv stood in the soft red light of the hanging paper lanterns. The Mizran Councillor appeared fully recovered from his ordeal in the mountains, his dark robes immaculate, dark hair combed carefully back, held in place with a dark blindfold. He was the image of imperial authority. And a leach. And a murderer. Kaden could feel Gabril tensing at his side, and he turned to fix the First Speaker with his gaze, then shook his head slowly. Adiv was flanked by half a dozen soldiers, and whatever Gabril's skills with those blades, he wasn't prepared to face a leach.

"I'm afraid that won't be possible, Councillor," the woman said. "As you know, we hold the identities of those inside Ciena's walls inviolate."

Kaden shifted his attention to the *leina* confronting Adiv, a tall, voluptuous woman with skin dark and lustrous as wet coal, her hair hanging in hundreds of delicate braids. She looked desperately vulnerable, standing before the armored soldiers in nothing more than a dress of diaphanous silk, but her face betrayed no fear.

She smiled, spreading her hands. "I'm sure you understand."

Adiv's jaw tightened. "I'm sure I do." He glanced around the garden, seeming to look through that blindfold of his from one pavilion to the next. Kaden kept still as the non-gaze passed over him, wondering for the first time whether Tan had killed all the *ak'hanath* back in the Bone Mountains. He realized he had no idea where the creatures had originally come from, whether Adiv had more, whether they were stalking him even now, scratching at the high walls of the temple, searching for a way in, a way over.

Finally Adiv turned back to the *leina*. "You know, Demivalle, that I have more men than these six."

He left the rest of the threat unvoiced, but the *leina*'s lips tightened a fraction.

"And *you* know, Councillor, that the citizens of Annur love my goddess. Many worship inside these walls, and the worshippers would be displeased with any disturbance."

"The citizens of Annur love Intarra, as well," Adiv replied. "And look what happened to Uinian."

Demivalle met his smile with one of her own. "Of course, Uinian was a traitor. I am not. I live to serve Annur and all her citizens, after serving my goddess, of course."

"You've always been clever with that tongue of yours, Valle, but you know as well as any that serving Annur is not the same as serving the Unhewn Throne."

"I wish all peace and pleasure upon the lords of our land." She cocked her head delicately to the side. "This is a . . . precarious time for the Dawn Palace. I would hate to see the current instability extended as a result of . . ." She paused longer this time, as though searching for the words. ". . . rash and unnecessary decisions."

Maybe it was her light, apologetic laugh, or the simple fact of seeing his will so clearly thwarted, but Adiv's face twisted into a snarl beneath his blindfold, and he leaned in close, seizing the *leina* by the arm, his fingers driving into her flesh.

"So we understand each other," he hissed, "I would remind you that what you have here is nothing more than a collection of pretty, perfumed whores. You hide behind the lust of Annur's powerful and rich as though that lust were loyalty. It is not. I will leave you for the moment, but if I discover you have lied to me, you may find that all this soft, decadent flesh you have so assiduously collected, all your beautiful boys and girls, will burn as briskly as your high walls."

If Demivalle was frightened by the threat, she didn't show it. Instead of drawing back from Adiv's grip, she pulled him closer in a mockery of true embrace.

"And in the interest of understanding," she whispered sweetly in his ear, the words soft, yet intended to carry to anyone else listening, "I would remind you that while you serve a man, I serve a goddess. It is a pity your eyes went bad so early, or you might see more clearly the power you confront."

"I could kill him," Gabril said, frowning at the flame flickering inside the porcelain lamp.

Morjeta shook her head vigorously. "No. You couldn't. Tarik Adiv is a cruel, vicious man, but he is not foolish. The six soldiers you saw tonight were the barest fraction of his strength."

"And he's a leach," Triste spat. "He can . . . do things."

Gabril shook his head in disgust. "Filthy scum."

Kaden took a deep breath, then blew it out slowly. After Adiv's departure, Morjeta had hurried them up the stairs to her chambers and double-bolted the doors while Triste pulled the curtains and lit more lamps. The temple, which had seemed like such a sanctuary for the past several days, now felt dangerous, sinister, a trap sliding slowly shut. He glanced around Morjeta's chamber, but there was little to see—delicately scented candles on the mantel; flowering jasmine in dark, elegant pots; a harp hung from a hook on one wall; and a scattering of parchment, quills, and ink jars scattered across a low table, the remnants of their long nights drafting the constitution. Nothing to suggest treachery. Nothing to hint that even here, in the heart of Ciena's temple, they were being watched.

"How did Adiv know I was here?" Kaden asked.

Triste stabbed a finger at the garden beyond the curtains. "There are hundreds of *leinas,*" she said, shaking her head with disgust. "Someone talked."

"What about all that about 'keeping identities inviolate'?" Kaden asked.

Morjeta pursed her lips. "Most of us serve the goddess above all." She spread her hands. "But despite the training and the oaths, *leinas* are human, with human hopes and flaws. They can be threatened or bribed. They can be manipulated to think they have no choices." She glanced at Triste, and a shadow of anguish passed across her face. "Demivalle is strict in her adherence to the oaths—this year already she has seen four *leinas* and a serving girl cut and put outside the walls for violating the trust of the goddess—but this temple houses hundreds, and she cannot be everywhere."

"We will move to my estate," Gabril said. "These Ishien would not follow you there, and this temple is no longer safe. Now that the councillor knows you are here, he will come back."

Morjeta hesitated, then shook her head. "He doesn't know. Not for certain. We've been careful to keep Kaden hooded and hidden at all times save inside my own rooms. At the most, Adiv has heard that my daughter has returned. You should be safe here, at least for a few more nights."

"He was searching for a man," Kaden pointed out.

"He was fishing," Morjeta said, "hoping Demivalle would let something slip. If he knew for certain that you were here, that I was shielding you, Ciena's walls would not keep you safe."

"There must be some way to stop him," Triste said, hands balling into fists, "to kill him."

"Tarik Adiv is not the problem," Kaden said quietly, shaking his head. "Not yet, at least."

Triste turned to him, aghast. "He tried to murder you once already. He threatened my mother and took me from the temple by force, and now he's back, hunting us again. How is he not the problem?"

"He is only an obstacle," Kaden replied, "if we decide to remain in the city. We could be gone tomorrow morning, by tonight, and he would have no way to follow us."

"You would run?" Gabril asked, face hardening. "And what of this empire you pledged to destroy? What of your constitution?"

Kaden met the First Speaker's angry glare. "I don't plan to run, but until we have devised a way to destroy the empire itself, it's irrelevant whether or not Tarik Adiv watches over the Dawn Palace. Irrelevant whether or not we kill him."

"Killing would be a good place to start," Triste said. "We can figure out the rest as we go along."

"No," Kaden said, shaking his head. "Killing Adiv will create an absence in the Dawn Palace, a brief period in which no one rules Annur—but absence is difficult to maintain. If our own council is not there to fill the empty space, then il Tornja, or Adare, or another of his minions will step in almost immediately."

"Unfortunately," Kiel said, "after our meeting tonight, forming a council looks unlikely."

"The nobles are fools," Gabril said, cracking the knuckles of one hand, then the other. "They would poison their own well to prevent others from drinking."

"What if you were able to offer them something?" Triste asked. "Promise them more, if they sign the constitution?"

"I don't have anything else to offer," Kaden said, spreading his hands.

"Future rights and prerogatives," Triste suggested, "in the new republic."

Kaden considered the idea a moment, then shook his head in frustration. "It was greed over the rights I was offering in the first place that choked off the agreement."

Morjeta had been staring at him, eyes bright in the lamplight. "It won't work. . . ." she whispered. "I thought that maybe . . ." She shook her head. "They aren't going to agree after all. I'm so sorry."

They fell silent at that, Gabril glaring moodily into the lamplight, Triste gnawing at her lip. Kaden studied them a moment, the thorn of a horrible new thought pricking at his mind, then looked away, watching the delicate curtains shift in the breeze. From the garden below, he could make out the light sound of music and laughter played over the deeper bass of moaning, the fervent cries of physical rapture. The weariness he'd felt just after returning from the warehouse settled on him once more, a heavy, soporific helplessness. These were his people, the patrons of the temple and the angry nobility alike, and yet sometimes they seemed more alien than the Csestriim.

He filled his mind with a *saama'an* of the meeting, studied various faces in the feeble lamplight. He could see the scene in perfect detail, but it meant little. He could stare at the faces for hours, watch the disaster unfold forward or backward, but he had no idea how to change the result. If it were a crumbling wall, or the broken axle of a cart, a wet clay pot on the spinning wheel or a goat's carcass to be carved, he would be able to discern the shape of the problem beneath the bright skin of the world, but he could find no pattern in the assembled aristocrats, no shape in the madness.

Exhaling slowly, he let the image go, watching instead as the oil lamp sputtered for a moment, the flame waving wildly before steadying itself. He understood how the lamp worked: oil and air, fuel and space, something and nothing. Starve it of oil—the flame died. Crowd it—the flame died. Kaden reached out, tested the heat, then settled his hand over the top of the lamp. The fire didn't quite reach his skin, but it hurt, hurt worse, then began to burn. The quick, desperate animal part of his brain screamed at him to pull back, to cradle it to his chest, but he silenced the beast and kept his hand in place, watching the pain but discarding the fear of pain.

It felt as though he'd been fighting and running forever, struggling against his foes when he had the strength, fleeing more often. And where had it landed him? Trapped inside a temple, his secrecy fraying, his plans thwarted, enemies circling. He stared at his hand. The skin beneath was seared, blistered, but the fire in the lamp had gone out. He lifted his palm slowly, watching the smoke break apart on the light breeze. The others were exclaiming, but he set the sound aside, following the track of his thought. All this time, he'd been trying to guard himself, his few friends, his family. . . . He turned his hand over, stared at the livid red flesh across the palm. The truth was, he couldn't protect anyone, not even himself. He'd failed at fighting. Failed at keeping his secrets. Failed at eluding Adiv and the Ishien both.

"Maybe it's time to stop fighting," he murmured, testing the idea aloud.

"What?" Triste asked.

He didn't look up, staring instead at the lines in his scorched flesh, studying them as he considered the various pieces of a new plan, rotating them like stones in his mind until they fit, locking into place.

He turned to Gabril. "I need to meet the council again."

The First Speaker frowned. "So soon? They will still be furious from tonight's fiasco."

"Not right away," Kaden replied. "Three days. On *my* ground this time."

Kiel raised his eyebrows. "Your ground?"

"The Shin chapterhouse," Kaden said. "It's neutral and discreet."

"The Shin chapterhouse," Kiel observed, "like this temple, will be watched by the Ishien."

Kaden paused at that, forced himself to hesitate, to smile. "I know. But there are other ways in. The abbot explained them to me when I spoke with him. Passages underground."

"Why risk these passages?" Gabril asked, shaking his head. "Why risk the place at all? I can secure another location easily, also neutral, one not watched by these foes of yours."

"The meeting has to take place at the chapterhouse. I have to show the nobles something."

Kiel studied him a moment. "The *kenta.*"

Kaden nodded.

"Why?" the Csestriim asked. "The gates have been your family's secret since the founding of the empire."

"It's the empire we're trying to replace," Kaden observed, carried along by the momentum of his own lie. "Triste suggested offering the nobility something they can't refuse, something in return for their participation in the republic. I intend to offer them the use of the *kenta.*"

"The gates would destroy them," Kiel said, narrowing his eyes.

"They don't know that. When they see me disappear, then return the same afternoon carrying fresh fruit from the markets of Olon, they'll understand the power. They'll sign whatever we put in front of them for a piece of it."

"And when they discover you've lied to them?"

"I'll tell them it takes months of training to safely use the gates. If we're all still alive then, we can worry about what comes next."

Kiel nodded. "It could work," he said, then paused, studying Kaden. "There's something you're not saying."

Kaden smoothed away the barbs of fear, forced himself to meet the Csestriim's gaze.

"There is," he agreed, then turned to Triste.

"I need you to take a note to the chapterhouse, to a monk named Iaapa."

"No!" Morjeta exploded, face aghast. "If it's watched, they'll take her! Absolutely not!"

"They'll watch her, but they won't take her," Kaden said. "Not until she's led them to me."

"They will!" the *leina* cried, gathering her daughter up in her arms. "You already explained to me what these men are like. They will torture her to find out where you are!"

Kaden shook his head. "They tried that already, at great length and with little success."

Triste shuddered at the memory, and her mother clutched her tighter.

"Why take the risk?" Kiel asked. "Why not send Gabril? The Ishien don't know him. They won't pay any attention to him at all."

Kaden hesitated, trying to decide how much to reveal. "I want them to notice," he said finally.

The girl disentangled herself from her mother slowly, then turned toward Kaden. "Why?" she asked, voice trembling with the single syllable.

"They'll follow you back here," he said, "but they won't be able to come inside the walls. At that point, they'll go back to the chapterhouse. They'll demand that Iaapa hand over the note that you'd been so conspicuously carrying."

"Why would a Shin abbot cooperate with these Ishien?" Gabril asked.

"Because Triste's going to ask him to. She's going to tell him that I asked it."

"And what," Kiel asked slowly, "does this mysterious note say?"

Kaden shrugged. "That I'm giving up. That I tried to take back my throne and failed. That I'm going back to Ashk'lan with another worshipper of the Blank God to restart the monastery there. That if any of his monks would like to join us, we would welcome them."

For several heartbeats no one spoke. Then Gabril started laughing. It was a warm, rich sound, and when Morjeta and Triste turned to him in confusion, he pointed across the table at Kaden.

"He may know nothing of knives, but his mind is keen as a blade."

"You think that when they read this note," Morjeta said finally, "that these Ishien will try to follow you back to your monastery?"

"For the chance to capture both Kiel and me?" Kaden asked. "I think they'd follow me all the way to Li."

"Only you are not going to Li," Kiel said. "Or to Ashk'lan."

Kaden shook his head, then turned to Triste. "There is a risk for you in delivering the message."

Fear filled her wide eyes, but she didn't hesitate. "I'll go."

"No," Morjeta protested. "Please."

Triste peeled away her mother's arms. "I'm going."

"What about the nobles?" Gabril asked. "They assembled once out of curiosity. They'll be reluctant to do so again."

Kaden nodded. "Explain to them that I plan to make my earlier offer more compelling. Also, make sure they dress discreetly. In fact, tell them to dress as monks."

"Monks?" Gabril asked. "Trust does not flow readily between them. As at our last meeting, they will not feel safe without steel in their hands."

Kaden nodded. "You'd be surprised what you can hide beneath a monk's robe. They can bring whatever weapons they want as long as they keep them hidden." He paused. "Can you write me a list of all the names?"

Gabril raised his eyebrows. "We've been over them already."

"I know. I want a chance to study them, to learn them by heart," Kaden replied. "This meeting is going to be difficult enough. I don't want to offend anyone by botching a name."

Gabril shrugged, then turned to Morjeta. "You have ink and brushes."

For a moment the woman seemed not to hear him, staring instead at Kaden as though seeing him for the first time. Then, just as Gabril seemed about to repeat himself, she nodded abruptly and left the room, returning moments later with an elaborate lacquered case, opening it on the table between them.

"Please," she said, gesturing to the inks and sheets of fine vellum. "Use whatever you need."

Gabril took one brush while Kaden selected another.

"While you're writing the names," he said, "I'll write a short note to each of our . . . friends explaining how to get into the chapterhouse unseen. If I seal them up, can you make sure they are delivered?"

Gabril nodded without glancing up from his writing. "It is simple enough."

"Thank you," Kaden said.

As he worked, he was careful to make sure no one in the room could see what he wrote. He thought he had finally discovered whom to trust, but he couldn't be certain, and it would not do for the wrong eyes to see that his notes to the nobility said nothing about meeting in the chapterhouse, that his letter to Iaapa had nothing to do with a return to Ashk'lan.

44

Valyn felt as though he'd been watching Balendin tear people apart for days, the shock of the violence matched only by the shock of seeing the leach free, striding up and down the far bank of the Black, the Urghul genuflecting before him as though he were a nomadic chieftain in his own right. Were it not for his fingers—still wrapped in bloody bandages—and his dark hair, dark skin, Valyn might have mistaken him for one of the horsemen.

It was impossible to be sure what had happened in the long days since he, Laith, and Talal rode south out of the Urghul camp, but the basic outlines were as clear as they were horrifying. As the flier suspected, Long Fist had double-crossed them. The Urghul chieftain had clearly decided there were better things to do with a Kettral-trained leach than cut him apart one joint at a time. Gwenna and the others, discovering the treachery, had managed to claw their way free, to get clear of the whole camp, to cross the Black, and arrive in Andt-Kyl in time to warn the town.

As for Balendin, the fact that he had turned on il Tornja, on Annur itself, wasn't so surprising. Given his well, his reliance on awe and terror for any arcane power, it was little surprise that the leach had thrown his lot in with the Urghul. The casual cruelty of the horsemen, the endless sacrifice and brutality, gave him the perfect opportunity to inflict pain and reap his sick reward from the terror of his captives. Back on the Islands he'd been forced to keep his torture and murder circumspect, forced to choose his time and his victims. Here, he had them lined up by the dozen, by the *hundred,* all those horrified eyes fixed upon him as he flayed the prisoners, and burned them, and tore them apart. For the Urghul, all that pain was a great sacrifice to Kwihna, but Valyn knew better. The sacrifices Balendin made were to himself.

"He's dangerous like this," Talal said quietly, after the sixth or seventh broken corpse was tossed aside.

"He's always been dangerous," Valyn replied, remembering Amie strung up in the dark garret back on Hook. Remembering Ha Lin. "People have always been wary of him. Even on the Islands: wary, angry, or afraid."

Talal shook his head. "That was nothing. This . . ." He sucked air between his teeth. "I have no idea what he can manage with the power. It must be flooding him."

"He can have the 'Kent-kissing power," Laith spat, "as long as it doesn't help him across the river."

And to Valyn's shocked relief, it did not. Hour after hour the Urghul went about their bloody sport without making anything but a few abortive efforts at crossing: two or three idiotic attempts to swim horses, a bizarre push to build a bridge by tossing a dozen logs into the channel and watching them bump up pointlessly against the old bridge pilings. By the time the sun began to set, the Urghul had made no real offensive at all.

And then they did.

An hour was all it took, half an hour, for the logs to build up. Valyn and his Wing could only watch, appalled, realizing along with the townsfolk what the Urghul intended. Somewhere, probably miles to the north, they'd found the timber that the townspeople had been logging all winter long. There would have been huge piles of it stacked at the side of the river, just waiting for the full summer floods to carry it down into Scar Lake. It wouldn't take more than a few dozen riders to loose it all, thousands upon thousands of logs. With so much weight in the river, there was no need for an engineer. The current built the bridge, forcing the logs up against the remnants of the old pilings and holding them in place.

In minutes the horsemen had gone from riding idly up and down the far bank to a full-blown charge across the precarious and shifting raft. The foremost riders foundered on the loosely packed logs, the legs of their panicked, screaming mounts plunging into the gaps. The river had turned into a deadly chaos of shifting trunks and thrashing, dying beasts, but the unseated Urghul pressed forward on foot, voices and spears both raised in defiance.

Valyn's eyes fixed on one woman with streaming braids and blood smeared over her face like paint. Her horse was gone, but she was darting forward, leaping nimbly from trunk to trunk, watching the logs, judging their movement, choosing her line. In other circumstances he would have

admired her poise, her patience—she would have made good Kettral material. Problem was, she'd nearly crossed the channel. A few more well-
timed leaps and she'd be into the mud flats on the near side. As though
sensing this herself, she paused atop the shifting dam and turned back,
waving her fellow warriors on, mouth pried wide with a scream he could
see, could almost hear, like a fine file drawn over glass.

Then an arrow took her through the shoulder, spinning her halfway
around, sending her tumbling into a gap between the logs. Valyn watched
as the trunks, forced on by the current, closed around her chest. She thrashed
desperately, heedless of the arrow wound, trying to claw her way free, but
there was no freedom to be had. The river flowed on implacably, crushing
her, then folding her under into the dark, invisible current.

If the dam had remained so precarious, the loggers would have had a
shot, but it was clear even in the gathering gloom that both the logs and
the water were working with the Urghul. More trunks piled up, stacking
closer and closer together, until the horsemen were crossing in groups of
three and four, sometimes keeping their saddles until the far bank. Valyn
shifted the long lens to Annick. Her right arm was a blur as she aimed and
shot, aimed and shot, too fast for Valyn himself to spot the relevant tar-
gets. Her face was turned away from him, but he could imagine her blue
eyes gone gray as slate in the twilight, the hard set of her jaw. The mud flats
gave her and her archers time, but the Urghul had numbers to spare and
more. With the dam firming up, even Annick couldn't hold them forever.

"Where in 'Shael's sweet name is Gwenna off to?" Laith muttered.

Valyn turned to find her darting north between the houses, away from
the fight. Didn't seem like Gwenna to run away.

"Getting more archers, maybe," Talal said.

"What archers?" Valyn asked, shaking his head. "Everyone who can
hold a bow is already on that barricade."

"We've got to go down," Laith said.

Valyn shook his head. "And do *what*? You don't even have a bow."

"I've got a pair of swords," Laith spat. "I've got my fucking fists."

"Your fists aren't going to turn that tide," Valyn growled. "Gwenna has
her mission, and we have ours."

"They need to fall back," Talal murmured. "They've lost the far channel. They need to fall back to the western island and blow the central
bridges."

Valyn turned back to the battle. At a glance, it wasn't obvious that the leach was right. Just a handful of riders had actually reached the barricade, and those were dispatched quickly enough by arrows and axes. As Valyn watched, Pyrre stepped from nowhere onto the highest log of the barrier, swung onto a horse behind the rider like a young woman going for a gallop with her gallant, hugging him close around the chest. Valyn caught a glimpse of steel in the starlight, and the man crumpled forward, then off, tumbling to the ground. Pyrre shrugged into better position on the horse's back, then kicked the mount north along the far side of the barricade, alone among the mass of Urghul. She charged directly into two more riders, leapt free as the horses went down in a tangle of thrashing limbs and hooves, landed atop the piled logs, then dropped down once more to cut the throats of the struggling Urghul.

It still looked like the villagers might hold, unless you glanced over to the far bank and saw the army pressing forward, unnumbered, spilling endlessly out of the shadows between the trees. The loggers were tough, but they weren't trained soldiers. Everyone had a breaking point, and when they broke, it would be a slaughter.

"Annick will pull them back," Valyn said, praying that it was true. The sniper had a good mind for tactics, but it wasn't at all clear she cared whether a few hundred loggers died on Urghul spears. She might have decided on some coldhearted sacrificial gambit known only to herself. "Annick will pull them back."

Talal pointed. "There."

The villagers were withdrawing. Not a rout, but a purposeful, single-file retreat westward through the village square and over the bridges joining the two islands. Annick stayed. Pyrre stayed. A few dozen hard-looking men and set-jawed women stayed, too, loosing arrows grimly into the massing horsemen, holding them while the others pulled back. The retreat seemed to take days, but it couldn't have been more than a few minutes before the loggers from the barricade had backed across the middle bridges onto the western island.

Meanwhile, scores of Urghul had gained the bank of the eastern island, their horses wallowing up through the mud flats or rearing at the barricade. That barricade was high enough to hold off the mounted riders for a few more moments, but it was going to be a close thing for those covering the retreat. A few Urghul had already dismounted to haul haphazardly on the logs. When they'd pried open a gap, the island was lost.

"Gwenna better have those central bridges rigged," Valyn said, his whole body tight as a bent bow. He ached to be down there, fighting shoulder to shoulder with his Wing against the Urghul tide, doing his part to hold back the menace. His fist clenched and unclenched mindlessly, searching for something to seize, to smash. Everything about holding his own position felt wrong, but if he descended, all reasonable hope of killing il Tornja went straight into the shitter. He could feel the claws of rage and readiness sunk deep in his flesh, tearing at him, but it was this moment that he had trained for. *Discipline,* Hendran wrote, *is the mind's leash on the body.*

"She'd better have those bridges rigged," he said again, forcing his fist to relax.

The explosion came, all right, a dull roar tearing through the damp fabric of the night, low at first, then abruptly sharp and percussive, a thousand thousand awful rents and ruptures piled on one another until Valyn felt he might go deaf with the sound. The middle bridges, however, didn't move, and it took him a heartbeat to realize that the explosion had come from the easternmost channel, from the packed dam of floating logs. Even as he stared, whole trunks, ten men high, were tossed into the air like so much kindling, raining down on the mud flats and the river alike, sending up great gouts of gray-white froth and spray, crushing Urghul and shattering their horses.

"Holy Hull," Talal breathed.

Valyn could only nod as the great balance of the log raft began to flex, then give way, the pilings that had originally blocked its passage suddenly and utterly obliterated. The riders who had been approaching the makeshift bridge just before it blew reined back their terrified mounts, scrabbling for the dubious safety of the shore while logs the size of a man's leg still clattered to earth, stabbing into the mud, cracking open on the harder ground beyond.

Laith let out a savage whoop, the sound lost in the greater chaos. "Gwenna, you vicious, redheaded *genius!*" he cheered. "That's our demo woman!" he shouted, seizing Valyn by the shoulder in his celebration, stabbing his finger at the wreckage of the bridge. "*She* did that!"

"But how?" Valyn asked slowly. "Where is she?"

Talal's face was sober. "The charge was triggered from beneath. You can see from the blow pattern."

"Which means she went under," Valyn said, staring at the insane mass of splintered logs, huge, jagged shards with the whole pent-up weight of the angry river behind them. The east channel was a churning wreckage of blasted bodies and spinning trunks. The channel had become Anan-shael's own sword. If Gwenna were there, and she had to be . . . "She's dead," Valyn said. The words left him hollow. "Gwenna's dead."

Laith stared for a second, then shoved him away. "You don't know that."

"We don't know *anything*," Valyn spat, "but use your fucking *eyes*." He stabbed a finger at the river. "Could *you* swim that out?"

"We don't *know*," Laith insisted. Then more quietly, "Even if she is dead, she did what she needed to do."

"Part of it," Valyn amended, pointing toward the center bridge. It felt like a heartless thing to say, but having too much heart in the middle of a battle was just a way to get dead. "She blew the dam, but the Urghul can still cross from the east island to the west."

Talal was staring through the long lens. "At a quick count, I put about three hundred on the east island."

"Making it an even fight at the bridge," Valyn said.

"An even fight," Talal said quietly, "except that it's three hundred of Long Fist's best and bravest against a bunch of loggers and a half dozen of il Tornja's scouts."

The new battle line was already forming up at the west end of the central bridge, just a hundred paces from the base of their tower. The loggers had erected another hasty barricade there as well, a waist-high wall of logs with archers spread out on either side. It was a good position. They could rake the Urghul on the bridge with arrows as they crossed, and the bridge itself made it difficult for the mounted riders to come at them more than two abreast.

A good spot, Valyn amended silently, *in the middle of a disastrous fucking mess.*

It had taken the Urghul less than an hour to cross the eastern channel and seize half the village. The loggers were making a good show of it, but they were poorly armed and, judging by their dangerously ragged ranks on the near shore, close to breaking. Gwenna's sacrifice had won them a momentary respite from the full weight of the Urghul force, but even that respite might not matter. As he watched, one rider managed to cross nearly the whole center span, crumbling just as he reached the barricade, an arrow in his eye. Annick's work, no doubt, but Annick couldn't shoot them all.

"Fuck this," Laith said. "I'm going down."

"Il Tornja—" Valyn began.

"Il Tornja is *your* 'Kent-kissing obsession," the flier spat. "*You* kill him."

All at once, Valyn's shame and helplessness, his resolve and uncertainty boiled over in a burning wash of black fury. Since the Wing was formed back on the Islands, Laith had done nothing but go with his gut, flying his way, fighting his way, ignoring orders when it suited him, and to Hull with whatever it did to the rest of the Wing. The son of a bitch seemed to think that just because he was quick with a joke and a pat on the back, everything would work out, that people would overlook all the damage caused by his recklessness. Valyn wanted to seize the flier by the throat and pound some discipline into him, and he half rose, moving toward him, when Talal put a hand on his shoulder.

"It might be best," the leach said quietly. "Two of us should be enough to finish il Tornja, and Annick and Pyrre could use some help down there, someone else to put a little backbone into the local folk."

Valyn remained in his half crouch for a moment, then spat over the edge of the tower and sat back. He looked at the flier and shook his head.

"Good luck," he said, voice cold as the dark water lapping the cliff below.

Laith considered him warily. "What do you want me to tell them down there? About you? What do you want me to tell Annick?"

Valyn hesitated. "Tell them I'm dead," he said finally.

The flier locked eyes with him a moment, then snorted in disgust. "Yeah, that fits. You might as well be."

†

It might have been a page from one of the textbooks back on the Islands, something from a chapter on morale, about the power of a single determined warrior to stiffen the resolve of an entire unit. Laith reached the bridge at a crucial point, just as a knot of horsemen were about to breach the barricade, and he threw himself into the fight with a fury, vaulting over the logs, hamstringing the first two horses, and splitting the skull of one of the fallen riders. Without glancing back to see who was following, the flier pressed on across, sliding between the horses, slitting tendons and throats with equal ease.

Annick and the other archers covered him, and moments later Pyrre appeared at his side. It seemed impossible that the two of them could hold the span against hundreds, but the Urghul were used to fighting on the wide steppe where they could use the speed of their horses and the length of their spears. The narrow space of the bridge worked against them, as did the darkness, and the constant rain of arrows. Laith and Pyrre turned back the assault, and then, while the Urghul withdrew in dismay, they retreated behind the barricade.

Valyn watched it all through the long lens, his stomach churning with a bilious mix of worry, fierce pride, and bitter resentment. Once again Laith had ignored orders and broken ranks, choosing to do just what suited him. He was a rogue, a renegade, a 'Shael-spawned menace . . . but then why, looking down on the vicious fight, did Valyn feel like the fraud and the failure? Professionals held to the mission. That mantra had been drilled into him ten thousand times. Professionals didn't go needlessly off script. And yet, lying on the cold roof, so close to the fight and so far away, he felt anything but professional. He wanted to scream, but the mission dictated silence, so he held his peace and watched.

Seven times the Urghul came, and seven times the villagers held them, Laith and Pyrre at the forefront, swords and knives a moonlit scribbling of quicksilver. Pyrre moved like a shadow between the mounted riders, never seeming to hurry, always just beneath the attacker's thrust, just to the side of it, pivoting or twisting to slide her knife into a neck or rib cage with all the delicacy of a dancer. Laith, on the other hand, was a whirlwind of blades, a maelstrom of savage hacking and slicing, a storm come among the Urghul. Valyn had seen the flier fight before, hundreds of times, but never like this. Laith moved as though possessed, unflagging, untiring, as though he could hold the bridge for days, months, as though nothing could cut him down.

Then the arrow took him through the lower back.

It was bound to happen sooner or later. The villagers weren't snipers. They were terrified. They couldn't see in the darkness like Kettral. Probably the man or woman who loosed the arrow didn't even see it strike, but Valyn saw it, saw the shaft punch in just below the ribs. Straight through the gut. Maybe the liver.

"No," Talal breathed next to him, seeing the same thing.

Valyn closed his eyes, but the sounds of screaming horses and dying men battered against his ears. Somewhere swaddled in that chorus of pain and death was Laith's voice. Valyn couldn't hear it, but knew how it sounded all the same, a defiant howl, a furious roar. He opened his lids again to see Laith on his feet, refusing to retreat, swinging his double blades in a narrowed ambit. Valyn wanted to bellow at the flier to get back, to fall behind the barricade, but the flier would never hear him. And Laith had never listened anyway.

Hot tears sheeted down Valyn's cheeks. His heart felt like a stone inside of him, like something that had never been alive.

As he watched, an Urghul spear took Laith through the chest, lifting him up, up. The horseman fell to one of Annick's arrows, but another of the Urghul was already there, leaning precariously over his horse's back to slash down with his sword into Laith's shoulder. Valyn forced himself to keep his eyes open, to witness, as though that would do any good, but even the witness was denied him. Drenched in blood, still clutching the spear sunk in his heart, Laith crumpled beneath the press of horses, then vanished from view.

"Laith." Valyn wasn't sure he'd said his friend's name aloud.

"May Ananshael be gentle with his soul," Talal murmured quietly.

Valyn shook his head. Madness filled the bridge, chaos and blood and pain—Ananshael's hand, and it was anything but gentle.

45

The Shin chapterhouse looked just as it had days earlier—featureless brick walls, shuttered windows, and a blank wooden door. Of course, it was hard to make out the details from behind the dust-streaked windows of the vacant house.

Behind him, in the wide, pine-paneled room, the members of his would-be council shifted warily. Gabril, Kiel, and Triste had been confused when Kaden led them there several hours earlier, forcing the back door open, then searching the inside of the house until he found the room he wanted, the one facing the square.

"Why are we here?" the First Speaker had asked, turning to take in the moldering space.

"This is where we're meeting the others," Kaden replied.

Gabril stared. "I told them to meet in the chapterhouse."

"And I told them, in the notes you delivered, to ignore that, to meet here."

Triste was shaking her head in confusion. "Why?"

"Because the chapterhouse isn't safe," Kaden replied. "It's easier to see than to explain. Here," he said, gesturing to the mouse-eaten furniture strewn across the room, "help me set these chairs up near the window so people have somewhere to sit."

As it turned out, most of the scions of Annur's great and powerful families, when they finally arrived, preferred to stand. If anything, they seemed to distrust one another more than at their previous meeting. Hands rarely strayed far from knives or swords, and everyone seemed to want a back to the wall. Only Kegellen had availed herself of a chair, subsiding into it with a contented sigh, then propping her feet on another. If she was content, however, the others were not.

"We have been here the better part of an hour," Tevis snapped finally, "and you have said nothing, done nothing, except stare out these 'Kent-kissing windows. I begin to lose my patience."

"I suspect," Kegellen replied languidly, "that you never had much to begin with." While the others had arrived in various approximations of monastic garb, Kegellen had made no effort to disguise herself. She wore a dress of the brightest yellow, fresh jasmine garlands around both wrists, and a headdress of peacock feathers that fluttered in the breeze. The ensemble struck Kaden as gaudy in the extreme, almost ludicrous, but he noticed that none of the others seated around the long table stared or laughed. The woman might have been all alone, fanning herself gently with an elegantly painted fan. She paused in the motion, then gestured toward the window.

"I, for one, appreciate the opportunity to look out over a quiet square. After all, it is these neighborhood squares, this one and scores like it scattered throughout the streets, that make up the true heart of our great city." She flicked the fan once more. "Look there at the tiny temple, or there, at that pale-skinned woman selling figs, or at the darling roses climbing the trellis outside the wine shop. . . ."

"I don't give a fuck for some pauper's wine shop," Tevis snapped. "Or for the 'Shael-spawned figs."

For once, Kaden found himself agreeing with the Nishan. The fig vendor and the wine merchant were irrelevant. It was the view over the square itself, and of the Shin chapterhouse in particular, that was crucial. He needed to see what was about to happen, and, more important, he needed *them* to see.

As he had hoped, Triste's trip to the chapterhouse two days prior had gone without incident. She knocked on the door, delivered the note penned in Kaden's own hand, and left. She said that she'd spent half the walk back to the Temple of Pleasure glancing over her shoulder and the other half running, but no one had accosted her, and as far as she could tell no one had followed her, either.

Kaden hoped that she was wrong.

For the twentieth time, he went over the plan. It would have been so much simpler to just *fight,* to attack the Ishien, then Adiv, then il Tornja and Adare, to keep attacking and attacking and attacking until his foes were dead or he was. It might even have been possible with Valyn's Wing at his back, but Valyn had never reached the meeting point. For all Kaden knew, Valyn had never escaped Assare. He put the grief from his mind, focusing on what mattered: he had no Kettral, no way to attack, nothing. It seemed too much to hope that he might take up that nothingness and use it as a weapon.

The memory of Gabril sparring in the courtyard of his palace filled Kaden's mind once more. He watched the motion of the robe as the soldiers circled, watched those long spears stab out, testing, probing. Gabril had offered no resistance—that was the whole point—letting the mistakes of his men lead them to their doom. Yielding, too, offered a way to victory. Of course, it could offer a quick path to death as well. Kaden took a deep breath, and turned back to the assembled aristocrats, wondering which path he had chosen.

"I've given Tarik Adiv your names," he said, keeping his voice level, calm.

Toward the back of the room, Kiel raised his eyebrows. Triste gasped. A snarl of shock, then a hiss went up from the assembled nobility, dismay and disbelief twisting their faces. After a moment, appalled stares gave way to exclamation and protest, accusatory fingers and a furious clamor of voices. Kaden forced himself to wait, to allow their anger to mount, to let the tension stretch to the point of breaking. For this to work, he needed them scared.

Tevis, however, looked anything but scared. "You worthless shit," he snarled, hand groping for the rapier at his belt. Gabril started to slide in front of Kaden, but Kaden waved him away, stepping forward to meet the Nishan's advance. Tevis's hand closed around his throat, cutting off the air. Kaden slowed his heart, forced his muscles to relax, glanced over the man's shoulder to lock eyes with Kegellen. Her gaze had gone hard at the revelation, but after a moment she waved a glittering hand.

"Set him down, Tevis," she said. "We had best learn the full extent of this foolishness. You can always tear his throat out later."

The nobleman pulled Kaden close to him, his eyes wide with fury, tendons in his neck strained to bursting, then tossed him to the floor. Kaden picked himself up slowly, surreptitiously testing the muscles of his neck. They were bruised, but he'd had worse dozens of times over at the hands of various *umials*. When he finally straightened, he found all eyes fixed on him, gazes sharp as spearpoints.

"Now," Kegellen continued, her voice deceptively mild, "why don't you explain to us just what sort of mischief you've been up to." She smiled.

Kaden gathered his thoughts. "I've made sure that Adiv knows I've returned to the city, made sure he knows your names and our intention of overthrowing the empire, our desire to install a republic in its place."

"It is hardly 'our' intention," said Azurtazine, tapping her long, painted nails against the surface of the table, "if I recall our last meeting correctly."

Kaden smiled. "I omitted that detail. Adiv believes we are of one mind, unified and ready to move against him."

"I knew I should have cut your throat in the warehouse," Tevis spat. "I don't intend to repeat the lapse."

"Cutting my throat now will do little to alleviate the problem," Kaden observed. "Adiv has your names already. He is unlikely to forget them."

"May I assume," Kegellen cut in, "that you've engaged in this little . . . stunt for some purpose other than your own amusement?"

"My purpose," Kaden replied evenly, "is to show you the truth."

Kegellen pouted. "Truth. Such a tricky word."

As though punctuating her remark, a great gong rang out, shivering the air, echoed across the rooftops by dozens more, all of them tolling the noon hour. Kaden turned to the window, gesturing toward the small square and the Shin chapterhouse beyond. It was time to see if his own quiet fight would play out as he'd hoped.

"Watch," he said, gesturing to the sunbaked plaza.

For a few heartbeats there was silence. On the cobbles below, men and women went about their midday chores and errands, calling out to one another in greeting or irritation.

"And what," Kegellen asked finally, "are we watching?"

Kaden's stomach clenched, his shoulders tensed. With an effort he smoothed away the worry. It wouldn't happen right away. Even after the noon gongs, some sort of pause was to be expected. He scanned the square below, searching for any sign, a hint of steel, the clank of armor. Nothing. What would be the consequence, he wondered, if he were wrong? So much hinged on his ability to inhabit the minds of men about whom he knew so little. The *beshra'an* had allowed him to track goats through the mountains, but Adiv was no goat. Matol was no goat. What if one or the other had seen through his trap? What if, even as he watched, they were deploying some elaborate scheme of their own?

Gabril took a step closer to him, face worried, hands on the pommels of his knives. Tevis was still standing, and even Kegellen was starting to look impatient. Kaden glanced back out into the courtyard, studying the front of the Shin chapterhouse. Nothing. Just blank brick and black smoke rising silently into the sky. Nothing. Nothing. And then, from across the small square, a column of fifty men burst into the light, a steel-shod ram at the fore. Kaden breathed out a low, unsteady breath, then held up a finger.

"There," he said.

The armed men crossed the square at a full run, shattering the door to the chapterhouse with the first blow. As the first six hauled the ram aside, others shoved forward into the breach, blades drawn. Even through the closed windows, Kaden could make out the sound of steel against steel, bellows of fighting, and then, moments later, the first screams of the wounded, of the dying.

"What in 'Shael's name . . ." Tevis demanded, eyes fixed on the attack.

"Those," Kaden said calmly, "are Tarik Adiv's men. The attackers."

"And who are they fighting?" Kegellen asked carefully.

"You," Kaden replied simply.

Tevis rounded on him, belt knife drawn. "Talk straight, Malkeenian, or you're done talking."

Kaden glanced down at the bright blade, forced himself to count ten heartbeats before answering. The whole thing could still collapse if it seemed as though he could be bullied by a large man with a knife.

"I gave Adiv your names, and told him we were meeting there," he gestured, "in the chapterhouse. He expects to find you disguised as monks. He believes, right now, that he is slaughtering you."

"Why?" Azurtazine cut in, shaking her head. "What's the point?"

"To show you," Kaden replied, "just how tenuous your position has become." He paused, looking over the group. Some were watching him, others staring at the blank wall of the chapterhouse, the brick and gaping darkness of the door hiding the vicious fight beyond.

"You hold your secret meetings," Kaden continued, "you plot and scheme and gripe, and you think yourselves safe behind your hoods and your money. You are not. Adiv, Adare, and il Tornja tolerate you only because they have more dangerous foes."

"They don't tolerate us," Azurtazine said, shaking her head. "They don't have any idea that we hate the empire. They don't even know who we are." She glanced at the doorway across the square. More soldiers were forcing their way forward into the darkness.

"And you thought they wouldn't find out?" Kaden asked, raising his eyebrows. "I've been in the city less than a week. I have no money, no connections, no men. I knew none of you before I arrived, and it took me a matter of days to learn your names, to expose you. If you think my sister and the *kenarang,* backed by the full might of Annur, wouldn't see you hanging for the ravens within a month, you are greater fools than I took you for."

An angry current passed through the room. It had been centuries since the families of the assembled aristocrats had wielded any real power, but the years had done nothing to blunt their pride. Kaden might have Intarra's eyes, but he lacked the throne, and, aside from Triste and Gabril, he was years younger than the next youngest person in the room. None of them, Bascan or Breatan, pale or dark, man or woman, appreciated being called a fool. On the other hand, the violence below was proving effective theater.

Even as Kaden turned, the shutters barring one of the second-story windows burst open and a man in monk's robes, sword clutched in one hand, face streaming with blood, fell roaring through the gap, landing with a sickening crunch on the stone below. Adiv's soldiers fell on him almost immediately, swords rising and falling in a savage butchery that left little but blood and bone smeared across the cobbles.

"By now," Kaden said, gesturing, "the soldiers are probably realizing that the men inside the chapterhouse are not you, that they were tricked. The realization is likely to fan the councillor's fury. He tried to take you all in one group, to cut the head from the conspiracy all at once. That failed, he will come to your inns and palaces, he will hunt you through the streets of Annur. If you slip the city walls, he will chase you back to your homes and see you burned or hanged."

"What is this?" Tevis demanded, face contorted with fury and confusion. "Your petulant revenge because we would not sign your paper?"

"On the contrary," Kaden replied. "It is a final chance. You would not play your stones, and so I have played them for you."

Kiel stepped forward from the back of the room, passing him the rolled constitution. Kaden took it, unfurled it, glanced over the words. Outside, the shouting and the screams had stopped. Silence filled the square, pressing against the windows like a storm.

"Individually, you are nothing. If you fight, you will die. If you run, you will die. Even if you escape the city, flee to your homes, and manage to raise a rebellion, my sister and her *kenarang* will march the legions and put it down." He paused, letting the fact sink in. "They cannot, however, put down a coordinated push from all of you at once. This"—he gestured to the page—"is both your sword and your shield."

For a moment no one moved, each trying to gauge the reactions of the others. Then Tevis surged to his feet.

"No!" he swore, reaching for his rapier, shoving his way past the table, cursing at Kegellen when his cloak caught on the arm of her chair. "You scheming Malkeenian fuck, I'll see you dead, I'll see you *flayed* before I so much as—"

The words fell off abruptly. Tevis's brow furrowed, and he looked down. One of the peacock feathers from Kegellen's hairpiece stuck incongruously from the hairy curls on his arm. The woman yawned as she drove the shaft of the feather deeper.

Tevis raised a hand, then, face baffled and rapidly turning blue, let it fall. He stared at Kaden, tongue lolling from his mouth, then down at Kegellen. When he finally fell, his face smashed into the table, tearing a gash across his purpled forehead. He thrashed twice on the wooden floor, then fell still.

Kegellen raised her eyebrows, nudged the corpse with a slippered foot, looked at Kaden, then over the small group.

"A man's entitled to his own opinions," she said with a shrug, "but not when they look likely to get me killed."

She returned her attention to Kaden. "Now, who were the poor souls inside the chapterhouse that those soldiers just slaughtered?"

"Not poor souls," Kaden replied. "A group known as the Ishien. A private foe of my own—one that betrayed me and people I held dear."

Kegellen flicked open her fan, watching him awhile above the delicate whir of the paper, then nodded.

"I, for one, am feeling a republican spirit stirring in my fat, jolly heart."

†

The signing of the constitution took only a matter of minutes. There were questions, of course, concerns, and demands, but the blood smeared on the stones of the square below and Tevis's corpse sprawled across the wooden floor muted any real objections. As Kaden had hoped, once the thing was done, once it was clear there would be no turning back, the nobles began to put aside their own bickering in the urgency of the moment. Only when the ink had finally dried, however, only once the others had departed to muster their own personal guards, their money, their friends, any allies they might have in the city, did Kaden finally sit.

"Why didn't you tell us?" Gabril asked, standing by the window. The sun was sinking toward the rooftops, and people had returned to the square, pointing fingers at the chapterhouse, pointing at the blood, exclaiming in loud, worried tones over the violence. "You thought one of us would reveal your secret?"

Triste and Kiel, too, had remained behind with him, and he eyed each of them in turn, gaze lingering on Triste. Finally he nodded.

"I thought I could trust all of you, but I couldn't be sure. The fewer people who know a thing . . ." He trailed off, spreading his hands.

Kiel pointed to the window. "It was the Ishien waiting inside the chapterhouse."

Kaden nodded. "We knew Matol would have the place watched. It was one of the only spots in the city I might go. They wouldn't take Triste, not until she led them to me, but as soon as she left, there was no reason not to burst in and demand the note that she had delivered."

Triste was shaking her head. "And it didn't say anything about Ashk'lan. It said we would be meeting there, in the chapterhouse, just the same way you told us in the temple."

Kaden nodded. "I needed the Ishien there when Adiv arrived. I needed them to kill each other."

"And the Shin?" Kiel asked.

"I don't know," Kaden said quietly. "For Matol to set the trap, he needed the monks out of the way. . . ."

Kiel raised his brows. "To Ekhard Matol, 'out of the way' usually means 'dead.'"

Kaden nodded reluctantly. It was a risk, and one he had no right to take for the monks. They were no part of the conspiracy, no part of the Ishien effort to hunt him down. Like the murdered brothers he had left behind in Ashk'lan, those here would have been devoted to quiet, peace, mindfulness, and tranquillity, and Kaden had brought the twin hammers of Ekhard Matol and Tarik Adiv on their sanctuary. He hoped the Ishien might have bound the men instead of killing them, but his hopes were scant protection to those inside. It was one of the reasons he had remained. He needed to see the bodies. To know for sure just how deeply his sacrificial knife had cut.

"And Adiv?" Gabril asked. "How did he come to suspect you were there?"

Kaden glanced at Triste again. She was staring at the blank floor where Tevis had fallen, but looked up as though she felt his eyes upon her. It was there, obvious to anyone who looked. The marvel was he hadn't seen it earlier.

"Morjeta," he said quietly.

Kiel frowned, then nodded. Gabril said nothing. Kaden kept his eyes on Triste. For a few heartbeats she just stood there, face blank.

"What?" she asked finally.

"Your mother," he said, as gently as he could. "She's the one who told Adiv we would be here. She's the one who gave him the names, who told him the people he'd be looking for would be dressed as monks but bearing blades."

Triste stared, then shook her head, slowly at first, then more violently. "No," she said, eyes blazing. *"No."*

Kaden nodded. "Yes."

It had taken him longer than it should have to piece it all together: the tension in Morjeta's face when Triste reappeared, her odd insistence on cooperation with the man who had seized her daughter, the very fact that she had *allowed* Triste to be taken in the first place. And then Adiv's unexpected arrival in the temple itself.

Oddly, the key had nothing to do with Morjeta at all. The whole thing had clicked into place only when Kaden watched Demivalle face down the Mizran Councillor. He had expected Adiv, with his title and the armed men at his back, to crush any resistance by the priestess. After all, that was the story of Triste's abduction: the councillor came, he issued threats, and the *leinas* handed her over. The story looked a good deal less likely after witnessing Demivalle's unflinching refusal to accommodate his demands.

The question was *why*? Why would Morjeta willingly give up her daughter? Why would she betray Kaden to the councillor? The answer was scrawled across Triste's face. Adiv's blindfold had obscured the resemblance, that and the fact that his skin was a few shades darker than Triste's, but when Kaden called those faces to mind, when he set them next to each other, there could be no mistaking the shape of the jaw, the elegant line of the nose. Adiv hadn't wrested an innocent girl from the iron grip of the Temple of Pleasure; he had taken his daughter.

"I don't think your mother meant to hurt you," he said carefully. "Tarik Adiv is one of the most powerful men in the kingdom. . . ." He hesitated, wondering whether or not to reveal the whole truth, then plunged ahead. "And he is your father."

Her face twisted with fear and revulsion, hands balled into fists at her side. For a moment she stood, a tower of mute fury and grief. Then, with a shriek, she hurled herself at Kaden. He caught her by the shoulders, but her fists rained down on him, pounding against his chest, his head. There was none of the inexplicable strength she had shown back in the Dead Heart, but the blows were powerful enough. As she sobbed, he pushed her back, forced her to stare into his eyes.

"She didn't betray *you*," he said. "Not when she gave you up the first time, and not now. She knows Adiv, she understands his power, his ruthlessness, and she's *frightened* for you, frightened that if she doesn't do something to stop me, he'll kill us both. She tried to help me, brought me to Gabril, helped to set up the meeting with the nobles. But when Adiv appeared in the temple, she quailed. It must have seemed the game was up, and she did what people so often do—she threw her lot in with what she hoped would be the winning side. She tried to protect herself and her daughter."

Slowly Triste's fury subsided, replaced by a blank hopelessness. Her hands dropped, and she backed away, not looking at him, not looking at anything.

"The list of names," Gabril said quietly.

Kaden nodded. He'd already memorized the list of the conspirators—it was a trivial matter—but he couldn't trust that Morjeta would remember them perfectly. He'd given her barely enough time with it, but when he returned, there was no doubt—the paper had moved ever so slightly. There was a new tension around the *leina*'s eyes. Her knuckles were white and bloodless where she clutched her skirts.

"Both of them," Triste said, her voice lost, flat.

"Both of them what?" Kaden asked.

"They both gave me up," she replied. "My mother gave me to . . . him. He gave me to you."

Kaden opened his mouth to reply, then realized he had no consolation to offer.

"Yes," he said quietly. "They gave you up."

46

Il Tornja tried to dissuade her.

"It's going to be a brutal march, Adare," he said, nodding out over the inky expanse of the lake. The sky was still full black, the stars undiminished by any hint of dawn, and yet the Army of the North and the Sons of Flame were already ranked in their marching columns, the men muttering to one another. They kept their voices low, in the way of people everywhere who speak before the sun has risen. "You can't ride," the *kenarang* went on. "The lake bottom won't support a horse, and if you give up halfway there, Ameredad can't spare more than a few men to guard you."

She bristled at the talk of giving up. "These are my soldiers," she replied stiffly. "They are marching to defend my empire. I will march with them."

"There is little you can do when we reach the Urghul."

"I can *be* there." Adare didn't know much about soldiering, but she'd read enough treatises on war to understand the importance of morale. "I can show them that I'm not going to hide while they lay down their lives."

And, she added silently, *I can keep an eye on you.*

She'd been forced to make common cause with the *kenarang,* but that didn't mean she trusted him, not even with Nira's hidden noose of fire tight around his neck.

Csestriim. Her mind still bucked at the notion, refused to truly accept it. She'd read thousands of pages about the Csestriim—treatises penned by scholars had who pored over their ancient cities, speculation by philosophers, religious tracts, and fantastic tales—but for all the ink spilled, none of it had seemed *real.* The fact that il Tornja, her father's killer, her former lover, the man who at that very moment stood at her side gazing north into the night, was thousands of years old, had worn hundreds of names and played dozens of roles through the millennia . . . it just seemed impossible.

"Adare . . ." he began.

"I'm going," she said. "Seventy miles. Thirty-five a day . . ."

"More, with the convolutions of the shoreline."

"I'm going."

He nodded, as though he had anticipated her stubbornness. How much of what she'd done had he anticipated? The question made her flesh crawl. She had no answer.

"At least," he pressed, "march with the Army of the North, with me."

Adare hesitated. The plan, hammered out between il Tornja and Vestan Ameredad while Adare looked on, was to split the armies. Ameredad would take the Sons up the eastern shore of the lake while il Tornja and the Army of the North moved along the west. The division meant that if the Urghul *did* try to slide down the sides of the lake, there would be a force to meet them whichever route they chose. Better, if the two armies were able to match pace—a big *if*—they'd have a chance to catch Long Fist between them. The arguments made good sense, but the division worried Adare. Ideally she would have been able to keep an eye on both Ameredad and il Tornja, but then, the world wasn't ideal.

"The Sons are mine," she said.

Il Tornja nodded. "Understood. But you are Emperor now. Which means the legions are yours as well. It would do the men good to see you among them. Ameredad is more than capable of leading his own soldiers."

Adare hesitated. It was a question, really, of who she could trust more. Or who she trusted least. Ameredad had nearly killed her, but of the two, il Tornja was by far the more dangerous. Which meant staying with il Tornja.

"All right," she said finally, "I'll stay with the legions."

He nodded, then waved over a messenger.

"Inform the commander of the Sons of Flame that the Emperor has decided to march with the Army of the North."

The man repeated the words back, saluted, then jogged east across the drying lake bed toward the assembled ranks of Intarra's faithful. Adare wondered how Lehav would take the news, then decided it didn't matter.

For a while they stood side by side in silence, an emperor who was not truly an emperor and a general who was far more than a general, watching the cold breeze ruffle the surface of the lake, shattering and shifting the reflected light of the stars.

"What happens if we don't get there in time?" she asked.

Il Tornja shrugged. "Andt-Kyl is a choke point across the Black," he replied. "It's the one place we know the Urghul *have* to go. If they get past it . . . we could be hunting them all over the north, chasing them down while they burn towns and murder Annurians from Breata to Katal."

"But the swamps," Adare said. "The lakes. If we can't move through this mess, how can they?"

"Oh, the terrain will slow them down for a while. It might take weeks for the army to break out of the Thousand Lakes, but they can split into dozens of bands, work their way through the wetlands at whatever pace they want. Once they break out onto solid, open ground, it's over. They have a mounted army. We don't."

"Well then," Adare said grimly, "we'd better get there in time."

And so, as the sun rose through the trees and the cool wind gusted south across the lake, Adare marched north, Ran il Tornja at her side, Fulton stalking a pace back, the long ranks of the Army of the North strung out along the narrow strip of dry lake bed between the trees and the lapping water.

That water seemed to go on forever, stretching north to where it hazed with the horizon. Seventy didn't look like much on the maps. Adare had covered ten times that distance since fleeing the Dawn Palace. Not, however, at the pace of the army quickstep, not hammering six or seven miles before the sun was even up. Her legs trembled, the arches of her feet ached, her shoulders had wound into a knot so tight it hurt to turn her head, and all she could see to the north was the endless line of dark firs marching away into the distance.

Rounding a sharp promontory sometime before dawn, she stumbled on the uneven stones littering the newly dried fringe of the lake. In a moment, Fulton was at her side, taking her elbow discreetly.

Adare shook him off.

"I'm fine," she said. "I'm fine."

"Of course, Your Radiance," he murmured, dropping his hand but remaining at her shoulder.

For a while they walked in silence, listening to the thousands of boots crunching behind them, to the clank of steel on steel as soldiers shifted their weapons. Adare glanced over. The Aedolian was wearing a quarter his weight in armor, well more than the most heavily laden legionary, but if the strain bothered him, he didn't show it. Hand on the pommel of his sword, eyes fixed resolutely ahead, he marched with all the strength of the younger men following behind. He was no longer as cadaverously thin as he had been in Olon, but the past months had left their marks on his face, in his graying hair.

"Thank you," Adare said quietly, surprised that she had spoken.

He turned to look at her. "For what, Your Radiance?"

"For coming after me," she replied. "For staying after . . . after what I did. At the Well . . ."

"No thanks are necessary, Your Radiance," he replied. "We all have our duty. Yours is to rule. Mine is to make sure you stay alive to do so."

"I just want you to know that I appreciate it—everything you've done for me."

He watched her for a while. "Please do not take this the wrong way, Your Radiance," he replied at last, "but it isn't for you."

Adare shook her head, confused.

It was a long time before Fulton spoke again. When he did, his voice was low, private, as though he'd forgotten she was there.

"I decided a long time ago what kind of man I wanted to be. I've sworn oaths to your family, but it is the promises a man makes to himself that he must keep."

She waited for him to say more, but he turned his eyes north, picked up the pace slightly, and walked on in silence, leaving Adare to her pain and her pondering. She was jealous of it, she realized, this unwavering fidelity to one's own code, the keeping of unspoken promises offered up in silence from the self to the self. She envied the Aedolian his ability to stay true to his convictions, and more, she envied him the convictions themselves. She had had convictions once, beliefs about justice and honor, right and wrong, but the slow turning of the world, like a mill wheel over grain, had ground them down to flour so fine that it slipped softly and silently between her fingers.

†

Dawn seemed a long time in coming. Valyn watched as the sky faded from black to bruise, from bruise to a wash of sallow yellow, dull as warmed-over wax, pale light suffusing the air above the serrated tops of the firs. By the time the sun finally rose, a blanched and pallid disc in the morning fog, the extent of the destruction below was already clear.

The eastern island, abandoned by the villagers the night before, still cracked and smoldered. The Urghul had put the homes, barns, and stables to the torch almost immediately, using the livid conflagration to light their assault on the central bridges. The houses had burned most of the night, white-hot at first, then orange, then red, glowing beams collapsing in on themselves every so often in a spray of sparks and a renewed hissing of embers. By morning the fires had ceded their light to the dull glow of the sun, but oily, acrid smoke still lingered in the air, and the hooves of the horses moving between the burned-out frames kicked up clouds of ash. Half a town destroyed in a single night. People's homes, their history . . .

Valyn didn't give a shit.

You could rebuild a house. An ax, a few good logs, a month to work— that was all it took. He stared at Laith's leg. It jutted out from beneath a fallen horse, the dead flier and dead beast alike tumbled onto the mud flats when the villagers finally managed to bring down the second bridge. That was all he could see of his friend: a boot and a few feet of dirty cloth, the fabric so worn and filthy that it looked brown rather than black. There were scores of bodies down there, Urghul and Annurian, twisted in all the various poses of dead. *Dancing with Ananshael,* the Kettral called it. It didn't look like dancing. It looked like death, and there was no rebuilding the dead, not with any number of axes or months.

That the loggers *had* brought down the bridge was just about the only bright spot in the murk of the morning. When Laith fell, the Urghul had redoubled their attack, heedless of the arrows rained on them, seemingly indifferent to the screaming of their horses as they crashed through the bridge rail and into the channel below. Even Pyrre was forced back behind the barricade, and for a few horrible minutes it looked as though the horsemen would break through. Then the loggers working beneath with their heavy felling axes managed to cut through the pilings and the whole western end of the span sagged, groaning as the wood bent beneath the strain, then snapped. It took half the barricade with it, but that didn't matter. Without a bridge to cross, the Urghul had no way to press their attack, and so, sometime around midnight, they fell back onto the eastern island, regrouping for the dawn.

"Balendin's there," Talal said, pointing through the smoke toward what had been the town square. "He's crossed the first channel."

Valyn raised the long lens. Gwenna's explosion had blasted out most of the log dam, but it was still possible to sneak across on foot, darting from one trunk to the next. The Urghul had been doing so all night, replenishing their numbers on the one island they held. It was a slow and painstaking process, one that forced them to leave their horses behind, but then, if they found a way to cross the central channel, it would be the numbers, not the horses that mattered.

Valyn focused on Balendin. There had been no sign of the leach all night. What he'd been doing during the last attack, Valyn had no idea, but there he was, arms stained past the elbows with blood, bison cloak wrapped around his shoulders, feathers in his hair twisting in the morning wind, eyes fixed firmly on the island to the west, where Valyn watched from atop his tower and the loggers prepared for the next assault.

Valyn shifted the long lens. "He brought his prisoners."

Talal nodded silently.

The captives—dozens of them—knelt in ragged ranks across what had been the northern end of the town square. Their wrists were bound and rough rope noosed their necks, linking one to the next, preventing anyone from running. None of them looked likely to try. Most kept their eyes on the mud, as though by shirking the gaze of their captors they might somehow escape notice. The faces of those few who did look up were filled with terror rather than defiance. They watched Balendin as he paced back and forth in the square with all the mindless helplessness of livestock waiting their turn at the slaughter.

A wave of dark disgust rose inside Valyn.

"Almost a hundred of them," he muttered, "and not one making any sort of play. Not one fighting back."

Talal shifted his eyes from the square to Valyn.

"They're not Kettral," the leach said quietly. "They don't know *how* to fight back."

He was right, but that didn't make the spectacle of several dozen men and women waiting meekly for their own horrific murders any easier to stomach. Valyn watched as two *ksaabe* cut an older man loose from the line, then dragged him forward to the center of the square. Balendin considered his captive for a moment, then smiled and drew his knife. The man began to pray, a frantic, repetitive plaint to Heqet that did nothing to stop the blade. Balendin took his right eye first, then his ear, then his shriveled cock.

"He's gathering his power," Valyn said, forcing himself to watch.

Talal nodded. "The question is: what's he going to do with it?"

They didn't need to wait long to find out. Balendin left his victim alive, barely—a defaced and disfigured creature thrashing weakly in the mud, a spectacle for the others to contemplate. Then he turned toward the center channel, raised one hand halfway, finger extended, and fixed his eyes on the shattered bridge. After a few heartbeats, it began to rise from the mud, twisting and contorting in midair like some massive wooden snake testing the morning breeze. The planks and logs shifted, grinding against one another, the whole thing undulating with Balendin's uncertainty. The leach didn't move. He didn't even seem to breathe, and after a few more heartbeats the bridge settled into place.

"Holy Hull," Valyn said.

Talal just stared.

The Urghul eyed the newly repaired bridge with trepidation, clearly as shocked and dismayed as the villagers on the west island. Then a horn began to sound, and another, and another, and the warriors began screaming, shaking spears and swords, swarming forward onto the resurrected decking.

"How long can he do that?" Valyn asked.

Talal hesitated. "I don't know. With all those prisoners fueling his well?" He shook his head. "Balendin took down Manker's tavern just drawing on one girl. Holding something up is harder than tearing it down, a lot harder, but he's got nearly a hundred people there, all terrified of him. Plus the people of Andt-Kyl." He shook his head. "He's probably leaching off us, even. At this distance, he can feel our hate, our anger."

"Annick . . ." Valyn began, but even as he watched, an arrow drove through the morning air toward the leach. Then, as though glancing off invisible steel, skittered away into the mud and rubble. Two more followed with no more effect. The corner of Balendin's mouth turned up.

"He's stronger than I realized," Talal said. "A lot stronger."

Valyn glanced down at the bridge. It was precarious, shifting and swaying with some unseen wind, and the Urghul couldn't cross as quickly as they would have liked. With enough arrows and enough backbone, the loggers would be able to hold them for a while. A little while. He turned to the lake. No sign of il Tornja or Adare. No sign of either army. From atop the tower, he could see at least ten miles south along both banks, which meant there would be no relief that morning.

"We have to stop him," Talal murmured.

"You can't stop him," Valyn said. "You can't even get close to him."

The leach frowned. "I don't need to get close to him. I just need to get close to his well."

Valyn hesitated. "The prisoners," he said slowly.

"The prisoners."

"You're going to try to free them?"

"No," Talal said, his face weary, defeated. "I'm going to try to kill them."

✝

"Gwenna."

The pain woke her as much as the voice, pain like a blade buried low in her back.

"Gwenna."

She shifted, cried out, then felt a strong hand clamp down on her mouth. When she tried to thrust it away, the pain lanced out into her wrist, shoulder, leg.

"It's Talal. Don't shout. The Urghul are right on top of us."

Talal. So she wasn't dead. That was a good thing. She tried to nod and the pain spiked up through her neck. She subsided against the mud and reconsidered. Maybe *alive* wasn't such a good thing after all.

"Did we . . ." she began, then started coughing, the spasm wracking her so viciously that she passed out all over again.

When she came to once more, she could see more clearly. She was inside somewhere, planks overhead blotting the sun. She could hear water. When she turned her head a fraction she realized she was *lying* in the 'Kent-kissing water. Talal was cradling her head, eyes wide with concern.

"You blew the bridge," he murmured. "It worked."

"Well, thank Hull for that," she said, her tongue fat and swollen in her mouth.

The leach grimaced. "There's more. Balendin got across. And a lot of Urghul. They're attacking the western island now."

Gwenna forced herself up on one elbow. The pain gouged at her in a dozen places, but she ground her teeth and closed her eyes until it subsided.

"Where are we?"

"Under one of the docks," he replied. "On the south shore of the eastern island."

"Thanks for coming after me."

He gave her a rueful smile. "I didn't. We thought you were dead."

"We?"

"Valyn and I."

She stared, trying to think past the pain and confusion. Talal was there, and Valyn, probably Laith, too, all of them in Andt-Kyl.

"What are you *doing* here?"

Talal opened his mouth to explain, then shook his head. "There's no time. I swam over because Balendin's using the captives, using their terror to hold up the center bridge."

Gwenna took a moment to absorb that. "All right," she said, levering herself into a seated position. "How do we stop him?"

The leach glanced down at her leg. "You're pretty beat up, Gwenna. That ankle's broken, and I pulled a jagged length of wood out of your back before you woke up. Another inch to the left, and you'd be dead."

She tested the flesh of her lower back weakly, finding a hastily wrapped field dressing. When she pressed down on the cloth, she almost passed out all over again.

"Just tell me the plan," she growled.

Talal shook his head helplessly. "Kill the captives. Balendin has himself shielded, but if I can get to them, if I can kill even half, I doubt he'll have the power to hold up the bridge."

"Kill half of them?" Gwenna asked, shaking her head weakly. "How are you planning to do that?"

"They're backed up to some burned-out buildings. I'll make my way through the rubble, slip in behind them, and start cutting throats. The Urghul aren't very well organized on this side. They don't expect an attack on their prisoners."

Gwenna stared, aghast. "They don't *need* to be fucking organized! You might kill five or six, Talal . . . ten at the outside, and then they'll be all over you. There's no cover in that 'Kent-kissing square, nowhere to hide."

Talal took a deep breath. "I know. But it's this, or we lose the town. Il Tornja's army is nowhere in sight. I don't understand Balendin's well nearly as well as I'd like, but even ten prisoners might make a difference. I have to try."

"Well, fuck," Gwenna said, shifting onto her knees. "I guess that makes two of us."

"No," Talal said, glancing at her broken ankle again. "You'll just slow me down."

"I might slow you down," she replied, gritting her teeth, "but I've got the explosives."

†

The armies were close—maybe nine miles off and marching at the double—but they might as well have been lazing around on the Godsway back in Annur for all the good they were able to do the people of Andt-Kyl. For the better part of an hour, Valyn had watched the Urghul swarm over Balendin's unnaturally supported bridge, pressing forward against the crumbling barricade at the far end. Three times they'd made it across, only to be driven back by il Tornja's scouts, Annick, and Pyrre, who seemed to be holding themselves in reserve to deal just with such breaches. Each time the Urghul managed to thrust through, the small knot of soldiers hammered them back, holding the line while the reeling loggers regained their footing and their confidence. They were saving the town, and with it the northern atrepies of the empire, while Valyn watched, hidden on the roof of the tower, holding to a discipline that felt crucial and evil at the same time.

He watched the Annurians beat back another attack, then cursed under his breath, jerking the long lens around to the south, studying the two armies once more. Judging from the standards, the Sons of Flame were to the east, while the Army of the North was working up the western shore. Il Tornja's group was making better time than the Intarran troops, but not enough better.

"Just *get* here," he muttered. "Just get here, you fucking bastard. *Get* here."

The words, of course, changed nothing. The army could only march as fast as it could march, and Valyn could only watch, first the battle below, then the distant troops, running the numbers over and over in his head, hating the answer every time he arrived at it.

Since slipping over the side of the roof nearly an hour earlier, Talal had disappeared. Valyn thought he'd seen the leach out in the lake, swimming toward the eastern island, but he'd lost track of him amongst the bobbing logs and hadn't been able to find him again. He swung the long lens over to Balendin. The corpses were piled around him now, eight or nine. As Valyn watched, one of the Urghul riders was gesturing urgently to the south. Balendin grimaced, then nodded, holding one hand out toward the central bridge as though to fix it in place, then turning toward the eastern shore. To Valyn's horror, the loose raft of logs bobbing between the pilings began to pack tighter, stacked by some invisible force.

Sweat streaked Balendin's face, but his jaw was set, and as Valyn stared the Urghul dragged out two more prisoners, a man and a woman, and began to tear the skin from their flesh. Balendin's lips moved as he directed the hideous ritual, and from the far shore the Urghul began to stream across the dam, no longer afoot, but on horse, riding straight over the island toward the central bridge and the loggers beyond.

Valyn searched the burned-out rubble desperately for Talal, stared until his eyes watered and his hands had twisted into claws around the long lens. There was no one. Nothing. Nothing but smoke, and embers, and death.

✝

The slowness hurt. It hurt because Gwenna could hear the loggers fighting for their lives on the far side of the bridge, the high, strident calls of people struggling and losing slowly. It hurt because she could glimpse, through the burned-out hulks of the buildings, the awful mutilation of Balendin's captives, the blood, and piss, and terror that she and Talal were too slow to prevent. And it hurt because just plain moving fucking hurt, and moving slowly just drew out the pain.

The cover was for shit, and Urghul were everywhere, afoot, on horse. Most were charging west, from one of Balendin's bloody bridges to the other, the endless parade of horseflesh and steel that couldn't end in anything but death for the people of Andt-Kyl. Enough, however, had spread out over the island, searching for 'Shael only knew what, that Gwenna and Talal were forced to hunch in shadowy corners for minutes at a time, to drag their way under still-smoldering beams and through rubble-filled cellar holes, all of which also hurt.

Gwenna would have cursed the fact that she couldn't actually stand on her broken ankle, but then, standing only would have got her killed quicker, and so she sucked up the pain, kept her belly in the mud and ash, and dragged herself forward on her elbows behind Talal.

It came as a shock when she lifted her head to find the hunched backs of the prisoners just a few paces off. She had no idea how long it had taken them to traverse the island—it felt like days—but the screaming and dying to the west meant the battle wasn't over yet. They weren't too late.

She turned her attention to the square. Balendin stood near the center, ringed with the dead and dying, his face a mask of rapture and rage, the vessels at his temples pulsing, sweat matting his hair to his scalp, slicking his cheeks. Gwenna ducked back down behind the low, broken wall that hid them from view.

"Why don't we just shoot him?" she hissed.

Talal shook his head. "Annick tried. He's shielded. We can't get at him."

Gwenna took a deep, shuddering breath. Between the pain, the disorientation, and the shock at finding herself alive at all, she hadn't allowed herself to consider what they were coming to do. It was the logical tactical decision. The *only* decision, as far as she could see. And it meant murdering scores of Annurians.

"What about a starshatter?" she asked, pulling the last remaining munition from her belt. "Will his shield stop that?"

Talal spread his hands hopelessly. "I don't know. I just . . . I don't know."

Gwenna's stomach clenched, and she forced down the urge to vomit. She could take a chance on Balendin, but they would only get the one chance. She risked another glance over the wall. A young man, no older than her, was groveling at Balendin's feet. His eyes were gouged out, and when he tried to scream the sound came out a gurgling, slithering mess. Someone had slit his tongue, she realized. And they were starting on his fingers.

"Sweet 'Shael," she said, sliding back behind the wall. "I don't know if I can do it."

Talal nodded grimly, hesitated, then extended his hand. "You light the wick. I'll throw it."

"It doesn't matter who fucking throws it," Gwenna spat.

The leach didn't flinch. "Yes," he said quietly. "It does. You don't have to do this alone. You light it. I'll throw it. We came here together, and we'll finish it together."

Suddenly, for no reason Gwenna could understand, she found herself weeping, the tears hot as coals on her cheeks.

"All right," she said, words choking in her throat. She fumbled for the striker, found it, made a flame, and pressed it to the wick. "Together," she said, passing the starshatter to Talal.

He took it, stared a moment at the burning wick as though it were a snake, closed his eyes, and mouthed a silent prayer. Then, with a roar, he stood from behind the wall and hurled it into the center of the doomed captives.

With a roar.

The last thing Gwenna thought before the starshatter exploded, tearing through bone and flesh, rending the bodies of dozens of helpless people like so much rotten meat, was that, until that moment, she'd never heard Talal raise his voice.

47

The histories were horseshit.

Adare had read about warfare in the histories. She had pored over the intricate maps of Annur's most famous battles, studying the neat lines of advance and retreat, committing to memory the most classic short pieces: Fleck's *Five Principles of Cavalry,* Venner's *Longbows and Flatbows,* Huel-Hang's *The Heart of a Conflict.* She'd been through Hendran's cryptic volume twice during the march north, grilling Fulton and Ameredad on the more obscure points. She didn't expect to become a battlefield commander, certainly not by reading a few old books, but she *had* hoped that her hasty study of war might help her to better understand the events churning around her, maybe even to save a few lives. The soldiers who had marched all this way to fight and die at her command deserved an emperor who would make an effort to understand what she had asked of them.

And so she had pored over the books until her lids drooped and the maps swam before her eyes only to discover here, now, in the midst of the furious battle for Andt-Kyl, that the books had told her less than nothing. The chaos in the streets of the tiny logging town seemed more like a riot than a battle. There were no disciplined blocks of men working in concert, no ordered sequence of attack and defense, no clear delineation between friend and foe. Instead, there was madness. The leather-clad loggers of the town ran in all directions, some cradling vicious wounds, some collapsed in doorways weeping, some hurling buckets of water on burning buildings, some charging down the street brandishing axes and crude spears, pointing and hollering in a direction that Adare desperately hoped was east.

Three times she had seen knots of Urghul horsemen—some no more than twenty paces distant—and three times Fulton had forced her to backtrack, to take a different route, his face grim as he spat orders at the Aedolians under his command, gesturing with his naked sword.

He had almost refused to let her into the town at all.

"You can only do two things in Andt-Kyl," he told her bluntly, staring at the smoking village from the western shore of the Black, where they had paused while il Tornja and the Army of the North pushed ahead. "You can get in the way, or you can die, Your Radiance."

"I need to see it," she had insisted.

"You can see it from here. It will make even less sense up close."

She stared at her Aedolian. "Are you defying me?"

"I am protecting you."

"There are other threats to my life and rule than an Urghul spear in the chest."

Fulton shook his head curtly. "That is why my order exists. Why I exist."

Adare blew out a frustrated breath. She had no doubts about Fulton's loyalty, but loyalty was not the same as judgment.

"Listen," she began, uncertain just how much she wanted to reveal. "The legions love il Tornja. Have you heard what the men say? He's invincible. He's unstoppable. Fearless. Brilliant—"

"Good qualities in a *kenarang*."

"You and I both know he is more than the *kenarang*. The true question is how *much* more he hopes to be."

Fulton narrowed his eyes. "I understood you had him in check, that your Mizran Councillor had . . . thwarted him."

Adare leaned close. "You saw exactly what I saw: a collar of flame. It was there for a few heartbeats, then it disappeared. Nira says she can keep il Tornja in check, but what do I know about a leach's kenning? What do you know?"

The Aedolian started to respond, but she cut him off.

"And even if it's true, even if we have il Tornja controlled, he's not the only danger. I'm new to the throne, Fulton. In fact, I've never even sat on the fucking thing. I'm young. I'm a woman. The Sons of Flame follow me because of what happened at the Everburning Well, but the legions follow il Tornja. If I'm going to win their support and loyalty, I need to prove myself something more than a callow young princess with more ambition than spine."

"Wading into a battle is no way to demonstrate your bravery."

"Unfortunately," Adare replied, "it is."

She gestured to the small town. Smoke rose over the far shore, but the nearest island appeared relatively untouched by the violence. At least, she hoped it was untouched. According to her scouts, il Tornja was in the tall stone tower that seemed to grow straight out of the cliffs on the island's southern coast. It looked close enough for her to reach.

"I have to go," she said again, willing Fulton to see the wisdom of her words, hoping desperately that they were, in fact, wise. "I have to go."

Fulton grimaced, flexed and unflexed his sword hand, then nodded curtly. "But once we cross the river, you obey me. If I tell you to move, you move. If I tell you to drop, you drop." He fixed her with a glare. "Do you understand? Your Radiance?"

Adare nodded. "I understand."

Despite the chaos raging in the streets, they reached the tower without any of the Aedolians being forced to bloody their blades. Il Tornja's own men stood at the base. Their eyes widened at the sight of the Emperor and her guard, but they bowed and moved aside. Only when Adare had stepped out of the light and madness into the cool, sepulchral dark of the tower did she realize she was trembling, her hands balled into aching fists at her side. She uncurled them slowly while Fulton ordered the other Aedolians to join the *kenarang*'s men at the entrance, then started climbing the spiral stair before he could notice her fear.

The stone of the tower dampened the worst of the sound—the clash of steel on steel, the screaming of men and horses—and Adare found herself climbing more slowly as she reached the top. When they approached the trapdoor at the top of the spiral, she paused, allowing Fulton to step past her, then followed him into the blinding light and battering noise of the battle.

She had expected a square room, something with windows to let out the light of Andt-Kyl's beacon, but there were no windows. She realized, as she blinked against the sun, that there weren't even walls. The top floor was open to the elements on all sides, a round stone pit six paces across at the center, blackened from the signal fires. Half a dozen stone pillars ringed the circumference, supporting a conical roof clearly intended to keep the worst of the rain and snow off the signal fire. Between the stone floor and the ceiling above, there was nothing but air, air opening onto a sheer drop in every direction.

Adare's stomach twisted. She wanted nothing more than to shrink back through the trapdoor into the relative silence and safety below. She, however, was the one who had insisted on coming, on being brave, being seen being brave, and after a moment she forced herself to take a step forward, to look at the full panorama of blood and suffering spread out below.

The bridges were gone, but the Urghul still crossed on felled logs, lashing their panicked mounts forward into the churning mass of gore and struggling bodies that had overtaken the two small islands. Adare stared. Every street and small square, every tiny alley, was packed with men, steel, and horseflesh. There was no way to make sense of the slaughter, no way to organize it. Two women, one in black, one in what looked like a fur coat slung over tattered red silk, fought back to back, ringed by a dozen riders. Adare stared. The black-clad one looked like little more than a girl, but she was holding the Urghul at bay somehow, twin blades spinning in her hands. As Adare watched, the horsemen forced them out of sight behind a burning building.

Fully half the town's houses were burning, bright and indifferent flame shimmering the air. A two-story log structure groaned as fire lapped the beams, then collapsed into the street, crushing a score of legionaries. Down by the river, the press forced soldiers into the turgid current where they flailed for a desperate moment before their armor dragged them under. Two streets over, a pair of Annurians hacked at the legs of a rearing horse while the rider plunged his spear downward over and over. The full fury of the struggle had not yet engulfed the tower, but men fought and died just a hundred paces distant.

This is battle, Adare told herself angrily. *Look at it.*

It didn't look like battle. It looked like mutual slaughter. She wanted to vomit.

"Your Radiance," Fulton said, extending an armored arm. "Please keep back from the edge. This is a dangerous place."

"I am not going to fall off the tower," she told him, trying to keep her voice firm, confident, turning her attention from the dead and dying to her immediate surroundings. Il Tornja sat at the very edge of the stone floor, just a few paces away. He had left all his guards below, but a dozen young men, battle messengers judging from their light armor, stood at attention, eyes moving nervously from il Tornja to the battle, then back. As Adare watched, two more runners burst up through the trapdoor, sweat streaming down their faces, chests heaving as they took their places at the end of the line. Blood dripped from the hand of the closest man, his blood or someone else's. Adare couldn't tell.

The *kenarang* himself might have been carved from stone. Unlike the famous generals whose paintings hung in halls of the Dawn Palace—men standing high in their stirrups or brandishing a sword from a rocky escarpment—il Tornja sat on the stone floor with his legs crossed beneath him, hands in his lap. He wore a sword buckled at his belt, but it remained sheathed. Adare couldn't see his face, but there was something about the man's absolute stillness that made her pause.

No, she reminded herself. *Not a man. A Csestriim.*

"The battle?" she asked, choosing her words carefully. "Is it going as planned?"

Il Tornja didn't turn, didn't speak. The wind shifted his hair, tugged at the collar of his cloak, but the general himself remained motionless. Adare glanced at the line of runners and signalmen. The nearest, a black-haired, wide-eyed youth, met her gaze, shook his head slightly, then pursed his lips. It took her a moment to realize he was mouthing the word "No." He looked almost as frightened of il Tornja as he did of the battle below.

Adare hesitated, then pushed her way forward. She hadn't risked the trip into town only to be cowed by her own *kenarang*. Csestriim or no, he still had Nira's collar around his neck, a deadly, invisible noose. One word from Adare and the old woman would kill him. Not that Nira was there. Even spry as she was, she couldn't have managed the forced march north. Adare tried to ignore the fact.

"*General,*" she said, stepping forward, taking il Tornja by the shoulder.

He turned his head.

"I said—"

The words withered in her mouth. She had locked gazes with her *kenarang* hundreds of times—over a shared pillow and a bared knife, in lust, love, and furious distrust—and she thought she understood the range of his emotion. She thought that she had fought past his lies and betrayals to finally understand something of the creature to whom she had tied her fate. Staring into his face, however, she realized for the first time the depth of her error.

Gone was the wry amusement she had seen so often, gone the wolfish hunger. All emotion had been scrubbed from those eyes, all expression Adare might have recognized as human . . . gone. His face was the face of a man, but for the first time she saw the mind behind in that unwavering stare: a mind cold and alien and unknowable as the dark space between midwinter stars. She wanted to shrink into her cloak, to turn away, to flee. For half a heartbeat, the terrifying drop from the tower seemed to offer escape rather than certain death.

"Stay," he said, the word quick as a knife nicking a vein. "But do not speak. It is a near thing, this contest."

"What—" she began, then faltered.

"I am what you kept alive to wage your wars. Now you will see why."

Adare nodded numbly. She felt that if she looked into the emptiness of those eyes a heartbeat longer her mind might unhinge. Far below, blood ran heavy as spring snowmelt in the town's crude gutters. The fight crashed up against the base of the tower. Men fought, and screamed, and died, but she no longer feared the battle. That, at least, was a fight between men, courage matched against courage, will against will. She was no warrior, but she could understand their hope, terror, and rage, emotions that seemed warm as summer rain, soft as a down bed when compared to the eyes of the creature beside her.

"One runner to the bridge," il Tornja said. He didn't turn to look at his messengers, nor did he raise a hand. "Tell them to abandon spears. Use swords."

A man darted through the trapdoor without a word.

Adare searched desperately in the madness for the Annurians holding what was left of the bridge, found them, finally. There couldn't have been more than two score, holding what looked like a desperate defensive position, their thicket of bristling long spears the only thing keeping the attacking Urghul at bay.

Fulton, following her gaze, shook his head slowly.

"They'll be slaughtered," Adare breathed. "Without spears, they'll be slaughtered."

She glanced at her Aedolian, hoping she was wrong, but he nodded grimly. "They need those spears."

"Most will die," il Tornja said, voice smooth as unscratched ice. "Some won't. Two runners," he went on. "One to the fourth street, one to the fifth. Archers on fourth to retreat. Archers on fifth to charge. Redirect the fourteenth squad to support that Kettral woman and her companion, the woman in red."

The runners saluted briskly, then bolted down the stairs.

"Kettral?" Adare asked, staring at the young girl in blacks she had seen earlier. "She's Kettral?"

"Yes," il Tornja replied flatly. "And she and the woman beside her are all that holds that entire street. That street anchors that flank. If they go down, we lose."

"Can they *do* that?" Adare asked, hands clenched at her side. "There are only two of them."

"They are doing it," the *kenarang* replied. Then, shifting his focus to a different quarter of the town, "Signal arrows. Two red. One green."

Bowmen stepped forward, lit oil-soaked rags at the tips of their arrows, waited for the unnatural flames to catch, fired high into the air, then stepped back without a word. Adare had no idea what the signals meant. She tried to find some corresponding movement in the battle below, found nothing but death and terror. Over by the burned-out bridge, the first messenger had reached the spearmen and convinced them to abandon their long shafts. As Fulton predicted, the Urghul pressed close, slaughtering the soldiers from the backs of their horses. After a few dozen heartbeats the entire position collapsed.

"They're *dying*," Adare protested.

"Yes," il Tornja replied.

"*Why?*"

He shook his head, the barest hint of a motion. "It's too complex."

Adare spent the hour that followed in a kind of horrified trance, watching as the *kenarang* sent runner after runner into the chaos below, listening as he uttered order after inscrutable order. *Hold this street, retreat into this alley, burn that building, charge.* Twice he sent soldiers into the fray to do nothing more than wave Annurian flags above their heads. He instructed his archers to light the docks on fire, despite the fact that there was no one on the docks. He even ordered several dozen troops in three different locations to surrender. None of it made any sense, not the insanity below nor il Tornja's response to it. He was like a madman commanding the troops at random, only there was no madness in those impossibly blank eyes, and despite the Urghul numbers, despite the fury with which they attacked again and again and again, despite the chaos engulfing the Annurian soldiers, he held the horsemen back.

Finally, as the sun began to settle in the sky, the *kenarang* rose smoothly and unexpectedly to his feet.

"It is finished," he said, gesturing over his shoulder, suddenly indifferent.

Adare stared at the carnage below. She could see no slackening of the battle, no shift in the violence. Exhausted soldiers heaved their weapons over and over into the flesh of their foes, screaming as they killed and were killed in turn. Il Tornja paid them no mind. Instead, he faced his signalmen and messengers, then bowed.

"You men have done well," he said as he straightened. "Thanks to you, the day is ours. You are dismissed."

It took the bowmen and messengers just a few moments to file back into the tower, leaving Adare alone on the roof with Fulton and il Tornja. When the trapdoor had clattered shut behind them, she turned to the general.

"What do you mean, it's over?" she demanded, voice cracking as she spoke.

"The battle is done. The rest is . . ." He paused. "You have seen a chicken struggle after the head is parted from the body?"

Adare nodded, horrified.

"This is that—a last spasm of blood and emotion. The real work is done."

She stared. "Where is Long Fist? The Urghul chieftain?"

"Not here." There was something in his voice, something Adare couldn't place. Not regret, certainly. Hunger, perhaps. A great hunger held in check. "He refused to take the field."

"It doesn't look done to me," Fulton growled. "Those horsemen are fifty paces from the tower."

Il Tornja shifted his gaze to the Aedolian. "That is why I am the *kenarang* and you are a guard."

"How do you *know*?" Adare demanded.

He fixed her with that hollow stare and once again she felt that dizzying vertigo, as though she teetered on the very lip of a bottomless well, as though if she fell forward, she would fall forever. Finally, he turned away, gesturing to the far bank.

"How many trees?" he asked.

Adare stared. "What?"

"The trees. How many are there?"

She shook her head, staring at the dark ranks of fir and pine. Even as she watched, the Urghul were slipping into the shadows between those trunks. Retreating, she realized. They were pulling back.

"I've no idea," she said. "Why does it even—"

"Two thousand six hundred and eight, between the mouth of the river and the stone point."

Adare stared.

"You've been counting trees this whole battle?"

He turned the empty pits of his eyes on her. "I don't need to count them, Adare. That is what I have tried to tell you. This thing you call thought, call reason, this plodding, deliberative mental process—it is . . . unnecessary to my kind."

"That doesn't make sense," she said. "Thought and reason were the essence of the Csestriim. All the histories agree."

He bent his face into a smile. "Ah. The histories." He raised a hand, held up two fingers. "How many?"

Adare stared. "What?"

"How many fingers am I holding up?"

She shook her head. "Two."

"How do you know?"

"I just—"

"Did you count?"

"Of course not. I just . . . see them."

The *kenarang* nodded. "In the same way, I just see"—he waved a hand at the slaughter taking place behind him—"all this."

For a while all she could do was watch dumbly as the men screamed and the blood flowed. Il Tornja's claim was too big, like being told there was another sky behind the sky.

"So we won?" she asked at last.

In an instant, the *kenarang* slipped back into his habitual wry smile. The horrifying emptiness drained from his eyes. "We?" he asked, amusement in his voice. "Yes, Your Radiance. We won."

The words should have been a relief, but when she thought a moment about what they meant, about what this general of hers could do, about how tenuously Adare herself understood the kenning that bound him to her will, his victory seemed suddenly sharp and cold, a knife in the dead of winter pressed against her ribs.

48

The armies arrived too late.

Not too late to fight the Urghul—there was fighting aplenty when the legions and the Sons of Flame finally caught the horsemen between them, streets washed in blood, men and women locked in furious battle just about everywhere Valyn looked—but too late to make a difference for Gwenna and Talal.

The vanguard of il Tornja's army arrived a little over an hour after the two Kettral set off the starshatter, killing half of Balendin's prisoners and maiming most of the rest. It was a horrific, gruesome spectacle, bodies and parts of bodies strewn about like meat in an untidy abattoir. Valyn had watched one man cradling his own severed leg as though it were a baby, weeping into his lap until he bled out and died. Of Gwenna and Talal there was no sign. It was possible they'd escaped, or been crushed beneath the remnants of the wall. Valyn had scanned the bloody ground for them, sweeping the long lens back and forth, staring at corpse after corpse, his heart growing heavier and heavier inside his chest.

The blast worked. That much was clear. It didn't kill Balendin, didn't even seem to hurt him, but it severed his connection with his well, and, as he turned in shock to stare at the rising smoke, at the mangled wreckage of his prisoners, the two bridges sagged, then collapsed into the dark water beneath, carrying dozens of riders with them.

Not that that ended the fight. If anything, the violence redoubled with the collapse of the bridges. Thousands of Urghul had forced their way onto the westernmost island before the spans went down, twice that number remained on the eastern island, and the far bank teemed with the rest of the enormous force. The trapped riders fought with a renewed savagery, understanding that their only hope of survival lay in a crushing victory, and the Annurian forces, outnumbered and exhausted from their march, reeled beneath the assault, struggling to form up in the unfamiliar terrain. It looked altogether possible that, despite the fallen bridges, despite the arrival of the imperial armies, the Urghul would still win.

Then il Tornja arrived on the roof of the signal tower.

Valyn had taken up the position initially because it offered the best sight lines over the town. From the tower, he could see both armies, consider their deployment, then choose the best angle of attack when the time came. That the *kenarang* might use the 'Kent-kissing thing as his command center had seemed too much to hope.

Valyn had watched, gut tight, as il Tornja rode down the muddy street, guards behind and before him. It was tempting to take the shot then. To kill the general in the midst of so much swirling chaos seemed almost trivial, and Valyn went so far as to level the wound-up flatbow and sight in on the man's forehead. It was Laith who stopped him. Laith and Gwenna and Talal. As far as Valyn knew, all three of them were dead somewhere in the twisted wreckage, all to hold back the Urghul. Finishing the battle was il Tornja's job, and Valyn would be shipped to 'Shael before he undercut his Wing's sacrifice. He eased his finger off the trigger. Adare said the man was a genius, and judging from the madness below he was going to need to be.

For most of the morning, Valyn lay still, hidden on the roof of the tower just a few feet from the *kenarang,* listening as he wove his inscrutable web. Despite a lifetime of military training, most of the orders made no sense at all to Valyn. Il Tornja abandoned points he could have held and held points he should have abandoned. He would send a runner with one message, then, moments later, contradict it with another runner or a signal arrow. He sent directives to let cornered Urghul escape, and more than once he gave direct orders that led to the capture of his own soldiers. And he killed men, killed them by the scores and by the hundreds, sacrificing entire units to Urghul traps that he could see clearly from the rooftops, sending men into fights they couldn't possibly win, demanding that they hold positions they couldn't possibly hold. It was insanity, utter insanity. And it worked.

Valyn had no idea how, but as the sun labored steadily higher, the Annurians began to win. There was no single victory that could account for it, no stunning charge or heroic stand. At least, not if you ignored the circle of death that surrounded Annick and Pyrre for hour after hour until they were pressed back behind a building and Valyn lost sight of them. In fact, he was hard-pressed to make any sense at all of the individual scenes of brutality and suffering playing out below.

He could, however, see the larger pattern as it emerged. The Annurians were pushing back the Urghul. Nothing startled the *kenarang,* nothing shocked him. Not the collapse of an entire company of archers, not the Urghul pressing up against the tower itself, not even Adare's unexpected arrival on the tower roof. Valyn tried to catch the man's smell. The world was awash in mud and blood and terror, but from il Tornja—nothing. He smelled like stone. Like snow. Like emptiness.

When the *kenarang* finally announced that the battle was over, all Valyn could do was stare. Men still screamed and died in the streets below, buildings still burned, steel still smashed against naked steel. It looked anything but over, and yet he could hear il Tornja rising to his feet below, could hear the messengers and signalmen departing down the stairwell, the trapdoor clattering shut behind them.

So, he thought, breathing out a slow, even breath, *it is time.*

He put his ear to the roof, listening to the people below. Adare and il Tornja continued to talk, and he could hear the Aedolian breathing, the grating of his armor as he shifted in place. The attack would have to be quick and brutal. Unfortunately, the *kenarang* had moved to the other side of the floor below. Valyn considered changing position before he struck, but the roof was warped and creaky. Any movement now would give him away. Striking from his current position would mean going through the Aedolian, but Valyn could cut his way through a guardsman. He would have preferred not to kill the man, but he would have preferred a lot of things.

The time for setting up and second-guessing was over. Just a few feet below and a couple paces distant stood the man who had murdered his father, the one responsible for the slaughter of Kaden's monks, for Amie's murder, and Ha Lin's. Valyn felt as though he'd been waiting forever, but the waiting was over. He took a deep breath, bared his teeth, and went.

The Aedolian managed to block the first blow, getting his armored forearm between his neck and Valyn's knife at the last moment. The man was smart. Instead of reaching for his own sword, a reaction that would have given Valyn the space and time necessary to finish him, he pressed forward, counting on his armor to block the knife, trying to bring his weight to bear as he lunged for Valyn's throat.

"Adare," he shouted roughly, eyes wide, lips turned back in a snarl. "Get back! Get *down*."

Someone had trained the Aedolian well. Most fighters instinctively limited their attacks, taking only the shots from which they thought they could recover safely. This man hurled himself forward with one intention only: clobbering Valyn back brutally enough to buy time for Adare to escape. It was a bold, brave attack. It was suicide. Valyn pivoted, knocking the Aedolian's hands clear, slipping inside his guard, driving the small dagger up into the unarmored space beneath the armpit. He twisted it hard, then spun away, pulling it free.

The guard collapsed, blood drooling from his lips, eyes glazing. Valyn tossed the knife to the ground behind him, drew his double blades, and fixed his eyes on the man across the fire pit.

If the *kenarang* was shocked by the attack, he didn't show it. Before Fulton's body hit the floor, his own blade had whispered from its sheath. He held it level between them in a type of hybrid low guard Valyn didn't recognize. Il Tornja's eyes flitted to the dead guardsman, to the trapdoor behind him, then back to Valyn. Valyn could smell Adare's grief and panic, could feel it deep in his lungs. From Ran il Tornja, however, there was nothing. He might have been made from the stone beneath his feet. The man looked calm, ready, which suited Valyn just fine. This was better than a bolt in the heart. He was looking forward to shattering that calm, to taking the bastard apart one finger at time.

"Valyn hui'Malkeenian," the *kenarang* said. His voice was smooth as brushed velvet.

Valyn opened his mouth to respond, but Adare shoved her way forward, putting herself between them, arms stretched out as though her slender hands could hold back the blades.

"No, Valyn!" she screamed, staring at the crumpled body of the guard. "Oh sweet 'Shael, Fulton!"

"He's dead," Valyn said, his own voice flat, emotionless.

"No," Adare said, stepping across the fire pit, collapsing to her knees beside the Aedolian. "No! *Why?*"

Valyn didn't look down, but he could hear her scrabbling pointlessly at the man's armor behind him, as though she could find the wound, could stanch the flow of blood.

"He might have been part of it," Valyn said, stepping forward. "A part of the plot. The men who came for Kaden were all Aedolians."

"He wasn't part of *anything*," she wailed. "All he did was try to keep me *safe*!"

"Well, he knew what he was signing up for." Maybe the man was guilty. Maybe he was innocent. It didn't matter. A lot of innocent people had died already.

"You've made a mistake, Valyn," il Tornja said, not lowering his guard.

Valyn took a half step to the left, and the *kenarang* turned with him, adjusting the angle of his blade. Valyn moved right, two steps, and again il Tornja adjusted, the movements subtle but precise. So. The man could keep his cool during an attack, and he knew how to fight.

"I've made plenty of mistakes," Valyn said. "But this isn't one of them. You murdered my father. You ripped out the heart of Annur, and I'm going to rip out yours."

"He just *saved* Annur!" Adare spat. "This fight, this battle, this whole fucking thing . . . we won because of him!"

"And now that we've won," Valyn said, keeping his eyes on the *kenarang,* testing his responses to changes in guard, posture, "we are finished with him."

"And what about you, Valyn?" il Tornja asked, cocking his head to the side. "Where have *you* been while we battled back the Urghul?" He gestured toward the fighting still raging below. "What role did you play in saving Annur?"

"I was waiting for you."

"And while you waited," Adare snarled from behind him, "people died. Were you huddled up there the whole time? This is about *more* than your own personal vendetta."

"Don't talk to me," Valyn said, trying to still the sudden trembling in his hands, "about watching people die." Memories of the night before filled his mind, of Laith fighting on the bridge, of the flier falling, spears buried in his flesh. "While you've been primping and playing emperor, I've been fighting my way across this whole fucking continent—"

"You were sent here," Adare protested, "by Long Fist. By the bastard who just attacked the empire."

"It doesn't matter," Valyn said. "I'm here. And I'm going to kill your pet general."

"In fact," Il Tornja said, "you may decide that it does matter. When you know the truth."

"What truth?" Valyn snarled.

More than anything, he wanted to be finished talking, but talking gave him time to probe, to test, to study the *kenarang*'s responses. Il Tornja was a swordsman as well as a general, that much was already clear. If Valyn was going to kill him, to be *sure* of killing him, he needed to know more. Somewhere behind him, Adare was still sobbing, still trying to stanch the hole in Fulton's flesh. Valyn blocked out her cries.

"You left the truth behind long ago," he said, moving as he spoke, studying il Tornja's response. "Left it when you killed my father."

"This is bigger than your father," the general said.

"Save your breath. Adare already fed me this line. We need you to defeat the Urghul, to defeat Long Fist . . ."

"And have you paused to wonder," il Tornja asked, "just where your friend Long Fist has been during this whole bloody battle?"

"Elsewhere," Valyn spat. "Who cares?"

"You might, if you hope to save Annur."

"We saved it already. Right here. The Urghul are broken."

Il Tornja smiled, a careless, easy expression. If he was nervous to be facing one of the Kettral, he didn't show it. "It might be more accurate to say that *I* saved it. Put up your blade for a moment and I'll tell you why. I'll explain where Long Fist is."

Valyn tested a low feint. Il Tornja stepped aside easily.

"He is in the Waist," the general said.

"That's impossible," Valyn said. "Unless he has a bird, he couldn't have made it out of the northern atrepies."

"He has something better than a bird," il Tornja replied slowly. "He has the *kenta*. I take it you've heard of the Csestriim gates? From your brother perhaps?"

Valyn tried not to stare, tried to keep his mind loose, ready. When the attack came, it would come fast.

"What I learned from my brother is that only the Shin can use the gates. I don't know much about Long Fist, but he's obviously not a monk."

"No," il Tornja said. "He is a god."

"Horseshit," Valyn spat, lunging forward, committing to the attack this time.

Il Tornja knocked it away.

"Unfortunately not."

"A god?" Adare asked, voice high and tight.

"Meshkent, to be precise." The *kenarang* raised his brows as he watched Valyn.

"Sweet Intarra's light," Adare breathed.

Valyn shook his head, fury at his sister's stupidity flaring up inside him. "He's *lying,* Adare. Meshkent . . ." For a moment words failed him. "What the fuck would Meshkent be doing here, taking part in some border dispute?"

"He hates you," il Tornja said simply. "Your empire. Our empire. Before Annur, there were a hundred tribes, a thousand spread across Vash and Eridroa making daily offerings of violence and pain to their bloody god. Your ancestors banished the practice."

"No," Valyn said, clenching his teeth. "*No.* I'm through with this, with hearing your excuses. You *killed my father.*"

Il Tornja nodded, but raised a conciliatory hand. "Let me explain."

"Explain?" Valyn spat, almost choking on the word. "*Explain?* So you can poison my mind the way you did my sister's? So you can turn me into your fawning little puppy? So you can explain to me how my father needed to die for the greater good of Annur? So you can tell me tales about some 'Kent-kissing god you claim to be fighting? Fuck you, and fuck your explanation!"

He struck just before the last word, lashing out with both blades in a double vane. It was just another test, another probe, but il Tornja turned it aside easily.

"You can't win, Valyn."

Valyn laughed at that, a sick, dead sound, even in his own ears. "Really?" He jerked his head behind him, where Adare still crouched over the corpse of the Aedolian. "That poor shit was one of your best. He was in full armor, and I killed him with a belt knife. You know how to handle your blade, but I'm *Kettral.*"

"Valyn," Adare pleaded. "We need him. You don't know everything. I didn't tell you everything!"

"You can tell me when he's dead."

He struck again, open fan sliding into horns twisting through the milling stone, one form becoming the next, his body more certain than his mind. Again, il Tornja blocked the attack, his one blade matching Valyn's two, and again Valyn stepped back. The man was better than good, in truth, as good as the best bladesmen back on the Islands. Valyn hadn't expected that, but it hardly mattered. He felt strong, ready, his slarn-tainted blood hot in his veins.

"I'll find an opening," he said. "Sooner or later."

"You *can't,* Valyn," Adare insisted, just at his ear now.

"Watch me," he said grimly.

Il Tornja's eyes darted to the left, to Adare, but before Valyn could turn, the knife plunged into his side, hot and freezing all at the same time, stealing the words.

For a moment he just stared, unable to make sense of the feeling. *How . . .* he thought, staring at il Tornja, trying not to lose his hold of his own blades, trying to keep his feet as his whole body began to crumple.

Adare, he realized as she wrenched herself away sobbing, taking what felt like half of his guts with her.

"You can't kill him, Valyn," she screamed. "I *need* him."

She went on shouting, Valyn's own belt knife still clutched in her hand, her knuckles white where they weren't sticky with his blood. She was screaming and screaming, something about murder and loyalty and the empire, her face twisted with grief and fury both.

Doesn't make sense. The thought drifted through his mind. *I wanted to save her.*

Before he could follow the idea, it broke apart like cloud on a windy day.

Shock. He was going into shock.

He tried to focus on the pain, to understand it. It gave him something to concentrate on, which helped to keep him from drifting into uncon-sciousness. *Below the lung,* a part of him thought. *Below the lung, or I'd be gurgling at each breath.* He dropped a sword and pressed the fingers of his free hand into the wound, almost fainting as pain lanced his side. *She got past the muscle, though. Probably in the liver.* Soldiers sometimes survived stab wounds to the liver. Not often. Legs like water beneath him, he stag-gered back almost to the lip of the tower.

"It's over, Valyn," il Tornja said, shaking his head. "Drop the other sword, and we'll patch you up."

Valyn shook his head weakly, clutching desperately to his remaining blade.

"No," he murmured. "It's not over."

"You can't fight, Valyn," Adare said, stretching out a bloody hand toward him, her eyes red, cheeks wet with tears. "Just put down the sword."

"You can't win," il Tornja said.

"I don't have to," Valyn replied.

The *kenarang* hesitated, then shook his head. "Meaning what?"

"Kaden," Valyn breathed.

Il Tornja nodded slowly. "Where is he? Is he determined to see me dead, the way you are?"

Valyn shook his head weakly, a smile stretching his lips. "Kaden is nothing like me," he said. "He isn't angry. He isn't rash. He is level as the sea before a storm." His legs trembled beneath him. "Kaden will not trust anyone. He will not make mistakes. He will wait as long as it takes and then, someday, when you are tired or relaxed, when you forget to bolt the door, when you're out riding, or signing papers, he will come for you. He's not like me. He will not fail."

The *kenarang*'s lips tightened.

"Valyn," Adare said. "You don't understand. It's not too late." She took a step forward.

"Yes," he said. "It is."

He had one more play left, one final thrust before he collapsed. With a roar, he hurled himself forward, hacking up and across. It was a desperate attack, and il Tornja treated it that way, knocking Valyn's blade aside, then flicking out with his own sword, a casual, almost contemptuous motion. Valyn jerked his head back, but too late, too late.

The blackness came before the burn, a darkness as absolute as anything in the pit of Hull's Hole. Then the fire, a searing line slashed across his face. His eyes, he realized dimly. The *kenarang* had slashed his eyes, blinding him.

Valyn stumbled, half fell, then pushed ahead with what meager strength remained, a single step into the darkness, then another, on and on until there was no more stone beneath his feet, until he was dropping helplessly, hopelessly toward the cold, dark water slapping at the rocks below.

49

The cloying air inside the Shin chapterhouse reeked of blood and death. It reminded Kaden of the slaughter of goats back in the Bone Mountains, only the slaughter of goats happened outside, in the clean air beneath the bright gaze of the sun. The small rooms of the chapterhouse admitted little light, and less air. In the struggle, someone had kicked a large pot of beans into the hearth, and the sludgy mix of wood, ash, and broth still smoked, filling the rooms until it was difficult to see, to breathe.

Bodies lay everywhere, dozens of them, twisted in broken postures, or seated against the stone walls as though sleeping. Some had been nearly hacked apart, flesh rent in wide, ragged wounds, some had been killed by tiny holes no larger around than Kaden's thumb.

"Adiv's men," he observed, frowning at the bodies. "Six or seven of them for every one of the others."

Kiel nodded. "The Ishien know their work, and they had prepared the ground for an ambush."

Triste stared about her, hand clasped over her nose and mouth to keep out the smell or to stop herself from retching. Since learning of her mother's betrayal, she hadn't said two words together. Kaden had wanted her to remain behind, to go with Gabril, but when he said that he intended to look for Adiv's body in the wreckage, she had insisted on coming, face hard as stone.

"He's my father," she'd said, "and if he's dead I want to see it with my own eyes."

The chances were slim. Kaden hadn't seen a quarter of the faces of the imperial soldiers, but it seemed unlikely that Adiv had involved himself in the attack. In fact, Kaden had insisted on waiting until dusk in case the councillor were secreted somewhere else in the square, watching the smoldering chapterhouse from his own hidden vantage. Certainly, as they explored the rooms, he saw no sign of Adiv. No sign, either, of Ekhard Matol.

The absence of both men worried Kaden, and as they pressed deeper into the chapterhouse, he felt the muscles of his chest grow tighter.

"Matol is a shrewd, dangerous fighter," Kiel said, as though hearing his thoughts. "It's possible he escaped."

"If Matol is still alive," Kaden replied, "then this whole thing failed."

"It brought the nobles over to your side," the Csestriim pointed out.

"That was only one part of the plan. I had hoped that Adiv and the Ishien would destroy each other. If they have not, if Matol is still alive, I have a problem. They will make a bid for control of the *kenta,* denying me the gates."

"It's possible he used the *kenta* here to escape," Kiel said. "It is part of the imperial rather than the Ishien network, but he knows of it."

Kaden nodded grimly. He'd already considered the possibility that the Ishien might escape through the gate—it was a flaw with the plan—but he'd hoped that their desire to capture him combined with the shock of Adiv's arrival would have stunned them long enough to break off any possibility of an orderly retreat. He had hoped that Matol himself would have been leading the ambush. More evidence of an old Shin truth: *Hope is a straight road to suffering.*

"Where is the *kenta?*" he asked.

Kiel crooked a finger at the floor. "Down."

Kaden hesitated. "Someone could be waiting there. They could have doubled back."

Triste, however, shoved past him. "I'm going," she said. "I need to see." And before he could reach her, she was running down the stairs.

†

They'd barely reached the basement when the attackers hit them. Kaden had tried to study each hollow as they passed, holding his lantern high, listening for the scuff of boot on stone. He'd heard nothing, seen nothing, and then a bright shattering pain erupted across the back of his head and he was falling forward, head striking against the stone wall, then the stone floor.

Blood flooded his mouth. He realized vaguely that he'd bitten into his tongue, but there was no time to worry about that. As his mind swayed, thought coalescing then scattering like a school of skittish fish, the fighting continued around him. Triste was screaming, and then suddenly silent. Kaden tried to rise to his feet, but something slammed him back down. A weight settled across the small of his back, grinding him into the floor. He opened his eyes to see Kiel struggling with an armed figure, and then, quick as thought, the Csestriim, too, was down.

It happened too fast for Kaden to have any idea what was going on, but there was no mistaking Ekhard Matol's face when the man crouched down beside him, his skin spattered with blood, eyes wide.

"You remember some of the things we did to your little whore here?" he asked, voice soft but savage. "The fire? The slivers of glass?"

Kaden kept his mouth shut, focused all his effort on shoving aside the red welter of pain, on seeing the dimensions of the trap that they had sprung. There were four figures in addition to Matol, one driving a boot into his back, the other leaning over Kiel a few steps away. Matol himself was holding the Csestriim *naczal* in his hands.

"Tan's spear," Kaden managed.

The Ishien shook his head. "Not anymore."

"Where is he? Is he all right?"

"You can ask him yourself when we're back in the Heart." The man chuckled. "'Course, he might have trouble answering you."

"Matol," one of the other men cut in, "we need to move." It had taken them only a few moments to bind Kiel's hands behind his back. The Csestriim swayed slightly, but he was doing better than Triste, who lay slumped in a heap where the wall met the floor. Matol scowled, then nodded. "Get the girl," he said, gesturing with the spear. "We'll be secure once we're through the *kenta*."

A moment later, Kaden felt himself hauled upward by the back of his shirt. The Ishien had made no effort to tie his hands—another measure of the contempt they felt for him—but a short knife appeared at his throat.

"Walk," Matol hissed.

Kaden walked.

They followed the corridor for a few dozen paces, turned into a smaller passageway, then descended another stairwell. When they reached a small room, stone walls rough cut and dripping, Matol pulled him up short.

"The *kenta* is just ahead. You might want to prepare yourself."

Kaden stared. The shock of the attack had so disordered his mind that any thought of reaching for the *vaniate* had been jarred free. Without the warning, he would have stepped through the gate and into his own obliteration.

"I don't know if I can," he said quietly.

At his side, Matol just snorted, then pressed the knife deep enough into his skin to draw blood.

"Ah, the *vaniate*," he mused. "The Shin methods are so much more . . . humane than ours, but they do have their limitations. You have to court the emptiness, woo it." He pursed his lips, shook his head in disgust. "Our way has fallen out of favor with the monks, but," he shrugged, "you can't argue with the result."

A few paces off, the *kenta* loomed out of the darkness, the slender arch of stone tossing back the lamplight at strange angles. The man hauling Triste—Kaden didn't recognize him—carried her through over his shoulder without a moment of hesitation. Kiel was shoved through a few heartbeats after. Kaden scrambled to find the wide empty space of the trance, reached for the bird that had guided him through before. As though frightened off by the chaos in his mind, the bird refused to alight. He called it, and it fled. He strained for the *vaniate,* and he failed.

Matol watched him with a hungry smile.

"Having a little bit of difficulty letting go? The calm not coming as easily as you'd hoped?"

As he spoke, he pressed the tip of the knife deeper. Kaden could feel his own blood trickling over the clavicle and down his chest.

"Don't let the pain distract you," Matol chuckled. "It would be a shame to lose your focus now."

The pain. Kaden dove into the sensation, leaning into the knife, pressing it farther into his neck until the bright ache lanced down his collar and shoulder, up into his jaw. Matol was shoving him toward the *kenta,* but Kaden closed his eyes, concentrating on that pain, watching it spread like a growing plant, green tendrils driving into the cracks of his mind, breaking apart the edifice of thought. Matol was saying something, but Kaden ignored it, letting the bright green pain lace through him until there was no emotion left, nothing but the wide blank of the *vaniate.*

Now, he realized. *It has to be now, right on the other side.*

He opened his eyes in time to see the *kenta* looming before him, then stepped through.

The Ishien were waiting on the other side, just a pace from the gate, but they were watching Kiel and Triste. Kaden gave them no time to respond.

He hurled himself forward, launching himself squarely into the nearest man's chest. He had just a heartbeat to hear Triste shouting, Matol cursing, both sounds devoid of meaning inside the emptiness of the *vaniate,* both voices almost lost in the gulls screaming overhead, the waves crashing against the cliffs below. He had half a heartbeat to feel the sun, hot as a slap to the skin, a quarter heartbeat in which his foe tried to shove him off while Kaden wrapped his arms tight and drove forward with his legs, pushing, pushing, until they were both falling through the next *kenta,* the one that Kiel had warned him led into the Dawn Palace.

The Ishien went through first, backward, somehow keeping his balance as Kaden strove to bring him down. Even as they moved, Kaden could feel the other man shifting, adjusting, dropping his weapon and bringing his hands to bear, starting a pivot that would end with a throw. Kaden had no doubt he would be on the ground in moments, his face pressed into the dirt, but the man didn't have moments. The hot sun winked out as they slipped through the invisible surface of the *kenta* into a stone chamber lit on all sides by torches, a stone chamber guarded by a dozen men, half of them with crossbows.

Silence reigned for a heartbeat. Then the first bolts leapt from the bows, outpacing the shouts of alarm that followed, the quick responses of reflex and fight moving so much faster than understanding. Several must have flown wide, but Kaden could feel at least two of the bolts punch into his adversary's flesh, jolting them both. The man didn't cry out, didn't so much as groan, but Kaden could feel him hesitate, sagging as the steel lodged tight. Emotion should have come over Kaden then— relief or fear or savage joy—but there was no emotion inside the emptiness. He had accomplished one goal. Many remained. Quickly, he pulled himself free of the corpse, considered the rounded *kenta* chamber, then stepped back through the gate into the blinding sun.

He'd been gone just a few heartbeats, but everything had changed. The man he'd dragged through the *kenta,* who was now lying dead on the other side in some secret chamber beneath the Dawn Palace, had been the one guarding Kiel. Which meant that, at least for the moment, the Csestriim was free. His wrists remained bound behind him, but that hadn't stopped him from moving to the *kenta* leading to the Shin chapterhouse, hadn't prevented him from kicking Matol's legs out from under him as he emerged.

It was a feeble attack, and the Ishien commander was already rising to his feet, teeth bared, but he had dropped Tan's *naczal,* and Kaden took it up, the shaft cool and smooth in his hands. The violence seemed to have jolted Triste fully awake, and she writhed in the arms of her captor like a caught wolf, screaming and scratching, biting and clawing. The Ishien was larger, but the same brutal strength with which the girl had broken Matol's hand back in the Dead Heart seemed to have surfaced once more.

Kaden circled them, cool and distant inside the *vaniate,* considering his options. The *naczal* was deadly in Tan's hands, but he wasn't even sure which end to strike with. Any effort to attack Triste's captor was just as likely to hurt her as it was to reach the Ishien. He watched, searching for an opening, seeing nothing but a flurry of arms and struggling flesh. It was no good. He wasn't Valyn or Pyrre. The monks hadn't possessed so much as a single sword. He'd stayed alive in Annur this long only by deflecting and dodging attacks, pitting the strength of one foe against another: Adiv's men against the Ishien, the aristocrats against the imperial guards, the soldiers on the other side of the *kenta* against whoever he had shoved through. The strategy had worked, until now. On the green circle of grass, cliffs dropping into the wide blue sea on every side, there was no more dodging to be had, no more deflecting. It was time to fight, and Kaden knew nothing of fighting.

"I've changed my mind," Matol said. "I'm not taking you back to rot with your teacher. I'm going to gut you right here."

He stooped, never taking his eyes from Kaden's face, to pick up the sword dropped by his lost companion. The other Ishien shifted, blades at the ready, faces closed. *The vaniate,* Kaden realized. He wasn't the only one acting from inside the trance. They *were all* inside the *vaniate,* all except Triste, who had redoubled her thrashing.

As Matol talked, Kiel slipped to Kaden's side.

"Cut me free," he said, glancing over his shoulder to the rope knotting his hands.

Matol pointed his sword at Kaden. "You murdered my man to help *this* inhuman scum, and you're still helping him, dancing when he says dance, like a demented puppet. I'm going to put this steel in your flesh, and I'm going to watch you squirm. You should thank me. I'm going to cut the strings."

Kaden ignored him, turning instead to slit the rope binding Kiel's wrists. The rough fiber parted effortlessly beneath the *naczal* blade. That made two of them free. Kaden hesitated, then handed the spear to Kiel.

"Can you use this?"

The Csestriim took it, sighted down the shaft. "It has been many centuries," he said, spinning the blade in a smooth, practiced motion, "but the memory is strong."

Kiel slid in front of Kaden, blocking Matol's advance, and suddenly the odds didn't look so long. Matol's jaw tightened. Evidently his reading of the scene mirrored Kaden's own.

"Billick," he said, turning to one of the remaining soldiers. "Get the others. They're just beyond the Cavaltin gate. You can be back in twenty breaths."

Kaden had no idea where Cavaltin was, or which *kenta* led to it, but it hardly mattered. Somewhere, somewhere close, more Ishien waited, maybe dozens more, heavily armed and ready. When they came, there would be no escape. It was just a fact, true as the sky above them was true. Billick charged across the green sward, passed through the *kenta,* then vanished. Triste chose that moment to twist in her captor's grasp, sink her teeth into his collar, and then, as he roared and jerked back, to wrench free.

Matol cursed, shook his head, then spat into the grass. Triste's panicked escape had thrown her almost directly into the man's path, and he stepped forward, raised his sword, then hacked down in a vicious arc. Kaden could only watch as the sword fell toward her head, but Kiel was quicker, sliding the *naczal* into the gap, deflecting Matol's blow into the dull earth. The Csestriim withdrew the spear, preparing another thrust, but before he could move, Triste staggered to her feet. Kaden expected her to flee, to hurl herself away from the blades, but instead she lunged forward into Matol, her face drawn with fear and fury, eyes wide as suns, hands clutching around his back, pulling him close even as she drove them both back.

"Get off me, you soulless whore," Matol spat. He twisted, but couldn't wrench free. With his sword arm trapped against his side, he couldn't bring the blade to bear.

"It is you," Triste murmured, "who abandoned your soul."

No, Kaden realized. *That isn't Triste.* The frightened child who had sobbed in his pavilion back in Ashk'lan was gone, replaced by the woman who had shattered Matol's wrist weeks earlier. The Ishien was older than her, taller and stronger, but Triste was bearing him up and back somehow, forcing him to give ground, her muscles bent to the task, tendons straining in her legs, the backs of her knees, her neck. Strangely, she was smiling, full lips parted with the effort of breath.

"I warned you," she said, voice lapidary as polished stone, "that this day would come."

Matol struggled and cursed and lost ground. She was forcing him toward the *kenta,* and for a moment Kaden thought he understood her plan, thought she intended to force him through into the hail of crossbow bolts as he had the other Ishien. The plan had worked once; it could work again. Only she was moving toward the wrong *kenta,* toward the gate that led back into the basement of the Shin chapterhouse.

"No, Triste," he shouted, gesturing to the palace gate, "the other one. The *other* one!"

She ignored him.

"You gave up your soul," she said. "You thought you had burned it out with your vicious rituals, your petty faith in the power of pain." She laughed, a full, throaty laugh. "Pain is so limited."

"I'll show you pain, bitch."

The two remaining Ishien moved toward the *kenta* and their commander, but Kiel was faster, stepping forward to block them, raising the *naczal.*

"I'll show you pain like you'd never believe," Matol snarled, dropping his sword, wrenching his hand free and scrabbling with it at her throat.

"You would be shocked, you weak little man, at what I believe."

Matol's fingers closed around her neck, but Triste just smiled, pulling him closer, then pressing her lips to his. Kaden stared as she wrapped him in her embrace, her eyes closed with something like rapture as she moved against him, hip to hip, mouth to mouth, like lovers in desperate ecstasy. The Ishien was still choking her even as his mouth opened to her kiss, responding to some animal call older than thought, older than hate. Triste clutching at his free arm, pressing it back, back through the space of the *kenta* . . .

Matol jerked as though stabbed, tried to shout, to pull away, but Triste's hand was locked on the back of his neck. He yanked his arm from the *kenta,* only there was no arm left, just a blank slab of flesh with two circles of bone at the center, butchered as though with an impossibly sharp cleaver. Bone and flesh. Then blood in a fountain.

Triste pulled back a moment, smiling as Matol flailed. "Don't think about the pain," she cooed, "think about the pleasure. You thought you had burned it out of your soul, but I am returning it to you." Then her lips were on his again, questing, probing, her chest pressed up against his chest as she forced him toward the gate once more. He took a step back, his leg passed the invisible plane, and he buckled, as though someone on the far side had kicked his foot out from under him.

Triste held him up, pulling him into her lips, her arms, her horrible embrace. The leg was gone. Both Matol and Triste were soaked in blood, and still she didn't let him go. Matol writhed inside her arms, but it was no longer clear he was trying to escape, no longer clear that he could. As Kaden stared, shock scratching at the edge of the *vaniate,* Triste slammed the Ishien leader up against the post of the *kenta,* forcing her body against his, sliding a hand down his breeches even as she pivoted him against the stone once more, pivoted him into the hungry emptiness of the gate. Matol's spine arched, his head craned back, his whole body convulsed, a series of awful, bone-wracking spasms, and then, finally, Triste let him fall. There was little left but the head and a sliver of torso. He looked more like a side of bloody beef than a man. Triste was drenched, as though she had stood for hours in a rain of blood, but she paid no attention to the red streaming down her face, dripping from her fingers. She stared at Matol, her face hard and unreadable, then licked the blood from her lips.

"Triste?" Kaden said, his mind still scrambling to make sense of what he'd seen.

She shook her head, eyes huge and blank. "What?"

Then, before he could respond, the Ishien were pouring through the gate on the far side of the island. There were at least a dozen, all in boiled wool and leather, all carrying blades and bows. A few faces Kaden recognized, others he did not. The numbers were what mattered. Triste could hardly yank all of them from the *vaniate,* could hardly drive all of them through the gates.

"Here," Billick called, gesturing. "Ring them in."

As the Ishien spread out, Kaden watched all chance of freedom slip away. No sorrow came with the realization of failure. No fear.

"Bring them down with bolts and arrows," the Ishien went on. "To the legs only. I want them crippled, not dead."

He glanced once at the mangled smear of flesh that had been Matol, then hefted his blade, as though testing its weight. They were taking their time, choosing their shots, but it wouldn't be long before the arrows flew.

"Behind the *kenta*," Kiel said, gesturing.

Kaden understood, retreating behind the gate with Triste just before the first hum of the bowstrings. A half-dozen arrows streaked toward them . . . then vanished into the emptiness of the *kenta*. The gate was a shield, but it was immobile. Even as he watched, the Ishien were spreading out, moving to the flanks. Over his shoulder, just a few paces behind, the island dropped away, cliffs plunging straight down into the shattered rocks and spray below. There would be no escape there.

"We have to go through," he said.

"The palace archers," Triste said, lips drawn back in a smile or a snarl. Face and hair dripping blood, she might have been some figure from nightmare, but inside the variate Kaden was beyond all nightmare.

"We're behind the gate now," Kaden said, mind humming. "We'll come out on the opposite side, putting the *kenta* between us and the palace guards. It'll shield us."

He glanced at Kiel, and the Csestriim nodded. "Until they adjust," he murmured.

"They're not taking me," Triste said, eyeing the Ishien with something like hunger. "They will never take me."

"Our odds on the other side of the gate are slim," Kiel said.

"They're slim either way," Kaden said. "Right now, confusion is our friend."

Before they could debate the matter further, Triste loosed a defiant scream, then hurled herself through the *kenta*.

Kaden hesitated, probing the boundary of the *vaniate*. It flexed beneath his mind's touch, like the surface of a pool of water when a leaf settles upon it, but the trance held. He took one more look at the Ishien, then followed.

The stone chamber was in chaos. Men were shouting orders at one another, waving weapons, pointing bows. The sound redoubled as Kaden emerged through the gate, reverberating off of the walls and low ceiling, the cries of anger, fear, and confusion battering him from all directions. The crossbowmen loosed another volley that passed harmlessly into the *kenta*. Kiel lowered the blade of the *naczal*, leveling it inches from the gate.

"The Ishien have a hard choice," he said, voice calm as though discussing the evening meal. "We're waiting on this side, the guards on the other, and they know it."

"There's only three of us," Kaden said.

"But we are *here*," Kiel replied. "Which gives us an edge."

For a few heartbeats, nothing happened. The palace soldiers struggled to reload and crank their weapons while their commander shouted pointless orders. Kaden scanned the tiny space for some escape, but there was nothing to find. The chamber was only ten paces across, and seemed to be far underground, the only exit a narrow corridor blocked by a line of soldiers and crossbowmen with swords at their hips.

The corridor or the *kenta*. The soldiers or the Ishien. There were no good choices. Kaden reached behind him, took a torch from its sconce on the wall. It was a foolish weapon, but felt better than facing all that steel with nothing in his hands.

"We wait for the Ishien," he said. "They'll absorb some of the attack. When they come through, we have to force our way back through the *kenta*, hope we can slip past whomever they left on the island."

Kiel nodded, but Triste didn't move. She was staring, bloody eyes fixed on something in the corridor, a shape moving in the darkness. Kaden squinted. It looked like another soldier, a lone man arriving from the barracks or halls above. Then he stepped forward into the light.

"My father," she snarled, hands balled into fists.

As usual, Adiv's blindfold did nothing to hinder the sense that he was looking at you, looking straight through you. The councillor studied them, then waved a hand at the soldiers under his command. "Advance," he said, voice hard. "Kill them."

The palace guards managed three or four steps before the first of the Ishien charged through the *kenta*. Unlike Kaden, they hadn't seen the ground, and they paused for a second just inside the gate. The guards, too, hesitated, then plunged ahead with a roar. The next moments were madness. Without the *kenta* shielding them from the worst of the violence, Kaden, Kiel, and Triste would have been cut to pieces almost immediately. Most of the Ishien met the palace attack, although two or three turned, searching for their quarry. Kiel stabbed one through the neck, and another through the hamstring, dropping him to the floor. Kaden thrust his torch into the fallen man's face, blocking out his scream, ignoring the stench of burning flesh.

"Fall back," Adiv was shouting, his voice somehow carrying above the chaos. *"Drop back!"*

Some of the guards retreated, while others, turning at the command, fell to the Ishien. There was a rumbling, Kaden realized, a low, implacable grinding of stone on stone, a sound he'd heard hundreds of times in the high mountains as the granite shifted against itself with the spring thaw, as great blocks sheared off from the cliffs, sliding down the crags, the terrible, thundering weight shattering trees and smashing boulders, crushing everything beneath. He glanced up to see the stone ceiling shifting, the carefully mortared blocks grinding against one another, fine powder sifting down into his eyes, filling his lungs.

"Back!" Adiv called again. Kaden could hear the voice clearly enough, but he could no longer make out the leach, hidden as he was by the rising dust and the darkness of the corridor. As he strained to see what was happening on the far side of the gate, an enormous stone, ten times the size of a man, tore free from the ceiling, smashing down into the Ishien, crushing two and trapping a third, blocking off the *kenta*.

Kaden turned to Kiel. "What's happening?"

The Csestriim's eyes were hard, intent. "The leach," he said. "He's trying to crush us."

Kaden stared. Several of the torches had guttered out, and the tops of the walls were trembling. There was no telling how much weight hung suspended above them, but the stone of the vaulted arch was dropping away seemingly everywhere, everywhere but right above them.

"Go," Triste growled, her voice thick with strain. Kaden turned. Her eyes were wide, lips parted, and her chest heaved as though she'd just sprinted the Circuit of Ravens. Sweat sheened her forehead and face. Matol's blood dripped. *"Go."*

Kaden glanced up. "I'm going, come on. This whole place is falling apart."

"I know, you fool." She groaned. "I'm holding it up."

There was no time to stare, no time to ask questions. Kaden seized her by the arm, thrust his torch before him into the half-lit darkness of choking stone dust, and dragged her forward. By the time they reached the door, the entire chamber was shaking, stones the size of his chest raining down like hail, shattering on the floor.

"Faster," Kiel said, sliding in front of them, *naczal* held at the ready.

The corridor, too, was collapsing, the grinding and shattering blotting out all other sound. Of Adiv and his men, there was no sign, just a hundred paces of straight stone hallway ending in a staircase. No guards. There was no need, when Adiv could pull the entire structure down on their heads, burying them in the rubble. As though in a trance, Triste stumbled forward behind Kiel. Kaden began to follow, when a fragment of stone caught him across the back, slamming his body to the floor and blasting apart the *vaniate*. Pain and fear flooded in, the hot red reek of his own mortality. Powerless to shout, he watched as Triste and Kiel reached the stairs, then started up, not realizing he'd fallen.

He took a breath, almost choked on the dust, then dragged in another. Each movement of his lungs sent a stabbing pain through his back. Something was broken—maybe a rib—but there was no time to dwell on it. Without Triste to support the ceiling, the corridor was coming apart. Grimly, Kaden thrust back the wash of feeling, dragging himself to his feet.

The forty-six steps were the longest of his life, but by the time he reached the upper landing, the tunnel had stopped shaking. He could hear the last stones smashing against the floor below, but the sound was muted, partly by distance, partly by a louder, more strident noise shoving it aside, drowning it out. Men were screaming in the hallway ahead, shouting and sobbing, voices bright with desperation. Kaden took a step forward, slipped, caught himself, then looked down. The stone was awash in blood. A few paces off, a soldier lay crumpled against the wall. Beyond him another, then another.

Dread mounting, Kaden limped ahead, forcing down the pain in his chest, trying to still the battering of his heart, trying to *think*. They were in the Dawn Palace, or beneath it. Adiv had marshaled his men, but someone was killing those men. Kiel had proven himself capable with the *naczal,* but it wasn't Kiel. Kaden stared at another corpse as he passed. The face had been utterly smashed, features caved into the back of the skull. No weapon could do that.

Triste. It had to be. When Adiv tried to tear down the tunnel, she had held it up. Like her father, she was a leach, a powerful leach, and something inside her had snapped.

He redoubled his pace, following the corridor around one corner, then another, pushing past dozens of bodies until the dank, cold scent of the stone began to give way to fresh air. He rounded a final bend and pulled up short. Thirty paces away, silhouetted by the bright blaze of the noonday sun, arms outstretched as though eager for some terrible embrace, Triste stood in an arch leading outside. Beyond her, Kaden could make out fire and smoke, could hear screams, but Triste herself remained motionless as stone. As Kaden stared, Adiv stepped from an alcove halfway down the corridor. He didn't spare a glance for Kaden. All his attention was focused on his daughter, and as he moved, the bare knife in his hand glinted with reflected sunlight.

Kaden threw himself into a lurching run. There was no point shouting a warning any more than there was trying to cover the sound of his approach—the violence beyond the doorway was deafening even inside the hall. It was a race, pure and simple, with Triste's life as the prize, and though Kaden knew nothing about fighting, nothing about war or politics, nothing about leaches or their powers, he knew how to run. He'd been running his whole life, running hungry, running in the dark, running hurt, and so, gritting his teeth, he ran.

He hit Adiv a few paces from the entrance, a few paces from Triste, slamming him to the floor. Agony scoured his back, but he ignored the agony. He had only moments, less than moments, before the leach turned on him and tore him apart. Kaden found the knife, tried to pull it to Adiv's throat. He was stronger than the councillor, but the other man had an animal's desperate tenacity, and Kaden could get no purchase on the handle.

He grimaced; then, steeling himself against the pain, he wrapped his fingers around the blade itself, feeling the keen edge bite into his flesh, tendon, bone. He ignored the blood and sudden stupid uselessness of the fingers, forcing the knife closer to Adiv, wrapping his legs around the leach's torso, dragging it closer, and closer.

The councillor cursed, snarled something, and suddenly Kaden felt himself losing the fight, as though a great invisible hand had lent its strength to Adiv's struggle. He was losing. He had no idea how to fight back against a kenning. Then, abruptly, the man went limp. Kaden stared, then shoved the leach aside to find Kiel standing over them, *naczal* buried in the councillor's back. A momentary surge of exultation flared up in him, but Kiel's expression doused it.

"Quickly," he said, reaching down to help Kaden to his feet. "It's Triste."

Kaden shook his head. "What?"

"She's killing them."

"Killing *who*?"

"Everyone."

By the time Kaden reached the doorway, it was all over. People were still sobbing, screaming, flames still lapped the sky, but Triste had dropped her arms. She stood like a marionette, as though her whole body were suspended by a single, impossibly thin string.

"Triste?" he said carefully, setting a hand gently on her shoulder.

She turned to him, eyes blank as cloud, but didn't respond.

"What did you do?" he asked.

"I don't know." The words were dark, leaden. "I don't know."

There was no fear in her tone, no worry, just a deep, unplumbed helplessness. Kaden took her face in his hands, looked into her eyes. There was nothing to see, and when he let his hands fall, she crumpled to the floor, folding in on herself. Kaden started to kneel, but Kiel waved him forward, toward the arch.

"You had best look," he said.

Kaden hesitated, then limped from shadow into sunlight. For a long time he had no idea what he was looking at. Kiel claimed the *kenta* let out inside the Dawn Palace, and the guardsmen below certainly seemed to confirm the idea, but Kaden didn't recognize the blackened, blasted courtyard before him. There were a few twisted trees, all on fire, scores of corpses, dozens more wounded and dying. The walls enclosing the small space were scorched, and at least one building was fully ablaze. It was only when he turned that he saw the twin towers, Yvonne's and the Crane, flanking him, while above and behind them, like a bright point lodged in the belly of the sky, stood Intarra's Spear.

He turned back to the courtyard. There was nothing to see but horror. Nothing to hear but the keening of the wounded and the clattering boots of more guardsmen drawing near. Kaden watched them burst into the small square, level their spears, then pause. He raised his eyes slowly, straightened his back. He had returned to his palace, to the home of his father, of his family. If he were going to die here, he would die with his eyes open. He would die on his feet.

The commander of the guards stared. Then, to Kaden's shock, dropped to his knees. Behind him, his men shifted in confusion. The air was thick with smoke and warped by the heat of the still-burning flames, but if he could see them, they could see him, and one by one, they saw. One by one, they fell to their knees, pressed foreheads against the bloody stone. For what seemed like a long time there was only the crackling of flame, the sobs of the mangled. Then, like the low rumble of a flooded river, the voices came:

"All hail the Scion of Light, the Long Mind of the World, Holder of the Scales, and Keeper of the Gates."

Kaden felt like choking, like vomiting. He wanted to fall to the stones and weep. But the Shin had taught him to stand even when his body flagged. They had taught him to look at the world without weeping.

"All hail," the voices continued, rising above the wind, above the flame, "he who holds back the darkness. All hail the Emperor."

50

Adare stood at the end of the dock, back to the still-burning desolation of Andt-Kyl's eastern island, eyes on the small boats quartering through the waves. There were half a dozen of them, and they'd been at it all morning, back and forth, back and forth, dropping their weighted nets, trolling the bottom, then pulling them up slick and glistening with small fish. They kept those fish, tossing them into wooden barrels before lowering the nets once more. Adare chafed at the delay, the distraction, but she could hardly fault them. She had given the fisherman of Andt-Kyl this task, had asked it of them at a time when such asking was hard. Their town still smoldered. Many of their dead remained unburied. The wounded—both the screaming and the silent—needed tending. And still she had asked these men to go out in their small boats, to trawl for bodies.

"You will want to search for your mothers and fathers swept into the lake, for your brothers and sisters," she had said, then added silently, shamefully, *And for my own.*

The fishermen had just glanced at each other, looked out over the waves, then nodded. Half of Andt-Kyl was in flames, including storerooms and root cellars stocked with the last of the winter's provisions, food intended to carry the townsfolk through to the harvest. It made a certain sense to take to the boats. The living would need to eat, and these men knew their business; they could do their usual work while they searched for the dead.

Adare stood on the docks all morning staring south, staring until her eyes ached with the strain, a stone settling in her stomach every time they pulled another sodden body from the water. She could tell, even half a mile distant, whether the corpse belonged to a logger or to one of the Urghul. The horsemen were stripped of valuables, then tossed unceremoniously into the hold to be burned ashore later—no sense dragging the same corpse out of the water a dozen times. The dead of Andt-Kyl, however, were laid gently on the decking. The living fishermen hovered over them, as though they were spirits slipping clear of the wet flesh. Adare couldn't hear anything at that distance, but from the angle of the heads, the stillness of the poses, she could imagine them praying.

She had tried to pray herself.

Intarra, she began, over and over, *Lady of Light, please . . .*

That same invocation, again and again. She never got any further. There was no way to know if the goddess was listening, if she cared, if she was even *real,* but none of that was the obstacle, not the true obstacle. There was always doubt in matters of faith, doubt that had never before, even at Adare's most skeptical, stopped her from praying. No, the reason she could not finish her prayer here, now, staring out over the blue-gray waves of the lake, watching the men in the small boats haul up struggling fish and the calm, unstruggling dead, was not a problem of the goddess, but of Adare herself. She couldn't end the prayer because she didn't know what to pray for.

Her brother was dead. She had killed him, or helped to. *Valyn,* she said silently, the name like a nail lodged in her mind. He was her brother, and she had killed him. The truth scalded, but it was the truth, and so, rather than turning away from the lake, rather than burying herself in the thousands of other matters that needed her attention, rather than drinking until she dropped, or talking until she forgot, or working with her hands until exhaustion delivered her into sleep, she stood at the end of the dock, rehearsing what she had done, saying over and over the name of a dead brother, trying and failing to pray.

"Your Radiance."

Lehav's voice behind her. The scuff of his boots on the wooden dock. She closed her eyes, measured out the last moments of her solitude in his approaching steps.

"The town?" she asked, when he paused at her shoulder. "Do they know yet how many died?"

"It's a mess," he replied grimly. "It's hard to know anything. Maybe half."

Half a town killed. Was that a victory, against the might of an Urghul army? A failure?

"What about the Sons?"

"We took a beating. Not as bad as the Army of the North. I heard you were atop the signal tower."

Adare nodded, still not looking at him.

"That was foolish," he said.

Before the battle she would have bridled at the comment, would have argued the point loudly and long, as she had done with Fulton. Fulton, who was dead. Dead because she had insisted on seeing the battle up close. She shook her head slowly.

"It seemed important."

A cold wind blew through the long pause that followed, nicking the waves, fueling the fires behind them.

"I will leave you," Lehav said finally. He did not leave.

Adare took a long, unsteady breath.

Intarra, she prayed inwardly, *Lady of Light.* She had tried so many times already to compose this prayer, had failed so many times that when the last words came, they surprised her: *Lady of Light, forgive me.*

She couldn't have said for what transgression she was begging forgiveness. She had failed her father and made common cause with his killer, had taken a leach as her councillor, had raised up an army to fight against armies of Annur, had stolen a throne from one brother and slid a knife between the ribs of another. . . .

It had all seemed so necessary.

Forgive me, she prayed again, again without entrusting the prayer to speech.

Sunlight shattered on the waves. It burned her eyes. Behind her, the flames still raged. Forgiveness, it seemed, lay far from the providence of fire. She watched a moment longer as the fishermen hauled another quiet body from the lake, then turned to Lehav.

He was studying her—his prophet, chosen of Intarra, Emperor of Annur—with dark, uncertain eyes.

"Let's go," said Adare hui'Malkeenian before he could speak again. "There is work to be done."

51

For a while, Kaden considered it.

He hadn't expected to end the day in the Dawn Palace, hadn't expected to be heralded as the Emperor of Annur, but then, as the Shin said, *To expect is to err.*

When he emerged into the burning square at the center of the Dawn Palace, when the guardsmen knelt before him, intoning the ancient formula that had preceded all Malkeenian rulers for generations, it seemed harder to refuse the honor than to accept it. Whatever play Adare had made for the throne, she was hundreds of miles away in Raalte and had made no formal declaration of her own intent. The citizens of Annur were confused, and Kaden, standing at the center of the empire, was best situated to turn that confusion to his advantage. It looked suddenly, shockingly simple to take the throne and declare himself his father's heir.

In the end, it was that very simplicity that made him hesitate. Ran il Tornja was not a simple thinker. Neither was Adare. Winning a single battle meant little in the larger war, and seizing the Unhewn Throne was a far cry from holding it. A single man, even a man inside the walls of the Dawn Palace, was too easy to topple, too easy to kill. They would expect him to seize the reins of power, and they would have plans in place to handle him when he did so. The events of the last day had seen Adiv killed and his force of loyalists gutted, but Kaden had no doubt that there were still people in the palace—ministers, guards, concubines—who would plant a blade in his back at a word from the *kenarang,* not to mention the enemies he would make with the members of his newly formed council.

Of course, even the ceding of imperial power was not a straightforward matter. Kaden spent the rest of the night just setting in motion the most basic wheels: sending messengers to the various nobles of the council;

talking down the dozens of ministers who gathered like ill-fed ravens, baffled that Kaden would surrender his titles and fearful that any transition would mean an end to their sinecures; reassuring the palace guard; arranging to conclusively seal off the *kenta* chamber; seeing to it that the scores of people killed by Triste's fury were properly washed, wrapped, and transported out of the palace for burial; instructing the palace staff to clean the wreckage strewn about the Jasmine Court; and then finally, just as the tip of Intarra's Spear began to glow with the pale light of the un-risen sun, collecting his newly forged council in the Hall of a Thousand Trees, unfurling the constitution before the sight of the entire court, and administering the oaths to defend and uphold the fledgling republic against all foes.

When the audience was finally over, Kaden felt ready to collapse on his feet, and there were still hundreds of questions to answer, thousands of tasks, tiny and enormous, that had to be addressed if the Annurian Republic were to have any hope of survival.

Kaden wiped his face with his hands as he exited the hall, as though he could scrub the weariness from his eyes, the cobwebs from his thoughts. Kiel and Gabril walked at his side.

"There is something you should know," the Csestriim said quietly, glancing over at Kaden as though gauging his readiness to hear a difficult truth.

Kaden stared at him, then waved him on.

"In preparing Adiv's body for the fires his blindfold was removed," Kiel said. "He could see. He has eyes."

"Just like any other man." Kaden shook his head.

"No," Kiel responded. "Not just like any other man. Tarik Adiv shared your burning irises."

Kaden stopped walking. For a long time he didn't move. There seemed no point. There were a thousand tasks ahead of him, none of which he understood.

"A relative," he said finally.

Kiel nodded. "Your family is old. There are many branches. Intarra's touch is strongest upon your own, but there are others."

Kaden had never considered the notion before, but it made a certain sense. If Sanlitun had known, he might have given Adiv a high post in the government out of some kind of loyalty. And Adiv himself . . . how would he have felt after a lifetime hiding his eyes while the Malkeenians flaunted their own? Bitter enough to turn on an emperor who had favored him?

Bitter enough to kill? Kaden shook his head. More questions and no answers.

"I should go to my father's study," he said. "Look over his papers before the council meets again. What do I have, a few hours?"

"What you should do," Kiel said, "is sleep."

Gabril nodded. "Work without rest and you will achieve nothing."

The First Speaker and the Csestriim had not left his side since the
Great Gate was thrown open and the council admitted to the deafening
tolling of the gongs. Kaden was grateful for the support, more than grateful, but after hours of talking, negotiation, and reassurance, he longed for
a few hours of silence, of solitude.

Gabril, as though sensing his thoughts, patted him on the shoulder.
"Come. We will see you to your chambers, and I will command the watch
at your door myself." If the First Speaker was exhausted after the long
night, he didn't show it. But then, the First Speaker hadn't spent the afternoon fighting for his life against Adiv, Matol, and the Ishien. Kaden started
to accept, then shook his head.

"There's Triste, too," he said. "I have to see her."

In the chaos following his emergence from the *kenta,* in his urgency to
see the council installed before any opposition could coalesce, Kaden had
allowed the girl to be led away, her eyes blank, baffled, and hopeless. The
palace guards had wanted to kill her on the spot, but Kaden stopped
them, insisting on her imprisonment instead. In truth, he had no idea
what to think about her final bloody massacre, no idea how to feel about
it. Certainly she had saved his life, both by holding up the tunnel as Adiv
sought to tear it down, and by killing the soldiers under the leach's command. It seemed, however, that something inside the girl had snapped,
some cord tethering her mind to the world. He had walked among the
bodies in the Jasmine Court, had looked at their faces. There were ministers among the number, and courtiers, one old woman, and at least three
children. They couldn't all have been a part of Adiv's plot. They weren't
all supporters of Adare and il Tornja.

The sight sickened and saddened him, both for the victims and for
Triste. Whatever fury had consumed her, whatever power had torn the
lives from five or six score Annurians, it was clear that she understood it
no better than anyone else. In the wake of the slaughter, he wanted nothing more than to sit with her, comfort her, try to understand just what had
happened and how—but there was no time. Instead, he had seen her

drugged with adamanth root, locked in a barred chamber inside the Crane, and placed under triple guard while he went about wrenching aside the final foundations of empire.

Now, before he slept, he owed her a visit. Gabril seemed to have other thoughts on the matter, and his jaw tightened as Kaden changed course for the Crane.

"Whatever your past with that woman, she is an abomination. She should be killed, not coddled."

"She's hardly being coddled," Kaden replied, his own voice harder than he'd intended. "She's locked away."

"Allowing a known leach to live is hardly a way to build support for the republic," Gabril said. "Especially a leach who only just now cut down hundreds of your subjects."

"They're not *my* subjects anymore," Kaden said. "And it will be the council, not me, who determines Triste's fate. It doesn't change the fact that she has been with me since this all started, has *saved* me more than once, and I intend to see her now, to offer her what comfort I can."

Gabril shook his head. "Then you go alone. I will be outside your quarters when you have finished with this folly."

"Not alone," Kiel said. "I will join you, if you allow."

Kaden nodded wearily, watching the First Speaker turn on his heel and stalk across the courtyard.

✝

At first Kaden thought the room was empty. Someone had drawn the heavy shutters without bothering to light the lamps, blocking out the faint blush of light seeping into the eastern sky. He could make out a small pallet at the far side of the room, two lacquered chairs, and a basin with water on a low table; the chamber was hardly a cell, but it was certainly a far cry from the other guest suites in the palace. The air was hot and stuffy, as though the window hadn't been open for months.

Kaden took a few tentative steps into the room as Kiel pulled the door shut behind them.

"Triste?" he called.

Silence.

He crossed to the window, unlatched the shutters, and pushed them open. When he turned he saw her, crouched between the pallet and the wall, arms clutching her knees to her chest, eyes staring at nothing. Despite the bowl of water, she had made no effort to scrub the blood from her face or hands. It had dried and cracked, making it seem as though her skin was sloughing away. Her dress, too, was black and heavy with blood. She paid no attention to any of it, staring blankly at a section of wall a few paces distant.

"Triste?" he said again, crossing toward her hesitantly. "Are you all right?"

Her body convulsed, shaking with something that was part sob, part bitter laugh.

"My mother is a traitor," she said without shifting her eyes or raising her voice. "She sold me to my father, who was a traitor and a leach. *I* am a leach and I just murdered I don't know how many people."

The bald statement of the facts brought Kaden up short. He wanted to offer some consolation, but had no idea what to say. As the silence stretched, she raised her eyes at last.

"When will I be executed?" The words held no fear. If anything, there was a note of hope in her voice.

Kaden shook his head slowly. "Triste . . . I . . . The council will decide, but I'm going to fight for you, fight to see you saved. Not all leaches are evil."

Her mouth dropped open in disbelief. "I saw the bodies, Kaden! The people I killed! A child with her head torn halfway off . . . A man holding his intestines in his arms . . . I *slaughtered them.*"

Kaden hesitated, then nodded. "You killed them, but you didn't *mean* to kill them. That's important."

"I didn't?" she asked, staring at him bleakly. "How do you know?"

"Do you remember what happened?" Kaden asked. "In the tunnel, back on the island with the *kenta*?"

She shook her head, a tiny defeated motion. "Parts. Glimpses. I remember fury. And blood." She paused, tears streaking her blood-soaked face. "And power. I'm a leach. A *leach*. Just like the Atmani."

"Maybe you are," Kaden said, "but there are worse things to be."

His years with the monks had ground out most reflexive aversion, but there was still something deep inside him, some vicious muscle trained in his early childhood, that recoiled at the thought. All the old words, like dumb fish rising to the light, floated into his mind: *foul, twisted, loathsome.* He looked at Triste, at the delicate arc of her neck, the fall of her hair onto her shoulders. It seemed cruel of Bedisa to weave something so vile into a being so beautiful.

Put it away, he told himself, taming the feeling that crouched, muttering, inside of him. At every point since he'd met her, Triste had been kind and generous. When events came to a head, when she fell into the hands of the Ishien, it had been Kaden who failed her, not the other way around. If she was a leach, she was a leach.

"It doesn't change who you are," he said, though as the words left his lips he remembered her pressing Matol up against the *kenta,* his hand at her throat, her lips pressed to his as she forced him struggling through the gate, remembered her standing, silhouetted, at the end of the corridor, her scream loud as the sun.

She raised her head. Firelight reflected in her streaked tears as though she were crying flame. "Who am I?" she whispered, eyes boring into him, both defiant and desperate.

Kaden shook his head helplessly, and for the first time, Kiel stepped forward, crouching a pace away from Triste, considering her carefully.

"Tell me everything," he said. "Start at the start."

"Why?"

"Because," the Csestriim replied, "you want to learn the truth. I have lived a long time, and seen more than you know."

Triste glanced at Kaden, then back at Kiel, and then the words were tumbling out of her, like water spilling over the lip of Umber's Pool back in the Bone Mountains, falling too fast and far to recall, pulled by a force as old and strong as the earth itself. Kiel listened in silence, nodding when Triste faltered, his face still as stone, eyes intent as she recounted it all: the flight through the mountains, her reading of the script in Assare, her impossible passage through the *kenta* and killing of Ekhard Matol, right up through her utter destruction of Adiv's guard.

"There's something wrong with me," she concluded finally, voice breaking. "Something awful and broken." She had managed to dam up her terror and grief, but Kaden could hear them pressing behind her low voice, a massive weight barely restrained. "I know things," she concluded. "Things I shouldn't know. I can *do* things. . . ." She trailed off, staring out the window.

Kiel glanced at Kaden, then returned his gaze to the girl.

"A remarkable account," he said. "Unique."

"I'm a leach," Triste said, circling back to where they began.

"Almost certainly," Kiel replied. "It would explain your ability to match pace with Kaden and Tan in the mountains, not to mention the fact that you just held up a hundred tons of stone. You are not just a leach, but an extremely powerful one."

Triste nodded helplessly, but Kiel pressed ahead.

"There is more."

Kaden nodded slowly. "Just being a leach wouldn't allow her to pass the *kenta,* would it?"

He hesitated, then shook his head. "No. Not that I've ever heard of." He turned to Triste. "How did you feel when you stepped through the gate?"

She frowned. "Terrified. Every single time. Confused and terrified."

Kiel nodded. "It should have destroyed you."

"And then there's the languages," Kaden said. "You didn't learn them in the temple."

Triste shook her head weakly. "I wanted to believe that, but . . . no." She paused, gazing out at the blank sky, eyes wide and lambent as the moon. "It's like there's . . . someone else."

Kaden narrowed his eyes. "Someone else?"

She grimaced, wrestling with the unspoken words. "Someone else . . . inside me. *She* could read the writing in Assare. . . ."

"She was the one who spoke after breaking Matol's hand back in the Heart," Kaden said. He summoned to mind the girl's words. *" 'Stoppered to your cries will be my ears, and dried to dust the wide lake of my mercy.' "*

Triste shuddered.

"Do you remember saying that?" he pressed.

"I don't . . ." She hesitated. "I'm not sure. It's like something I dreamed and then forgot."

"It doesn't sound like you," Kiel observed. "Different syntax. Different idiom."

Triste looked from Kaden to Kiel, then back again. "What does it *mean*?" she asked. "How can I not be myself?"

Kaden shook his head. The Shin would have torn apart the question as predicated on incoherence. The very words *I* and *self* were mired in error, referring to nothing more than illusion, a shifting amalgamation of senses and perceptions with no core, no foundation, no indivisible essence. And yet, the thing that made the illusion so deceptive, so persuasive, was its very coherence. For Triste's self to shift, to shatter . . . the monks had never spoken of such a thing.

"This other . . . aspect," Kiel said carefully, "she seems to emerge only under certain conditions." He ticked them off on his fingers. "The flight through the mountains. The attack in Assare. Your assault on Matol. Conditions of extreme stress."

"Like my mind is broken," she said. "Like something broke it."

Kiel nodded, but Kaden shook his head.

"Broken suggests two halves from a shattered whole," he said, then indicated her with a vague hand, "but there's nothing missing from you now. You're a whole person. And what Kiel's calling the other aspect doesn't seem like an aspect. She's confident, angry. She seems to have a memory of her own, abilities of her own. There might be some bleeding between the two of you, but you both seem whole, distinct. Like another soul was somehow planted in your body."

The whole thing seemed impossible if Kaden paused to consider it, but Triste's eyes blazed.

"Who is she?"

Kiel shook his head. "It doesn't seem like you can know. There may be some . . . seepage between the two of you, but not enough for you to remember or understand."

Triste's lips tightened. "Ask her."

Kaden shook his head. "That's what they were doing back at the Heart," he said. "That was the whole point of the torture. Matol demanded to know who you were a dozen times, and all he ended up with was a broken hand."

"But," Kiel pointed out, "Matol was a foe. Tan was a foe. Maybe she would talk to us. To you."

"Ask her," Triste said.

"All right," Kaden said, frowning. "The next time she . . . emerges, I'll ask."

Triste shook her head grimly. "Now."

"It won't work," Kiel said. "You can't just call her out."

"Yes," Triste said, seizing the knife from Kaden's belt and pressing it to her stomach, "I can."

Kaden and Kiel both started forward, but she was already driving the knife into her flesh, slowly but steadily, the cloth of the robe and the skin beneath parting under the pressure. Her face twisted in pain and Kaden extended a hand, but Kiel held him back.

"Come out here, you bitch," she spat, voice hoarse and ragged. "Get the fuck *out.*"

"She'll kill herself," Kaden said, body tight as a bowstring.

"It is her mind," Kiel replied, "and her body. Her choice."

Kaden hesitated. The first inch of the knife had disappeared, and blood soaked her dress, drenching the gruesome fabric. Her lips had gone dark as night, and her eyes rolled in her head, but she kept her white-knuckled grip on the knife, the slow, relentless pressure.

It's over, Kaden thought, horrified at what he had allowed to happen. *It's over.*

Then the knife stopped, and her eyes, rather than lolling blankly in their sockets, went abruptly sharp as nails, driving into Kaden.

"Fools," she spat, voice strong as a great river in full flood. "You must keep this child from her idiocy. If she destroys this body, you will, all of you, suffer beyond your paltry imagining."

Kaden stared. "What . . ." he began.

Triste shook her head impatiently. "Your world teeters. My husband, power-maddened, roams nearly at will. An ocean of misery rises, and I am trapped," she glanced down at her body, "inside this flesh."

Kaden found himself shrinking before that gaze. He wanted to close his eyes, to cover his ears, to flee. Instead, he forced himself to lean closer.

"Who are you?" he asked softly.

The woman looked at him a moment, and then, to his surprise, released the knife, raised a hand, and ran a finger along his cheek. "The monks worked hard to cut you off from me, Kaden hui'Malkeenian. But you are a man, and even the Great Emptiness cannot sever you utterly from my touch."

A welter of emotions rose up in Kaden, fear and wonder undiluted by his years of training, the feelings taking him in their grip as powerfully as they had when he was a small child. There was something new there, as well, something hot and cold at once, burning from the tip of her finger where it touched his skin down through his heart into his very core, filling him with heat.

"Who are you?" he asked again, his voice a husky whisper.

"I am the joy in your heart," she said, smiling grimly, "and the pleasure in your loins. I am the mother of everything you have labored to deny."

She held Kaden's gaze a moment, then glanced off to the side, as though listening to a new wind approaching across the water. "She is as strong as she is foolish, this vessel of mine," she said with a grimace, then locked her eyes on Kaden once more. "The *obviate,*" she said, voice bent with urgency. "You must perform it. Keep her safe until the *obviate,* for if she dies while I am trapped inside, my hand will vanish from this world and you will sink beneath a wide sea of suffering."

"Who are you?" Kaden asked again, although a terrible thought was growing inside him.

The woman smiled, the moment suspended seemingly forever, then plunged her face into her hands, sobbing. When she spoke again, it was with Triste's voice, trembling and terrified.

"Who is she?" she moaned. "Holy Hull, who *is* she?"

Kaden shook his head, the answer too large to voice.

It was Kiel who replied. "She is your goddess," he said gently. "The one you have named Ciena."

Triste stared. "That's impossible."

"No," he said. "The gods took human form during the Csestriim wars."

"But why?" Kaden asked, his voice hoarse. "Even if it's true, why now?" He shook his head. "I don't know."

"What does it *mean*?" Triste demanded.

"It means," Kiel replied, staring at the blank wall, "that something interesting has begun."

Triste glanced down at her blood-slick hands, then up at the Csestriim, her eyes wide, terrified. *"Interesting?"* she demanded, voice fraying with panic. "How is this *interesting*? It's *horrifying*!"

The Csestriim studied her awhile, then nodded. "Yes. That seems accurate. For those of you who can feel horror, it will be horrifying."

52

Seamless dark.
Cold. Then creeping heat.
Low hum of insects.
Lapping water.
Pain like a blanket.
Then, worse than the pain, memory.
Laith holding the bridge, then falling.
Gwenna and Talal standing as they hurled a starshatter into Balendin's prisoners, then falling.
Adare burying the blade in his side, il Tornja slicing him across the face, all sight extinguished, then Valyn himself falling, smashing into the water at the tower's base.

Failure bitter as blood in his mouth, and the darkness, unrelenting and absolute, clamped down around him like a vise.

Valyn raised his head from the mud, then let it fall. How he had washed up on the shore of the lake he couldn't say. He remembered swimming, his body going through the dumb bestial motions that had been trained into the fibers of his muscle, remembered floating when he was too tired to swim, then swimming some more. Why, he had no idea. Habit. Stubbornness. Cowardice.

He raised a trembling hand toward his eyes, desperate for the truth and terrified of it. The pain burned so bright he could almost see by it. He could endure the pain, but at the thought of a life lived in darkness—constant, unrelieved darkness blacker than the deepest pit of Hull's Hole—his heart quailed.

He slid the tips of his fingers over his eyes, yanked back at the stabbing pain, then forced his hand to the wound once more. The gash started at his temple and sliced clean across both eyes and the bridge of his nose. The skin wept blood and, when he steeled himself enough to test the eyeballs, he found that they were cut cleanly as half-sliced eggs. He jerked his hand away once more, rolled onto his side, vomited into the mud, and lay still.

Fir needles sifted the wind.

Smoke, thick and sickening.

A twist in his innards where Adare had planted the knife.

Though she had torn the blade free, he could feel the queasy shift of his own slick viscera.

"Might as well know the worst," he muttered. His own words felt lighter than ash in his ears, sounded like something already dead.

Fingers slick with blood, he probed the wound, driving his hand in past the second knuckle, pushing through skin and muscle, hunting the worst until he passed out, darkness in his mind rising up to meet the great, encircling dark beyond.

When he came to, he knew he was going to die.

The contours of his wound were wrong. There was too much blood. The steel had sliced thin walls that were not to be sliced. He drew the knowledge around him like a warm cloak, closed bloody lids over the ruin of his eyes, and slept.

†

Cold.

Low call of an owl.

Dark beyond dark.

"Come on, 'Shael," he muttered, teeth chattering. "Come *on*."

Ananshael's absence.

His whole body shaking, Valyn hauled himself from the frigid mud.

"There's got to be a warmer place to die," he groaned, crawling forward on hands and knees, groping blindly for some pile of leaves and needles, some swath of moss where he could lie down, finally, and quit.

No, he realized with a sudden shock. Not blindly.

As always, he could hear a thousand sounds, could feel the ten thousand strands of the air itself eddy around his scrabbling fingers, but there was more. His mind remained dark, but there were . . . layers to the darkness, shapes that were not shapes, form etched into the formless void left by his stolen sight.

Hemlock boughs?

Rotted pine?

The swift flick of a bat's wing in passage?

He didn't see them—there was nothing to see in the unending dark—he *knew* them.

Bruised and baffled, he tested the wound at his side. It continued to weep blood. It should have killed him, but he was not dead.

"How?" he demanded of the darkness.

No reply, just the slap of chop on the rock, the leaves shifting in the breeze, and beneath, the distant sobbing and cries left behind by the battle.

"How?" he demanded again, forcing himself to his feet.

As if in reply, threaded on the wind: the long, low cry of the owl.

Valyn closed his eyes and breathed. The wound at his side stretched, then tore, but he kept breathing in, hauling the cold night air into his lungs until he felt that he would burst, tasting it as it passed his tongue, drawing it through his nose, in and in, sifting the smells.

Moss and rotted leaves, balsam and wet rock, dead fish farther off, and smoke and steel and thousands of gallons of blood slicked on the lake. *Deeper.* Horseflesh, dead and alive, vomit and piss, festering wounds . . . *Deeper.* A thousand thousand hair-thin strands shifting and tangling until . . .

There.

Leather and sweat. Whisper of nitre. Anger.

Gwenna.

Copper and steel, wet wool and wariness.

Talal.

Blood and cold, resin and steel.

Annick.

Alive. All three. Though how he knew he could not say.

Lungs burning, he blew out the great breath, sagging into a pine's jagged limbs.

When he had the strength, he tried a step, another, then tripped on an unseen snag and pitched forward. Pain like lightning up his arm. He stood again, stumbled a few steps, *knew* too late a tree stood in his way even as the broken branch bit into his shoulder, tossing him to the uneven ground.

It was pointless. The whole fucking thing was pointless. He couldn't smell anyone, not at this distance. Certainly couldn't sort his own Wing from the scents scribbled across his mind. He couldn't see. His eyes were gone.

"You're losing your mind," he screamed, heedless of who might hear. "You don't even know how to die." His eyes wept hot blood. "Quit with the fucking bullshit. Just *quit*! Just lie *down*!"

Again, the owl's cry.

He listened to it fade, then shook his head.

"I'm done," he said dully, the rage gone, snuffed out. Everything hurt. Everything wanted to quit. His hands hung wooden and useless at his sides. "I'm through getting up. I'm done."

He took a long, unsteady breath, stared at the dark shapes sculpted from the deeper darkness, clamped a hand over the wound at his side, and got up.

GODS AND RACES, AS UNDERSTOOD BY THE CITIZENS OF ANNUR

RACES

Nevariim—Immortal, beautiful, bucolic. Foes of the Csestriim. Extinct thousands of years before the appearance of humans. Likely apocryphal.

Csestriim—Immortal, vicious, emotionless. Responsible for the creation of civilization and the study of science and medicine. Destroyed by humans. Extinct thousands of years.

Human—Identical in appearance to the Csestriim, but mortal, subject to emotion.

THE OLD GODS, IN ORDER OF ANTIQUITY

Blank God, the—The oldest, predating creation. Venerated by the Shin monks.

Ae—Consort to the Blank God, the Goddess of Creation, responsible for all that is.

Astar'ren—Goddess of Law, Mother of Order and Structure. Called the Spider by some, although the adherents of Kaveraa also claim that title for their own goddess.

Pta—Lord of Chaos, disorder, and randomness. Believed by some to be a simple trickster, by others, a destructive and indifferent force.

Intarra—Lady of Light, Goddess of Fire, starlight, and the sun. Also the patron of the Malkeenian Emperors of Annur, who claim her as a distant ancestor.

Hull—The Owl King, the Bat, Lord of the Darkness, Lord of the Night, aegis of the Kettral, patron of thieves.

Bedisa—Goddess of Birth, she who weaves the souls of all living creatures.

Ananshael—God of Death, the Lord of Bones, who unknits the weaving of his consort, Bedisa, consigning all living creatures to oblivion. Worshipped by the Skullsworn in Rassambur.

Ciena—Goddess of Pleasure, believed by some to be the mother of the young gods.

Meshkent—The Cat, the Lord of Pain and Cries, consort of Ciena, believed by some to be the father of the young gods. Worshipped by the Urghul, some Manjari, and the jungle tribes.

THE YOUNG GODS, ALL COEVAL WITH HUMANITY

Eira—Goddess of Love and mercy.

Maat—Lord of Rage and hate.

Kaveraa—Lady of Terror, Mistress of Fear.

Heqet—God of Courage and battle.

Orella—Goddess of Hope.

Orilon—God of Despair.